28

SCIENCE FICTION
STORIES OF
H. G. WELLS

DOVER PUBLICATIONS, INC.

Library of Congress Catalog Card Number: 52-13264

Manufactured in the United States of America

Dover Publications, Inc.
180 Varick Street
New York 14, New York

CONTENTS

28
SCIENCE FICTION
STORIES OF
H. G. WELLS

MEN LIKE GODS

CHAPTER THE FIRST

MR. BARNSTAPLE TAKES A HOLIDAY

§ 1

MR. BARNSTAPLE found himself in urgent need of a holiday, and he had no one to go with and nowhere to go. He was overworked. And he was tired of home.

He was a man of strong natural affections; he loved his family extremely so that he knew it by heart, and when he was in these jaded moods it bored him acutely. His three sons, who were all growing up, seemed to get leggier and larger every day; they sat down in the chairs he was just going to sit down in; they played him off his own pianola; they filled the house with hoarse, vast laughter at jokes that one couldn't demand to be told; they cut in on the elderly harmless flirtations that had hitherto been one of his chief consolations in this vale; they beat him at tennis; they fought playfully on the landings, and fell downstairs by twos and threes with an enormous racket. Their hats were everywhere. They were late for breakfast. They went to bed every night in a storm of uproar: "Haw, Haw, Haw—*bump!*" And their mother seemed to like it. They all cost money, with a cheerful disregard of the fact that everything had gone up except Mr. Barnstaple's earning power. And when he said a few plain truths about Mr. Lloyd George at meal times, or made the slightest attempt to raise the tone of the table talk above the level of the silliest persiflage, their attention wandered ostentatiously. . . .

1

At any rate it *seemed* ostentatiously.

He wanted badly to get away from his family to some place where he could think of its various members with quiet pride and affection, and otherwise not be disturbed by them. . . .

And also he wanted to get away for a time from Mr. Peeve. The very streets were becoming a torment to him, he wanted never to see a newspaper or newspaper placard again. He was obsessed by apprehensions of some sort of financial and economic smash that would make the great war seem a mere incidental catastrophe. This was because he was sub-editor and general factotum of the *Liberal,* that well-known organ of the more depressing aspects of advanced thought, and the unvarying pessimism of Mr. Peeve, his chief, was infecting him more and more. Formerly it had been possible to put up a sort of resistance to Mr. Peeve by joking furtively about his gloom with the other members of the staff, but now there were no other members of the staff: they had all been retrenched by Mr Peeve in a mood of financial despondency. Practically, now, nobody wrote regu-larly for the *Liberal* except Mr. Barnstaple and Mr. Peeve. So Mr. Peeve had it all his own way with Mr. Barnstaple. He would sit hunched up in the editorial chair, with his hands deep in his trouser pockets, taking a gloomy view of everything, sometimes for two hours together. Mr. Barn staple's natural tendency was towards a modest hopefulness and a belief in progress, but Mr. Peeve held very strongly that a belief in progress was at least six years out of date, and that the brightest hope that remained to liberalism was for a good Day of Judgment soon. And having finished the copy of what the staff, when there was a staff, used to call his weekly indigest, Mr. Peeve would depart and leave Mr. Barnstaple to get the rest of the paper together for the next week.

Even in ordinary times Mr. Peeve would have been hard enough to live with; but the times were not ordinary, they were full of disagreeable occurrences that made his melancholy anticipations all too plausible. The great coal lock out had been going on for a month, and seemed to foreshadow the commercial ruin of England; every morning brought intelli gence of fresh outrages from Ireland, unforgivable and unforgettable outrages; a prolonged drought threatened the harvests of the world; the League of Nations, of which Mr. Barnstaple had hoped enormous things in the great days of President Wilson, was a melancholy and self-satisfied futility; everywhere there was conflict, everywhere unreason; seven eights of the world seemed to be sinking down towards chronic disorder and social dissolution. Even without Mr. Peeve it would have been difficult enough to have made headway against the facts.

Mr. Barnstaple was, indeed, ceasing to secrete hope, and for such types as he, hope is the essential solvent without which there is no digesting life. His hope had always been in liberalism and generous liberal effort, but he was begin- ning to think that liberalism would never do anything more for ever than sit hunched up with its hands in its pockets grumbling and peeving at the activities of baser but more energetic men. Whose scrambling activities would inevitably wreck the world.

Night and day now, Mr. Barnstaple was worrying about the world at large. By night even more than by day, for sleep was leaving him. And he was haunted by a dreadful craving to bring out a number of the *Liberal* of his very own—to alter it all after Mr. Peeve had gone away, to cut out all the dyspeptic stuff, the miserable empty girding at this wrong and that, the gloating on cruel and unhappy things, the exaggeration of the simple, natural, human misdeeds of Mr. Lloyd George, the appeals to Lord Grey, Lord Robert

Cecil, Lord Lansdowne, the Pope, Queen Anne, or the Emperor Frederick Barbarossa (it varied from week to week), to arise and give voice and form to the young aspirations of a world reborn, and, instead, to fill the number with—Utopia! to say to the amazed readers of the *Liberal:* Here are things that have to be done! Here are the things we are going to do! What a blow it would be for Mr. Peeve at his Sunday breakfast! For once, too astonished to secrete abnormally, he might even digest that meal!

But this was the most foolish of dreaming. There were the three young Barnstaples at home and their need for a decent start in life to consider. And beautiful as the thing was as a dream, Mr. Barnstaple had a very unpleasant conviction that he was not really clever enough to pull such a thing off. He would make a mess of it somehow. . . .

One might jump from the frying-pan into the fire. The *Liberal* was a dreary, discouraging, ungenerous paper, but anyhow it was not a base and wicked paper.

Still, if there was to be no such disastrous outbreak it was imperative that Mr. Barnstaple should rest from Mr. Peeve for a time. Once or twice already he had contradicted him. A row might occur anywhen. And the first step towards resting from Mr. Peeve was evidently to see a doctor. So Mr. Barnstaple went to a doctor.

"My nerves are getting out of control," said Mr. Barnstaple. "I feel horribly neurasthenic."

"You are suffering from neurasthenia," said the doctor.

"I dread my daily work."

"You want a holiday."

"You think I need a change?"

"As complete a change as you can manage."

"Can you recommend any place where I could go?"

"Where do you want to go?"

"Nowhere definite. I thought you could recommend——"

"Let some place attract you—and go there. Do nothing to force your inclinations at the present time."

Mr. Barnstaple paid the doctor the sum of one guinea, and armed with these instructions prepared to break the news of his illness and his necessary absence to Mr. Peeve when-ever the occasion seemed ripe for doing so.

§ 2

For a time this prospective holiday was merely a fresh addition to Mr. Barnstaple's already excessive burthen of worries. To decide to get away was to find oneself face to face at once with three apparently insurmountable problems: How to get away? Whither? And since Mr Barnstaple was one of those people who tire very quickly of their own company: With whom? A sharp gleam of furtive scheming crept into the candid misery that had recently become Mr. Barnstaple's habitual expression. But then, no one took much notice of Mr. Barnstaple's expressions.

One thing was very clear in his mind. Not a word of this holiday must be breathed at home. If once Mrs. Barnstaple got wind of it, he knew exactly what would happen. She would, with an air of competent devotion, take charge of the entire business. "You must have a *good* holiday," she would say. She would select some rather distant and expensive resort in Cornwall or Scotland or Brittany, she would buy a lot of outfit, she would have afterthoughts to swell the luggage with inconvenient parcels at the last moment, and she would bring the boys. Probably she would arrange for one or two groups of acquaintances to come to the same place to "liven things up." If they did they were certain to bring the worst sides of their natures with them and to develop into the most indefatigable of bores. There would be no conversation. There would be much unreal laughter. There would be endless games. . . . *No!*

But how is a man to go away for a holiday without his wife getting wind of it? Somehow a bag must be packed and smuggled out of the house. . . .

The most hopeful thing about Mr. Barnstaple's position from Mr. Barnstaple's point of view was that he owned a small automobile of his very own. It was natural that this car should play a large part in his secret plannings. It seemed to offer the easiest means of getting away; it converted the possible answer to Whither? from a fixed and definite place into what mathematicians call, I believe, a locus; and there was something so companionable about the little beast that it did to a slight but quite perceptible extent answer the question, With whom? It was a two-seater. It was known in the family as the Foot Bath, Colman's Mustard, and the Yellow Peril. As these names suggest, it was a low, open car of a clear yellow colour. Mr. Barnstaple used it to come up to the office from Sydenham because it did thirty-three miles to the gallon and was ever so much cheaper than a season ticket. It stood up in the court under the office window during the day. At Sydenham it lived in a shed of which Mr. Barnstaple carried the only key. So far he had managed to prevent the boys from either driving it or taking it to pieces. At times Mrs. Barnstaple made him drive her about Sydenham for her shopping, but she did not really like the little car because it exposed her to the elements too much and made her dusty and dishevelled. Both by reason of all that it made possible and by reason of all that it debarred, the little car was clearly indicated as the medium for the needed holiday. He drove very badly, but he drove very carefully; and though it sometimes stopped and refused to proceed, it did not do, or at any rate it had not so far done as most other things did in Mr. Barnstaple's life, which was to go due east when he turned the steering wheel west. So that it gave him an agreeable sense of mastery.

In the end Mr. Barnstaple made his decisions with great rapidity. Opportunity suddenly opened in front of him. Thursday was his day at the printer's, and he came home on Thursday evening feeling horribly jaded. The weather kept obstinately hot and dry. It made it none the less distressing that this drought presaged famine and misery for half the world. And London was in full season, smart and grinning: if anything it was a sillier year than 1913, the great tango year, which, in the light of subsequent events, Mr. Barnstaple had hitherto regarded as the silliest year in the world's history. The *Star* had the usual batch of bad news along the margin of the sporting and fashionable intelligence that got the displayed space. Fighting was going on between the Russians and Poles, and also in Ireland, Asia Minor, the Indian frontier, and Eastern Siberia. There had been three new horrible murders. The miners were still out, and a big engineering strike was threatened. There had been only standing room in the down train and it had started twenty minutes late.

He found a note from his wife explaining that her cousins at Wimbledon had telegraphed that there was an unexpected chance of seeing the tennis there with Mademoiselle Lenglen and all the rest of the champions, and that she had gone over with the boys and would not be back until late. It would do their game no end of good, she said, to see some really first-class tennis. Also it was the servants' social that night. Would he mind being left alone in the house for once? The servants would put him out some cold supper before they went.

Mr. Barnstaple read this note with resignation. While he ate his supper, he ran his eyes over a pamphlet a Chinese friend had sent him to show how the Japanese were deliberately breaking up what was left of the civilization and education of China.

It was only as he was sitting and smoking a pipe in his little back garden after supper that he realized all that being left alone in the house meant for him.

Then suddenly he became very active. He rang up Mr. Peeve, told him of the doctor's verdict, explained that the affairs of the *Liberal* were just then in a particularly leavable state, and got his holiday. Then he went to his bedroom and packed up a hasty selection of things to take with him in an old Gladstone bag that was not likely to be immediately missed, and put this in the dickey of his car. After which he spent some time upon a letter which he addressed to his wife and put away very carefully in his breast pocket.

Then he locked up the car-shed and composed himself in a deck chair in the garden with his pipe and a nice thoughtful book on the Bankruptcy of Europe, so as to look and feel as innocent as possible before his family came home.

When his wife returned he told her casually that he believed he was suffering from neurasthenia, and that he had arranged to run up to London on the morrow and consult a doctor in the matter.

Mrs. Barnstaple wanted to choose him a doctor, but he got out of that by saying that he had to consider Peeve in the matter and that Peeve was very strongly set on the man he had already in fact consulted. And when Mrs. Barnstaple said that she believed they *all* wanted a good holiday, he just grunted in a non-committal manner.

In this way Mr. Barnstaple was able to get right away from his house with all the necessary luggage for some weeks' holiday, without arousing any insurmountable opposition. He started next morning Londonward. The traffic on the way was gay and plentiful, but by no means troublesome, and the Yellow Peril was running so sweetly that she might almost have been named the Golden Hope. In Camberwell he turned into the Camberwell New Road and made his

way to the post office at the top of Vauxhall Bridge Road.
There he drew up. He was scared but elated by what he
was doing. He went into the post office and sent his wife
a telegram. "Dr. Pagan," he wrote, "says solitude and rest
urgently needed so am going off Lake District recuperate
have got bag and things expecting this letter follows."

Then he came outside and fumbled in his pocket and
produced and posted the letter he had written so carefully
overnight. It was deliberately scrawled to suggest neurasthenia at an acute phase. Dr. Pagan, it explained, had ordered
an immediate holiday and suggested that Mr. Barnstaple
should "wander north." It would be better to cut off all
letters for a few days, or even a week or so. He would not
trouble to write unless something went wrong. No news
would be good news. Rest assured all would be well. As
soon as he had a certain address for letters he would wire
it, but only very urgent things were to be sent on.

After this he resumed his seat in his car with such a sense
of freedom as he had never felt since his first holidays from
his first school. He made for the Great North Road, but at
the traffic jam at Hyde Park Corner he allowed the policeman
to turn him down towards Knightsbridge, and afterwards at
the corner where the Bath Road forks away from the Oxford
Road an obstructive van put him into the former. But it
did not matter very much. Any way led to Elsewhere and
he could work northward later.

§ 3

The day was one of those days of gay sunshine that were
characteristic of the great drought of 1921. It was not in
the least sultry. Indeed there was a freshness about it that
blended with Mr. Barnstaple's mood to convince him that
there were quite agreeable adventures before him. Hope
had already returned to him. He knew he was on the way

out of things, though as yet he had not the slightest suspicion
how completely out of things the way was going to take
him. It would be quite a little adventure presently to stop
at an inn and get some lunch, and if he felt lonely as he
went on he would give somebody a lift and talk. It would
be quite easy to give people lifts because so long as his
back was generally towards Sydenham and the *Liberal* office,
it did not matter at all now in which direction he went.

A little way out of Slough he was passed by an enormous
grey touring car. It made him start and swerve. It came
up alongside him without a sound, and though according
to his only very slightly inaccurate speedometer, he was
doing a good twenty-seven miles an hour, it had passed
him in a moment. Its occupants, he noted, were three gentlemen and a lady. They were all sitting up and looking
backward as though they were interested in something that
was following them. They went by too quickly for him to
note more than that the lady was radiantly lovely in an
immediate and indisputable way, and that the gentleman
nearest to him had a peculiarly elfin yet elderly face.

Before he could recover from the *eclat* of this passage a
car with the voice of a prehistoric saurian warned him that
he was again being overtaken. This was how Mr. Barnstaple liked being passed. By negotiation. He slowed down,
abandoned any claim to the crown of the road, and made
encouraging gestures with his hand. A large, smooth, swift
Limousine availed itself of his permission to use the thirty
odd feet or so of road to the right of him. It was carrying a
fair load of luggage, but except for a young gentleman with
an eye-glass who was sitting beside the driver, he saw nothing
of its passengers. It swept around a corner ahead in the
wake of the touring car.

Now even a mechanical foot-bath does not like being
passed in this lordly fashion on a bright morning on the open

road. Mr. Barnstaple's accelerator went down and he came round that corner a good ten miles per hour faster than his usual cautious practice. He found the road quite clear ahead of him.

Indeed he found the road much too clear ahead of him. It stretched straight in front for perhaps a third of a mile. On the left were a low, well-trimmed hedge, scattered trees, level fields, some small cottages lying back, remote poplars, and a distant view of Windsor Castle. On the right were level fields, a small inn, and a background of low, wooded hills. A conspicuous feature in this tranquil landscape was the board advertisment of a riverside hotel at Maidenhead. Before him was a sort of heat flicker in the air and two or three little dust whirls spinning along the road. And there was not a sign of the grey touring car and not a sign of the Limousine.

It took Mr. Barnstaple the better part of two seconds to realize the full astonishment of this fact. Neither to right nor left was there any possible side road down which either car could have vanished. And if they had already got round the further bend, then they must be travelling at the rate of two or three hundred miles per hour!

It was Mr. Barnstaple's excellent custom whenever he was in doubt to slow down. He slowed down now. He went on at a pace of perhaps fifteen miles an hour, staring open-mouthed about the empty landscape for some clue to this mysterious disappearance. Curiously enough he had no feeling that he himself was in any sort of danger.

Then his car seemed to strike something and skidded. It skidded round so violently that for a moment or so Mr. Barnstaple lost his head. He could not remember what ought to be done when a car skids. He recalled something vaguely about steering in the direction in which the car is skidding, but he could not make out in the excitement of the moment in what direction the car was skidding.

Afterwards he remembered that at this point he heard a sound. It was exactly the same sound, coming as the climax of an accumulating pressure, sharp like the snapping of a lute string, which one hears at the end—or beginning—of insensibility under anaesthetics.

He had seemed to twist round towards the hedge on the right, but now he found the road ahead of him again. He touched his accelerator and then slowed down and stopped. He stopped in the profoundest astonishment.

This was an entirely different road from the one he had been upon half a minute before. The hedges had changed, the trees had altered, Windsor Castle had vanished, and—a small compensation—the big Limousine was in sight again. It was standing by the roadside about two hundred yards away.

CHAPTER THE SECOND

THE WONDERFUL ROAD

§ 1

FOR a time Mr. Barnstaple's attention was very unequally divided between the Limousine, whose passengers were now descending, and the scenery about him. This latter was indeed so strange and beautiful that it was only as people who must be sharing his admiration and amazement and who therefore might conceivably help to elucidate and relieve his growing and quite overwhelming perplexity, that the little group ahead presently arose to any importance in his consciousness.

The road itself, instead of being the packed together pebbles and dirt smeared with tar with a surface of grit, dust, and animal excrement, of a normal English high road, was apparently made of glass, clear in places as still water and in places milky or opalescent, shot with streaks of soft colour or glittering richly with clouds of embedded golden flakes. It was perhaps twelve or fifteen yards wide. On either side was a band of greensward, of a finer grass than Mr. Barnstaple had ever seen before—and he was an expert and observant mower of lawns—and beyond this a wide border of flowers. Where Mr. Barnstaple sat agape in his car and perhaps for thirty yards in either direction this border was a mass of some unfamiliar blossom of forget-me-not blue. Then the colour was broken by an increasing number of tall, pure white spikes that finally ousted the blue altogether from the bed. On the opposite side of the way these same spikes were mingled with masses of plants bearing seed pods equally strange to Mr. Barnstaple, which varied through a series of blues and mauves and purples to an intense crimson. Beyond this gloriously coloured foam of flowers spread flat meadows on which creamy cattle were grazing. Three close at hand, a little startled perhaps by Mr. Barnstaple's sudden apparition, chewed the cud and regarded him with benevolently speculative eyes. They had long horns and dewlaps like the cattle of South Europe and India. From these benign creatures Mr. Barnstaple's eyes went to a long line of flame-shaped trees, to a colonade of white and gold, and to a background of snow-clad mountains. A few tall, white clouds were sailing across a sky of dazzling blue. The air impressed Mr. Barnstaple as being astonishingly clear and sweet.

Except for the cows and the little group of people standing by the Limousine Mr. Barnstaple could see no other living creatures at all. The motorists were standing still and staring about them. A sound of querulous voices came to him.

A sharp crepitation at his back turned Mr. Barnstaple's attention round. By the side of the road in the direction from which conceivably he had come were the ruins of what appeared to be a very recently demolished stone house. Beside it were two large apple trees freshly twisted and riven, as if by some explosion, and out of the centre of it came a column of smoke and this sound of things catching fire. And the contorted lines of these shattered apple trees helped Mr. Barnstaple to realize that some of the flowers by the wayside near at hand were also bent down to one side as if by the passage of a recent violent gust of wind. Yet he had heard no explosion nor felt any wind.

He stared for a time and then turned as if for an explanation to the Limousine. Three of these people were now coming along the road towards him, led by a tall, slender, grey-headed gentleman in a felt hat and a long motoring dust-coat. He had a small upturned face with a little nose that scarce sufficed for the springs of his gilt glasses. Mr. Barnstaple restarted his engine and drove slowly to meet them.

As soon as he judged himself within hearing distance he stopped and put his head over the side of the Yellow Peril with a question. At the same moment the tall, grey-headed gentleman asked practically the same question.

"Can you tell me at all, Sir, where we *are?*"

§ 2

"Five minutes ago," said Mr. Barnstaple, "I should have said we were on the Maidenhead Road. Near Slough."

"Exactly!" said the tall gentleman in earnest argumentative tones. "Exactly! And I maintain that there is not the slightest reason for supposing that we are not still on the Maidenhead Road."

The challenge of the dialectician rang in his voice.

"It doesn't *look* like the Maidenhead Road," said Mr. Barnstaple.

"Agreed! But are we to judge by appearances or are we to judge by the direct continuity of our experience? The Maidenhead Road led to this, was in continuity with this, and therefore I hold that this is the Maidenhead Road."

"Those mountains?" considered Mr. Barnstaple.

"Windsor Castle ought to be there," said the tall gentleman brightly as if he gave a point in a gambit.

"Was there five minutes ago," said Mr. Barnstaple.

"Then obviously those mountains are some sort of a camouflage," said the tall gentleman triumphantly, "and the whole of this business is, as they say nowadays, a put-up thing."

"It seems to be remarkably well put up," said Mr. Barnstaple.

Came a pause during which Mr. Barnstaple surveyed the tall gentleman's companions. The tall gentleman he knew perfectly well. He had seen him a score of times at public meetings and public dinners. He was Mr. Cecil Burleigh, the great Conservative leader. He was not only distinguished as a politician; he was eminent as a private gentleman, a philosopher and a man of universal intelligence. Behind him stood a short thick-set, middle aged young man, unknown to Mr. Barnstaple, the natural hostility of whose appearance was greatly enhanced by an eye-glass. The third member of the little group was also a familiar form, but for a time Mr. Barnstaple could not place him. He had a clean-shaven, round, plump face and a well-nourished person, and his costume suggested either a High Church clergyman or a prosperous Roman Catholic priest.

The young man with the eye-glass now spoke in a kind of impotent falsetto. "I came down to Taplow Court by road not a month ago and there was certainly nothing of this sort on the way then."

"I admit there are difficulties," said Mr. Burleigh with gusto. "I admit there are considerable difficulties. Still, I venture to think my main proposition holds."

"*You* don't think this is the Maidenhead Road?" said the gentleman with the eye-glass flatly to Mr. Barnstaple.

"It seems too perfect for a put-up thing," said Mr. Barnstaple with a mild obstinacy.

"But, my dear Sir!" protested Mr. Burleigh, "this road is *notorius* for nursery seedsmen, and sometimes they arrange the most astonishing displays. As an advertisement."

"Then why don't we go straight on to Taplow Court now?" asked the gentleman with the eye-glass.

"Because," said Mr. Burleigh, with the touch of asperity natural when one has to insist on a fact already clearly known, and obstinately overlooked, "Rupert insists that we are in some other world. And won't go on. That is why. He has always had too much imagination. He thinks that things that don't exist **can** exist. And now he imagines himself in

some sort of scientific romance and out of our world altogether. In another dimension. I sometimes think it would
have been better for all of us if Rupert had taken to writing
romances—instead of living them. If you, as his secretary,
think that you will be able to get him on to Taplow in time
for lunch with the Windsor people——"

Mr. Burleigh indicated by a gesture ideas for which he
found words inadequate.

Mr. Barnstaple had already noted a slow-moving, intent,
sandy-complexioned figure in a grey top hat with a black
band that the caricaturists had made familiar, exploring the
flowery tangle beside the Limousine. This then must be no
less well-known person than Rupert Catskill, the Secretary
of State for War. For once Mr. Barnstaple found himself
in entire agreement with this all too adventurous politician.
This *was* another world. Mr. Barnstaple got out of his car
and addressed himself to Mr. Burleigh. "I think we may
get a lot of light upon just where we are, Sir; if we explore
this building which is burning here close at hand. I thought
just now that I saw a figure lying on the slope close behind
it. If we could catch one of the hoaxers——"

He left his sentence unfinished because he did not believe for a moment that they were being hoaxed. Mr.
Burleigh had fallen very much in his opinion in the last
five minutes.

All four men turned their faces to the smoking ruin.

"It's a very extraordinary thing that there isn't a soul in
sight," remarked the eye glass gentleman searching the
horizon.

"Well, I see no harm whatever in finding out what is
burning," said Mr. Burleigh and led the way, upholding an
intelligent, anticipatory face towards the wrecked house
between the broken trees.

But before he had gone a dozen paces the attention of

the little group was recalled to the Limousine by a loud scream of terror from the lady who had remained seated therein.

§ 3

"Really this is too much!" cried Mr. Burleigh with a note of genuine exasperation. "There must surely be police regulations to prevent this kind of thing."

"It's out of some travelling menagerie," said the gentleman with the eye-glass. "What ought we to do?"

"It looks tame," said Mr. Barnstaple, but without any impulse to put his theory to the test.

"It might easily frighten people very seriously," said Mr. Burleigh. And lifting up a bland voice he shouted: "Don't be alarmed, Stella! It's probably quite tame and harmless. Don't *irritate* it with that sunshade. It might fly at you. Stel-*la!*"

"It" was a big and beautifully-marked leopard which had come very softly out of the flowers and sat down like a great cat in the middle of the glass road at the side of the big car. It was blinking and moving its head from side to side rhythmically, with an expression of puzzled interest, as the lady, in accordance with the best traditions of such cases, opened and shut her parasol at it as rapidly as she could. The chauffeur had taken cover behind the car. Mr. Rupert Catskill stood staring, knee-deep in flowers, apparently only made aware of the creature's existence by the same scream that had attracted the attention of Mr. Burleigh and his companions.

Mr. Catskill was the first to act, and his act showed his mettle. It was at once discreet and bold. "Stop flopping that sunshade, Lady Stella," he said. "Let me—I will—catch its eye."

He made a detour round the car so as to come face to

face with the animal. Then for a moment he stood, as it were, displaying himself, a resolute little figure in a grey frock coat and a black-banded top hat. He held out a cautious hand, not too suddenly for fear of startling the creature. *"Poossy!"* he said.

The leopard, relieved by the cessation of Lady Stella's sunshade, regarded him with interest and curiosity. He drew closer. The leopard extended its muzzle and sniffed.

"If it will only let me stroke it," said Mr. Catskill, and came within arm's length.

The beast sniffed the extended hand with an expression of incredulity. Then with a suddenness that sent Mr. Catskill back several paces, it sneezed. It sneezed again much more violently, regarded Mr. Catskill reproachfully for a moment, and then leapt lightly over the flower-bed and made off in the direction of the white and golden colonnade. The grazing cattle in the field, Mr. Barnstaple noted, watched its passage without the slightest sign of dismay.

Mr. Catskill remained in a slightly expanded state in the middle of the road. "No animal," he remarked, "can stand up to the steadfast gaze of the human eye. Not one. It is a riddle for your materialist. . . . Shall we join Mr. Cecil, Lady Stella? He seems to have found something to look at down there. The man in the little yellow car may know where he is. Hm?"

He assisted the lady to get out of the car and the two came on after Mr. Barnstaple's party, which was now again approaching the burning house. The chauffeur, evidently not wishing to be left alone with the Limousine in this world of incredible possibilities, followed as closely as respect permitted.

CHAPTER THE THIRD

THE BEAUTIFUL PEOPLE

§ 1

THE fire in the little house did not seem to be making headway. The smoke that came from it was much less now han when Mr. Barnstaple had first observed it. As they came close they found a quantity of twisted bits of bright metal and fragments of broken glass among the shattered masonry. The suggestion of exploded scientific apparatus was very strong. Then almost simultaneously the entire party became aware of a body lying on the grassy slope behind the ruin. It was the body of a man in the prime of life, naked except for a couple of bracelets and a necklace and girdle, and blood was oozing from his mouth and nostrils. With a kind of awe Mr. Barnstaple knelt down beside this prostrate figure and felt its still heart. He had never seen so beautiful a face and body before.

"Dead," he whispered.

"Look!" cried the shrill voice of the man with the eye-glass. "Another!"

He was pointing to something that was hidden from Mr. Barnstaple by a piece of wall. Mr. Barnstaple had to get up and climb over a heap of rubble before he could see this second find. It was a slender girl, clothed as little as the man. She had evidently been flung with enormous violence against the wall and killed instantaneously. Her face was quite undistorted although her skull had been crushed in from behind; her perfect mouth and green-grey eyes were a little open and her expression was that of one who is still thinking out some difficult but interesting problem. She did not seem in the least dead but merely disregardful. One hand still grasped a copper implement with a handle of glass. The other lay limp and prone.

For some seconds nobody spoke. It was as if they all feared to interrupt the current of her thoughts.

Then Mr. Barnstaple heard the voice of the priestly gentleman speaking very softly behind him. "What a *perfect* form!" he said.

"I admit I was wrong," said Mr. Burleigh with deliberation. "I have been wrong. . . . These are no earthly people. Manifestly. And *ergo,* we are not on earth. I cannot imagine what has happened nor where we are. In the face of sufficient evidence I have never hesitated to retract an opinion. This world we are in is not our world. It is something——"

He paused. "It is something very wonderful indeed."

"And the Windsor party," said Mr. Catskill without any apparent regret, "must have its lunch without us."

"But then," said the clerical gentleman, "what world *most* we in, and how did we get here?"

"Ah! *there,* said Mr. Burleigh, blandly, "you go altogether beyond my poor powers of guessing. We are here in some world that is singularly like our world and singularly unlike it. It must be in some way related to our world or we could not be here. But how it can be related is, I confess, a hopeless mystery to me. Maybe we are in some other dimension of space than those we wot of. But my poor head whirls at the thought of these dimensions. I am—— I am *mazed—mazed.*"

"Einstein," injected the gentleman with the eye-glass compactly and with evident self-satisfaction.

"Exactly!" said Mr. Burleigh. "Einstein might make it clear to us. Or dear old Haldane might undertake to explain it and fog us up with that adipose Hegelianism of his. But I am neither Haldane nor Einstein. Here we are in some world which is, for all practical purposes, including the purposes of our week-end engagements, Nowhere. Or if you prefer the Greek of it, we are in Utopia. And as I do not see that there is any manifest way out of it again, I suppose the thing we have to do as rational creatures is to make the best of it. And watch our opportunities. It is certainly a very lovely world. The loveliness is even greater than the wonder. And there are human beings here—with minds. I judge from all this material lying about, it is a world in which experimental chemistry is pursued—pursued indeed to the bitter end—under almost idyllic conditions. Chemistry— and nakedness. I feel bound to confess that whether we are to regard these two people who have apparently just blown themselves up here, as Greek gods or as naked savages, seems to me to be altogether a question of individual taste. I admit a bias for the Greek god—and goddess."

"Except that it is a little difficult to think of two dead immortals," squeaked the gentleman of the eye-glass in the tone of one who scores a point.

Mr. Burleigh was about to reply, and to judge from his ruffled expression his reply would have been of a disciplinary nature. But instead he exclaimed sharply and turned round to face two newcomers. The whole party had become aware of them at the same moment. Two stark Appollos stood over the ruin and were regarding our Earthlings with an astonish- ment at least as great as that they created.

One spoke, and Mr. Barnstaple was astonished beyond measure to find understandable words reverberating in his mind.

"Red Gods!" cried the Utopian. "What things are you? And how did you get into the world?"

(English! It would have been far less astounding if they

had spoken Greek. But that they should speak any known language was a matter for incredulous amazement.)

§ 2

Mr. Cecil Burleigh was the least disconcerted of the party. "Now," he said, "we may hope to learn something definite— face to face with rational and articulate creatures."

He cleared his throat, grasped the lapels of his long dust coat with two long nervous hands, and assumed the duties of spokesman. "We are quite unable, gentlemen, to account for our presence here," he said. "We are as puzzled as you are. We have discovered ourselves suddenly in your world instead of our own."

"You come from another world?"

"Exactly. A quite different world. In which we have all our natural and proper places. We were travelling in that world of ours in—Ah!—certain vehicles, when suddenly we discovered ourselves here. Intruders, I admit, but, I can assure you, innocent and unpremeditated intruders."

"You do not know how it is that Arden and Greenlake have failed in their experiment and how it is that they are dead?"

"If Arden and Greenlake are the names of these two beautiful young people here, we know nothing about them except that we found them lying as you see them when we came from the road hither to find out or, in fact, to in-quire——"

He cleared his throat and left his sentence with a floating end.

The Utopian, if we may for convenience call him that, who had first spoken, looked now at his companion and seemed to question him mutely. Then he turned to the Earthlings again. He spoke and again those clear tones rang, not—so it seemed to Mr. Barnstaple—in his ears but within his head.

"It will be well if you and your friends do not trample this wreckage. It will be well if you all return to the road. Come with me. My brother here will put an end to this burning and do what needs to be done to our brother and sister. And afterwards this place will be examined by those who understand the work that was going on here."

"We must throw ourselves entirely upon your hospitality," said Mr. Burleigh. "We are entirely at your disposal. This encounter, let me repeat, was not of our seeking."

"Though we should certainly have sought it if we had known of its possibility," said Mr. Catskill, addressing the world at large and glancing at Mr. Barnstaple as if for confirmation. "We find this world of yours—*most* attractive."

"At the first encounter," the gentleman with the eye-glass endorsed, "a *are* attractive world."

As they returned through the thick growing flowers to the road, in the wake of the Utopian and Mr. Burleigh, Mr. Barnstaple found Lady Stella rustling up beside him. Her words, in this setting of pure wonder, filled him with amazement at their serene and invincible ordinariness. "Haven't we met before somewhere—at lunch or something—Mr.— Mr.——?"

Was all this no more than a show? He stared at her blankly for a moment before supplying her with:

"Barnstaple."

"Mr. Barnstaple?"

His mind came into line with hers.

"I've never had that pleasure, Lady Stella. Though, of course, I know you—I know you very well from your photographs in the weekly illustrated papers."

"Did you hear what it was that Mr. Cecil was saying just now? About this being Utopia?"

"He said we might *call* it Utopia."

"So like Mr. Cecil. But is it Utopia?—*really* Utopia?"

"I've always longed so to be in Utopia," the lady went on without waiting for Mr. Barnstaple's reply to her question. "What splendid young men these two Utopians appear to be! They must, I am sure, belong to its aristocracy—in spite of their—informal—costume. Or even because of it." . . .

Mr. Barnstaple had a happy thought. "I have also recognized Mr. Burleigh and Mr. Rupert Catskill, Lady Stella, but I should be so glad if you would tell me who the young gentleman with the eyeglass is, and the clerical gentleman. They are close behind us."

Lady Stella imparted her information in a charmingly confidential undertone. "The eyeglass," she murmured, "is—I am going to spell it—F.R.E.D.D.Y. M.U.S.H. Taste Good taste. He is awfully clever at finding out young poets and all that sort of literary thing. And he's Rupert's secretary. If there is a literary Academy, they say, he's certain to be in it. He's dreadfully critical and sarcastic. We were going to Taplow for a perfectly intellectual week-end, quite like the old times. So soon as the Windsor people had gone again, that is. . . . Mr. Gosse was coming and Max Beerbohm —and everyone like that. But nowadays something always happens. Always. . . . The unexpected—almost excessively. . . . The clerical collar"—she glanced back to judge whether she was within earshot of the gentleman under discussion— "is Father Amerton, who is so dreadfully outspoken about the sins of society and all *that* sort of thing. It's odd, but out of the pulpit he's inclined to be shy and quiet and a little awkward with the forks and spoons. Paradoxical, isn't it?"

"Of *course!*" cried Mr. Barnstaple. "I remember him now. I knew his face but I couldn't place it. Thank you so much, Lady Stella."

§ 3

There was something very reassuring to Mr. Barnstaple in the company of these famous and conspicuous people and particularly in the company of Lady Stella. She was indeed heartening: she brought so much of the dear old world with her, and she was so manifestly prepared to subjugate this new world to its standards at the earliest possible opportunity. She fended off much of the wonder and beauty that had threatened to submerge Mr. Barnstaple altogether. Meeting her and her company was in itself for a man in his position a minor but considerable adventure that helped to bridge the gulf of astonishment between the humdrum of his normal experiences and this all too bracing Utopian air. It solidified, it—if one may use the word in such connexion—it *degraded* the luminous splendour about him towards complete credibility that it should also be seen and commented on by her and by Mr. Burleigh, and viewed through the appraising monocle of Mr. Freddy Mush. It brought it within range of the things that get into the newspapers. Mr. Barnstaple alone in Utopia might have been so completely overawed as to have been mentally overthrown. This easy-mannered brown skinned divinity who was now exchanging questions with Mr. Burleigh was made mentally accessible by that great man's intervention.

Yet it was with something very like a catching of the breath that Mr. Barnstaple's attention reverted from the Limousine people to this noble-seeming world into which he and they had fallen. What sort of beings really were these men and women of a world where ill-bred weeds, it seemed, had ceased to thrust and fight amidst the flowers, and where leopards void of feline malice looked out with friendly eyes upon the passerby?

It was astounding that the first two inhabitants they had found in this world of subjugated nature should be lying dead, victims, it would seem, of some hazardous experiment. It was still more astonishing that this other pair who called themselves the brothers of the dead man and woman, should betray so little grief or dismay at the tragedy. There had been no emotional scene at all, Mr. Barnstaple realized, no consternation or weeping. They were evidently much more puzzled and interested than either horrified or distressed.

The Utopian who had remained in the ruin, had carried out the body of the girl to lay it beside her companion's, and he had now, Mr. Barnstaple saw, returned to a close scrutiny of the wreckage of the experiment.

But now more of these people were coming upon the scene. They had aeroplanes in this world, for two small ones, noiseless and swift in their flight as swallows, had landed in the fields near by. A man had come up along the road on a machine like a small two-wheeled two-seater with its wheels in series, bicycle fashion; lighter and neater it was than any earthly automobile and mysteriously able to stand up on its two wheels while standing still. A burst of laughter from down the road called Mr. Barnstaple's attention to a group of these Utopians who had apparently found something exquisitely ridiculous in the engine of the Limousine. Most of these people were as scantily clothed and as beautifully built as the two dead experimentalists, but one or two were wearing big hats of straw, and one who seemed to be an older woman of thirty or more wore a robe of white bordered by an intense red line. She was speaking now to Mr. Burleigh.

Although she was a score of yards away, her speech presented itself in Mr. Barnstaple's mind with great distinctness.

"We do not even know as yet what connexion your coming into our world may have with the explosion that has just happened here or whether, indeed, it has any connexion. We want to inquire into both these things. It

will be reasonable, we think, to take you and all the possessions you have brought with you to a convenient place
for a conference not very far from here. We are arranging
for machines to take you thither. There perhaps you will
eat. I do not know when you are accustomed to eat?"

"Refreshment," said Mr. Burleigh, rather catching at the
idea. "Some refreshment would certainly be acceptable before very long. In fact, had we not fallen so sharply out
of our own world into yours, by this time we should have
been lunching—lunching in the best of company."

"Wonder and lunch," thought Mr. Barnstaple. Man is
a creature who must eat by necessity whether he wonder
or no. Mr. Barnstaple perceived indeed that he was already
hungry and that the air he was breathing was a keen and
appetizing air.

The Utopian seemed struck by a novel idea. "Do you
eat several times a day? What sort of things do you eat?"

"Oh! Surely! They're *not* vegetarians!" cried Mr. Mush
sharply in a protesting parenthesis, dropping his eyeglass
from its socket.

They were all hungry. It showed upon their faces.

"We are all accustomed to eat several times a day," said
Mr. Burleigh. "Perhaps it would be well if I were to give
you a brief resume of our dietary. There may be differences.
We begin, as a rule, with a simple cup of tea and the thinnest
slice of bread-and-butter brought to the bedside. Then comes
breakfast." . . . He proceeded to a masterly summary of his
gastronomic day, giving clearly and attractively the particulars
of an English breakfast, eggs to be boiled four and a half
minutes, neither more or less, lunch with any light wine,
tea rather a social rally than a serious meal, dinner, in some
detail, the occasional resort to supper. It was one of those
clear statements which would have rejoiced the House of
Commons, light, even gay, and yet with a trace of earnestness.

The Utopian woman regarded him with deepening interest as he proceeded. "Do you all eat in this fashion?" she asked.

Mr. Burleigh ran his eye over his party. "I cannot answer for Mr.—Mr.——?"

"Barnstaple. . . . Yes, I eat in much the same fashion."

For some reason the Utopian woman smiled at him. She had very pretty brown eyes, and though he liked her to smile he wished that she had not smiled in the way she did.

"And you sleep?" she asked.

"From six to ten hours, according to circumstances," said Mr. Burleigh.

"And you make love?"

The question perplexed and to a certain extent shocked our Earthlings. What exactly did she mean? For some moments no one framed a reply. Mr. Barnstaple's mind was filled with a hurrying rush of strange possibilities.

Then Mr. Burleigh, with his fine intelligence and the quick evasiveness of a modern leader of men, stepped into the breach. "Not habitually, I can assure you," he said. "Not habitually."

The woman with the red-bordered robe seemed to think this over for a swift moment. Then she smiled faintly.

"We must take you somewhere where we can talk of all these things," she said. "Manifestly you come from some strange other world. Our men of knowledge must get to-gether with you and exchange ideas."

§ 4

At half-past ten that morning Mr. Barnstaple had been motoring along the main road through Slough, and now at half-past one he was soaring through wonderland with his own world half forgotten. "Marvellous," he repeated. "Marvellous. I knew that I should have a good holiday. But *this, this*——*!*"

He was extraordinarily happy with the bright unclouded happiness of a perfect dream. Never before had he enjoyed the delights of an explorer in new lands, never before had he hoped to experience these delights. Only a few weeks before he had written an article for the *Liberal* lamenting the "End of the Age of Exploration," an article so thoroughly and aimlessly depressing that it had pleased Mr. Peeve extremely. He recalled that exploit now with but the faintest twinge of remorse.

The Earthling party had been distributed among four small aeroplanes and as Mr. Barnstaple and his companion, Father Amerton, rose in the air, he looked back to see the automobiles and luggage being lifted with astonishing ease into two lightly built lorries. Each lorry put out a pair of glittering arms and lifted up its automobile as a nurse might lift up a baby.

By contemporary earthly standards of safety Mr. Barnstaple's aviator flew very low. There were times when he passed between trees rather than over them, and this, even if at first it was a little alarming, permitted a fairly close inspection of the landscape. For the earlier part of the journey it was garden pasture with grazing creamy cattle and patches of brilliantly coloured vegetation of a nature unknown to Mr. Barnstaple. Amidst this cultivation narrow tracks, which may have been foot or cycle tracks, threaded their way. Here and there ran a road bordered with flowers and shaded by fruit trees.

There were few houses and no towns or villages at all. The houses varied very greatly in size, from little isolated buildings which Mr. Barnstaple thought might be elegant summer-houses or little temples, to clusters of roofs and turrets which reminded him of country chateaux or suggested extensive farming or dairying establishments. Here and there people were working in the fields or going to and fro on foot or on machines, but the effect of the whole was of an extremely underpopulated land.

It became evident that they were going to cross the range of snowy mountains that had so suddenly blotted the distant view of Windsor Castle from the landscape.

As they approached these mountains, broad stretches of golden corn-land replaced the green of the pastures and then the cultivation became more diversified. He noted unmistakable vineyards on sunny slopes, and the number of workers visible and the habitations multiplied. The little squadron of aeroplanes flew up a broad valley towards a pass so that Mr. Barnstaple was able to scrutinize the mountain scenery. Came chestnut woods and at last pines. There were Cyclopean turbines athwart the mountain torrents and long, low, many windowed buildings that might serve some industrial purpose. A skilfully graded road with exceedingly bold, light and beautiful viaducts mounted towards the pass. There were more people, he thought, in the highland country than in the levels below, though still far fewer than he would have seen upon any comparable countryside on earth.

Ten minutes of craggy desolation with the snow-fields of a great glacier on one side intervened before he descended into the upland valley on the Conference Place where presently he alighted. This was a sort of lap in the mountain, terraced by masonry so boldly designed that it seemed a part of the geological substance of the mountain itself. It faced towards a wide artificial lake retained by a stupendous dam from the lower reaches of the valley. At intervals along this dam there were great stone pillars dimly suggestive of seated figures. He glimpsed a wide plain beyond, which reminded him of the valley of the Po, and then as he descended the straight line of the dam came up to hide this further vision.

Upon these terraces, and particularly upon the lower ones,

were groups and clusters of flowerlike buildings, and he distinguished paths and steps and pools of water as if the whole place were a garden.

The aeroplanes made an easy landing on a turfy expanse. Close at hand was a graceful chalet that ran out from the shores of the lake over the water and afforded mooring to a flotilla of gaily coloured boats. . . .

It was Father Amerton who had drawn Mr. Barnstaple's attention to the absence of villages. He now remarked that there was no church in sight and that nowhere had they seen any spires or belfries. But Mr. Barnstaple thought that some of the smaller buildings might be temples or shrines. "Religion may take different forms here," he said.

"And how few babies or little children are visible!" Father Amerton remarked. "Nowhere have I seen a mother with her child."

"On the other side of the mountains there was a place like the playing field of a big school. There were children there and one or two older people dressed in white."

"I saw that. But I was thinking of babes. Compare this with what one would see in Italy.

"The most beautiful and desirable young women," added the reverend gentleman; *"most* desirable—and not a sign of maternity!"

Their aviator, a sun-tanned blond with very blue eyes, helped them out of the machine, and they stood watching the descent of the other members of their party. Mr. Barnstaple was astonished to note how rapidly he was becoming familiarized with the colour and harmony of this new world; the strangest things in the whole spectacle now were the figures and clothing of his associates. Mr. Rupert Catskill in his celebrated grey top hat, Mr. Mush with his preposterous eye-glass, the peculiar long slenderness of Mr. Burleigh, and the square leather-clad lines of Mr. Burleigh's chauffeur, struck him as being far more incredible than the graceful Utopian forms about him.

The aviator's interest and amusement enhanced Mr. Barn-staple's perception of his companion's oddity. And then came a wave of profound doubt.

"I suppose this is *really* real," he said to Father Amerton.

"Really real! What else can it be?"

"I suppose we are not dreaming all this."

"Are your dreams and my dreams likely to coincide?"

"Yes; but there are quite impossible things—absolutely impossible things."

"As, for instance?"

"Well, how is it that these people are speaking to us in English—modern English?"

"I never thought of that. It is rather incredible. They don't talk in English to one another."

Mr. Barnstaple stared in round-eyed amazement at Father Amerton, struck for the first time by a still more incredible fact. "They don't talk in *anything* to one another," he said. "And we haven't noticed it until this moment!"

CHAPTER THE FOURTH

THE SHADOW OF EINSTEIN FALLS ACROSS THE STORY
BUT PASSES LIGHTLY BY

§ 1

EXCEPT for that one perplexing fact that all these Utopians had apparently a complete command of idiomatic English, Mr. Barnstaple found his vision of this new world developing with a congruity that no dream in his experience had ever possessed. It was so coherent, so orderly, that less and less was it like a strange world at all and more and more like an arrival in some foreign but very highly civilized country.

Under the direction of the brown-eyed woman in the scarlet-edged robe, the Earthlings were established in their quarters near the Conference Place in the most hospitable and comfortable fashion conceivable. Five or six youths and girls made it their business to initiate the strangers in the little details of Utopian domesticity. The separate buildings in which they were lodged had each an agreeable little dressing room, and the bed, which had sheets of the finest linen and a very light puffy coverlet, stood in an open loggia—too open Lady Stella thought, but then as she said, "One feels so safe here." The luggage appeared and the valises were identified as if they were in some hospitable earthly mansion.

But Lady Stella had to turn two rather too friendly youths out of her apartment before she could open her dressing-bag and administer refreshment to her complexion.

A few minutes later some excitement was caused by an outbreak of wild laughter and the sounds of an amiable but hysterical struggle that came from Lady Stella's retreat. The girl who had remained with her had displayed a quite femminine interest in her equipment and had come upon a particularly charming and diaphanous sleeping suit. For some obscure reason this secret daintiness amused the young Utopian extremely, and it was with some difficulty that Lady Stella restrained her from putting the garment on and dancing out in it for a public display. "Then *you* put it on," the girl insisted.

"But you don't understand," cried Lady Stella. "It's almost—*sacred!* It's for nobody to see—*ever*.

"But *why?*" the Utopian asked, puzzled beyond measure.

Lady Stella found an answer impossible.

The light meal that followed was by terrestrial standards an entirely satisfactory one. The anxiety of Mr. Freddy Mush was completely allayed: there were cold chicken and ham and a very pleasant meat pate. There were also rather coarsegrained but most palatable bread, pure butter, an exquisite salad, fruit, cheese of the Gruyere type, and a light white wine which won from Mr. Burleigh the tribute that "Moselle never did anything better."

"You find our food very like your own?" asked the woman in the red-trimmed robe.

"Eckquithit quality," said Mr. Mush with his mouth rather full.

"Food has changed very little in the last three thousand years. People had found out all the best things to eat long before the Age of Confusion."

"It's too real to be real," Mr. Barnstaple repeated to himself. "Too real to be real."

He looked at his companions, elated, interested and eating with appreciation.

If it wasn't for the absurdity of these Utopians speaking English with a clearness that tapped like a hammer inside

his head Mr. Barnstaple would have had no doubt whatever
of his reality.

No servants waited at the clothless stone table; the woman
in the white and scarlet robe and the two aviators shared
the meal and the guests attended to each other's requirements. Mr. Burleigh's chauffeur was for modestly shrinking
to another table until the great statesman reassured him
with: "Sit down there, Penk. Next to Mr. Mush." Other
Utopians with friendly but keenly observant eyes upon the
Earthlings came into the great pillared veranda in which the
meal had been set, and smiled and stood about or sat down.
There were no introductions and few social formalities.

"All this is most reassuring," said Mr. Burleigh. "Most
reassuring. I'm bound to say these beat the Chatsworth
peaches. Is that cream, my dear Rupert, in the little brown
jar in front of you? . . . I guessed as much. If you are sure
you can spare it, Rupert. . . . Thank you."

§ 2

Several of the Utopians made themselves known by name
to the Earthlings. All their voices sounded singularly alike
to Mr. Barnstaple and the words were as clear as print.
The brown-eyed woman's name was Lychnis. A man with
a beard who might perhaps, Mr. Barnstaple thought, have
been as old as forty, was either Urthred or Adam or Edom,
the name for all its sharpness of enunciation had been very
difficult to catch. It was as if large print *hesitated*. Urthred
conveyed that he was an ethnologist and historian and that
he desired to learn all that he possibly could about the ways
of our world. He impressed Mr. Barnstaple as having the
easy carriage of some earthly financier or great newspaper
proprietor rather than the diffidence natural in our own
everyday world to a merely learned man. Another of their
hosts, Serpentine, was also, Mr. Barnstaple learnt with sur-

prise, for his bearing too was almost masterful, a scientific man. He called himself something that Mr. Barnstaple could not catch. First it sounded like "atomic mechanician," and then oddly enough it sounded like "molecular chemist." And then Mr. Barnstaple heard Mr. Burleigh say to Mr. Mush, "He said 'physio-chemist, didn't he?"

"I thought he just called himself a materialist," said Mr. Mush.

"I thought he said he weighed things," said Lady Stella.

"Their intonation is peculiar," said Mr. Burleigh. "Sometimes they are almost too loud for comfort and then there is a kind of gap in the sounds." . . .

When the meal was at an end the whole party removed to another little building that was evidently planned for classes and discussions. It had a semi-circular apse round which ran a series of white tablets which evidently functioned at times as a lecturer's blackboard, since there were black and coloured pencils and cloths for erasure lying on a marble ledge at a convenient height below the tablets. The lecturer could walk from point to point of this semi-circle as he talked. Lychnis, Urthred, Serpentine and the Earthlings seated themselves on a semicircular bench below this lecturer's track, and there was accommodation for about eighty or a hundred people upon the seats before them. All these were occupied, and beyond stood a number of graceful groups against a background of rhododendronlike bushes, between which Mr. Barnstaple caught glimpses of grassy vistas leading down to the shining waters of the lake.

They were going to talk over this extraordinary irruption into their world. Could anything be more reasonable than to talk it over? Could anything be more fantastically impossible?

"Odd that there are no swallows," said Mr. Mush suddenly in Mr. Barnstaple's ear. "I wonder why there are no swallows."

Mr. Barnstaple's attention went to the empty sky. "No gnats nor flies perhaps," he suggested. It was odd that he had not missed the swallows before.

"Sssh!" said Lady Stella. "He's beginning."

§ 3

This incredible conference began. It was opened by the man named Serpentine, and he stood before his audience and seemed to make a speech. His lips moved, his hands assisted his statements; his expression followed his utterance. And yet Mr. Barnstaple had the most subtle and indefensible doubt whether indeed Serpentine was speaking. There was something odd about the whole thing. Sometimes the thing said sounded with a peculiar resonance in his head; sometimes it was indistinct and elusive like an object seen through troubled waters; sometimes though Serpentine still moved his fine hands and looked towards his hearers, there were gaps of absolute silence—as if for brief intervals Mr. Barnstaple had gone deaf. . . . Yet it was a discourse; it held together and it held Mr. Barnstaple's attention.

Serpentine had the manner of one who is taking great pains to be as simple as possible with a rather intricate question. He spoke, as it were, in propositions with a pause between each. "It had long been known," he began, "that the possible number of dimensions, like the possible number of anything else that could be enumerated, was unlimited!"

Yes, Mr. Barnstaple had got that, but it proved too much for Mr. Freddy Mush.

"Oh, Lord!" he said. "Dimensions!" and dropped his eye-glass and became despondently inattentive.

"For most practical purposes," Serpentine continued, "the particular universe, the particular system of events, in which we found ourselves and of which we formed part, could

be regarded as occurring in a space of three rectilinear dimensions and as undergoing translation, which translation
was in fact duration, through a fourth dimension, *time*. Such
a system of events was necessarily a gravitational system."

"Er!" said Mr. Burleigh sharply. "Excuse me! I don't
see that."

So he, at any rate, was following it too.

"Any universe that endures must necessarily gravitate,"
Serpentine repeated, as if he were asserting some self-evident
fact.

"For the life of me I can't see that," said Mr. Burleigh
after a moment's reflection.

Serpentine considered him for a moment. "It is so," he
said, and went on with his discourse. Our minds, he continued, had been evolved in the form of this practical conception of things, they accepted it as true, and it was only
by great efforts of sustained analysis that we were able to
realize that this universe in which we lived not only extended
but was, as it were, slightly bent and contorted, into a
number of other long unsuspected spatial dimensions. It
extended beyond its three chief spatial dimensions into these
others just as a thin sheet of paper, which is practically two
dimensional, extended not only by virtue of its thickness but
also of its crinkles and curvature into a third dimension.

"Am I going deaf?" asked Lady Stella in a stage whisper.
"I can't catch a word of all this."

"Nor I," said Father Amerton.   ·

Mr. Burleigh made a pacifying gesture towards these
unfortunates without taking his eyes off Serpentine's face.
Mr. Barnstaple knitted his brows, clasped his knees, knotted
his fingers, held on desperately.

He *must* be hearing—of course he was hearing!

Serpentine proceeded to explain that just as it would be
possible for any number of practically two-dimensional

universes to lie side by side, like sheets of paper, in a three dimensional space, so in the many dimensional space about which the ill-equipped human mind is still slowly and painfully acquiring knowledge, it is possible for an innumerable quantity of practically three-dimensional universes to lie, as it were, side by side and to undergo a roughly parallel movement through time. The speculative work of Lonestone and Cephalus had long since given the soundest basis for the belief that there actually were a very great number of such space-and-time universes, parallel to one another and resembling each other, nearly but not actually, much as the leaves of a book might resemble one another. All of them would have duration, all of them would be gravitating systems——

(Mr. Burleigh shook his head to show that still he didn't see it.)

—And those lying closest together would most nearly resemble each other. How closely they now had an opportunity of learning. For the daring attempts of those two great geniuses, Arden and Greenlake, to use the— *(inaudible)* —thrust of the atom to rotate a portion of the Utopian material universe in that dimension, the F dimension, into which it had long been known to extend for perhaps the length of a man's arm, to rotate this fragment of Utopian matter, much as a gate is swung on its hinges, had manifestly been altogether succesful. The gate had swung back again, bringing with it a breath of close air, a storm of dust, and, to the immense amazement of Utopia, three sets of visitors from an unknown world.

"Three?" whispered Mr. Barnstaple, doubtfully. "Did he say *three?"*

[Serpentine disregarded him.]

"Our brother and sister have been killed by some unexpected release of force, but their experiment has opened a way that now need never be closed again, out of the present spatial limitations of Utopia into a whole vast folio of hitherto unimagined worlds. Close at hand to us, even as Lonestone guessed ages ago, nearer to us, as he put it, than the blood in our hearts——"

("Nearer to us than breathing and closer than hands and feet," Father Amerton misquoted, waking up suddenly. "But what is he talking about? I don't catch it.")

"—we discover another planet, much the same size as ours to judge by the scale of its inhabitants, circulating, we may certainly assume, round a sun like that in our skies, a planet bearing life and being slowly subjugated; even as our own is being subjugated, by intelligent life which has evidently evolved under almost exactly parallel conditions to those of our own evolution. This sister universe to ours is, so far as we may judge by appearances, a little retarded in time in relation to our own. Our visitors wear something very like the clothing and display physical characteristics resembling those of our ancestors during the last Age of Confusion. . . .

"We are not yet justified in supposing that their history has been strictly parallel to ours. No two particles of matter are alike; no two vibrations. In all the dimensions of being, in all the universes of God, there has never been and there can never be an exact repetition. That we have come to realize is the one impossible thing. Nevertheless, this world you call Earth is manifestly very near and like to this universe of ours. . . .

"We are eager to learn from you Earthlings, to check our history, which is still very imperfectly known, by your experiences, to show you what we know, to make out what may be possible and desirable in intercourse and help between the people of your planet and ours. We, here, are the merest beginners in knowledge; we have learnt as yet scarcely anything more than the immensity of the things that we have yet to learn and do. In a million kindred things our two worlds may perhaps teach each other and help each other. . . .

"Possibly there are streaks of heredity in your planet that have failed to develop or that have died out in ours. Possibly there are elements or minerals in one world that are rare or wanting in the other. . . . The structure of your atoms (?) . . . our worlds may intermarry (?) . . . to their common invigoration. . . ."

He passed into the inaudible just when Mr. Barnstaple was most moved and most eager to follow what he was saying. Yet a deaf man would have judged he was still speaking.

Mr. Barnstaple met the eye of Mr. Rupert Catskill, as distressed and puzzled as his own. Father Amerton's face was buried in his hands. Lady Stella and Mr. Mush were whispering softly together; they had long since given up any pretence of listening.

"Such," said Serpentine, abruptly becoming audible again, "is our first rough interpretation of your apparition in our world and of the possibilities of our interaction. I have put our ideas before you as plainly as I can. I would suggest that now one of you tell us simply and plainly what *you* conceive to be the truth about your world in relation to ours."

CHAPTER THE FIFTH

THE GOVERNANCE AND HISTORY OF UTOPIA

§ 1

CAME a pause. The Earthlings looked at one another and their gaze seemed to converge upon Mr. Cecil Burleigh. That statesman feigned to be unaware of the general expectation. "Rupert," he said. "Won't *you?*"

"I reserve my comments," said Mr. Catskill.

"Father Amerton, you are accustomed to treat of other worlds."

"Not in your presence, Mr. Cecil. No."

"But what am I to tell them?"

"What you think of it," said Mr. Barnstaple.

"Exactly," said Mr. Catskill. "Tell them what you think of it."

No one else appeared to be worthy of consideration. Mr. Burleigh rose slowly and walked thoughtfully to the centre of the semicircle. He grasped his coat lapels and remained for some moments with face downcast as if considering what he was about to say. "Mr. Serpentine," he began at last, raising a candid countenance and regarding the blue sky above the distant lake through his glasses. "Ladies and Gentlemen——"

He was going to make a speech!—as though he was at a Primrose League garden party—or Geneva. It was preposterous and yet, what else was there to be done?

"I must confess, Sir, that although I am by no means a novice at public speaking, I find myself on this occasion somewhat at a loss. Your admirable discourse, Sir, simple,

43

direct, lucid, compact, and rising at times to passages of of unaffected eloquence, has set me a pattern that I would fain follow—and before which, in all modesty, I quail. You ask me to tell you as plainly and clearly as possible the outline facts as we conceive them about this kindred world out of which with so little premeditation we have come to you. So far as my poor powers of understanding or discussing such recondite matters go, I do not think I can better or indeed supplement in any way your marvellous exposition of the mathematical aspects of the case. What you have told us embodies the latest, finest thoughts of terrestrial science and goes, indeed, far beyond our current ideas. On certain matters, in, for example, the relationship of time and gravitation, I feel bound to admit that I do not go with you, but that is rather a failure to understand your position than any positive dissent. Upon the broader aspects of the case there need be no difficulties between us. We accept your main propositions unreservedly; namely, that we con-ceive ourselves to be living in a parallel universe to yours, on a planet the very brother of your own, indeed quite amazingly like yours, having regard to all the possible con-trasts we might have found here. We are attracted by and strongly disposed to accept your view that our system is, in all probability, a little less seasoned and mellowed by the touch of time than yours, short perhaps by some hundreds or some thousands of years of your experiences. Assuming this, it is inevitable, Sir, that a certain humility should mingle in our attitude towards you. As your juniors it becomes us not to instruct but to learn. It is for us to ask: What have you done? To what have you reached? rather than to display to you with an artless arrogance all that still remains for us to learn and do. . . ."

"No!" said Mr. Barnstaple to himself but half audibly. "This is a dream.   . If it were anyone else. . . ."

He rubbed his knuckles into his eyes and opened them again, and there he was still, sitting next to Mr. Mush in the midst of these Olympian divinities. And Mr. Burleigh, that polished sceptic, who never believed, who was never astonished, was leaning forward on his toes and speaking, speaking, with the assurance of a man who has made ten thousand speeches. He could not have been more sure of himself and his audience in the Guildhall in London. And they were understanding him! Which was absurd!

There was nothing to do but to fall in with this stupendous absurdity—and sit and listen. Sometimes Mr. Barnstaple's mind wandered altogether from what Mr. Burleigh was saying. Then it returned and hung desperately to his discourse. In his halting, parliamentary way, his hands trifling with his glasses or clinging to the lapels of his coat, Mr. Burleigh was giving Utopia a brief account of the world of men, seeking to be elementary and lucid and reasonable, telling them of states and empires, of wars and the Great War, of economic organization and disorganization, of revolutions and Bolshevism, of the terrible Russian famine that was beginning, of the difficulties of finding honest statesmen and officials, and of the unhelpfulness of newspapers, of all the dark and troubled spectacle of human life. Serpentine had used the term "the Last Age of Confusion," and Mr. Burleigh had seized upon the phrase and was making much of it. . . .

It was a great oratorical impromptu. It must have gone on for an hour, and the Utopians listened with keen, attentive faces, now and then nodding their acceptance and recognition of this statement or that. "Very like," would come tapping into Mr. Barnstaple's brain. "With us also—in the Age of Confusion."

At last Mr. Burleigh, with the steady deliberation of an old parliamentary hand, drew to his end. Compliments.

He bowed. He had done. Mr. Mush startled everyone by a vigorous hand-clapping in which no one else joined.

The tension in Mr. Barnstaple's mind had become intolerable. He leapt to his feet.

§ 2

He stood making those weak propitiatory gestures that come so naturally to the inexperienced speaker. "Ladies and Gentlemen," he said. "Utopians, Mr. Burleigh! I crave your pardon for a moment. There is a little matter. Urgent."

For a brief interval he was speechless.

Then he found attention and encouragement in the eye of Urthred.

"Something I don't understand. Something incredible—I mean, incompatible. The little rift. Turns everything into a fantastic phantasmagoria."

The intelligence in Urthred's eye was very encouraging. Mr. Barnstaple abandoned any attempt to address the company as a whole, and spoke directly to Urthred.

"You live in Utopia, hundreds of thousands of years in advance of us. How is it that you are able to talk contemporary English—to use exactly the same language that we do? I ask you, how is that? It is incredible. It jars. It makes a dream of you. And yet you are not a dream? It makes me feel—almost—insane."

Urthred smiled pleasantly. "We *don't* speak English," he said.

Mr. Barnstaple felt the ground slipping from under his feet. "But I *hear* you speaking English," he said.

"Nevertheless we do not speak it," said Urthred.

He smiled still more broadly. "We don't—for ordinary purposes—speak anything."

Mr. Barnstaple, with his brain resigning its functions, maintained his pose of deferential attention.

"Ages ago," Urthred continued, "we certainly used to speak languages. We made sounds and we heard sounds. People used to think, and then chose and arranged words and uttered them. The hearer heard, noted, and retranslated the sounds into ideas. Then, in some manner which we still do not understand perfectly, people began to *get* the idea before it was clothed in words and uttered in sounds. They began to hear in their minds, as soon as the speaker had arranged his ideas and before he put them into word symbols even in his own mind. They knew what he was going to say before he said it. This direct transmission presently became common; it was found out that with a little effort most people could get over to each other in this fashion to some extent, and the new mode of communication was developed systematically.

"That is what we do now habitually in this world. We think directly *to* each other. We determine to convey the thought and it is conveyed at once—provided the distance is not too great. We use sounds in this world now only for poetry and pleasure and in moments of emotion or to shout at a distance, or with animals, not for the transmission of ideas from human mind to kindred human mind any more. When I think to you, the thought, *so far as it finds corresponding ideas and suitable words in your mind,* is reflected in your mind. My thought clothes itself in words in your mind, which words you seem to hear—and naturally enough in your own language and your own habitual phrases. Very probably the members of your party are hearing what I am saying to you, each with his own individual difference of vocabulary and phrasing."

Mr. Barnstaple had been punctuating this discourse with sharp intelligent nods, coming now and then to the verge of interruption. Now he broke out with: "And that is why occasionally—as for instance when Mr. Serpentine made his wonderful explanation just now—when you soar into ideas of which we haven't even a shadow in our minds, we just hear nothing at all."

"Are there such gaps?" asked Urthred.

"Many, I fear—for all of us," said Mr. Burleigh.

"It's like being deaf in spots," said Lady Stella. "Large spots."

Father Amerton nodded agreement.

"And that is why we cannot be clear whether you are called Urthred or Adam, and why I have found myself confusing Arden and Greentrees and Forest in my mind."

"I hope that now you are mentally more at your ease?" said Urthred.

"Oh, quite," said Mr. Barnstaple. "Quite. And all things considered, it is really very convenient for us that there should be this method of transmission. For otherwise I do not see how we could have avoided weeks of linguistic bother, first principles of our respective grammars, logic, significs, and so forth, boring stuff for the most part, before we could have got to anything like our present under-standing."

"A very good point indeed," said Mr. Burleigh, turning round to Mr. Barnstaple in a very friendly way. "A very good point indeed. I should never have noted it if you had not called my attention to it. It is quite extraordinary; I had not noted anything of this—this difference. I was occupied, I am bound to confess, by my own thoughts. I supposed they were speaking English. Took it for granted."

§ 3

It seemed to Mr. Barnstaple that this wonderful experience was now so complete that there remained nothing more to wonder at except its absolute credibility. He sat in this beautiful little building looking out upon dreamland flowers and the sunlit lake amidst this strange mingling of week-end English costumes and this more than Olympian nudity that had already ceased to startle him, he listened and occasionally participated in the long informal conversation that now ensued. It was a discussion that brought to light the most amazing and fundamental differences of moral and social outlook. Yet everything had now assumed a reality that made it altogether natural to suppose that he would presently go home to write about it in the *Liberal* and tell his wife, as much as might seem advisable at the time, about the manners and costumes of this hitherto undiscovered world. He had not even a sense of intervening distances. Sydenham might have been just around the corner.

Presently two pretty young girls made tea at an equipage among the rhododendra and brought it round to people. Tea! It was what we should call China tea, very delicate, and served in little cups without handles, Chinese fashion, but it was real and very refreshing tea.

The earlier curiosities of the Earthlings turned upon methods of government. This was perhaps natural in the presence of two such statesmen as Mr. Burleigh and Mr. Catskill.

"What form of government do you have?" asked Mr. Burleigh. "Is it a monarchy or an autocracy or a pure democracy? Do you separate the executive and the legislative? And is there one central government for all your planet, or are there several governing centres?"

It was conveyed to Mr. Burleigh and his companions with some difficulty that there was no central government in Utopia at all.

"But surely," said Mr. Burleigh, "there is someone or something, some council or bureau or what not, somewhere, with which the final decision rests in cases of collective action for the common welfare? Some ultimate seat and organ of sovereignty, it seems to me, there *must* be." . . .

No, the Utopians declared, there was no such concentration of authority in their world. In the past there had been, but it had long since diffused back into the general body of the community. Decisions in regard to any particular matter were made by the people who knew most about that matter.

"But suppose it is a decision that has to be generally observed? A rule affecting the public health, for example? Who would enforce it?"

"It would not need to be enforced. Why should it?"

"But suppose someone refused to obey your regulation?"

"We should inquire why he or she did not conform. There might be some exceptional reason."

"But failing that?"

"We should make an inquiry into his mental and moral health."

"The mind doctor takes the place of the policeman," said Mr. Burleigh.

"I should prefer the policeman," said Mr. Rupert Catskill.

"You *would,* Rupert," said Mr. Burleigh as who should say: *"Got* you that time."

"Then do you mean to say," he continued, addressing the Utopians with an expression of great intelligence, "that your affairs are all managed by special bodies or organizations— one scarcely knows what to call them—without any co-ordination of their activities?"

"The activities of our world," said Urthred, "are all co-ordinated to secure the general freedom. We have a number of intelligences directed to the general psychology of the race and to the interaction of one collective function upon another."

"Well, isn't that group of intelligences a governing class?" said Mr. Burleigh.

"Not in the sense that they exercise any arbitrary will," said Urthred. "They deal with general relations, that is all. But they rank no higher, they have no more precedence on that account than a philosopher has over a scientific specialist."

"This is a republic indeed!" said Mr. Burleigh. "But how it works and how it came about I cannot imagine. Your state is probably a highly socialistic one?"

"You live still in a world in which nearly everything except the air, the high roads, the high seas and the wildner-ness is privately owned?"

"We do," said Mr. Catskill. "Owned—and competed for."

"We have been through that stage. We found at last that private property in all but very personal things was an intolerable nuisance to mankind. We got rid of it. An artist or a scientific man has complete control of all the material he needs, we all own our tools and appliances and have rooms and places of our own, but there is no property for trade or speculation. All this militant property, this property of manœuvre, has been quite got rid of. But how we got rid of it is a long story. It was not done in a few years. The exaggeration of private property was an entirely natural and necessary stage in the development of human nature. It led at last to monstrous results, but it was only through these monstrous and catastrophic results that men learnt the need and nature of the limitations of private property."

Mr. Burleigh had assumed an attitude which was obviously habitual to him. He sat very low in his chair with his long legs crossed in front of him and the thumb and fingers of one hand placed with meticulous exactness against those of the other.

"I must confess," he said, "that I am most interested in the peculiar form of Anarchism which seems to prevail here. Unless I misunderstand you completely every man attends to his own business as the servant of the state. I take it you have—you must correct me if I am wrong—a great number of people concerned in the production and distribution and preparation of food; they inquire, I assume, into the needs of the world, they satisfy them and they are law unto themselves in their way of doing it. They conduct researches, they make experiments. Nobody compels, obliges, restrains or prevents them. ("People talk to them about it," said Urthred with a faint smile.) And again others produce and manufacture and study metals for all mankind and are also a law unto themselves. Others again see to the habitability of your world, plan and arrange these delightful habitations, say who shall use them and how they shall be used. Others pursue pure science. Others experiment with sensory and imaginative possibilities and are artists. Others again teach."

"They are very important," said Lychnis.

"And they all do it in harmony—and due proportion. Without either a central legislature or executive. I will admit that all this seems admirable—but impossible. Nothing of the sort has ever been even suggested yet in the world from which we come."

"Something of the sort was suggested long ago by the Guild Socialists," said Mr. Barnstaple.

"Dear me!" said Mr. Burleigh. "I know very little about the Guild Socialists. Who were they? Tell me."

Mr. Barnstaple tacitly declined that task. "The idea is quite familiar to our younger people," he said. "Laski calls it the pluralistic state, as distinguished from the monistic state in which sovereignty is concentrated. Even the Chinese have it. A Pekin professor, Mr. S. C. Chang, has written a pamphlet on what he calls 'Professionalism.' I read it only a few weeks ago. He sent it to the office of the *Liberal*. He points out how undesirable it is and how unnecessary for China to pass through a phase of democratic politics on the western model. He wants China to go right straight on to a collateral independence of functional classes, mandarins, industrials, agricultural workers and so forth, much as we seem to find it here. Though that of course involves an educational revolution. Decidedly the germ of what you call Anarchism here is also in the air we come from."

"Dear me!" said Mr. Burleigh, looking more intelligent and appreciative than ever. "And is that so? I had *no* idea——!"

§ 4

The conversation continued desultory in form and yet the exchange of ideas was rapid and effective. Quite soon, as it seemed to Mr. Barnstaple, an outline of the history of Utopia from the Last Age of Confusion onward shaped itself in his mind.

The more he learnt of that Last Age of Confusion the more it seemed to resemble the present time on earth. In those days Utopians had worn abundant clothing and lived in towns quite after the earthly fashion. A fortunate conspiracy of accidents rather than any set design had opened for them some centuries of opportunity and expansion. Climatic phases and political chances had smiled upon the race after a long period of recurrent shortage, pestilence and destructive warfare. For the first time the Utopians had been able to explore the whole planet on which they lived, and these explorations had brought great virgin areas under the axe, the spade and the plough. There had been an enormous increase in real wealth and in leisure and liberty. Many thousands of people were lifted out of the normal squalor of human life to positions in which they could, if they chose, think and act with unprecedented freedom. A few, a sufficient few, did. A vigorous development of scientific inquiry began and, trailing after it a multitude of ingenious inventions, produced a great enlargement of practical human power.

There had been previous outbreaks of the scientific intelligence in Utopia, but none before had ever occured in such favourable circumstances or lasted long enough to come to abundant practical fruition. Now in a couple of brief centuries the Utopians, who had hitherto crawled about their planet like sluggish ants or travelled parasitically on larger and swifter animals, found themselves able to fly rapidly or speak instantaneously to any other point on the planet. They found themselves, too, in possession of mechanical power on a scale beyond all previous experience, and not simply of mechanical power; physiological and then psychological science followed in the wake of physics and chemistry, and extraordinary possibilities of control over his own body and over his social life dawned upon the Utopian. But these things came, when at last they did come, so rapidly and confusingly that it was only a small minority of people who realized the possibilities, as distinguished from the concrete achievements, of this tremendous expansion of knowledge. The rest took the novel inventions as they came, haphazard, with as little adjustment as possible of their thoughts and ways of living to the new necessities these novelties implied.

The first response of the general population of Utopia to the prospect of power, leisure and freedom thus opened out to it, was proliferation. It behaved just as senselessly and mechanically as any other animal or vegetable species would have done. It bred until it had completely swamped the ampler opportunity that had opened before it. It spent the great gifts of science as rapidly as it got them in a mere insensate multiplication of the common life. At one time in the last Age of Confusion the population of Utopia had mounted to over two thousand million. . . .

"But what is it now?" asked Mr. Burleigh.

About two hundred and fifty million, the Utopians told him. That had been the maximum population that could live a fully developed life upon the surface of Utopia. But now with increasing resources the population was being increased.

A gasp of horror came from Father Amerton. He had been dreading this realization for some time. It struck at his moral foundations. "And you dare to *regulate* increase! You control it! Your woman consent to bear children as they are needed—or refrain!"

"Of course," said Urthred. "Why not?"

"I feared as much," said Father Amerton, and leaning forward he covered his face with his hands murmuring, "I felt this in the atmosphere! The human stud farm! Refusing to create souls! The *wickedness* of it! Oh, my God!"

Mr. Burleigh regarded the emotion of the reverend gentleman through his glasses with a slightly shocked expression. He detested catchwords. But Father Amerton stood for very valuable conservative elements in the community. Mr. Burleigh turned to the Utopian again. "That is extremely interesting," he said. "Even at present our earth contrives to carry a population of at least five times that amount."

"But twenty millions or so will starve this winter, you told us a little while ago—in a place called Russia. And only a very small proportion of the rest are leading what even you would call full and spacious lives?"

"Nevertheless the contrast is striking," said Mr. Burleigh.

"It is terrible!" said Father Amerton.

The overcrowding of the planet in the Last Age of Confusion was, these Utopians insisted, the fundamental evil out of which all the others that afflicted the race arose. An overwhelming flood of new-comers poured into the world

and swamped every effort the intelligent minority could make
to educate a sufficient proportion of them to meet the demands
of the new and still rapidly changing conditions of life.
And the intelligent minority was not itself in any position
to control the racial destiny. These great masses of population
that had been blundered into existence, swayed by damaged
and decaying traditions and amenable to the crudest suggestions, were the natural prey and support of every
adventurer with a mind blatant enough and a conception
of success coarse enough to appeal to them. The economic
system, clumsily and convulsively reconstructed to meet the
new conditions of mechanical production and distribution,
became more and more a cruel and impudent exploitation
of the multitudinous congestion of the common man by the
predatory and acquisitive few. That all too common common
man was hustled through misery and subjection from his
cradle to his grave; he was cajoled and lied to, he was
bought, sold and dominated by an impudent minority, bolder
and no doubt more energetic, but in all other respects no
more intelligent than himself. It was difficult, Urthred said,
for a Utopian nowadays to convey the monstrous stupidity,
wastefulness and vulgarity to which these rich and powerful
men of the Last Age of Confusion attained.

("We will not trouble you," said Mr. Burleigh.
"Unhappily—we know. . . . We know. Only too well do
we know.")

Upon this festering, excessive mass of population disasters
descended at last like wasps upon a heap of rotting fruit.
It was its natural, inevitable destiny. A war that affected
nearly the whole planet dislocated its flimsy financial system
and most of its economic machinery beyond any possibility
of repair. Civil wars and clumsily conceived attempts at
social revolution continued the disorganization. A series of
years of bad weather accentuated the general shortage. The

exploiting adventurers, too stupid to realize what had happened, continued to cheat and hoodwink the commonalty and burke any rally of honest men, as wasps will continue to eat even after their bodies have been cut away. The effort to make passed out of Utopian life, triumphantly superseded by the effort to get. Production dwindled down towards the vanishing point. Accumulated wealth vanished. An overwhelming system of debt, a swarm of creditors, morally incapable of helpful renunciation, crushed out all fresh initiative,

The long diastole in Utopian affairs that had begun with the great discoveries, passed into a phase of rapid systole. What plenty and pleasure was still possible in the world was filched all the more greedily by the adventurers of finances and speculative business. Organized science had long since been commercialized, and was "applied" now chiefly to a hunt for profitable patents and the forestalling of necessary supplies. The neglected lamp of pure science waned, flickered and seemed likely to go out again altogether, leaving Utopia in the beginning of a new series of Dark Ages like those before the age of discovery began. . . .

"It is really *very* like a gloomy diagnosis of our own outlook," said Mr. Burleigh. "Extraordinarily like. How Dean Inge would have enjoyed all this!"

"To an infidel of his stamp, no doubt, it would seem most enjoyable," said Father Amerton a little incoherently.

These comments annoyed Mr. Barnstaple, who was urgent to hear no more.

"And then," he said to Urthred, "what happened?"

§ 5

What happened, Mr. Barnstaple gathered, was a deliberate change in Utopian thought. A growing number of people were coming to understand that amidst the powerful and easily released forces that science and organization had brought within reach of man, the old conception of social life in the state, as a limited and legalized struggle of men and women to get the better of one another, was becoming too dangerous to endure, just as the increased dreadfulness of modern weapons was making the separate sovereignty of nations too dangerous to endure. There had to be new ideas and new conventions of human association if history was not to end in disaster and collapse.

All societies were based on the limitation by laws and taboos and treaties of the primordial fierce combativeness of the ancestral man ape; that ancient spirit of self-assertion had now to undergo new restrictions commensurate with the new powers and dangers of the race. The idea of competition to possess, as the ruling idea of intercourse, was, like some ill-controlled furnace, threatening to consume the machine it had formerly driven. The idea of creative service had to replace it. To that idea the human mind and will had to be turned if social life was to be saved. Propositions that had seemed, in former ages, to be inspired and exalted idealism began now to be recognized not simply as sober psychological truth but as practical and urgently necessary truth. In explaining this Urthred expressed himself in a manner that recalled to Mr. Barnstaple's mind certain very familiar phrases; he seemed to be saying that whosoever would save his life should lose it, and that whosoever would give his life should thereby gain the whole world.

Father Amerton's thoughts, it seemed, were also responding in the same manner. For he suddenly interrupted with: "But what you are saying is a quotation!"

Urthred admitted that he had a quotation in mind, a passage from the teachings of a man of great poetic power who had lived long ago in the days of spoken words.

He would have proceeded, but Father Amerton was too

excited to let him do so. "But who was this teacher?" he asked. "Where did he live? How was he born? How did he die?"

A picture was flashed upon Mr. Barnstaple's consciousness of a solitary-looking pale-faced figure, beaten and bleeding, surrounded by armoured guards, in the midst of a thrusting, jostling, sun-bit crowd which filled a narrow, high walled street. Behind, some huge ugly implement was borne along, dipping and swaying with the swaying of the multitude. . . .

"Did he die upon the cross in *this* world also?" cried Father Amerton. "Did he die upon the Cross?"

This prophet in Utopia they learnt had died very painfully, but not upon the Cross. He had been tortured in some way, but neither the Utopians nor these particular Earthlings had sufficient knowledge of the technicalities of torture to get any idea over about that, and then apparently he had been fastened upon a slowly turning wheel and exposed until he died. It was the abominable punishment of a cruel and conquering race, and it had been inflicted upon him because his doctrine of universal service had alarmed the rich and dominant who did not serve. Mr. Barnstaple had a momentary vision of a twisted figure upon that wheel of torture in the blazing sun. And, marvellous triumph over death! out of a world that could do such a deed had come this great peace and universal beauty about him!

But Father Amerton was pressing his questions. "But did you not realize who he was? Did not this world suspect?"

A great many people thought that this man was a God. But he had been accustomed to call himself merely a son of God or a son of Man.

Father Amerton stuck to his point. "But you worship him now?"

"We follow his teaching because it was wonderful and true," said Urthred.

"But worship?"

"No."

"But does nobody worship? There *were* those who worshipped him?"

There were those who worshipped him. There were those who quailed before the stern magnificence of his teaching and yet who had a tormenting sense that he was right in some profound way. So they played a trick upon their own uneasy consciences by treating him as a magical god instead of as a light to their souls. They interwove with his execution ancient traditions of sacrificial kings. Instead of receiving him frankly and clearly and making him a part of their understandings and wills they pretended to eat him mystically and make him a part of their bodies. They turned his wheel into a miraculous symbol, and tney confused it with the equator and the sun and the ecliptic and indeed with anything else that was round. In cases of ill-luck, ill-health or bad weather it was believed to be very helpful for the believer to describe a circle in the air with the forefinger.

And since this teacher's memory was very dear to the ignorant multitude because of his gentleness and charity, it was seized upon by cunning and aggressive types who constituted themselves champions and exponents of the wheel, who grew rich and powerful in its name, led peoples into great wars for its sake and used it as a cover and justification for envy, hatred, tyranny and dark desires. Until at last men said that had that ancient prophet come again to Utopia, his own triumphant wheel would have crushed and destroyed him afresh. . . .

Father Amerton seemed inattentive to this communication. He was seeing it from another angle. "But surely," he said, "there is a remnant of believers still! Despised perhaps—but a remnant?"

There was no remnant. The whole world followed that Teacher of Teachers, but no one worshipped him. On some old treasured buildings the wheel was still to be seen carved, often with the most fantastic decorative elaborations. And in museums and collections there were multitudes of pictures, images, charms and the like.

"I don't understand this," said Father Amerton. "It's too terrible. I am at a loss. I do not understand."

§ 6

A fair and rather slender man with a delicately beautiful face whose name Mr. Barnstaple was to learn later, was Lion, presently took over from Urthred the burthen of explaining and answering the questions of the Earthlings.

He was one of the educational co-ordinators in Utopia. He made it clear that the change over in Utopian affairs had been no sudden revolution. No new system of laws and customs, no new method of economic co-operation based on the idea of universal service to the common good, had sprung abruptly into being complete and finished. Throughout a long period, before and during the Last Age of Confusion, the foundations of the new state were laid by a growing multitude of inquirers and workers, having no set plan or preconceived method, but brought into unconscious co-operation by a common impulse to service and a common lucidity and veracity of mind. It was only towards the climax of the Last Age of Confusion in Utopia that psychological science began to develop with any vigour, comparable to the vigour of the development of geographical and physical science during the preceding centuries. And the social and economic disorder which was checking experimental science and crippling the organized work of the universities was stimulating inquiry into the process of human association and making it desperate and fearless.

The impression given Mr. Barnstaple was not of one of those violent changes which our world has learnt to call revolutions, but of an increase of light, a dawn of new ideas, in which the things of the old order went on for a time with diminishing vigour until people began as ·a matter of common sense to do the new things in the place of old.

The beginnings of the new order were in discussions, books and psychological laboratories; the soil in which it grew was found in schools and colleges. The old order gave small rewards to the schoolmaster, but its dominant types were too busy with the struggle for wealth and power to take much heed of teaching: it was left to any man or woman who would give thought and labour without much hope of tangible rewards, to shape the world anew in the minds of the young. And they did so shape it. In a world ruled ostensibly by adventurer politicians, in a world where men came to power through floundering business enterprises and financial cunning, it was presently being taught and under' stood that extensive private property was socially a nuisance, and that the state could not do its work properly nor edu' cation produce its proper results, side by side with a class of irresponsible rich people. For, by their very nature, they assailed, they corrupted, they undermined every state under' taking; their flaunting existences distorted and disguised all the values of life. They had to go, for the good of the race.

"Didn't they fight?" asked Mr. Catskill pugnaciously.

They had fought irregularly but fiercely. The fight to delay or arrest the coming of the universal scientific state, the educational state, in Utopia, had gone on as a conscious struggle for nearly five centuries. The fight against it was the fight of greedy, passionate, prejudiced and self'seeking men against the crystallization into concrete realities of this new idea of association for service. It was fought wherever ideas were spread; it was fought with dismissals and threats and boycotts and storms of violence, with lies and false accusations, with prosecutions and imprisonments, with lynching-rope, tar and feathers, paraffin, bludgeon and rifle, bomb and gun.

But the service of the new idea that had been launched into the world never failed; it seized upon the men and women it needed with compelling power. Before the scientific state was established in Utopia more than a million martyrs had been killed for it, and those who had suffered lesser wrongs were beyond all reckoning. Point after point was won in education, in social laws, in economic method. No date could be fixed for the change. A time came when Utopia perceived that it was day and that a new order of things had replaced the old. . . .

"So it must be," said Mr. Barnstaple, as though Utopia were not already present about him. "So it must be."

A question was being answered. Every Utopian child is taught to the full measure of its possibilities and directed to the work that is indicated by its desires and capacity. It is born well. It is born of perfectly healthy parents; its mother has chosen to bear it after due thought and preparation. It grows up under perfectly healthy conditions; its natural impulses to play and learn are gratified by the subtlest educational methods; hands, eyes and limbs are given every opportunity of training and growth; it learns to draw, write, express itself, use a great variety of symbols to assist and extend its thought. Kindness and civility become ingrained habits, for all about it are kind and civil. And in particular the growth of its imagination is watched and encouraged. It learns the wonderful history of its world and its race, how man has struggled and still struggles out of his earlier animal narrowness and egotism towards an empire over being that is still but faintly apprehended through dense veils of ignorance. All its desires are made fine; it learns from poetry, from example and the love of those about it to lose its solicitude for itself in love; its sexual passions are turned against its selfishness, its curiosity flowers into scientific passion, combativeness is set to fight disorder, its inherent pride and ambition are directed towards an honorable share in the common achievement. It goes to the work that attracts it and chooses what it will do.

If the individual is indolent there is no great loss, there is plenty for all in Utopia, but then it will find no lovers, nor will it ever bear children, because no one in Utopia loves those who have neither energy nor distinction. There is much pride of the mate in Utopian love. And there is no idle rich "society" in Utopia, nor games and shows for the mere looker-on. There is nothing for the mere looker-on. It is a pleasant world indeed for holidays, but not for those who would continuously do nothing.

For centuries now Utopian science has been able to discriminate among births, and nearly every Utopian alive would have ranked as an energetic creative spirit in former days. There are few dull and no really defective people in Utopia; the idle strains, the people of lethargic dispositions or weak imaginations, have mostly died out; the melancholic type has taken its dismissal and gone; spiteful and malignant characters are disappearing. The vast majority of Utopians are active, sanguine, inventive, receptive and good-tempered.

"And you have not even a parliament?" asked Mr. Burleigh, still incredulous.

Utopia has no parliament, no politics, no private wealth, no business competition, no police nor prisons, no lunatics, no defectives nor cripples, and it has none of these things because it has schools and teachers who are all that schools and teachers can be. Politics, trade and competition are the methods of adjustment of a crude society. Such methods of adjustment have been laid aside in Utopia for more than a thousand years. There is no rule nor government needed by adult Utopians because all the rule and government they need they have had in childhood and youth.

Said Lion: *"Our education is our government."*

CHAPTER THE SIXTH

SOME EARTHLY CRITICISMS

§ 1

AT times during that memorable afternoon and evening it seemed to Mr. Barnstaple that he was involved in nothing more remarkable than an extraordinary dialogue about government and history, a dialogue that had in some inexplicable way become spectacular; it was as if all this was happening only in his mind; and then the absolute reality of his adventure would return to him with overwhelming power and his intellectual interest fade to inattention in the astounding strangeness of his position. In these latter phases he would find his gaze wandering from face to face of the Utopians who surrounded him, resting for a time on some exquisite detail of the architecture of the building and then coming back to these divinely graceful forms.

Then incredulously he would revert to his fellow Earthlings.

Not one of these Utopian faces but was as candid, earnest and beautiful as the angelic faces of an Italian painting. One woman was strangely like Michael Angelo's Delphic Sibyl. They sat in easy attitudes, men and women together, for the most part concentrated on the discussion, but every now and then Mr. Barnstaple would meet the direct scrutiny of a pair of friendly eyes or find some Utopian face intent upon the costume of Lady Stella or the eye-glass of Mr. Mush.

Mr. Barnstaple's first impression of the Utopians had been that they were all young people; now he perceived that many of these faces had a quality of vigorous maturity. None showed any of the distinctive marks of age as this world notes them, but both Urthred and Lion had lines of experience about eyes and lips and brow.

The effect of these people upon Mr. Barnstaple mingled stupefaction with familiarity in the strangest way. He had a feeling that he had always known that such a race could exist and that this knowledge had supplied the implicit standard of a thousand judgments upon human affairs, and at the same time he was astonished to the pitch of incredulity to find himself in the same world with them. They were at once normal and wonderful in comparison with himself and his companions who were, on their part, at the same time queer and perfectly matter-of-fact.

And together with a strong desire to become friendly and intimate with these fine and gracious persons, to give himself to them and to associate them with himself by service and reciprocal acts, there was an awe and fear of them that made him shrink from contact with them and quiver at their touch. He desired their personal recognition of himself as a fellow and companion so greatly that his sense of his own ungraciousness and unworthiness overwhelmed him. He wanted to bow down before them. Beneath all the light and loveliness of things about him lurked the intolerable premonition of his ultimate rejection from this new world.

So great was the impression made by the Utopians upon Mr. Barnstaple, so entirely did he yield himself up to his joyful acceptance of their grace and physical splendour, that for a time he had no attention left over to note how different from his own were the reactions of several of his Earthling companions. The aloofness of the Utopians from the queerness, grotesqueness and cruelty of normal earthly life, made him ready for the most uncritical approval of their institutions and ways of life.

It was the behaviour of Father Amerton which first awakened him to the fact that it was possible to disapprove of these wonderful people very highly and to display a very considerable hostility to them. At first Father Amerton had kept a round-faced, round-eyed wonder above his round collar; he had shown a disposition to give the lead to anyone who chose to take it, and he had said not a word until the naked beauty of dead Greenlake had surprised him into an expression of unclerical appreciation. But during the journey to the lakeside and the meal and the opening arrangements of the conference there was a reaction, and this first naive and deferential astonishment gave place to an attitude of resistance and hostility. It was as if this new world which had begun by being a spectacle had taken on the quality of a proposition which he felt he had either to accept or confute. Perhaps it was that the habit of mind of a public censor was too strong for him and that he could not feel normal again until he began to condemn. Perhaps he was really shocked and distressed by the virtual nudity of these lovely bodies about him. But he began presently to make queer grunts and coughs, to mutter to himself, and to betray an increasing incapacity to keep still.

He broke out first into an interruption when the question of population was raised. For a little while his intelligence prevailed over this emotional stir when the prophet of the wheel was discussed, but then his gathering preoccupations resumed their sway.

"I must speak out," Mr. Barnstaple heard him mutter. "I must speak out."

Now suddenly he began to ask questions. "There are some things I want to have clear," he said. "I want to know what moral state this so-called Utopia is in. Excuse me!"

He got up. He stood with wavering hands, unable for a moment to begin. Then he went to the end of the row of seats and placed himself so that his hands could rest on the back of a seat. He passed his fingers through his hair and he seemed to be inhaling deeply. An unwonted animation came into his face, which reddened and began to shine. A horrible suspicion crossed the mind of Mr. Barnstaple that so it was he must stand when he began those weekly sermons of his, those fearless denunciations of almost everything, in the church of Saint Barnabas in the West. The suspicion deepened to a still more horrible certainty.

"Friends, Brothers of this new world—I have certain things to say to you that I cannot delay saying. I want to ask you some soul-searching questions. I want to deal plainly with you about some plain and simple but very fundamental matters. I want to put things to you frankly and as man to man, not being mealy-mouthed about urgent if delicate things. Let me come without parley to what I have to say. I want to ask you if, in this so-called state of Utopia, you still have and respect and honour the most sacred thing in social life. Do you still respect the marriage bond?"

He paused, and in the pause the Utopian reply came through to Mr. Barnstaple: "In Utopia there are no bonds."

But Father Amerton was not asking questions with any desire for answers; he was asking questions pulpit-fashion.

"I want to know," he was booming out, "if that holy union revealed to our first parents in the Garden of Eden holds good here, if that sanctified lifelong association of one man and one woman, in good fortune and ill fortune, excluding every other sort of intimacy, is the rule of your lives. I want to know——"

"But he *doesn't* want to know," came a Utopian intervention.

"——if that shielded and guarded dual purity——"

Mr. Burleigh raised a long white hand. "Father Amerton," he protested, *"please."*

The hand of Mr. Burleigh was a potent hand that might still wave towards preferment. Few things under heaven could stop Father Amerton when he was once launched upon one of his soul storms, but the hand of Mr. Burleigh was among such things.

"——has followed another still more precious gift and been cast aside here and utterly rejected of men? What is it, Mr. Burleigh?"

"I wish you would not press this matter further just at present, Father Amerton. Until we have learnt a little more. Institutions are, manifestly, very different here. Even the institution of marriage may be different."

The preacher's face lowered. "Mr. Burleigh," he said, "I *must*. If my suspicions are right, I want to strip this world forthwith of its hectic pretence to a sort of health and virtue."

"Not much stripping required," said Mr. Burleigh's chauffeur, in a very audible aside.

A certain testiness became evident in Mr. Burleigh's voice.

"Then ask questions," he said. "Ask questions. Don't orate, please. They don't want us to orate."

"I've asked my question," said Father Amerton sulkily with a rhetorical glare at Urthred, and remained standing.

The answer came clear and explicit. In Utopia there was no compulsion for men and women to go about in indissoluble pairs. For most Utopians that would be inconvenient. Very often men and women, whose work brought them closely together, were lovers and kept very much together, as Arden and Greenlake had done. But they were not obliged to do that.

There had not always been this freedom. In the old crowded days of conflict, and especially among the agricultural workers and employed people of Utopia, men and women who had been lovers were bound together under severe penalties for life. They lived together in a small home which the woman kept in order for the man, she was his servant and bore him as many children as possible, while he got food for them. The children were desired be-cause they were soon helpful on the land or as wage-earners. But the necessities that had subjugated women to that sort of pairing had passed away.

People paired indeed with their chosen mates, but they did so by an inner necessity and not by any outward com-pulsion.

Father Amerton had listened with ill-concealed impatience. Now he jumped with: "Then I was right, and you have abolished the family?" His finger pointed at Urthred made it almost a personal accusation.

No. Utopia had not abolished the family. It had enlarged and glorified the family until it embraced the whole world. Long ago that prophet of the wheel, whom Father Amerton seemed to respect, had preached that very enlargement of the ancient narrowness of home. They had told him while he preached that his mother and his brethren stood without and claimed his attention. But he would not go to them. He had turned to the crowd that listened to his words: "Behold my mother and my brethren!"

Father Amerton slapped the seat-back in front of him loudly and startlingly. "A quibble," he cried, "a quibble! Satan too can quote the scriptures."

It was clear to Mr. Barnstaple that Father Amerton was not in complete control of himself. He was frightened by what he was doing and yet impelled to do it. He was too excited to think clearly or control his voice properly, so that he shouted and boomed in the wildest way. He was "letting himself go" and trusting to the habits of the pulpit of Saint Barnabas to bring him through.

"I perceive now how you stand. Only too well do I perceive how you stand. From the outset I guessed how things were with you. I waited—I waited to be perfectly sure, before I bore my testimony. But it speaks for itself— the shamelessness of your costume, the licentious freedom of your manners! Young men and women, smiling, joining hands, near to caressing, when averted eyes, averted eyes, are the least tribute you could pay to modesty! And this vile talk—of lovers loving—without bonds or blessings, without rules or restraint. What does it mean? Whither does it lead? Do not imagine because I am a priest, a man pure and virginal in spite of great temptations, do not imagine that I do not understand! Have I no vision of the secret places of the heart? Do not the wounded sinners, the broken potsherds, creep to me with their pitiful confessions? And I will tell you plainly whither you go and how you stand! This so-called freedom of yours is nothing but license. Your so-called Utopia, I see plainly, is nothing but a hell of unbridled indulgence! Unbridled indulgence!"

Mr. Burleigh held up a protesting hand, but Father Amerton's eloquence soared over the obstruction.

He beat upon the back of the seat before him. "I will bear my witness," he shouted. "I will bear my witness. I will make no bones about it. I refuse to mince matters I tell you. You are all living—in promiscuity! That is the word for it. In animal promiscuity! In *bestial* promiscuity!"

Mr. Burleigh had sprung to his feet. He was holding up his two hands and motioning the London Boanerges to sit down. "No, no!" he cried. "You must *stop*, Mr. Amerton. Really, you must stop. You are being insulting. You do not understand. Sit *down*, please. I insist."

"Sit down and hold your peace," said a very clear voice. "Or you will be taken away."

Something made Father Amerton aware of a still figure at his elbow. He met the eyes of a lithe young man who was scrutinizing his build as a portrait painter might scrutinize a new sitter. There was no threat in his bearing, he stood quite still, and yet his appearance threw an extraord' inary quality of evanescence about Father Amerton. The great preacher's voice died in his throat.

Mr. Burleigh's bland voice was lifted to avert a conflict. "Mr. Serpentine, Sir, I appeal to you and apologize. He is not fully responsible. We others regret the interruption— the incident. I pray you, please do not take him away, whatever taking away may mean. I will answer personally for his good behaviour. . . . *Do* sit down, Mr. Amerton, *please; now;* or I shall wash my hands of the whole business."

Father Amerton hesitated.

"My time will come," he said and looked the young man in the eyes for a moment and then went back to his seat.

Urthred spoke quietly and clearly. "You Earthlings are difficult guests to entertain. This is not all. . . . Manifestly this man's mind is very unclean. His sexual imagination is evidently inflamed and diseased. He is angry and anxious to insult and wound. And his noises are terrific. To morrow he must be examined and dealt with."

"How?" said Father Amerton, his round face suddenly grey. "How do you mean—*dealt* with?"

"Please do not talk," said Mr. Burleigh. *"Please* do not talk any more. You have done quite enough mischief. . . ."

For the time the incident seemed at an end, but it had left a queer little twinge of fear in Mr. Barnstaple's heart. These Utopians were very gentlemannered and gracious people indeed, but just for a moment the hand of power had seemed to hover over the Earthling party. Sunlight and beauty were all about the visitors, nevertheless they were strangers and quite helpless strangers in an unknown world.

The Utopian faces were kindly and their eyes curious and in a manner friendly, but much more observant than friendly. It was as if they looked across some impassable gulf of difference.

And then Mr. Barnstaple in the midst of his distress met the brown eyes of Lychnis, and they were kindlier than the eyes of the other Utopians. She, at least, understood the fear that had come to him, he felt, and she was willing to reassure him and be his friend. Mr. Barnstaple looked at her, feeling for the moment much as a stray dog might do who approaches a doubtfully amiable group and gets a friendly glance and a greeting.

§ 2

Another mind that was also in active resistance to Utopia was that of Mr. Freddy Mush. He had no quarrel indeed with the religion or morals or social organization of Utopia He had long since learnt that no gentleman of serious æsthetic pretensions betrays any interest whatever in such matters. His perceptions were by hypothesis too fine for them. But presently he made it clear that there had been something very ancient and beautiful called the "Balance of Nature" which the scientific methods of Utopia had destroyed. What this Balance of Nature of his was, and how it worked on earth, neither the Utopians nor Mr. Barnstaple were able to understand very clearly. Under cross-examination Mr. Mush grew pink and restive and his eye-glass flashed defensively. "I hold by the swallows," he repeated. "If you can't see my point about that I don't know what else I can say."

He began with the fact and reverted to the fact that there were no swallows to be seen in Utopia, and there were no gnats nor midges. There had been an enormous deliberate reduction of insect life in Utopia, and that had seriously affected every sort of creature that was directly or indirectly dependent upon insect life. So soon as the new state of affairs was securely established in Utopia and the educational state working, the attention of the Utopian community had been given to the long-cherished idea of a systematic extermination of tiresome and mischievous species. A careful inquiry was made into the harmfulness and the possibility of eliminating the house-fly for example, wasps and hornets, various species of mice and rats, rabbits, stinging-nettles. Ten thousand species, from disease-germ to rhinoceros and hyena, were put upon their trial. Every species found was given an advocate. Of each it was asked: What good is it? What harm does it do? How can it be extirpated? What else may go with it if it goes? Is it worth while wiping it out of existence? Or can it be mitigated and retained? And even when the verdict was death final and complete, Utopia set about the business of extermination with great caution. A reserve would be kept and was in many cases still being kept, in some secure isolation, of every species condemned.

Most infectious and contagious fevers had been completely stamped out; some had gone very easily; some had only been driven out of human life by proclaiming a war and subjecting the whole population to discipline. Many internal and external parasites of man and animals had also been got rid of completely. And further, there had been a great cleansing of the world from noxious insects, from weeds and vermin and hostile beasts. The mosquito had gone, the house-fly, the blow-fly, and indeed a great multitude of flies had gone; they had been driven out of life by campaigns involving an immense effort and extending over many generations. It had been infinitely more easy to get rid of such big annoyances as the hyena and the wolf than to abolish these smaller pests. The attack upon the flies had involved the virtual rebuilding of a large proportion of Utopian houses and a minute cleansing of them all throughout the planet.

The question of what else would go if a certain species went was one of the most subtle that Utopia had to face. Certain insects, for example, were destructive and offensive grubs in the opening stage of their lives, were evil as cater-pillar or pupa and then became either beautiful in themselves or necessary to the fertilization of some useful or exquisite flowers. Others offensive in themselves were a necessary irreplaceable food to pleasant and desirable creatures. It was not true that swallows had gone from Utopia, but they had become extremely rare; and rare too were a number of little insectivorous birds, the fly-catcher for example, that harlequin of the air. But they had not died out altogether; the extermination of insects had not gone to that length; sufficient species had remained to make some districts still habitable for these delightful birds.

Many otherwise obnoxious plants were a convenient source of chemically complex substances that were still costly or tedious to make synthetically, and so had kept a restricted place in life. Plants and flowers, always simpler and more plastic in the hands of the breeder and hybridizer than animals, had been enormously changed in Utopia. Our Earthlings were to find a hundred sorts of foliage and of graceful and scented blossoms that were altogether strange to them. Plants, Mr. Barnstaple learnt, had been trained and bred to make new and unprecedented secretions, waxes, gums, essential oils and the like, of the most desirable quality.

There had been much befriending and taming of big animals; the larger carnivora, combed and cleaned, reduced to a milk dietary, emasculated in spirit and altogether be-catted, were pets and ornaments in Utopia. The almost extinct elephant had increased again and Utopia had saved her giraffes. The brown bear had always been disposed to sweets and vegetarianism and had greatly improved in intelli-gence. The dog had given up barking and was comparatively rare. Sporting dogs were not used nor small pet animals.

Horses Mr. Barnstaple did not see, but as he was a very modern urban type he did not miss them very much and he did not ask any questions about them while he was actually in Utopia. He never found out whether they had or had not become extinct.

As he heard on his first afternoon in that world of this revision and editing, this weeding and cultivation of the kingdoms of nature by mankind, it seemed to him to be the most natural and necessary phase in human history. "After all," he said to himself, "it was a good invention to say that man was created a gardener."

And now man was weeding and cultivating his own strain. . . .

The Utopians told of eugenic beginnings, of a new and surer decision in the choice of parents, of an increasing in the science of heredity; and as Mr. Barnstaple contrasted the firm clear beauty of face and limb that every Utopian displayed with the carelessly assembled features and bodily disproportions of his earthly associates, he realized that already, with but three thousand years or so of advantage, these Utopians were passing beyond man towards a nobler humanity. They were becoming different in kind.

§ 3

They were different in kind.

As the questions and explanations and exchanges of that afternoon went on, it became more and more evident to Mr. Barnstaple that the difference of their bodies was as nothing to the differences of their minds. Innately better to begin with, the minds of these children of light had grown up uninjured by any such tremendous frictions, concealments, ambiguities and ignorances as cripple the growing mind of an Earthling. They were clear and frank and direct. They had never developed that defensive suspicion of the teacher, that resistance to instruction, which is the natural response to teaching that is half aggression. They were beautifully unwary in their communications. The ironies, concealments, insincerities, vanities and pretensions of earthly conversation seemed unknown to them. Mr. Barnstaple found this mental nakedness of theirs as sweet and refreshing as the mountain air he was breathing. It amazed him that they could be so patient and lucid with beings so underbred.

Underbred was the word he used in his mind. Himself, he felt the most underbred of all; he was afraid of these Utopians; snobbish and abject before them, he was like a mannerless earthy lout in a drawing-room, and he was bitterly ashamed of his own abjection. All the other Earthlings except Mr. Burleigh and Lady Stella betrayed the defensive spite of consciously inferior creatures struggling against that consciousness.

Like Father Amerton, Mr. Burleigh's chauffeur was evidently greatly shocked and disturbed by the unclothed condition of the Utopians; his feelings expressed themselves by gestures, grimaces and an occasional sarcastic comment such as "I *don't* think!" or "What O!" These he addressed for the most part to Mr. Barnstaple, for whom, as the owner of a very little old car, he evidently mingled feelings of profound contempt and social fellowship. He would also direct Mr. Barnstaple's attention to anything that he considered remarkable in bearing or gesture, by means of a peculiar stare and grimace combined with raised eyebrows. He had a way of pointing with his mouth and nose that Mr. Barnstaple under more normal circumstances might have found entertaining.

Lady Stella, who had impressed Mr. Barnstaple at first as a very great lady of the modern type, he was now beginning to feel was on her defence and becoming rather too ladylike. Mr. Burleigh however retained a certain aristocratic sublimity. He had been a great man on earth for all his life and it was evident that he saw no reason why he should not be accepted as a great man in Utopia. On earth he had done little and had been intelligently receptive with the happiest results. That alert, questioning mind of his, free of all persuasions, convictions or revolutionary desires, fell with the utmost ease into the pose of a distinguished person inspecting, in a sympathetic but entirely non-committal manner, the institutions of an alien state. "Tell me," that engaging phrase, laced his conversation.

The evening was drawing on; the clear Utopian sky was glowing with the gold of sunset and a towering mass of cloud above the lake was fading from pink to a dark purple, when Mr. Rupert Catskill imposed himself upon Mr. Barnstaple's attention. He was fretting in his place. "I have something to say," he said. "I have something to say."

Presently he jumped up and walked to the centre of the semicircle from which Mr. Burleigh had spoken earlier in the afternoon. "Mr. Serpentine," he said, "Mr. Burleigh. There are a few things I should be glad to say—if you can give me this opportunity of saying them."

§ 4

He took off his grey top hat, went back and placed it on his seat and returned to the centre of the apse. He put back his coat tails, rested his hands on his hips, thrust his head forward, regarded his audience for a moment with an expression half cunning, half defiant, muttered something inaudible and began.

His opening was not prepossessing. There was some slight

impediment in his speech, the little brother of a lisp, against which his voice beat gutturally. His first few sentences had an effect of being jerked out by unsteady efforts. Then it became evident to Mr. Barnstaple that Mr. Catskill was expressing a very definite point of view, he was offering a reasoned and intelligible view of Utopia. Mr. Barnstaple disagreed with that criticism, indeed he disagreed with it violently, but he had to recognize that it expressed an under-standable attitude of mind.

Mr. Catskill began with a sweeping admission of the beauty and order of Utopia. He praised the "glowing health" he saw "on every cheek," the wealth, tranquillity and comfort of Utopian life. They had "tamed the forces of nature and subjugated them altogether to one sole end, to the material comfort of the race."

"But Arden and Greenlake?" murmured Mr. Barnstaple.

Mr. Catskill did not hear or heed the interruption. "The first effect, Mr. Speaker—Mr. Serpentine, I *should* say—the first effect upon an earthly mind is overwhelming. Is it any wonder"—he glanced at Mr. Burleigh and Mr. Barnstaple—"is it any wonder that admiration has carried some of us off our feet? Is it any wonder that for a time your almost magic beauty has charmed us into forgetting much that is in our own natures—into forgetting deep and mysterious impulses, cravings, necessities, so that we have been ready to say, 'Here at last is Lotus Land. Here let us abide, let us adapt ourselves to this planned and ordered splendour and live our lives out here and die.' I, too, Mr.—Mr. Serpentine, succumbed to that magic for a time. But only for a time. Already, Sir, I find myself full of questionings." . . .

His bright, headlong mind had seized upon the fact that every phase in the weeding and cleaning of Utopia from pests and parasites and diseases had been accompanied by the possibility of collateral limitations and losses; or perhaps it would be juster to say that that fact had seized upon his mind. He ignored the deliberation and precautions that had accompanied every step in the process of making a world securely healthy and wholesome for human activity. He assumed there had been losses with every gain, he went on to exaggerate these losses and ran on glibly to the inevitable metaphor of throwing away the baby with its bath—inevitable, that is, for a British parliamentarian. The Utopians, he declared, were living lives of extraordinary ease, safety and "may I say so—indulgence" ("They work," said Mr. Barnstaple), but with a thousand annoyances and disagreeables gone had not something else greater and more precious gone also? Life on earth was, he admitted, insecure, full of pains and anxieties, full indeed of miseries and distresses and anguish, but also, and indeed by reason of these very things, it had moments of intensity, hopes, joyful surprises, escapes, attainments, such as the ordered life of Utopia could not possibly afford. "You have been getting away from conflicts and distresses. Have you not also been getting away from the living and quivering realities of life?"

He launched out upon a eulogy of earthly life. He extolled the vitality of life upon earth as though there were no signs of vitality in the high splendour about him. He spoke of the "thunder of our crowded cities," of the "urge of our teeming millions," of the "broad tides of commerce and industrial effort and warfare" that "swayed and came and went in the hives and harbours of our race."

He had the knack of the plausible phrase and that imaginative touch which makes for eloquence. Mr. Barnstaple forgot that slight impediment and the thickness of the voice that said these things. Mr. Catskill boldly admitted all the earthly evils and dangers that Mr. Burleigh had retailed. Everything that Mr. Burleigh had said was true. All that he had said fell indeed far short of the truth. Famine we knew, and pestilence. We suffered from a thousand diseases that Utopia had eliminated. We were afflicted by a thousand afflictions that were known to Utopia now only by ancient tradition. "The rats gnaw and the summer flies persecute and madden. At times life reeks and stinks. I admit it, Sir, I admit it. We go down tar below your extremest experiences into discomforts and miseries, anxieties and anguish of soul and body, into bitterness, terror and despair. Yea. But do we not also go higher? I challenge you with that. What can you know in this immense safety of the intensity, the frantic, terror driven intensity, of many of our efforts? What can you know of reprieves and interludes and escapes? Think of our many happinesses beyond your ken! What do you know here of the sweet early days of convalescence? Of going for a holiday out of disagreeable surroundings? Of taking some great risk to body or fortune and bringing it off? Of winning a bet against enormous odds? Of coming out of prison? And, Sir, it has been said that there are those in our world who have found a fascination even in pain itself. Because our life is dreadfuller, Sir, it has, and it must have, moments that are infinitely brighter than yours. It is titanic, Sir, where this is merely tidy. And we are inured to it and hardened by it. We are tempered to a finer edge. That is the point to which I am coming. Ask us to give up our earthly disorder, our miseries and distresses, our high death-rates and our hideous diseases, and at the first question every man and woman in the world would say. Yes! Willingly, Yes!' At the first question, Sir!"

Mr. Catskill held his audience for a moment on his extended finger.

"And then we should begin to take thought. We should ask, as you say your naturalists asked about your flies and suchlike offensive small game, we should ask, 'What goes with it? What is the price?' And when we learnt that the price was to surrender that intensity of life, that tormented energy, that pickled and experienced toughness, that rat-like, wolf-like toughness our perpetual struggle engenders, we should hesitate. We should hesitate. In the end, Sir, I believe, I hope and believe, indeed I pray and believe, we should say, 'No!' We should say, 'No!' "

Mr. Catskill was now in a state of great cerebral exaltation. He was making short thrusting gestures with his clenched fist. His voice rose and fell and boomed; he swayed and turned about, glanced for the approval of his fellow Earthlings, flung stray smiles at Mr. Burleigh.

This idea that our poor wrangling, nerveless, chance-driven world was really a fierce and close-knit system of powerful reactions in contrast with the evening serenities of a made and finished Utopia, had taken complete possession of his mind. "Never before, Sir, have I. realized, as I realize now, the high, the terrible and adventurous destinies of our earthly race. I look upon this Golden Lotus Land of yours, this devine perfected land from which all conflict has been banished——"

Mr. Barnstaple caught a faint smile on the face of the woman who had reminded him of the Delphic Sibyl.

"——and I admit and admire its order and beauty as some dusty and resolute pilgrim might pause, on his exalted and mysterious quest, and admit and admire the order and beauty of the pleasant gardens of some prosperous Sybarite. And like that pilgrim I may beg leave, Sir, to question the wisdom of your way of living. For I take it, Sir, that it is now a proven thing that life and all the energy and beauty of life are begotten by struggle and competition and conflict; we were moulded and wrought in hardship, and so, Sir, were you. And yet you dream here that you have eliminated conflict for ever. Your economic state, I gather, is some form of socialism; you have abolished competition in all the businesses of peace. Your political state is one universal unity; you have altogether cut out the bracing and ennobling threat and the purging and terrifying experience of war. Everything is ordered and provided for. Everything is secure. Everything is secure, Sir, except for one thing. . . .

"I grieve to trouble your tranquillity, Sir, but I must breathe the name of that one forgotten thing— *degeneration!* What is there here to prevent degeneration? Are you preventing degeneration?

"What penalties are there any longer for indolence? What rewards for exceptional energy and effort? What is there to keep men industrious, what watchful, when there is no personal loss but only some remote danger or inquiry to the community? For a time by a sort of inertia you may keep going. You may seem to be making a success of things. I admit it, you *do* seem to be making a success of things. Autumnal glory! Sunset splendour! *While about you in universes parallel to yours, parallel races still toil, still suffer, still complete and eliminate and gather strength and energy!*"

Mr. Catskill flourished his hand at the Utopians in rhetorical triumph.

"I would not have you think, Sir, that these criticisms of your world are offered in a hostile spirit. They are offered in the most amiable and helpful spirit. I am the skeleton, but the most friendly and apologetic skeleton, at your feast. I ask my searching and disagreeable question because I must. Is it indeed the wise way that you have chosen? You have sweetness and light—and leisure. Granted. But if there is all this multitude of Universes, of which you have told us, · Mr. Serpentine, so clearly and illuminatingly, and if one may suddenly open into another as ours has done into yours, I would ask you most earnestly how safe is your sweetness, your light and your leisure? We talk here, separated by we know not how flimsy a partition from innumerable worlds. And at that thought, Sir, it seems to me that as I stand here in the great golden calm of this place I can almost hear the trampling of hungry myriads as fierce and persistent as rats or wolves, the snarling voices of races inured to every pain and cruelty, the threat of terrible heroisms and pitiless aggressions. . . ."

He brought his discourse to an abrupt end. He smiled faintly; it seemed to Mr. Barnstaple that he triumphed over Utopia. He stood with hands on his hips and, as if he bent his body by that method, bowed stiffly. "Sir," he said with that ghost of a lisp of his, his eye on Mr. Burleigh, "I have said my say."

He turned about and regarded Mr. Barnstaple for a moment with his face screwed up almost to the appearance of a wink. He nodded his head, as if he tapped a nail with a hammer, jerked himself into activity, and returned to his proper place.

§ 5

Urthred did not so much answer Mr. Catskill as sit, elbow on knee and chin on hand, thinking audibly about him.

"The gnawing vigour of the rat," he mused, "the craving pursuit of the wolf, the mechanical persistence of wasp and fly and disease germ, have gone out of our world. That is true. We have obliterated that much of life's devouring forces. And lost nothing worth having. Pain, filth, indignity for ourselves—or any creatures; they have gone or they go. But it is not true that competition has gone from our world. Why does he say it has? Everyone here works to his or her utmost—for service and distinction. None may cheat himself out of toil or duty as men did in the age of confusion, when the mean and acquisitive lived and bred in luxury upon the heedlessness of more generous types. Why does he say we degenerate? He has been told better already.

The indolent and inferior do not procreate here. And why should he threaten us with fancies of irruptions from other, fiercer, more barbaric worlds? It is we who can open the doors into such other universes or close them as we choose. Because we know. We can go to them—when we know enough we shall—but they cannot come to us. There is no way but knowledge out of the cages of life. . . . What is the matter with the mind of this man?

"These Earthlings are only in the beginnings of science. They are still for all practical ends in that phase of fear and taboos that came also in the development of Utopia before confidence and understanding. Out of which phase our own world struggled during the Last Age of Confusion. The minds of these Earthlings are full of fears and prohibitions, and though it has dawned upon them that they may possibly control their universe, the thought is too terrible yet for them to face. They avert their minds from it. They still want to go on thinking, as their fathers did before them, that the universe is being managed for them better than they can control it for themselves. Because if that is so, they are free to obey their own violent little individual motives. Leave things to God, they cry, or leave them to Competition."

"Evolution was our blessed word," said Mr. Barnstaple, deeply interested.

"It is all the same thing—God, or Evolution, or what you will—so long as you mean a Power beyond your own which excuses you from your duty. Utopia says, 'Do not leave things at all. Take hold.' But these Earthlings still lack the habit of looking at reality—undraped. This man with the white linen fetter round his neck is afraid even to look upon men and women as they are. He is disgustingly excited by the common human body. This man with the glass lens before his left eye struggles to believe that there is a wise old Mother Nature behind the appearances of things, keeping a Balance. It was fantastic to hear about his Balance of Nature. Cannot he with two eyes and a lens see better than that? This last man who spoke so impressively, thinks that this old Beldame Nature is a limitless source of will and energy if only we submit to her freaks and cruelties and imitate her most savage moods, if only we sufficiently thrust and kill and rob and ravish one another. . . . He too preaches the old fatalism and believes it is the teaching of science. . . .

"These Earthlings do not yet dare to see what our Mother Nature is. At the back of their minds is still the desire to abandon themselves to her. They do not see that except for our eyes and wills, she is purposeless and blind. She is not awful, she is horrible. She takes no heed to our standards, nor to any standards of excellence. She made us by accident; all her children are bastards—undesired; she will cherish or expose them, pet or starve or torment without rhyme or reason. She does not heed, she does not care. She will lift us up to power and intelligence, or debase us to the mean feebleness of the rabbit or the slimy white filthiness of a thousand of her parasitic inventions. There must be good in her because she made all that is good in us—but also there is endless evil. Do not you Earthlings see the dirt of her, the cruelty, the insane indignity of much of her work?"

"Phew! Worse than 'Nature red in tooth and claw,'" murmured Mr. Freddy Mush.

"These things are plain," mused Urthred. "If they dared to see."

"Half the species of life in our planet also, half and more than half of all the things alive, were ugly or obnoxious, inane, miserable, wretched, with elaborate diseases, helplessly ill-adjusted to Nature's continually fluctuating conditions, when first we took this old Hag, our Mother, in hand. We have, after centuries of struggle, suppressed her nastier fancies, and washed her and combed her and taught her to respect and heed the last child of her wantonings—Man. With Man came Logos, the Word and the Will into our universe, to watch it and fear it, to learn it and cease to fear it, to know it and comprehend it and master it. So that we of Utopia are no longer the beaten and starved children of Nature, but her free and adolescent sons. We have taken over the Old Lady's Estate. Every day we learn a little better how to master this little planet. Every day our thoughts go out more surely to our inheritance, the stars. And the deeps beyond and beneath the stars."

"You have reached the stars?" cried Mr. Barnstaple.

"Not yet. Not even the other planets. But very plainly the time draws near when those great distances will cease to restrain us. . . ."

He paused. "Many of us will have to go out into the deeps of space. . . . And never return. . . . Giving their lives. . . .

"And into these new spaces—countless brave men. . . ."

Urthred turned towards Mr. Catskill. "We find your frankly expressed thoughts particularly interesting to-day. You help us to understand the past of our own world. You help us to deal with an urgent problem that we will presently explain to you. There are thoughts and ideas like yours in our ancient literature of two or three thousand years ago, the same preaching of selfish violence as though it was a virtue. Even then intelligent men knew better, and you yourself might know better if you were not wilfully set in wrong opinions. But it is plain to see from your manner and bearing that you are very wilful indeed in your opinions.

"You are not, you must realize, a very beautiful person, and probably you are not very beautiful in your pleasures and proceedings. But you have super-abundant energy, and so it is natural for you to turn to the excitements of risk and escape, to think that the best thing in life is the sensation of conflict and winning. Also in the economic confusion of such a world as yours there is an intolerable amount of toil that must be done, toil so disagreeable that it makes everyone of spirit anxious to thrust away as much of it as possible and to claim exemption from it on account of nobility, gallantry or good fortune. People in your world no doubt persuade themselves very easily that they are justifiably exempted, and you are under that persuasion. You live in a world of classes. Your badly trained mind has been under no necessity to invent its own excuses; the class into which you were born had all its excuses ready for you. So it is you take the best of everything without scruple and you adventure with life, chiefly at the expense of other people, with a mind trained by all its circumstances to resist the idea that there is any possible way of human living that can be steadfast and disciplined and at the same time vigorous and happy. You have argued against that persuasion all your life as though it were your personal enemy. It is your personal enemy; it condemns your way of life altogether, it damns you utterly for your adventures.

"Confronted now with an ordered and achieved beauty of living you still resist; you resist to escape dismay; you argue that this world of ours is unromantic, wanting in intensity, decadent, feeble. Now—in the matter of physical strength, grip hands with that young man who sits beside you."

Mr. Catskill glanced at the extended hand and shook his head knowingly. "You go on talking," he said.

"Yet when I tell you that neither our wills nor our bodies are as feeble as yours, your mind resists obstinately. You will not believe it. If for a moment your mind admits it, afterwards it recoils to the system of persuasions that protect your self-esteem. Only one of you accepts our world at all, and he does so rather because he is weary of yours than willing of ours. So I suppose it has to be. Yours are Age of Confusion minds, trained to conflict, trained to insecurity and secret self-seeking. In that fashion Nature and your state have taught you to live and so you must needs live until you die. Such lessons are to be unlearnt only in ten thousand generations, by the slow education of three thousand years.

"And we are puzzled by the question, what are we to do with you? We will try our utmost to deal fairly and friendly with you if you will respect our laws and ways.

"But it will be very difficult, we know, for you. You do not realize yet how difficult your habits and preconceptions will make it for you. Your party so far has behaved very reasonably and properly, in act if not in thought. But we have had another experience of Earthling ways to-day of a much more tragic kind. Your talk of fiercer, barbaric worlds breaking in upon us has had its grotesque parallel in reality to-day. It is true; there is something fierce and ratlike and dangerous about Earthly men. You are not the only Earthlings who came to Utopia through this gate that swung open for a moment to-day. There are others——"

"Of course!" said Mr. Barnstaple. "I should have guessed it! That third lot!"

"There is yet another of these queer locomotive machines of yours in Utopia."

"The grey car!" said Mr. Barnstaple to Mr. Burleigh. "It wasn't a hundred yards ahead of you."

"Raced us from Hounslow," said Mr. Burleigh's driver. "Real hot stuff."

Mr. Burleigh turned to Mr. Freddy Mush. "I think you said you recognised someone?"

"Lord Barralonga, Sir, almost to a certainty, and I *think* Miss Greeta Grey."

"There were two other men," said Mr. Barnstaple.

"They will complicate things," said Mr. Burleigh.

"They do complicate things," said Urthred. "They have killed a man."

"A Utopian?"

"These other people—there are five of them—whose names you seem to know, came into Utopia just in front of your two vehicles. Instead of stopping as you did when they found themselves on a new strange road, they seem to have quickened their pace very considerably. They passed some men and women and they made extraordinary gestures to them and abominable noises produced by an instrument specially designed for that purpose. Further on they encountered a silver cheetah and charged at it and ran right over it, breaking its back. They do not seem to have paused to see what became of it. A young man named Gold came out into the road to ask them to stop. But their machine is made in the most fantastic way, very complex and very foolish. It is quite unable to stop short suddenly. It is not driven by a single engine that is completely controlled. It has a complicated internal conflict. It has a sort of engine that drives it forward by a complex cogged gear on the axle of the hind wheels and it has various clumsy stopping contrivances by means of friction at certain points. You can apparently drive the engine at the utmost speed and at the same time jam the wheels to prevent them going round. When this young man stepped forward in front of them, they were quite unable to stop. They may have tried to do so. They say they did. Their machine swerved dangerously and struck him with its side.

"And killed him?"

"And killed him instantly. His body was horribly injured. . . . But they did not stop even for that. They slowed down and had a hasty consultation, and then seeing that

people were coming they set their machine in motion again
and made off. They seem to have been seized with a panic
fear of restraint and punishment. Their motives are very
difficult to understand. At any rate they went on. They
rode on and on into our country for some hours. An
aeroplane was presently set to follow them and another to
to clear the road in front of them. It was very difficult to
clear the road because neither our people nor our animals
understand such vehicles as theirs—nor such behaviour. In
the afternoon they got among mountains and evidently found
our roads much too smooth and difficult for their machine.
It made extraordinary noises as though it was gritting its
teeth, and emitted a blue vapour with an offensive smell.
At one corner where it should have stopped short, it skated
about and slid suddenly sideways and rolled over a cliff and
fell for perhaps twice the height of a man into a torrent.

"And they were killed?" asked Mr. Burleigh, with, as
it seemed to Mr. Barnstaple, a touch of eagerness in his
voice.

"Not one of them."

"Oh!" said Mr. Burleigh, "then what happened?"

"One of them has a broken arm and another is badly
cut about the face. The other two men and the woman are
uninjured except for fright and shock. When our people
came up to them the four men held their hands above their
heads. Apparently they feared they would be killed at once
and did this as an appeal for mercy."

"And what are you doing with them?"

"We are bringing them here. It is better we think to keep
all you Earthlings together. At present we cannot imagine
what must be done to you. We want to learn from you and
we want to be friendly with you if it is possible. It has
been suggested that you should be returned to your world.
In the end that may be the best thing to do. But at present

we do not know enough to do this certainly. Arden and Greenlake, when they made the attempt to rotate a part of our matter through the F dimension, believed that they would rotate it in empty space in that dimension. The fact that you were there and were caught into our universe, is the most unexpected thing that has happened in Utopia for a thousand years."

CHAPTER THE SEVENTH

THE BRINGING IN OF LORD BARRALONGA'S PARTY

§ 1

THE conference broke up upon this announcement, but Lord Barralonga and his party were not brought to the Conference Gardens until long after dark. No effort was made to restrain or control the movements of the Earthlings. Mr. Burleigh walked down to the lake with Lady Stella and the psychologist whose name was Lion, asking and answering questions. Mr. Burleigh's chauffeur wandered rather disconsolately, keeping within hail of his employer. Mr. Rupert Catskill took Mr. Mush off by the arm as if to give him instructions.

Mr. Barnstaple wanted to walk about alone to recall and digest the astounding realizations of the afternoon and to accustom himself to the wonder of this beautiful world, so beautiful and now in the twilight so mysterious also, with its trees and flowers becoming dim and shapeless notes of pallor and blackness and with the clear forms and gracious proportions of its buildings melting into a twilight indistinctness.

The earthliness of his companions intervened between him and this world into which he felt he might otherwise have been accepted and absorbed. He was in it, but in it only as a strange and discordant intruder. Yet he loved it already, and desired it and was passionately anxious to become a part of it. He had a vague but very powerful feeling that if only he could get away from his companions, if only in some way he could cast off his earthly clothing and everything upon him that marked him as earthly and linked him to earth, he would by the very act of casting that off become himself native to Utopia, and then that this tormenting sense, this bleak distressing strangeness would vanish out of his mind. He would suddenly find himself a Utopian in nature and reality, and it was Earth that would become the incredible dream, a dream that would fade at last completely out of his mind.

For a time however Father Amerton's need of a hearer prevented any such detachment from earthly thoughts and things. He stuck close to Mr. Barnstaple and maintained a stream of questions and comments that threw over this Utopian scene the quality of some Earl's Court exhibition that the two of them were visiting and criticizing together. It was evidently so provisional, so disputable and unreal to him, that at any moment Mr. Barnstaple felt he would express no astonishment if a rift in the scenery suddenly let in the clatter of the Earl's Court railway station or gave a glimpse of the conventional Gothic spire of St. Barnabas in the West.

At first Father Amerton's mind was busy chiefly with the fact that on the morrow he was to be "dealt with" on account of the scene in the conference. "How **can** they deal with me?" he said for the fourth time.

"I beg your pardon," said Mr. Barnstaple. Every time Mr. Amerton began speaking Mr. Barnstaple said, "I beg your pardon," in order to convey to him that he was interrupting a train of thought. But every time Mr. Barnstaple said, "I beg your pardon," Mr. Amerton would merely remark "You ought to consult someone about your hearing," and then go on with what he had to say.

"How can I be *dealt with?*" he asked of Mr. Barnstaple and the circumambient dusk. "How can I be dealt with?"

"Oh! psycho-analysis or something of that sort," said Mr.

Barnstaple.

"It takes two to play at that game," said Father Amerton, but it seemed to Mr. Barnstaple with a slight flavour of relief in his tone. "Whatever they ask me, whatever they suggest to me, I will not fail—I will bear my witness."

"I have no doubt they will find it hard to suppress you," said Mr. Barnstaple bitterly. . . .

For a time they walked among the tall sweet-smelling, white-flowered shrubs in silence. Now and then Mr. Barnstaple would quicken or slacken his pace with the idea of increasing his distance from Father Amerton but quite mechanically Father Amerton responded to these efforts. "Promiscuity," he began again presently. "What other word could you use?"

"I really beg your pardon," said Mr. Barnstaple.

"What other word could I have used *but* 'promiscuity'? What else could one expect—with people running about in this amazing want of costume, but the morals of the monkeys' cage? They admit that our institution of marriage is practically unknown to them!"

"It's a different world," said Mr. Barnstaple irritably. "A different world."

"The Laws of Morality hold good for every conceivable world."

"But in a world in which people propagated by fission and there was no sex?"

"Morality would be simpler but it would be the same morality." . . .

Presently Mr. Barnstaple was begging his pardon again.

"I was saying that this is a lost world."

"It doesn't *look* lost," said Mr. Barnstaple.

"It has rejected and forgotten Salvation."

Mr. Barnstaple put his hands into his pockets and began to whistle the barcarolle from "The Tales of Hoffman," very softly to himself. Would Father Amerton never leave him? Could nothing be done with Father Amerton? At the old shows at Earl's Court there used to be wire baskets for waste paper and cigarette ends and bores generally. If one could only tip Father Amerton suddenly into some such receptacle!

"Salvation has been offered them, and they have rejected it and well nigh forgotten it. And that is why we have been sent to them. We have been sent to them to recall them to the One Thing that Matters, to the One Forgotten Thing. Once more we have to raise the healing symbol as Moses raised it in the Wilderness. Ours is no light mission. We have been sent into this Hell of sensuous materialism——"

"Oh, *Lord!*" said Mr. Barnstaple, and relapsed into the barcarolle. . . .

"I *beg* your pardon," he exclaimed again presently.

"Where is the Pole Star? What has happened to the Wain?"

Mr. Barnstaple looked up.

He had not thought of the stars before, and he looked up prepared in this fresh Universe to see the strangest constellations. But just as the life and size of the planet they were on ran closely parallel to the earth's so he beheld above him a starry vault of familiar forms. And just as the Utopian world failed to be altogether parallel to its sister universe, so did these constellations seem to be a little out in their drawing. Orion, he thought, straddled wider and with a great unfamiliar nebula at one corner, and it was true—the Wain was flattened out and the pointers pointed to a great void in the heavens.

"Their Pole Star gone! The Pointers, the Wain askew! It is symbolical," said Father Amerton.

It was only too obviously going to be symbolical. Mr. Barnstaple realized that a fresh storm of eloquence was imminent from Father Amerton. At any cost he felt this nuisance must be abated.

§ 2

On earth Mr. Barnstaple had been a passive victim to bores of all sorts, delicately and painfully considerate of the mental limitations that made their insensitive pressure possible. But the free air of Utopia had already mounted to his head and released initiatives that his excessively deferential recognition of others had hitherto restrained. He had had enough of Father Amerton; it was necessary to turn off Father Amerton, and he now proceeded to do so with a simple directness that surprised himself.

"Father Amerton," he said, "I have a confession to make to you."

"Ah!" cried Father Amerton. "Please—anything?"

"You have been walking about with me and shouting at my ears until I am strongly impelled to murder you."

"If what I have said has struck home——"

"It hasn't struck home. It has been a tiresome, silly, deafening jabber in my ears. It wearies me indescribably. It prevents my attending to the marvellous things about us. I see exactly what you mean when you say that there is no Pole Star here and that that is symbolical. Before you begin I appreciate the symbol, and a very obvious, weak and ultimately inaccurate symbol it is. But you are one of those obstinate spirits who believe in spite of all evidence that the eternal hills are still eternal and the fixed stars fixed for ever. I want you to understand that I am entirely out of sympathy with all this stuff of yours. You seem to embody all that is wrong and ugly and impossible in Catholic teaching. I agree with these Utopians that there is something wrong with your mind about sex, in all probability a nasty twist given to it in early life, and that what you keep saying and hinting about sexual life here is horrible and outrageous. And I am equally hostile to you and exasperated and repelled by you when you speak of religion proper. You make religion disgusting just as you make sex disgusting. You are a dirty priest. What *you* call Christianity is a black and ugly superstition, a mere excuse for malignity and persecution. It is an outrage upon Christ. If you are a Christian, then most passionately I declare myself *not* a Christian. But there are other meanings for Christianity than those you put upon it, and in another sense this Utopia here is Christian beyond all dreaming. Utterly beyond your understanding. We have come into this glorious world, which, compared to our world, is like a bowl of crystal compared to an old tin can, and you have the insufferable impudence to say that we have been sent hither as missionaries to teach them—God knows what!"

"God *does* know what," said Father Amerton, a little taken aback, but coming up very pluckily.

"Oh!" cried Mr. Barnstaple, and was for a moment speechless.

"Listen to me, my Friend," said Father Amerton, catching at his sleeve.

"Not for my life!" cried Mr. Barnstaple, recoiling. "See! Down that vista, away there on the shore of the lake, those black figures are Mr. Burleigh, Mr. Mush and Lady Stella. They brought you here. They belong to your party and you belong to them. If they had not wanted your company you would not have been in their car. Go to them. I will not have you with me any longer. I refuse you and reject you. That is your way. This, by this little building, is mine. Don't follow me, or I will lay hands on you and bring in these Utopians to interfere between us. . . . Forgive my plainness, Mr. Amerton. But get away from me! Get away from me!"

Mr. Barnstaple turned, and seeing that Father Amerton stood hesitating at the parting of the ways, took to his heels and ran from him.

He fled along an alley behind tall hedges, turned sharply to the right and then to the left, passed over a high bridge that crossed in front of a cascade that flung a dash of spray in his face, blundered by two couples of lovers who whispered softly in the darkling, ran deviously across flower-studded turf, and at last threw himself down breathless upon the steps that led up to a terrace that looked towards lake and mountains, and was adorned, it seemed in the dim light, with squat stone figures of seated vigilant animals and men.

"Ye merciful stars!" cried Mr. Barnstaple. "At last I am alone."

He sat on these steps for a long time with his eyes upon the scene about him, drinking in the satisfying realization that for a brief interval at any rate, with no earthly presence to intervene, he and Utopia were face to face.

§ 3

He could not call this world the world of his dreams because he had never dared to dream of any world so closely shaped to the desires and imaginations of his heart. But surely this world it was, or a world the very fellow of it, that had lain deep beneath the thoughts and dreams of thousands of sane and troubled men and women in the world of disorder from which he had come. It was no world of empty peace, no such golden decadence of indulgence as Mr. Catskill tried to imagine it; it was a world, Mr. Barnstaple perceived, intensely militant, conquering and to conquer, prevailing over the obduracy of force and matter, over the lifeless separations of empty space and all the antagonistic mysteries of being.

In Utopia in the past, obscured by the superficial exploits

of statesmen like Burleigh and Catskill and the competition
of traders and exploiters every whit as vile and vulgar as
their earthly compeers, the work of quiet and patient thinkers
and teachers had gone on and the foundations which sustained
this serene intensity of activity had been laid. How few of
these pioneers had ever felt more than a transitory gleam
of the righteous loveliness of the world their lives made
possible!

And yet even in the hate and turmoil and distresses of
the Days of Confusion there must have been earnest enough
of the exquisite and glorious possibilities of life. Over the
foulest slums the sunset called to the imaginations of men,
and from mountain ridges, across great valleys, from cliffs
and hill-sides and by the uncertain and terrible splendours
of the sea, men must have had glimpses of the inconceivable
and attainable magnificence of being. Every flower petal,
every sunlit leaf, the vitality of young things, the happy
moments of the human mind transcending itself in art, all
these things must have been material for hope, incentive to
effort. And now at last—this world!

Mr. Barnstaple lifted up his hands like one who worships
to the friendly multitude of the stars above him.

"I have seen," he whispered. "I have seen."

Little lights and soft glows of illumination were coming
out here and there over this great park of flowerlike buildings and garden spaces that sloped down towards the lake.
A circling aeroplane, itself a star, hummed softly overhead.

A slender girl came past him down the steps and paused
at the sight of him.

"Are you one of the Earthlings?" came the question, and
a beam of soft light shone momentarily upon Mr. Barnstaple from the bracelet on her arm.

"I came to-day," said Mr. Barnstaple, peering up at her.

"You are the man who came alone in a little machine of

tin, with rubber air-bags round the wheels, very rusty underneath, and painted yellow. I have been looking at it."

"It is not a bad little car," said Mr. Barnstaple.

"At first we thought the priest came in it with you."

"He is no friend of mine."

"There were priests like that in Utopia many years ago. They caused much mischief among the people."

"He was with the other lot," said Mr. Barnstaple. "For their week-end party I should think him—rather a mistake."

She sat down a step or so above him.

"It is wonderful that you should come here out of your world to us. Do you find this world of ours very wonderful? I suppose many things that seem quite commonplace to me because I have been born among them seem wonderful to you."

"You are not very old?"

"I am eleven. I am learning the history of the Ages of Confusion, and they say your world is still in an Age of Confusion. It is just as though you came to us out of the past—out of history. I was in the Conference and I was watching your face. You love this present world of ours— at least you love it much more than your other people do."

"I want to live all the rest of my life in it."

"I wonder if that is possible?"

"Why should it not be possible? It will be easier than sending me back. I should not be very much in the way. I should only be here for twenty or thirty years at the most, and I would learn everything I could and do everything I was told."

"But isn't there work that you have to do in your own world?"

Mr. Barnstaple made no answer to that. He did not seem to hear it. It was the girl who presently broke the silence.

"They say that when we Utopians are young, before our minds and characters are fully formed and matured, we are very like the men and women of the Age of Confusion. We are moré egotistical then, they tell us; life about us is still so unknown, that we are adventurous and romantic. I suppose I am egotistical yet—and adventerous. And it does still seem to me that in spite of many terrible and dreadful things there was much that must have been wildly exciting and desirable in that past—which is still so like your present. What can it have been like to have been a general entering a conquered city? Or a prince being crowned? Or to be rich and able to astonish people by acts of power and benevolence? Or to be a martyr led out to die for some splendid misunderstood cause?"

"These things sound better in stories and histories than in reality," said Mr. Barnstaple after due consideration. "Did you hear Mr. Rupert Catskill, the last of the Earthlings to make a speech?"

"He thought romantically—but he did not look romantic."

"He has lived most romantically. He has fought bravely in wars. He has been a prisoner and escaped wonderfully from prison. His violent imaginations have caused the deaths of thousands of people. And presently we shall see another romantic adventurer in this Lord Barralonga they are bring-ing hither. He is enormously rich and he tries to astonish people with his wealth—just as you have dreamt of astonishing people."

"Are they not astonished?"

"Romance is not reality," said Mr. Barnstaple. "He is one of a number of floundering, corrupting rich men who are a weariness to themselves and an intolerable nuisance to the rest of the world. They want to do vulgar showy things. This man Barralonga was an assistant to a photogra-pher and something of an actor when a certain invention called moving pictures came into our world. He became a great prospector in the business of showing these pictures, partly by accident, partly by the unscrupulous cheating of various inventors. Then he launched out into speculations in shipping and in a trade we carry on in our world in frozen meat brought from great distances. He made food costly for many people and impossible for some, and so he grew rich. For in our world men grow wealthy by inter-cepting rather than by serving. And having become ignobly rich, certain of our politicians, for whom he did some timely services, ennobled him by giving him the title of Lord. Do you understand the things I am saying? Was your Age of Confusion so like ours? *You did not know it was so ugly.* Forgive me if I disillusion you about the Age of Confusion and its romantic possibilities. But I have just stepped out of the dust and disorder and noise of its indiscipline, out of limitation, cruelties and distresses, out of weariness in which hope dies. . . . Perhaps if my world attracts you you may yet have an opportunity of adventuring out of all this into its disorders. . . . That will be an adventure indeed. . . . Who knows what may happen between our worlds? . . . But you will not like it, I am afraid. You cannot imagine how dirty our world is. . . . Dirt and disease, these are in the trailing skirts of all romance. . . ."

A silence fell between them; he followed his own thoughts and the girl sat and wondered over him.

At length he spoke again.

"Shall I tell you what I was thinking of when you spoke to me?"

"Yes?"

"Your world is the consummation of a million ancient dreams. It is wonderful! It is wonder, high as heaven. But it is a great grief to me that two dear friends of mine cannot be here with me to see what I am seeing. It is queer how strong the thought of them is in my mind. One has passed now beyond all the universes, alas;—but the other is still in my world. You are a student, my dear; everyone of your world, I suppose, is a student here, but in our world students are a class apart. We three were happy together because we were students and not yet caught into the mills of senseless toil, and we were none the less happy perhaps because we were miserably poor and often hungry together. We used to talk and dispute together and in our students' debating society, discussing the disorders of our world and how some day they might be bettered. Was there, in your Age of Confusion, that sort of eager, hopeful, poverty-struck student life?"

"Go on," said the girl with her eyes intent on his dim profile. "In old novels I have read of just that hungry dreaming student world."

"We three agreed that the supreme need of our time was education. We agreed that was the highest service we could join. We all set about it in our various ways, I the least useful of the three. My friends and I drifted a little apart. They edited a great monthly periodical that helped to keep the world of science together, and my friend, serving a careful and grudging firm of publishers, edited school books for them, conducted an educational paper, and also inspected schools for our university. He was too heedless of pay and profit ever to become even passably well off though these publishers profited greatly by his work; his whole life was a continual service of toil for teaching; he did not take as much as a month's holiday in any year in his life. While he lived I thought little of the work he was doing, but since he died I have heard from teachers whose schools he inspected, and from book writers whom he advised, of the incessant high quality of his toil and the patience and sympathy of his work. On such lives as his this Utopia in

which your sweet life is opening is founded; on such lives
our world of earth will yet build its Utopia. But the life
of this friend of mine ended abruptly in a way that tore
my heart. He worked too hard and too long through a crisis
in which it was inconvenient for him to take a holiday. His
nervous system broke down with shocking suddenness, his
mind gave way, he passed into a phase of acute melancholia
and—died. For it is perfectly true, old Nature has neither
righteousness nor pity. This happened a few weeks ago.
That other old friend and I, with his wife, who had been
his tireless helper, were chief among the mourners at his
funeral. To-night the memory of that comes back to me
with extraordinary vividness. I do not know how you dispose of your dead here, but on earth the dead are mostly
buried in the earth."

"We are burnt," said the girl.

"Those who are liberal-minded in our world burn also.
Our friend was burnt, and we stood and took our part in
a service according to the rites of our ancient religion in
which we no longer believed, and presently we saw his coffin,
covered with wreathes of flowers, slide from before us out
of our sight through the gates that led to the furnaces of
the crematorium, and as it went, taking with it so much of
my youth, I saw that my other dear old friend was sobbing,
and I too was wrung to the pitch of tears to think that so
valiant and devoted and industrious a life should end, as it
seemed, so miserably and thanklessly. The priest had been
reading a long contentious discourse by a theological writer
named Paul, full of bad argument by analogy and weak
assertions. I wished that instead of the ideas of this ingenious
ancient we could have had some discourse upon the real
nobility of our friend, on the pride and intensity of his work
and on his scorn for mercenary things. All his life he had
worked with unlimited devotion for such a world as this,

and yet I doubt if he had ever had any realization of the clearer, nobler life for man than his life of toil and the toil of such lives as his, were making sure and certain in the days to come. He lived by faith. He lived too much by faith. There was not enough sunlight in his life. If I could have him here now—and that other dear friend who grieved for him so bitterly; if I could have them both here; if I could give up my place here to them so that they could see, as I see, the real greatness of their lives reflected in these great consequences of such lives as theirs—then, then I could rejoice in Utopia indeed. . . . But I feel now as if I had taken my old friend's savings and was spending them on myself. . . ."

Mr. Barnstaple suddenly remembered the youth of his hearer. "Forgive me, my dear child, for running on in this fashion. But your voice was kind."

The girl's answer was to bend down and brush his extended hand with her soft lips.

Then suddenly she sprang to her feet. "Look at that light," she said, "among the stars!"

Mr. Barnstaple stood up beside her.

"That is the aeroplane bringing Lord Barralonga and his party; Lord Barralonga who killed a man today! Is he a very big, strong man—ungovernable and wonderful?"

Mr. Barnstaple, struck by a sudden doubt, looked sharply at the sweet upturned face beside him.

"I have never seen him. But I believe he is a youngish, baldish, undersized man, who suffers very gravely from a disordered liver and kidneys. This has prevented the dissipation of his energies upon youthful sports and pleasures and enabled him to concentrate upon the acquisition of property. And so he was able to buy the noble title that touches your imagination. Come with me and look at him."

The girl stood still and met his eyes. She was eleven years

old and she was as tall as he was.

"But was there no romance in the past?"

"Only in the hearts of the young. And it died."

"But is there no romance?"

"Endless romance—and it has all to come. It comes for you."

§ 4

The bringing in of Lord Barralonga and his party was something of an anti-climax to Mr. Barnstaple's wonderful day. He was tired and, quite unreasonably, he resented the invasion of Utopia by these people.

The two parties of Earthlings were brought together in a brightly lit hall near the lawn upon which the Barralonga aeroplane had come down. The new-comers came in in a group together, blinking, travel-worn and weary-looking. But it was evident they were greatly relieved to encounter other Earthlings in what was to them a still intensely puzzling experience. For they had had nothing to compare with the calm and lucid discussion of the Conference Place. Their lapse into this strange world was still an incomprehensible riddle for them.

Lord Barralonga was the owner of the gnome-like face that had looked out at Mr. Barnstaple when the large grey car had passed him on the Maidenhead Road. His skull was very low and broad above his brows so that he reminded Mr. Barnstaple of the flat stopper of a glass bottle. He looked hot and tired, he was considerably dishevelled as if from a struggle, and one arm was in a sling; his little brown eyes were as alert and wary as those of a wicked urchin in the hands of a policeman. Sticking close to him like a familiar spirit was a small, almost jockey-like chauffeur, whom he addressed as "Ridley." Ridley's face also was marked by the stern determination of a man in a difficult position not in any manner to give himself away. His left cheek and ear had been cut in the automobile smash and were liberally adorned with sticking plaster. Miss Greeta Grey, the lady of the party, was a frankly blonde beauty in a white flannel tailor-made suit. She was extraordinarily unruffled by the circumstances in which she found herself; it was as if she had no sense whatever of their strangeness. She carried herself with the habitual hauteur of a beautiful girl almost professionally exposed to the risk of unworthly advances. Anywhere.

The other two people of the party were a grey-faced, grey-clad American, also very wary-eyed, who was, Mr. Barnstaple learnt from Mr. Mush, Hunker, the Cinema King, and a thoroughly ruffled-looking Frenchman, a dark, smartly dressed man, with an imperfect command of English, who seemed rather to have fallen into Lord Barralonga's party than to have belonged to it properly. Mr. Barnstaple's mind leapt to the conclusion, and nothing occurred afterwards to change his opinion, that some interest in the cinematograph had brought this gentleman within range of Lord Barralonga's hospitality and that he had been caught, as a foreigner may so easily be caught, into the embrace of a thoroughly uncongenial week-end expedition.

As Lord Barralonga and Mr. Hunker came forward to greet Mr. Burleigh and Mr. Catskill, this Frenchman addressed himself to Mr. Barnstaple with the enquiry whether he spoke French.

"I cannot understand," he said. "We were to have gone to Viltshire—Wiltshire, and then one 'orrible thing has happen after another. What is it we have come to and what sort of people are all these people who speak most excellent French? Is it a joke of Lord Barralonga, or a dream, or what has happen to us?"

Mr. Barnstaple attempted some explanation.

"Another dimension," said the Frenchman, "another worl'. That is all very well. But I have my business to attend to in London. I have no need to be brought back in this way to France, some sort of France, some other France in some other worl'. It is too much of a joke altogether."

Mr. Barnstaple attempted some further exposition. It was clear from his interlocutor's puzzled face that the phrases he used were too difficult. He turned helplessly to Lady Stella and found her ready to undertake the task. "This lady," he said, "will be able to make things plain to you. Lady Stella, this is Monsieur——"

"Emile Dupont," the Frenchman bowed. "I am what you call a journalist and publicist. I am interested in the cinematograph from the point of view of education and propaganda. It is why I am here with his Lordship Barralonga."

French conversation was Lady Stella's chief accomplishment. She sailed into it now very readily. She took over the elucidation of M. Dupont, and only interrupted it to tell Miss Greeta Grey how pleasant it was to have another woman with her in this strange world.

Relieved of M. Dupont, Mr. Barnstaple stood back and surveyed the little group of Earthlings in the centre of the hall and the circle of tall, watchful Utopians about them and rather aloof from them. Mr. Burleigh was being distantly cordial to Lord Barralonga, and Mr. Hunker was saying what a great pleasure it was to him to meet "Britain's foremost statesman." Mr. Catskill stood in the most friendly manner beside Barralonga; they knew each other well; and Father Amerton exchanged comments with Mr. Mush. Ridley and Penk, after some moments of austere regard, had gone apart to discuss the technicalities of the day's experience in undertones. Nobody paid any attention to Mr. Barnstaple.

It was like a meeting at a railway station. It was like a

reception. It was utterly incredible and altogether common place. He was weary. He was saturated and exhausted by wonder.

"Oh, I am going to my bed!" he yawned suddenly. "I am going to my little bed."

He made his way through the friendly-eyed Utopians out into the calm starlight. He nodded to the strange nebula at the corner of Orion as a weary parent might nod to importunate offspring. He would consider it again in the morning. He staggered drowsily through the gardens to his own particular retreat.

He disrobed and went to sleep as immediately and profoundly as a tired child.

CHAPTER THE EIGHTH

EARLY MORNING IN UTOPIA

§ 1

MR. BARNSTAPLE awakened slowly out of profound slumber.

He had a vague feeling that a very delightful and wonderful dream was slipping from him. He tried to keep on with the dream and not to open his eyes. It was about a great world of beautiful people who had freed themselves from a thousand earthly troubles. But it dissolved and faded from his mind. It was not often nowadays that dreams came to Mr. Barnstaple. He lay very still with his eyes closed, reluctantly coming awake to the affairs of every day.

The cares and worries of the last fortnight resumed their sway. Would he ever be able to get away for a holiday by himself? Then he remembered that he had already got his valise stowed away in the Yellow Peril. But surely that was not last night; that was the night before last, and he had started—he rememberd now starting and the little thrill of getting through the gate before Mrs. Barnstaple suspected anything. He opened his eyes and fixed them on a white ceiling, trying to recall that journey. He remembered turning into the Camberwell New Road and the bright exhilaration of the morning, Vauxhall Bridge and that nasty tangle of traffic at Hyde Park Corner. He always maintained that the west of London was far more difficult for motoring than the east. Then—had he gone to Uxbridge? No. He recalled the road to Slough and then came a blank in his mind.

What a very good ceiling this was! Not a crack nor a

stain!

But how had he spent the rest of the day? He must have got somewhere because here he was in a thoroughly comfortable bed—an excellent bed. With a thrush singing. He had always maintained that a good thrush could knock spots off a nightingale, but this thrush was a perfect Caruso. And another answering it! In July! Pangbourne and Caversham were wonderful places for nightingales. In June. But this was July—and thrushes. . . . Across these drowsy thoughtphantoms came the figure of Mr. Rupert Catskill, hands on hips, face and hand thrust forward speaking, saying astonishing things. To a naked seated figure with a grave intent face. And other figures. One with a face like the Delphic Sibyl. Mr. Barnstaple began to remember that in some way he had got himself mixed up with a weekend party at Taplow Court. Now had this speech been given at Taplow Court? At Taplow Court they wear clothes. But perhaps the aristocracy in retirement and privacy——?

Utopia? . . . But was it possible?

Mr. Barnstaple sat up in his bed in a state of extreme amazement. "Impossible!" he said. He was lying in a little loggia half open to the air. Between the slender pillars of fluted glass he saw a range of snowtopped mountains, and in the foreground a great cluster of tall spikes bearing deep red flowers. The bird was still singing—a glorified thrush, in a glorified world. Now he remembered everything. Now it was all clear. The sudden twisting of the car, the sound like the snapping of a fiddle string and—Utopia! Now he had it all, from the sight of sweet dead Greenlake to the bringing in of Lord Barralonga under the strange unfamiliar stars. It was no dream. He looked at his hand on the exquisitely fine coverlet. He felt his rough chin. It was a world real enough for shaving—and for a very definite readiness for breakfast. Very—for he had missed his supper.

And as if in answer to his thought a smiling girl appeared ascending the steps to his sleeping-place and bearing a little tray. After all, there was much to be said for Mr. Burleigh. To his swift statesmanship it was that Mr. Barnstaple owed this morning cup of tea.

"Good morning," said Mr. Barnstaple.

"Why not?" said the young Utopian, and put down his tea and smiled at him in a motherly fashion and departed.

"Why not a good morning, I suppose," said Mr. Barnstaple and meditated for a moment, chin on knees, and then gave his attention to the bread-and-butter and tea.

§ 2

The little dressing-room in which he found his clothes lying just as he had dumped them overnight, was at once extraordinarily simple and extraordinarily full of interest for Mr. Barnstaple. He paddled about it humming as he examined it.

The bath was much shallower than an ordinary earthly bath; apparently the Utopians did not believe in lying down and stewing. And the forms of everything were different, simpler and more graceful. On earth he reflected art was largely wit. The artist had a certain limited selection of obdurate materials and certain needs, and his work was a clever reconciliation of the obduracy and the necessity and of the idiosyncrasy of the substance to the æsthetic preconceptions of the human mind. How delightful, for example, was the earthly carpenter dealing cleverly with the grain and character of this wood or that. But here the artist had a limitless control of material, and that element of witty adaptation had gone out of his work. His data were the human mind and body. Everything in this little room was unobtrusively but perfectly convenient—and difficult to misuse. If you splashed too much a thoughtful outer rim tidied things up for you.

In a tray by the bath was a very big fine sponge. So either Utopians still dived for sponges or they grew them or trained them (who could tell?) to come up of their own accord.

As he set out his toilet things a tumbler was pushed off a glass shelf on to the floor and did not break. Mr. Barnstaple in an experimental mood dropped it again and still it did not break.

He could not find taps at first though there was a big washing basin as well as a bath. Then he perceived a number of studs on the walls with black marks that might be Utopian writing. He experimented. He found very hot water and then very cold water filling his bath, a fountain of probably soapy warm water, and other fluids,—one with an odour of pine and one with a subdued odour of chlorine. The Utopian characters on these studs set him musing for a time; they were the first writing he had seen; they appeared to be word characters, but whether they represented sounds or were greatly simplified hieroglyphics he could not imagine. Then his mind went off at a tangent in another direction because the only metal apparent in this dressing-room was gold. There was, he noted, an extraordinary lot of gold in the room. It was set and inlaid in gold. The soft yellow lines gleamed and glittered. Gold evidently was cheap in Utopia. Perhaps they knew how to make it.

He roused himself to the business of his toilet. There was no looking glass in the room, but when he tried what he thought was the handle of a cupboard door, he found himself opening a triple full-length mirror. Afterwards he was to discover that there were no displayed mirrors in Utopia; Utopians, he was to learn, thought it indecent to be reminded of themselves in that way. The Utopian method was to scrutinize oneself, see that one was all right and then forget oneself for the rest of the day. He stood now surveying his pyjamad and unshaven self with extreme disfavour. Why do respectable citizens favour such ugly pink-striped pyjamas? When he unpacked his nail brush and tooth brush, shaving brush and washing glove, they seemed to him to have the coarseness of a popular burlesque. His tooth brush was a particularly ignoble instrument. He wished now he had bought a new one at the chemist's shop near Victoria Station.

And what nasty queer things his clothes were!

He had a fantastic idea of adopting Utopian ideas of costume, but a reflective moment before his mirror restrained him. Then he remembered that he had packed a silk tennis shirt and flannels. Suppose he wore those, without a collar stud or tie—and went barefooted?

He surveyed his feet. As feet went on earth they were not unsightly feet. But on earth they had been just wasted.

§ 3

A particularly clean and radiant Mr. Barnstaple, white-clad, bare-necked and bare-footed, presently emerged into the Utopian sunrise. He smiled, stretched his arms and took a deep breath of the sweet air. Then suddenly his face became hard and resoulute.

From another little sleeping house not two hundred yards away Father Amerton was emerging. Intuitively Mr. Barnstaple knew he meant either to forgive or be forgiven for the overnight quarrel. It would be a matter of chance whether he would select the role of offender or victim; what was certain was that he would smear a dreary mess of emotional personal relationship over the jewel-like clearness and brightness of the scene. A little to the right of Mr. Barnstaple and in front of him were wide steps leading down towards the lake. Three strides and he was going down these steps two at a time. It may have been his hectic fancy, but it seemed to him that he heard the voice of Father Amerton, "Mr. Barn—staple," in pursuit.

Mr. Barnstaple doubled and doubled again and crossed a bridge across an avalanche gully, a bridge with huge masonry in back and roof and with delicate pillars of prismatic glass towards the lake. The sunlight entangled in these pillars broke into splashes of red and blue and golden light. Then at a turfy corner gay with blue gentians, he narrowly escaped a collision with Mr. Rupert Catskill. Mr. Catskill was in the same costume that he had worn on the previous day except that he was without his grey top hat. He walked with his hands clasped behind him.

"Hullo!" he said. "What's the hurry? We seem to be the first people up."

"I saw Father Amerton——"

'That accounts for it. You were afraid of being caught up in a service, Matins or Prime or whatever he calls it. Wise man to run. He shall pray for the lot of us. Me too."

He did not wait for any endorsement from Mr. Barnstaple, but went on talking.

"You have slept well? What did you think of the old fellow's answer to my speech. Eh? Evasive cliches. When in doubt, abuse the plaintiff's attorney. We don't agree with him because we have bad hearts."

"What old fellow do you mean?"

"The worthy gentleman who spoke after me."

"Urthred! But he's not forty."

"He's seventy-three. He told us afterwards. They live long here, a lingering business. Our lives are fitful hectic fever from their point of view. But as Tennsyon said, 'Better fifty years of Europe than a cycle of Cathay!' H'm? He evaded my points. This is Lotus Land, Sunset Land; we shan't be thanked for disturbing its slumbers."

"I doubt their slumbers."

"Perhaps the Socialist bug has bit you too. Yes—I see it has! Believe me this is the most complete demonstration of decadence it would be possible to imagine. Complete. And we shall disturb their—slumbers, never fear. Nature, you will see, is on our side—in a way no one has thought of yet."

"But I don't see the decadence," said Mr. Barnstaple.

"None so blind as those who won't see. It's everywhere. Their large flushed pseudo-health. Like fatted cattle. And their treatment of Barralonga. They don't know how to treat him. They don't even arrest him. They've never arrested anyone for a thousand years. He careers through their land, killing and slaying and frightening and disturbing and they're flabbergasted, Sir, simply flabbergasted. It's like a dog run-ning amuck in a world full of sheep. If he hadn't had a side-slip I believe he would be hooting and snorting and careering along now—killing people. They've lost the instinct of social defence."

"I wonder."

"A very good attitude of mind. If indulged in, in modera-tion. But when your wondering is over, you will begin to see that I am right. M'm? Ah! There on that terrace! Isn't that my Lord Barralonga and his French acquaintance? It is. Inhaling the morning air. I think with your permission I will go on and have a word with them. Which way did you say Father Amerton was? I don't want to disturb his de-votions. This way? Then if I go to the right——"

He grimaced amiably over his shoulder.

§ 4

Mr. Barnstaple came upon two Utopians gardening.

They had two light silvery wheelbarrows, and they were cutting out old wood and overblown clusters from a line of thickets that sprawled over a rough-heaped ridge of rock and foamed with crimson and deep red roses. These gardeners had great leather gauntlets and aprons of tanned skin, and they carried hooks and knives.

Mr. Barnstaple had never before seen such roses as they were tending here; their fragrance filled the air. He did not know that double roses could be got in mountains; bright red single sorts he had seen high up in Switzerland, but not such huge loose-flowered monsters as these. They dwarfed their leaves. Their wood was in long, thorny, snaky-red streaked stems that writhed wide and climbed to the rocky lumps over which they grew. Their great petals fell like red snow and like drifting moths and like blood upon the soft soil that sheltered amidst the brown rocks.

"You are the first Utopians I have actually seen at work," he said.

"This isn't our work," smiled the nearer of the two, a fair-haired, freckled, blue-eyed youth. "But as we are for these roses we have to keep them in order."

"Are they your roses?"

"Many people think these double mountain roses too much trouble and a nuisance with their thorns and sprawling branches, and many people think only the single sorts of roses ought to be grown in these high places and that this lovely sort ought to be left to die out up here. Are you for our roses?"

"Such roses as these?" said Mr. Barnstaple. "Altogether."

"Good! Then just bring me up my barrow closer for all this litter. We're responsible for the good behaviour of all this thicket reaching right down there almost to the water."

"And you have to see to it yourselves?"

"Who else?"

"But couldn't you get someone—pay someone to see to

it for you?"

"Oh, hoary relic from the ancient past!" the young man replied. "Oh, fossil ignoramus from a barbaric universe! Don't you realize that there is no working class in Utopia? It died out fifteen hundred years or so ago. Wages-slavery, pimping and so forth are done with. We read about them in books. Who loves the rose must serve the rose—himself."

"But you work."

"Not for wages. Not because anyone else loves or desires something else and is too lazy to serve it or get it himself. We work, part of the brain, part of the will, of Utopia."

"May I ask at what?"

"I explore the interior of our planet. I study high-pressure chemistry. And my friend——"

He interrogated his friend, whose dark face and brown eyes appeared suddenly over a foam of blossom "I do Food."

"A cook?"

"Of sorts. Just now I am seeing to your Earthling dietary. It's most interesting and curious—but I should think rather destructive. I plan your meals. . . . I see you look anxious, but I saw to your breakfast last night." He glanced at a minute wrist-watch under the gauntlet of his gardening glove. "It will be ready in about an hour. How was the early tea?"

"Excellent," said Mr. Barnstaple.

"Good," said the dark young man. "I did my best. I hope the breakfast will be as satisfactory. I had to fly two hundred kilometres for a pig last night and kill it and cut it up myself, and find out how to cure it. Eating bacon has gone out of fashion in Utopia. I hope you will find my rashers satisfactory."

"It seems very rapid curing—for a rasher," said Mr. Barnstaple. "We could have done without it."

"Your spokesman made such a point of it."

The fair young man struggled out of the thicket and wheeled his barrow away. Mr. Barnstaple wished the dark young man "Good morning."

"Why shouldn't it be?" asked the dark young man.

§ 5

He discovered Ridley and Penk approaching him. Ridley's face and ear were still adorned with sticking-plaster and his bearing was eager and anxious. Penk followed a little way behind him, holding one hand to the side of his face. Both were in their professional dress, white-topped caps, square-cut leather coats and black gaiters; they had made no concessions to Utopian laxity.

Ridley began to speak as soon as he judged Mr. Barnstaple was within earshot.

"You don't 'appen to know, Mister, where these 'ere decadents shoved our car?"

"I thought your car was all smashed up."

"Not a Rolls-Royce—not like that. Wind-screen, mud-guards and the on-footboards perhaps. We went over sideways. I want to 'ave a look at it. And I didn't turn the petrol off. The carburettor was leaking a bit. My fault. I 'adn't been careful enough with the strainer. If she runs out of petrol, where's one to get more of it in this blasted Elysium? I ain't seen a sign anywhere. I know if I don't get that car into running form before Lord Barralonga wants it there's going to be trouble."

Mr. Barnstaple had no idea where the cars were.

" 'Aven't you a car of your own?" asked Ridley reproachfully.

"I have. But I've never given it a thought since I got out of it."

"Owner-driver," said Ridley bitterly.

"Anyhow, I can't help you find your cars. Have you

asked any of the Utopians?"

"Not us. We don't like the style of 'em," said Ridley. "They'll tell you."

"And watch us—whatever we do to our cars. They don't get a chance of looking into a Rolls-Royce every day in the year. Next thing we shall have them driving off in 'em. I don't like the place, and I don't like these people. They're queer. They ain't decent. His lordship says they're a lot of degenerates, and it seems to me his lordship is about right. I ain't a Puritan, but all this running about without clothes is a bit too thick for me. I wish I knew where they'd stowed those cars."

Mr. Barnstaple was considering Penk. "You haven't hurt your face?" he asked.

"Nothing to speak of," said Penk. "I suppose we ought to be getting on."

Ridley looked at Penk and then at Mr. Barnstaple. "He's had a bit of a contoosion," he remarked, a faint smile breaking through his sourness.

"We better be getting on if we're going to find those cars," said Penk.

A grin of intense enjoyment appeared upon Ridley's face. " 'E's bumped against something."

"Oh—*shut it!*" said Penk.

But the thing was too good to keep back. "One of these girls 'it 'im."

"What do you mean?" said Mr. Barnstaple. "You haven't been taking liberties——?"

"I 'ave *not,*" said Penk. "But as Mr. Ridley's been so obliging as to start the topic I suppose I got to tell wot 'appened. It jest illustrates the uncertainties of being among a lot of arf-savage, arf-crazy people, like we got among."

Ridley smiled and winked at Mr. Barnstaple. "Regular 'ard clout she gave 'im. Knocked him over. 'E put 'is 'and

on 'er shoulder and *clop!* over 'e went. Never saw anything like it."

"Rather unfortunate," said Mr. Barnstaple.

"It all 'appened in a second like."

"It's a pity it happened."

"Don't you go making any mistake about it, Mister, and
don't you go running off with any false ideas about it," said
Penk. "I don't want the story to get about—it might do
me a lot of 'arm with Mr. Burleigh. Pity Mr. Ridly couldn't
'old 'is tongue. What provoked her I do not know. She
came into my room as I was getting up, and she wasn't what
you might call wearing anything, and she looked a bit saucy,
to my way of thinking, and—well, something came into my
head to say to her, something—well, just the least little bit
sporty, so to speak. One can't always control one's thoughts
—can one? A man's a man. If a man's expected to be
civil in his private thoughts to girls without a stitch, so to
speak—*well!* I dunno. I really do not know. It's against
nature. I never said it, whatever it was I thought of. Mr.
Ridley 'ere will bear me out. I never said a word to her.
I 'adn't opened my lips when she hit me. Knocked me over,
she did—like a ninepin. Didn't even seem angry about it.
A 'ook-'it—sideways. It was surprise as much as anything
floored me."

"But Ridley says you touched her."

"Laid me 'and on 'er shoulder perhaps, in a sort of
fatherly way. As she was turning to go—not being sure
whether I wasn't going to speak to her, I admit. And there
you are! If I'm to get into trouble because I was wantonly
'it——"

Penk conveyed despair of the world by an eloquent gesture.

Mr. Barnstaple considered. "I shan't make trouble," he
said. "But all the same I think we must all be very careful
with these Utopians. Their ways are not our ways."

"Thank God!" said Ridley. "The sooner I get out of this world back to Old England, the better I shall like it."

He turned to go.

"You should 'ear 'is lordship," said Ridley over his shoulder. " 'E says it's just a world of bally degenerates—rotten degenerates—in fact, if you'll excuse me—§ § * ! * ! * † * † ! degenerates. Eh? That about gets 'em."

"The young woman's arm doesn't seem to have been very degenerate," said Mr. Barnstaple, standing the shock bravely.

"Don't it?" said Ridley bitterly. "That's all *you* know. Why! if there's one sign more sure than another about degeneration it's when women take to knocking men about. It's against instink. In any respectable decent world such a thing couldn't possibly 'ave 'appened. No 'ow!"

"No—'ow," echoed Penk.

"In *our* world, such a girl would jolly soon 'ave 'er lesson. Jolly soon. See?"

But Mr. Barnstaple's roving eye had suddenly discovered Father Amerton approaching very rapidly across a wide space of lawn and making arresting gestures. Mr. Barnstaple perceived he must act at once.

"Now here's someone who will certainly be able to help you find your cars, if he cares to do so. He's a most helpful man—Father Amerton. And the sort of views he has about women are the sort of views you have. You are bound to get on together. If you will stop him and put the whole case to him—plainly and clearly. . . ."

He set off at a brisk pace towards the lake shore.

He could not be far now from the little summer-house that ran out over the water against which the gaily coloured boats were moored.

If he were to get into one of these and pull out into the lake he would have Father Amerton at a very serious disadvantage. Even if that good man followed suit. One cannot have a really eloquent emotional scene when one is pulling hard in pursuit of another boat.

§ 6

As Mr. Barnstaple untied the bright white canoe with the big blue eye painted at its prow that he had chosen, Lady Stella appeared on the landing-stage. She came out of the pavilion that stood over the water, and something in her quick movement as she emerged suggested to Mr. Barn-staple's mind that she had been hiding there. She glanced about her and spoke very eagerly. "Are you going to row out upon the lake, Mr. Barnstaple? May I come?"

She was attired, he noted, in a compromise between the Earthly and the Utopian style. She was wearing what might have been either a very simple custard-coloured tea robe or a very sophisticated bath wrap; it left her slender, pretty arms bare and free except for a bracelet of amber and gold, and on her bare feet—and they were unusually shapely feet—were sandals. Her head was bare, and her dark hair very simply done with a little black and gold fillet round it that suited her intelligent face. Mr. Barnstaple was an ignoramus about feminine costume, but he appreciated the fact that she had been clever in catching the Utopian note.

He helped her into the canoe. "We will paddle right out—a good way," she said with another glance over her shoulder, and sat down.

For a long time Mr. Barnstaple paddled straight out so that he had nothing before him but sunlit water and sky, the low hills that closed in the lake towards the great plain, the huge pillars of the distant dam, and Lady Stella. She affected to be overcome by the beauty of the Conference garden slope with its houses and terraces behind him, but he could see that she was not really looking at the scene as a whole, but searching it restlessly for some particular object or person.

She made conversational efforts, on the loveliness of the morning and on the fact that birds were singing—"in July."

"But here it is not necessarily July," said Mr. Barnstaple.

"How stupid of me! Of course not."

"We seem to be in a fine May."

"It is probably very early," she said. "I forgot to wind my watch."

"Oddly enough we seem to be at about the same hours in our two worlds," said Mr. Barnstaple. "My wrist watch says Seven."

"No," said Lady Stella, answering her own thoughts and with her eyes on the distant gardens. "That is a Utopian girl. Have you met any others—of our party—this morning?"

Mr. Barnstaple brought the canoe round so that he too could look at the shore. From here they could see how perfectly the huge terraces and avalanche walls and gullies mingled and interwove with the projecting ribs and cliffs of the mountain masses behind. The shrub tangles passed up into hanging pinewoods; the torrents and cascades from the snowfield above were caught and distributed amidst the emerald slopes and gardens of the Conference Park. The terraces that retained the soil and held the whole design spread out on either hand to a great distance and were continued up into the mountain substance; they were built of a material that ranged through a wide variety of colours from a deep red to a purple-veined white, and they were diversified by great arches over torrents and rock gullies, by huge round openings that spouted water and by cascades of steps. The buildings of the place were distributed over these terraces and over the grassy slopes they contained, singly or in groups and clusters, buildings of purple and blue and white as light and delicate as the Alpine flowers about them. For some moments Mr. Barnstaple was held silent by this scene, and then he attended to Lady Stella's question. "I met Mr. Rupert Catskill and the two chauffeurs," he said, "and I saw Father Amerton and Lord Barralonga and M. Dupont in the distance. I've seen nothing of Mr. Mush or Mr. Burleigh."

"Mr. Cecil won't be about for hours yet. He will lie in bed until ten or eleven. He always takes a good rest in the morning when there is any great mental exertion before him."

The lady hesitated and then asked: "I suppose you haven't seen Miss Greeta Grey?"

"No," said Mr. Barnstaple. "I wasn't looking for our people. I was just strolling about—and avoiding somebody."

"The censor of manners and costumes?"

"Yes. . . . That, in fact, is why I took to this canoe."

The lady reflected and decided on a confidence.

"I was running away from someone too."

"Not the preacher?"

"Miss Grey!"

Lady Stella apparently went off at a tangent. "This is going to be a very difficult world to stay in. These people have very delicate taste. We may easily offend them."

"They are intelligent enough to understand."

"Do people who understand necessarily forgive? I've always doubted that proverb."

Mr. Barnstaple did not wish the conversation to drift away into generalities, so he paddled and said nothing.

"You see, Miss Grey used to play Phryne in a Revue."

"I seem to remember something about it. There was a fuss in the newspapers."

"That perhaps gave her a bias."

Three long sweeps with the paddle.

"But this morning she came to me and told me that she

was going to wear complete Utopian costume."

"Meaning?"

"A little rouge and face powder. It doesn't suit her the least little bit, Mr. Bastaple. It's a faux pas. It's indecent. But she's running about the gardens——. She might meet anyone. It's lucky Mr. Cecil isn't up. If she meets Father Amerton——! But it's best not to think of that. You see, Mr. Bastaple, these Utopians and their sun-brown bodies— and everything, are in the picture. They don't embarrass me. But Miss Grey——. An earthly civilized woman taken out of her clothes *looks* taken out of her clothes. Peeled. A sort of *bleached* white. That nice woman who seems to hover round us, Lychnis, when she advised me what to wear, never for one moment suggested anything of the sort. . . . But, of course, I don't know Miss Grey well enough to talk to her and besides, one never knows how a woman of that sort is going to take a thing. . . ."

Mr. Barnstaple stared shoreward. Nothing was to be seen of an excessively visible Miss Greeta Grey. Then he had a conviction. "Lychnis will take care of her," he said.

"I hope she will. Perhaps, if we stay out here for a time——"

"She will be looked after," said Mr. Barnstaple. "But I think Miss Grey and Lord Barralonga's party generally are going to make trouble for us. I wish they hadn't come through with us."

"Mr. Cecil thinks that," said Lady Stella.

"Naturally we shall all be thrown very much together and judged in a lump."

"Naturally," Lady Stella echoed.

She said no more for a little while. But it was evident that she had more to say. Mr. Barnstaple paddled slowly.

"Mr. Bastable," she began presently.

Mr. Barnstaple's paddle became still.

"Mr. Bastable—are you *afraid?*"

Mr. Barnstaple judged himself. "I have been too full of wonder to be afraid."

Lady Stella decided to confess. "I *am* afraid," she said. "I wasn't at first. Everything seemed to go so easily and simply. But in the night I woke up—horribly afraid."

"No," considered Mr. Barnstaple. "No. It hasn't taken me like that—yet. . . . Perhaps it will."

Lady Stella leant forward and spoke confidentially, watching the effect of her words on Mr. Barnstaple. "These Utopians—I thought at first they were just simple, healthy human beings, artistic and innocent. But they are not, Mr. Bastable. There is something hard and complicated about them, something that goes beyond us and that we don't understand. And they don't care for us. They look at us with heartless eyes. Lychnis is kind, but hardly any of the others are the least bit kind. And I think they find us inconvenient."

Mr. Barnstaple thought it over. "Perhaps they do. I have been so preoccupied with admiration—so much of this is fine beyond dreaming—that I have not thought very much how we effected them. But—yes—they seem to be busy about other things and not very attentive to us. Except the ones who have evidently been assigned to watch and study us. And Lord Barralonga's headlong rush through the country must certainly have been inconvenient."

"He killed a man."

"I know."

They remained thoughtfully silent for some moments.

"And there are other things," Lady Stella resumed. "They think quite differently from our way of thinking. I believe they despise us already. I noted something. . . . Last evening you were not with us by the lake when Mr. Cecil asked them about their philosophy. He told them things about

Hegel and Bergson and Lord Haldane and his own wonderful
scepticism. He opened out—unusually. It was very interesting—to me. But I was watching Urthred and Lion and in
the midst of it I saw—I am convinced—they were talking
to each other in that silent way they have, about something
quite different. They were just *shamming* attention. And
when Freddy Mush tried to interest them in Neo-Georgian
poetry and the effect of the war upon literature, and how
he hoped that they had something *half* as beautiful as the
Iliad in Utopia, though he confessed he couldn't believe they
had, they didn't even pretend to listen. They did not answer
him at all. . . . Our minds don't matter a bit to them."

"In these subjects. They are three thousand years further
on. But we might be interesting as learners."

"Would it have been interesting to have taken a Hottentot
about London explaining things to him—after one had got
over the first fun of showing off his ignorance? Perhaps
it would. But I don't think they want us here very much
and I don't think they are going to like us very much, and
I don't know what they are likely to do to us if we give
too much trouble. And so I am afraid."

She broke out in a new place. "In the night I was
reminded of my sister Mrs. Kelling's monkeys.

"It's a mania with her. They run about the gardens and
come into the house and the poor things are always in
trouble. They don't quite know what they may do and what
they may not do; they all look frightfully worried and they
get slapped and carried to the door and thrown out and
all sorts of things like that. They spoil things and make
her guests uneasy. You never seem to know what a
monkey's going to do. And everybody hates to have them
about except my sister. And she keeps on scolding them.
'Come *down,* Jacko! Put that *down,* Sadie!'"

Mr. Barnstaple laughed. "It isn't going to be quite so

bad as that with us, Lady Stella. We are not monkeys."

She laughed too. "Perhaps it isn't. But all the same—in the night—I felt it might be. We are inferior creatures. One has to admit it. . . . "

She knitted her brows. Her pretty face expressed great intellectual effort. "Do you realize how we are cut off? . . . Perhaps you will think it silly of me Mr. Bastable, but last night before I went to bed I sat down to write to my sister a letter and tell her all about things while they were fresh in my mind. And suddenly I realized I might as well write to—Julius Cæsar."

Mr. Barnstaple hadn't thought of that.

"That's a thing I can't get out of my head, Mr. Bastable— no letters, no telegrams, no newspapers, no Bradshaw in Utopia. All the things we care for really—— All the people we live for. Cut off! I don't know for how long. But completely cut off. . . . How long are they likely to keep us here?"

Mr. Barnstaple's face became speculative.

"Are you *sure* they can ever send us back?" the lady asked.

"There seems to be some doubt. But they are astonishingly clever people."

"It seemed so easy coming here—just as if one walked round a corner—but, of course, properly speaking we are out of space and time. . . . More out of it even than dead people. . . . The North Pole or Central Africa is a whole universe nearer home than we are. . . . It's hard to grasp that. In this sunlight it all seems so bright and familiar. . . . Yet last night there were moments when I wanted to scream. . . ."

She stopped short and scanned the shore. Then very deliberately she sniffed.

Mr. Barnstaple became aware of a peculiarly sharp and

appetising smell drifting across the water to him.

"Yes," he said.

"It's breakfast bacon!" cried Lady Stella with a squeak in her voice.

"Exactly as Mr. Burleigh told them," said Mr. Barnstaple mechanically turning the canoe shoreward.

"Breakfast bacon! That's the most reassuring thing that has happened yet. . . . Perhaps after all it was silly to feel frightened. And there they are signalling to us!" She waved her arm.

"Greeta in a white robe—as you prophesied—and Mr. Mush in a sort of toga talking to her. . . . Where could he have got that toga?"

A faint sound of voices calling reached them.

"Com—*ing!*" cried Lady Stella.

"I hope I haven't been pessimistic," said Lady Stella. "But I felt *horrid* in the night."

QUARANTINE CRAG

CHAPTER THE FIRST

THE EPIDEMIC

§ 1

THE shadow of the great epidemic in Utopia fell upon our little band of Earthlings in the second day after their irruption. For more than twenty centuries the Utopians had had the completest freedom from the infectious and contagious disease of all sorts. Not only had the graver epidemic fevers and all sorts of skin diseases gone out of the lives of animals and men, but all the minor infections of colds, coughs, influenzas and the like had also been mastered and ended. By isolation, by the control of carriers, and so forth, the fatal germs had been cornered and obliged to die out.

And there had followed a corresponding change in the Utopian physiology. Secretions and reactions that had given the body resisting power to infection had diminished; the energy that produced them had been withdrawn to other more serviceable applications. The Utopian physiology, relieved of these merely defensive necessities, had simplified itself and become more direct and efficient. This cleaning up of infections was such ancient history in Utopia that only those who specialized in the history of pathology understood anything of the miseries mankind had suffered under from this source, and even these specialists do not seem to have had any idea of how far the race had lost its former resistance to infection. The first person to think of this lost resisting power seems to have been Mr. Rupert

Catskill. Mr. Barnstaple recalled that when they had met early on the first morning of their stay in the Conference Gardens, he had been hinting that Nature was in some unexplained way on the side of the Earthlings.

If making them obnoxious was being on their side then certainly Nature was on their side. By the evening of the second day after their arrival nearly everybody who had been in contact with the Earthlings, with the exception of Lychnis, Serpentine and three or four others who had retained something of their ancestral antitoxins, was in a fever with cough, sore throat, aching bones, headache and such physical depression and misery as Utopia had not known for twenty centuries. The first inhabitant of Utopia to die was that leopard which had sniffed at Mr. Ruppert Catskill on his first arrival. It was found unaccountably dead on the second morning after that encounter. In the afternoon of the same day one of the girls who had helped Lady Stella to unpack her bags sickened suddenly and died. . . .

Utopia was even less prepared for the coming of these disease germs than for the coming of the Earthlings who brought them. The monstrous multitude of general and fever hospitals, doctors, drug shops, and so forth, that had existed in the last Age of Confusion had long since passed out of memory; there was a surgical service for accidents and a watch kept upon the health of the young, and there were places of rest at which those who were extremely old were assisted, but there remained scarcely anything of the hygienic organization that had formerly struggled against disease. Abruptly the Utopian intelligence had to take up again a tangle of problems long since solved and set aside, to improvise forgotten apparatus and organizations for disinfection and treatment, and to return to all the disciplines of the war against diseases that had marked an epoch in its history twenty centuries before. In one respect indeed that war had left Utopia with certain permanent advantages. Nearly all the insect disease carriers had been exterminated, and rats and mice and the untidier sorts of small bird had passed out the problem of sanitation. That set very definite limits to the spread of the new infections and to the nature of the infections that could be spread. It enabled the Earth-lings only to communicate such ailments as could be breathed across an interval, or conveyed by a contaminating touch. Though not one of them was ailing at all, it became clear that someone among them had brought latent measles into the Utopian universe, and that three or four of them had liberated a long suppressed influenza. Themselves too tough to suffer, they remained at the focus of these two epidemics, while their victims coughed and sneezed and kissed and whispered them about the Utopian planet. It was not until the afternoon of the second day after the irruption that Utopia realized what had happened, and set itself to deal with this relapse into barbaric solicitudes.

§ 2

Mr. Barnstaple was probably the last of the Earthlings to hear of the epidemic. He was away from the rest of the party upon an expedition of his own.

It was early clear to him that the Utopians did not intend to devote any considerable amount of time or energy to the edification of their Earthling visitors. After the *eclaircissement* of the afternoon of the irruption there were no further attempts to lecture to the visitors upon the constitution and methods of Utopia and only some very brief questioning upon the earthly state of affairs. The Earthlings were left very much together to talk things out among themselves. Several Utopians were evidently entrusted with their comfort and well-being, but they did not seem to think that their functions extended to edification. Mr. Barnstaple found much to irritate him in the ideas and comments of several of his associates, and so he obeyed his natural inclination to explore Utopia for himself. There was something that stirred his imagination in the vast plain below the lake that he had glimpsed before his aeroplane descended into the valley of the Conference, and on his second morning he had taken a little boat and rowed out across the lake to examine the dam that retained its waters and to get a view of the great plain from the parapet of the dam.

The lake was much wider than he had thought it and the dam much larger. The water was crystalline clear and very cold, and there were but few fish in it. He had come out immediately after his breakfast, but it was near midday before he had got to the parapet of the great dam and could look down the lower valley to the great plain.

The dam was built of huge blocks of red and gold-veined rock, but steps at intervals gave access to the roadway along its crest. The great seated figures which brooded over the distant plain had been put there, it would seem, in a mood of artistic light-heartedness. They sat as if they watched or thought, vast rude shapes, half mountainous, half human. Mr. Barnstaple guessed them to be perhaps two hundred feet high; by pacing the distance between two of them and afterwards counting the number of them, he came to the conclusion that the dam was between seven and ten miles long. On the far side it dropped sheerly for perhaps five hundred feet, and it was sustained by a series of enormous buttresses that passed almost insensibly into native rock. In the bays between these buttresses hummed great batteries of water turbines, and then, its first task done, the water dropped foaming and dishevelled and gathered in another broad lake retained by a second great dam two miles or so away and perhaps a thousand feet lower. Far away was a third lake and a third dam and then the plain. Only three or four minute-looking Utopians were visible amidst all this Titanic engineering.

Mr. Barnstaple stood, the smallest of objects, in the shadow of a brooding Colossus, and peered over these nearer things at the hazy levels of the plain beyond.

What sort of life was going on there? The relationship of plain to mountain reminded him very strongly of the Alps and the great plain of Northern Italy, down into which he had walked as the climax of many a summer holiday in his youth. In Italy he knew that those distant levels would be covered with clustering towns and villages and carefully irrigated and closely cultivated fields. A dense population would be toiling with an ant-like industry in the production of food; for ever increasing its numbers until those inevitable consequences of overcrowding, disease and pestilence, es-tablished a sort of balance between the area of the land and the number of families scraping at it for nourishment. As a toiling man can grow more food than he can actually eat, and as virtuous women can bear more children than the land can possibly employ, a surplus of landless population would be gathered in wen-like towns and cities, engaged there in legal and financial operations against the agriculturalist or in the manufacture of just plausible articles for sale.

Ninety-nine out of every hundred of this population would be concentrated from childhood to old age upon the difficult task which is known as "getting a living." Amidst it, sustained by a pretence of magical propitiations, would rise shrines and temples, supporting a parasitic host of priests and monks and nuns. Eating and breeding, the simple routines of the common life since human societies began, complications of food-getting, elaborations of acquisitiveness and a tribute paid to fear; such would be the spectacle that anv warm and fertile stretch of earth would still display. There would be gleams of laughter and humor there, brief interludes of holiday, flashes of youth before its extinction in adult toil; but a driven labour, the spite and hates of overcrowding, the eternal uncertainty of destitution, would dominate the scene. Decrepitude would come by sixty; women would be old and worn out by forty. But this Utopian plain below, sunlit and fertile though it was, was under another law. Here that common life of mankind, its ancient traditions, its hoary jests and tales repeated generation after generation, its seasonal festivals, its pious fears and spasmodic indul-gences, its limited yet incessant and pitifully childish hoping, and its abounding misery and tragic futility had come to an end. It had passed for ever out of this older world. That high tide of common living had receded and vanished while the soil was still productive and the sun still shone.

It was with something like awe that Mr. Barnstaple realized how clean a sweep had been made of the common life in a mere score of centuries, how boldly and dreadfully the mind of man had taken hold, soul and body and destiny, of the life and destiny of the race. He knew himself now for the creature of transition he was, so deep in the habits of the old, so sympathetic with the idea of the new that has still but scarcely dawned on earth. For long he had known how intensely he loathed and despised that reeking peasant life which is our past; he realized now for the first time, how profoundly he feared the high austere Utopian life which lies before us. This world he looked out upon seemed very clean and dreadful to him. What were they doing upon those distant plains? What daily life did they lead there?

He knew enough of Utopia now to know that the whole land would be like a garden, with every natural tendency to beauty seized upon and developed and every innate ugliness corrected and overcome. These people could work and struggle for loveliness, he knew, for his two rose growers had taught him as much. And to and fro the food folk and the housing people and those who ordered the general life went, keeping the economic machine running so smoothly that one heard nothing of the jangling and jarring and internal breakages that constitute the dominant melody in our Earth's affairs. The ages of economic disputes and experiments had come to an end; the right way to do things had been found. And the population of this Utopia, which had shrunken at one time to only two hundred million, was now increasing again to keep pace with the constant increase in human resources. Having freed itself from a thousand evils that would otherwise have grown with its growth, the race could grow indeed.

And down there under the blue haze of the great plain almost all those who were not engaged in the affairs of food and architecture, health, education and the correlation of activities, were busied upon creative work; they were continually exploring the world without or the world within, through scientific research and artistic creation. They were continually adding to their collective power over life or to the realized worth of life.

Mr. Barnstaple was accustomed to think of our own world as a wild rush of inventions and knowledge, but all the progress of earth for a hundred years could not compare, he knew, with the forward swing of these millions of associated intelligences in one single year. Knowledge swept forward here and darkness passed as the shadow of a cloud passes on a windy day. Down there they were assaying the minerals that lie in the heart of their planet, and weaving a web to capture the sun and the stars. Life marched here; it was terrifying to think with what strides. Terrifying—because at the back of Mr. Barnstaple's mind, as at the back of so many intelligent minds in our world still, had been the persuasion that presently everything would be known and the scientific process come to an end. And then we should be happy for ever after.

He was not really acclimatized to progress. He had always thought of Utopia as a tranquillity with everything settled for good. Even to-day it seemed tranquil under that level haze, but he knew that this quiet was the steadiness of a mill race, which seems almost motionless in its quiet onrush until a bubble or a fleck of foam or some stick or leaf shoots along it and reveals its velocity.

And how did it feel to be living in Utopia? The lives of the people must be like the lives of very successful artists or scientific workers in this world, a continual refreshing discovery of new things, a constant adventure into the unknown and untried. For recreation they went about their planet, and there was much love and laughter and friendship in Utopia and an abundant easy informal social life. Games that did not involve bodily exercise, those substitutes of the half-witted for research and mental effort, had gone entirely out of life, but many active games were played for the sake of fun and bodily vigour. . . . It must be a good life for those who had been educated to live it, indeed a most enviable life.

And pervading it all must be the happy sense that it mattered; it went on to endless consequences. And they loved no doubt—subtly and deliciously—but perhaps a little hardly. Perhaps in those distant plains there was not much pity for tenderness. Bright and lovely beings they were—in no way pitiful. There would be no need for those qualities. . . .

Yet the woman Lychnis looked kind. . . .

Did they keep faith or need to keep faith as earthly lovers do? What was love like in Utopia? Lovers still whispered in the dusk. . . . What was the essence of love? A preference, a sweet pride, a delightful gift won, the most exquisite reassurance of body and mind. . . .

What could it be like to love and be loved by one of these Utopian women?—to have her glowing face close to one's own —to be quickened into life by her kiss? . . .

Mr. Barnstaple sat in his flannels, barefooted, in the shadow of a stone Colossus. He felt like some minute stray insect perched upon the big dam. It seemed to him that it was impossible that this triumphant Utopian race could ever fall back again from its magnificent attack upon the dominion of all things. High and tremendously this world had clambered and was still clambering. Surely it was safe now in its attainment. Yet all this stupendous security and mastery of nature had come about in the little space of three thousand years. . . .

The race could have altered fundamentally in that brief interval. Essentially it was still a stone-age race, it was not twenty thousand years away from the days when it knew nothing of metals and could not read nor write. Deep in its nature, arrested and undeveloped, there still lay the seeds of anger and fear and dissension. There must still be many uneasy and insubordinate spirits in this Utopia. Eugenics had scarcely begun here. He remembered the keen sweet face of the young girl who had spoken to him in the starlight on the night of his arrival, and the note of romantic eagerness in her voice when she had asked if Lord Barralonga was not a very vigorous and cruel man.

Did the romantic spirit still trouble imaginations here? Possibly only adolescent imaginations.

Might not some great shock or some phase of confusion still be possible to this immense order? Might not its system of education become wearied by its task of discipline and fall a prey to the experimental spirit? Might not the unforeseen be still lying in wait for this race? Suppose there should prove to be an infection in Father Amerton's religious fervour or Rupert Catskill's incurable craving for fantastic enterprises!

No! It was inconceivable. The achievement of this world was too calmly great and assured.

Mr. Barnstaple stood up and made his way down the steps of the great dam to where, far below, his little skiff floated like a minute flower-petal upon the clear water.

§ 3

He became aware of a considerable commotion in the Conference places.

There were more than thirty aeroplanes circling in the air and descending and ascending from the park, and a great number of big white vehicles were coming and going by the pass road. Also people seemed to be moving briskly among the houses, but it was too far off to distinguish what they were doing. He stared for a time and then got into his little boat.

He could not watch what was going on as he returned across the lake because his back was towards the slopes, but once an aeroplane came down very close to him, and he saw its occupant looking at him as he rowed. And once when he rested from rowing and sat around to look he saw what he thought was a litter carried by two men.

As he drew near the shore a boat put off to meet him. He was astonished to see that its occupants were wearing what looked like helmets of glass with white pointed visors. He was enormously astonished and puzzled.

As they approached their message resonated into his mind "Quarantine. You have to go into quarantine. You Earthlings have started an epidemic and it is necessary to put you into quarantine."

Then these glass helmets must be a sort of gas mask.

When they came alongside him he saw that this was so. They were made of highly flexible and perfectly translucent material. . . .

§ 4

Mr. Barnstaple was taken past some sleeping loggias where Utopians were lying in beds, while others who wore gas masks waited upon them. He found that all the Earthlings and all their possessions, except their cars, were assembled in the hall of the first day's Conference. He was told that the whole party was to be removed to a new place where they could be isolated and treated.

The only Utopians with the party were two who wore gas masks and lounged in the open portico in attitudes disagreeably suggestive of sentries or custodians.

The Earthlings sat about in little groups among the seats, except Mr. Rupert Catskill, who was walking up and down in the apse talking. He was hatless, flushed and excited, with his hair in some disorder.

"It's what I foresaw would happen all along," he repeated. "Didn't I tell you Nature was on our side? Didn't I say it?"

Mr. Burleigh was shocked and argumentative. "For the life of me I can't see the logic of it," he declared. "Here are we—absolutely the only perfectly immune people here—and we—*we* are to be isolated."

"They say they catch things from us," said Lady Stella.

"Very well," said Mr. Burleigh, making his point with his long white hand. "Very well, then let *them* be isolated! This is—Chinese; this is topsy turvy. I'm disappointed in them."

"I suppose it's their world," said Mr. Hunker, "and we've got to do things their way."

Mr. Catskill concentrated upon Lord Barralonga and the two chauffeurs. "I welcome this treatment. I welcome it."

"What's your idea, Rupert?" said his lordship. "We lose our freedom of action."

"Not at all," said Mr. Catskill. "Not at all. We gain it. We are to be isolated. We are to be put by ourselves in some island or mountain. Well and good. Well and good. This is only the beginning of our adventures. We shall see what we shall see."

"But how?"

"Wait a little. Until we can speak more freely. . . . These are panic measures. This pestilence is only in its opening stage. Everything is just beginning. Trust me."

Mr. Barnstaple sat sulkily by his valise, avoiding the challenge of Mr. Catskill's eye.

CHAPTER THE SECOND

THE CASTLE ON THE CRAG

§ 1

THE quarantine place to which the Earthlings were taken must have been at a very considerable distance from the place of the Conference, because they were nearly six hours upon their journey, and all the time they were flying high and very swiftly. They were all together in one flying ship; it was roomy and comfortable, and could have held perhaps four times as many passengers. They were accompanied by about thirty Utopians in gas-masks, among whom were two women. The aviators wore dresses of a white fleecy substance that aroused the interest and envy of both Miss Grey and Lady Stella. The flying ship passed down the valley and over the great plain and across a narrow sea and another land with a rocky coast and dense forests, and across a great space of empty sea. There was scarcely any shipping to be seen upon this sea at all; it seemed to Mr. Barnstaple that no earthly ocean would be so untravelled; only once or twice did he see very big drifting vessels quite unlike any earthly ships, huge rafts or platforms they seemed to be rather than ships, and once or twice he saw what was evidently a cargo boat—one with rigged masts and sails. And the air was hardly more frequented. After he was out of sight of land he saw only three aeroplanes until the final landfall.

They crossed a rather thickly inhabited, very delightful-looking coastal belt and came over what was evidently a rainless desert country, given over to mining and to vast engineering operations. Far away were very high snowy mountains, but the aeroplane descended before it came to these. For a time the Earthlings were flying over enormous heaps of slaggy accumulations, great mountains of them, that seemed to be derived from a huge well-like excavation that went down into the earth to an unknown depth. A tremendous thunder of machinery came out of this pit and much smoke. Here there were crowds of workers, and they seemed to be living in camps among the debris. Evidently the workers came to this place merely for spells of work; there were no signs of homes. The aeroplane of the Earth-lings skirted this region and flew on over a rocky and almost treeless desert deeply cut by steep gorges of the canyon type. Few people were to be seen, but there were abundant signs of engineering activity. Every torrent, every cataract was working a turbine, and great cables followed the cliffs of the gorges and were carried across the desert spaces. In the wider places of the gorges there were pine woods and a fairly abundant vegetation.

The high crag which was their destination stood out, an almost completely isolated headland, in the fork between two convergent canyons. It towered up to a height of perhaps two thousand feet above the foaming clash of the torrents below, a great mass of pale greenish and purple rocks, jagged and buttressed and cleft deeply by joint planes and white crystalline veins. The gorge on one side of it was much steeper than that on the other, it was overhung indeed as to be darkened like a tunnel, and here within a hundred feet or so of the brow a slender metallic bridge had been flung across the gulf. Some yards above it were projections that might have been the remains of an earlier bridge of stone. Behind, the crag fell steeply for some hundreds of feet to a long slope covered with a sparse vegetation which rose again to the main masses of the mountain, a wall of cliffs with a level top.

It was on this slope that the aeroplane came down alongside of three or four smaller machines. The crag was surmounted by the tall ruins of an ancient castle, within the circle of whose walls clustered a number of buildings which had recently harboured a group of chemical students. Their researches, which had been upon some question of atomic structure quite incomprehensible to Mr. Barnstaple, were finished now and the place had become vacant. Their laboratory was still stocked with apparatus and material; and water and power were supplied to it from higher up the gorge by means of pipes and cables. There was also an abundant store of provisions. A number of Utopians were busily adapting the place to its new purpose of isolation and disinfection when the Earthlings arrived.

Serpentine appeared in the company of a man in a gas-mask whose name was Cedar. This Cedar was a cytologist, and he was in charge of the arrangements for this improvised sanatorium.

Serpentine explained that he himself had flown to the crag in advance, because he understood the equipment of the place and the research that had been going on there, and because his knowledge of the Earthlings and his com-parative immunity to their infections made him able to act as an intermediary between them and the medical men who would now take charge of their case. He made these explanations to Mr. Burleigh, Mr. Barnstaple, Lord Barralonga and Mr. Hunker. The other Earthlings stood about in small groups beside the aeroplane from which they had alighted, regarding the castellated summit of the crag, the scrubby bushes of the bleak upland about them, and the towering cliffs of the adjacent canyons with no very favourable expressions.

Mr. Catskill had gone apart nearly to the edge of the

great canyon, and was standing with his hands behind his back in an attitude almost Napoleonic, lost in thought, gazing down into those sunless depths. The roar of the unseen waters below, now loud, now nearly inaudible, quivered in the air.

Miss Greeta Grey had suddenly produced a Kodak camera; she had been reminded of its existence when packing for this last journey, and she was taking a snapshot of the entire party.

Cedar said that he would explain the method of treatment he proposed to follow, and Lord Barralonga called "Rupert!" to bring Mr. Catskill into the group of Cedar's hearers.

Cedar was as explicit and concise as Urthred had been. It was evident, he said, that the Earthlings were the hosts of a variety of infectious organisms which were kept in check in their bodies by immunizing counter substances, but against which the Utopians had no defences ready and could hope to secure immunity only after a painful and disastrous epidemic. The only way to prevent this epidemic devastating their whole planet indeed, was firstly to gather together and cure all the cases affected, which was being done by converting the Conference Park into a big hospital, and next to take the Earthlings in hand and isolate them absolutely from the Utopians until they could be cleaned of their infections. It was, he confessed, an inhospitable thing to do to the Earthlings, but it seemed the only possible thing to do, to bring them into this peculiarly high and dry desert air and there to devise methods for their complete physical cleansing. If that was possible it would be done, and then the Earthlings would again be free to go and come as they pleased in Utopia.

"But suppose it is not possible?" said Mr. Catskill abruptly.

"I think it will be."

"But if you fail?"

Cedar smiled at Serpentine. "Physical research is taking up the work in which Arden and Greenlake were foremost, and it will not be long before we are able to repeat their experiment. And then to reverse it."

"With us as your raw material?"

"Not until we are fairly sure of a safe landing for you."

"You mean," said Mr. Mush, who had joined the circle about Cedar and Serpentine, "that you are going to send us back?"

"If we cannot keep you," said Cedar, smiling.

"Delightful prospect!" said Mr. Mush, unpleasantly. "To be shot across space in a gun. Experimentally."

"And may I ask," came the voice of Father Amerton, "may I ask the nature of this *treatment* of yours, these experiments of which we are to be the—guinea pigs, so to speak. Is it to be anything in the nature of vaccination?"

"Injections," explained Mr. Barnstaple.

"I have hardly decided yet," said Cedar. "The problem raises questions this world has forgotten for ages."

"I may say at once that I am a confirmed anti-vaccinationist," said Father Amerton. "Absolutely. Vaccination is an outrage on nature. If I had any doubts before I came into this world of—of *vitiation,* I have no doubts now. Not a doubt! If God had meant us to have these serums and ferments in our bodies he would have provided more natural and dignified means of getting them there than a squirt."

Cedar did not discuss the point. He went on to further apologies. For a time he must ask the Earthlings to keep within certain limits, to confine themselves to the crag and the slopes below it as far as the mountain cliffs. And further, it was impossible to set young people to attend to them as had hitherto been done. They must cook for themselves and see to themselves generally. The appliances were all to be found above upon the crest of the crag and he and Serpentine would make any explanations that were needful. They would find there was ample provisions for them.

"Then are we to be left alone here?" asked Mr. Catskill.

"For a time. When we have our problem clearer we will come again and tell you what we mean to do."

"Good," said Mr. Catskill. "Good."

"I wish I hadn't sent my maid by train," said Lady Stella.

"I have come to my last clean collar," said M. Dupont with a little humorous grimace. "It is no joke this week-end with Lord Barralonga."

Lord Barralonga turned suddenly to his particular minion. "I believe that Ridley has the makings of a very good cook."

"I don't mind trying my hand," said Ridley. "I've done most things—and once I used to look after a steam car."

"A man who can keep one of those—those things in order can do anything," said Mr. Penk with unusual emotion. "I've no objection to being a temporary general utility along of Mr. Ridley. I began my career in the pantry and I ain't ashamed to own it."

"If this gentleman will show us the gadgets," said Mr. Ridley, indicating Serpentine.

"Exactly," said Mr. Penk.

"And if all of us give as little trouble as possible," said Miss Greeta bravely.

"I think we shall be able to manage," said Mr. Burleigh to Cedar. "If at first you can spare us a little advice and help."

§ 2

Cedar and Serpentine remained with the Earthlings upon Quarantine Crag until late in the afternoon. They helped to prepare a supper and set it out in the courtyard of the castle. They departed with a promise to return on the morrow, and the Earthlings watched them and their accompanying aeroplanes soar up into the sky.

Mr. Barnstaple was surprised to find himself distressed at their going. He had a feeling that mischief was brewing amongst his companions and that the withdrawal of these Utopians removed a check upon this mischief. He had helped Lady Stella in the preparation of an omelette; he had to carry back a dish and a frying pan to the kitchen after it was served, so that he was the last to seat himself at the supper table. He found the mischief he dreaded well afoot.

Mr. Catskill had finished his supper already and was standing with his foot upon a bench orating to the rest of the company.

"I ask you, Ladies and Gentlemen," Mr. Catskill was saying; "I ask you: Is not Destiny writ large upon this day's adventure? Not for nothing was this place a fortress in ancient times. Here it is ready to be a fortress again. M'm—a fortress. . . . In such an adventure as will make the stories of Cortez and Pizarro pale their ineffectual fires!"

"My dear Rupert!" cried Mr. Burleigh. "What have you got into that head of yours now?"

Mr. Catskill waved two fingers dramatically. "The conquest of a world!"

"Good God!" cried Mr. Barnstaple. "Are you mad?"

"As Clive," said Mr. Catskill, "or Sultan Baber when he marched to Panipat."

"It's a tall proposition," said Mr. Hunker, who seemed to have had his mind already prepared for these suggestions, "but I'm inclined to give it a hearing. The alternative so far as I can figure it out is to be scoured and whitewashed inside and out and then fired back into our world—with a chance of hitting something hard on the way. You tell them, Mr. Catskill."

"Tell them," said Lord Barralonga, who had also been prepared. "It's a gamble, I admit. But there's situations when one has to gamble—or be gambled with. I'm all for the active voice."

"It's a gamble—certainly," said Mr. Catskill. "But upon this narrow peninsula, upon this square mile or so of territory, the fate, Sir, of two universes awaits decision. This is no time for the faint heart and the paralysing touch of discretion. Plan swiftly—act swiftly. . . ."

"This is simply *thrilling!*" cried Miss Greeta Grey, clasping her hands about her knees and smiling radiantly at Mr. Mush.

"These people," Mr. Barnstaple interrupted, "are three thousand years ahead of us. We are like a handful of Hottentots in a showman's van at Earl's Court, planning the conquest of London."

Mr. Catskill, hands on hips, turned with extraordinary good humour upon Mr. Barnstaple. "Three thousand years away from us—*yes!* Three thousand years ahead of us—*no!* That is where you and I join issue. You say these people are super-men. M'm—super-men. . . . I say they are degenerate men. Let me call your attention to my reasons for this belief—in spite of their beauty, their very considerable material and intellectual achievements and so forth. Ideal people, I admit. . . . What then? . . . My case is that they have reached a summit—and passed it, that they are going on by inertia and that they have lost the power not only of resistance to disease—that weakness we shall see develop more and more—but also of meeting strange and distressing emergencies. They are gentle. Altogether too gentle. They are ineffectual. They do not know what to do. Here is Father Amerton. He disturbed that first meeting in the most insulting way. (You know you did, Father Amerton. I'm not blaming you. You are morally—sensitive. And there were things to outrage you.) He was threatened—as a little boy is threatened by a feeble old woman. Something was to be done to him. Has anything been done to him?"

"A man and a woman came and talked to me," said Father Amerton.

"And what did you do?"

"Simply confuted them. Lifted up my voice and confuted them."

"What did they say?"

"What *could* they say?"

"We all thought tremendous things were going to be done to poor Father Amerton. Well, and now take a graver case. Our friend Lord Barralonga ran amuck with his car—and killed a man. M'm. Even at home they'd have endorsed your license you know. And fined your man. But here? . . . The thing has scarcely been mentioned since. Why? Because they don't know what to say about it or do about it. And now they have put us here and begged us to be good. Until tney are ready to come and try experiments upon us and inject things into us and I don't know what. And if we submit, Sir, if we submit, we lose one of our greatest powers over these people, our power of at once giving and resisting malaise, and in addition, I know not what powers of initiative that may very well be associated with that physiological toughness of which we are to be robbed. They may trifle with our ductless glands. But science tells us that these very glands secrete our personalities. Mentally, morally we shall be dissolved. If we submit, Sir—if we submit. But suppose we do not submit; what then?"

"Well," said Lord Barralonga, "what then?"

"They will not know what to do. Do not be deceived by any outward shows of beauty and prosperity. These people are living, as the ancient Peruvians were living in the time of Pizarro, in an enervating dream. They have drunken the debilitating draught of Socialism, and as in

ancient Peru, there is no health nor power of will left in
them any more. A handful of resolute men and women who
can dare—may not only dare but triumph in the face of
such a world. And thus it is I lay my plans before you."

"You mean to jump this entire Utopian planet?" said
Mr. Hunker.

"Big order," said Lord Barralonga.

"I mean, Sir, to assert the rights of a more vigorous form
of social life over a less vigorous form of social life. Here
we are—in a fortress. It is a real fortress and quite de-
fensible. While you others have been unpacking, Barralonga
and Hunker and I have been seeing to that. There is a
sheltered well so that if need arises we can get water from
the canyon below. The rock is excavated into chambers
and shelters; the wall on the land side is sound and high,
glazed so that it cannot be scaled. This great archway can
easily be barricaded when the need arises. Steps go down
through the rock to that little bridge which can if necessary
be cut away. We have not yet explored all the excavations.
In Mr. Hunker we have a chemist—he was a chemist before
the movie picture claimed him as its master—and he says
there is ample material in the laboratory for a store of bombs.
This party, I find, can muster five revolvers with ammunition.
I scarcely dared hope for that. We have food for many days."

"Oh! This is ridiculous!" cried Mr. Barnstaple standing
up and then sitting down again. "This is preposterous! To
turn on these friendly people! But they can blow this little
headland to smithereens whenever they want to."

"Ah!" said Mr. Catskill and held him with his out-stretched
finger. "We've thought of that. But we can take a leaf
from the book of Cortez—who, in the very centre of Mexico,
held Montezuma as his prisoner and hostage. We too will
have our hostage. Before we lift a finger——. First our
hostage. . . ."

"Aerial bombs!"

"Is there such a thing in Utopia? Or such an idea? And again—we must have our hostage."

"Somebody of importance," said Mr. Hunker.

"Cedar and Serpentine are both important people," said Mr. Burleigh in tones of disinterested observation.

"But surely, Sir, you do not countenance this schoolboy's dream of piracy!" cried Mr. Barnstaple, sincerely shocked.

"Schoolboys!" cried Father Amerton. "A cabinet minister, a peer and a great entrepreneur!"

"My dear Sir," said Mr. Burleigh, "we are, after all, only envisaging eventualities. For the life of me, I do not see why we should not thresh out these possibilities. Though I pray to Heaven we may never have to realize them. You were saying, Rupert—

"We have to establish ourselves here and assert our independence and make ourselves *felt* by these Utopians."

" 'Ear, 'ear!" said Mr. Ridley cordially. "One or two I'd like to make feel personally."

"We have to turn this prison into a capitol, into the first foothold of mankind in this world. It is like a foot thrust into a reluctant door that must never more close upon our race."

"It is closed," said Mr. Barnstaple. "Except by the mercy of these Utopians we shall never see our world again. And even with their mercy it is doubtful."

"That's been keeping me awake nights," said Mr. Hunker.

"It's an idea that must have occurred to all of us," said Mr. Burleigh.

"And it's an idea that's so thundering disagreeable that one hasn't cared to talk about it," said Lord Barralonga.

"I never 'ad it until this moment," said Penk. "You don't reely mean to say, Sir, *we can't get back?*"

"Things will be as they will be," said Mr. Burleigh.

"That is why I am anxious to hear Mr. Catskill's ideas."

Mr. Catskill rested his hands on his hips and his manner became very solemn. "For once," he said, "I am in agreement with Mr. Barnaby. I believe that the chances are *against* our ever seeing the dear cities of our world again."

"I felt that," said Lady Stella, with white lips. "I *knew* that two days ago."

"And so behold my week-end expand to an eternity!" said M. Dupont, and for a time no one said another word.

"It's as if——" Penk said at last. "Why! One might be dead!"

"But I *murst* be back," Miss Greeta Grey broke out abruptly, as one who sets aside a foolish idea. "It's absurd. I have to go on at the Alhambra on September the 2nd. It's imperative. We came here quite easily; it's ridiculous to say I can't go back in the same way."

Lord Barralonga regarded her with affectionate malignity. "You wait," he said.

"But I murst!" she sang.

"There's such things as impossibilities—even for Miss Greeta Grey."

"Charter a special aeroplane!" she said. "Anything."

He regarded her with an elfin grin and shook his head.

"My dear man," she said, "you've only seen me in a holiday mood, so far. Work is serious."

"My dear girl, that Alhambra of yours is about as far from us now as the Court of King Nebuchadnezzar. . . . It can't be done."

"But it *murst,*" she said in her queenly way. "And that's all about it."

§ 3

Mr. Barnstaple got up from the table and walked apart

to where a gap in the castle wall gave upon the darkling wilderness without. He sat down there. His eyes went from the little group talking around the supper table to the sunlit crest of the cliffs across the canyon and to the wild and lonely mountain slopes below the headland. In this world he might have to live out the remainder of his days.

And those days might not be very numerous if Mr. Catskill had his way. Sydenham, and his wife and the boys were indeed as far—"as the Court of King Nebuchadnezzar."

He had scarcely given his family a thought since he had posted his letter at Victoria. Now he felt a queer twinge of desire to send them some word or token—if only he could. Queer that they would never hear from him or of him again! How would they get on without him? Would there be any difficulty about the account at the bank? Or about the insurance money? He had always intended to have a joint and several account with his wife at the bank, and he had never quite liked to do it. Joint and several. . . . A thing every man ought to do. . . . His attention came back to Mr. Catskill unfolding his plans.

"We have to make up our minds to what may be a prolonged, a very prolonged stay here. Do not let us deceive ourselves upon that score. It may last for years—it may last for generations."

Something struck Penk in that. "I don't 'ardly see," he said, "how that can be—*generations?*"

"I am coming to that," said Mr. Catskill.

"Un'appily," said Mr. Penk, and became profoundly restrained and thoughtful with his eyes on Lady Stella.

"We have to remain, a little alien community, in this world until we dominate it, as the Romans dominated the Greeks, and until we master its science and subdue it to our purpose. That may mean a long struggle. It may mean a very long struggle indeed. And meanwhile we must

maintain ourselves as a community; we must consider ourselves a colony, a garrison, until that day of reunion comes.
We must hold our hostages, Sir, and not only our hostages.
It may be necessary for our purpose, and if it is necessary
for our purpose, so be it—to get in others of these Utopians,
to catch them young, before this so-called education of
theirs unfits them for our purpose, to train them in the
great traditions of our Empire and our race."

Mr. Hunker seemed on the point of saying something
but refrained.

M. Dupont got up sharply from the table, walked four
paces away, returned and stood still, watching Mr. Catskill.

"Generations?" said Mr. Penk.

"Yes," said Mr. Catskill. "Generations. For here we are
strangers—strangers, like that other little band of adventurers
who established their citadel five-and-twenty centuries ago
upon the Capitol beside the rushing Tiber. This is our
Capitol. A greater Capitol—of a greater Rome—in a vaster
world. And like that band of Roman adventurers we too
may have to reinforce our scanty numbers at the expense
of the Sabines about us, and take to ourselves servants and
helpers and—*mates!* No sacrifice is too great for the high
possibilities of this adventure."

M. Dupont seemed to nerve himself for the sacrifice.

"Duly married," injected Father Amerton.

"Duly married," said Mr. Catskill in parenthesis. "And
so, Sir, we will hold out here and maintain ourselves and
dominate this desert countryside and spread our prestige and
our influence and our spirit into the inert body of this
decadent Utopian world. Until at last we are able to master
the secret that Arden and Greenlake were seeking and
recover the way back to our own people, opening to the
crowded millions of our Empire——"

§ 4

"Just a moment," said Mr. Hunker. "Just a moment! About this empire——!"

"Exactly," said M. Dupont, recalled abruptly from some romantic day-dream. "About your Empire——!"

Mr. Catskill regarded them thoughtfully and defensively. "When I say Empire I mean it in the most general sense."

"Exactly," snapped M. Dupont.

"I was thinking generally of our—Atlantic civilization."

"Before, Sir, you go on to talk of Anglo-Saxon unity and the English-speaking race," said M. Dupont, with a rising note of bitterness in his voice, "permit me to remind you, Sir, of one very important fact that you seem to be overlooking. The language of Utopia, Sir, is French. I want to remind you of that. I want to recall it to your mind. I will lay no stress here on the sacrifices and martyrdoms that France has endured in the cause of Civilization——"

The voice of Mr. Burleigh interrupted. "A very natural misconception. But, if you will pardon the correction, the language of Utopia is *not* French."

Of course, Mr. Barnstaple reflected, M. Dupont had not heard the explanation of the language difficulty.

"Permit me, Sir, to believe the evidence of my ears," the Frenchman replied with dignified politeness. "These Utopians, I can assure you, speak French and nothing but French—and very excellent French it is."

"They speak no language at all," said Mr. Burleigh.

"Not even English?" sneered M. Dupont.

"Not even English."

"Not League of Nations, perhaps? But—Bah! Why do I argue? They speak French. Not even a Bosch would deny it. It needs an Englishman——"

A beautiful wrangle, thought Mr. Barnstaple. There was no Utopian present to undeceive M. Dupont and he stuck to his belief magnificently. With a mixture of pity and derision and anger, Mr. Barnstaple listened to this little band of lost human beings, in the twilight of a vast, strange and possibly inimical world, growing more and more fierce and keen in a dispute over the claims of their three nations to "dominate" Utopia, claims based entirely upon greeds and misconceptions. Their voices rose to shouts and sank to passionate intensity as their life-long habits of national egotism reasserted themselves. Mr. Hunker would hear nothing of any "Empire"; M. Dupont would hear of nothing but the supreme claim of France. Mr. Catskill twisted and turned. To Mr. Barnstaple this conflict of patriotic prepossessions seemed like a dog-fight on a sinking ship. But at last Mr. Catskill, persistent and ingenious, made headway against his two antagonists.

He stood at the end of the table explaining that he had used the word Empire loosely, apologizing for using it, explaining that when he said Empire he had all Western Civilization in mind. "When I said it," he said, turning to Mr. Hunker, "I meant a common brotherhood of understanding." He faced towards M. Dupont. "I meant our tried and imperishable Entente."

"There are at least no Russians here," said M. Dupont. "And no Germans."

"True," said Lord Barralonga. "We start ahead of the Hun here, and we can keep ahead."

"And I take it," said Mr. Hunker, "that Japanese are barred."

"No reason why we shouldn't start clean with a complete colour bar," reflected Lord Barralonga. "This seems to me a White Man's World."

"At the same time," said M. Dupont, coldly and insistently, "you will forgive me if I ask you for some clearer definition of our present relationship and for some guarantee, some effective guarantee, that the immense sacrifices France has made and still makes in the cause of civilized life, will receive their proper recognition and their due reward in this adventure. . . .

"I ask only for justice," said M. Dupont.

§ 5

Indignation made Mr. Barnstaple bold. He got down from his perch upon the wall and came up to the table.

"Are you mad," he said, "or am I?

"This squabble over flags and countries and fanciful rights and deserts—it is hopeless folly. Do you not realize even now the position we are in?"

His breath failed him for a moment and then he resumed.

"Are you incapable of thinking of human affairs except in terms of flags and fighting and conquest and robbery? Cannot you realize the proportion of things and the quality of this world into which we have fallen? As I have said already, we are like some band of savages in a show at Earl's Court, plotting the subjugation of London. We are like suppressed cannibals in the heart of a great city dreaming of a revival of our ancient and forgotten filthiness. What are our chances in this fantastic struggle?"

Mr. Ridley spoke reprovingly. "You're forgetting every-think you just been told. Everythink. Arf their population is laid out with 'flu and measles. And there's no such thing as a 'ealthy fighting will left in all Utopia."

"Precisely," said Mr. Catskill.

"Well, suppose you have chances? If that makes your scheme the more hopeful, it also makes it more horrible. Here we are lifted out of the troubles of our time to a vision, to a reality, of civilization such as our world can only hope to climb to in scores of centuries! Here is a world at peace, splendid, happy, full of wisdom and hope!

If our puny strength and base cunning can contrive it, we are to shatter it all! We are proposing to wreck a world! I tell you it is not an adventure. It is a crime. It is an abomination. I will have no part in it. I am against you in this attempt."

Father Amerton would have spoken but Mr. Burleigh arrested him by a gesture.

"What would *you* have us do?" asked Mr. Burleigh.

"Submit to their science. Learn what we can from them. In a little while we may be cured of our inherent poisons and we may be permitted to return from this outlying desert of mines and turbines and rock, to those gardens of habitation we have as yet scarcely seen. There we too may learn something of civilization. . . . In the end we may even go back to our own disordered world—with knowledge, with hope and help, missionaries of a new order."

"But why——?" began Father Amerton.

Again Mr. Burleigh took the word. "Everything you say," he remarked, "rests on unproven assumptions. You choose to see this Utopia through rose-tinted glasses. We others—for it is"—he counted—"eleven to one against you—see things without such favourable preconceptions."

"And may I ask, Sir," said Father Amerton, springing to his feet and hitting the table a blow that set all the glasses talking. "May I ask who *you* are, to set yourself up as a judge and censor of the common opinion of mankind? For I tell you, Sir, that here in this lonely and wicked and strange world, we here, we twelve, do represent mankind. We are the advance guard, the pioneers—in the new world that God has given us, even as He gave Canaan to Israel His chosen, three thousand years ago. Who are *you*——"

"Exactly," said Penk. "Who are you?"

And Mr. Ridley reinforced him with a shout: "Oo the 'ell are *you?*"

Mr. Barnstaple had no platform skill to meet so direct an attack. He stood helpless. Astonishingly Lady Stella came to his rescue.

"That isn't fair, Father Amerton," she said. "Mr. Barnstaple, whoever he is, has a perfect right to express his own opinion."

"And having expressed it," said Mr. Catskill, who had been walking up and down on the other side of the table to that on which Mr. Barnstaple stood, "Mm, having expressed it, to allow us to proceed with the business at hand. I suppose it was inevitable that we should find the conscientious objector in our midst—even in Utopia. The rest of us, I take it, are very much of one mind about our situation."

"We are," said Mr. Mush, regarding Mr. Barnstaple with a malevolent expression.

"Very well. Then I suppose we must follow the precedents established for such cases. We will not ask Mr.—Mr. Bastaple to share the dangers—and the honours—of a combatant. We will ask him merely to do civilian work of a helpful nature——"

Mr. Barnstaple held up his hand. "No," he said. "I am not disposed to be helpful. I do not recognize the analogy of the situation to the needs of the Great War, and, anyhow, I am entirely opposed to this project—this brigandage of a civilization. You cannot call me a conscientious objector to fighting, because I do not object to fighting in a just cause. But this adventure of yours is not a just cause. . . . I implore you, Mr. Burleigh, you who are not merely a politician, but a man of culture and a philosopher, to reconsider what it is we are being urged towards—towards acts of violence and mischief from which there will be no drawing back!"

"Mr. Barnstaple," said Mr. Burleigh with grave dignity

and something like a note of reproach in his voice, "I *have* considered. But I think I may venture to say that I am a man of some experience, some traditional experience, in human affairs. I may not altogether agree with my friend Mr. Catskill. Nay! I will go further and say that in many respects I do *not* agree with him. If I were the autocrat here I would say that we have to offer these Utopians resistance—for our self-respect—but not to offer them the violent and aggressive resistance that he contemplates. I think we could be far more subtle, far more elaborate and far more successful than Mr. Catskill is likely to be. But that is my own opinion. Neither Mr. Hunker nor Lord Barralonga, nor Mr. Mush nor M. Dupont shares it. Nor do Mr.—our friends, the ah!—technical engineers here share it. And what I do perceive to be imperative upon our little band of Earthlings, lost here in a strange universe, is *unity of action*. Whatever else betide, dissension must not betray us. We must hold together and act together as one body. Discuss if you will, when there is any time for discussion, but in the end *decide*. And having decided abide loyally by the decision. Upon the need of securing a hostage or two I have no manner of doubt whatever. Mr. Catskill is right."

Mr. Barnstaple was a bad debater. "But these Utopians are as human as we are," he said. "All that is most sane and civilized in ourselves is with them."

Mr. Ridley interrupted in a voice designedly rough. "Oh Lord!" he said. "We can't go on jawing 'ere for ever. It's sunset, and Mr.—this gentleman 'as 'ad 'is' say, and more than is say. We ought to have our places and know what is expected of us before night. May I propose that we elect Mr. Catskill our Captain with full military powers."

"I second that," said Mr. Burleigh with grave humility

"Perhaps M. Dupont," said Mr. Catskill, "will act with

me as associated Captain, representing our glorious ally, his own great country."

"In the absence of a more worthy representative," acquiesced M. Dupont, "and to see that French interests are duly respected."

"And if Mr. Hunker would act as my lieutenant? . . . Lord Barralonga will be our quartermaster and Father Amerton our chaplain and censor. Mr. Burleigh, it goes without saying, will be our civil head."

Mr. Hunker coughed. He frowned with the expression of one who makes a difficult explanation. "I won't be exactly lieutenant," he said. "I'll take no official position. I've a sort of distaste for—foreign entanglements. I'll be a looker on—who helps. But I think you will find you can count on me, Gentlemen—when help is needed."

Mr. Catskill seated himself at the head of the table and indicated the chair next to his for M. Dupont. Miss Greeta Grey seated herself on his other hand between him and Mr. Hunker. Mr. Burleigh remained in his place, a chair or so from Mr. Hunker. The rest came and stood round the Captain except Lady Stella and Mr. Barnstaple.

Almost ostentatiously Mr. Barnstaple turned his back on the new command. Lady Stella, he saw, remained seated far down the table, looking dubiously at the little crowd of people at the end. Then her eyes went to the desolate mountain crest beyond.

She shivered violently and stood up. "It's going to be very cold here after sunset," she said, with nobody heeding her. "I shall go and unpack a wrap."

She walked slowly to her quarters and did not reappear.

§ 6

Mr. Barnstaple did not want to seem to listen to this Council of War. He walked to the wall of the old castle and up a flight of stone steps and along the rampart to the peak of the headland. Here the shattering and beating sound of the waters in the two convergent canyons was very loud.

There was still a bright upper rim of sunlit rock on the mountain face behind, but all the rest of the world was now in a deepening blue shadow, and a fleecy white mist was gathering in the canyons below and hiding the noisy torrents. It drifted up almost to the level of the little bridge that spanned the narrower canyon to a railed stepway from the crest on the further side. For the first time since he had arrived in Utopia Mr. Barnstaple felt a chill in the air. And loneliness like a pain.

Up the broader of the two meeting canyons some sort of engineering work was going on and periodic flashes lit the drifting mist. Far away over the mountains a solitary aeroplane, very high, caught the sun's rays ever and again and sent down quivering flashes of dazzling golden light, and then, as it wheeled about, vanished again in the deepening blue.

He looked down into the great courtyard of the ancient castle below him. The modern buildings in the twilight looked like phantom pavilions amidst the archaic masonry. Someone had brought a light, and Captain Rupert Catskill, the new Cortez, was writing orders, while his Commando stood about him.

The light shone on the face and shoulders and arms of Miss Greeta Grey; she was peering over the Captain's arm to see what he was writing. And as Mr. Barnstaple looked he saw her raise her hand suddenly to conceal an involuntary yawn.

CHAPTER THE THIRD

MR. BARNSTAPLE AS A TRAITOR TO MANKIND

§ 1

MR. BARNSTAPLE spent a large part of the night sitting upon his bed and brooding over the incalculable elements of the situation in which he found himself.

What could he do? What ought he do? Where did his loyalty lie? The dark traditions and infections of the Earth had turned his wonderful encounter into an ugly and dangerous antagonism far too swiftly for him to adjust his mind to the new situation. Before him now only two possibilities seemed open. Either the Utopians would prove themselves altogether the stronger and the wiser and he and all his fellow pirates would be crushed and killed like vermin, or the desperate ambitions of Mr. Catskill would be realized and they would become a spreading sore in the fair body of this noble civilization, a band of robbers and destroyers, dragging Utopia year by year and age by age back to terrestrial conditions. There seemed only one escape from the dilemma; to get away from this fastness to the Utopians, to reveal the whole scheme of the Earthlings to them, and to throw himself and his associates upon their mercy. But this must be done soon, before the hostages were seized and bloodshed began.

But in the first place it might be very difficult now to get away from the Earthling band. Mr. Catskill would already have organized watchers and sentinels, and the peculiar position of the Crag exposed every avenue of escape. And in the next place Mr. Barnstaple had a life-long habit of mind which predisposed him against tale-bearing and dissentient action. His school training had moulded him into subservience to any group or gang in which he found himself; his form, his side, his house, his school, his club, his party, and so forth. Yet his intelligence and his limitless curiosities had always been opposed to these narrow conspiracies against the world at large. His spirit had made him an uncomfortable rebel throughout his whole earthly existence. He loathed political parties and political leaders, he despised and rejected nationalism and imperialism and all the tawdry loyalties associated with them; the aggressive conqueror, the grabbing financier, the shoving business man, he hated as he hated wasps, rats, hyenas, sharks, fleas, nettles, and the like: all his life he had been a citizen of Utopia exiled upon Earth. After his fashion he had sought to serve Utopia. Why should he not serve Utopia now? Because his band was a little and desperate band, that was no reason why he should serve the things he hated. If they were a desperate crew, the fact remained that they were also, as a whole, an evil crew. There is no reason why liberalism should degenerate into a morbid passion for minorities. . . .

Only two persons among the Earthlings, Lady Stella and Mr. Burleigh, held any of his sympathy. And he had his doubts about Mr. Burleigh. Mr. Burleigh was one of those strange people who seem to understand everything and feel nothing. He impressed Mr. Barnstaple as being intelligently irresponsible. Wasn't that really more evil than being unintelligently adventurous like Hunker or Barralonga?

Mr. Barnstaple's mind returned from a long excursion in ethics to the realities about him. To-morrow he would survey the position and make his plans, and perhaps in the twilight he would slip away.

It was entirely in his character to defer action in this way for the better part of the day. His life had been one of deferred action almost from the beginning.

§ 2

But events could not wait for Mr. Barnstaple.

He was called at dawn by Penk, who told him that henceforth the garrison would be aroused every morning by an electric hooter he and Ridley had contrived. As Penk spoke a devastating howl from this contrivance inaugurated the new era. He handed Mr. Barnstaple a slip of paper torn from a note-book on which Mr. Catskill had written:—

"Non-comb Barnaby. To assist Ridley prepare breakfast, lunch and dinner, times and menu on mess-room wall, clear away and wash up smartly and at other times to be at disposal of Lt. Hunker, in chemical laboratory for experimenting and bomb-making. Keep laboratory clean."

"That's your job," said Penk. "Ridley's waitin' for you."

"Well," said Mr. Barnstaple, and got up. It was no use precipitating a quarrel if he was to escape. So he went to the scarred and bandaged Ridley, and they produced a very good imitation of a British military kitchen in that great raw year, 1914.

Everyone was turned out to breakfast at half-past six by a second solo on the hooter. The men were paraded and inspected by Mr. Catskill, with M. Dupont standing beside him; Mr. Hunker stood parallel with these two and a few yards away; all the other men fell in except Mr. Burleigh, who was to be civil commander in Utopia, and was, in that capacity, in bed, and Mr. Barnstaple the non-combatant. Miss Greeta Grey and Lady Stella sat in a sunny corner of the courtyard sewing at a flag. It was to be a blue flag with a white star, a design sufficiently unlike any existing national flag to avoid wounding the patriotic susceptibilities of any of the party. It was to represent the Earthling League of Nations.

After the parade the little garrison dispersed to its various posts and duties, M. Dupont assumed the chief command, and Mr. Catskill, who had watched all night, went to lie down. He had the Napoleonic quality of going off to sleep for an hour or so at any time in the day.

Mr. Penk went up to the top of the castle, where the hooter was installed, to keep a look out.

There were some moments to be snatched between the time when Mr. Barnstaple had finished with Ridley and the time when Hunker would discover his help was available, and this time he devoted to an inspection of the castle wall on the side of the slopes. While he was standing on the old rampart, weighing his chances of slipping away that evening in the twilight, an aeroplane appeared above the crag and came down upon the nearer slope. Two Utopians descended, talked with their aviator for a time, and then turned their faces towards the fastness of the Earthlings.

A single note of the hooter brought out Mr. Catskill upon the rampart beside Mr. Barnstaple. He produced a field-glass and surveyed the approaching figures.

"Serpentine and Cedar," he said, lowering his field-glass. "And they come alone. Good."

He turned round and signalled with his hand to Penk, who responded with two short whoops of his instrument. This was the signal for a general assembly.

Down below in the courtyard appeared the rest of the Allied force and Mr. Hunker and fell in with a reasonable imitation of discipline.

Mr. Catskill passed Mr. Barnstaple without taking any notice of him, joined M. Dupont, Mr. Hunker and their subordinates below and proceeded to instruct them in his plans for the forthcoming crisis. Mr. Barnstaple could not hear what was said. He noted with sardonic disapproval that each man as Mr. Catskill finished with him, clicked his heels together and saluted. Then at a word of command they dispersed to their posts.

There was a partly ruined flight of steps leading down from the general level of the courtyard through this great archway in the wall that gave access to and from the slopes below. Ridley and Mush went down to the right of these steps and placed themselves below a projecting mass of masonry so as to be hidden from anyone approaching from below. Father Amerton and Mr. Hunker concealed them-selves similarly to the left. Father Amerton, Mr. Barnstaple noted, had been given a coil of rope, and then his roving eye discovered Mr. Mush glancing at a pistol in his hand and then replacing it in his pocket. Lord Barralonga took up a position for himself some steps above Mr. Mush and produced a revolver which he held in his one efficient hand. Mr. Catskill remained at the head of the stairs. He also was holding a revolver. He turned to the citadel, considered the case of Penk for a moment, and then motioned him down to join the others. M. Dupont, armed with a stout table leg, placed himself at Mr. Catskill's right hand.

For a time Mr. Barnstaple watched these dispositions without any realization of their significance. Then his eyes went from the crouching figures within the castle to the two unsuspecting Utopians who were coming up towards them, and he realized that in a couple of minutes Serpentine and Cedar would be struggling in the grip of their captors. . . .

He perceived he had to act. And this had been a con-templative critical life with no habit of decision.

He found himself trembling violently.

§ 3

He still desired some mediatory intervention even in these fatal last moments. He raised an arm and cried "Hi!" as much to the Earthlings below as to the Utopians without.

No one noticed either his gesture or his feeble cry.

Then his will seemed to break through a tangle of obstacles to one simple idea. Serpentine and Cedar must not be seized. He was amazed and indignant at his own vacillation. Of course they must not be seized! This foolery must be thwarted forthwith. In four strides he was on the wall above the archway and now he was shouting loud and clear. "Danger!" he shouted. "Danger" and again "Danger!"

He heard Catskill's cry of astonishment and then a pistol bullet whipped through the air close to him.

Serpentine stopped short and looked up, touched Cedar's arm and pointed.

"These Earthlings want to imprison you. Don't come here! Danger!" yelled Mr. Barnstaple waving his arms and "*pat, pat, pat,*" Mr. Catskill experienced the disappointments of revolver shooting.

Serpentine and Cedar were turning back—but slowly and hesitatingly.

For a moment Mr. Caskill knew not what to do. Then he flung himself down the steps, crying, "After them! Stop them! Come on!"

"Go back!" cried Mr. Barnstaple to the Utopians. "Go back! Quickly! Quickly!"

Came a clatter of feet from below and then the eight men who constituted the combatant strength of the Earthling forces in Utopia emerged from under the archway running towards the two astonished Utopians. Mr. Mush led, with Ridley at his heels; he was pointing his revolver and shouting. Next came M. Dupont zealous and active. Father Amerton brought up the rear with the rope.

"Go back!" screamed Mr. Barnstaple, with his voice breaking.

Then he stopped shouting and watched—with his hands

clenched.

The aviator was running down the slope from his machine to the assistance of Serpentine and Cedar. And above out of the blue two other aeroplanes had appeared.

The two Utopians disdained to hurry and in a few seconds their pursuers had come up with them. Hunker, Ridley and Mush led the attack. M. Dupont, flourishing his stick, was abreast with them, but running out to the right as though he intended to get between them and the aviator. Mr. Catskill and Penk were a little behind the leading three; the one-armed Barralonga was perhaps ten yards behind and Father Amerton had halted to re-coil his rope more conveniently.

There seemed to be a moment's parley and then Serpentine had moved quickly as if to seize Hunker. A pistol cracked and then another went off rapidly three times. "Oh God!" cried Mr. Barnstaple. "Oh God!" as he saw Serpentine throw up his arms and fall backward, and then Cedar had grasped and lifted up Mush and hurled him at Mr. Catskill and Penk, bowling both of them over into one indistinguishable heap. With a wild cry M. Dupont closed in on Cedar but not quickly enough. His club shot into the air as Cedar parried his blow, and then the Utopian stooped, caught him by a leg, overthrew him lifted him and whirled him round as one might whirl a rabbit, to inflict a stunning blow on Mr. Hunker.

Lord Barralonga ran back some paces and began shooting at the approaching aviator.

The confusion of legs and arms on the ground became three separate people again. Mr. Catskill shouting directions, made for Cedar, followed by Penk and Mush and, a moment after, by Hunker and Dupont. They clung to Cedar as hounds will cling to a boar. Time after time he flung them off him. Father Amerton hovered unhelpfully with his rope.

For some moments Mr. Barnstaple's attention was concentrated upon this swaying and staggering attempt to overpower Cedar, and then he became aware of other Utopians running down the slope to join the fray. . . . The other two aeroplanes had landed.

Mr. Catskill realized the coming of these reinforcements almost as soon as Mr. Barnstaple. His shouts of "Back! Back to the castle!" reached Mr. Barnstaple's ears. The Earthlings scattered away from the tall dishevelled figure, hesitated, and began to walk and then run back towards the Castle.

And then Ridley turned and very deliberately shot Cedar, who clutched at his breast and fell into a sitting position.

The Earthlings retreated to the foot of the steps that led up through the archway into the castle, and stood there in a panting, bruised and ruffled group. Fifty yards away Serpentine lay still, the aviator whom Barralonga had shot writhed and moaned, and Cedar sat up with blood upon his chest trying to feel his back. Five other Utopians came hurrying to their assistance.

"What is all this firing?" said Lady Stella, suddenly at Mr. Barnstaple's elbow.

"Have they caught their hostages?" asked Miss Greeta Grey.

"For the life of me!" said Mr. Burleigh, who had come out upon the wall a yard or so away, "this ought never to have happened. How did this get— *muffed*, Lady Stella?"

"I called out to them," said Mr. Barnstaple.

"*You*—called—out to them!" said Mr. Burleigh incredulous.

"Treason I did not calculate upon," came the wrathful voice of Mr. Catskill ascending out of the archway.

§ 4

For some moments Mr. Barnstaple made no attempt to escape the danger that closed in upon him. He had always lived a life of very great security and with him, as with so many highly civilized types, the power of apprehending personal danger was very largely atrophied. He was a spectator by temperament and training alike. He stood now as if he looked at himself, the central figure of a great and hopeless tragedy. The idea of flight came belatedly, in a reluctant and apologetic manner in his mind.

"Shot as a traitor," he said aloud. "Shot as a traitor."

There was that bridge over the narrow gorge. He might still get over that, if he went for it at once. If he was quick—quicker than they were. He was too intelligent to dash off for it; that would certainly have set the others running. He walked along the wall in a leisurely fashion past Mr. Burleigh, himself too civilized to intervene. In a quickening stroll he gained the steps that led to the citadel. Then he stood still for a moment to survey the situation. Catskill was busy setting sentinels at the gate. Perhaps he had not thought yet of the little bridge and imagined that Mr. Barnstaple was at his disposal at any time that suited him. Up the slope the Utopians were carrying off the dead or wounded men.

Mr. Barnstaple ascended the steps as if buried in thought and stood on the citadel for some seconds, his hands in his trouser pockets, as if he surveyed the view. Then he turned to the winding staircase that went down to a sort of guard-room below. As soon as he was surely out of sight he began to think and move very quickly.

The guard-room was perplexing. It had five doors, any one of which except the one by which he had just entered the room, might lead down to the staircase. Against one, however, stood a pile of neat packing-cases. That left three to choose from. In each case stone steps ran down to a landing and a turning place. He stood hesitating at the third and noted that a cold draught came blowing up it. Surely that meant that this went down to the cliff face, or whence came the air? Surely this was it!

Should he shut the doors he had opened? No! Leave them all open.

He heard a clatter coming down the staircase from the citadel. Softly and swiftly he ran down the steps and halted for a second at the corner landing. He was compelled to stop and listen to the movements of his pursuers. "This is the door to the bridge, Sir!" he heard Ridley cry, and then he heard Catskill say, "The Tarpeian Rock," and Barralonga, "Exactly! Why should we waste a cartridge? .Are you sure this goes to the bridge, Ridley?"

The footsteps pattered across the guard-room and passed —down one of the other staircases

"A reprieve!" whispered Mr. Barnstaple and then stopped aghast.

He was trapped! The staircase they were on was the staircase to the bridge!

They would go down as far the bridge and as soon as they got to it they would see that he was neither on it nor on the steps on the opposite side of the gorge and that therefore he could not possibly have escaped. They would certainly bar that way either by closing and fastening any door there might be or, failing such a barrier, by setting a sentinel, and then they would come back and hunt for him at their leisure.

What was it Catskill had been saying? The Tarpeian Rock? . . .

Horrible!

They musn't take him alive. . .

He must fight like a rat in a corner and oblige them to shoot him. . . .

He went on down the staircase. It became very dark and then grew light again. It ended in an ordinary big cellar,

which may once have been a gun-pit or magazine. It was
fairly well lit by two unglazed windows cut in the rock.
It now contained a store of provisions. Along one side
stood an array of the flask-like bottles that were used for
wine in Utopia; along the other was a miscellany of packing-
cases and cubes wrapped in gold-leaf. He lifted one of the
glass flasks by its neck. It would make an effective club.
Suppose he made a sort of barrier of the packing cases across
the entrance and stood beside it and clubbed the pursuers
as they came in! Glass and wine would smash over their
skulls. . . . It would take time to make the barrier. . . . He
chose and carried three of the larger flasks to the doorway
where they would be handy for him. Then he had an
inspiration and looked at the window.

He listened at the door of the staircase for a time. Not
a sound came from above. He went to the window and
and lay down in the deep embrasure and wriggled forward
until he could see out and up and down. The cliff below
fell sheer; he could have spat on to the brawling torrent
fifteen hundred feet perhaps below. The crag here was
made up of almost vertical strata which projected and
receded; a big buttress hid almost all of the bridge except
the far end which seemed to be about twenty or thirty yards
lower than the opening from which Mr. Barnstaple was
looking. Mr. Catskill appeared upon this bridge, very small
and distant, scrutinizing the rocky stair-way beyond the
bridge. Mr. Barnstaple withdrew his head hastily. Then
very discreetly he peeped again. Mr. Catskill was no longer
to be seen. He was coming back.

To business! There was not much time.

In his earlier days before the great war had made travel
dear and uncomfortable Mr. Barnstaple had done some rock
climbing in Switzerland and he had also had some experience
in Cumberland and Wales. He surveyed now the rocks close

at hand with an intelligent expertness. They were cut by almost horizontal joint planes into which there had been a considerable infiltration chiefly of white crystalline material. This stuff, which he guessed was calcite, had weathered more rapidly than the general material of the rock, leaving a series of irregular horizontal grooves. With luck it might be possible to work along the cliff face, turn the buttress and scramble to the bridge.

And then came an even more hopeful idea. He could easily get along the cliff face to the first recess, flatten himself there, and remain until the Earthlings had searched his cellar. After they had searched he might creep back to the cellar. Even if they looked out of the window they would not see him and even if he left finger marks and so forth in the embrasure, they would be likely to conclude that he had either jumped or fallen down the crag into the gorge below. But at first it might be slow work negotiating the cliff face. . . . And this would cut him off from his weapons, the flasks. . . .

But the idea of hiding in the recess had taken a strong hold upon his imagination. Very cautiously he got out of the window, found a handhold, got his feet on to his ledge and began to work his way along towards his niche.

But there were unexpected difficulties, a gap of nearly five yards in the handhold—nothing. He had to flatten himself and trust to his feet, and for a time he remained quite still in that position.

Further on was a rotten lump of the vein mineral and it broke away under him very disconcertingly, but happily his fingers had a grip and the other foot was firm. The detached crystals slithered down the rock face for a moment and then made no further sound. They had dropped into the void. For a time he was paralysed.

"I'm not in good form," whispered Mr. Barnstaple. "I'm

not in good form."

He clung motionless and prayed.

With an effort he resumed his traverse.

He was at the very corner of the recess when some faint noise drew his eyes to the window from which he had emerged. Ridley's face was poked out slowly and cautiously, his eyes red and fierce among his white bandages.

§ 5

He did not at first see Mr. Barnstaple. "Gawd!" he said when he did so and withdrew his head hastily.

Came a sound of voices saying indistinguishable things.

Some inappropriate instinct kept Mr. Barnstaple quite still, though he could have got into cover in the recess quite easily before Mr. Catskill looked out revolver in hand.

For some moments they stared at each other in silence.

"Come back or I shoot," said Mr. Catskill unconvincingly.

"Shoot!" said Mr. Barnstaple after a moments reflection.

Mr. Catskill craned his head out and stared down into the shadowy blue depths of the canyon. "It isn't necessary," he answered. "We have to save cartridges."

"You haven't the guts," said Mr. Barnstaple.

"It's not quite that," said Mr. Catskill.

"No," said Mr. Barnstaple, "it isn't. You are funda-mentally a civilized man."

Mr. Catskill scowled at him without hostility.

"You have a very good imagination," Mr. Barnstaple reflected. "The trouble is that you have been so damnably educated. What is the trouble with you? You are be-Kiplinged. Empire and Anglo-Saxon and boy-scout and sleuth are the stuff in your mind. If I had gone to Eton I might have been the same as you are, I suppose."

"Harrow," corrected Mr. Catskill.

"A perfectly *beastly* public school. Suburban place where

the boys wear chignons and straw haloes. I might have
guessed Harrow. But it's queer I bear you no malice. Given
decent ideas you might have been very different from what
you are. If I had been your schoolmaster—— But it's too
late now."

"It is," said Mr. Rupert Catskill smiling genially and
cocked his eye down into the canyon.

Mr. Barnstaple began to feel for his ledge round the
corner with one foot.

"Don't go for a minute," said Mr. Catskill. "I'm not
going to shoot."

A voice from within, probably Lord Barralonga's, said
something about heaving a rock at Mr. Barnstaple. Someone
else, probably Ridley, approved ferociously.

"Not without due form of trial," said Mr. Catskill over
his shoulder. His face was inscrutable, but a fantastic idea
began to run about in Mr. Barnstaple's mind that Mr. Catskill
did not want to have him killed. He had thought about
things and he wanted him now to escape—to the Utopians
and perhaps rig up some sort of settlement with them.

"We intend to try you, Sir," said Mr. Catskill. "We
intend to try you. We cite you to appear."

Mr. Catskill moistened his lips and considered. "The
court will sit almost at once." His little bright brown eyes
estimated the chances of Mr. Barnstaple's position very
rapidly. He craned towards the bridge. "We shall not
waste time over our procedure," he said. "And I have little
doubt of our verdict. We shall condemn you to death.
So—there you are, Sir. I doubt if we shall be more than
a quarter of an hour before your fate is legally settled."

He glanced up trying to see the crest of the crag. "We
shall probably throw rocks," he said.

"*Moriturus te saluo*," said Mr. Barnstaple with an air of
making a witty remark. "If you will forgive me I will go

on now to find a more comfortable position."

Mr. Catskill remained looking hard at him.

"I've never borne you any ill-will," said Mr. Barnstaple. "Had I been your schoolmaster everything might have been different. Thanks for the quarter of an hour more you give me. And if by any chance——"

"Exactly," said Mr. Catskill.

They understood one another.

When Mr. Barnstaple stepped round the bend into the recess Mr. Catskill was still looking out and Lord Barralonga was faintly audible advocating the immediate heaving of rocks.

§ 6

The ways of the human mind are past finding out. From desperation Mr. Barnstaple's mood had passed to exhilaration. His first sick horror of climbing above this immense height had given place now to an almost boyish assurance. His sense of immediate death had gone. He was appreciating this adventure, indeed he was enjoying it, with an entire disregard now of how it was to end.

He made fairly good time until he got to the angle of the buttress, though his arms began to ache rather badly, and then he had a shock. He had now a full view of the bridge and up the narrow gorge. The ledge he was working along did not run to the bridge at all. It ran a good thirty feet below it. And what was worse, between himself and the bridge were two gullies and chimneys of uncertain depth. At this discovery he regretted for the first time that he had not stayed in the cellar and made a fight for it there.

He had some minutes of indecision—with the ache in his arms increasing.

He was roused from his inaction by what he thought at first was the shadow of a swift flying bird on the rock.

Presently it returned. He hoped he was not to be assailed by birds. He had read a story—but never mind that now.

Then came a loud crack overhead, and he glanced up to see a lump of rock which had just struck a little bulge above him, fly to fragments. From which incident he gathered firstly that the court had delivered an adverse verdict rather in advance of Mr. Catskill's time, and secondly that he was visible from above. He resumed his traverse towards the shelter of the gully with feverish energy.

The gully was better than he expected, a chimney; difficult, he thought, to ascend, but quite practicable downward. It was completely overhung. And perhaps a hundred feet below there was a sort of step in it that gave a quite broad recess, sheltered from above and with room enough for a man to sprawl on it if he wanted to do so. There would be rest for Mr. Barnstaple's arms, and without any needless delay he clambered down to it and abandoned himself to the delightful sensation of not holding on to anything. He was out of sight and out of reach of his Earthling pursuers.

In the back of the recess was a trickle of water. He drank and began to think of food and to regret that he had not brought some provision with him from the store in the cellar. He might have opened one of those gold-leaf-covered cubes or pocketed a small flask of wine. Wine would be very heartening just now. But it did not do to think of that. He stayed for a long time, as it seemed to him, on his precious shelf, scrutinizing the chimney below very carefully. It seemed quite practicable for a long way down. The sides became very smooth, but they seemed close enough together to get down with his back against one side and his feet against the other.

He looked at his wrist-watch. It was still not nine o'clock in the morning—it was about ten minutes to nine. He had been called by Ridley before half past five. At half-past six he had been handing out breakfast in the courtyard. Serpentine and Cedar must have appeared about eight o'clock. In about ten minutes Serpentine had been murdered. Then the flight and the pursuit. How quickly things had happened! . . .

He had all day before him. He would resume his descent at half past nine Until then he would rest. . . . It was absurd to feel hungry yet. . . .

He was climbing again before half-past nine. For perhaps a hundred feet it was easy. Then by imperceptible degrees the gully broadened. He only realized it when he found himself slipping. He slipped, struggling furiously, for perhaps twenty feet, and then fell outright another ten and struck a rock and was held by a second shelf much broader than the one above. He came down on it with a jarring concussion and rolled—happily he rolled inward. He was bruised, but not seriously hurt. "My luck," he said. "My luck holds good."

He rested for a time, and then, confident that things would be all right, set himself to inspect the next stage of his descent. It was with a sort of incredulity that he discovered the chimney below his shelf was absolutely unclimbable. It was just a straight, smooth rock on either side for twenty yards at least and six feet wide. He might as well fling himself over at once as try to get down that. Then he saw that it was equally impossible to retrace his steps. He could not believe it; it seemed too silly. He laughed as one might laugh if one found one's own mother refusing to recognize one after a day's absence.

Then abruptly he stopped laughing.

He repeated every point in his examination. He fingered the smooth rocks about him. "But this is absurd," he said breaking out into a cold perspiration. There was no way out of this corner into which he had so painfully and laboriously got himself. He could neither go on nor go back. He was caught. His luck had given out.

§ 7

At midday by his wrist watch Mr. Barnstaple was sitting in his recess as a weary invalid suffering from some incurable disease might sit up in an arm-chair during a temporary respite from pain, with nothing to do and no hope before him. There was not one chance in ten thousand that any-thing could happen to release him from this trap into which he had clambered. There was a trickle of water at the back but no food, not even a grass blade to nibble. Unless he saw fit to pitch himself over into the gorge, he must starve to death. . . . It would perhaps be cold at nights but not cold enough to kill him.

To this end he had come then out of the worried journalism of London and the domesticities of Sydenham.

Queer journey it was that he and the Yellow Peril had made!—Camberwell, Victoria, Hounslow, Slough, Utopia, the mountain paradise, a hundred fascinating and tantalizing glimpses of a world of real happiness and order, that long, long aeroplane flight half round a world. . . . And now—death.

The idea of abbreviating his sufferings by jumping over had no appeal for him. He would stay here and suffer such suffering as there might be before the end. And three hundred yards away or so were his fellow Earthlings, also awaiting their fate. . . . It was amazing. It was prosaic. . . .

After all to this or something like this most humanity had to come.

Sooner or later people had to lie and suffer, they had to think and then think feverishly and then weakly, and so fade to a final cessation of thought.

On the whole, he thought, it was preferable to die in this fashion, preferable to a sudden death, it was worth while to look death in the face for a time, to have leisure to write *finis* in one's mind, to think over life and such living as one had done and to think it over with a detachment, an independence, that only an entire inability to alter one jot of it now could give.

At present his mind was clear and calm; a bleak serenity like a clear winter sky possessed him. There was suffering ahead, he knew, but he did not believe it would be intolerable suffering. If it proved intolerable the canyon yawned below. In that respect this shelf or rock was a better death bed than most, a more convenient death bed. Your sick bed presented pain with a wide margin, set it up for your too complete examination. But to starve was not so very dreadful, he had read; hunger and pain there would be, most distressful about the third day, and after that one became feeble and did not feel so much. It would not be like the torture of many cancer cases or the agony of brain fever; it would not be one tithe as bad as that. Lonely it would be. But is one much less lonely on a death-bed at home? They come and say, "There! there!" and do little serviceable things—but are there any other interchanges? . . . You go your solitary way, speech and movement and the desire to speak or move passing from you, and their voices fade. . . . Everywhere death is a very solitary act, a going apart. . . .

A younger man would probably have found this loneliness in the gorge very terrible, but Mr. Barnstaple had outlived the intenser delusions of companionship. He would have liked a last talk with his boys and to have put his wife into a good frame of mind, but even these desires were perhaps more sentimental than real. When it came to talks with his boys he was apt to feel shy. As they had come to have personalities of their own and to grow through adolescence, he had felt more and more that talking intimately to them was an invasion of their right to grow up along their own lines. And they too he felt were shy with him, defensively shy. Perhaps later on sons came back to a man—that was a later on that he would never know now. But he wished he could have let them know what had happened to him. That troubled him. It would set him right in their eyes, it would perhaps be better for their characters, if they did not think—as they were almost bound to think—that he had run away from them or lapsed mentally or even fallen into bad company and been made away with. As it was they might be worried and ashamed, needlessly, or put to expense to find out where he was, and that would be a pity.

One had to die. Many men had died as he was going to die, fallen into strange places, lost in dark caverns, marooned on desert islands, astray in the Australian bush, imprisoned and left to perish. It was good to die without great anguish or insult. He thought of the myriads of men who had been crucified by the Romans—was it eight thousand or was it ten thousand of the army of Spartacus that they killed in that fashion along the Appian Way?—of negroes hung in chains to starve, and of an endless variety of such deaths. Shocking to young imaginations such things were and more fearful in thought than in reality. It is all a matter of a little more pain or a little less pain—but God will not have any great waste of pain. Cross, wheel, electric chair or bed of suffering—the thing is, *you die and have done.*

It was pleasant to find that one could think stoutly of these things. It was good to be caught and to find that one was not frantic. And Mr. Barnstaple was surprised to find how little he cared, now that he faced the issue closely, whether he was immortal or whether he was not. He was quite prepared to find himself immortal or at least not ending with death, in whole or in part. It was ridiculous to be dogmatic and say that a part, an impression, of his conscience and even of his willing life might not go on in some fashion. But he found it impossible to imagine how that could be. It was unimaginable. It was not to be anticipated. He had no fear of that continuation. He had no thought nor fear of the possibility of punishment or cruelty. The universe had at times seemed to him to be very carelessly put together, but he had never believed that it was the work of a malignant imbecile. It impressed him as immensely careless but not as dominatingly cruel. He had been what he had been, weak and limited and sometimes silly, but the punishment of these defects lay in the defects themselves.

He ceased to think about his own death. He began to think of life generally, its present lowliness, its valiant aspiration. He found himself regretting bitterly that he was not to see more of this Utopian world, which was in so many respects so near an intimation of what our own world may become. It had been very heartening to see human dreams and human ideals vindicated by realization, but it was distressing to have had the vision snatched away while he was still only beginning to examine it. He found himself asking questions that had no answers for him, about economics, about love and struggle. Anyhow, he was glad to have seen as much as he had. It was good to have been purged by this vision and altogether lifted out of the dreary hopelessness of Mr. Peeve, to have got life into perspective again.

The passions and conflicts and discomforts of A.D. 1921 were the discomforts of the fever of an uninoculated world. The Age of Confusion on the Earth also would, in its own time, work itself out, thanks to a certain obscure indomitable righteousness in the blood of the human type. Squatting in a hole in the cliff of the great crag, with unclimbable heights

and depths above him and below, chilly, hungry and uncomfortable, this thought was a profound comfort to the strangely
constituted mind of Mr. Barnstaple.

But how miserably had he and his companions failed to rise
to the great occasions of Utopia ! No one had raised an effectual hand to restrain the puerile imaginations of Mr. Catskill and the mere brutal aggressiveness of his companions.
How invincibly had Father Amerton headed for the role of
the ranting, hating, persecuting, quarrel-making priest. How
pitifully weak and dishonest Mr. Burleigh—and himself
scarcely better! disapproving always and always in ineffective opposition. What an unintelligent beauty-cow that
woman Greeta Grey was, receptive, acquisitive, impenetrable to any idea of what was due to her as a yielding female.
Lady Stella was of finer clay, but fired to no service. Women,
he thought, had not been well-represented in this chance
expedition, just one waster and one ineffective. Was that
a fair sample of Earth's womankind?

All the use these Earthlings had had for Utopia was to
turn it back as speedily as possible to the aggressions, sub-
jugations, cruelties and disorders of the Age of Confusion
to which they belonged. Serpentine and Cedar, the man of
scientific power and the man of healing, they had sought to
make hostages to disorder, and failing that they had killed or
sought to kill them.

They had tried to bring back Utopia to the state of Earth,
and indeed but for the folly, malice and weakness of men
Earth was now Utopia. Old Earth was Utopia now, a garden
and a glory, the Earthly Paradise, except that it was trampled
to dust and ruin by its Catskills, Hunkers, Barralongas, Rid-
leys, Duponts, and their kind. Against their hasty trampling
folly nothing was pitted, it seemed, in the whole wide world
at present but the whinings of the Peeves, the acquiescent
disapproval of the Burleighs and such immeasurable inef-

fectiveness as his own protest. And a few writers and teachers who produced results at present untraceable.

Once more Mr. Barnstaple found himself thinking of his old friend, the school inspector and school-book writer, who had worked so steadfastly and broken down and died so pitifully. He had worked for Utopia all his days. Were there hundreds or thousands of such Utopians yet on earth ? What magic upheld them?

"I wish I could get some message through to them," said Mr. Barnstaple, "to hearten them."

For it was true, though he himself had to starve and die like a beast fallen into a pit, nevertheless Utopia triumphed and would triumph. The grabbers and fighters, the persecutors and patriots, the lynchers and boycotters and all the riff-raff of short-sighted human violence, crowded on to final defeat. Even in their lives they know no happiness, they drive from excitement to excitement and from gratification to exhaustion. Their enterprises and successes, their wars and glories, flare and pass. Only the true thing grows, the truth, the clear idea, year by year and age by age, slowly and invincibly as a diamond grows amidst the darkness and pressures of the earth, or as the dawn grows amidst the guttering lights of some belated orgy.

What would be the end of those poor little people up above there ? Their hold on life was even more precarious than his own, for he might lie and starve here slowly for weeks before his mind gave its last flicker. But they had openly pitted themselves against the might and wisdom of Utopia, and even now the ordered power of that world must be closing in upon them. He still had a faint irrational remorse for his betrayal of Catskill's ambush. He smiled now at the passionate conviction he had felt at the time that if once Catskill could capture his hostages, Earth might prevail over Utopia. That conviction had rushed him into action.

His weak cries had seemed to be all that was left to avert this monstrous disaster. But suppose he had not been there at all, or suppose he had obeyed the lingering instinct of fellowship that urged him to fight with the others; what then?

When he recalled the sight of Cedar throwing Mush about as one might throw a lap-dog about, and the height and shape of Serpentine, he doubted whether even upon the stairs in the archway it would have been possible for the Earthlings to have overpowered these two. The revolvers would have come into use just as they had come into use upon the slope, and Catskill would have got no hostages but only two murdered men.

How unutterably silly the whole scheme of Catskill had been ! But it was no sillier than the behavior of Catskill, Burleigh and the rest of the world's statesmen had been on earth, during the last few years. At times during the agony of the great war it had seemed that Utopia drew near to earth. The black clouds and smoke of these dark years had been shot with the light of strange hopes, with the promise of a world reborn. But the nationalists, financiers, priests and patriots, had brought all those hopes to nothing. They had trusted to old poisons and infections and to the weak resistances of the civilized spirit. They had counted their weapons and set their ambushes and kept their women busy sewing flags of discord. . . .

For a time they had killed hope, but only for a time. For Hope, the redeemer of mankind, there is a perpetually resurrection.

"Utopia will win," said Mr. Barnstaple and for a time he he sat listening to a sound he had heard before without heeding it very greatly, a purring throb in the rocks about him, like the running of some great machine. It grew louder and faded down to the imperceptible again.

His thoughts came back to his erstwhile companions. He

hoped they were not too miserable or afraid up there. He was particularly desirous that something should happen to keep up Lady Stella's courage.   He worried affectionately about Lady Stella. For the rest it would be as well if they remained actively combative to the end. Possibly they were all toiling at some preposterous and wildly hopeful defensive scheme of Catskill's. Except Mr. Burleigh who would be resting—con-vinced that for him at least there would still be a gentle-manly way out. And probably not much afraid if there wasn't Amerton and possibly Mush might lapse into a religious re-vival—that would irritate the others a little, or possibly even provide a mental opiate for Lady Stella and Miss Greeta Grey. Then for Penk there was wine in the cellar. . . .

They would follow the laws of their being, they would do the things that nature and habit would require of them. What else was possible ?

Mr. Barnstaple plunged into a metaphysical gulf. . . .

Presently he caught himself looking at his wrist watch. It was twenty minutes past twelve.   He was looking at his watch more and more frequently—or time was going more and more slowly. . . . Should he wind his watch or let it run down ? He was already feeling very hungry. That could not be real hunger yet; it must be his imagination getting out of his natural control.

CHAPTER THE FOURTH

THE END OF QUARANTINE CRAG

§ 1

MR. BARNSTAPLE awoke slowly and reluctantly from a dream about cookery. He was Soyer, the celebrated chef of the Reform Club, and he was inventing and tasting new dishes. But in the pleasant way of dreamland he was not only Soyer, but at the same time he was a very clever Utopian biologist and also God Almighty. So that he could not only make new dishes, but also make new vegetables and meats to go into them. He was particularly interested in a new sort of fowl, the Chateaubriand breed of fowls, which was to combine the rich quality of very good beefsteak with the size and delicacy of a fowl's breast. And he wanted to stuff it with a blend of pimento, onion and mushroom —except that the mushroom wasn't quite the thing. The mushrooms—he tasted them—indeed just the least little modification. And into the dream came an assistant cook, several assistant cooks, all naked as Utopians, bearing fowls from the pantry and saying that they had not kept, they had gone "high" and they were going higher. In order to illustrate this idea of their going higher these assistant cooks lifted the fowls above their heads and then began to climb the walls of the kitchen, which were rocky and for a kitchen remarkably close together. Their figures became dark. They were thrown up in black outline against the luminous steam arising from a cauldron of boiling soup. It was boiling soup, and yet it was cold soup and cold steam.

Mr. Barnstaple was awake.

In the place of luminous steam there was mist, brightly moonlit mist, filling the gorge. It threw up the figures of the two Utopians in black silhouette. . . .

What Utopians?

His mind struggled between dreaming and waking. He started up rigidly attentive. They moved with easy gestures, quite unaware of his presence so close to them. They had already got a thin rope ladder fixed to some point overhead, but how they had managed to do this he did not know. One still stood on the shelf, the other swayed above him stretched across the gully clinging to the rope with his feet against the rock. The head of a third figure appeared above the edge of the shelf. It swayed from side to side. He was evidently coming up by a second rope ladder. Some sort of discussion was in progress. It was borne in upon Mr. Barnstaple that this last comer thought that he and his companions had clambered high enough, but that the uppermost man insisted they should go higher. In a few moments the matter was settled.

The uppermost Utopian became very active, lunged upward, swung out and vanished by jerks out of Mr. Barnstaple's field of view. His companions followed him and one after the other was lost to sight, leaving nothing visible but the convulsively agitated rope ladder and a dangling rope that they seemed to be dragging up the crag with them.

Mr. Barnstaple's taut muscles relaxed. He yawned silently, stretched his painful limbs and stood up very cautiously. He peered up the gully. The Utopians seemed to have reached the shelf above and to be busy there . The rope that had dangled became taut. They were hauling up something from below. It was a large bundle, possibly of tools or weapons or material wrapped in something that deadened its impacts against the rock. It jumped into view, hung spinning for a moment and was then snatched upward as the Utopians took in a fresh reef of rope. A period of silence followed.

He heard a metallic clang and then, thud, thud, a dull intermittent hammering. Then he jumped back as the end of a thin rope, apparently running over a pulley, dropped past him. The sounds from above now were like filing and then some bits of rock fell past him into the void.

§ 2

He did not know what to do. He was afraid to call to these Utopians and make his presence known to them. After the murder of Serpentine he was very doubtful how a Utopian would behave to an Earthling found hiding in a dark corner.

He examined the rope ladder that had brought these Utopians to his level. It was held by a long spike the end of which was buried in the rock at the side of the gully. Possibly this spike had been fired at the rock from below while he was asleep. The ladder was made up of straight lengths and rings at intervals of perhaps two feet. It was of such light material that he would have doubted its capacity to bear a man if he had not seen the Utopians upon it. It occurred to him that he might descend by this now and take his chances with any Utopians who might be below. He could not very well bring himself to the attention of these three Utopians above except by some sudden and startling action which might provoke sudden and unpleasant responses, but if he appeared first clambering slowly from above any Utopians beneath would have time to realize and consider the fact of his proximity before they dealt with him. And also he was excessively eager to get down from this dreary ledge.

He gripped a ring, thrust a leg backwards over the edge of the shelf, listened for some moments to the little noises of the three workers above him, and then began his descent.

It was an enormous descent. Presently he found himself regretting that he had not begun counting the rings of the ladder. He must already have handed himself down hundreds. And still when he craned his neck to look down, the dark gulf yawned below. It had become very dark now. The moonlight did not cut down very deeply into the canyon and the faint reflection from the thin mists above was all there was to break the blackness. And even overhead the moonlight seemed to be passing.

Now he was near the rock, now it fell away and the rope ladder seemed to fall plumb into lightless bottomless space. He had to feel for each ring, and his bare feet and hands were already chafed and painful. And a new and disagreeable idea had come into his head—that some Utopian might presently come rushing up the ladder. But he would get notice of that because the rope would tighten and quiver, and he would be able to cry out, "I am an Earthling coming down. I am a harmless Earthling."

He began to cry out these words experimentally. The gorge re-echoed them, and there was no answering sound.

He became silent again, descending grimly and as steadily as possible, because now an intense desire to get off this infernal rope ladder and rest his hot hands and feet was overmastering every other motive.

Clang, clang and a flash of green light.

He became rigid peering into the depths of the canyon. Came the green flash again. It revealed the depths of the gorge, still as it seemed an immense distance below him. And up the gorge—something; he could not grasp what it was during that momentary revelation. At first he thought it was a huge serpent writhing its way down the gorge, and then he concluded it must be a big cable that was being brought along the gorge by a handful of Utopians. But how the three or four figures he had indistinctly seen could move this colossal rope he could not imagine. The head of this cable serpent seemed to be lifting itself obliquely up the cliff. Perhaps it was being dragged up by ropes he had not observed. He waited for a third flash, but none came. He listened. He could hear nothing but a throbbing sound he had already noted before, like the throbbing of an engine running very smoothly.

He resumed his descent.

When at last he reached a standing place it took him by surprise. The rope ladder fell past it for some yards and ended. He was swaying more and more and beginning to realize that the rope ladder came to an end, when he perceived the dim indication of a nearly horizontal gallery cut along the rock face. He put out a foot and felt an edge and swung away out from it. He was now so weary and exhausted that for a time he could not relinquish his grip on the rope ladder and get a footing on the shelf. At last he perceived how this could be done. He released his feet and gave himself a push away from the rock with them. He swung back into a convenient position for getting a foothold. He repeated this twice, and then had enough confidence to abandon his ladder and drop on to the shelf. The ladder dangled away from him into the darkness and then came wriggling back to tap him playfully and startlingly on the shoulder blade.

The gallery he found himself in seemed to follow a great vein of crystalline material, along the cliff face. Borings as high as a man ran into the rock. He peered and felt his way along the gallery for a time. Manifestly if this was a mine there would be some way of ascending to it and descending from it into the gorge. The sound of the torrent was much louder now, and he judged he had perhaps come down two-thirds of the height of the crag. He was inclined to wait for daylight. The illuminated dial of his wrist-watch told him it was now four o'clock. It would not be long before dawn. He found a comfortable face of rock for his back and squatted down.

Dawn seemed to come very quickly, but in reality he dozed away the interval. When he glanced at his watch again it was half-past five.

He went to the edge of the gallery and peered up the gorge to where he had seen the cable. Things were pale and dim and very black and white, but perfectly clear. The walls of the canyon seemed to go up for ever and vanish at last in cloud. He had a glimpse of a Utopian below, who was presently hidden by the curve of the gorge. He guessed that the great cable must have been brought so close up to the Quarantine Crag as to be invisible to him.

He could find no down-going steps from the gallery, but some thirty or forty yards off were five or six cable ways running at a steep angle from the gallery to the opposite side of the gorge. They looked very black and distinct. He went along to them. Each was a carrier cable on which ran a small carrier trolley with a big hook below. Three of the carrier cables were empty, but on two the trolley was hauled up. Mr. Barnstaple examined the trolleys and found a catch retained them. He turned over one of these catches and the trolley ran away promptly, nearly dropping him into the gulf. He saved himself by clutching the carrier cable. He watched the trolley swoop down like a bird to a broad stretch of sandy beach on the other side of the torrent and come to rest there. It seemed all right. Trembling violently, he turned to the remaining trolley.

His nerves and will were so exhausted now that it was a long time before he could bring himself to trust to the hook of the remaining trolley and to release its catch. Then smoothly and swiftly he swept across the gorge to the beach below. There were big heaps of crystalline mineral on this beach and a cable—evidently for raising it—came down out of the mists above from some invisible crane, but not a Utopian was in sight. He relinquished his hold and dropped safely on his feet. The beach bordered down stream and he walked along it close to the edge of the torrent.

The light grew stronger as he went. The world ceased to be a world of greys and blacks; colour came back to things. Everything was heavily bedewed. And he was hungry and almost intolerably weary. The sand changed in its nature and became soft and heavy for his feet. He felt he could walk no further. He must wait for help. He sat down on a rock and looked up towards Quarantine Crag towering overhead.

§ 3

Sheer and high the great headland rose like the prow of some gigantic ship behind the two deep blue canyons; a few wisps and layers of mist still hid from Mr. Barnstaple its crest and the little bridge across the narrower gorge. The sky above between the streaks of mist was now an intense blue. And even as he gazed the mists swirled and dissolved, the rays of the rising sun smote the old castle to blinding gold, and the fastness of the Earthlings stood out clear and bright.

The bridge and the castle were very remote, and all that part of the crag was like a little cap on the figure of a tall upstanding soldier. Round beneath the level of the bridge at about the height at which the three Utopians had worked or were still working ran something dark, a rope-like band. He jumped to the conclusion that this must be the cable he had seen lit up by those green flashes in the night. Then he noted a peculiar body upon the crest of the more open of the two gorges. It was an enormous vertical coil, a coil flattened into a disc, which had appeared on the edge of the cliff opposite to Coronation Crag. Less plainly seen because of a projecting mass of rock, was a similar coil in the narrower canyon close to the steps that led up from the little bridge. Two or three Utopians, looking very small because they were so high and very squat because they were so foreshortened, were moving along the cliff edge and handling something that apparently had to do with these coils.

Mr. Barnstaple stared at these arrangements with much the same uncomprehending stare as that with which some savage who had never heard a shot fired in anger might watch the loading of a gun.

Came a familiar sound, faint and little. It was the hooter of Quarantine Castle sounding the reveille. And almost simultaneously the little Napoleonic figure of Mr. Rupert Catskill emerged against the blue. The head and shoulders of Penk rose and halted and stood at attention behind him. The captain of the Earthlings produced his field glasses and surveyed the coils through them.

"I wonder what he makes of them," said Mr. Barnstaple.

Mr. Catskill turned and gave some direction to Penk, who saluted and vanished.

A click from the nearer gorge jerked his attention back to the little bridge. It had gone! His eye dropped and caught it up within a few yards of the water. He saw the water splash and the metal framework crumple up and dance two steps and lie still, and then a moment later the crash and clatter of the fall reached his ears.

"Now who did that?" asked Mr. Barnstaple and Mr. Catskill answered his question by going hastily to that corner of the castle and staring down. Manifestly therefore it was the Utopians who had cut the bridge.

Mr. Catskill was joined almost immediately by Mr. Hunker and Lord Barralonga. Their gestures suggested an animated discussion.

The sunlight was creeping by imperceptible degrees down the front of Quarantine Crag. It had now got down to the cable that encircled the crest; in the light this shone with a coppery sheen. The three Utopians who had awakened Mr. Barnstaple in the night became visible descending the rope ladder very rapidly. And once more Mr. Barnstaple was aware of that humming sound he had heard ever and again during the night, but now it was much louder and it sounded everywhere about him, in the air, in the water, in the rocks and in his bones.

Abruptly something black and spear-shaped appeared beside the little group of Earthlings above. It seemed to jump up beside them, it paused and jumped again half the height of a man and jumped again. It was a flag being hauled up a flag staff, that Mr. Barnstaple had not hitherto observed. It reached the top of the staff and hung limp.

Then some eddy in the air caught it. It flapped out for a moment, displayed a white star on a blue ground and dropped again.

This was the flag of Earth—this was the flag of the crusade to restore the blessings of competition, conflict and warfare to Utopia. Beneath it appeared the head of Mr. Burleigh, examining the Utopian coils through his glasses.

§ 4

The throbbing and humming in Mr. Barnstaple's ears grew rapidly louder and rose acutely to an extreme intensity. Suddenly great flashes of violet light leapt across from coil to coil, passing through Quarantine Castle as though it was not there.

For a moment longer it *was* there.

The flag flared out madly and was torn from its staff. Mr. Burleigh lost his hat. A half length of Mr. Catskill became visible struggling with his coat tails which had blown up and enveloped his head. At the same time Mr. Barnstaple saw the Castle rotating upon the lower part of the crag, exactly as though some invisible giant had seized the upper tenth of the headland and was twisting it round.

And then it vanished.

As it did so, a great column of dust poured up into its place; the waters in the gorge sprung into the air in tall fountains and were splashed to spray, and a deafening thud smote Mr. Barnstaple's ears. Aerial powers picked him up and tossed him a dozen yards and he fell amidst a rain of dust and stones and water. He was bruised and stunned.

"My God!" he cried, "My God," and struggled to his knees, feeling violently sick.

He had a glimpse of the crest of Quarantine Crag, truncated as neatly as though it had been cheese cut with a sharp knife. And then fatigue and exhaustion had their way with him and he sprawled forward and lay insensible

BOOK THE THIRD

A NEOPHYTE IN UTOPIA

CHAPTER THE FIRST

THE PEACEFUL HILLS BESIDE THE RIVER

§ 1

"GOD has made more universes than there are pages in all the libraries of earth; man may learn and grow for ever amidst the multitude of his worlds."

Mr. Barnstaple had a sense of floating from star to star and from plane to plane, through an incessant variety and wonder of existences. He passed over the edge of being; he drifted for ages down the faces of immeasurable cliffs; he travelled from everlasting to everlasting in a stream of innumerable little stars. At last came a phase of profound restfulness. There was a sky of level clouds, warmed by the light of a declining sun, and a skyline of gently undulating hills, golden grassy upon their crests and carrying dark purple woods and thickets and patches of pale yellow like ripening corn upon their billowing slopes. Here and there were domed buildings and terraces, flowering gardens and little villas and great tanks of gleaming water.

There were many trees like the eucalyptus—only that they had darker leaves—upon the slopes immediately below and round and about him; and all the land fell at last towards a very broad valley down which a shining river wound leisurely in great semi-circular bends until it became invisible in the evening haze.

A slight movement turned his eyes to discover Lychnis seated beside him. She smiled at him and put her finger on her lips. He had a vague desire to address her, and smiled faintly and moved his head. She got up and slipped away from him past the head of his couch. He was too feeble and incurious to raise his head and look to see where she had gone. But he saw that she had been sitting at a white table on which was a silver bowl full of intensely blue flowers, and the colour of the flowers held him and diverted his first faint impulse of curiosity.

He wondered whether. colours were really brighter in this Utopian world or whether something in the air quickened and clarified his apprehension.

Beyond the table were the white pillars of the loggia. A branch of one of these eucalyptus-like trees with leaves bronze black, came very close outside.

And there was music. It was a little trickle of sound, that dripped and ran, a mere unobtrusive rivulet of little clear notes upon the margin of his consciousness, the song of some fairyland Debussy.

Peace. . . .

§ 2

He was awake again.

He tried hard to remember.

He had been knocked over and stunned in some manner too big and violent for his mind to hold as yet.

Then people had stood about him and talked about him. He remembered their feet. He must have been lying on his face with his face very close to the ground. Then they had turned him over, and the light of the rising sun had been blinding in his eyes.

Two gentle goddesses had given him some restorative in a gorge at the foot of high cliffs. He had been carried in a woman's arms as a child is carried. After that there were cloudy and dissolving memories of a long journey, a long flight through the air. There was something next to this, a vision of huge complicated machinery that did not join on to anything else. For a time his mind held this up in an interrogative fashion and then dropped it wearily. There had been voices in consultation, the prick of an injection and some gas that he had had to inhale. And sleep—or sleeps, spells of sleep interspersed with dreams. . . .

Now with regard to that gorge; how had he got there?

The gorge—in another light—with Utopians who struggled with a great cable.

Suddenly hard and clear came the vision of the headland of Coronation Crag towering up against the bright blue morning sky, and then the crest of it grinding round, with its fluttering flags and its dishevelled figures, passing slowly and steadily, as some great ship passes out of a dock, with its flags and passengers into the invisible and unknown. All the wonder of his great adventure returned to Mr. Barnstaple's mind.

§ 3

He sat up in a state of interrogation and Lychnis reappeared at his elbow.

She seated herself on his bed close to him, shook up some pillows behind him and persuaded him to lie back upon them. She persuaded him that he was cured of some illness and no longer infectious, but that he was still very weak. Of what illness? he asked himself. More of the immediate past bcame clear to him.

"There was an epidemic," he said. "A sort of mixed epidemic—of all our infections."

She smiled reassuringly. It was over. The science and organization of Utopia had taken the danger by the throat and banished it. Lychnis, however, had had nothing to do with the preventive and cleansing work that had ended the career of these invading microbes so speedily; her work had been the help and care of the sick. Something came through to the intelligence of Mr. Barnstaple that made him think that she was faintly sorry that this work of pity was no longer necessary. He looked up into her beautiful and kindly eyes and met her friendly solicitude. She was not sorry Utopia was cured again; that was incredible; but it seemed to him that she was sorry that she could no longer spend herself in need of assistance.

"What became of those people on the rock?" he asked. "What became of the other Earthlings?"

She did not know. They had been cast out of Utopia, she thought.

"Back to earth?"

She did not think they had gone back to the earth. They had perhaps gone into yet another universe. But she did not know. She was one of those who had no mathematical apti-tudes, and physico-chemical science and the complex theories of dimensions that interested so many people in Utopia were outside her circle of ideas. She believed that the crest of Coronation Crag had been swung out of the Utopian uni-verse altogether. A great number of people were now so intensely interested in this experimental work upon the un-explored dimensions into which physical processes might be swung, but these matters terrified her. Her mind recoiled from them as one recoils from the edge of a cliff. She did not want to think where the Earthlings had gone, what deeps they had reeled over, what immensities they had seen and swept down into. Such thoughts opened dark gulfs be-neath her feet where she had thought everything fixed and secure. She was a conservative in Utopia. She loved life as it was and as it had been. She had given herself to the care of Mr. Barnstaple when she had found that he had escaped the fate of the other Earthlings, and she had not troubled very greatly about the particulars of that fate. She had avoided thinking about it.

"But where are they? Where have they gone?"

She did not know.

She conveyed to him haltingly and imperfectly her own halting and unsympathetic ideas of these new discoveries that had inflamed the Utopian imagination. The crucial moment had been the experiment of Arden and Greenlake that had brought the Earthlings into Utopia. That had been the first rupture of the hitherto invincible barriers that had held their universe in three spatial dimensions. That had opened these abysses. That had been the moment of release for all the new work that now filled Utopia. That had been the first achievement of practical results from an intricate network of theory and deduction. It sent Mr. Barnstaple's mind back to the humbler discoveries of earth, to Franklin snapping the captive lightning from his kite and Galvani, with his dancing frog's legs, puzzling over the miracle that brought electricity into the service of men. But it had taken a century and a half for electricity to make any sensible changes in human life because the earthly workers were so few and the ways of the world so obstructive and slow and spiteful. In Utopia to make a novel discovery was to light an intellectual conflagration. Hundreds of thousands of experimentalists in free and open co-operation were now working along the fruitful lines that Arden and Greenlake had made manifest. Every day, every hour now, new and hitherto fantastic possibilities of inter-spatial relationship were being made plain to the Utopians.

Mr. Barnstaple rubbed his head and eyes with both hands and then lay back, blinking at the great valley below him, growing slowly golden as the sun sank. He felt himself to be the most secure and stable of beings at the very center of a sphere of glowing serenity. And that effect of an immense tranquillity was a delusion; that still evening peace was woven of incredible billions of hurrying and clashing atoms.

All the peace and fixity that man has ever known or will ever know is but the smoothness of the face of a torrent that flies along with incredible speed from cataract to cataract. Time was when men could talk of everlasting hills. To-day a schoolboy knows that they dissolve under the frost and wind and rain and pour seaward, day by day and hour by hour. Time was when men could speak of Terra Firma and feel the earth fixed, adamantine beneath their feet. Now they know that it whirls through space eddying about a spinning, blindly driven sun amidst a sheeplike drift of stars. And this fair curtain of appearance before the eyes of Mr. Barnstaple, this still and level flush of sunset and the great cloth of starry space that hung behind the blue; that too was now to be pierced and torn and rent asunder. . . .

The extended fingers of his mind closed on the things that concerned him most.

"But where are my people?" he asked. "Where are their bodies? Is it just possible they are still alive?"

She could not tell him.

He lay thinking. . . . It was natural that he should be given into the charge of a rather backward-minded woman. The active-minded here had no more use for him in their lives than active-minded people on earth have for pet animals. She did not want to think about these spatial relations at all; the subject was too difficult for her; she was one of Utopia's educational failures. She sat beside him with a divine sweetness and tranquillity upon her face, and he felt his own judgment upon her like a committed treachery. Yet he wanted to know very badly the answer to his question.

He supposed the crest of Coronation Crag had been twisted round and flung off into some outer space. It was

unlikely that this time the Earthlings would strike a convenient planet again. In all probability they had been
turned off into the void, into the interstellar space of some
unknown universe. . . .

What would happen then? They would freeze. The air
would instantly diffuse right out of them. Their own
gravitation would flatten them out, crush them together,
collapse them! At least they would have no time to suffer.
A gasp, like some one flung into ice-cold water. . . .

He contemplated these possibilities.

"Flung out!" he said aloud. "Like a cageful of mice
thrown over the side of a ship!"

"I don't understand," said Lychnis, turning to him.

He appealed to her. "And now—tell me. What is to
become of me?"

§ 4

For a time Lychnis gave him no answer. She sat with
her soft eyes upon the blue haze into which the great river
valley had now dissolved. Then she turned to him with
a question:

"You want to stay in this world?"

"Surely any Earthling would want to stay in this world.
My body has been purified. Why should I not stay?"

"It seems a good world to you?"

"Loveliness, order, health, energy and wonder; it has all
the good things for which my world groans and travails."

"And yet our world is not content."

"I could be contented."

"You are tired and weak still."

"In this air I could grow strong and vigorous. I could
almost grow young in this world. In years, as you count
them here, I am still a young man."

Again she was silent for a time. The mighty lap of the

landscape was filled now with indistinguishable blue, and beyond the black silhouettes of the trees upon the hillside only the skyline of the hills was visible against the yellow green and pale yellow of the evening sky. Never had Mr. Barnstaple seen so peaceful a nightfall. But her words denied that peace. "Here," she said, "there is no rest. Every day men and women awake and say: What new thing shall we do to-day? What shall we change?"

"They have changed a wild planet of disease and disorder into a sphere of beauty and safety. They have made the wilderness of human motives bear union and knowledge and power."

"And research never rests, and curiosity and the desire for more power and still more power consumes all our world."

"A healthy appetite. I am tired now, as weak and weary and soft as though I had just been born; but presently when I have grown stronger I too may share in that curiosity and take a part in these great discoveries that now set Utopia astir. Who knows?"

He smiled at her kind eyes.

"You will have much to learn," he said.

She seemed to measure her own failure as she said these words.

Some sense of the profound differences that three thousand years of progress might have made in the fundamental ideas and ways of thinking of the race dawned upon Mr. Barnstaple's mind. He remembered that in Utopia he heard only the things he could understand, and that all that found no place in his terrestrial circle of ideas was inaudible to his mind. The gulfs of misunderstanding might be wider and deeper than he was assuming. A totally illiterate Gold Coast negro trying to master thermo-electricity would have set himself a far more hopeful task.

"After all it is not the new discoveries that I want to

share," he said; "quite possibly they are altogether beyond me; it is this perfect beautiful daily life, this life of all the dreams of my own time come true, that I want. I just want to be alive here. That will be enough for me."

"You are weak and tired yet," said Lychnis. "When you are stronger you may face other ideas."

"But what other ideas——?"

"Your mind may turn back to your own world and your own life."

"Go back to Earth!"

Lychnis looked out at the twilight again for a while before she turned to him with, "You are an Earthling born and made. What else can you be?"

"What else can I be?" Mr. Barnstaple's mind rested upon that, and he lay feeling rather than thinking amidst its implications as the pinpoint lights of Utopia pricked the darkling blue below and ran into chains and groups and coalesced into nebulous patches.

He resisted the truth below her words. This glorious world of Utopia, perfect and assured, poised ready for tremendous adventures amidst untravelled universes, was a world of sweet giants and uncompanionable beauty, a world of enterprises in which a door muddy-witted, weak-willed Earthling might neither help nor share. They had plundered their planet as one empties a purse; they thrust out their power amidst the stars. . . . They were kind. They were very kind. . . . But they were different. . . .

CHAPTER THE SECOND

A LOITERER IN A LIVING WORLD

§ 1

IN a few days Mr. Barnstaple had recovered strength of body and mind. He no longer lay in bed in a loggia, filled with self-pity and the beauty of a world subdued; he went about freely and was soon walking long distances over the Utopian countryside, seeking acquaintances and learning more and more of this wonderland of accomplished human desires.

For that is how it most impressed him. Nearly all the greater evils of human life had been conquered; war, pestilence and malaise, famine and poverty had been swept out of human experience. The dreams of artists, of perfected and lovely bodies and of a world transfigured to harmony and beauty had been realized; the spirits of order and organization ruled triumphant. Every aspect of human life had been changed by these achievements.

The climate of this Valley of Rest was bland and sunny like the climate of South Europe, but nearly everything characteristic of the Italian or Spanish scene had gone. Here were no bent and aged crones carrying burthens, no chatter-ing pursuit by beggars, no ragged workers lowering by the wayside. The puny terracing, the distressing accumulations of hand cultivation, the gnarled olives, hacked vines, the little patches of grain or fruit, and the grudged litigious irrigation of those primitive conditions, gave place to sweep-ing schemes of conservation, to a broad and subtle handling of slope and soil and sunshine. No meagre goats nor sheep, child-tended, cropped among the stones, no tethered cattle ate their apportioned circles of herbage and no more. There were no hovels by the wayside, no shrines with tortured, blood-oozing images, no slinking misbegotten curs nor beaten beasts sweating and panting between their overloaded panniers at the steeper places of rutted, rock-strewn and dung-strewn roads. Instead the great smooth indestructible ways swept in easy gradients through the land, leaping gorges and crossing valleys upon wide-arched viaducts, piercing cathedral-like aisles through the hillsides, throwing off bastions to command some special splendour of the land. Here were resting places and shelters, stairways clambering to pleasant arbours and summer-houses where friends might talk and lovers shelter and rejoice. Here were groves and avenues of such trees as he had never seen before. For on earth as yet there is scarcely such a thing as an altogether healthy fully grown tree, nearly all our trees are bored and consumed by parasites, rotten and tumorous with fungi, more gnarled and crippled and disease-twisted even than mankind.

The landscape had absorbed the patient design of five-and-twenty centuries. In one place Mr. Barnstaple found great works in progress; a bridge was being replaced, not because it was outworn, but because someone had produced a bolder, more delightful design.

For a time he did not observe the absence of telephonic or telegraphic communication; the posts and wires that mark a modern countryside had disappeared. The reasons for that difference he was to learn later. Nor did he at first miss the railway, the railway station and the wayside inn. He perceived that the frequent buildings must have specific functions, that people came and went from them with an appearance of interest and preoccupation, that from some of them seemed to come a hum and whir of activity; work of many sorts was certainly in progress; but his ideas of the mechanical organization of this new world were too

vague and tentative as yet for him to attempt to fix any
significance to this sort of place or that. He walked agape
like a savage in a garden.

He never came to nor saw any towns. The reason for
any such close accumulations of human beings had largely
disappeared. In certain places, he learnt, there were
gatherings of people for studies, mutual stimulation, or
other convenient exchanges, in great series of communicating
buildings; but he never visited any of these centres.

And about this world went the tall people of Utopia,
fair and wonderful, smiling or making some friendly gesture
as they passed him but giving him little chance for questions
or intercourse. They travelled swiftly in machines upon the
high road or walked, and ever and again the shadow of
a silent soaring aeroplane would pass over him. He went
a little in awe of these people and felt himself a queer
creature when he met their eyes. For like the gods of
Greece and Rome theirs was a cleansed and perfected
humanity, and it seemed to him that they were gods. Even
the great tame beasts that walked freely about this world
had a certain divinity that checked the expression of Mr.
Barnstaple's friendliness.

§ 2

Presently he found a companion for his rambles, a boy
of thirteen, a cousin of Lychnis, named Crystal. He was
a curly-headed youngster, brown-eyed as she was; and he
was reading history in a holiday stage of his education.

So far as Mr. Barnstaple could gather the more serious
part of his intellectual training was in mathematical work
interrelated to physical and chemical science, but all that
was beyond an Earthling's range of ideas. Much of this
work seemed to be done in cooperation with other boys,
and to be what we should call research on earth. Nor could

Mr. Barnstaple master the nature of some other sort of study which seemed to turn upon refinements of expression. But the history brought them together. The boy was just learn-ing about the growth of the Utopian social system out of the efforts and experiences of the Ages of Confusion. His imagination was alive with the tragic struggles upon which the present order of Utopia was founded, he had a hundred questions for Mr. Barnstaple, and he was full of explicit information which was destined presently to sink down and become part of the foundations of his adult mind. Mr. Barnstaple was as good as a book to him, and he was as good as a guide to Mr. Barnstaple. They went about together talking upon a footing of the completest equality, this rather exceptionally intelligent Earthling and this Utopian stripling, who topped him by perhaps an inch when they stood side by side.

The boy had the broad facts of Utopian history at his fingers' ends. He could explain and find an interest in explaining how artificial and upheld the peace and beauty of Utopia still were. Utopians were in essence, he said, very much what their ancestors had been in the beginnings of the newer stone age, fifteen thousand or twenty thousand years ago. They were still very much what Earthlings had been in the corresponding period. Since then there had been only 600 or 700 generations and no time for any very fundamental changes in the race. There had not been even a general admixture of races. On Utopia as on earth there had been dusky and brown peoples, and they remained distinct. The various races mingled socially but did not interbreed very much; rather they purified and intensified their racial gifts and beauties. There was often very passionate love between people of contrasted race, but rarely did such love come to procreation. There had been a certain deliberate elimination of ugly, malignant, narrow, stupid and gloomy types during the past dozen centuries or so; but except for the fuller realization of his latent possibilities, the common man in Utopia was very little different from the ordinary energetic and able people of a later stone-age or early bronze-age community. They were infinitely better nourished, trained and educated, and mentally and physically their condition was clean and fit, but they were the same flesh and nature as we are.

"But," said Mr. Barnstaple, and struggled with that idea for a time. "Do you mean to tell me that half the babies born on earth to-day might grow to be such gods as these people I meet?"

"Given our air, given our atmosphere."

"Given your heritage."

"Given our freedom."

In the past of Utopia, in the Age of Confusion, Mr. Barnstaple had to remember, everyone had grown up with a crippled or a thwarted will, hampered by vain restrictions or misled by plausible delusions. Utopia still bore it in mind that human nature was fundamentally animal and savage and had to be adapted to social needs, but Utopia had learnt the better methods of adaption—after endless failures of compulsion, cruelty and deception. "On Earth we tame our animals with hot irons and our fellow men by violence and fraud," said Mr. Barnstaple, and described the schools and books, newspapers and public discussions of the early twentieth century to his incredulous companion. "You cannot imagine how beaten and fearful even decent people are upon Earth. You learn of the Age of Confusion in your histories but you do not know what the realities of a bad mental atmosphere, an atmosphere of feeble laws, hates and superstitions, are. As night goes round the Earth always there are hundreds of thousands of people who should be sleeping, lying awake, fearing a bully, fearing a cruel competition, dreading lest they cannot make good, ill of some illness they cannot comprehend, distressed by some irrational quarrel, maddened by some thwarted instinct or some suppressed and perverted desire." . . .

Crystal admitted that it was hard to think now of the Age of Confusion in terms of misery. Much of the every-day misery of Earth was now inconceivable. Very slowly Utopia had evolved its present harmony of law and custom and education. Man was no longer crippled and compelled; it was recognized that he was fundamentally an animal and that his daily life must follow the round of appetites satisfied and instincts released. The daily texture of Utopian life was woven of various and interesting foods and drinks, of free and entertaining exercise and work, of sweet sleep and of the interest and happiness of fearless and spiteless love-making. Inhibition was at a minimum. But where the power of Utopian education began was after the animal had been satisfied and disposed of. The jewel on the reptile's head that had brought Utopia out of the confusions of human life, was curiosity, the play impulse, prolonged and expanded in adult life into an insatiable appetite for knowledge and an habitual creative urgency. All Utopians had become as little children, learners and makers.

It was strange to hear this boy speaking so plainly and clearly of the educational process to which he was being subjected, and particularly to find he could talk so frankly of love.

An earthly bashfulness almost prevented Mr. Barnstaple from asking, "But you—— You do not make Love?"

"I have had curiosities," said the boy, evidently saying what he had been taught to say. "But it is not necessary nor becoming to make love too early in life nor to let desire take hold of one. It weakens youth to become too early possessed by desire—which often will not leave one again.

It spoils and cripples the imagination. I want to do good work as my father has done before me."

Mr. Barnstaple glanced at the beautiful young profile at his side and was suddenly troubled by memories of a certain study number four at school, and of some ugly phases of his adolescence, the stuffy, secret room, the hot and ugly fact. He felt a beastlier Earthling than ever. "Heigho!" he sighed. "But this world of yours is as starlight and as sweet as cold water on a dusty day."

"Many people I love," said the boy, "but not with passion. Some day that will come. But one must not be too eager and anxious to meet passionate love or one might make-believe and give or snatch at a sham. . . . There is no hurry. No one will prevent me when my time comes. All good things come to one in this world in their own good time."

But work one does not wait for; one's work, since it concerns one's own self only, one goes to meet. Crystal thought very much about the work that he might do. It seemed to Mr. Barnstaple that work, in the sense of uncongenial toil, had almost disappeared from Utopia. Yet all Utopia was working. Everyone was doing work that fitted natural aptitudes and appealed to the imagination of the worker. Everyone worked happily and eagerly—as those people we call geniuses do on our Earth.

For suddenly Mr. Barnstaple found himself telling Crystal of the happiness of the true artist, of the true scientific worker, of the original man even on earth as it is to-day. They, too, like the Utopians do work that concerns themselves and is in their own nature for great ends. Of all Earthlings they are the most enviable.

"If such men are not happy on earth," said Mr. Barnstaple, "it is because they are touched with vulgarity and still heed the soiled successes and honours and satisfactions of vulgar men, still feel neglect and limitation that should concern them no more. But to him who has seen the sun shine in Utopia surely the utmost honour and glory of earth can signify no more and be no more desirable than the complimentary spittle of the chieftain and a string of barbaric beads."

§ 3

Crystal was still of an age to be proud of his *savoir faire*. He showed Mr. Barnstaple his books and told him of his tutors and exercises.

Utopia still made use of printed books; books were still the simplest, clearest way of bringing statement before a tranquil mind. Crystal's books were very beautifully bound in flexible leather that his mother had tooled for him very prettily, and they were made of hand-made paper. The lettering was some fluent phonetic script that Mr. Barnstaple could not understand. It reminded him of Arabic; and frequent sketches, outline maps and diagrams were interpo' for whom he prepared a sort of exercise report, and he lated. Crystal was advised in his holiday reading by a tutor supplemented his reading by visits to museums; but there was no educational museum convenient in the Valley of Peace for Mr. Barnstaple to visit.

Crystal had passed out of the opening stage of education which was carried on, he said, upon large educational estates given up wholly to the lives of children. Education up to eleven or twelve seemed to be much more carefully watched and guarded and taken care of in Utopia than upon eart'ı. Shocks to the imagination, fear and evil suggestions were warded off as carefully as were infection and physical disaster; by eight or nine the foundations of a Utopian character were surely laid, habits of cleanliness, truth, candour and helpfulness, confidence in the world, fearlessness and a sense of belonging to the great purpose of the race.

Only after nine or ten did the child go outside the garden of its early growth and begin to see the ordinary ways of the world. Until that age the care of the children was largely in the hands of nurses and teachers, but after that time the parents became more of a factor than they had been in a youngster's life. It was always a custom for the parents of a child to be near and see that child in its nursery days, but just when earthly parents tended to separate from their children as they went away to school or went into business, Utopian parentage grew to be something closer. There was an idea in Utopia that between parent and child there was a necessary temperamental sympathy; children looked forward to the friendship and company of their parents, and parents looked forward to the interest of their children's adolescence, and though a parent had practically no power over a son or daughter, he or she took naturally the position of advocate, adviser and sympathetic friend The friendship was all the franker and closer because of that lack of power, and all the easier because age for age the Utopians were so much younger and fresher-minded than Earthlings. Crystal it seemed had a very great passion for his mother. He was very proud of his father, who was a wonderful painter and designer; but it was his mother who possessed the boy's heart.

On his second walk with Mr. Barnstaple he said he was going to hear from his mother, and Mr. Barnstaple was shown the equivalent of correspondence in Utopia. Crystal carried a little bundle of wires and light rods; and presently coming to a place where a pillar stood in the midst of a lawn he spread this affair out like a long cat's cradle and tapped a little stud in the pillar with a key that he carried on a light gold chain about his neck. Then he took up a receiver attached to his apparatus, and spoke aloud and listened and presently heard a voice.

It was a very pleasant woman's voice; it talked to Crystal for a time without interruption, and then Crystal talked back, and afterwards there were other voices, some of which Crystal answered and some which he heard without replying. Then he gathered up his apparatus again.

This Mr. Barnstaple learnt was the Utopian equivalent of letter and telephone. For in Utopia, except by previous arrangement, people do not talk together on the telephone. A message is sent to the station of the district in which the recipient is known to be, and there it waits until he chooses to tap his accumulated messages. And any that one wishes to repeat can be repeated. Then he talks back to the senders and dispatches any other messages he wishes. The transmission is wireless. The little pillars supply electric power for transmission or for any other purpose the Utopians require. For example, the gardeners resort to them to run their mowers and diggers and rakes and rollers.

Far away across the valley Crystal pointed out the district station at which this correspondence gathered and was dispersed. Only a few people were on duty, there; almost all the connexions were automatic. The messages came and went from any part of the planet.

This set Mr. Barnstaple going upon a long string of questions.

He discovered for the first time that the message organization of Utopia had a complete knowledge of the whereabouts of every soul upon the planet. It had a record of every living person and it knew in what message district he was. Everyone was indexed and noted.

To Mr. Barnstaple, accustomed to the crudities and dishonesties of earthly governments, this was an almost terrifying discovery. "On earth that would be the means of unending blackmail and tyranny," he said. "Everyone

would lie open to espionage. We had a fellow at Scotland
Yard. If he had been in your communication department
he would have made life in Utopia intolerable in a week.
You cannot imagine the nuisance he was." . . .

Mr. Barnstaple had to explain to Crystal what blackmail
meant. It was like that in Utopia to begin with, Crystal
said. Just as on earth so in Utopia there was the same
natural disposition to use knowledge and power to the disadvantage of one's fellows, and the same jealousy of having
one's personal facts known. In the Stone Age in Utopia
men kept their true names secret and could only be spoken
of by nicknames. They feared magic abuses. "Some savages
still do that on earth," said Mr. Barnstaple. It was only
very slowly that Utopians came to trust doctors and dentists
and only very slowly that doctors and dentists became trust-
worthy. It was a matter of scores of centuries before the
chief abuses of the confidences and trusts necessary to a
modern social organization could be effectively corrected.

Every young Utopian had to learn the Five Principles of
Liberty, without which civilization is impossible. The first
was the Principle of Privacy. This is that all individual
personal facts are private between the citizen and the public
organization to which he entrusts them, and can be used
only for his convenience and with his sanction. Of course
all such facts are available for statistical uses, but not as
individual personal facts. And the second principle is the
Principle of Free Movement. A citizen, subject to the due
discharge of his public obligations, may go without permission or explanation to any part of the Utopian planet.
All the means of transport are freely at his service. Every
Utopian may change his surroundings, his climate and his
social atmosphere as he will. The third principle is the
Principle of Unlimited Knowledge. All that is known in
Utopia, except individual personal facts about living people,

is on record and as easily available as a perfected series of indices, libraries, museums, and inquiry offices can make it. Whatever the Utopian desires to know he may know with the utmost clearness, exactness and facility so far as his powers of knowing and his industry go. Nothing is kept from him and nothing is misrepresented to him. And that brought Mr. Barnstaple to the fourth Principle of Liberty, which was that Lying is the Blackest Crime.

Crystal's definition of Lying was a sweeping one; the inexact statement of facts, even the suppression of a material fact, was lying.

"Where there are lies there cannot be freedom."

Mr. Barnstaple was mightily taken by this idea. It seemed at once quite fresh to him and one that he had always unconsciously entertained. Half the difference between Utopia and our world he asserted lay in this, that our atmosphere was dense and poisonous with lies and shams.

"When one comes to think of it," said Mr. Barnstaple, and began to expatiate to Crystal upon all the falsehoods of human life. The fundamental assumptions of earthly associations were still largely lies, false assumptions of necessary and unavoidable difference in flags and nationality, pretences of function and power in monarchy; impostures of organized learning, religious and moral dogmas and shams. And one must live in it; one is a part of it. You are restrained, taxed, distressed and killed by these insane unrealities. "Lying the Primary Crime! How simple that is! how true and necessary it is! That dogma is the funda-mental distinction of the scientific world-state from all preceding states." And going on from that Mr. Barnstaple launched out into a long and loud tirade against the sup-pression and falsifications of earthly newspapers.

It was a question very near his heart. The London newspapers had ceased to be impartial vehicles of news;

they omitted, they mutilated, they misstated. They were no better than propaganda rags. Rags! *Nature,* within its field, was shiningly accurate and full, but that was a purely scientific paper; it did not touch the everyday news. The Press, he held, was the only possible salt of contemporary life, and if the salt had lost its savour——!

The poor man was orating as though he was back at his Sydenham breakfast-table after a bad morning's paper.

"Once upon a time Utopia was in just such a tangle," said Crystal consolingly. "But there is a proverb, 'Truth comes back where once she has visited.' You need not trouble so much as you do. Some day even your press may grow clear."

"How do *you* manage about newspapers and criticism?" said Mr. Barnstaple.

Crystal explained that there was a complete distinction between news and discussion in Utopia. There were houses —one was in sight—which were used as reading rooms. One went to these places to learn the news. Thither went the reports of all the things that were happening on the planet, things found, things discovered, things done. The reports were made as they were needed; there were no advertisement contracts to demand the same bulk of news every day. For some time Crystal said the reports had been very full and amusing about the Earthlings, but he had not been reading the paper for many days because of the interest in history the Earthling affair had aroused in him. There was always news of fresh scientific discoveries that stirred the imagination. One frequent item of public interest and excitement was the laying out of some wide scheme of research. The new spatial work that Arden and Greenlake had died for was producing much news. And when people died in Utopia it was the custom to tell the story of their lives. Crystal promised to take Mr. Barnstaple to a news place and entertain him by reading him some of the Utopian descriptions of earthly life which had been derived from the Earthlings, and Mr. Barnstaple asked that when this was done he might also hear about Arden and Greenlake, who had been not only great discoverers, but great lovers, and of Serpentine and Cedar, for whom he had conceived an intense admiration. Utopian news lacked of course the high spice of an earthly newspaper; the intriguing murders and amusing misbehaviours, the entertaining and exciting consequences of sexual ignorance and sexual blunderings, the libel cases and detected swindles, the great processional movements of Royalty across the general traffic, and the romantic fluctuations of the stock exchange and sport. But where the news of Utopia lacked liveliness, the liveliness of discussion made up for it. For the Fifth Principle of Liberty in Utopia was Free Discussion and Criticism.

Any Utopian was free to criticise and discuss anything in the whole universe provided he told no lies about it directly or indirectly; he could be as respectful or disrespectful as he pleased; he could propose anything however subversive. He could break into poetry or fiction as he chose. He could express himself in any literary form he liked or by sketch or caricature as the mood took him. Only he must refrain from lying; that was the one rigid rule of controversy. He could get what he had to say printed and distributed to the news rooms. There it was read or neglected as the visitors chanced to approve of it or not. Often if they liked what they read they would carry off a copy with them. Crystal had some new fantastic fiction about the exploration of space among his books; imaginative stories that boys were reading very eagerly; they were pamphlets of thirty or forty pages printed on a beautiful paper that he said was made directly from flax and certain reeds. The librarians noted what books and papers were read and taken away, and these they replaced with fresh copies. The piles that went unread were presently reduced to one or two copies and the rest went back to the pulping mills. But many of the poets and philosophers and story-tellers whose imaginations found no wide popularity were nevertheless treasured and their memories kept alive by a few devoted admirers.

§ 4

"I am not at all clear in my mind about one thing," said Mr. Barnstaple. "I have seen no coins and nothing like money pass in this world. By all outward appearance this might be a Communism such as was figured in a book we used to value on Earth, a book called *News from Nowhere* by an Earthling named William Morris. It was a graceful impossible book. In that dream everyone worked for the joy of working and took what he needed. But I have never believed in Communism because I recognize as here in Utopia you seem to recognize, the natural fierceness and greediness of the untutored man. There is joy in creation for others to use, but no natural joy in unrequited service. The sense of justice to himself is greater in man than the sense of service. Somehow here you must balance the work anyone does for Utopia against what he destroys or consumes. How do you do it?"

Crystal considered. "There were Communists in Utopia in the Last Age of Confusion. In some parts of our planet they tried to abolish money suddenly and violently and brought about great economic confusion and want and misery. To step straight to communism failed—very tragically. And yet Utopia to-day is practically a communism, and except by way of curiosity I have never had a coin in my hand in all my life."

In Utopia just as upon earth, he explained, money came

as a great discovery; as a method of freedom. Hitherto, before the invention of money, all service between man and man had been done through bondage or barter. Life was a thing of slavery and narrow choice. But money opened up the possibility of giving a worker a free choice in his reward. It took Utopia three thousand years and more to realize that possibility. The idea of money abounded in pitfalls and was easily corruptible; Utopia floundered its way to economic lucidity through long centuries of credit and debt, false and debased money; extravagant usury and every possibility of speculative abuse. In the matter of money more than in any other human concern, human cunning has set itself most vilely and treacherously to prey upon human necessity. Utopia once carried, as earth carries now, a load of parasitic souls, speculators, forestallers, gamblers and bargain-pressing Shylocks, exacting every conceivable advantage out of the weaknesses of the monetary system; she had needed centuries of economic sanitation. It was only when Utopia had got to the beginnings of world-wide political unity and when there were sufficiently full statistics of world resources and world production, that human society could at last give the individual worker the assurance of a coin of steadfast significance, a coin that would mean for him to-day or to-morrow or at any time the certainty of a set quantity of elemental values. And with peace throughout the planet and increasing social stability, interest, which is the measure of danger and uncertainty, dwindled at last to nothing. Banking became a public service perforce, because it no longer offered profit to the individual banker. "Rentier classes," Crystal conveyed, "are not a permanent element in any community. They mark a phase of transition between a period of insecurity and no interest. They are a dawn phenomenon."

Mr. Barnstaple digested this statement after an interval

of incredulity. He satisfied himself by a few questions that young Utopia really had some idea of what a rentier class was, what its moral and imaginative limitations were likely to be and the role it may have played in the intellectual development of the world by providing a class of independent minds.

"Life is intolerant of all independent classes," said Crystal, evidently repeating an axiom. "Either you must earn or you must rob. . . . We have got rid of robbing."

The youngster still speaking by his book went on to explain how the gradual disuse of money came about. It was an outcome of the general progressive organization of the economic system, the substitution of collective enterprises for competitive enterprises and of wholesale for retail dealing. There had been a time in Utopia when money changed hands at each little transaction and service. One paid money if one wanted a newspaper or a match or a bunch of flowers or a ride on a street conveyance. Everybody went about the world with pockets full of small coins paying on every slight occasion. Then as economic science became more stable and exact the methods of the club and the covering subscription extended. People were able to buy passes that carried them by all the available means of transport for a year or for ten years or for life. The State learnt from clubs and hostels to provide matches, newspapers, stationery and transport for a fixed annual charge. The same inclusive system spread from small and incidental things to great and essential matters, to housing and food and even clothing. The State postal system, which knew where every Utopian citizen was, was presently able in conjunction with the public banking system to guarantee his credit in any part of the world. People ceased to draw coin for their work; the various departments of service, and of economic, educational and scientific activity would credit the individual with his earnings in the public bank and debit him with his customary charges for all the normal services of life.

"Something of this sort is going on on earth even now," said Mr. Barnstaple. "We use money in the last resort, but a vast volume of our business is already a matter of book-keeping."

Centuries of unity and energy had given Utopia a very complete control of many fountains of natural energy upon the planet, and this was the heritage of every child born therin. He was credited at his birth with a sum sufficient to educate and maintain him up to four-or five-and-twenty, and then he was expected to choose some occupation to replenish his account.

"But if he doesn't?" said Mr. Barnstaple.

"Everyone does."

"But if he didn't?"

"He'd be miserable and uncomfortable. I've never heard of such a case. I suppose he'd be discussed. Psychologists might examine him. . . . But one must do something."

"But suppose Utopia had no work for him to do?"

Crystal could not imagine that. "There is always something to be done."

"But in Utopia once, in the old times, you had unemployment?"

"That was part of the Confusion. There was a sort of hypertrophy of debt; it had become paralysis. Why, when they had unemployment at that same time there was neither enough houses nor food nor clothing. They had unemployment and shortage at one and the same time. It is incredible."

"Does everyone earn about the same amount of pay?"

"Energetic and creative people are often given big grants if they seem to need the help of others or a command of natural resources. . . . And artists sometimes grow rich if their work is much desired."

"Such a gold chain as yours you had to buy?"

"From the maker in his shop. My mother bought it."

"Then there are shops?"

"You shall see some. Places where people go to see new and delightful things."

"And if an artist grows rich, what can he do with his money?"

"Take time and material to make some surpassingly beautiful thing to leave the world. Or collect and help with the work of other artists. Or do whatever else he pleases to teach and fine the common sense of beauty in Utopia. Or just do nothing. . . . Utopia can afford it—if he can."

§ 5

"Cedar and Lion," said Mr. Barnstaple, "explained to the rest of us how it is that your government is as it were broken up and dispersed among the people who have special knowledge of the matters involved. The balance between interests, we gathered, was maintained by those who studied the general psychology and the educational organization of Utopia. At first it was very strange to our earthly minds that there should be nowhere a pretended omniscience and a practical omnipotence, that is to say a sovereign thing, a person or an assembly whose *fiat* was final. Mr. Burleigh and Mr. Catskill thought that such a thing was absolutely necessary, and so, less surely, did I. 'Who will decide?' was their riddle. They expected to be taken to see the President or the Supreme Council of Utopia. I suppose it seems to you the most natural of things that there should be nothing of the sort, and that a question should go simply and naturally to the man who knows best about it."

"Subject to free criticism," said Crystal.

"Subject to the same process that has made him eminent

and responsible. But don't people thrust themselves forward even here—out of vanity. And don't people get thrust forward in front of the best—out of spite?"

"There is plenty of spite and vanity in every Utopian soul," said Crystal. "But people speak very plainly and criticism is very searching and free. So that we learn to search our motives before we praise or question."

"What you say and do shows up here plainly at its true value," said Mr. Barnstaple. "You cannot throw mud in the noise and darkness unchallenged or get a false claim acknowledged in the disorder."

"Some years ago there was a man, an artist, who made a great trouble about the work of my father. Often artistic criticism is very bitter here, but he was bitter beyond measure. He caricatured my father and abused him incessantly. He followed him from place to place. He tried to prevent the allocation of material to him. He was quite ineffective. Some people answered him, but for the most part he was disregarded. . . ."

The boy stopped short.

"Well?"

"He killed himself. He could not escape from his own foolishness. Everyone knew what he had said and done. . . ."

"But in the past there were kings and councils and conferences in Utopia," said Mr. Barnstaple, returning to the main point.

"My books teach me that our state could have grown up in no other way. We had to have these general dealers in human relationship, politicians and lawyers, as a necessary stage in political and social development. Just as we had to have soldiers and policemen to save people from mutual violence. It was only very slowly that politicians and lawyers came to admit the need for special knowledge in the things they had to do. Politicians would draw boundaries without any proper knowledge of ethnology or economic geography, and lawyers decide about will and purpose with the crudest knowledge of psychology. They produced the most pre- posterous and unworkable arrangements in the gravest fashion."

"Like Tristram Shandy's parish bull—which set about begetting the peace of the world at Versailles," said Mr. Barnstaple.

Crystal looked puzzled.

"A complicated allusion to a purely earthly matter," said Mr. Barnstaple. "This complete diffusion of the business of politics and law among the people with knowledge, is one of the most interesting things of all to me in this world. Such a diffusion is beginning upon earth. The people who understand world-health for instance are dead against politi- cal and legal methods, and so are many of our best economists. And most people never go into a law court, and wouldn't dream of doing so upon business of their own, from their cradles to their graves. What became of your politicians and lawyers? Was there a struggle?"

"As light grew and intelligence spread they became more and more evidently unnecessary. They met at last only to appoint men of knowledge as assessors and so forth, and after a time even these appointments became foregone con- clusions. Their activities melted into the general body of criticism and discussion. In places there are still old buildings that used to be council chambers and law courts. The last politician to be elected to a legislative assembly died in Utopia about a thousand years ago. He was an eccentric and garrulous old gentleman; he was the only candidate and one man voted for him, and he insisted upon assembling in solitary state and having all his speeches and proceedings taken down in shorthand. Boys and girls who were learning

stenography used to go to report him. Finally he was dealt
with as a mental case."

"And the last judge?"

"I have not learnt about the last judge," said Crystal.
"I must ask my tutor. I suppose there was one, but I
suppose nobody asked him to judge anything. So he probably
got something more respectable to do."

§ 6

"I begin to apprehend the daily life of this world," said
Mr. Barnstaple. "It is a life of demi-gods, very free, strongly
individualized, each following an individual bent, each con-
tributing to great racial ends. It is not only cleanly naked
and sweet and lovely but full of personal dignity. It is,
I see, a practical communism, planned and led up to through
long centuries of education and discipline and collectivist
preparation. I had never thought before that socialism could
exalt and ennoble the individual and individualism degrade
him, but now I see plainly that here the thing is proved.
In this fortunate world—it is indeed the crown of all its
health and happiness—there is no Crowd. The old world,
the world to which I belong, was and in my universe alas
still is, the world of the Crowd, the world of that detestable
crawling mass of un-featured, infected human beings.

"You have never seen a Crowd, Crystal; and in all your
happy life you never will. You have never seen a Crowd
going to a football match or a race meeting or a bull-fight
or a public execution or the like crowd joy; you have never
watched a Crowd wedge and stick in a narrow place or hoot
or howl in a crisis. You have never watched it stream
sluggishly along the streets to gape at a King, or yell for
a war, or yell quite equally for a peace. And you have
never seen the Crowd, struck by some Panic breeze, change
from Crowd proper to Mob and begin to smash and hunt.

All the Crowd celebrations have gone out of this world; all the Crowd's gods, there is no Turf here, no Sport, no war demonstrations, no Coronations and Public Funerals, no great shows, but only your little theatres. . . . Happy Crystal! who will never see a Crowd!"

"But I have seen Crowds," said Crystal.

"Where?"

"I have seen cinematograph films of Crowds, photographed thirty centuries ago and more. They are shown in our history museums. I have seen Crowds streaming over downs after a great race meeting, photographed from an aeroplane, and Crowds rioting in some public square and being dispersed by the police. Thousands and thousands of swarming people. But it is true what you say. There are no more crowds in Utopia. Crowds and the crowd-mind have gone for ever."

§ 7

When after some days Crystal had to return to his mathematical studies, his departure left Mr. Barnstaple very lonely. He found no other companion. Lychnis seemed always near him and ready to be with him, but her want of active intellectual interests, so remarkable in this world of vast intellectual activities, estranged him from her. Other Utopians came and went, friendly, amused, polite, but intent upon their own business. They would question him curiously, attend perhaps to a question or so of his own, and depart with an air of being called away.

Lychnis, he began to realize, was one of Utopia's failures. She was a lingering romantic type and she cherished a great sorrow in her heart. She had had two children whom she had loved passionately. They were adorably fearless, and out of foolish pride she had urged them to swim out to sea and they had been taken by a current and drowned. Their father had been drowned in attempting their rescue and

Lychnis had very nearly shared their fate. She had been rescued. But her emotional life had stopped short at that point, had, as it were, struck an attitude and remained in it. Tragedy possessed her. She turned her back on laughter and gladness and looked for distress. She had rediscovered the lost passion of pity, first pity for herself and then a desire to pity others. She took no interest any more in vigorous and complete people, but her mind concentrated upon the consolation to be found in consoling pain and distress in others. She sought her healing in healing them. She did not want to talk to Mr. Barnstaple of the brightness of Utopia; she wanted him to talk to her of the miseries of earth and of his own miseries. That she might sympathize. But he would not tell her of his own miseries because indeed, such was his temperament, he had none; he had only exasperations and regrets.

She dreamt, he perceived, of being able to come to earth and give her beauty and tenderness to the sick and poor. Her heart went out to the spectacle of human suffering and weakness. It went out to these things hungrily and desirously. . . .

Before he detected the drift of her mind he told her many things about human sickness and poverty. But he spoke of these matters not with pity but indignation, as things that ought not to be. And when he perceived how she feasted on these things he spoke of them hardly and cheerfully as things that would presently be swept away. "But they will still have suffered," she said. . . .

Since she was always close at hand, she filled for him perhaps more than her legitimate space in the Utopian spectacle. She lay across it like a shadow. He thought very frequently about her and about the pity and resentment against life and vigour that she embodied. In a world of fear, weakness, infection, darkness and confusion, pity, the

act of charity, the alms and the refuge, the deed of stark
devotion, might show indeed like sweet and gracious
presences; but in this world of health and brave enterprises,
pity betrayed itself a vicious desire. Crystal, Utopian youth,
was as hard as his name. When he had slipped one day on
some rocks and twisted and torn his ankle, he had limped
but he had laughed. When Mr. Barnstaple was winded on
a steep staircase Crystal was polite rather than sympathetic.
So Lychnis had found no confederate in the dedication of
her life to sorrow; even from Mr. Barnstaple she could win
no sympathy. He perceived that indeed so far as temperament went he was a better Utopian than she was. To him
as to Utopia it seemed rather an occasion for gladness than
sorrow that her man and her children had met death
fearlessly. They were dead; a brave stark death; the waters
still glittered and the sun still shone. But her loss had
revealed some underlying racial taint in her, something very
ancient in the species, something that Utopia was still breeding out only very slowly, the dark sacrificial disposition that
bows and responds to the shadow. It was strange and yet
perhaps it was inevitable that Mr. Barnstaple should meet
again in Utopia that spirit which Earth knows so well, the
spirit that turns from the Kingdom of Heaven to worship
the thorns and the nails, which delights to represent its
God, not as the Resurrection and the Life but as a woeful
and defeated cadaver.

She would talk to him of his sons as if she envied him
because of the loss of her own, but all she said reminded
him of the educational disadvantages and narrow prospects
of his boys and how much stouter and finer and happier
their lives would have been in Utopia. He would have
risked drowning them a dozen times to have saved them
from being clerks and employees of other men. Even by
earthly standards he felt now that he had not done his best

by them; he had let many things drift in their lives and in the lives of himself and his wife that he now felt he ought to have controlled. Could he have his time over again he felt that he would see to it that his sons took a livelier interest in politics and science and were not so completely engulfed in the trivialities of suburban life, in tennis playing, amateur theatricals, inane flirtations and the like. They were good boys in substance he felt, but he had left them to their mother; and he had left their mother too much to herself instead of battling with her for the sake of his own ideas. They were living trivially in the shadow of one great catastrophe and with no security against another; they were living in a world of weak waste and shabby insufficiency. And his own life also had been—weak waste.

His life at Sydenham began to haunt him. "I criticized everything but I altered nothing," he said. "I was as bad as Peeve. Was I any more use in that world than I am in this? But on Earth we are all wasters. . . ."

He avoided Lychnis for a day or so and wandered about the valley alone. He went into a great reading-room and fingered books he could not read; he was suffered to stand in a workshop, and he watched an artist make a naked girl of gold more lovely than any earthly statue and melt her again dissatisfied; here he came upon men building, and here was work upon the fields, here was a great shaft in the hill-side and something deep in the hill that flashed and scintillated strangely; they would not let him go in to it; he saw a thousand things he could not understand. He began to feel as perhaps a very intelligent dog must sometimes feel in the world of men, only that he had no master and no instincts that could find a consolation in canine abjection. The Utopians went about their business in the day-time, they passed him smiling and they filled him with intolerable envy. They knew what to do. They belonged. They went by in twos and threes in the evening, communing together and sometimes singing together. Lovers would pass him, their sweetly smiling faces close together, and his loneliness became an agony of hopeless desires.

Because, though he fought hard to keep it below the threshold of his consciousness, Mr. Barnstaple desired greatly to love and be loved in Utopia. The realization that no one of these people could ever conceive of any such intimacy of body or spirit with him was a humiliation more fundamental even than his uselessness. The loveliness of the Utopian girls and women who glanced at him curiously or passed him with a serene indifference, crushed down his self-respect and made the Utopian world altogether intolerable to him. Mutely, unconsciously, these Utopian goddesses concentrated upon him the uttermost abasement of caste and race inferiority. He could not keep his thoughts from love where everyone it seemed had a lover, and in this Utopian world love for him was a thing grotesque and inconceivable. . . .

Then one night as he lay awake distressed beyond measure by the thought of such things, an idea came to him whereby it seemed to him he might restore his self-respect and win a sort of citizenship in Utopia.

So that they might even speak of him and remember him with interest and sympathy.

CHAPTER THE THIRD

THE SERVICE OF THE EARTHLING

§ 1

THE man to whom Mr. Barnstaple, after due inquiries, went to talk to was named Sungold. He was probably very old, because there were lines of age about his eyes and over his fine brow. He was a ruddy man, bearded with an auburn beard that had streaks of white, and his eyes were brown and nimble under his thick eyebrows. His hair had thinned but little and flowed back like a mane, but its copper-red colour had gone. He sat at a table with papers spread before him, making manuscript notes. He smiled at Mr. Barnstaple, for he had been expecting him, and indicated a seat for him with his stout and freckled hand. Then he waited smilingly for Mr. Barnstaple to begin.

"This world is one triumph of the desire for order and beauty in men's minds," said Mr. Barnstaple. "But it will not tolerate one useless soul in it. Everyone is happily active. Everyone but myself. . . . I belong nowhere. I have nothing to do. And no one—is related to me."

Sungold moved his head lightly to show that he understood.

"It is hard for an Earthling, with an earthly want of training, to fall into any place here. Into any usual work or any usual relationship. One is—a stranger. . . . But it is still harder to have no place at all. In the new work, of which I am told you know most of anyone and are indeed the centre and regulator, it has occurred to me that I might be of some use, that I might indeed be as good as a Utopian.

. . . If so, I want to be of use. You may want someone
just to risk death—to take the danger of going into some
strange place—someone who desires to serve Utopia—and
who need not have skill or knowledge—or be a beautiful or
able person?"

Mr. Barnstaple stopped short.

Sungold conveyed the completest understanding of all that
was in Mr. Barnstaple's mind.

Mr. Barnstaple sat interrogative while for a time Sungold
thought.

Then words and phrases began to string themselves together in Mr. Barnstaple's mind.

Sungold wondered if Mr. Barnstaple understood either the
extent or the limitations of the great discoveries that were
now being made in Utopia. Utopia, he said, was passing
into a phase of intense intellectual exaltation. New powers
and possibilities intoxicated the imagination of the race, and
it was indeed inconceivable that an unteachable and perplexed Earthling could be anything but distressed and uncomfortable amidst the vast strange activities that must now
begin. Even many of their own people, the more backward
Utopians, were disturbed. For centuries Utopian philosophers
and experimentalists had been criticizing, revising and recon-
structing their former instinctive and traditional ideas of
space and time, of form and substance, and now very rapidly
the new ways of thinking were becoming clear and simple
and bearing fruit in surprising practical applications. The
limitations of space which had seemed for ever insurmountable
were breaking down; they were breaking down in a strange
and perplexing way but they were breaking down. It was
now theoretically possible, it was rapidly becoming prac-
ticably possible, to pass from the planet Utopia to which
the race had hitherto been confined, to other points in its
universe of origin, that is to say to remote planets and

distant stars. . . . That was the gist of the present situation.

"I cannot imagine that," said Mr. Barnstaple.

"You cannot imagine it," Sungold agreed, quite cordially.
"But it is so. A hundred years ago it was inconceivable—
here."

"Do you get there by some sort of backstairs in another
dimension?" said Mr. Barnstable.

Sungold considered this guess. It was a grotesque image,
he said, but from the point of view of an Earthling it would
serve. That conveyed something of its quality. But it was
so much more wonderful. . . .

"A new and astounding phase has begun for life here.
We learnt long ago the chief secrets of happiness upon this
planet. Life is good in this world. You find it good? . . .
For thousands of years yet it will be our fastness and our
home. But the wind of a new adventure blows through our
life. All this world is in a mood like striking camp in the
winter quarters when spring approaches."

He leant over his papers towards Mr. Barnstaple, and held
up a finger and spoke audible words as if to make his meaning plainer. It seemed to Mr. Barnstaple that each word
translated itself into English as he spoke it. At any rate
Mr. Barnstaple understood. "The collision of our planet
Utopia with your planet Earth was a very curious accident,
but an unimportant accident, in this story. I want you to
understand that. Your universe and ours are two out of
a great number of gravitation-time universes, which are
translated together through the inexhaustible infinitude of
God. They are similar throughout, but they are identical
in nothing. Your planet and ours happen to be side by
side, so to speak, but they are not travelling at exactly the
same pace nor in a strictly parallel direction. They will
drift apart again and follow their several destinies. When

Arden and Greenlake made their experiment the chances of their hitting anything in your universe were infinitely remote. They had disregarded it, they were merely rotating some of our matter out of and then back into our universe. You fell into us—as amazingly for us as for you. The importance of our discoveries for us lies in our own universe and not in yours. We do not want to come into your universe nor have more of your world come into ours. You are too like us, and you are too dark and troubled and diseased—you are too contagious—and we, we cannot help you yet because we are not gods but men."

Mr. Barnstaple nodded.

"What could Utopians do with the men of Earth? We have no strong instinct in us to teach or dominate other adults. That has been bred out of us by long centuries of equality and free co-operation. And you would be too numerous for us to teach and much of your population would be grown up and set in bad habits. Your stupidities would get in our way, your quarrels and jealousies and traditions, your flags and religions and all your embodied spites and suppressions, would hamper us in everything we should want to do. We should be impatient with you, unjust, overbearing. You are too like us for us to be patient with your failures. It would be hard to remember constantly how ill-bred you were. In Utopia we found out long ago that no race of human beings was sufficiently great, subtle, and powerful to think and act for any other race. Perhaps already you are finding out the same thing on Earth as your races come into closer contact. And much more would this be true between Utopia and Earth. From what I know of your people and their ignorance and obstinacies it is clear our people would despise you; and contempt is the cause of all injustice. We might end by exterminating you. . . . But why should we make that possible? . . . We must leave you alone. We cannot trust ourselves with you. . . . Believe me this is the only reasonable course for us."

Mr. Barnstaple assented silently.

You and I—two individuals—can be friends and understand."

"What you say is true," said Mr. Barnstaple. "It is true. But it grieves me it is true. . . . Greatly. . . . Nevertheless, I gather, I at least may be of service in Utopia?"

"You can."

"How?"

"By returning to your own world."

Mr. Barnstaple thought for some moments. It was what he had feared. But he had offered himself. "I will do that."

"By attempting to return, I should say. There is risk. You may be killed."

"I must take that."

"We want to verify all the data we have of the relations of our universe to yours. We want to reverse the experiment of Arden and Greenlake and see if we can return a living being to your world. We are almost certain now that we can do so. And that human being must care for us enough and care for his own world enough to go back and give us a sign that he has got there."

Mr. Barnstaple spoke huskily. "I can do that," he said.

"We can put you into that machine of yours and into the clothes you wore. You can be made again exactly as you left your world."

"Exactly. I understand."

"And because your world is vile and contentious and yet has some strangely able brains in it, here and there, we do not want your people to know of us, living so close to you—for we shall be close to you yet for some hundreds of years at least—we do not want them to know for fear that they should come here presently, led by some poor silly genius of a scientific man, come in their greedy, foolish, breeding swarms, hammering at our doors, threatening our lives, and spoiling our high adventures, and so have to be beaten off and killed like an invasion of rats or parasites."

"Yes," said Mr. Barnstaple. "Before men can come to Utopia, they must learn the way here. Utopia, I see, is only a home for those who have learnt the way."

He paused and answered some of his own thoughts. "When I have returned," he said, "shall I begin to forget Utopia?"

Sungold smiled and said nothing.

"All my days the nostalgia of Utopia will distress me."

"And uphold you."

"I shall take up my earthly life at the point where I laid it down, but—on Earth—I shall be a Utopian. For I feel that having offered my service and had it accepted, that I am no longer an outcast in Utopia. I belong. . . ."

"Remember you may be killed. You may die in the trial."

"As it may happen."

"Well—Brother!"

The friendly paw took Mr. Barnstaple's and pressed it and the deep eyes smiled.

"After you have returned and given us your sign, several of the other Earthlings may also be sent back."

Mr. Barnstaple sat up. *"But!"* he gasped. His voice rose high in amazement. "I thought they were hurled into the blank space of some outer universe and altogether destroyed!"

"Several were killed. They killed themselves by rushing down the side of the old fortress in the outer darkness as the Crag rotated. The men in leather. The man you call Long Barrow——"

"Barralonga?"

"Yes. And the man who shrugged his shoulders and said, 'What would you?' The others came back as the rotation was completed late in the day—asphyxiated and frozen but not dead. They have been restored to life, and we are puzzled now how to dispose of them. . . . They are of no use whatever in this world. They encumber us."

"It is only too manifest," said Mr. Barnstaple.

"The man you call Burleigh seems to be of some importance in your earthly affairs. We have searched his mind. His powers of belief are very small. He believes in very little but the life of a cultivated wealthy gentleman who holds a position of modest distinction in the councils of a largely fictitious empire. It is doubtful if he will believe in the reality of any of this experience. We will make sure anyhow that he thinks it has been an imaginative dream. He will consider it too fantastic to talk about because it is plain he is already very afraid of his imagination. He will find himself back in your world a few days after you reach it and he will make his way to his own home unobtrusively. He will come next after you. You will see him reappear in political affairs. Perhaps a little wiser."

"It might well be," said Mr. Barnstaple.

"And—what are the sounds of his name?—Rupert Catskill; he too will return. Your world would miss him."

"Nothing will make *him* wiser," said Mr. Barnstaple with conviction.

"Lady Stella will come."

"I am glad she has escaped. She will say nothing about Utopia. She is very discreet."

"The priest is mad. His behaviour became offensive and obscene and he is under restraint."

"What did he do?"

"He made a number of aprons of black silk and set out

with them to attack our young people in an undignified manner."

"You can send him back," said Mr. Barnstaple after reflection.

"But will your world allow that sort of thing?"

'*We* call that sort of thing Purity," said Mr. Barnstaple. "But of course if you like to keep him. . . ."

"He shall come back," said Sungold.

"The others you can keep," said Mr. Barnstaple. "In fact you will have to keep them. Nobody on Earth will trouble about them very much. In our world there are so many people that always a few are getting lost. As it is, returning even the few you propose to do may excite attention. Local people may begin to notice all these wanderers coming from nowhere in particular and asking their way home upon the Maidenhead road. They may give way under questions. . . . You cannot send any more. Put the rest on an island. Or something of that sort. I wish I could advise you to keep the priest also. But many people would miss him. They would suffer from suppressed Purity and begin to behave queerly. The pulpit of St. Barnabas satisfies a recognised craving. And it will be quite easy to persuade him that Utopia is a dream and delusion. All priests believe that naturally of all Utopias. He will think of it, if he thinks of it at all, as—what would he call it—as a moral nightmare."

§ 2

Their business was finished, but Mr. Barnstaple was loth to go.

He looked Sungold in the eye and found something kindly there.

"You have told me all that I have to do," he said, "and it is fully time that I went away from you, for any moment in your life is more precious than a day of mine. Yet because I am to go soon and so obediently out of this vast and splendid world of yours back to my native disorders, I could find it in my heart to ask you to unbend if you could, to come down to me a little, and to tell me simply and plainly of the greater days and greater achievements that are now dawning upon this planet. You speak of your being able presently to go out of this Utopia to remote parts in your universe. That perplexes my mind. Probably I am unfitted to grasp that idea, but it is very important to me. It has been a belief in our world that at last there must be an end to life because our sun and planets are cooling, and there seems no hope of escape from the little world upon which we have arisen. We were born with it and we must die with it. That robbed many of us of hope and energy. for why should we work for progress in a world that must freeze and die?"

Sungold laughed. "Your philosophers concluded too soon."

He sprawled over the table towards his hearer and looked him earnestly in the face.

"Your Earthly science has been going on for how long?"

"Two hundred—three hundred years."

Sungold held up two fingers. "And men? How many men?"

"A few hundred who mattered in each generation."

"We have gone on for three thousand years now, and a hundred million good brains have been put like grapes into the wine-press of science. And we know to-day—how little we know. There is never an observation made but a hundred observations are missed in the making of it; there is never a measurement but some impish truth mocks us and gets away from us in the margin of error. I know something of where your scientific men are, all power to the poor savages!

because I have studied the beginnings of our own science in the long past of Utopia. How can I express our distances? Since those days we have examined and tested and tried and retried a score of new ways of thinking about space, of which time is only a specialized form. We have forms of expression that we cannot get over to you so that things that used to seem difficult and paradoxical to you, lose all their difficulty in our minds. It is hard to convey to you. We think in terms of a space in which the space and time system, in terms of which you think, is only a specialized case. So far as our feelings and instincts and daily habits go we too live in another such system as you do—but not so far as our knowledge goes, not so far as our powers go. Our minds have exceeded our lives—as yours will. We are still flesh and blood, still hope and desire, we go to and fro and look up and down, but things that seemed remote are brought near, things that were inaccessible bow down, things that were insurmountable lie under the hollows of our hands."

"And you do not think your race nor, for the matter of that, ours, need ever perish?"

"Perish! We have hardly begun!"

The old man spoke very earnestly. Unconsciously he parodied Newton. "We are like little children who have been brought to the shores of a limitless ocean. All the knowledge we have gathered yet in the few score generations since first we began to gather knowledge, is like a small handful of pebbles gathered upon the shore of that limitless sea.

"Before us lies knowledge, endlessly, and we may take and take, and as we take, grow. We grow in power, we grow in courage. We renew our youth. For mark what I say, our worlds grow younger. The old generations of apes and sub-men before us had aged minds; their narrow reluctant wisdom was the meagre profit, hoarded and stale and sour, of innumerable lives. They dreaded new things; so bitterly did they value the bitterly won old. But to learn is, at length, to become young again, to be released, to begin afresh. Your world, compared with ours, is a world of unteachable encrusted souls, of bent and droning traditions, of hates and injuries and such-like unforgettable things. But some day you too will become again like little children, and it will be you who will find your way through to us—to us, who will be waiting for you. Two universes will meet and embrace, to beget a yet greater universe. . . . You Earthlings do not begin to realize yet the significance of life. Nor we Utopians—scarcely more. . . . Life is still only a promise, still waits to be born, out of such poor stirrings in the dust as we. . . .

"Some day here and everywhere, Life of which you and I are but anticipatory atoms and eddies, life will awaken indeed, one and whole and marvellous, like a child awaking to concsious life. It will open its drowsy eyes and stretch itself and smile, looking the mystery of God in the face as one meets the morning sun. We shall be there then, all that matters of us, you and I. . . .

"And it will be no more than a beginning, no more than a beginning. . . ."

CHAPTER THE FOURTH

THE RETURN OF THE EARTHLING

§ 1

TOO soon the morning came when Mr. Barnstaple was to look his last upon the fair hills of Utopia and face the great experiment to which he had given himself. He had been loth to sleep and he had slept little that night, and in the early dawn he was abroad, wearing for the last time the sandals and the light white robe that had become his Utopian costume. Presently he would have to struggle into socks and boots and trousers and collar; the strangest gear. It would choke him, he felt, and he stretched his bare arms to the sky and yawned and breathed his lungs full. The valley below still drowsed beneath a coverlet of fleecy mists; he turned his face uphill, the sooner to meet the sun.

Never before had he been out among the Utopian flowers at such an early hour; it was amusing to see how some of the great trumpets still drooped asleep and how many of the larger blossoms were furled and hung. Many of the leaves too were wrapped up, as limp as new hatched moths. The gossamer spiders had been busy and everything was very wet with dew. A great tiger came upon him suddenly out of a side path and stared hard at him for some moments with round yellow eyes. Perhaps it was trying to remember the forgotten instincts of its breed.

Some way up the road he passed under a vermilion archway and went up a flight of stone stairs that promised to bring him earlier to the crest.

A number of friendly little birds, very gaily coloured,

flew about him for a time, and one perched impudently upon his shoulder, but when he put up his hand to caress it it evaded him and flew away. He was still ascending the staircase when the sun rose. It was as if the hillside slipped off a veil of grey and blue and bared the golden beauty of its body.

Mr. Barnstaple came to a landing place upon the staircase and stopped, and stood very still watching the sunrise search and quicken the brooding deeps of the valley below.

Far away, like an arrow shot from east to west, appeared a line of dazzling brightness on the sea.

§ 2

"Serenity," he murmured. "Beauty. All the works of men—in perfect harmony . . . minds brought to harmony. . . ."

According to his journalistic habit he tried over phrases. "An energetic peace . . . confusions dispersed . . . A world of spirits, crystal clear. . . ."

What was the use of words?

For a time he stood quite still listening, for from some slope above a lark had gone heavenward, spraying sweet notes. He tried to see that little speck of song and was blinded by the brightening blue of the sky.

Presently the lark came down and ceased. Utopia was silent, except for a burst of childish laughter somewhere on the hillside below.

It dawned upon Mr. Barnstaple how peaceful was the Utopian air in comparison with the tormented atmosphere of Earth. Here was no yelping and howling of tired or irritated dogs, no braying, bellowing, squealing and distressful outcries of uneasy beasts, no farmyard clamour, no shouts of anger, no barking and coughing, no sounds of hammering, beating, sawing, grinding, mechanical hooting, whistling, screaming and the like, no clattering of distant trains, clanking of automobiles or other ill-contrived mechanisms; the tiresome and ugly noises of many an unpleasant creature were heard no more. In Utopia the ear like the eye was at peace. The air which at once been a mud of felted noises was now—a purified silence. Such sounds as one heard lay upon it like beautiful printing on a generous sheet of fine paper.

His eyes returned to the landscape below as the last fleecy vestiges of mist dissolved away. Water-tanks, roads, bridges, buildings, embankments, colonnades, groves, gardens, channels, cascades and fountains grew multitudinously clear, framed under a branch of dark foliage from a white-stemmed tree that gripped a hold among the rocks at his side.

"Three thousand years ago this was a world like ours. . . . Think of it—in a hundred generations. . . . In three thousand years we might make our poor waste of an Earth, jungle and desert, slag-heap and slum, into another such heaven of beauty and power. . . .

"Worlds they are—similar, but not the same. . . .

"If I could tell them what I have seen! . . .

"Suppose all men could have this vision of Utopia. . . .

"They would not believe it if I told them. No. . . .

"They would bray like asses at me and bark like dogs! . . . They will have no world but their own world. It hurts them to think of any world but their own. Nothing can be done that has not been done already. To think otherwise would be humiliation. . . . Death, torture, futility—anything but humiliation! So they must sit among their weeds and excrement, scratching and nodding sagely at one another, hoping for a good dog-fight and to gloat upon pain and effort they do not share, sure that mankind stank, stinks and must always stink, that stinking is very pleasant indeed, and that there is nothing new under the sun. . . ."

His thoughts were diverted by two young girls who came running one after the other up the staircase. One was dark even to duskiness and her hands were full of blue flowers; the other who pursued her, was a year or so younger and golden fair. They were full of the limitless excitement of young animals at play. The former one was so intent upon the other that she discovered Mr. Barnstaple with a squeak of surprise after she had got to his landing. She stared at him with a quick glance of inquiry, flashed into impudent roguery, flung two blue flowers in his face and was off up the steps above. Her companion, intent on capture, flew by. They flickered up the staircase like two butterflies of buff and pink; halted far above and came together for a momentary consultation about the stranger, waved hands to him and vanished.

Mr. Barnstaple returned their greeting and remained cheered.

§ 3

The view-point to which Lychnis had directed Mr. Barnstaple stood out on the ridge between the great valley in which he had spent the last few days and a wild and steep glen down which ran a torrent that was destined after some hundred miles of windings to reach the river of the plain. The view-point was on the crest of a crag, it had been built out upon great brackets so that it hung sheer over a bend in the torrent below; on the one hand was mountainous scenery and a rich and picturesque foam of green vegetation in the depths, on the other spread the broad garden spaces of a perfected landscape. For a time Mr. Barnstaple scrutinized this glen into which he looked for the first time. Five hundred feet or so below him, so that he felt that he could have dropped a pebble upon its outstretched wings, a buzzard was soaring.

Many of the trees below he thought must be fruit trees, but they were too far off to see distinctly. Here and there he could distinguish a footpath winding up among the trees and rocks, and among the green masses were little pavilions in which he knew the wayfarer might rest and make tea for himself and find biscuits and such-like refreshment, and possibly a couch and a book. The whole world, he knew, was full of such summer-houses and kindly shelters. . . .

After a time he went back to the side of his view-place up which he had come, and regarded the great valley that went out towards the sea. The word Pisgah floated through his mind. For indeed below him was the Promised Land of human desires. Here at last, established and secure, were peace, power, health, happy activity, length of days and beauty. All that we seek was found here and every dream was realized.

How long would it be yet—how many centuries or thousands of years—before a man would be able to stand upon some high place on earth also and see mankind triumphant and wholly and for ever at peace? . . .

He folded his arms under him upon the parapet and mused profoundly.

There was no knowledge in this Utopia of which Earth had not the germs, there was no power used here that Earthlings might not use. Here, but for ignorance and darkness and the spites and malice they permit, was Earth to-day. . . .

Toward such a world as this Utopia Mr. Barnstaple had been striving weakly all his life. If the experiment before him succeeded, if presently he found himself alive again on Earth, it would still be towards Utopia that his life would be directed. And he would not be alone. On Earth there must be thousands, tens of thousands, perhaps hundreds of thousands, who were also struggling in their minds and acts to find a way of escape for themselves and for their children from the disorders and indignities of the Age of Confusion, hundreds of thousands who wanted to put an end to wars and waste, to heal and educate and restore, to set up the banner of Utopia over the shams and divisions that waste mankind.

"Yes, but we fail," said Mr. Barnstaple and walked fretfully to and fro. "Tens and hundreds of thousands of men and women! And we achieve so little! Perhaps every young man and every young woman has had some dream at least of serving and bettering the world. And we are scattered and wasted, and the old things and the foul things, customs, delusions, habits, tolerated treasons, base immedi-acies, triumph over us!"

He went to the parapet again and stood with his foot on a seat, his elbow on his knee and his chin in his han, staring at the loveliness of this world he was to leave so soon. . . .

"We could do it."

And suddenly it was borne in upon Mr. Barnstaple that he belonged now soul and body to the Revolution, to the Great Revolution that is afoot on Earth; that marches and will never desist nor rest again until old Earth is one city and Utopia set up therein. He knew clearly that this Revolution is life, and that all other living is a trafficking of life with death. And as this crystallized out in his mind he knew instantly that so presently it would crystallize out in the minds of countless others of those hundreds of thousands of men and women on Earth whose minds are set towards Utopia.

He stood up. He began walking to and fro. "We shall do it," he said.

Earthly thought was barely awakened as yet to the task

and possibilities before mankind. All human history so far had been no more than the stirring of a sleeper, a gathering discontent, a rebellion against the limitations set upon life, the unintelligent protest of thwarted imaginations. All the conflicts and insurrections and revolutions that had ever been on Earth were but indistinct preludes of the revolution that had still to come. When he had started out upon this fantastic holiday Mr. Barnstaple realized he had been in a mood of depression; earthly affairs had seemed utterly confused and hopeless to him; but now from the view-point of Utopia achieved, and with his health renewed, he could see plainly enough how steadily men on earth were feeling their way now, failure after failure, towards the opening drive of the final revolution. He could see how men in his own lifetime had been struggling out of such entanglements as the lie of monarchy, the lies of dogmatic religion and dogmatic morality towards public self-respect and cleanness of mind and body. They struggled now also towards international charity and the liberation of their common economic life from a network of pretences, dishonesties and impostures. There is confusion in all struggles; retractions and defeats; but the whole effect seen from the calm height of Utopia was one of steadfast advance. . . . .

There were blunders, there were set-backs, because the forces of revolution still worked in the twilight. The great effort and the great failure of the socialist movement to create a new state in the world had been contemporaneous with Mr. Barnstaple's life; socialism had been the gospel of his boyhood; he had participated in its hopes, its doubts, its bitter internal conflicts. He had seen the movement losing sweetness and gathering force in the narrowness of the Marxist formulæ. He had seen it sacrifice its constructive power for militant intensity. In Russia he had marked its ability to overthrow and its inability to plan or build. Like every liberal spirit in the world he had shared the chill of Bolshevik presumption and Bolshevik failure, and for a time it had seemed to him that this open bankruptcy of a great creative impulse was no less and no more than a victory for reaction, that it gave renewed life to all the shams, impostures, corruptions, traditional anarchies and ascendencies, that restrain and cripple human life. . . . But now from this high view-point in Utopia he saw clearly that the Phœnix of Revolution flames down to ashes only to be born again. While the noose is fitted round the Teacher's neck the youths are reading his teaching. Revolutions arise and die; the Great Revolution comes incessantly and inevitably.

The time was near—and in what life was left to him, he himself might help to bring it nearer—when the forces of that last and real revolution would work no longer in the twilight but in the dawn, and a thousand sorts of men and women now far apart and unorganized and mutually antagonistic would be drawn together by the growth of a common vision of the world desired. The Marxist had wasted the forces of revolution for fifty years; he had had no vision; he had had only a condemnation for established things. He had estranged all scientific and able men by his pompous affectation of the scientific; he had terrified them by his intolerant orthodoxy; his delusion that all ideas are begotten by material circumstances had made him negligent of education and criticism. He had attempted to build social unity on hate and rejected every other driving force for the bitterness of a class war. But now, in its days of doubt and exhaustion, vision was returning to Socialism, and the dreary spectacle of a proletarian dictatorship gave way once more to Utopia, to the demand for a world fairly and righteously at peace, its resources husbanded and exploited for the common good, its every citizen freed not only from servitude but from ignorance, and its surplus energies directed steadfastly to the increase of knowledge and beauty. The attainment of that vision by more and more minds was a thing now no longer to be prevented. Earth would tread the path Utopia had trod. She too would weave law, duty and education into a larger sanity than man had ever known. Men also would presently laugh at the things they had feared, and brush aside the impostures that had overawed them and the absurdities that had tormented and crippled their lives. And as this great revolution was achieved and earth wheeled into daylight, the burthen of human miseries would lift, and courage oust sorrow from the hearts of men. Earth, which was now no more than a wilderness, sometimes horrible and at best picturesque, a wilderness interspersed with weedy scratchings for food and with hovels and slums and slag heaps, Earth too would grow rich with loveliness and fair as this great land was fair. The sons of Earth also, purified from disease, sweet-minded and strong and beautiful, and high viaducts, its wide slopes of sunlit cultivation, its would go proudly about their conquered planet and lift their daring to the stars.

"Given the will," said Mr. Barnstaple. "Given only the will." . . .

§ 4

From some distant place came the sound of a sweet-toned bell striking the hour.

The time for the service to which he was dedicated was drawing near. He must descend and be taken to the place where the experiment was to be made.

He took one last look at the glen and then went back to the broad prospect of the great valley, with its lakes and tanks and terraces, its groves and pavilions, its busy buildings universal gracious amenity. "Farewell, Utopia," he said, and was astonished to discover how deeply his emotions were stirred.

"Dear Dream of Hope and Loveliness, Farewell!"

He stood quite still in a mood of sorrowful deprivation too deep for tears.

It seemed to him that the spirit of Utopia bent down over him like a goddess, friendly, adorable—and inaccessible.

His very mind stood still.

"Never," he whispered at last, "for me. . . . Except to serve. . . . No. . . ."

Presently he began to descend the steps that wound down from the view-point. For a time he noted little of the things immediately about him. Then the scent of roses invaded his attention, and he found himself walking down a slanting pergola covered with great white roses and very active with little green birds. He stopped short and looked up at the leaves, light-saturated, against the sky. He put up his hands and drew down one of the great blossoms until it touched his cheek.

§ 5

They took Mr. Barnstaple back by aeroplane to the point upon the glassy road where he had first come into Utopia. Lychnis came with him and Crystal, who was curious to see what would be done.

A group of twenty or thirty people, including Sungold, awaited him. The ruined laboratory of Arden and Green-lake had been replaced by fresh buildings, and there were additional erections on the further side of the road; but Mr. Barnstaple could recognize quite clearly the place where Mr. Catskill had faced the leopard and where Mr. Burleigh had accosted him. Several new kinds of flowers were now out, but the blue blossoms that had charmed him on arrival still prevailed. His old car, the Yellow Peril, looking now the clumsiest piece of ironmongery conceivable, stood in the road. He went and examined it. It seemed to be in perfect order; it had been carefully oiled and the petrol tank was full.

In a little pavilion were his bag and all his earthly clothes. They were very clean and they had been folded and pressed, and he put them on. His shirt seemed tight across his chest and his collar decidedly tight, and his coat cut him a little under the arms. Perhaps these garments had shrunken when they were disinfected. He packed his bag and Crystal put it in the car for him.

Sungold explained very simply all that Mr. Barnstaple had to do. Across the road, close by the restored laboratory, stretched a line as thin as gossamer. "Steer your car to that and break it," he said. "That is all you have to do. Then take this red flower and put it down exactly where your wheel tracks show you have entered your own world."

Mr. Barnstaple was left beside the car. The Utopians went back twenty or thirty yards and stood in a circle about him. For a few moments everyone was still.

§ 6

Mr. Barnstaple got into his car, started his engine, let it throb for a minute and then put in the clutch. The yellow car began to move towards the line of gossamer. He made a gesture with one hand which Lychnis answered. Sungold and others of the Utopians also made friendly movements. But Crystal was watching too intently for any gesture.

"Good-bye, Crystal!" cried Mr. Barnstaple, and the boy responded with a start.

Mr. Barnstaple accelerated, set his teeth and, in spite of his will to keep them open, shut his eyes as he touched the gossamer line. Came that sense again of unendurable tension and that sound like the snapping of a bow-string. He had an irresistible impulse to stop—go back. He took his foot from the accelerator, and the car seemed to fall a foot or so and stopped so heavily and suddenly that he was jerked forward against the steering wheel. The oppression lifted. He opened his eyes and looked about him.

The car was standing in a field from which the hay had recently been carried. He was tilted on one side because of a roll in the ground. A hedge in which there was an open black gate, separated this hay-field from the high road. Close at hand was a board advertisement of some Maidenhead hotel. On the far side of the road were level fields against a background of low wooded hills. Away to the left was a little inn. He turned his head and saw Windsor Castle in the remote distance rising above poplar-studded meadows. It was not, as his Utopians had promised him, the exact spot of his departure from our Earth, but it was certainly less than a hundred yards away.

He sat still for some moments, mentally rehearsing what he had to do. Then he started the Yellow Peril again and drove it close up to the black gate.

He got out and stood with the red flower in his hand. He had to go back to the exact spot at which he had re-entered this universe and put that flower down there. It would be quite easy to determine that point by the track the car had made in the stubble. But he felt an extraordinary reluctance to obey these instructions. He wanted to keep this flower. It was the last thing, the only thing, he had now from that golden world. That and the sweet savour on his hands.

It was extraordinary that he had brought no more than this with him. Why had he not brought a lot of flowers? Why had they giving him nothing, no little thing, out of all their wealth of beauty? He wanted intensely to keep this flower. He was moved to substitute a spray of honeysuckle from the hedge close at hand. But then he remembered that that would be infected stuff for them. He must do as he was told. He walked back along the track of his car to its beginning, stood for a moment hesitating, tore a single petal from that glowing bloom, and then laid down the rest of the great flower carefully in the very centre of his track. The petal he put in his pocket. Then with a heavy heart he went back slowly to his car and stood beside it, watching that star of almost luminous red.

His grief and emotion were very great. He was bitterly sorrowful now at having left Utopia.

It was evident the great drought was still going on, for the field and the hedges were more parched and brown than he had ever seen an English field before. Along the road lay a thin cloud of dust that passing cars continually renewed. This old world seemed to him to be full of unlovely sights the honking of distant cars, the uproar of a train, a thirsty and sounds and odours already half forgotten. There was cow mourning its discomfort; there was the irritation of dust in his nostrils and the smell of sweltering tar; there was barbed wire in the hedge near by and along the top of the black gate, and horse-dung and scraps of dirty paper at his feet. The lovely world from which he had been driven had shrunken now to a spot of shining scarlet.

Something happened very quickly. It was as if a hand appeared for a moment and took the flower. In a moment it had gone. A little eddy of dust swirled and drifted and sank. . . .

It was the end.

At the thought of the traffic on the main road Mr. Barnstaple stooped down so as to hide his face from the passersby. For some minutes he was unable to regain his self-control. He stood with his arm covering his face, leaning against the shabby brown hood of his car. . . .

At last this gust of sorrow came to an end and he could get in again, start up the engine and steer into the main road.

He turned eastward haphazard. He left the black gate open behind him. He went along very slowly for as yet he had formed no idea of whither he was going. He began to think that probably in this old world of ours he was being sought for as a person who had mysteriously disappeared. Someone might discover him and he would become the focus of a thousand impossible questions. That would be very tiresome and disagreeable. He had not thought of this in Utopia. In Utopia it had seemed quite possible that he could come back into Earth unobserved. Now on earth that confidence seemed foolish. He saw ahead of him the board of a modest tea-room. It occurred that he might alight there, see a newspaper, ask a discreet question or so, and find out what had been happening to the world and whether he had indeed been missed.

He found a table already laid for tea under the window. In the centre of the room a larger table bore an aspidistra in a big green pot and a selection of papers, chiefly out-of-date illustrated papers. But there was also a copy of the morning's *Daily Express*.

He seized upon this eagerly, fearful that he would find it full of the mysterious disappearance of Mr. Burleigh, Lord Barralonga, Mr. Rupert Catskill, Mr. Hunker, Father Amerton, and Lady Stella, not to mention the lesser lights . . . Gradually as he turned it over his fears vanished. There was not a word about any of them!

"But surely," he protested to himself, now clinging to his idea, "their friends must have missed them!"

He read through the whole paper. Of one only did he find mention and that was the last name he would have expected to find—Mr. Freddy Mush. The Princess de Modena-Frascati *(nee* Higgisbottom) Prize for English literature had been giving away to nobody in particular by Mr. Graceful Gloss owing to "the unavoidable absence of Mr. Freddy Mush abroad."

The problem of why there had been no hue and cry for the others opened a vast field of worldly speculation to Mr. Barnstaple in which he wandered for a time. His mind went back to that bright red blossom lying among the cut stems of the grass in the mown field and to the hand that had seemed to take it. With that the door that had opened so marvellously between that strange and beautiful world and our own had closed again.

Wonder took possession of Mr. Barnstaple's mind. That dear world of honesty and health was beyond the utmost boundaries of our space, utterly inaccessible to him now for evermore; and yet, as he had been told, it was but one of countless universes that move together in time, that lie against one another, endlessly like the leaves of a book. And all of them are as nothing in the endless multitudes of systems and dimensions that surround them. "Could I but rotate my arm out of the limits set to it," one of the Utopians had said to him; "I could thrust it into a thousand universes." . . .

A waitress with his teapot recalled him to mundane things.

The meal served to him seemed tasteless and unclean. He drank the queer brew of the tea because he was thirsty but he ate scarcely a mouthful.

Presently he chanced to put his hand in his pocket and touched something soft. He drew out the petal he had torn from the red flower. It had lost its glowing red, and as he held it out in the stuffy air of the room it seemed to writhe as if shrivelled and blackened; its delicate scent gave place to a mawkish odour.

"Manifestly," he said. "I should have expected this."

He dropped the lump of decay on his plate, then picked

it up again and thrust it into the soil in the pot of the aspidistra.

He took up the *Daily Express* again and turned it over, trying to recover his sense of this world's affairs.

§ 7

For a long time Mr. Barnstaple meditated over the *Daily Express* in the tea-room at Colnebrook. His thoughts went far so that presently the newspaper slipped to the ground unheeded. He roused himself with a sigh and called for his bill. Paying, he became aware of a pocket-book still full of pound notes. "This will be the cheapest holiday I have ever had," he thought. "I've spent no money at all." He inquired for the post-office, because he had a telegram to send.

Two hours later he stopped outside the gate of his little villa at Sydenham. He set it open—the customary bit of stick with which he did this was in its usual place—and steered the Yellow Peril with the dexterity of use and went past the curved flower-bed to the door of his shed. Mrs. Barnstaple appeared in the porch.

"William! You're back at last?"

"Yes, I'm back. You got my telegram?"

"Ten minutes ago. Where have you been all this time? It's more than a month."

"Oh! just drifting about and dreaming. I've had a wonderful time."

"You ought to have written. You really ought to have written. . . . You *did*, William. . . ."

"I didn't bother. The doctor said I wasn't to bother. I told you. Is there any tea going? Where are the boys?"

"The boys are out. Let me make you some fresh tea." She did so and came and sat down in the cane chair in front of him and the tea-table. "I'm glad to have you back. Though I could scold you. . . ."

"You're looking wonderfully well," she said. "I've never seen your skin so clear and brown."

"I've been in good air all the time."

"Did you get to the Lakes?"

"Not quite. But it's been good air everywhere. Healthy air."

"You never got lost?"

"Never."

"I had ideas of you getting lost—losing your memory. Such things happen. You didn't?"

"My memory's as bright as a jewel."

"But where did you go?"

"I just wandered and dreamt. Lost in a day-dream. Often I didn't ask the name of the place where I was staying. I stayed in one place and then in another. I never asked their names. I left my mind passive. Quite passive. I've had a tremendous rest—from everything. I've hardly given a thought to politics or money or social questions—at least, the sort of thing *we* call social questions—or any of these worries, since I started. . . . Is that this week's *Liberal?*"

He took it, turned it over, and at last tossed it on to the sofa. "Poor old Peeve," he said. "Of course I must leave that paper. He's like wall-paper on a damp wall. Just blotches and rustles and fails to stick. . . . Gives me mental rheumatics."

Mrs. Barnstaple stared at him doubtfully. "But I always thought that the *Liberal* was such a safe job."

"I don't want a safe job now. I can do better. There's other work before me. . . . Don't you worry. I can take hold of things surely enough after this rest. . . . How are the boys?"

"I'm a little anxious about Frankie."

Mr. Barnstaple had picked up the *Times*. An odd

advertisement in the Agony column had caught his eye. It ran: "Cecil. Your absence exciting remark. Would like to know what you wish us to tell people. Write fully Scotch address. Di. ill with worry. All instructions will be followed."

"I beg your pardon, my dear?" he said putting the paper aside.

"I was saying that he doesn't seem to be settling down to business. He doesn't like it. I wish you could have a good talk with him. He's fretting because he doesn't *know* enough. He says he wants to be a science student at the Polytechnic and go on learning things."

"Well, he can. Sensible boy! I didn't think he had it in him. I meant to have a talk to him. But this meets me half-way. Certainly he shall study science."

"But the boy has to earn a living."

"That will come. If he wants to study science he shall."

Mr. Barnstaple spoke in a tone that was altogether new to Mrs. Barnstaple, a tone of immediate, quiet and assured determination. It surprised her still more that he should use this tone without seeming to be aware that he had used it.

He bit his slice of bread and butter, and she could see that something in the taste surprised and displeased him. He glanced doubtfully at the remnant of the slice in his hand. "Of course," he said. "London butter. Three days' wear. Left about. Funny how quickly one's taste alters."

He picked up the *Times* again and ran his eye over its columns.

"This world is really very childish," he said. "Very. I had forgotten. Imaginary Bolshevik plots. Sinn Fein proclamations. The Prince. Poland. Obvious lies about the Chinese. Obvious lies about Egypt. People pulling Wickham Steed's leg. Shampious article about Trinity

Sunday. The Hitchin murder. . . . H'm!—rather a nasty one. . . . The Pomfort Rembrandt. . . . Insurance. . . . Letter from indignant peer about Death Duties. . . . Dreary Sport. Boating, Tennis, Schoolboy cricket. Collapse of Harrow! As though such things were of the slightest importance! . . . How silly it is—all of it! It's like coming back to the quarrels of servants and the chatter of children."

He found Mrs. Barnstaple regarding him intently. "I haven't seen a paper from the day I started until this morning," he explained.

He put down the paper and stood up. For some minutes Mrs. Barnstaple had been doubting whether she was not the victim of an absurd hallucination. Now she realized that she was in the presence of the most amazing fact she had ever observed.

"Yes," she said. "It is so. Don't move! Keep like that. I know it sounds ridiculous, William, but you have grown taller. It's not simply that your stoop has gone. You have grown, oh!—two or three inches."

Mr. Barnstaple stared at her, and then held out his arm. Certainly he was showing an unusual length of wrist. He tried to judge whether his trousers had also the same grown-out-of look.

Mrs. Barnstaple came up to him almost respectfully. She stood beside him and put her shoulder against his arm. "Your shoulder used to be exactly level with mine," she said. "See where we are now!"

She looked up into his eyes. As though she was very glad indeed to have him back with her.

But Mr. Barnstaple remained lost in thought. "It must be the extreme freshness of the air. I have been in some wonderful air. . . . Wonderful! . . . But at my age! To have grown! And I *feel* as though I'd grown, inside and out, mind and body. . . ."

Mrs. Barnstaple presently began to put the tea-things together for removal.

"You seem to have avoided the big towns."

"I did."

"And kept to the country roads and lanes."

"Practically. . . . It was all new country to me. Beautiful. . . . Wonderful. . . ."

His wife still watched him.

"You must take *me* there some day," she said. "I can see that it has done you a world of good."

THE EMPIRE OF THE ANTS

§ 1

WHEN Captain Gerilleau received instructions to take his new gunboat, the *Benjamin Constant*, to Badama on the Batemo arm of the Guaramadema and there assist the inhabitants against a plague of ants, he suspected the authorities of mockery. His promotion had been romantic and irregular, the affections of a prominent Brazilian lady and the captain's liquid eyes had played a part in the process, and the *Diario* and *O Futuro* had been lamentably disrespectful in their comments. He felt he was to give further occasion for disrespect.

He was a Creole, his conceptions of etiquette and discipline were pure-blooded Portuguese, and it was only to Holroyd, the Lancashire engineer who had come over with the boat, and as an exercise in the use of English—his "th" sounds were very uncertain—that he opened his heart.

"It is in effect," he said, "to make me absurd! What can a man do against ants? Dey come, dey go."

"They say," said Holroyd, "that these don't go. That chap you said was a Sambo——"

"Zambo—it is a sort of mixture of blood."

"Sambo. He said the people are going!"

The captain smoked fretfully for a time. "Dese tings 'ave to happen," he said at last. "What is it? Plagues of ants and suchlike as God wills. Dere was a plague in Trinidad—the little ants that carry leaves. Orl der orange-trees, all der mangoes! What does it matter? Sometimes ant armies come into your houses—fighting ants; a different sort. You go and they clean the house. Then you come back again;—the house is clean, like new! No cockroaches, no fleas, no jiggers in the floor."

269

"That Sambo chap," said Holroyd, "says these are a different sort of ant."

The captain shrugged his shoulders, fumed, and gave his attention to a cigarette.

Afterwards he reopened the subject. "My dear 'Olroyd, what am I to do about dese infernal ants?"

The captain reflected. "It is ridiculous," he said. But in the afternoon he put on his full uniform and went ashore, and jars and boxes came back to the ship and subsequently he did. And Holroyd sat on deck in the evening coolness and smoked profoundly and marvelled at Brazil. They were six days up the Amazon, some hundreds of miles from the ocean, and east and west of him there was a horizon like the sea, and to the south nothing but a sand-bank island with some tufts of scrub. The water was always running like a sluice, thick with dirt, animated with crocodiles and hovering birds, and fed by some inexhaustible source of tree trunks; and the waste of it, the headlong waste of it, filled his soul. The town of Alemquer, with its meagre church, its thatched sheds for houses, its discoloured ruins of ampler days, seemed a little thing lost in this wilderness of Nature, a sixpence dropped on Sahara. He was a young man, this was his first sight of the tropics, he came straight from England, where Nature is hedged, ditched, and drained into the perfection of submission, and he had suddenly discovered the insignificance of man. For six days they had been steaming up from the sea by unfrequented channels, and man had been as rare as a rare butterfly. One saw one day a canoe, another day a distant station, the next no men at all. He began to perceive that man is indeed a rare animal, having but a precarious hold upon this land.

He perceived it more clearly as the days passed, and he made his devious way to the Batemo, in the company of this remarkable commander, who ruled over one big gun, and was forbidden to waste his ammunition. Holroyd was learning Spanish industriously, but he was still in the present tense and substantive stage of speech, and the only other person who had any words of English was a negro stoker, who had them all wrong. The second in command was a Portuguese, da Cunha, who spoke French, but it was a different sort of French from the French Holroyd had learned in Southport, and their intercourse was confined to politenesses and simple propositions about the weather. And the weather, like everything else in this amazing new world, the weather had no human aspect, and was hot by night and hot by day, and the air steam, even the wind was hot steam, smelling of vegetation in decay: and the alligators and the strange birds, the flies of many sorts and sizes, the beetles, the ants, the snakes and monkeys seemed to wonder what man was doing in an atmosphere that had no gladness in its sunshine and no coolness in its night. To wear clothing was intolerable, but to cast it aside was to scorch by day and expose an ampler area to the mosquitoes by night; to go on deck by day was to be blinded by glare and to stay below was to suffocate. And in the daytime came certain flies, extremely clever and noxious about one's wrist and ankle. Captain Gerilleau, who was Holroyd's sole distraction from these physical distresses, developed into a formidable bore, telling the simple story of his heart's affections day by day, a string of anonymous women, as if he was telling beads. Sometimes he suggested sport, and they shot at alligators, and at rare intervals they came to human aggregations in the waste of trees, and stayed for a day or so, and drank and sat about; and, one night, danced with Creole girls, who found Holroyd's poor elements of Spanish, without either past tense or future, amply sufficient for their purposes. But these were mere luminous chinks in the long grey passage of the streaming river, up which the throbbing engines beat. A certain liberal heathen deity, in the shape of a demi-john, held seductive court aft, and, it is probable, forward.

But Gerilleau learned things about the ants, more things and more, at this stopping-place and that, and became interested in his mission.

"Dey are a new sort of ant," he said. "We have got to be—what do you call it?—entomologie? Big. Five centimetres! Some bigger! It is ridiculous. We are like the monkeys—sent to pick insects. . . . But dey are eating up the country."

He burst our indignantly. "Suppose—suddenly, there are complications with Europe. Here am I—soon we shall be above the Rio Negro—and my gun, useless!"

He nursed his knee and mused.

"Dose people who were dere at de dancing place, dey 'ave come down. Dey 'ave lost all they got. De ants come to deir house one afternoon. Everyone run out. You know when de ants come one must—everyone runs out and they go over the house. If you stayed they'd eat you. See? Well, presently dey go back; dey say, 'The ants 'ave gone.' . . . De ants 'aven't gone. Dey try to go in—de son, 'e goes in. De ants fight."

"Swarm over him?"

"Bite 'im. Presently he comes out again—screaming and running. He runs past them to the river. See? He get into de water and drowns de ants—yes." Gerilleau paused, brought his liquid eyes close to Holroyd's face, tapped Holroyd's knee with his knuckle. "That night he dies, just as if he was stung by a snake."

"Poisoned—by the ants?"

"Who knows?" Gerilleau shrugged his shoulders. "Perhaps they bit him badly. . . . When I joined dis service I joined to fight men. Dese things, dese ants, dey come and go. It is no business for men."

After that he talked frequently of the ants to Holroyd, and whenever they chanced to drift against any speck of humanity in that waste of water and sunshine and distant trees, Holroyd's improving knowledge of the language enabled him to recognise the ascendant word Saüba, more and more completely dominating the whole.

He perceived the ants were becoming interesting, and the nearer he drew to them the more interesting they became. Gerilleau abandoned his old themes almost suddenly, and the Portuguese lieutenant became a conversational figure; he knew something about the leaf-cutting ant, and expanded his knowledge. Gerilleau sometimes rendered what he had to tell to Holroyd. He told of the little workers that swarm and fight, and the big workers that command and rule, and how these latter always crawled to the neck and how their bite drew blood. He told how they cut leaves and made fungus beds, and how their nests in Caracas are sometimes a hundred yards across. Two days the three men spent disputing whether ants have eyes. The discussion grew dangerously heated on the second afternoon, and Holroyd saved the situation by going ashore in a boat to catch ants and see. He captured various specimens and returned, and some had eyes and some hadn't. Also, they argued, do ants bite or sting?

"Dese ants," said Gerilleau, after collecting information at a rancho, "have big eyes. They don't run about blind—not as most ants do. No! Dey get in corners and watch what you do."

"And they sting?" asked Holroyd.

"Yes. Dey sting. Dere is poison in the sting." He meditated. "I do not see what men can do against ants. Dey come and go."

"But these don't go."

"They will," said Gerilleau.

Past Tamandu there is a long low coast of eighty miles without any population, and then one comes to the confluence of the main river and the Batemo arm like a great lake, and then the forest came nearer, came at last intimately near. The character of the channel changes, snags abound, and the *Benjamin Constant* moored by a cable that night, under the very shadow of dark trees. For the first time for many days came a spell of coolness, and Holroyd and Gerilleau sat late, smoking cigars and enjoying this delicious sensation. Gerilleau's mind was full of ants and what they could do. He decided to sleep at last, and lay down on a mattress on deck, a man hopelessly perplexed; his last words, when he already seemed asleep, were to ask, with a flourish of despair: "What can one do with ants? . . . De whole thing is absurd."

Holroyd was left to scratch his bitten wrists, and meditate alone.

He sat on the bulwark and listened to the changes in

Gerilleau's breathing until he was fast asleep, and then the ripple and lap of the stream took his mind, and brought back that sense of immensity that had been growing upon him since first he had left Para and come up the river. The monitor showed but one small light, and there was first a little talking forward and then stillness. His eyes went from the dim black outlines of the middle works of the gunboat towards the bank, to the black overwhelming mysteries of forest, lit now and then by a fire-fly, and never still from the murmur of alien and mysterious activities. . . .

It was the inhuman immensity of this land that astonished and oppressed him. He knew the skies were empty of men, the stars were specks in an incredible vastness of space; he knew the ocean was enormous and untamable, but in England he had come to think of the land as man's. In England it is indeed man's, the wild things live by sufferance, grow on lease, everywhere the roads, the fences, and absolute security run. In an atlas, too, the land is man's, and all coloured to show his claim to it—in vivid contrast to the universal independent blueness of the sea. He had taken it for granted that a day would come when everywhere about the earth, plough and culture, light tramways, and good roads, and ordered security, would prevail. But now, he doubted.

This forest was interminable, it had an air of being invincible, and Man seemed at best an infrequent precarious intruder. One travelled for miles amidst the still, silent struggle of giant trees, of strangulating creepers, of assertive flowers, everywhere the alligator, the turtle, and endless varieties of birds and insects seemed at home, dwelt irreplaceably—but Man, Man at most held a footing upon resentful clearings, fought weeds, fought beasts and insects for the barest foothold, fell a prey to snake and beast, insect and fever, and was presently carried away. In many places down the river he had been manifestly driven back, this deserted creek or that preserved the name of a *casa*, and here and there ruinous white walls and a shattered tower enforced the lesson. The puma, the jaguar, were more the masters here. . . .

Who were the real masters?

In a few miles of this forest there must be more ants than there are men in the whole world! This seemed to Holroyd a perfectly new idea. In a few thousand years men had emerged from barbarism to a stage of <u>civilisation</u> that made them feel lords of the future and masters of the earth! But what was to prevent the ants evolving also? Such ants as one knew lived in little communities of a few thousand individuals, made no concerted efforts against the greater world. But they had a language, they had an intelligence! Why should things stop at that any more than men had stopped at the barbaric stage? Suppose presently the ants began to store knowledge, just as men had done by means of books and records, use weapons, form great empires, sustain a planned and <u>organised</u> war?

Things came back to him that Gerilleau had gathered about these ants they were approaching. They used a poison like the poison of snakes. They obeyed greater leaders even as the leaf-cutting ants do. They were carnivorous, and where they came they stayed. . . .

The forest was very still. The water lapped incessantly against the side. About the lantern overhead there eddied a noiseless whirl of phantom moths.

Gerilleau stirred in the darkness and sighed. "What can one *do?*" he murmured, and turned over and was still again.

Holroyd was roused from meditations that were becoming sinister by the hum of a mosquito.

§ 2

The next morning Holroyd learned they were within forty kilometres of Badama, and his interest in the banks intensified. He came up whenever an opportunity offered to examine his surroundings. He could see no signs of human occupation whatever, save for a weedy ruin of a house and the green-stained façade of the long-deserted monastery at Mojú, with a forest tree growing out of a vacant window space, and great creepers netted across its vacant portals.

Several flights of strange yellow butterflies with semi-transparent wings crossed the river that morning, and many alighted on the monitor and were killed by the men. It was towards afternoon that they came upon the derelict cuberta.

She did not at first appear to be derelict; both her sails were set and hanging slack in the afternoon calm, and there was the figure of a man sitting on the fore planking beside the shipped sweeps. Another man appeared to be sleeping face downwards on the sort of longitudinal bridge these big canoes have in the waist. But it was presently apparent, from the sway of her rudder and the way she drifted into the course of the gun-boat, that something was out of order with her. Gerilleau surveyed her through a field-glass, and became interested in the queer darkness of the face of the sitting man, a red-faced man he seemed, without a nose—crouching he was rather than sitting, and the longer the captain looked the less he liked to look at him, and the less able he was to take his glasses away.

But he did so at last, and went a little way to call up Holroyd. Then he went back to hail the cuberta. He hailed her again, and so she drove past him. *Santa Rosa* stood out clearly as her name.

As she came by and into the wake of the monitor, she pitched a little, and suddenly the figure of the crouching man collapsed as though all its joints had given way. His hat fell off, his head was not nice to look at, and his body flopped lax and rolled out of sight behind the bulwarks.

"*Caramba!*" cried Gerilleau, and resorted to Holroyd forthwith.

Holroyd was halfway up the companion. "Did you see dat?" said the captain.

"Dead!" said Holroyd. "Yes. You'd better send a boat aboard. There's something wrong."

"Did you—by any chance—see his face?"

"What was it like?"

"It was—ugh!—I have no words." And the captain suddenly turned his back on Holroyd and became an active and strident commander.

The gunboat came about, steamed parallel to the erratic course of the canoe, and dropped the boat with Lieutenant da Cunha and three sailors to board her. Then the curiosity of the captain made him draw up almost alongside as the lieutenant got aboard, so that the whole of the *Santa Rosa*, deck and hold, was visible to Holroyd.

He saw now clearly that the sole crew of the vessel was these two dead men, and though he could not see their faces, he saw by their outstretched hands, which were all of ragged flesh, that they had been subjected to some strange exceptional process of decay. For a moment his attention concentrated on those two enigmatical bundles of dirty clothes and laxly flung limbs, and then his eyes went forward to discover the open hold piled high with trunks and cases, and aft, to where the little cabin gaped inexplicably empty. Then he became aware that the planks of the middle decking were dotted with moving black specks.

His attention was riveted by these specks. They were all walking in directions radiating from the fallen man in a manner—the image came unsought to his mind—like the crowd dispersing from a bull-fight.

He became aware of Gerilleau beside him. "Capo," he said, "have you your glasses? Can you focus as closely as those planks there?"

Gerilleau made an effort, grunted, and handed him the glasses.

There followed a moment of scrutiny. "It's ants," said the Englishman, and handed the focussed field-glass back to Gerilleau.

His impression of them was of a crowd of large black ants, very like ordinary ants except for their size, and for the fact that some of the larger of them bore a sort of clothing of grey. But at the time his inspection was too brief for particulars. The head of Lieutenant da Cunha appeared over the side of the cuberta, and a brief colloquy ensued.

"You must go aboard," said Gerilleau.

The lieutenant objected that the boat was full of ants.

"You have your boots," said Gerilleau.

The lieutenant changed the subject. "How did these men die?" he asked.

Captain Gerilleau embarked upon speculations that Holroyd could not follow, and the two men disputed with a certain increasing vehemence. Holroyd took up the field-glass and resumed his scrutiny, first of the ants and then of the dead man amidships.

He has described these ants to me very particularly.

He says they were as large as any ants he has ever seen, black and moving with a steady deliberation very different from the mechanical fussiness of the common ant. About one in twenty was much larger than its fellows, and with an exceptionally large head. These reminded him at once of the master workers who are said to rule over the leaf-cutter ants; like them they seemed to be directing and coördinating the general movements. They tilted their bodies back in a manner altogether singular as if they made some use of the fore feet. And he had a curious fancy that he was too far off to verify, that most of these ants of both kinds were wearing accoutrements, had things strapped about their bodies by bright white bands like white metal threads. . . .

He put down the glasses abruptly, realising that the question of discipline between the captain and his subordinate had become acute.

"It is your duty," said the captain, "to go aboard. It is my instructions."

The lieutenant seemed on the verge of refusing. The head of one of the mulatto sailors appeared beside him.

"I believe these men were killed by the ants," said Holroyd abruptly in English.

The captain burst into a rage. He made no answer to Holroyd. "I have commanded you to go aboard," he screamed to his subordinate in Portuguese. "If you do not go aboard forthwith it is mutiny—rank mutiny. Mutiny and cowardice! Where is the courage that should animate us? I will have you in irons, I will have you shot like a dog," He began a torrent of abuse and curses, he danced to and fro. He shook his fists, he behaved as if beside himself with rage, and the lieutenant, white and still, stood looking at him. The crew appeared forward, with amazed faces.

Suddenly, in a pause of this outbreak, the lieutenant came to some heroic decision, saluted, drew himself together and clambered upon the deck of the cuberta.

"Ah!" said Gerilleau, and his mouth shut like a trap. Holroyd saw the ants retreating before da Cunha's boots. The Portuguese walked slowly to the fallen man, stooped down, hesitated, clutched his coat and turned him over. A black swarm of ants rushed out of the clothes, and da Cunha stepped back very quickly and trod two or three times on the deck.

Holroyd put up the glasses. He saw the scattered ants about the invader's feet, and doing what he had never seen ants doing before. They had nothing of the blind movements of the common ant; they were looking at him—as a rallying crowd of men might look at some gigantic monster that had dispersed it.

"How did he die?" the captain shouted.

Holroyd understood the Portuguese to say the body was too much eaten to tell.

"What is there forward?" asked Gerilleau.

The lieutenant walked a few paces, and began his answer in Portuguese. He stopped abruptly and beat off something from his leg. He made some peculiar steps as if he was trying to stamp on something invisible, and went quickly towards the side. Then he controlled himself, turned about, walked deliberately forward to the hold, clambered up to the foredecking, from which the sweeps are worked, stooped for a time over the second man, groaned audibly, and made his way back and aft to the cabin, moving very rigidly. He turned and began a conversation with his captain, cold and respectful in tone on either side, contrasting vividly with the wrath and insult of a few moments before. Holroyd gathered only fragments of its purport.

He reverted to the field-glasses, and was surprised to find

the ants had vanished from all the exposed surfaces of the deck. He turned towards the shadows beneath the decking, and it seemed to him they were full of watching eyes.

The cuberta, it was agreed, was derelict, but too full of ants to put men aboard to sit and sleep: it must be towed. The lieutenant went forward to take in and adjust the cable, and the men in the boat stood up to be ready to help him. Holroyd's glasses searched the canoe.

He became more and more impressed by the fact that a great if minute and furtive activity was going on. He perceived that a number of gigantic ants—they seemed nearly a couple of inches in length—carrying oddly-shaped burthens for which he could imagine no use—were moving in rushes from one point of obscurity to another. They did not move in columns across the exposed places, but in open, spaced-out lines, oddly suggestive of the rushes of modern infantry advancing under fire. A number were taking cover under the dead man's clothes, and a perfect swarm was gathering along the side over which da Cunha must presently go.

He did not see them actually rush for the lieutenant as he returned, but he has no doubt they did make a concerted rush. Suddenly the lieutenant was shouting and cursing and beating at his legs. "I'm stung!" he shouted, with a face of hate and accusation towards Gerilleau.

Then he vanished over the side, dropped into his boat, and plunged at once into the water. Holroyd heard the splash.

The three men in the boat pulled him out and brought him aboard, and that night he died.

§ 3

Holroyd and the captain came out of the cabin in which the swollen and contorted body of the lieutenant lay and stood together at the stern of the monitor, staring at the sinister vessel they trailed behind them. It was a close, dark night that had only phantom flickerings of sheet lightinng to illuminate it. The cuberta, a vague black triangle, rocked about in the steamer's wake, her sails bobbing and flapping, and the black smoke from the funnels, spark-lit ever and again, streamed over her swaying masts.

Gerilleau's mind was inclined to run on the unkind things the lieutenant had said in the heat of his last fever.

"He says I murdered 'im," he protested. "It is simply absurd. Someone 'ad to go aboard. Are we to run away from these confounded ants whenever they show up?"

Holroyd said nothing. He was thinking of a disciplined rush of little black shapes across bare sunlit planking.

"It was his place to go," harped Gerilleau. "He died in the execution of his duty. What has he to complain of? Murdered!... But the poor fellow was—what is it?—demented. He was not in his right mind. The poison swelled him.... U'm."

They came to a long silence.

"We will sink that canoe—burn it."

"And then?"

The inquiry irritated Gerilleau. His shoulders went up, his hands flew out at right angles from his body. "What is one to *do?*" he said, his voice going up to an angry squeak.

"Anyhow," he broke out vindictively, "every ant in dat cuberta!—I will burn dem alive!"

Holroyd was not moved to conversation. A distant ululation of howling monkeys filled the sultry night with foreboding sounds, and as the gunboat drew near the black mysterious banks this was reinforced by a depressing clamour of frogs.

"What is one to *do?*" the captain repeated after a vast interval, and suddenly becoming active and savage and blasphemous, decided to burn the *Santa Rosa* without further delay. Everyone aboard was pleased by that idea, everyone helped with zest; they pulled in the cable, cut it, and dropped the boat and fired her with tow and kerosene, and soon the cuberta was crackling and flaring merrily amidst the immensities of the tropical night. Holroyd watched the mounting yellow flare against the blackness, and the livid flashes of sheet lightning that came and went above the forest summits, throwing them into momentary silhouette, and his stoker stood behind him watching also.

The stoker was stirred to the depths of his linguistics. "*Saüba* go pop, pop," he said, "Wahaw!" and laughed richly.

But Holroyd was thinking that these little creatures on the decked canoe had also eyes and brains.

The whole thing impressed him as incredibly foolish and wrong, but—what was one to *do?* This question came back enormously reinforced on the morrow, when at last the gunboat reached Badama.

This place, with its leaf-thatch-covered houses and sheds, its creeper-invaded sugar-mill, its little jetty of timber and canes, was very still in the morning heat, and showed never a sign of living men. Whatever ants there were at that distance were too small to see.

"All the people have gone," said Gerilleau, "but we will do one thing anyhow. We will 'oot and vissel."

So Holroyd hooted and whistled.

Then the captain fell into a doubting fit of the worst kind. "Dere is one thing we can do," he said presently.

"What's that?" said Holroyd.

" 'Oot and vissel again."

So they did.

The captain walked his deck and gesticulated to himself. He seemed to have many things on his mind. Fragments of speeches came from his lips. He appeared to be addressing some imaginary public tribunal either in Spanish or Portuguese. Holroyd's improving ear detected something about ammunition. He came out of these preoccupations suddenly into English. "My dear 'Olroyd!" he cried, and broke off with "But what *can* one do?"

They took the boat and the field-glasses, and went close in to examine the place. They made out a number of big ants, whose still postures had a certain effect of watching them, dotted about the edge of the rude embarkation jetty. Gerilleau tried ineffectual pistol shots at these. Holroyd thinks he distinguished curious earthworks running between the nearer houses, that may have been the work of the insect conquerors of those human habitations. The explorers pulled past the jetty, and became aware of a human skeleton wearing a loin cloth, and very bright and clean and shining, lying beyond. They came to a pause regarding this. . . .

"I 'ave all dose lives to consider," said Gerilleau suddenly.

Holroyd turned and stared at the captain, realising slowly that he referred to the unappetising mixture of races that constituted his crew.

"To send a landing party—it is impossible—impossible. They will be poisoned, they will swell, they will swell up and abuse me and die. It is totally impossible. . . . If we land, I must land alone, alone, in thick boots and with my life in my hand. Perhaps I should live. Or again—I might not land. I do not know. I do not know."

Holroyd thought he did, but he said nothing.

"De whole thing," said Gerilleau suddenly, " 'as been got up to make me ridiculous. De whole thing!"

They paddled about and regarded the clean white skeleton from various points of view, and then they returned to the gunboat. Then Gerilleau's indecisions became terrible. Steam was got up, and in the afternoon the monitor went on up the river with an air of going to ask somebody something, and by sunset came back again and anchored. A thunderstorm gathered and broke furiously, and then the night became beautifully cool and quiet and everyone slept on deck. Except Gerilleau, who tossed about and muttered. In the dawn he awakened Holroyd.

"Lord!" said Holroyd, "what now?"

"I have decided," said the captain.

"What—to land?" said Holroyd, sitting up brightly.

"No!" said the captain, and was for a time very reserved. "I have decided," he repeated, and Holroyd manifested symptoms of impatience.

"Well,—yes," said the captain, "*I shall fire de big gun!*"

And he did! Heaven knows what the ants thought of it, but he did. He fired it twice with great sternness and ceremony. All the crew had wadding in their ears, and there was an effect of going into action about the whole affair, and first they hit and wrecked the old sugar-mill, and then they smashed the abandoned store behind the jetty. And then Gerilleau experienced the inevitable reaction.

"It is no good," he said to Holroyd; "no good at all. No sort of bally good. We must go back—for instructions. Dere will be de devil of a row about dis ammunition—oh! de *devil* of a row! You don't know, 'Olroyd. . . ."

He stood regarding the world in infinite perplexity for a space.

"But what else was there to *do?*" he cried.

In the afternoon the monitor started down stream again, and in the evening a landing party took the body of the lieutenant and buried it on the bank upon which the new ants have so far not appeared. . . .

§ 4

I heard this story in a fragmentary state from Holroyd not three weeks ago.

These new ants have got into his brain, and he has come back to England with the idea, as he says, of "exciting people" about them "before it is too late." He says they threaten British Guiana, which cannot be much over a trifle of a thousand miles from their present sphere of activity, and that the Colonial Office ought to get to work upon them at once. He declaims with great passion: "These are intelligent ants. Just think what that means!"

There can be no doubt they are a serious pest, and that the Brazilian Government is well advised in offering a prize of five hundred pounds for some effectual method of extirpation. It is certain too that since they first appeared in the hills beyond Badama, about three years ago, they have achieved extraordinary conquests. The whole of the south bank of the Batemo River, for nearly sixty miles, they have in their effectual occupation; they have driven men out completely, occupied plantations and settlements, and boarded and captured at least one ship. It is even said they have in some inexplicable way bridged the very considerable Capuarana arm and pushed many miles towards the Amazon itself.

There can be little doubt that they are far more reasonable and with a far better social organisation than any previously known ant species; instead of being in dispersed societies they are organised into what is in effect a single nation; but their peculiar and immediate formidableness lies not so much in this as in the intelligent use they make of poison against their larger enemies. It would seem this poison of theirs is closely akin to snake poison, and it is highly probable they actually manufacture it, and that the larger individuals among them carry the needle-like crystals of it in their attacks upon men.

Of course it is extremely difficult to get any detailed information about these new competitors for the sovereignty of the globe. No eye-witnesses of their activity, except for such glimpses as Holroyd's, have survived the encounter. The most extraordinary legends of their prowess and capacity are in circulation in the region of the Upper Amazon, and grow daily as the steady advance of the invader stimulates men's imaginations through their fears. These strange little creatures are credited not only with the use of implements and a knowledge of fire and metals and with organised feats of engineering that stagger our Northern minds—unused as we are to such feats as that of the Saübas of Rio de Janeiro, who in 1841 drove a tunnel under Parahyba where it is as wide as the Thames at London Bridge—but with an organised and detailed method of record and communication analogous to our books. So far their action has been a steady progressive settlement, involving the flight or slaughter of every human being in the new areas they invade. They are increasing rapidly in numbers, and Holroyd at least is firmly convinced that they will finally dispossess man over the whole of tropical South America.

And why should they stop at tropical South America?

Well, there they are, anyhow. By 1911 or thereabouts, if they go on as they are going, they ought to strike the Capuarana Extension Railway, and force themselves upon the attention of the European capitalist.

By 1920 they will be halfway down the Amazon. I fix 1950 or '60 at the latest for the discovery of Europe.

THE LAND IRONCLADS*

THE young lieutenant lay beside the war correspondent and admired the idyllic calm of the enemy's lines through his field-glass.

"So far as I can see," he said at last, "one man."

"What's he doing?" asked the war correspondent.

"Field-glass at us," said the young lieutenant.

"And this is war!"

"No," said the young lieutenant; "it's Bloch."

"The game's a draw."

"No! They've got to win or else they lose. A draw's a win for our side."

They had discussed the political situation fifty times or so, and the war correspondent was weary of it. He stretched out his limbs. "Aaai s'pose it *is* !" he yawned.

Flut !

"What was that?"

"Shot at us."

The war correspondent shifted to a slightly lower position. "No one shot at him," he complained.

"I wonder if they think we shall get so bored we shall go home?"

The war correspondent made no reply.

"There's the harvest, of course. . . ."

They had been there a month. Since the first brisk movements after the declaration of war things had gone slower and slower, until it seemed as though the whole machine of events must have run down. To begin with, they had had almost a scampering time; the invader had come across the frontier on the very dawn of the war in half-a-dozen parallel columns

*First published in December 30, 1903.

behind a cloud of cyclists and cavalry, with a general air of coming straight on the capital, and the defender horsemen had held him up, and peppered him and forced him to open out to outflank, and had then bolted to the next position in the most approved style, for a couple of days, until in the afternoon, bump! they had the invader against their prepared lines of defence. He did not suffer so much as had been hoped and expected: he was coming on, it seemed, with his eyes open, his scouts winded the guns, and down he sat at once without the shadow of an attack and began grubbing trenches for himself, as though he meant to sit down there to the very end of time. He was slow, but much more wary than the world had been led to expect, and he kept convoys tucked in and shielded his slow-marching infantry sufficiently well to prevent any heavy adverse scoring.

"But he ought to attack," the young lieutenant had insisted.

"He'll attack us at dawn, somewhere along the lines. You'll get the bayonets coming into the trenches just about when you can see," the war correspondent had held until a week ago.

The young lieutenant winked when he said that.

When one early morning the men the defenders sent to lie out five hundred yards before the trenches, with a view to the unexpected emptying of magazines into any night attack, gave way to causeless panic and blazed away at nothing for ten minutes, the war correspondent understood the meaning of that wink.

"What would you do if you were the enemy?" said the war correspondent, suddenly.

"If I had men like I've got now?"

"Yes."

"Take those trenches."

"How?"

"Oh—dodges! Crawl out halfway at night before moonrise and get into touch with the chaps we send out. Blaze at 'em if they tried to shift, and so bag some of 'em in the daylight. Learn that patch of ground by heart, lie all day in squatty holes, and come on nearer next night. There's a bit over there, lumpy ground, where they could get across to rushing distance—easy. In a night or so. It would be a mere game for our fellows; it's what they're made for. . . . Guns? Shrapnel and stuff wouldn't stop good men who meant business."

"Why don't *they* do that?"

"Their men aren't brutes enough; that's the trouble. They're a crowd of devitalised townsmen, and that's the truth of the matter. They're clerks, they're factory hands, they're students, they're civilised men. They can write, they can talk, they can make and do all sorts of things, but they're poor amateurs at war. They've got no physical staying power, and that's the whole thing. They've never slept in the open one night in their lives; they've never drunk anything but the purest water-company water; they've never gone short of three meals a day since they left their feeding-bottles. Half their cavalry never cocked leg over horse till it enlisted six months ago. They ride their horses as though they were bicycles—you watch 'em! They're fools at the game, and they know it. Our boys of fourteen can give their grown men points. . . . Very well——"

The war correspondent mused on his face with his nose between his knuckles.

"If a decent civilisation," he said, "cannot produce better men for war than——"

He stopped with belated politeness. "I mean——"

"Than our open-air life," said the young lieutenant.

"Exactly," said the war correspondent. "Then civilisation has to stop."

"It looks like it," the young lieutenant admitted.

"Civilisation has science, you know," said the war correspondent. "It invented and it makes the rifles and guns and things you use."

"Which our nice healthy hunters and stockmen and so on, rowdy-dowdy cowpunchers and nigger-whackers, can use ten times better than—— *What's that?*"

"What?" said the war correspondent, and then seeing his

companion busy with his field-glass he produced his own: "Where?" said the war correspondent, sweeping the enemy's lines.

"It's nothing," said the young lieutenant, still looking.

"What's nothing?"

The young lieutenant put down his glass and pointed. "I thought I saw something there, behind the stems of those trees. Something black. What it was I don't know."

The war correspondent tried to get even by intense scrutiny.

"It wasn't anything," said the young lieutenant, rolling over to regard the darkling evening sky, and generalised: "There never will be anything any more for ever. Unless——"

The war correspondent looked inquiry.

"They may get their stomachs wrong, or something— living without proper drains."

A sound of bugles came from the tents behind. The war correspondent slid backward down the sand and stood up. "Boom!" came from somewhere far away to the left. "Halloa!" he said, hesitated, and crawled back to peer again. "Firing at this time is jolly bad manners."

The young lieutenant was uncommunicative for a space.

Then he pointed to the distant clump of trees again. "One of our big guns. They were firing at that," he said.

"The thing that wasn't anything?"

"Something over there, anyhow."

Both men were silent, peering through their glasses for a space. "Just when it's twilight," the lieutenant complained. He stood up.

"I might stay here a bit," said the war correspondent.

The lieutenant shook his head. "There's nothing to see," he apologised, and then went down to where his little squad of sun-brown, loose-limbed men had been yarning in the trench. The war correspondent stood up also, glanced for a moment at the businesslike bustle below him, gave perhaps twenty seconds to those enigmatical trees again, then turned his face towards the camp.

He found himself wondering whether his editor would consider the story of how somebody thought he saw something black behind a clump of trees, and how a gun was fired at this illusion by somebody else, too trivial for public consumption.

"It's the only gleam of a shadow of interest," said the war correspondent, "for ten whole days."

"No," he said presently; "I'll write that other article, 'Is War Played Out?'"

He surveyed the darkling lines in perspective, the tangle of trenches one behind another, one commanding another, which the defender had made ready. The shadows and mists swallowed up their receding contours, and here and there a lantern gleamed, and here and there knots of men were busy about small fires. "No troops on earth could do it," he said. . . .

He was depressed. He believed that there were other things in life better worth having than proficiency in war; he believed that in the heart of civilisation, for all its stresses, its crushing concentrations of forces, its injustice and suffering, there lay something that might be the hope of the world; and the idea that any people by living in the open air, hunting perpetually, losing touch with books and art and all the things that intensify life, might hope to resist and break that great development to the end of time, jarred on his civilised soul.

Apt to his thought came a file of the defender soldiers and passed him in the gleam of a swinging lamp that marked the way.

He glanced at their red-lit faces, and one shone out for a moment, a common type of face in the defender's ranks: ill-shaped nose, sensuous lips, bright clear eyes full of alert cunning, slouch hat cocked on one side and adorned with the peacock's plume of the rustic Don Juan turned soldier, a hard brown skin, a sinewy frame, an open, tireless stride, and a master's grip on the rifle.

The war correspondent returned their salutations and went on his way.

"Louts," he whispered. "Cunning, elementary louts. And they are going to beat the townsmen at the game of war!"

From the red glow among the nearer tents came first one

and then half-a-dozen hearty voices, bawling in a drawling unison the words of a particularly slab and sentimental patriotic song.

"Oh, *go* it!" muttered the war correspondent, bitterly.

§ 2

It was opposite the trenches called after Hackbone's Hut that the battle began. There the ground stretched broad and level between the lines, with scarcely shelter for a lizard, and it seemed to the startled, just-awakened men who came crowding into the trenches that this was one more proof of that inexperience of the enemy of which they had heard so much. The war correspondent would not believe his ears at first, and swore that he and the war artist, who, still imperfectly roused, was trying to put on his boots by the light of a match held in his hand, were the victims of a common illusion. Then, after putting his head in a bucket of cold water, his intelligence came back as he towelled. He listened. "Gollys!" he said; "that's something more than scare firing this time. It's like ten thousand carts on a bridge of tin."

There came a sort of enrichment to that steady uproar. "Machine-guns!"

Then, "Guns!"

The artist, with one boot on, thought to look at his watch, and went to it hopping.

"Half an hour from dawn," he said. "You were right about their attacking, after all. . . ."

The war correspondent came out of the tent, verifying the presence of chocolate in his pocket as he did so. He had to halt for a moment or so until his eyes were toned down to the night a little. "Pitch!" he said. He stood for a space to season his eyes before he felt justified in striking out for a black gap among the adjacent tents. The artist coming out behind him fell over a tent-rope. It was half-past two o'clock in the morning of the darkest night in time, and against a sky of dull black silk the enemy was talking search-lights, a wild jabber of search-lights. "He's trying to blind our riflemen," said the war correspondent with a flash, and waited for the artist and then set off with a sort of discreet haste again. "Whoa!" he said, presently. "Ditches!"

They stopped.

"It's the confounded search-lights," said the war correspondent.

They saw lanterns going to and fro, near by, and men falling in to march down to the trenches. They were for following them, and then the artist began to get his night eyes. "If we scramble this," he said, "and it's only a drain, there's a clear run up to the ridge." And that way they took. Lights came and went in the tents behind, as the men turned out, and ever and again they came to broken ground and staggered and stumbled. But in a little while they drew near the crest. Something that sounded like the impact of a tremendous railway accident happened in the air above them, and the shrapnel bullets seethed about them like a sudden handful of hail. "Right-ho!" said the war correspondent, and soon they judged they had come to the crest and stood in the midst of a world of great darkness and frantic glares, whose principal fact was sound.

Right and left of them and all about them was the uproar, an army-full of magazine fire, at first chaotic and monstrous, and then, eked out by little flashes and gleams and suggestions, taking the beginnings of a shape. It looked to the war correspondent as though the enemy must have attacked in line and with his whole force—in which case he was either being or was already annihilated.

"Dawn and the dead," he said, with his instinct for headlines. He said this to himself, but afterwards by means of shouting he conveyed an idea to the artist. "They must have meant it for a surprise," he said.

It was remarkable how the firing kept on. After a time he began to perceive a sort of rhythm in this inferno of noise. It would decline—decline perceptibly, droop towards something that was comparatively a pause—a pause of inquiry. "Aren't you all dead yet?" this pause seemed to say. The flickering fringe of rifle-flashes would become attenuated and broken, and the whack-bang of the enemy's big guns two miles away there would come up out of the deeps. Then suddenly, east or west of them, something would startle the rifles to a frantic outbreak again.

The war correspondent taxed his brain for some theory of conflict that would account for this, and was suddenly aware that the artist and he were vividly illuminated. He could see the ridge on which they stood, and before them in black outline a file of riflemen hurrying down towards the nearer trenches. It became visible that a light rain was falling, and farther away towards the enemy was a clear space with men —"our men?"—running across it in disorder. He saw one of those men throw up his hands and drop. And something else black and shining loomed up on the edge of the beam-coruscating flashes; and behind it and far away a calm, white eye regarded the world. "Whit, whit, whit," sang something in the air, and then the artist was running for cover, with the war correspondent behind him. Bang came shrapnel, bursting close at hand as it seemed, and our two men were lying flat in a dip in the ground, and the light and everything had gone again, leaving a vast note of interrogation upon the light.

The war correspondent came within bawling range. "What the deuce was it? Shooting our men down!"

"Black," said the artist, "and like a fort. Not two hundred yards from the first trench."

He sought for comparisons in his mind. "Something between a big blockhouse and a giant's dishcover," he said.

"And they were running!" said the war correspondent.

"You'd run if a thing like that, with a search-light to help it, turned up like a prowling nightmare in the middle of the night."

They crawled to what they judged the edge of the dip and lay regarding the unfathomable dark. For a space they could distinguish nothing, and then a sudden convergence of the search-lights of both sides brought the strange thing out again.

In that flickering pallor it had the effect of a large and clumsy black insect, an insect the size of an iron-clad cruiser, crawling obliquely to the first line of trenches and firing shots out of port-holes in its side. And on its carcass the bullets must have been battering with more than the passionate violence of hail on a roof of tin.

Then in the twinkling of an eye the curtain of the dark had fallen again and the monster had vanished, but the crescendo of musketry marked its approach to the trenches.

They were beginning to talk about the thing to each other, when a flying bullet kicked dirt into the artist's face, and they decided abruptly to crawl down into the cover of the trenches. They had got down with an unobtrusive persistence into the second line, before the dawn had grown clear enough for anything to be seen. They found themselves in a crowd of expectant riflemen, all noisily arguing about what would happen next. The enemy's contrivance had done execution upon the outlying men, it seemed, but they did not believe it would do any more. "Come the day and we'll capture the lot of them," said a burly soldier.

"Them?" said the war correspondent.

"They say there's a regular string of 'em, crawling along the front of our lines. . . . Who cares?"

The darkness filtered away so imperceptibly that at no moment could one declare decisively that one could see. The search-lights ceased to sweep hither and thither. The enemy's monsters were dubious patches of darkness upon the dark, and then no longer dubious, and so they crept out into distinctness. The war correspondent, munching chocolate absent-mindedly, beheld at last a spacious picture of battle under the cheerless sky, whose central focus was an array of fourteen or fifteen huge clumsy shapes lying in perspective on the very edge of the first line of trenches, at intervals of perhaps three hundred yards, and evidently firing down upon the crowded riflemen. They were so close in that the defender's guns had ceased, and only the first line of trenches was in action.

The second line commanded the first, and as the light grew, the war correspondent could make out the riflemen who were fighting these monsters, crouched in knots and crowds behind the transverse banks that crossed the trenches against the eventuality of an enfilade. The trenches close to the big machines were empty save for the crumpled suggestions of dead and wounded men; the defenders had been driven right and left as soon as the prow of a land ironclad had loomed up over the front of the trench. The war correspondent produced his field-glass, and was immediately a centre of inquiry from the soldiers about him.

They wanted to look, they asked questions, and after he had announced that the men across the traverses seemed unable to advance or retreat, and were crouching under cover rather than fighting, he found it advisable to loan his glasses to a burly and incredulous corporal. He heard a strident voice and found a lean and sallow soldier at his back talking to the artist.

"There's chaps down there caught," the man was saying. "If they retreat they got to expose themselves, and the fire's too straight. . . ."

"They aren't firing much, but every shot's a hit."

"Who?"

"The chaps in that thing. The men who're coming up———"

"Coming up where?"

"We're evacuating them trenches where we can. Our chaps are coming back up the zigzags. . . . No end of 'em hit. . . . But when we get clear our turn'll come. Rather! Those things won't be able to cross a trench or get into it; and before they can get back our guns'll smash 'em up. Smash 'em right up. See?" A brightness came into his eyss. "Then we'll have a go at the beggars inside," he said. . . .

The war correspondent thought for a moment, trying to realise the idea. Then he set himself to recover his field-glass from the burly corporal. . . .

The daylight was getting clearer now. The clouds were lifting, and a gleam of lemon-yellow amidst the level masses to the east portended sunrise. He looked again at the land ironclad. As he saw it in the bleak, grey dawn, lying obliquely upon the slope and on the very lip of the foremost trench, the suggestion of a stranded vessel was very strong indeed. It might have been from eighty to a hundred feet long—it was about two hundred and fifty yards away—its vertical side was ten feet high or so, smooth for that height, and then with a complex patterning under the eaves of its flattish turtle cover. This patterning was a close interlacing of portholes, rifle barrels, and telescope tubes—sham and real—indistinguishable one from the other. The thing had come into such a position as to enfilade the trench, which was empty now, so far as he could see, except for two or three crouching knots of men and the tumbled dead. Behind it, across the plain, it had scored the grass with a train of linked impressions, like the dotted tracings sea-things leave in sand. Left and right of that track dead men and wounded men were scattered—men it had picked off as they fled back from their advanced positions in the search-light glare from the invader's lines. And now it lay with its head projecting a little over the trench it had won, as if it were a single sentient thing planning the next phase of its attack.

He lowered his glasses and took a more comprehensive view of the situation. These creatures of the night had evidently won the first line of trenches and the fight had come to a pause. In the increasing light he could make out by a stray shot or a chance exposure that the defender's marksmen were lying thick in the second and third line of trenches up towards the low crest of the position, and in such of the zigzags as gave them a chance of a converging fire. The men about him were talking of guns. "We're in the line of the big guns at the crest, but they'll soon shift one to pepper them," the lean man said, reassuringly.

"Whup," said the corporal.

"Bang! bang! bang! Whir-r-r-r!" it was a sort of nervous jump, and all the rifles were going off by themselves. The war correspondent found himself and the artist, two idle men crouching behind a line of preoccupied backs, of industrious men discharging magazines. The monster had moved. It continued to move regardless of the hail that splashed its skin with bright new specks of lead. It was singing a mechanical little ditty to itself, "Tuf-tuf, tuf-tuf, tuf-tuf," and squirting out little jets of steam behind. It had humped itself up, as a limpet does before it crawls; it had lifted its skirt and displayed along the length of it—*feet !* They were thick, stumpy feet, between knobs and buttons in shape—flat, broad things, reminding one of the feet of elephants or the legs of caterpillars; and then, as the skirt rose higher, the war correspondent, scrutinising the thing through his glasses again, saw that these feet hung, as it were, on the rims of wheels. His thoughts whirled back to Victoria Street, Westminster, and he saw himself in the piping times of peace, seeking matter for an interview.

"Mr.—Mr. Diplock," he said; "and he called them Pedrails. . . . Fancy meeting them here!"

The marksman beside him raised his head and shoulders in a speculative mood to fire more certainly—it seemed so natural to assume the attention of the monster must be distracted by this trench before it—and was suddenly knocked backwards by a bullet through his neck. His feet flew up, and he vanished out of the margin of the watcher's field of vision. The war correspondent grovelled tighter, but after a glance behind him at a painful little confusion, he resumed his fieldglass, for the thing was putting down its feet one after the other, and hoisting itself farther and farther over the trench. Only a bullet in the head could have stopped him looking just then.

The lean man with the strident voice ceased firing to turn and reiterate his point. "They can't possibly cross," he bawled. "They——"

"Bang! Bang! Bang! Bang!"—drowned everything.

The lean man continued speaking for a word or so, then gave it up, shook his head to enforce the impossibility of anything crossing a trench like the one below, and resumed business once more.

And all the while that great bulk was crossing. When the war correspondent turned his glass on it again it had bridged the trench, and its queer feet were rasping away at the farther bank, in the attempt to get a hold there. It got its hold. It continued to crawl until the greater bulk of it was over the trench—until it was all over. Then it paused for a moment, adjusted its skirt a little nearer the ground, gave an unnerving "toot, toot," and came on abruptly at a pace of, perhaps, six miles an hour straight up the gentle slope towards our observer.

The war correspondent raised himself on his elbow and looked a natural inquiry at the artist.

For a moment the men about him stuck to their position and fired furiously. Then the lean man in a mood of precipitancy slid backwards, and the war correspondent said "Come along" to the artist, and led the movement along the trench.

As they dropped down, the vision of a hillside of trench being rushed by a dozen vast cockroaches disappeared for a space, and instead was one of a narrow passage, crowded with men, for the most part receding, though one or two turned or halted. He never turned back to see the nose of the monster creep over the brow of the trench; he never even troubled to keep in touch with the artist. He heard the "whit" of bullets about him soon enough, and saw a man before him stumble and drop, and then he was one of a furious crowd fighting to get into a transverse zigzag ditch that enabled the defenders to get under cover up and down the hill. It was like a theatre panic. He gathered from signs and fragmentary words that on ahead another of these monsters had also won to the second trench.

He lost his interest in the general course of the battle for a space altogether; he became simply a modest egotist, in a mood of hasty circumspection, seeking the farthest rear, amidst a dispersed multitude of disconcerted riflemen similarly employed. He scrambled down through trenches, he took his courage in both hands and sprinted across the open, he had moments of panic when it seemed madness not to be quadrupedal, and moments of shame when he stood up and faced about to see how the fight was going. And he was one of many thousand very similar men that morning. On the ridge he halted in a knot of scrub, and was for a few minutes almost minded to stop and see things out.

The day was now fully come. The grey sky had changed to

blue, and of all the cloudy masses of the dawn there remained only a few patches of dissolving fleeciness. The world below was bright and singularly clear. The ridge was not, perhaps, more than a hundred feet or so above the general plain, but in this flat region it sufficed to give the effect of extensive view. Away on the north side of the ridge, little and far, were the camps, the ordered wagons, all the gear of a big army; with officers galloping about and men doing aimless things. Here and there men were falling in, however, and the cavalry was forming up on the plain beyond the tents. The bulk of men who had been in the trenches were still on the move to the rear, scattered like sheep without a shepherd over the farther slopes. Here and there were little rallies and attempts to wait and do—something vague; but the general drift was away from any concentration. There on the southern side was the elaborate lacework of trenches and defences, across which these iron turtles, fourteen of them spread out over a line of perhaps three miles, were now advancing as fast as a man could trot, and methodically shooting down and breaking up any persistent knots of resistance. Here and there stood little clumps of men, outflanked and unable to get away, showing the white flag, and the invader's cyclist infantry was advancing now across the open, in open order but unmolested to complete the work of the machines. Surveyed at large, the defenders already looked a beaten army. A mechanism that was effectually ironclad against bullets, that could at a pinch cross a thirty-foot trench, and that seemed able to shoot out rifle-bullets with unerring precision, was clearly an inevitable victor against anything but rivers, precipices, and guns.

He looked at his watch. "Half-past four! Lord! What things can happen in two hours. Here's the whole blessed army being walked over, and at half-past two——

"And even now our blessed louts haven't done a thing with their guns!"

He scanned the ridge right and left of him with his glasses. He turned again to the nearest land ironclad, advancing now obliquely to him and not three hundred yards away, and

then scanned the ground over which he must retreat if he was
not to be captured.

"They'll do nothing," he said, and glanced again at the
enemy.

And then from far away to the left came the thud of a gun,
followed very rapidly by a rolling gun-fire.

He hesitated and decided to stay.

§ 3

The defender had relied chiefly upon his rifles in the event
of an assault. His guns he kept concealed at various points
upon and behind the ridge ready to bring them into action
against any artillery preparations for an attack on the part
of his antagonist. The situation had rushed upon him with
the dawn, and by the time the gunners had their guns ready
for motion, the land ironclads were already in among the foremost trenches. There is a natural reluctance to fire into one's
own broken men, and many of the guns, being intended simply to fight an advance of the enemy's artillery, were not in
positions to hit anything in the second line of trenches. After
that the advance of the land ironclads was swift. The defender-
general found himself suddenly called upon to invent a new
sort of warfare, in which guns were to fight alone amidst
broken and retreating infantry. He had scarcely thirty minutes in which to think it out. He did not respond to the call,
and what happened that morning was that the advance of
the land ironclads forced the fight, and each gun and battery
made what play its circumstances dictated. For the most
part it was poor play.

Some of the guns got in two or three shots, some one or
two, and the percentage of misses was unusually high. The
howitzers, of course, did nothing. The land ironclads in each
case followed much the same tactics. As soon as a gun came
into play the monster turned itself almost end-on, so as to
minimise the chances of a square hit, and made not for the
gun, but for the nearest point on its flank from which the
gunners could be shot down. Few of the hits scored were

very effectual; only one of the things was disabled, and that was the one that fought the three batteries attached to the brigade on the left wing. Three that were hit when close upon the guns were clean shot through without being put out of action. Our war correspondent did not see that one momentary arrest of the tide of victory on the left; he saw only the very ineffectual fight of half-battery 96B close at hand upon his right. This he watched some time beyond the margin of safety.

Just after he heard the three batteries opening up upon his left he became aware of the thud of horses' hoofs from the sheltered side of the slope, and presently saw first one and then two other guns galloping into position along the north side of the ridge, well out of sight of the great bulk that was now creeping obliquely towards the crest and cutting up the lingering infantry beside it and below, as it came.

The half-battery swung round into line—each gun describing its curve—halted, unlimbered, and prepared for action. . . .

"Bang!"

The land ironclad had become visible over the brow of the hill, and just visible as a long black back to the gunners. It halted, as though it hesitated.

The two remaining guns fired, and then their big antagonist had swung round and was in full view, end-on, against the sky, coming at a rush.

The gunners became frantic in their haste to fire again. They were so near the war correspondent could see the expression of their excited faces through his field-glass. As he looked he saw a man drop, and realised for the first time that the ironclad was shooting.

For a moment the big black monster crawled with an accelerated pace towards the furiously active gunners. Then, as if moved by a generous impulse, it turned its full broadside to their attack, and scarcely forty yards away from them. The war correspondent turned his field-glass back to the gunners and perceived it was now shooting down the men about the guns with the most deadly rapidity.

Just for a moment it seemed splendid, and then it seemed horrible. The gunners were dropping in heaps about their guns. To lay a hand on a gun was death. "Bang!" went the gun on the left, a hopeless miss, and that was the only second shot the half-battery fired. In another moment half-a-dozen surviving artillerymen were holding up their hands amidst a scattered muddle of dead and wounded men, and the fight was done.

The war correspondent hesitated between stopping in his scrub and waiting for an opportunity to surrender decently, or taking to an adjacent gully he had discovered. If he surrendered it was certain he would get no copy off; while, if he escaped, there were all sorts of chances. He decided to follow the gully, and take the first offer in the confusion beyond the camp of picking up a horse.

§ 4

Subsequent authorities have found fault with the first land ironclads in many particulars, but assuredly they served their purpose on the day of their appearance. They were essentially long, narrow, and very strong steel frameworks carrying the engines, and borne upon eight pairs of big pedrail wheels, each about ten feet in diameter, each a driving wheel and set upon long axles free to swivel round a common axis. This arrangement gave them the maximum of adaptability to the contours of the ground. They crawled level along the ground with one foot high upon a hillock and another deep in a depression, and they could hold themselves erect and steady sideways upon even a steep hillside. The engineers directed the engines under the command of the captain, who had look-out points at small ports all round the upper edge of the adjustable skirt of twelve-inch iron-plating which protected the whole affair, and who could also raise or depress a conning-tower set about the port-holes through the centre of the iron top cover. The riflemen each occupied a small cabin of peculiar construction, and these cabins were slung along the sides of and before and behind the great main framework, in a manner suggestive of the slinging of the seats of an Irish jaunting-car. Their rifles, however, were very different pieces of apparatus from the simple mechanisms in the hands of their adversaries.

These were in the first place automatic, ejected their cartridges and loaded again from a magazine each time they fired, until the ammunition store was at an end, and they had the most remarkable sights imaginable, sights which threw a bright little camera-obscura picture into the light-tight box in which the rifleman sat below. This camera-obscura picture was marked with two crossed lines, and whatever was covered by the intersection of these two lines, that the rifle hit. The sighting was ingeniously contrived. The rifleman stood at the table with a thing like an elaboration of a draughtsman's dividers in his hand, and he opened and closed these dividers, so that they were always at the apparent height—if it was an ordinary-sized man—of the man he wanted to kill. A little twisted strand of wire like an electric-light wire ran from this implement up to the gun, and as the dividers opened and shut the sights went up or down. Changes in the clearness of the atmosphere, due to changes of moisture, were met by an ingenious use of that meteorologically sensitive substance, catgut, and when the land ironclad moved forward the sights got a compensatory deflection in the direction of its motion. The rifleman stood up in his pitch-dark chamber and watched the little picture before him. One hand held the dividers for judging distance, and the other grasped a big knob like a door-handle. As he pushed this knob about the rifle above swung to correspond, and the picture passed to and fro like an agitated panorama. When he saw a man he wanted to shoot he brought him up to the cross lines, and then pressed a finger upon a little push like an electric bell-push, conveniently placed in the centre of the knob. Then the man was shot. If by any chance the rifleman missed his target he moved the knob a trifle, or readjusted his dividers, pressed the push, and got him the second time.

This rifle and its sights protruded from a port-hole, exactly like a great number of other port-holes that ran in a triple

row under the eaves of the cover of the land ironclad. Each
port-hole displayed a rifle and sight in dummy, so that the
real ones could only be hit by a chance shot, and if one was,
then the young man below said "Pshaw!" turned on an electric light, lowered the injured instrument into his camera, replaced the injured part, or put up a new rifle if the injury was
considerable.

You must conceive these cabins as hung clear above the
swing of the axles, and inside the big wheels upon which the
great elephant-like feet were hung, and behind these cabins
along the centre of the monster ran a central gallery into
which they opened, and along which worked the big compact
engines. It was like a long passage into which this throbbing
machinery had been packed, and the captain stood about the
middle, close to the ladder that led to his conning-tower, and
directed the silent, alert engineers—for the most part by
signs. The throb and noise of the engines mingled with the
reports of the rifles and the intermittent clangour of the bullet
hail upon the armour. Ever and again he would touch the
wheel that raised his conning-tower, step up his ladder until
his engineers could see nothing of him above the waist, and
then come down again with orders. Two small electric lights
were all the illumination of this space—they were placed to
make him most clearly visible to his subordinates; the air was
thick with the smell of oil and petrol, and had the war correspondent been suddenly transferred from the spacious dawn
outside to the bowels of this apparatus he would have thought
himself fallen into another world.

The captain, of course, saw both sides of the battle. When
he raised his head into his conning-tower there were the dewy
sunrise, the amazed and disordered trenches, the flying and
falling soldiers, the depressed-looking groups of prisoners, the
beaten guns; when he bent down again to signal "half speed,"
"quarter speed," "half circle round toward the right," or
what not, he was in the oil-smelling twilight of the ill-lit engine-room. Close beside him on either side was the mouthpiece
of a speaking-tube, and ever and again he would direct one
side or other of his strange craft to "concentrate fire forward

on gunners," or to "clear out trench about a hundred yards on our right front."

He was a young man, healthy enough but by no means sun-tanned, and of a type of feature and expression that prevails in His Majesty's Navy: alert, intelligent, quiet. He and his engineers and his riflemen all went about their work, calm and reasonable men. They had none of that flapping strenuousness of the half-wit in a hurry, that excessive strain upon the blood-vessels, that hysteria of effort which is so frequently regarded as the proper state of mind for heroic deeds.

For the enemy these young engineers were defeating they felt a certain qualified pity and a quite unqualified contempt. They regarded these big, healthy men they were shooting down precisely as these same big, healthy men might regard some inferior kind of nigger. They despised them for making war; despised their bawling patriotisms and their emotionality profoundly; despised them, above all, for the petty cunning and the almost brutish want of imagination their method of fighting displayed. "If they *must* make war," these young men thought, "why in thunder don't they do it like sensible men?" They resented the assumption that their own side was too stupid to do anything more than play their enemy's game, that they were going to play this costly folly according to the rules of unimaginative men. They resented being forced to the trouble of making man-killing machinery; resented the alternative of having to massacre these people or endure their truculent yappings; resented the whole unfathomable imbecility of war.

Meanwhile, with something of the mechanical precision of a good clerk posting a ledger, the riflemen moved their knobs and pressed their buttons. . . .

The captain of Land Ironclad Number Three had halted on the crest close to his captured half-battery. His lined-up prisoners stood hard by and waited for the cyclists behind to come for them. He surveyed the victorious morning through his conning-tower.

He read the general's signals. "Five and Four are to keep

among the guns to the left and prevent any attempt to recover them. Seven and Eleven and Twelve, stick to the guns you have got; Seven, get into position to command the guns taken by Three. Then we're to do something else, are we? Six and One, quicken up to about ten miles an hour and walk round behind that camp to the levels near the river—we shall bag the whole crowd of them," interjected the young man. "Ah, here we are! Two and Three, Eight and Nine, Thirteen and Fourteen, space out to a thousand yards, wait for the word, and then go slowly to cover the advance of the cyclist infantry against any charge of mounted troops. That's all right. But where's Ten? Halloa! Ten to repair and get movable as soon as possible. They've broken up Ten!"

The discipline of the new war machines was business-like rather than pedantic, and the head of the captain came down out of the conning-tower to tell his men. "I say, you chaps there. They've broken up Ten. Not badly, I think; but anyhow, he's stuck."

But that still left thirteen of the monsters in action to finish up the broken army.

The war correspondent stealing down his gully looked back and saw them all lying along the crest and talking fluttering congratulatory flags to one another. Their iron sides were shining golden in the light of the rising sun.

§ 5

The private adventures of the war correspondent terminated in surrender about one o'clock in the afternoon, and by that time he had stolen a horse, pitched off it, and narrowly escaped being rolled upon; found the brute had broken its leg, and shot it with his revolver. He had spent some hours in the company of a squad of dispirited riflemen, had quarrelled with them about topography at last, and gone off by himself in a direction that should have brought him to the banks of the river and didn't. Moreover, he had eaten all his chocolate and found nothing in the whole world to drink. Also, it had become extremely hot. From behind a broken, but attractive, stone wall he had seen far away in the distance the defender-horsemen trying to charge cyclists in open order, with land ironclads outflanking them on either side. He had discovered that cyclists could retreat over open turf before horsemen with a sufficient margin of speed to allow of frequent dismounts and much terribly effective sharp-shooting; and he had a sufficient persuasion that those horsemen, having charged their hearts out, had halted just beyond his range of vision and surrendered. He had been urged to sudden activity by a forward movement of one of those machines that had threatened to enfilade his wall. He had discovered a fearful blister on his heel.

He was now in a scrubby gravelly place, sitting down and meditating on his pocket-handkerchief, which had in some extraordinary way become in the last twenty-four hours extremely ambiguous in hue. "It's the whitest thing I've got," he said.

He had known all along that the enemy was east, west, and south of him, but when he heard land ironclads Numbers One and Six talking in their measured, deadly way not half a mile to the north he decided to make his own little unconditional peace without any further risks. He was for hoisting his white flag to a bush and taking up a position of modest obscurity near it until someone came along. He became aware of voices, clatter, and the distinctive noises of a body of horse, quite near, and he put his handkerchief in his pocket again and went to see what was going forward.

The sound of firing ceased, and then as he drew near he heard the deep sounds of many simple, coarse, but hearty and noble-hearted soldiers of the old school swearing with vigour.

He emerged from his scrub upon a big level plain, and far away a fringe of trees marked the banks of the river.

In the centre of the picture was a still intact road bridge, and a big railway bridge a little to the right. Two land ironclads rested, with a general air of being long, harmless sheds, in a pose of anticipatory peacefulness right and left of the picture, completely commanding two miles and more of the river levels. Emerged and halted a few yards from the scrub was the remainder of the defenders' cavalry, dusty, a little disordered, and obviously annoyed, but still a very fine show of men. In the middle distance three or four men and horses were receiving medical attendance, and nearer a knot of officers regarded the distant novelties in mechanism with profound distaste. Every one was very distinctly aware of the twelve other ironclads, and of the multitude of townsmen soldiers on bicycles or afoot, encumbered now by prisoners and captured war-gear but otherwise thoroughly effective, who were sweeping like a great net in their rear.

"Checkmate," said the war correspondent, walking out into the open. "But I surrender in the best of company. Twenty-four hours ago I thought war was impossible—and these beggars have captured the whole blessed army! Well! Well!" He thought of his talk with the young lieutenant. "If there's no end to the surprises of science, the civilised people have it, of course. As long as their science keeps going they will necessarily be ahead of open-country men. Still. . . ." He wondered for a space what might have happened to the young lieutenant.

The war correspondent was one of those inconsistent people who always want the beaten side to win. When he saw all these burly, sun-tanned horsemen, disarmed and dismounted and lined up; when he saw their horses unskilfully led away by the singularly not equestrian cyclists to whom they had surrendered; when he saw these truncated Paladins watching this scandalous sight, he forgot altogether that he had called these men "cunning louts" and wished them beaten not four-and-twenty hours ago. A month ago he had seen that regiment in its pride going forth to war, and had been told of its terrible prowess, how it could charge in open order with each man firing from his saddle, and sweep before it anything else that ever came out to battle in any sort of order, foot or horse. And it had had to fight a few score of young men in atrociously unfair machines!

"Manhood *versus* Machinery" occurred to him as a suitable headline. Journalism curdles all one's mind to phrases.

He strolled as near the lined-up prisoners as the sentinels seemed disposed to permit, and surveyed them and compared their sturdy proportions with those of their lightly built captors.

"Smart degenerates," he muttered. "Anæmic cockneydom."

The surrendered officers came quite close to him presently, and he could hear the colonel's high-pitched tenor. The poor gentleman had spent three years of arduous toil upon the best material in the world perfecting that shooting from the saddle charge, and he was inquiring with phrases of blasphemy, natural in the circumstances, what one could be expected to do against this suitably consigned ironmongery.

"Guns," said some one.

"Big guns they can walk round. You can't shift big guns to keep pace with them, and little guns in the open they rush. I saw 'em rushed. You might do a surprise now and then— assassinate the brutes, perhaps——"

"You might make things like 'em."

"What? *More* ironmongery? Us? . . ."

"I'll call my article," meditated the war corrsependent, "'Mankind *versus* Ironmongery,' and quote the old boy at the beginning."

And he was much too good a journalist to spoil his contrast by remarking that the half-dozen comparatively slender young men in blue pyjamas who were standing about their victorious land ironclad, drinking coffee and eating biscuits, had also in their eyes and carriage something not altogether degraded below the level of a man.

THE COUNTRY OF THE BLIND

THREE hundred miles and more from Chimborazo, one hundred from the snows of Cotopaxi, in the wildest wastes of Ecuador's Andes, there lies that mysterious mountain valley, cut off from the world of men, the Country of the Blind. Long years ago that valley lay so far open to the world that men might come at last through frightful gorges and over an icy pass into its equable meadows; and thither indeed men came, a family or so of Peruvian half-breeds fleeing from the lust and tyranny of an evil Spanish ruler. Then came the stupendous outbreak of Mindobamba, when it was night in Quito for seventeen days, and the water was boiling at Yagua-chi and all the fish floating dying even as far as Guayaquil; everywhere along the Pacific slopes there were landslips and swift thawings and sudden floods, and one whole side of the old Arauca crest slipped and came down in thunder, and cut off the Country of the Blind for ever from the exploring feet of men. But one of these early settlers had chanced to be on the hither side of the gorges when the world had so terribly shaken itself, and he perforce had to forget his wife and his child and all the friends and possessions he had left up there, and start life over again in the lower world. He started it again but ill, blindness overtook him, and he died of punishment in the mines; but the story he told begot a legend that lingers along the length of the Cordilleras of the Andes to this day.

He told of his reason for venturing back from that fastness, into which he had first been carried lashed to a llama, beside a vast bale of gear, when he was a child. The valley, he said, had in it all that the heart of man could desire—sweet water, pasture, an even climate, slopes of rich brown soil with tangles of a shrub that bore an excellent fruit, and on one side great hanging forests of pine that held the avalanches high. Far overhead, on three sides, vast cliffs of grey-green rock were capped by cliffs of ice; but the glacier stream came not to them but flowed away by the farther slopes, and only now and then huge ice masses fell on the valley side. In this valley it neither rained nor snowed, but the abundant springs gave a rich green pasture, that irrigation would spread over all the valley space. The settlers did well indeed there. Their beasts did well and multiplied, and but one thing marred their happiness. Yet it was enough to mar it greatly. A strange disease had come upon them, and had made all the children born to them there—and indeed, several older children also —blind. It was to seek some charm or antidote against this plague of blindness that he had with fatigue and danger and difficulty returned down the gorge. In those days, in such cases, men did not think of germs and infections but of sins; and it seemed to him that the reason of this affliction must lie in the negligence of these priestless immigrants to set up a shrine so soon as they entered the valley. He wanted a shrine—a handsome, cheap, effectual shrine—to be erected in the valley; he wanted relics and such-like potent things of faith, blessed objects and mysterious medals and prayers. In his wallet he had a bar of native silver for which he would not account; he insisted there was none in the valley with something of the insistence of an inexpert liar. They had all clubbed their money and ornaments together, having little need for such treasure up there, he said, to buy them holy help against their ill. I figure this dim-eyed young mountaineer, sunburnt, gaunt, and anxious, hat-brim clutched feverishly, a man all unused to the ways of the lower world, telling this story to some keen-eyed, attentive priest before the great convulsion; I can picture him presently seeking to return with pious and infallible remedies against that trouble, and the infinite dismay with which he must have faced the tumbled vastness where the gorge had once come out. But the rest of his story of mischances is lost to me, save that I know of his evil death after several years. Poor stray from that remoteness! The stream that had once made the gorge now bursts from the mouth of a rocky cave, and the legend his poor, ill-told story set going developed into the legend of a race of blind men somewhere "over there" one may still hear to-day.

And amidst the little population of that now isolated and forgotten valley the disease ran its course. The old became groping and purblind, the young saw but dimly, and the children that were born to them saw never at all. But life was very easy in that snow-rimmed basin, lost to all the world, with neither thorns nor briars, with no evil insects nor any beasts save the gentle breed of llamas they had lugged and thrust and followed up the beds of the shrunken rivers in the gorges up which they had come. The seeing had become purblind so gradually that they scarcely noted their loss. They guided the sightless youngsters hither and thither until they knew the whole valley marvellously, and when at last sight died out among them the race lived on. They had even time to adapt themselves to the blind control of fire, which they made carefully in stoves of stone. They were a simple strain of people at the first, unlettered, only slightly touched with the Spanish civilisation, but with something of a tradition of the arts of old Peru and of its lost philosophy. Generation followed generation. They forgot many things; they devised many things. Their tradition of the greater world they came from became mythical in colour and uncertain. In all things save sight they were strong and able; and presently the chance of birth and heredity sent one who had an original mind and who could talk and persuade among them, and then afterwards another. These two passed, leaving their effects, and the little community grew in numbers and in understanding, and met and settled social and economic problems that arose. Generation followed generation. There came a time when a child was born who was fifteen generations from that ancestor who went out of the valley with a bar of silver to seek God's aid, and who never returned. Thereabouts it chanced that a man came into this community from the outer world. And this is the story of that man.

He was a mountaineer from the country near Quito, a man who had been down to the sea and had seen the world, a reader of books in an original way, an acute and enterprising man, and he was taken on by a party of Englishmen who had come out to Ecuador to climb mountains, to replace one of their three Swiss guides who had fallen ill. He climbed here and he climbed there, and then came the attempt on Parascotopetl, the Matterhorn of the Andes, in which he was lost to the outer world. The story of the accident has been written a dozen times. Pointer's narrative is the best. He tells how the party worked their difficult and almost vertical way up to the very foot of the last and greatest precipice, and how they built a night shelter amidst the snow upon a little shelf of rock, and, with a touch of real dramatic power, how presently they found Nunez had gone from them. They shouted, and there was no reply; shouted and whistled, and for the rest of that night they slept no more.

As the morning broke they saw the traces of his fall. It seems impossible he could have uttered a sound. He had slipped eastward towards the unknown side of the mountain; far below he had struck a steep slope of snow, and ploughed his way down it in the midst of a snow avalanche. His track went straight to the edge of a frightful precipice, and beyond that everything was hidden. Far, far below, and hazy with distance, they could see trees rising out of a narrow, shut-in valley—the lost Country of the Blind. But they did not know it was the lost Country of the Blind, nor distinguish it in any way from any other narrow streak of upland valley. Unnerved by this disaster, they abandoned their attempt in the afternoon, and Pointer was called away to the war before he could make another attack. To this day Parascotopetl lifts an unconquered crest, and Pointer's shelter crumbles unvisited amidst the snows.

And the man who fell survived.

At the end of the slope he fell a thousand feet, and came down in the midst of a cloud of snow upon a snow slope even steeper than the one above. Down this he was whirled, stunned and insensible, but without a bone broken in his body; and then at last came to gentler slopes, and at last rolled out and lay still, buried amidst a softening heap of the white masses that had accompanied and saved him. He came to himself with a dim fancy that he was ill in bed; then realised his position with a mountaineer's intelligence, and worked himself loose, and after a rest or so, out until he saw the stars. He rested flat upon his chest for a space, wondering where he was and what had happened to him. He explored his limbs, and discovered that several of his buttons were gone and his coat turned over his head. His knife had gone from his pocket and his hat was lost, though he had tied it under his chin. He recalled that he had been looking for loose stones to raise his piece of the shelter wall. His ice-axe had disappeared.

He decided he must have fallen, and looked up to see, exaggerated by the ghastly light of the rising moon, the tremendous flight he had taken. For a while he lay, gazing blankly at that vast pale cliff towering above, rising moment by moment out of a subsiding tide of darkness. Its phantasmal mysterious beauty held him for a space, and then he was seized with a paroxysm of sobbing laughter. . . .

After a great interval of time he became aware that he was near the lower edge of the snow. Below, down what was now a moonlit and practicable slope, he saw the dark and broken appearance of rock-strewn turf. He struggled to his feet, aching in every joint and limb, got down painfully from the heaped loose snow about him, went downward until he was on the turf, and there dropped rather than lay beside a boulder, drank deep from the flask in his inner pocket, and instantly fell asleep. . . .

He was awakened by the singing of birds in the trees far below.

He sat up and perceived he was on a little alp at the foot of a vast precipice, that was grooved by the gully down which he and his snow had come. Over against him another wall of rock reared itself against the sky. The gorge between these precipices ran east and west and was full of the morning sunlight, which lit to the westward the mass of fallen mountain that closed the descending gorge. Below him it seemed there was a precipice equally steep, but behind the snow in the gully he found a sort of chimney-cleft dripping with snow-water down which a desperate man might venture. He found it easier than it seemed, and came at last to another desolate alp, and then after a rock climb of no particular difficulty to a steep slope of trees. He took his bearings and turned his face up the gorge, for he saw it opened out above upon green meadows, among which he now glimpsed quite distinctly a cluster of stone huts of unfamiliar fashion. At times his progress was like clambering along the face of a wall, and after a time the rising sun ceased to strike along the gorge, the voices of the singing birds died away, and the air grew cold and dark about him. But the distant valley with its houses was all the brighter for that. He came presently to talus, and among the rocks he noted—for he was an observant man—an unfamiliar fern that seemed to clutch out of the crevices with intense green hands. He picked a frond or so and gnawed its stalk and found it helpful.

About midday he came at last out of the throat of the gorge into the plain and the sunlight. He was stiff and weary; he sat down in the shadow of a rock, filled up his flask with water from a spring and drank it down, and remained for a time resting before he went on to the houses.

They were very strange to his eyes, and indeed the whole aspect of that valley became, as he regarded it, queerer and more unfamiliar. The greater part of its surface was lush green meadow, starred with many beautiful flowers, irrigated with extraordinary care, and bearing evidence of systematic cropping piece by piece. High up and ringing the valley about was a wall, and what appeared to be a circumferential water-channel, from which the little trickles of water that fed the meadow plants came, and on the higher slopes above this flocks of llamas cropped the scanty herbage. Sheds, apparently shelters or feeding-places for the llamas, stood against the boundary wall here and there. The irrigation streams ran together into a main channel down the centre of the valley, and this was enclosed on either side by a wall breast high. This gave a singularly urban quality to this secluded place, a quality that was greatly enhanced by the fact that a number of paths paved with black and white stones, and each with a curious little kerb at the side, ran hither and thither in an orderly manner. The houses of the central village were quite unlike the casual and higgledy-piggledy agglomeration of the mountain villages he knew; they stood in a continuous row on either side of a central street of astonishing cleanness; here and there their parti-coloured facade was pierced by a door, and not a solitary window broke their even frontage. They were parti-coloured with extraordinary irregularity; smeared with a sort of plaster that was sometimes grey, sometimes drab, sometimes slate-coloured or dark brown; and it was the sight of this wild plastering first brought the word "blind" into the thoughts of the explorer. "The good man who did that," he thought, "must have been as blind as a bat."

He descended a steep place, and so came to the wall and channel that ran about the valley, near where the latter spouted out its surplus contents into the deeps of the gorge in a thin and wavering thread of cascade. He could now see a number of men and women resting on piled heaps of grass, as if taking a siesta, in the remoter part of the meadow, and nearer the village a number of recumbent children, and then nearer at hand three men carrying pails on yokes along a little path that ran from the encircling wall towards the houses. These latter were clad in garments of llama cloth and boots and belts of leather, and they wore caps of cloth with back and ear flaps. They followed one another in single file, walking slowly and yawning as they walked, like men who have been up all night. There was something so reassuringly prosperous and respectable in their bearing that after a moment's hesitation Núñez stood forward as conspicuously as possible upon his rock, and gave vent to a mighty shout that echoed round the valley.

The three men stopped, and moved their heads as though they were looking about them. They turned their faces this way and that, and Núñez gesticulated with freedom. But they did not appear to see him for all his gestures, and after a time, directing themselves towards the mountains far away to the right, they shouted as if in answer. Núñez bawled again, and then once more, and as he gestured ineffectually the word "blind" came up to the top of his thoughts. "The fools must be blind," he said.

When at last, after much shouting and wrath, Núñez crossed the stream by a little bridge, came through a gate in the wall, and approached them, he was sure that they were blind. He was sure that this was the Country of the Blind of which the legends told. Conviction had sprung upon him, and a sense of great and rather enviable adventure. The three stood side by side, not looking at him, but with their ears directed towards him, judging him by his unfamiliar steps. They stood close together like men a little afraid, and he could see their eyelids closed and sunken, as though the very balls beneath had shrunk away. There was an expression near awe on their faces.

"A man," one said, in hardly recognisable Spanish—"a man it is—a man or a spirit—coming down from the rocks."

But Núñez advanced with the confident steps of a youth who enters upon life. All the old stories of the lost valley and the Country of the Blind had come back to his mind, and through his thoughts ran this old proverb, as if it were a refrain—

"In the Country of the Blind the One-eyed Man is King."

"In the Country of the Blind the One-eyed Man is King."

And very civilly he gave them greeting. He talked to them and used his eyes.

"Where does he come from, brother Pedro?" asked one.

"Down out of the rocks."

"Over the mountains I come," said Núñez, "out of the country beyond there—where men can see. From near Bogota, where there are a hundred thousands of people, and where the city passes out of sight."

"Sight?" muttered Pedro. "Sight?"

"He comes," said the second blind man, "out of the rocks."

The cloth of their coats Núñez saw was curiously fashioned, each with a different sort of stitching.

They startled him by a simultaneous movement towards

him, each with a hand outstretched. He stepped back from the advance of these spread fingers.

"Come hither," said the third blind man, following his motion and clutching him neatly.

And they held Núñez and felt him over, saying no word further until they had done so.

"Carefully," he cried, with a finger in his eye, and found they thought that organ, with its fluttering lids, a queer thing in him. They went over it again.

"A strange creature, Correa," said the one called Pedro. "Feel the coarseness of his hair. Like a llama's hair."

"Rough he is as the rocks that begot him," said Correa, investigating Núñez's unshaven chin with a soft and slightly moist hand. "Perhaps he will grow finer." Núñez struggled a little under their examination, but they gripped him firm.

"Carefully," he said again.

"He speaks," said the third man. "Certainly he is a man."

"Ugh!" said Pedro, at the roughness of his coat.

"And you have come into the world?" asked Pedro.

"*Out* of the world. Over mountains and glaciers; right over above there, halfway to the sun. Out of the great big world that goes down, twelve days' journey to the sea."

They scarcely seemed to heed him. "Our fathers have told us men may be made by the forces of Nature," said Correa. "It is the warmth of things and moisture, and rottenness—rottenness."

"Let us lead him to the elders," said Pedro.

"Shout first," said Correa, "lest the children be afraid. This is a marvellous occasion."

So they shouted, and Pedro went first and took Núñez by the hand to lead him to the houses.

He drew his hand away. "I can see," he said.

"See?" said Correa.

"Yes, see," said Núñez, turning towards him, and stumbled against Pedro's pail.

"His senses are still imperfect," said the third blind man. "He stumbles, and talks unmeaning words. Lead him by the hand."

"As you will," said Núñez, and was led along, laughing.

It seemed they knew nothing of sight.

Well, all in good time he would teach them.

He heard people shouting, and saw a number of figures gathering together in the middle roadway of the village.

He found it tax his nerve and patience more than he had anticipated, that first encounter with the population of the Country of the Blind. The place seemed larger as he drew near to it, and the smeared plasterings queerer, and a crowd of children and men and women (the women and girls, he was pleased to note, had some of them quite sweet faces, for all that their eyes were shut and sunken) came about him, holding on to him, touching him with soft, sensitive hands, smelling at him, and listening at every word he spoke. Some of the maidens and children, however, kept aloof as if afraid, and indeed his voice seemed coarse and rude beside their softer notes. They mobbed him. His three guides kept close to him with an effect of proprietorship, and said again and again, "A wild man out of the rocks."

"Bogotá," he said. "Bogotá. Over the mountain crests."

"A wild man—using wild words," said Pedro. "Did you hear that—*Bogotá*? His mind is hardly formed yet. He has only the beginnings of speech."

A little boy nipped his hand. "Bogotá!" he said mockingly.

"Ay! A city to your village, I come from the great world—where men have eyes and see."

"His name's Bogotá," they said.

"He stumbled," said Correa, "stumbled twice as we came hither."

"Bring him to the elders."

And they thrust him suddenly through a doorway into a room as black as pitch, save at the end there faintly glowed a fire. The crowd closed in behind him and shut out all but the faintest glimmer of day, and before he could arrest himself he had fallen headlong over the feet of a seated man. His arm, out-flung, struck the face of someone else as he went down; he felt the soft impact of features and heard a cry of anger, and for a moment he struggled against a number of hands that clutched him. It was a one-sided fight. An inkling of the situation came to him, and he lay quiet.

"I fell down," he said; "I couldn't see in this pitchy darkness."

There was a pause as if the unseen persons about him tried to understand his words. Then the voice of Correa said: "He is but newly formed. He stumbles as he walks and mingles words that mean nothing with his speech."

Others also said things about him that he heard or understood imperfectly.

"May I sit up?" he asked, in a pause. "I will not struggle against you again."

They consulted and let him rise.

The voice of an older man began to question him, and Núñez found himself trying to explain the great world out of which he had fallen, and the sky and mountains and sight and such-like marvels, to these elders who sat in darkness in the Country of the Blind. And they would believe and understand nothing whatever he told them, a thing quite outside his expectation. They would not even understand many of his words. For fourteen generations these people had been blind and cut off from all the seeing world; the names for all the things of sight had faded and changed; the story of the outer world was faded and changed to a child's story; and they had ceased to concern themselves with anything beyond the rocky slopes above their circling wall. Blind men of genius had arisen among them and questioned the shreds of belief and tradition they had brought with them from their seeing days, and had dismissed all these things as idle fancies, and replaced them with new and saner explanations. Much of their imagination had shrivelled with their eyes, and they had made for themselves new imaginations with their ever more sensitive ears and finger-tips. Slowly Núñez realised this; that his expectation of wonder and reverence at his origin and his gifts was not to be borne out; and after his poor attempt to explain sight to them had been set aside as the confused version of a new-made being describing the marvels of his incoherent sensations, he subsided, a little dashed, into listening to their instruction. And the eldest of the blind men explained to him life and philosophy and religion, how that the world (meaning their valley) had been first an empty hollow in the rocks, and then had come, first, inanimate things without the gift of touch, and llamas and a few other creatures that had little sense, and then men, and at last angels, whom one could hear singing and making fluttering sounds, but whom no one could touch at all, which puzzled Núñez greatly until he thought of the birds.

He went on to tell Núñez how this time had been divided into the warm and the cold, which are the blind equivalents of day and night, and how it was good to sleep in the warm and work during the cold, so that now, but for his advent, the whole town of the blind would have been asleep. He said Núñez must have been specially created to learn and serve the wisdom they had acquired, and for that all his mental incoherency and stumbling behaviour he must have courage and do his best to learn, and at that all the people in the doorway murmured encouragingly. He said the night—for the blind call their day night—was now far gone, and it behooved everyone to go back to sleep. He asked Núñez if he knew how to sleep, and Núñez said he did, but that before sleep he wanted food.

They brought him food—llama's milk in a bowl, and rough salted bread—and led him into a lonely place to eat out of their hearing, and afterwards to slumber until the chill of the mountain evening roused them to begin their day again. But Núñez slumbered not at all.

Instead, he sat up in the place where they had left him, resting his limbs and turning the unanticipated circumstances of his arrival over and over in his mind.

Every now and then he laughed, sometimes with amusement, and sometimes with indignation.

"Unformed mind!" he said. "Got no senses yet! They little know they've been insulting their heaven-sent king and master. I see I must bring them to reason. Let me think—let me think."

He was still thinking when the sun set.

Núñez had an eye for all beautiful things, and it seemed to him that the glow upon the snowfields and glaciers that rose about the valley on every side was the most beautiful thing he had ever seen. His eyes went from that inaccessible glory to the village and irrigated fields, fast sinking into the twilight, and suddenly a wave of emotion took him, and he thanked God from the bottom of his heart that the power of sight had been given him.

He heard a voice calling to him from out of the village.

"Ya ho there, Bogotá! Come hither!"

At that he stood up smiling. He would show these people once and for all what sight would do for a man. They would seek him, but not find him.

"You move not, Bogotá," said the voice.

He laughed noiselessly, and made two stealthy steps aside from the path.

"Trample not on the grass, Bogotá; that is not allowed."

Núñez had scarcely heard the sound he made himself. He stopped, amazed.

The owner of the voice came running up the piebald path towards him.

He stepped back into the pathway. "Here I am," he said.

"Why did you not come when I called you?" said the blind man. "Must you be led like a child? Cannot you hear the path as you walk?"

Núñez laughed. "I can see it," he said.

"There is no such word as *see*," said the blind man, after a pause. "Cease this folly, and follow the sound of my feet."

Núñez followed, a little annoyed.

"My time will come," he said.

"You'll learn," the blind man answered. "There is much to learn in the world."

"Has no one told you, 'In the Country of the Blind the One-eyed Man is King'?"

"What is blind?" asked the blind man carelessly over his shoulder.

Four days passed, and the fifth found the King of the Blind still incognito, as a clumsy and useless stranger among his subjects.

It was, he found, much more difficult to proclaim himself than he had supposed, and in the meantime, while he meditated his *coup d'état*, he did what he was told and learned the manners and customs of the Country of the Blind. He found working and going about at night a particularly irksome thing, and he decided that that should be the first thing he would change.

They led a simple, laborious life, these people, with all the elements of virtue and happiness, as these things can be understood by men. They toiled, but not oppressively; they had food and clothing sufficient for their needs; they had days and seasons of rest; they made much of music and singing, and there was love among them, and little children.

It was marvellous with what confidence and precision they went about their ordered world. Everything, you see, had been made to fit their needs; each of the radiating paths of the valley area had a constant angle to the others, and was distinguished by a special notch upon its kerbing; all obstacles and irregularities of path or meadow had long since been cleared away; all their methods and procedure arose naturally from their special needs. Their senses had become marvellously acute; they could hear and judge the slightest gesture of a man a dozen paces away—could hear the very beating of his heart. Intonation had long replaced expression with them, and touches gesture, and their work with hoe and spade and fork was as free and confident as garden work can be. Their sense of smell was extraordinarily fine; they could distinguish individual differences as readily as a dog can, and they went about the tending of the llamas, who lived among the rocks above and came to the wall for food and shelter, with ease and confidence. It was only when at last Núñez sought to assert himself that he found how easy and confident their movements could be.

He rebelled only after he had tried persuasion.

He tried at first on several occasions to tell them of sight.

"Look you here, you people," he said. "There are things you do not understand in me."

Once or twice one or two of them attended to him; they sat with faces downcast and ears turned intelligently towards him, and he did his best to tell them what it was to see. Among his hearers was a girl, with eyelids less red and sunken than the others, so that one could almost fancy she was hiding eyes, whom especially he hoped to persuade. He spoke of the beauties of sight, of watching the mountains, of the sky and the sunrise, and they heard him with amused incredulity that presently became condemnatory. They told him there were indeed no mountains at all, but that the end of the rocks where the llamas grazed was indeed the end of the world; thence sprang a cavernous roof of the universe, from which the dew and the avalanches fell; and when he maintained stoutly the world had neither end nor roof such as they supposed, they said his thoughts were wicked. So far as he could describe sky and clouds and stars to them it seemed to them a hideous void, a terrible blankness in the place of the smooth roof to things in which they believed—it was an article of faith with them that the cavern roof was exquisitely smooth to the touch. He saw that in some manner he shocked them, and gave up that aspect of the matter altogether, and tried to show them the practical value of sight. One morning he saw Pedro in the path called Seventeen and coming towards the central houses, but still too far off for hearing or scent, and he told them as much. "In a little while," he prophesied, "Pedro will be here." An old man remarked that Pedro had no business on Path Seventeen, and then, as if in confirmation, that individual as he drew near turned and went transversely into Path Ten, and so back with nimble paces towards the outer wall. They mocked Núñez when Pedro did not arrive, and afterwards, when he asked Pedro questions to clear his character, Pedro denied and outfaced him, and was afterwards hostile to him.

Then he induced them to let him go a long way up the sloping meadows towards the wall with one complacent individual, and to him he promised to describe all that happened among the houses. He noted certain goings and comings, but the things that really seemed to signify to these people happened inside of or behind the windowless houses—the only things they took note of to test him by—and of these he could see or tell nothing; and it was after the failure of this attempt, and the ridicule they could not repress, that he resorted to force. He thought of seizing a spade and suddenly smiting one or two of them to earth, and so in fair combat showing the advantage of eyes. He went so far with that resolution as to seize his spade, and then he discovered a new thing about himself, and that was that it was impossible for him to hit a blind man in cold blood.

He hesitated, and found them all aware that he snatched up the spade. They stood alert, with their heads on one side, and bent ears towards him for what he would do next.

"Put that spade down," said one, and he felt a sort of helpless horror. He came near obedience.

Then he thrust one backwards against a house wall, and fled past him and out of the village.

He went athwart one of their meadows, leaving a track of trampled grass behind his feet, and presently sat down by the side of one of their ways. He felt something of the buoyancy that comes to all men in the beginning of a fight, but more perplexity. He began to realise that you cannot even fight happily with creatures who stand upon a different mental basis to yourself. Far away he saw a number of men carrying spades and sticks come out of the street of houses, and advance in a spreading line along the several paths towards him. They advanced slowly, speaking frequently to one another, and ever and again the whole cordon would halt and sniff the air and listen.

The first time they did this Núñez laughed. But afterwards he did not laugh.

One struck his trail in the meadow grass, and came stooping and feeling his way along it.

For five minutes he watched the slow extension of the cordon, and then his vague disposition to do something forthwith became frantic. He stood up, went a pace or so towards the circumferential wall, turned, and went back a little way. There they all stood in a crescent, still and listening.

He also stood still, gripping his spade very tightly in both hands. Should he charge them?

The pulse in his ears ran into the rhythm of "In the Country of the Blind the One-eyed Man is King!"

Should he charge them?

He looked back at the high and unclimbable wall behind— unclimbable because of its smooth plastering, but withal pierced with many little doors, and at the approaching line of seekers. Behind these, others were now coming out of the street of houses.

Should he charge them?

"Bogotá!" called one. "Bogotá! where are you?"

He gripped his spade still tighter, and advanced down the meadows towards the place of habitations, and directly he moved they converged upon him. "I'll hit them if they touch me," he swore; "by Heaven, I will. I'll hit." He called aloud, "Look here, I'm going to do what I like in this valley. Do you hear? I'm going to do what I like and go where I like!"

They were moving in upon him quickly, groping, yet moving rapidly. It was like playing blind man's buff, with everyone blindfolded except one. "Get hold of him!" cried one. He found himself in the arc of a loose curve of pursuers. He felt suddenly he must be active and resolute.

"You don't understand," he cried in a voice that was meant to be great and resolute, and which broke. "You are blind, and I can see. Leave me alone!"

"Bogotá! Put down that spade, and come off the grass!"

The last order, grotesque in its urban familiarity, produced a gust of anger.

"I'll hurt you," he said, sobbing with emotion. "By Heaven, I'll hurt you. Leave me alone!"

He began to run, not knowing clearly where to run. He ran from the nearest blind man, because it was a horror to hit him. He stopped, and then made a dash to escape from their closing ranks. He made for where a gap was wide, and the men on either side, with a quick perception of the approach of his paces, rushed in on one another. He sprang forward, and then saw he must be caught, and *swish!* the spade had struck. He felt the soft thud of hand and arm, and the man was down with a yell of pain, and he was through.

Through! And then he was close to the street of houses again, and blind men, whirling spades and stakes, were running with a sort of reasoned swiftness hither and thither.

He heard steps behind him just in time, and found a tall man rushing forward and swiping at the sound of him. He lost his nerve, hurled his spade a yard wide at his antagonist, and whirled about and fled, fairly yelling as he dodged another.

He was panic-stricken. He ran furiously to and fro, dodging when there was no need to dodge, and in his anxiety to see on every side of him at once, stumbling. For a moment he was down and they heard his fall. Far away in the circumferential wall a little doorway looked like heaven, and he set off in a wild rush for it. He did not even look round at his pursuers until it was gained, and he had stumbled across the bridge, clambered a little way among the rocks, to the surprise and dismay of a young llama, who went leaping out of sight, and lay down sobbing for breath.

And so his *coup d'etat* came to an end.

He stayed outside the wall of the valley of the Blind for two nights and days without food or shelter, and meditated upon the unexpected. During these meditations he repeated very frequently and always with a profounder note of derision the exploded proverb: "In the Country of the Blind the One-Eyed Man is King." He thought chiefly of ways of fighting and conquering these people, and it grew clear that for him no practicable way was possible. He had no weapons, and now it would be hard to get one.

The canker of civilisation had got to him even in Bogotá, and he could not find it in himself to go down and assassinate a blind man. Of course, if he did that, he might then dictate terms on the threat of assassinating them all. But—sooner or later he must sleep! . . .

He tried also to find food among the pine trees, to be comfortable under pine boughs while the frost fell at night, and—with less confidence—to catch a llama by artifice in order to try to kill it—perhaps by hammering it with a stone —and so finally, perhaps, to eat some of it. But the llamas had a doubt of him and regarded him with distrustful brown eyes, and spat when he drew near. Fear came on him the second day and fits of shivering. Finally he crawled down to the wall of the Country of the Blind and tried to make terms. He crawled along by the stream, shouting, until two blind men came out to the gate and talked ro him.

"I was mad," he said. "But I was only newly made."

They said that was better.

He told them he was wiser now, and repented of all he had done.

Then he wept without intention, for he was very weak and ill now, and they took that as a favourable sign.

They asked him if he still thought he could "*see*."

"No," he said. "That was folly. The word means nothing— less than nothing!"

They asked him what was overhead.

"About ten times ten the height of a man there is a roof above the world—of rock—and very, very smooth." . . . He burst again into hysterical tears. "Before you ask me any more, give me some food or I shall die."

He expected dire punishments, but these blind people were capable of toleration. They regarded his rebellion as but one more proof of his general idiocy and inferiority; and after they had whipped him they appointed him to do the simplest and heaviest work they had for anyone to do, and he, seeing no other way of living, did submissively what he was told.

He was ill for some days, and they nursed him kindly. That refined his submission. But they insisted on his lying in the dark, and that was a great misery. And blind philosophers came and talked to him of the wicked levity of his mind, and reproved him so impressively for his doubts about the lid of rock that covered their cosmic casserole that he almost doubted whether indeed he was not the victim of hallucination in not seeing it overhead.

So Núñez became a citizen of the Country of the Blind, and these people ceased to be a generalised people and became individualities and familiar to him, while the world beyond the mountains became more and more remote and unreal. There was Yacob, his master, a kindly man when not annoyed; there was Pedro, Yacob's nephew; and there was Medinasaroté, who was the youngest daughter of Yacob. She was little esteemed in the world of the Blind, because she had a clear-cut face, and lacked that satisfying, glossy smoothness that is the blind man's ideal of feminine beauty; but Núñez thought her beautiful at first, and presently the most beautiful thing in the whole creation. Her closed eyelids were not sunken and red after the common way of the valley, but lay as though they might open again at any moment; and she had long eyelashes, which were considered a grave disfigurement. And her voice was strong, and did not satisfy the acute hearing of the valley swains. So that she had no lover.

There came a time when Núñez thought that, could he win her, he would be resigned to live in the valley for all the rest of his days.

He watched her; he sought opportunities of doing her little services, and presently he found that she observed him. Once at a rest-day gathering they sat side by side in the dim starlight, and the music was sweet. His hand came upon hers and he dared to clasp it. Then very tenderly she returned his pressure. And one day, as they were at their meal in the darkness, he felt her hand very softly seeking him, and as it chanced the fire leaped then and he saw the tenderness of her face.

He sought to speak to her.

He went to her one day when she was sitting in the summer moonlight spinning. The light made her a thing of silver and mystery. He sat down at her feet and told her he loved her, and told her how beautiful she seemed to him. He had a lover's voice, he spoke with a tender reverence that came near to awe, and she had never before been touched by adoration. She made him no definite answer, but it was clear his words pleased her.

After that he talked to her whenever he could take an opportunity. The valley became the world for him, and the world beyond the mountains where men lived in sunlight seemed no more than a fairy tale he would some day pour into her ears. Very tentatively and timidly he spoke to her of sight.

Sight seemed to her the most poetical of fancies, and she listened to his description of the stars and the mountains and her own sweet white-lit beauty as though it was a guilty indulgence. She did not believe, she could only half understand, but she was mysteriously delighted, and it seemed to him that she completely understood.

His love lost its awe and took courage. Presently he was for demanding her of Yacob and the elders in marriage, but she became fearful and delayed. And it was one of her elder sisters who first told Yacob that Medina-sarote and Núñez were in love.

There was from the first very great opposition to the marriage of Núñez and Medina-sarote; not so much because they valued her as because they held him as a being apart, an idiot, incompetent thing below the permissible level of a man. Her sisters opposed it bitterly as bringing discredit on them all; and old Yacob, though he had formed a sort of liking for his clumsy, obedient serf, shook his head and said the thing could not be. The young men were all angry at the idea of corrupting the race, and one went so far as to revile and strike Núñez. He struck back. Then for the first time he found an advantage in seeing, even by twilight, and after that fight was over no one was disposed to raise a hand against him. But they still found his marriage impossible.

Old Yacob had a tenderness for his last little daughter, and was grieved to have her weep upon his shoulder.

"You see, my dear, he's an idiot. He has delusions; he can't do anything right."

"I know," wept Medina-sarote. "But he's better than he

was. He's getting better. And he's strong, dear father, and kind—stronger and kinder than any other man in the world. And he loves me—and, Father, I love him."

Old Yacob was greatly distressed to find her inconsolable, and, besides—what made it more distressing—he liked Núñez for many things. So he went and sat in the windowless council-chamber with the other elders and watched the trend of the talk, and said, at the proper time, "He's better than he was. Very likely, some day, we shall find him as sane as ourselves."

Then afterwards one of the elders, who thought deeply, had an idea. He was the great doctor among these people, their medicine-man, and he had a very philosophical and inventive mind, and the idea of curing Núñez of his peculiarities appealed to him. One day when Yacob was present he returned to the topic of Núñez.

"I have examined Bogotá," he said, "and the case is clearer to me. I think very probably he might be cured."

"That is what I have always hoped," said old Yacob.

"His brain is affected," said the blind doctor.

The elders murmured assent.

"Now, *what* affects it?"

"Ah!" said old Yacob.

"*This,*" said the doctor, answering his own question. "Those queer things that are called the eyes, and which exist to make an agreeable soft depression in the face, are diseased, in the case of Bogotá, in such a way as to affect his brain. They are greatly distended, he has eyelashes, and his eyelids move, and consequently his brain is in a state of constant irritation and distraction."

"Yes?" said old Yacob. "Yes?"

"And I think I may say with reasonable certainty that, in order to cure him completely, all that we need do is a simple and easy surgical operation—namely, to remove these irritant bodies."

"And then he will be sane?"

"Then he will be perfectly sane, and a quite admirable citizen."

"Thank Heaven for science!" said old Yacob, and went forth at once to tell Núñez of his happy hopes.

But Núñez's manner of receiving the good news struck him as being cold and disappointing.

"One might think," he said, "from the tone you take, that you did not care for my daughter."

It was Medina-saroté who persuaded Núñez to face the blind surgeons.

"*You* do not want me," he said, "to lose my gift of sight?"

She shook her head.

"My world is sight."

Her head drooped lower.

"There are the beautiful things, the beautiful little things— the flowers, the lichens among the rocks, the lightness and softness on a piece of fur, the far sky with its drifting down of clouds, the sunsets and the stars. And there is *you*. For you alone it is good to have sight, to see your sweet, serene face, your kindly lips, your dear, beautiful hands folded together. . . . It is these eyes of mine you won, these eyes that hold me to you, that these idiots seek. Instead, I must touch you, hear you, and never see you again. I must come under that roof of rock and stone and darkness, that horrible roof under which your imagination stoops. . . . No; you would not have me do that?"

A disagreeable doubt had arisen in him. He stopped, and left the thing a question.

"I wish," she said, "sometimes——" She paused.

"Yes?" said he, a little apprehensively.

"I wish sometimes—you would not talk like that."

"Like what?"

"I know it's pretty—it's your imagination. I love it, but now——"

He felt cold. "*Now?*" he said faintly.

She sat still.

"You mean—you think—I should be better, better per-haps——"

He was realising things very swiftly. He felt anger, indeed, anger at the dull course of fate, but also sympathy for her lack of understanding—a sympathy near akin to pity.

"*Dear*," he said, and he could see by her whiteness how intensely her spirit pressed against the things she could not say. He put his arms about her, he kissed her ear, and they sat for a time in silence.

"If I were to consent to this?" he said at last, in a voice that was very gentle.

She flung her arms about him, weeping wildly. "Oh, if you would," she sobbed, "if only you would!"

For a week before the operation that was to raise him from his servitude and inferiority to the level of a blind citizen, Núñez knew nothing of sleep, and all through the warm sunlit hours, while the others slumbered happily, he sat brooding or wandered aimlessly, trying to bring his mind to bear on his dilemma. He had given his answer, he had given his consent, and still he was not sure. And at last work-time was over, the sun rose in splendour over the golden crests, and his last day of vision began for him. He had a few minutes with Medina-saroté before she went apart to sleep.

"To-morrow," he said, "I shall see no more."

"Dear heart!" she answered, and pressed his hands with all her strength.

"They will hurt you but little," she said; "and you are going through this pain—you are going through it, dear lover, for *me*. . . . Dear, if a woman's heart and life can do it, I will repay you. My dearest one, my dearest with the tender voice, I will repay."

He was drenched in pity for himself and her.

He held her in his arms, and pressed his lips to hers, and looked on her sweet face for the last time. "Good-bye!" he whispered at that dear sight, "good-bye!"

And then in silence he turned away from her.

She could hear his slow retreating footsteps, and something in the rhythm of them threw her into a passion of weeping.

He had fully meant to go to a lonely place where the meadows were beautiful with white narcissus, and there remain until the hour of his sacrifice should come, but as he went he lifted up his eyes and saw the morning, the morning like an angel in golden armour, marching down the steeps. . . .

It seemed to him that before this splendour he, and this blind world in the valley, and his love, and all, were no more than a pit of sin.

He did not turn aside as he had meant to do, but went on, and passed through the wall of the circumference and out upon the rocks, and his eyes were always upon the sunlit ice and snow.

He saw their infinite beauty, and his imagination soared over them to the things beyond he was now to resign for ever.

He thought of that great free world he was parted from, the world that was his own, and he had a vision of those further slopes, distance beyond distance, with Bogotá, a place of multitudinous stirring beauty, a glory by day, a luminous mystery by night, a place of palaces and fountains and statues and white houses, lying beautifully in the middle distance. He thought how for a day or so one might come down through passes, drawing ever nearer and nearer to its busy streets and ways. He thought of the river journey, day by day, from great Bogotá to the still vaster world beyond, through towns and villages, forest and desert places, the rushing river day by day, until its banks receded and the big steamers came splashing by, and one had reached the sea—the limitless sea, with its thousand islands, its thousands of islands, and its ships seen dimly far away in their incessant journeyings round and about that greater world. And there, unpent by mountains, one saw the sky—the sky, not such a disc as one saw it here, but an arch of immeasurable blue, a deep of deeps in which the circling stars were floating. . . .

His eyes scrutinised the great curtain of the mountains with a keener inquiry.

For example, if one went so, up that gully and to that chimney there, then one might come out high among those stunted pines that ran round in a sort of shelf and rose still higher and higher as it passed above the gorge. And then? That talus might be managed. Thence perhaps a climb might be found to take him up to the precipice that came below the snow; and if that chimney failed, then another farther to the east might serve his purpose better. And then? Then one would be out upon the amber-lit snow there, and halfway up to the crest of those beautiful desolations.

He glanced back at the village, then turned right round and regarded it steadfastly.

He thought of Medina-saroté, and she had become small and remote.

He turned again towards the mountain wall, down which the day had come to him.

Then very circumspectly he began to climb.

When sunset came he was no longer climbing, but he was far and high. He had been higher, but he was still very high. His clothes were torn, his limbs were blood-stained, he was bruised in many places, but he lay as if he were at his ease, and there was a smile on his face.

From where he rested the valley seemed as if it were in a pit and nearly a mile below. Already it was dim with haze and shadow, though the mountain summits around him were things of light and fire. The mountain summits around him were things of light and fire, and the little details of the rocks near at hand were drenched with subtle beauty—a vein of green mineral piercing the grey, the flash of crystal faces here and there, a minute, minutely beautiful orange lichen close beside his face. There were deep mysterious shadows in the gorge, blue deepening into purple, and purple into a luminous darkness, and overhead was the illimitable vastness of the sky. But he heeded these things no longer, but lay quite inactive there, smiling as if he were satisfied merely to have escaped from the valley of the Blind in which he had thought to be King.

The glow of the sunset passed, and the night came, and still he lay peacefully contented under the cold stars.

THE STOLEN BACILLUS

"THIS again," said the Bacteriologist, slipping a glass slide under the microscope, "is a preparation of the celebrated Bacillus of cholera—the cholera germ."

The pale-faced man peered down the microscope. He was evidently not accustomed to that kind of thing, and held a limp white hand over his disengaged eye. "I see very little," he said.

"Touch this screw," said the Bacteriologist; "perhaps the microscope is out of focus for you. Eyes vary so much. Just the fraction of a turn this way or that."

"Ah! now I see," said the visitor. "Not so very much to see after all. Little streaks and shreds of pink. And yet those little particles, those mere atomies, might multiply and devastate a city! Wonderful!"

He stood up, and releasing the glass slip from the microscope, held it in his hand towards the window. "Scarcely visible," he said, scrutinising the preparation. He hesitated. "Are these—alive? Are they dangerous now?"

"Those have been stained and killed," said the Bacteriologist. "I wish, for my own part, we could kill and stain every one of them in the universe."

"I suppose," the pale man said with a slight smile, "that you scarcely care to have such things about you in the living —in the active state?"

"On the contrary, we are obliged to," said the Bacteriologist. "Here, for instance——" He walked across the room and took up one of several sealed tubes. "Here is the living thing. This is a cultivation of the actual living disease bacteria." He hesitated. "Bottled cholera, so to speak."

A slight gleam of satisfaction appeared momentarily in the face of the pale man. "It's a deadly thing to have in your possession," he said, devouring the little tube with his eyes. The Bacteriologist watched the morbid pleasure in his visitor's expression. This man, who had visited him that afternoon with a note of introduction from an old friend, interested him from the very contrast of their dispositions. The lank black hair and deep grey eyes, the haggard expression and nervous manner, the fitful yet keen interest of his visitor were a novel change from the phlegmatic deliberations of the ordinary scientific worker with whom the Bacteriologist chiefly associated. It was perhaps natural, with a hearer evidently so impressionable to the lethal nature of his topic, to take the most effective aspect of the matter.

He held the tube in his hand thoughtfully. "Yes, here is the pestilence imprisoned. Only break such a little tube as this into a supply of drinking-water, say to these minute particles of life that one must needs stain and examine with the highest powers of the microscope even to see, and that one can neither smell nor taste—say to them, 'Go forth, increase and multiply, and replenish the cisterns,' and death—mysterious, untraceable death, death swift and terrible, death full of pain and indignity—would be released upon this city, and go hither and thither seeking his victims. Here he would take the husband from the wife, here the child from its mother, here the statesman from his duty, and here the toiler from his trouble. He would follow the water-mains, creeping along streets, picking out and punishing a house here and a house there where they did not boil their drinking-water, creeping into the wells of the mineral-water makers, getting washed into salad, and lying dormant in ices. He would wait ready to be drunk in the horse-troughs, and by unwary children in the public fountains. He would soak into the soil, to reappear in springs and wells at a thousand unexpected places. Once start him at the water supply, and before we could ring him in, and catch him again, he would have decimated the metropolis."

He stopped abruptly. He had been told rhetoric was his weakness.

"But he is quite safe here, you know—quite safe."

The pale-faced man nodded. His eyes shone. He cleared his throat. "These Anarchist—rascals," said he, "are fools, blind fools—to use bombs when this kind of thing is attainable. I think——"

A gentle rap, a mere light touch of the finger-nails was heard at the door. The Bacteriologist opened it. "Just a minute, dear," whispered his wife.

When he re-entered the laboratory his visitor was looking at his watch. "I had no idea I had wasted an hour of your time," he said. "Twelve minutes to four. I ought to have left here by half-past three. But your things were really too interesting. No, positively I cannot stop a moment longer. I have an engagement at four."

He passed out of the room reiterating his thanks, and the Bacteriologist accompanied him to the door, and then returned thoughtfully along the passage to his laboratory. He was musing on the ethnology of his visitor. Certainly the man was not a Teutonic type nor a common Latin one. "A morbid product, anyhow, I am afraid," said the Bacteriologist to himself. "How he gloated on those cultivations of disease-germs!" A disturbing thought struck him. He turned to the bench by the vapour-bath, and then very quickly to his writing-table. Then he felt hastily in his pockets, and then rushed to the door. "I may have put it down on the hall table," he said.

"Minnie!" he shouted hoarsely in the hall.

"Yes, dear," came a remote voice.

"Had I anything in my hand when I spoke to you, dear, just now?"

Pause.

"Nothing, dear, because I remember——"

"Blue ruin!" cried the Bacteriologist, and incontinently ran to the front door and down the steps of his house to the street.

Minnie, hearing the door slam violently, ran in alarm to the window. Down the street a slender man was getting into a cab. The Bacteriologist, hatless, and in his carpet slippers, was running and gesticulating wildly towards this group. One slipper came off, but he did not wait for it. "He has gone *mad!*" said Minnie; "it's that horrid science of his"; and, opening the window, would have called after him. The slender man, suddenly glancing round, seemed struck with the same idea of mental disorder. He pointed hastily to the Bacteriologist, said something to the cabman, the apron of the cab slammed, the whip swished, the horse's feet clattered, and in a moment cab, and Bacteriologist hotly in pursuit, had receded up the vista of the roadway and disappeared round the corner.

Minnie remained straining out of the window for a minute. Then she drew her head back into the room again. She was dumbfounded. "Of course he is eccentric," she meditated. "But running about London—in the height of the season, too—in his socks!" A happy thought struck her. She hastily put her bonnet on, seized his shoes, went into the hall, took down his hat and light overcoat from the pegs, emerged upon the doorstep, and hailed a cab that opportunely crawled by. "Drive me up the road and round Havelock Crescent, and see if we can find a gentleman running about in a velveteen coat and no hat."

"Velveteen coat, ma'am, and no 'at. Very good, ma'am." And the cabman whipped up at once in the most matter-of-fact way, as if he drove to this address every day in his life.

Some few minutes later the little group of cabmen and loafers that collects round the cabmen's shelter at Haverstock Hill were startled by the passing of a cab with a ginger-coloured screw of a horse, driven furiously.

They were silent as it went by, and then as it receded— "That's 'Arry 'Icks. Wot's *he* got?" said the stout gentleman known as Old Tootles.

"He's a-using his whip, he is, *to* rights," said the ostler boy.

"Hullo!" said poor old Tommy Byles; "here's another bloomin' loonatic. Blowed if there ain't."

"It's old George," said old Tootles, "and he's drivin' a loonatic, *as* you say. Ain't he a-clawin' out of the keb? Wonder if he's after 'Arry 'Icks?"

The group round the cabmen's shelter became animated. Chorus: "Go it, George!" "It's a race." "You'll ketch 'em!" "Whip up!"

"She's a goer, she is!" said the ostler boy.

"Strike me giddy!" cried old Tootles. "Here! *I'm* a-goin' to begin in a minute. Here's another comin'. If all the kebs in Hampstead ain't gone mad this morning!"

"It's a fieldmale this time," said the ostler boy.

"She's a followin' *him*," said old Tootles. "Usually the other way about."

"What's she got in her 'and?"

"Looks like a 'igh 'at."

"What a bloomin' lark it is! Three to one on old George," said the ostler boy. "Nexst!"

Minnie went by in a perfect roar of applause. She did not like it but she felt that she was doing her duty, and whirled on down Haverstock Hill and Camden Town High Street with her eyes ever intent on the animated back view of old George, who was driving her vagrant husband so incomprehensively away from her.

The man in the foremost cab sat crouched in the corner, his arms tightly folded, and the little tube that contained such vast possibilities of destruction gripped in his hand. His mood was a singular mixture of fear and exultation. Chiefly he was afraid of being caught before he could accomplish his purpose, but behind this was a vaguer but larger fear of the awfulness of his crime. But his exultation far exceeded his fear. No Anarchist before him had ever approached this conception of his. Ravachol, Vaillant, all those distinguished persons whose fame he had envied dwindled into insignificance beside him. He had only to make sure of the water supply, and break the little tube into a reservoir. How brilliantly he had planned it, forged the letter of introduction and got into the laboratory, and how brilliantly he had seized his opportunity! The world should hear of him at last. All those people who had sneered at him, neglected him, preferred other people to him, found his company undesirable, should consider him at last. Death, death, death! They had always treated him as a man of no importance. All the world had been in a conspiracy to keep him under. He would teach them yet what it is to isolate a man. What was this familiar

street? Great Saint Andrew's Street, of course! How fared
the chase? He craned out of the cab. The Bacteriologist was
scarcely fifty yards behind. That was bad. He would be
caught and stopped yet. He felt in his pocket for money, and
found half-a-sovereign. This he thrust up through the trap
in the top of the cab into the man's face. "More," he shouted,
"if only we get away."

The money was snatched out of his hand. "Right you are,"
said the cabman, and the trap slammed, and the lash lay
along the glistening side of the horse. The cab swayed, and
the Anarchist, half-standing under the trap, put the hand
containing the little glass tube upon the apron to preserve his
balance. He felt the brittle thing crack, and the broken half
of it rang upon the floor of the cab. He fell back into the
seat with a curse, and stared dismally at the two or three
drops of moisture on the apron.

He shuddered.

"Well! I suppose I shall be the first. *Phew!* Anyhow, I shall
be a Martyr. That's something. But it is a filthy death,
nevertheless. I wonder if it hurts as much as they say."

Presently a thought occurred to him—he groped between
his feet. A little drop was still in the broken end of the tube,
and he drank that to make sure. It was better to make sure.
At any rate, he would not fail.

Then it dawned upon him that there was no further need
to escape the Bacteriologist. In Wellington Street he told the
cabman to stop, and got out. He slipped on the step, and his
head felt queer. It was rapid stuff this cholera poison. He
waved his cabman out of existence, so to speak, and stood on
the pavement with his arms folded upon his breast awaiting
the arrival of the Bacteriologist. There was something tragic
in his pose. The sense of imminent death gave him a certain
dignity. He greeted his pursuer with a defiant laugh.

"Vive l'Anarchie! You are too late, my friend. I have
drunk it. The cholera is abroad!"

The Bacteriologist from his cab beamed curiously at him
through his spectacles. "You have drunk it! An Anarchist!
I see now." He was about to say something more, and then

checked himself. A smile hung in the corner of his mouth. He opened the apron of his cab as if to descend, at which the Anarchist waved him a dramatic farewell and strode off towards Waterloo Bridge, carefully jostling his infected body against as many people as possible. The Bacteriologist was so preoccupied with the vision of him that he scarcely manifested the slightest surprise at the appearance of Minnie upon the pavement with his hat and shoes and overcoat. "Very good of you to bring my things," he said, and remained lost in contemplation of the receding figure of the Anarchist.

"You had better get in," he said, still staring. Minnie felt absolutely convinced now that he was mad, and directed the cabman home on her own responsibility. "Put on my shoes? Certainly, dear," said he, as the cab began to turn, and hid the strutting black figure, now small in the distance, from his eyes. Then suddenly something grotesque struck him, and he laughed. Then he remarked, "It is really very serious, though."

"You see, that man came to my house to see me, and he is an Anarchist. No—don't faint, or I cannot possibly tell you the rest. And I wanted to astonish him, not knowing he was an Anarchist, and took up a cultivation of that new species of Bacterium I was telling you of, that infest, and I think cause, the blue patches upon various monkeys; and like a fool, I said it was Asiatic cholera. And he ran away with it to poison the water of London, and he certainly might have made things look blue for this civilised city. And now he has swallowed it. Of course, I cannot say what will happen, but you know it turned that kitten blue, and the three puppies—in patches, and the sparrow—bright blue. But the bother is, I shall have all the trouble and expense of preparing some more.

"Put on my coat on this hot day! Why? Because we might meet Mrs. Jabber. My dear, Mrs. Jabber is not a draught. But why should I wear a coat on a hot day because of Mrs. ——? Oh! *very* well."

THE FLOWERING OF THE
STRANGE ORCHID

THE buying of orchids always has in it a certain speculative flavour. You have before you the brown shrivelled lump of tissue, and for the rest you must trust your judgment, or the auctioneer, or your good-luck, as your taste may incline. The plant may be moribund or dead, or it may be just a respectable purchase, fair value for your money, or perhaps— for the thing has happened again and again—there slowly unfolds before the delighted eyes of the happy purchaser, day after day, some new variety, some novel richness, a strange twist of the labellum, or some subtler colouration or unexpected mimicry. Pride, beauty, and profit blossom together on one delicate green spike, and, it may be, even immortality. For the new miracle of Nature may stand in need of a new specific name, and what so convenient as that of its discoverer? "Johnsmithia"! There have been worse names.

It was perhaps the hope of some such happy discovery that made Winter-Wedderburn such a frequent attendant at these sales—that hope, and also, maybe, the fact that he had nothing else of the slightest interest to do in the world. He was a shy, lonely, rather ineffectual man, provided with just enough income to keep off the spur of necessity, and not enough nervous energy to make him seek any exacting employment. He might have collected stamps or coins, or translated Horace, or bound books, or invented new species of diatoms. But, as it happened, he grew orchids, and had one ambitious little hothouse.

"I have a fancy," he said over his coffee, "that something is going to happen to me to-day." He spoke—as he moved and thought—slowly.

"Oh, don't say *that!*" said his housekeeper—who was also

his remote cousin. For "something happening" was a euphemism that meant only one thing to her.

"You misunderstand me. I mean nothing unpleasant . . . though what I do mean I scarcely know.

"To-day," he continued, after a pause, "Peters' are going to sell a batch of plants from the Andamans and the Indies. I shall go up and see what they have. It may be I shall buy something good, unawares. That may be it."

He passed his cup for his second cupful of coffee.

"Are those the things collected by that poor young fellow you told me of the other day?" asked his cousin as she filled his cup.

"Yes," he said, and became meditative over a piece of toast.

"Nothing ever does happen to me," he remarked presently, beginning to think aloud. "I wonder why? Things enough happen to other people. There is Harvey. Only the other week—on Monday he picked up sixpence, on Wednesday his chicks all had the staggers, on Friday his cousin came home from Australia, and on Saturday he broke his ankle. What a whirl of excitement!—compared to me."

"I think I would rather be without so much excitement," said his housekeeper. "It can't be good for you."

"I suppose it's troublesome. Still . . . you see, nothing ever happens to me. When I was a little boy I never had accidents. I never fell in love as I grew up. Never married. . . . I wonder how it feels to have something happen to you, something really remarkable.

"That orchid-collector was only thirty-six—twenty years younger than myself—when he died. And he had been married twice and divorced once; he had had malarial fever four times, and once he broke his thigh. He killed a Malay once, and once he was wounded by a poisoned dart. And in the end he was killed by jungle-leeches. It must have all been very troublesome, but then it must have been very interesting, you know—except, perhaps, the leeches."

"I am sure it was not good for him," said the lady, with conviction.

"Perhaps not." And then Wedderburn looked at his watch. "Twenty-three minutes past eight. I am going up by the quarter to twelve train, so that there is plenty of time. I think I shall wear my alpaca jacket—it is quite warm enough—and my grey felt hat and brown shoes. I suppose——"

He glanced out of the window at the serene sky and sunlit garden, and then nervously at his cousin's face.

"I think you had better take an umbrella if you are going to London," she said in a voice that admitted of no denial. "There's all between here and the station coming back."

When he returned he was in a state of mild excitement. He had made a purchase. It was rare that he could make up his mind quickly enough to buy, but this time he had done so.

"There are Vandas," he said, "and a Dendrobe and some Palæonophis." He surveyed his purchases lovingly as he consumed his soup. They were laid out on the spotless tablecloth before him, and he was telling his cousin all about them as he slowly meandered through his dinner. It was his custom to live all his visits to London over again in the evening for her and his own entertainment.

"I knew something would happen to-day. And I have bought all these. Some of them—some of them—I feel sure, do you know, that some of them will be remarkable. I don't know how it is, but I feel just as sure as if someone had told me that some of these will turn out remarkable.

"That one"—he pointed to a shrivelled rhizome—"was not identified. It may be a Palæonophis—or it may not. It may be a new species, or even a new genus. And it was the last that poor Batten ever collected."

"I don't like the look of it," said his housekeeper. "It's such an ugly shape."

"To me it scarcely seems to have a shape."

"I don't like those things that stick out," said his housekeeper.

"It shall be put away in a pot to-morrow."

"It looks," said the housekeeper, "like a spider shamming dead."

Wedderburn smiled and surveyed the root with his head on one side. "It is certainly not a pretty lump of stuff. But you can never judge of these things from their dry appearance. It may turn out to be a very beautiful orchid indeed. How busy I shall be to-morrow! I must see to-night just exactly what to do with these things, and to-morrow I shall set to work.

"They found poor Batten lying dead, or dying, in a man-grove swamp—I forget which," he began again presently, "with one of these very orchids crushed up under his body. He had been unwell for some days with some kind of native fever, and I suppose he fainted. These mangrove swamps are very unwholesome. Every drop of blood, they say, was taken out of him by the jungle-leeches. It may be that very plant that cost him his life to obtain."

"I think none the better of it for that."

"Men must work though women may weep," said Wedder-burn with profound gravity.

"Fancy dying away from every comfort in a nasty swamp! Fancy being ill of fever with nothing to take but chlorodyne and quinine—if men were left to themselves they would live on chlorodyne and quinine—and no one round you but horrible natives! They say the Andaman islanders are most disgusting wretches—and, anyhow, they can scarcely make good nurses, not having the necessary training. And just for people in England to have orchids!"

"I don't suppose it was comfortable, but some men seem to enjoy that kind of thing," said Wedderburn. "Anyhow, the natives of his party were sufficiently civilised to take care of all his collection until his colleague, who was an ornithologist, came back again from the interior; though they could not tell the species of the orchid and had let it wither. And it makes these things more interesting."

"It makes them disgusting. I should be afraid of some of the malaria clinging to them. And just think, there has been a dead body lying across that ugly thing! I never thought of that before. There! I declare I cannot eat another mouthful of dinner."

"I will take them off the table if you like, and put them in the window-seat. I can see them just as well there."

The next few days he was indeed singularly busy in his steamy little hothouse, fussing about with charcoal, lumps of teak, moss, and all the other mysteries of the orchid cultivator. He considered he was having a wonderfully eventful time. In the evening he would talk about these new orchids to his friends, and over and over again he reverted to his expectation of something strange.

Several of the Vandas and the Dendrobium died under his care, but presently the strange orchid began to show signs of life. He was delighted and took his housekeeper right away from jam-making to see it at once, directly he made the discovery.

"That is a bud," he said, "and presently there will be a lot of leaves there, and those little things coming out here are aërial rootlets."

"They look to me like little white fingers poking out of the brown," said his housekeeper. "I don't like them."

"Why not?"

"I don't know. They look like fingers trying to get at you. I can't help my likes and dislikes."

"I don't know for certain, but I don't *think* there are any orchids I know that have aërial rootlets quite like that. It may be my fancy, of course. You see they are a little flattened at the ends."

"I don't like 'em," said his housekeeper, suddenly shivering and turning away. "I know it's very silly of me—and I'm very sorry, particularly as you like the thing so much. But I can't help thinking of that corpse."

"But it may not be that particular plant. That was merely a guess of mine."

His housekeeper shrugged her shoulders. "Anyhow I don't like it," she said.

Wedderburn felt a little hurt at her dislike to the plant. But that did not prevent his talking to her about orchids generally, and this orchid in particular, whenever he felt inclined.

"There are such queer things about orchids," he said one day; "such possibilities of surprises. You know, Darwin studied their fertilisation, and showed that the whole structure of an ordinary orchid-flower was contrived in order that moths might carry the pollen from plant to plant. Well, it seems that there are lots of orchids known the flower of which cannot possibly be used for fertilisation in that way. Some of the Cypripediums, for instance; there are no insects known that can possibly fertilise them, and some of them have never been found with seed."

"But how do they form new plants?"

"By runners and tubers, and that kind of outgrowth. That is easily explained. The puzzle is, what are the flowers for?"

"Very likely," he added, "*my* orchid may be something extraordinary in that way. If so I shall study it. I have often thought of making researches as Darwin did. But hitherto I have not found the time, or something else has happened to prevent it. The leaves are beginning to unfold now. I do wish you would come and see them!"

But she said that the orchid-house was so hot it gave her the headache. She had seen the plant once again, and the aërial rootlets, which were now some of them more than a foot long, had unfortunately reminded her of tentacles reaching out after something; and they got into her dreams, growing after her with incredible rapidity. So that she had settled to her entire satisfaction that she would not see that plant again, and Wedderburn had to admire its leaves alone. They were of the ordinary broad form, and a deep glossy green, with splashes and dots of deep red towards the base. He knew of no other leaves quite like them. The plant was placed on a low bench near the thermometer, and close by was a simple arrangement by which a tap dripped on the hot-water pipes and kept the air steamy. And he spent his afternoons now with some regularity meditating on the approaching flowering of this strange plant.

And at last the great thing happened. Directly he entered the little glass house he knew that the spike had burst out, although his great *Palæonophis Lowii* hid the corner where his new darling stood. There was a new odour in the air, a rich, intensely sweet scent, that overpowered every other in that crowded, steaming little greenhouse.

Directly he noticed this he hurried down to the strange orchid. And, behold! the trailing green spikes bore now three great splashes of blossom, from which this overpowering sweetness proceeded. He stopped before them in an ecstasy of admiration.

The flowers were white, with streaks of golden orange upon the petals; the heavy labellum was coiled into an intricate projection, and a wonderful bluish purple mingled there with the gold. He could see at once that the genus was altogether a new one. And the insufferable scent! How hot the place was! The blossoms swam before his eyes.

He would see if the temperature was right. He made a step towards the thermometer. Suddenly everything appeared unsteady. The bricks on the floor were dancing up and down. Then the white blossoms, the green leaves behind them, the whole greenhouse, seemed to sweep sideways, and then in a curve upward.

*   *   *   *   *

At half-past four his cousin made the tea, according to their invariable custom. But Wedderburn did not come in for his tea.

"He is worshipping that horrid orchid," she told herself, and waited ten minutes. "His watch must have stopped. I will go and call him."

She went straight to the hothouse, and, opening the door, called his name. There was no reply. She noticed that the air was very close, and loaded with an intense perfume. Then she saw something lying on the bricks between the hot-water pipes.

For a minute, perhaps, she stood motionless.

He was lying, face upward, at the foot of the strange orchid. The tentacle-like aërial rootlets no longer swayed freely in the air, but were crowded together, a tangle of grey ropes, and stretched tight with their ends closely applied to his chin and neck and hands.

She did not understand. Then she saw from under one of the exultant tentacles upon his cheek there trickled a little thread of blood.

With an inarticulate cry she ran towards him, and tried to pull him away from the leech-like suckers. She snapped two of these tentacles, and their sap dripped red.

Then the overpowering scent of the blossom began to make her head reel. How they clung to him! She tore at the tough ropes, and he and the white inflorescence swam about her. She felt she was fainting, knew she must not. She left him and hastily opened the nearest door, and, after she had panted for a moment in the fresh air, she had a brilliant inspiration. She caught up a flower-pot and smashed in the windows at the end of the greenhouse. Then she reëntered. She tugged now with renewed strength at Wedderburn's motic ss body, and brought the strange orchid crashing to the floor. It still clung with the grimmest tenacity to its victim. In a frenzy, she lugged it and him into the open air.

Then she thought of tearing through the sucker rootlets one by one, and in another minute she had released him and was dragging him away from the horror.

He was white and bleeding from a dozen circular patches.

The odd-job man was coming up the garden, amazed at the smashing of glass, and saw her emerge, hauling the inanimate body with red-stained hands. For a moment he thought impossible things.

"Bring some water!" she cried, and her voice dispelled his fancies. When, with unnatural alacrity, he returned with the water, he found her weeping with excitement, and with Wedderburn's head upon her knee, wiping the blood from his face.

"What's the matter?" said Wedderburn, opening his eyes feebly, and closing them again at once.

"Go and tell Annie to come out here to me, and then go for Doctor Haddon at once," she said to the odd-job man so soon as he brought the water; and added, seeing he hesitated, "I will tell you all about it when you come back."

Presently Wedderburn opened his eyes again, and, seeing

that he was troubled by the puzzle of his position, she explained to him, "You fainted in the hothouse."

"And the orchid?"

"I will see to that," she said..

Wedderburn had lost a good deal of blood, but beyond that he had suffered no very great injury. They gave him brandy mixed with some pink extract of meat, and carried him upstairs to bed. His housekeeper told her incredible story in fragments to Dr. Haddon. "Come to the orchid-house and see," she said.

The cold outer air was blowing in through the open door, and the sickly perfume was almost dispelled. Most of the torn aërial rootlets lay already withered amidst a number of dark stains upon the bricks. The stem of the inflorescence was broken by the fall of the plant, and the flowers were growing limp and brown at the edges of the petals. The doctor stooped towards it, then saw that one of the aërial rootlets still stirred feebly, and hesitated.

The next morning the strange orchid still lay there, black now and putrescent. The door banged intermittently in the morning breeze, and all the array of Wedderburn's orchids was shrivelled and prostrate. But Wedderburn himself was bright and garrulous upstairs in the glory of his strange adventure.

IN THE AVU OBSERVATORY

THE observatory at Avu, in Borneo, stands on the spur of the mountain. To the north rises the old crater, black at night against the unfathomable blue of the sky. From the little circular building, with its mushroom dome, the slopes plunge steeply downward into the black mysteries of the tropical forest beneath. The little house in which the observer and his assistant live is about fifty yards from the observatory, and beyond this are the huts of their native attendants.

Thaddy, the chief observer, was down with a slight fever. His assistant, Woodhouse, paused for a moment in silent contemplation of the tropical night before commencing his solitary vigil. The night was very still. Now and then voices and laughter came from the native huts, or the cry of some strange animal was heard from the midst of the mystery of the forest. Nocturnal insects appeared in ghostly fashion out of the darkness, and fluttered round his light. He thought, perhaps, of all the possibilities of discovery that still lay in the black tangle beneath him; for to the naturalist the virgin forests of Borneo are still a wonderland full of strange questions and half-suspected discoveries. Woodhouse carried a small lantern in his hand, and its yellow glow contrasted vividly with the infinite series of tints between lavender-blue and black in which the landscape was painted. His hands and face were smeared with ointment against the attacks of the mosquitoes.

Even in these days of celestial photography, work done in a purely temporary erection, and with only the most primitive appliances in addition to the telescope, still involves a very large amount of cramped and motionless watching. He sighed as he thought of the physical fatigues before him, stretched himself, and entered the observatory.

The reader is probably familiar with the structure of an

ordinary astronomical observatory. The building is usually cylindrical in shape, with a very light hemispherical roof capable of being turned round from the interior. The telescope is supported upon a stone pillar in the centre, and a clock-work arrangement compensates for the earth's rotation, and allows a star once found to be continuously observed. Be-sides this, there is a compact tracery of wheels and screws about its point of support, by which the astronomer adjusts it. There is, of course, a slit in the movable roof which follows the eye of the telescope in its survey of the heavens. The observer sits or lies on a sloping wooden arrangement, which he can wheel to any part of the observatory as the position of the telescope may require. Within it is advisable to have things as dark as possible, in order to enhance the brilliance of the stars observed.

The lantern flared as Woodhouse entered his circular den, and the general darkness fled into black shadows behind the big machine, from which it presently seemed to creep back over the whole place again as the light waned. The slit was a profound transparent blue, in which six stars shone with tropical brilliance, and their light lay, a pallid gleam, along the black tube of the instrument. Woodhouse shifted the roof, and then proceeding to the telescope, turned first one wheel and then another, the great cylinder slowly swinging into a new position. Then he glanced through the finder, the little companion telescope, moved the roof a little more, made some further adjustments, and set the clockwork in motion. He took off his jacket, for the night was very hot, and pushed into position the uncomfortable seat to which he was condemned for the next four hours. Then with a sigh he resigned himself to his watch upon the mysteries of space.

There was no sound now in the observatory, and the lantern waned steadily. Outside there was the occasional cry of some animal in alarm or pain, or calling to its mate, and the inter-mittent sounds of the Malay and Dyak servants. Presently one of the men began a queer chanting song, in which the others joined at intervals. After this it would seem that they turned in for the night, for no further sound came from their direction, and the whispering stillness became more and more profound.

The clockwork ticked steadily. The shrill hum of a mosquito explored the place and grew shriller in indignation at Woodhouse's ointment. Then the lantern went out and all the observatory was black.

Woodhouse shifted his position presently, when the slow movement of the telescope had carried it beyond the limits of his comfort.

He was watching a little group of stars in the Milky Way, in one of which his chief had seen or fancied a remarkable colour variability. It was not a part of the regular work for which the establishment existed, and for that reason perhaps Woodhouse was deeply interested. He must have forgotten things terrestrial. All his attention was concentrated upon the great blue circle of the telescope field—a circle powdered, so it seemed, with an innumerable multitude of stars, and all luminous against the blackness of its setting. As he watched he seemed to himself to become incorporeal, as if he too were floating in the ether of space. Infinitely remote was the faint red spot he was observing.

Suddenly the stars were blotted out. A flash of blackness passed, and they were visible again.

"Queer," said Woodhouse. "Must have been a bird."

The thing happened again, and immediately after the great tube shivered as though it had been struck. Then the dome of the observatory resounded with a series of thundering blows. The stars seemed to sweep aside as the telescope—which had been unclamped—swung round and away from the slit in the roof.

"Great Scott!" cried Woodhouse. "What's this?"

Some huge vague black shape, with a flapping something like a wing, seemed to be struggling in the aperture of the roof. In another moment the slit was clear again, and the luminous haze of the Milky Way shone warm and bright.

The interior of the roof was perfectly black, and only a scraping sound marked the whereabouts of the unknown creature.

Woodhouse had scrambled from the seat to his feet. He was trembling violently and in a perspiration with the suddenness of the occurrence. Was the thing, whatever it was, inside or out? It was big, whatever else it might be. Something shot across the skylight, and the telescope swayed. He started violently and put his arm up. It was in the observatory, then, with him. It was clinging to the roof, apparently. What the devil was it? Could it see him?

He stood for perhaps a minute in a state of stupefaction. The beast, whatever it was, clawed at the interior of the dome, and then something flapped almost into his face, and he saw the momentary gleam of starlight on a skin like oiled leather. His water-bottle was knocked off his little table with a smash.

The sense of some strange bird-creature hovering a few yards from his face in the darkness was indescribably unpleasant to Woodhouse. As his thought returned he concluded that it must be some night-bird or large bat. At any risk he would see what it was, and pulling a match from his pocket, he tried to strike it on the telescope seat. There was a smoking streak of phosphorescent light, the match flared for a moment, and he saw a vast wing sweeping towards him, a gleam of grey-brown fur, and then he was struck in the face and the match knocked out of his hand. The blow was aimed at his temple, and a claw tore sideways down to his cheek. He reeled and fell, and he heard the extinguished lantern smash. Another blow followed as he fell. He was partly stunned, he felt his own warm blood stream out upon his face. Instinctively he felt his eyes had been struck at, and, turning over on his face to protect them, tried to crawl under the protection of the telescope.

He was struck again upon the back, and he heard his jacket rip, and then the thing hit the roof of the observatory. He edged as far as he could between the wooden seat and the eye-piece of the instrument, and turned his body round so that it was chiefly his feet that were exposed. With these he could at least kick. He was still in a mystified state. The strange beast banged about in the darkness, and presently clung to the telescope, making it sway and the gear rattle. Once it flapped near him, and he kicked out madly and felt a soft body with his feet. He was horribly scared now. It must be a big thing to swing the telescope like that. He saw for a moment the outline of a head black against the starlight, with sharply-pointed upstanding ears and a crest between them. It seemed to him to be as big as a mastiff's. Then he began to bawl out as loudly as he could for help.

At that the thing came down upon him again. As it did so his hand touched something beside him on the floor. He kicked out, and the next moment his ankle was gripped and held by a row of keen teeth. He yelled again, and tried to free his leg by kicking with the other. Then he realised he had the broken water-bottle at his hand, and, snatching it, he struggled into a sitting posture, and feeling in the darkness towards his foot, gripped a velvety ear, like the ear of a big cat. He had seized the water-bottle by its neck and brought it down with a shivering crash upon the head of the strange beast. He repeated the blow, and then stabbed and jabbed with the jagged end of it, in the darkness, where he judged the face might be.

The small teeth relaxed their hold, and at once Woodhouse pulled his leg free and kicked hard. He felt the sickening feel of fur and bone giving under his boot. There was a tearing bite at his arm, and he struck over it at the face, as he judged, and hit damp fur.

There was a pause; then he heard the sound of claws and the dragging of a heavy body away from him over the observatory floor. Then there was silence, broken only by his own sobbing breathing, and a sound like licking. Everything was black except the parallelogram of the blue skylight with the luminous dust of stars, against which the end of the telescope now appeared in silhouette. He waited, as it seemed, an interminable time.

Was the thing coming on again? He felt in his trouser-pocket for some matches, and found one remaining. He tried to strike this, but the floor was wet, and it spat and went out. He cursed. He could not see where the door was situated.

In his struggle he had quite lost his bearings. The strange beast, disturbed by the splutter of the match, began to move again. "Time!" called Woodhouse, with a sudden gleam of mirth, but the thing was not coming at him again. He must have hurt it, he thought, with the broken bottle. He felt a dull pain in his ankle. Probably he was bleeding there. He wondered if it would support him if he tried to stand up. The night outside was very still. There was no sound of anyone moving. The sleepy fools had not heard those wings battering upon the dome, nor his shouts. It was no good wasting strength in shouting. The monster flapped its wings and startled him into a defensive attitude. He hit his elbow against the seat, and it fell over with a crash. He cursed this, and then he cursed the darkness.

Suddenly the oblong patch of starlight seemed to sway to and fro. Was he going to faint? It would never do to faint. He clenched his fists and set his teeth to hold himself together. Where had the door got to? It occurred to him he could get his bearings by the stars visible through the skylight. The patch of stars he saw was in Sagittarius and south-eastward; the door was north—or was it north by west? He tried to think. If he could get the door open he might retreat. It might be the thing was wounded. The suspense was beastly. "Look here!" he said, "if you don't come on, I shall come at you."

Then the thing began clambering up the side of the observatory, and he saw its black outline gradually blot out the skylight. Was it in retreat? He forgot about the door, and watched as the dome shifted and creaked. Somehow he did not feel very frightened or excited now. He felt a curious sinking sensation inside him. The sharply-defined patch of light, with the black form moving across it, seemed to be growing smaller and smaller. That was curious. He began to feel very thirsty, and yet he did not feel inclined to get anything to drink. He seemed to be sliding down a long funnel.

He felt a burning sensation in his throat, and then he perceived it was broad daylight, and that one of the Dyak servants was looking at him with a curious expression. Then there was the top of Thaddy's face upside down. Funny fellow, Thaddy, to go about like that! Then he grasped the situation better, and perceived that his head was on Thaddy's knee, and Thaddy was giving him brandy. And then he saw the eyepiece of the telescope with a lot of red smears on it. He began to remember.

"You've made this observatory in a pretty mess," said Thaddy.

The Dyak boy was beating up an egg in brandy. Woodhouse took this and sat up. He felt a sharp twinge of pain. His ankle was tied up, so were his arm and the side of his face. The smashed glass, red-stained, lay about the floor, the telescope seat was overturned, and by the opposite wall was a dark pool. The door was open, and he saw the grey summit of the mountain against a brilliant background of blue sky.

"Pah!" said Woodhouse. "Who's been killing calves here? Take me out of it."

Then he remembered the Thing, and the fight he had had with it.

"What *was* it?" he said to Thaddy—"The Thing I fought with?"

"*You* know that best," said Thaddy. "But, anyhow, don't worry yourself now about it. Have some more to drink."

Thaddy, however, was curious enough, and it was a hard struggle between duty and inclination to keep Woodhouse quiet until he was decently put away in bed, and had slept upon the copious dose of meat-extract Thaddy considered advisable. They then talked it over together.

"It was," said Woodhouse, "more like a big bat than anything else in the world. It had sharp, short ears, and soft fur, and its wings were leathery. Its teeth were little, but devilish sharp, and its jaw could not have been very strong or else it would have bitten through my ankle."

"It has pretty nearly," said Thaddy.

"It seemed to me to hit out with its claws pretty freely. That is about as much as I know about the beast. Our conversation was intimate, so to speak, and yet not confidential."

"The Dyak chaps talk about a Big Colugo, a Klang-utang

—whatever that may be. It does not often attack man, but I suppose you made it nervous. They say there is a Big Colugo and a Little Colugo, and a something else that sounds like gobble. They all fly about at night. For my own part I know there are flying foxes and flying lemurs about here, but they are none of them very big beasts."

"There are more things in heaven and earth," said Woodhouse—and Thaddy groaned at the quotation—"and more particularly in the forests of Borneo, than are dreamt of in our philosophies. On the whole, if the Borneo fauna is going to disgorge any more of its novelties upon me, I should prefer that it did so when I was not occupied in the observatory at night and alone."

A STORY OF THE STONE AGE

I. Ugh-lomi and Uya

THIS story is of a time beyond the memory of man, before the beginning of history, a time when one might have walked dryshod from France (as we call it now) to England, and when a broad and sluggish Thames flowed through its marshes to meet its father Rhine, flowing through a wide and level country that is under water in these latter days, and which we know by the name of the North Sea. In that remote age the valley which runs along the foot of the Downs did not exist, and the south of Surrey was a range of hills, fir-clad on the middle slopes, and snow-capped for the better part of the year. The cores of its summits still remain as Leith Hill, and Pitch Hill, and Hindhead. On the lower slopes of the range, below the grassy spaces where the wild horses grazed, were forests of yew and sweet-chestnut and elm, and the thickets and dark places hid the grizzly bear and the hyæna, and the grey apes clambered through the branches. And still lower amidst the woodland and marsh and open grass along the Wey did this little drama play itself out to the end that I have to tell. Fifty thousand years ago it was, fifty thousand years—if the reckoning of geologists is correct.

And in those days the spring-time was as joyful as it is now, and sent the blood coursing in just the same fashion. The afternoon sky was blue with piled white clouds sailing through it, and the southwest wind came like a soft caress. The new-come swallows drove to and fro. The reaches of the river were spangled with white ranunculus, the marshy places were starred with lady's-smock and lit with marshmallow wherever the regiments of the sedges lowered their swords, and the northward moving hippopotami, shiny black monsters, sporting clumsily, came floundering and blundering

360

through it all, rejoicing dimly and possessed with one clear idea, to splash the river muddy.

Up the river and well in sight of the hippopotami, a number of little buff-coloured animals dabbled in the water. There was no fear, no rivalry, and no enmity between them and the hippopotami. As the great bulks came crashing through the reeds and smashed the mirror of the water into silvery splashes, these little creatures shouted and gesticulated with glee. It was the surest sign of high spring. "Boloo!" they cried. "Baayah. Boloo!" They were the children of the men folk, the smoke of whose encampment rose from the knoll at the river's bend. Wild-eyed youngsters they were, with matted hair and little broad-nosed impish faces, covered (as some children are covered even nowadays) with a delicate down of hair. They were narrow in the loins and long in the arms. And their ears had no lobes, and had little pointed tips, a thing that still, in rare instances, survives. Stark-naked vivid little gipsies, as active as monkeys and as full of chatter, though a little wanting in words.

Their elders were hidden from the wallowing hippopotami by the crest of the knoll. The human squatting-place was a trampled area among the dead brown fronds of Royal Fern, through which the crosiers of this year's growth were unrolling to the light and warmth. The fire was a smouldering heap of char, light grey and black, replenished by the old women from time to time with brown leaves. Most of the men were asleep—they slept sitting with their foreheads on their knees. They had killed that morning a good quarry, enough for all, a deer that had been wounded by hunting dogs; so that there had been no quarrelling among them, and some of the women were still gnawing the bones that lay scattered about. Others were making a heap of leaves and sticks to feed Brother Fire when the darkness came again, that he might grow strong and tall therewith, and guard them against the beasts. And two were piling flints that they brought, an armful at a time, from the bend of the river where the children were at play.

None of these buff-skinned savages were clothed, but some

wore about their hips rude girdles of adder-skin or crackling, undressed hide, from which depended little bags, not made, but torn from the paws of beasts, and carrying the rudely-dressed flints that were men's chief weapons and tools. And one woman, the mate of Uya the Cunning Man, wore a wonderful necklace of perforated fossils—that others had worn before her. Beside some of the sleeping men lay the big antlers of the elk, with the tines chipped to sharp edges, and long sticks, hacked at the ends with flints into sharp points. There was little else save these things and the smouldering fire to mark these human beings off from the wild animals that ranged the country. But Uya the Cunning did not sleep, but sat with a bone in his hand and scraped busily thereon with a flint, a thing no animal would do. He was the oldest man in the tribe, beetle-browed, prognathous, lank-armed; he had a beard and his cheeks were hairy; and his chest and arms were black with thick hair. And by virtue both of his strength and cunning he was master of the tribe, and his share was always the most and the best.

Eudena had hidden herself among the alders, because she was afraid of Uya. She was still a girl, and her eyes were bright and her smile pleasant to see. He had given her a piece of the liver, a man's piece, and a wonderful treat for a girl to get; but as she took it the other woman with the necklace had looked at her, an evil glance, and Ugh-lomi had made a noise in his throat. At that, Uya had looked at him long and steadfastly, and Ugh-lomi's face had fallen. And then Uya had looked at her. She was frightened and she had stolen away, while the feeding was still going on, and Uya was busy with the marrow of a bone. Afterwards he had wandered about as if looking for her. And now she crouched among the alders, wondering mightily what Uya might be doing with the flint and the bone. And Ugh-lomi was not to be seen.

Presently a squirrel came leaping through the alders, and she lay so quiet the little man was within six feet of her before he saw her. Whereupon he dashed up a stem in a hurry and began to chatter and scold her. "What are you doing here," he asked, "away from the other men beasts?" "Peace," said Eudena, but he only chattered more, and then she began to break off the little black cones to throw at him. He dodged and defied her, and she grew excited and rose up to throw better, and then she saw Uya coming down the knoll. He had seen the movement of her pale arm amidst the thicket— he was very keen-eyed.

At that she forgot the squirrel and set off through the alders and reeds as fast as she could go. She did not care where she went so long as she escaped Uya. She splashed nearly knee-deep through a swampy place, and saw in front of her a slope of ferns—growing more slender and green as they passed up out of the light into the shade of the young chestnuts. She was soon amidst the trees—she was very fleet of foot, and she ran on and on until the forest was old and the vales great, and the vines about their stems where the light came were thick as young trees, and the ropes of ivy stout and tight. On she went, and she doubled and doubled again, and then at last lay down amidst some ferns in a hollow place near a thicket, and listened with her heart beating in her ears.

She heard footsteps presently rustling among the dead leaves, far off, and they died away and everything was still again, except the scandalising of the midges—for the evening was drawing on—and the incessant whisper of the leaves. She laughed silently to think the cunning Uya should go by her. She was not frightened. Sometimes, playing with the other girls and lads, she had fled into the wood, though never so far as this. It was pleasant to be hidden and alone.

She lay a long time there, glad of her escape, and then she sat up listening.

It was a rapid pattering growing louder and coming towards her, and in a little while she could hear grunting noises and the snapping of twigs. It was a drove of lean grisly wild swine. She turned about her, for a boar is an ill fellow to pass too closely, on account of the sideway slash of his tusks, and she made off slantingly through the trees. But the patter came nearer, they were not feeding as they wandered, but going fast—or else they would not overtake her—and she caught the limb of a tree, swung on to it, and ran up the stem with something of the agility of a monkey.

Down below the sharp bristling backs of the swine were already passing when she looked. And she knew the short, sharp grunts they made meant fear. What were they afraid of? A man? They were in a great hurry for just a man.

And then, so suddenly it made her grip on the branch tighten involuntarily, a fawn started in the brake and rushed after the swine. Something else went by, low and grey, with a long body, she did not know what it was, indeed she saw it only momentarily through the interstices of the young leaves; and then there came a pause.

She remained stiff and expectant, as rigid almost as though she was a part of the tree she clung to, peering down.

Then, far away among the trees, clear for a moment, then hidden, then visible knee-deep in ferns, then gone again, ran a man. She knew it was young Ugh-lomi by the fair colour of his hair, and there was red upon his face. Somehow his frantic flight and that scarlet mark made her feel sick. And then nearer, running heavily and breathing hard, came another man. At first she could not see, and then she saw, foreshortened and clear to her, Uya, running with treat strides and his eyes staring. He was not going after Ugh-lomi. His face was white. It was Uya—*afraid!* He passed, and was still loud hearing, when something else, something large and with grizzled fur, swinging along with soft swift strides, came rushing in pursuit of him.

Eudena suddenly became rigid, ceased to breathe, her clutch convulsive, and her eyes starting.

She had never seen the thing before, she did not even see him clearly now, but she knew at once it was the Terror of the Woodshade. His name was a legend, the children would frighten one another, frighten even themselves with his name, and run screaming to the squatting-place. No man had ever killed any of his kind. Even the mighty mammoth feared his anger. It was the grizzly bear, the lord of the world as the world went then.

As he ran he made a continuous growling grumble. "Men

in my very lair! Fighting and blood. At the very mouth of my lair. Men, men, men. Fighting and blood." For he was the lord of the wood and of the caves.

Long after he had passed she remained, a girl of stone, staring down through the branches. All her power of action had gone from her. She gripped by instinct with hands and knees and feet. It was some time before she could think, and then only one thing was clear in her mind, that the Terror was between her and the tribe—that it would be impossible to descend.

Presently, when her fear was a little abated, she clambered into a more comfortable position, where a great branch forked. The trees rose about her, so that she could see nothing of Brother Fire, who is black by day. Birds began to stir, and things that had gone into hiding for fear of her movements crept out. . . .

After a time the taller branches flamed out at the touch of the sunset. High overhead the rooks, who were wiser than men, went cawing home to their squatting-places among the elms. Looking down, things were clearer and darker. Eudena thought of going back to the squatting-place; she let herself down some way, and then the fear of the Terror of the Wood-shade came again. While she hesitated a rabbit squealed dismally, and she dared not descend farther.

The shadows gathered, and the deeps of the forest began stirring. Eudena went up the tree again to be nearer the light. Down below the shadows came out of their hiding places and walked abroad. Overhead the blue deepened. A dreadful stillness came, and then the leaves began whispering.

Eudena shivered and thought of Brother Fire.

The shadows now were gathering in the trees, they sat on the branches and watched her. Branches and leaves were turned to ominous, quiet black shapes that would spring on her if she stirred. Then the white owl, flitting silently, came ghostly through the shades. Darker grew the world and darker, until the leaves and twigs against the sky were black, and the ground was hidden.

She remained there all night, an age-long vigil, straining

her ears for the things that went on below in the darkness, and keeping motionless lest some stealthy beast should discover her. Man in those days was never alone in the dark, save for such rare accidents as this. Age after age he had learnt the lesson of its terror—a lesson we poor children of his have nowadays painfully to unlearn. Eudena, though in age a woman, was in heart like a little child. She kept as still, poor little animal, as a hare before it is started.

The stars gathered and watched her—her one grain of comfort. In one bright one she fancied there was something like Ugh-lomi. Then she fancied it *was* Ugh-lomi. And near him, red and duller, was Uya, and as the night passed Ugh-lomi fled before him up the sky.

She tried to see Brother Fire, who guarded the squatting-place from beasts, but he was not in sight. And far away she heard the mammoths trumpeting as they went down to the drinking-place, and once some huge bulk with heavy paces hurried along, making a noise like a calf, but what it was she could not see. But she thought from the voice it was Yaaa, the rhinoceros, who stabs with his nose, goes always alone, and rages without cause.

At last the little stars began to hide, and then the larger ones. It was like all the animals vanishing before the Terror. The Sun was coming, lord of the sky, as the grizzly was lord of the forest. Eudena wondered what would happen if one star stayed behind. And then the sky paled to the dawn.

When the daylight came the fear of lurking things passed, and she could descend. She was stiff, but not so stiff as you would have been, dear young lady (by virtue of your upbringing), and as she had not been trained to eat at least once in three hours, but instead had often fasted three days, she did not feel uncomfortably hungry. She crept down the tree very cautiously, and went her way stealthily through the wood, and not a squirrel sprang or deer started but the terror of the grizzly bear froze her marrow.

Her desire was now to find her people again. Her dread of Uya the Cunning was consumed by a greater dread of loneliness. But she had lost her direction. She had run heedlessly overnight, and she could not tell whether the squatting-place was sunward or where it lay. Ever and again she stopped and listened. And at last, very far away, she heard a measured chinking. It was so faint even in the morning stillness that she could tell it must be far away. But she knew the sound was that of a man sharpening a flint.

Presently the trees began to thin out, and then came a regiment of nettles barring the way. She turned aside, and then she came to a fallen tree that she knew, with a noise of bees about it. And so presently she was in sight of the knoll, very far off, and the river under it, and the children and the hippopotami just as they had been yesterday, and the thin spire of smoke swaying in the morning breeze. Far away by the river was the cluster of alders where she had hidden. And at the sight of that the fear of Uya returned, and she crept into a thicket of bracken, out of which a rabbit scuttled, and lay awhile to watch the squatting-place.

The men were mostly out of sight, saving Wau, the flint-chopper; and at that she felt safer. They were away hunting food, no doubt. Some of the women, too, were down in the stream, stooping intent, seeking mussels, crayfish, and water-snails, and at the sight of their occupation Eudena felt hungry. She rose, and ran through the fern, designing to join them. As she went she heard a voice among the bracken calling softly. She stopped. Then suddenly she heard a rustle behind her, and turning saw Ugh-lomi rising out of the fern. There were streaks of brown blood and dirt on his face, and his eyes were fierce, and the white stone of Uya, the white Fire Stone, that none but Uya dared to touch, was in his hand. In a stride he was beside her, and gripped her arm. He swung her about, and thrust her before him towards the woods. "Uya," he said, and waved his arms about. She heard a cry, looked back, and saw all the women standing up, and two wading out of the stream. Then came a nearer howling, and the old woman with the beard, who watched the fire on the knoll, was waving her arms, and Wau, the man who had been chipping the flint, was getting to his feet. The little children too were hurrying and shouting.

"Come!" said Ugh-lomi, and dragged her by the arm.

She still did not understand.

"Uya has called the death word," said Ugh-lomi, and she glanced back at the screaming curve of figures, and understood.

Wau and all the women and children were coming towards them, a scattered array of buff, shock-headed figures, howling, leaping, and crying. Over the knoll two youths hurried. Down among the ferns to the right came a man, heading them off from the wood. Ugh-lomi left her arm, and the two began running side by side, leaping the bracken and stepping clear and wide. Eudena, knowing her fleetness and the fleetness of Ugh-lomi, laughed aloud at the unequal chase. They were an exceptionally straight-limbed couple for those days.

They soon cleared the open, and drew near the wood of chestnut-trees again—neither afraid now because neither was alone. They slackened their pace, already not excessive. And suddenly Eudena cried and swerved aside, pointing, and looking up through the tree-stems. Ugh-lomi saw the feet and legs of men running towards him. Eudena was already running off at a tangent. And as he, too, turned to follow her they heard the voice of Uya coming through the trees, and roaring out his rage at them.

Then terror came in their hearts, not the terror that numbs, but the terror that makes one silent and swift. They were cut off now on two sides. They were in a sort of corner of pursuit. On the right hand, and near by them, came the men swift and heavy, with bearded Uya, antler in hand, leading them; and on the left, scattered as one scatters corn, yellow dashes among the fern and grass, ran Wau and the women; and even the little children from the shallow had joined the chase. The two parties converged upon them. Off they went, with Eudena ahead.

They knew there was no mercy for them. There was no hunting so sweet to these ancient men as the hunting of men. Once the fierce passion of the chase was lit, the feeble beginnings of humanity in them were thrown to the winds. And

Uya in the night had marked Ugh-lomi with the death word. Ugh-lomi was the day's quarry, the appointed feast.

They ran straight—it was their only chance—taking whatever ground came in the way—a spread of stinging nettles, an open glade, a clump of grass out of which a hyæna fled snarling. Then woods again, long stretches of shady leaf-mould and moss under the green trunks. Then a stiff slope, tree-clad, and long vistas of trees, a glade, a succulent green area of black mud, a wide-open space again, and then a clump of lacerating brambles, with beast tracks through it. Behind them the chase trailed out and scattered, with Uya ever at their heels. Eudena kept the first place, running light and with her breath easy, for Ugh-lomi carried the Fire Stone in his hand.

It told on his pace—not at first, but after a time. His footsteps behind her suddenly grew remote. Glancing over her shoulder as they crossed another open space, Eudena saw that Ugh-lomi was many yards behind her and Uya close upon him, with antler already raised in the air to strike him down. Wau and the others were but just emerging from the shadow of the woods.

Seeing Ugh-lomi in peril, Eudena ran sideways, looking back, threw up her arms and cried aloud, just as the antler flew. And young Ugh-lomi, expecting this and understanding her cry, ducked his head, so that the missile merely struck his scalp lightly, making but a trivial wound, and flew over him. He turned forthwith, the quartzite Fire Stone in both hands, and hurled it straight at Uya's body as he ran loose from the throw. Uya shouted, but could not dodge it. It took him under the ribs, heavy and flat, and he reeled and went down without a cry. Ugh-lomi caught up the antler—one tine of it was tipped with his own blood—and came running on again with a red trickle just coming out of his hair.

Uya rolled over twice, and lay a moment before he got up, and then he did not run fast. The colour of his face was changed. Wau overtook him, and then others, and he coughed and laboured in his breath. But he kept on.

At last the two fugitives gained the bank of the river, where the stream ran deep and narrow, and they still had fifty yards in hand of Wau, the foremost pursuer, the man who made the smiting stones. He carried one, a large flint, the shape of an oyster and double the size, chipped to a chisel edge, in either hand.

They sprang down the steep bank into the stream, rushed through the water, swam the deep current in two or three strokes, and came out wading again, dripping and refreshed, to clamber up the farther bank. It was undermined, and with willows growing thickly therefrom, so that it needed clambering. And while Eudena was still among the silvery branches and Ugh-lomi still in the water—for the antler had encumbered him—Wau came up against the sky on the opposite bank, and the smiting stone, thrown cunningly, took the side of Eudena's knee. She struggled to the top and fell.

They heard the pursuers shout to one another, and Ugh-lomi climbing to her and moving jerkily to mar Wau's aim, felt the second smiting stone graze his ear, and heard the water splash below him.

Then it was Ugh-lomi, the stripling, proved himself to have come to man's estate. For running on, he found Eudena fell behind, limping, and at that he turned, and crying savagely and with a face terrible with sudden wrath and trickling blood, ran swiftly past her back to the bank, whirling the antler round his head. And Eudena kept on, running stoutly still, though she must needs limp at every step, and the pain was already sharp.

So that Wau, rising over the edge and clutching the straight willow branches, saw Ugh-lomi towering over him, gigantic against the blue; saw his whole body swing round, and the grip of his hands upon the antler. The edge of the antler came sweeping through the air, and he saw no more. The water under the osiers whirled and eddied and went crimson six feet down the stream. Uya following stopped knee-high across the stream, and the man who was swimming turned about.

The other men who trailed after—they were none of them very mighty men (for Uya was more cunning than strong, brooking no sturdy rivals)—slackened momentarily at the sight of Ugh-lomi standing there above the willows, bloody and terrible, between them and the halting girl, with the huge antler waving in his hand. It seemed as though he had gone into the water a youth, and come out of it a man full grown.

He knew what there was behind him. A broad stretch of grass, and then a thicket, and in that Eudena could hide. That was clear in his mind, though his thinking powers were too feeble to see what should happen thereafter. Uya stood knee-deep, undecided and unarmed. His heavy mouth hung open, showing his canine teeth, and he panted heavily. His side was flushed and bruised under the hair. The other man beside him carried a sharpened stick. The rest of the hunters came up one by one to the top of the bank, hairy, long-armed men clutching flints and sticks. Two ran off along the bank down stream, and then clambered to the water, where Wau had come to the surface struggling weakly. Before they could reach him he went under again. Two others threatened Ugh-lomi from the bank.

He answered back, shouts, vague insults, gestures. Then Uya, who had been hesitating, roared with rage, and whirling his fists plunged into the water. His followers splashed after him.

Ugh-lomi glanced over his shoulder and found Eudena already vanished into the thicket. He would perhaps have waited for Uya, but Uya preferred to spar in the water below him until the others were beside him. Human tactics in those days, in all serious fighting, were the tactics of the pack. Prey that turned at bay they gathered around and rushed. Ugh-lomi felt the rush coming, and hurling the antler at Uya, turned about and fled.

When he halted to look back from the shadow of the thicket he found only three of his pursuers had followed him across the river, and they were going back again. Uya, with a bleeding mouth, was on the farther side of the stream again, but lower down, and holding his hand to his side. The others were in the river dragging something to shore. For a time at least the chase was intermitted.

Ugh-lomi stood watching for a space, and snarled at the sight of Uya. Then he turned and plunged into the thicket.

In a minute, Eudena came hastening to join him, and they went on hand in hand. He dimly perceived the pain she suffered from the cut and bruised knee, and chose the easier ways. But they went on all that day, mile after mile, through wood and thicket, until at last they came to the chalk-land, open grass with rare woods of beech, and the birch growing near water, and they saw the Wealden mountains nearer, and groups of horses grazing together. They went circumspectly, keeping always near thicket and cover, for this was a strange region—even its ways were strange. Steadily the ground rose, until the chestnut forests spread wide and blue below them, and the Thames marshes shone silvery, high and far. They saw no men, for in those days men were still only just come into this part of the world, and were moving but slowly along the river-ways. Towards evening they came on the river again, but now it ran in a gorge, between high cliffs of white chalk that sometimes overhung it. Down the cliffs was a scrub of birches and there were many birds there. And high up the cliff was a little shelf by a tree, whereon they clambered to pass the night.

They had had scarcely any food; it was not the time of year for berries, and they had no time to go aside to snare or waylay. They tramped in a hungry, weary silence, gnawing at twigs and leaves. But over the surface of the cliffs were a multitude of snails, and in a bush were the freshly-laid eggs of a little bird, and then Ugh-lomi threw at and killed a squirrel in a beech-tree, so that at last they fed well. Ugh-lomi watched during the night, his chin on his knees; and he heard young foxes crying hard by, and the noise of mammoths down the gorge, and the hyænas yelling and laughing far away. It was chilly, but they dared not light a fire. Whenever he dozed, his spirit went abroad, and straightway met with the spirit of Uya, and they fought. And always Ugh-lomi was paralysed so that he could not smite nor run, and then he would awake suddenly. Eudena, too, dreamt evil things of Uya, so that they both awoke with the fear of him in their hearts, and by the light of the dawn they saw a woolly rhinoceros go blundering down the valley.

During the day they caressed one another and were glad of the sunshine, and Eudena's leg was so stiff she sat on the ledge all day. Ugh-lomi found great flints sticking out of the cliff face, greater than any he had seen, and he dragged some to the ledge and began chipping, so as to be armed against Uya when he came again. And at one he laughed heartily, and Eudena laughed, and they threw it about in derision. It had a hole in it. They stuck their fingers through it, it was very funny indeed. Then they peeped at one another through it. Afterwards, Ugh-lomi got himself a stick, and thrusting by chance at this foolish flint, the stick went in and stuck there. He had rammed it in too tightly to withdraw it. That was still stranger—scarcely funny, terrible almost, and for a time Ugh-lomi did not greatly care to touch the thing. It was as if the flint had bit and held with its teeth. But then he got familiar with the odd combination. He swung it about, and perceived that the stick with the heavy stone on the end struck a better blow than anything he knew. He went to and fro swinging it, and striking with it; but later he tired of it and threw it aside. In the afternoon he went up over the brow of the white cliff, and lay watching by a rabbit-warren until the rabbits came out to play. There were no men thereabouts, and the rabbits were heedless. He threw a smiting stone he had made and got a kill.

That night they made a fire from flint sparks and bracken fronds, and talked and caressed by it. And in their sleep Uya's spirit came again, and suddenly, while Ugh-lomi was trying to fight vainly, the foolish flint on the stick came into his hand, and he struck Uya with it, and behold! it killed him. But afterwards came other dreams of Uya—for spirits take a lot of killing, and he had to be killed again. Then after that the stone would not keep on the stick. He awoke tired and rather gloomy, and was sulky all the forenoon, in spite of Eudena's kindliness, and instead of hunting he sat chipping a sharp edge to the singular flint, and looking strangely at her. Then he bound the perforated flint on to the stick with strips of rabbit skin. And afterwards he walked up and down the ledge, striking with it, and muttering to himself, and thinking of Uya. It felt very fine and heavy in the hand.

Several days, more than there was any counting in those days, five days, it may be, or six, did Ugh-lomi and Eudena stay on that shelf in the gorge of the river, and they lost all fear of men, and their fire burnt redly of a night. And they were very merry together; there was food every day, sweet water, and no enemies. Eudena's knee was well in a couple of days, for those ancient savages had quick-healing flesh. Indeed, they were very happy.

On one of those days Ugh-lomi dropped a chunk of flint over the cliff. He saw it fall, and go bounding across the river bank into the river, and after laughing and thinking it over a little he tried another. This smashed a bush of hazel in the most interesting way. They spent all the morning dropping stones from the ledge, and in the afternoon they discovered this new and interesting pastime was also possible from the cliff-brow. The next day they had forgotten this delight. Or at least, it seemed they had forgotten.

But Uya came in dreams to spoil the paradise. Three nights he came fighting Ugh-lomi. In the morning after these dreams Ugh-lomi would walk up and down, threatening him and swinging the axe, and at last came the night after Ugh-lomi brained the otter, and they had feasted. Uya went too far. Ugh-lomi awoke, scowling under his heavy brows, and he took his axe, and extending his hand towards Eudena he bade her wait for him upon the ledge. Then he clambered down the white declivity, glanced up once from the foot of it and flourished his axe, and without looking back again went striding along the river bank until the overhanging cliff at the bend hid him.

Two days and nights did Eudena sit alone by the fire on the ledge waiting, and in the night the beasts howled over the cliffs and down the valley, and on the cliff over against her the hunched hyænas prowled black against the sky. But no evil thing came near her save fear. Once, far away, she heard the roaring of a lion, following the horses as they came northward over the grass lands with the spring. All the time she waited—the waiting that is pain.

And the third day Ugh-lomi came back, up the river. The plumes of a raven were in his hair. The first axe was red-stained, and had long dark hairs upon it, and he carried the necklace that had marked the favourite of Uya in his hand. He walked in the soft places, giving no heed to his trail. Save a raw cut below his jaw there was not a wound upon him. "Uya!" cried Ugh-lomi exultant, and Eudena saw it was well. He put the necklace on Eudena, and they ate and drank together. And after eating he began to rehearse the whole story from the beginning, when Uya had cast his eyes on Eudena, and Uya and Ugh-lomi, fighting in the forest, had been chased by the bear, eking out his scanty words with abundant panto-mime, springing to his feet and whirling the stone axe round when it came to the fighting. The last fight was a mighty one, stamping and shouting, and once a blow at the fire that sent a torrent of sparks up into the night. And Eudena sat red in the light of the fire, gloating on him, her face flushed and her eyes shining, and the necklace Uya had made about her neck. It was a splendid time, and the stars that look down on us looked down on her, our ancestor—who has been dead now these fifty thousand years.

II.   The Cave Bear

In the days when Eudena and Ugh-lomi fled from the people of Uya towards the fir-clad mountains of the Weald, across the forests of sweet-chestnut and the grass-clad chalk-land, and hid themselves at last in the gorge of the river be-tween the chalk cliffs, men were few and their squatting-places far between. The nearest men to them were those of the tribe, a full day's journey down the river, and up the mountains there were none. Man was indeed a newcomer to this part of the world in that ancient time, coming slowly along the rivers, generation after generation, from one squatting place to another, from the south-westward. And the animals that held the land, the hippopotamus and rhinoceros of the river valleys, the horses of the grass plains, the deer and swine of the woods, the grey apes in the branches, the cattle of the uplands, feared him but little—let alone the mammoths in the mountains and the elephants that came through the land in the summer-time out of the south. For why should they fear him, with but the rough, chipped flints that he had not learnt to haft and which he threw but ill, and the poor spear of sharpened wood, as all the weapons he had against hoof and horn, tooth and claw?

Andoo, the huge cave bear, who lived in the cave up the gorge, had never even seen a man in all his wise and respectable life, until midway through one night, as he was prowling down the gorge along the cliff edge, he saw the glare of Eudena's fire upon the ledge, and Eudena red and shining, and Ugh-lomi, with a gigantic shadow mocking him upon the white cliff, going to and fro, shaking his mane of hair, and waving the axe of stone—the first axe of stone—while he chanted of the killing of Uya. The cave bear was far up the gorge, and he saw the thing slanting-ways and far off. He was so surprised he stood quite still upon the edge, sniffing the novel odour of burning bracken, and wondering whether the dawn was coming up in the wrong place.

He was the lord of the rocks and caves, was the cave bear, as his slighter brother, the grizzly, was lord of the thick woods below, and as the dappled lion—the lion of those days was dappled—was lord of the thorn-thickets, reed-beds, and open plains. He was the greatest of all meat-eaters; he knew no fear, none preyed on him, and none gave him battle; only the rhinoceros was beyond his strength. Even the mammoth shunned his country. This invasion perplexed him. He noticed these new beasts were shaped like monkeys, and sparsely hairy like young pigs. "Monkey and young pig," said the cave bear. "It might not be so bad. But that red thing that jumps, and the black thing jumping with it yonder! Never in my life have I seen such things before!"

He came slowly along the brow of the cliff towards them, stopping thrice to sniff and peer, and the reek of the fire grew stronger. A couple of hyænas also were so intent upon the thing below that Andoo, coming soft and easy, was close upon them before they knew of him or he of them. They stared guiltily and went lurching off. Coming round in a wheel, a hundred yards off, they began yelling and calling him names to revenge themselves for the start they had had. "Ya-ha!" they cried. "Who can't grub his own burrow? Who eats roots like a pig? . . . Ya-ha!" for even in those days the hyæna's manners were just as offensive as they are now.

"Who answers the hyæna?" growled Andoo, peering through the midnight dimness at them, and then going to look at the cliff edge.

There was Ugh-lomi still telling his story, and the fire getting low, and the scent of the burning hot and strong.

Andoo stood on the edge of the chalk cliff for some time, shifting his vast weight from foot to foot, and swaying his head to and fro, with his mouth open, his ears erect and twitching, and the nostrils of his big, black muzzle sniffing. He was very curious, was the cave bear, more curious than any of the bears that live now, and the flickering fire and the incomprehensible movements of the man, let alone the intrusion into his indisputable province, stirred him with a sense of strange new happenings. He had been after red deer fawn that night, for the cave bear was a miscellaneous hunter, but this quite turned him from that enterprise.

"Ya-ha!" yelled the hyænas behind. "Ya-ha-ha!"

Peering through the starlight, Andoo saw there were now three or four going to and fro against the grey hillside. "They will hang about me now all the night. . . . until I kill," said Andoo. "Filth of the world!" And mainly to annoy them, he resolved to watch the red flicker in the gorge until the dawn came to drive the hyæna scum home. And after a time they vanished, and he heard their voices, like a party of Cockney beanfeasters, away in the beech-woods. Then they came slinking near again. Andoo yawned and went on along the cliff, and they followed. Then he stopped and went back.

It was a splendid night, beset with shining constellations, the same stars, but not the same constellations we know, for since those days all the stars have had time to move into new places. Far away across the open space beyond where the heavy-shouldered, lean-bodied hyænas blundered and howled, was a beech-wood, and the mountain slopes rose beyond, a dim mystery, until their snow-capped summits came out white and cold and clear, touched by the first rays of the yet unseen moon. It was a vast silence, save when the yell of the hyænas flung a vanishing discordance across its peace, or when from down the hills the trumpeting of the new-come elephants came faintly on the faint breeze. And below now, the red flicker had dwindled and was steady, and shone a deeper red, and Ugh-lomi had finished his story and was preparing to sleep, and Eudena sat and listened to the strange voices of unknown beasts, and watched the dark eastern sky growing deeply luminous at the advent of the moon. Down below, the river talked to itself, and things unseen went to and fro.

After a time the bear went away, but in an hour he was back again. Then, as if struck by a thought, he turned, and went up the gorge. . . .

The night passed, and Ugh-lomi slept on. The waning moon rose and lit the gaunt white cliff overhead with a light that was pale and vague. The gorge remained in a deeper shadow and seemed all the darker. Then by imperceptible degrees, the day came stealing in the wake of the moonlight. Eudena's eyes wandered to the cliff brow overhead once, and then again. Each time the line was sharp and clear against the sky, and yet she had a dim perception of something lurking there. The red of the fire grew deeper and deeper, grey scales spread upon it, its vertical column of smoke became more and more visible, and up and down the gorge things that had been unseen grew clear in a colourless illumination. She may have dozed.

Suddenly she started up from her squatting position, erect and alert, scrutinising the cliff up and down.

She made the faintest sound, and Ugh-lomi too, light-sleeping like an animal, was instantly awake. He caught up his axe and came noiselessly to her side.

The light was still dim, the world now all in black and dark grey, and one sickly star still lingered overhead. The ledge they were on was a little grassy space, six feet wide, perhaps, and twenty feet long, sloping outwardly, and with a handful of St. John's wort growing near the edge. Below it the soft white rock fell away in a steep slope of nearly fifty feet to the thick bush of hazel that fringed the river. Down the river this slope increased, until some way off a thin grass held its own right up to the crest of the cliff. Overhead, forty or fifty feet of rock bulged into the great masses characteristic of chalk, but at the end of the ledge a gully, a precipitous groove of discoloured rock, slashed the face of the cliff, and gave a footing to a scrubby growth, by which Eudena and Ugh-lomi went up and down.

They stood as noiseless as startled deer, with every sense expectant. For a minute they heard nothing, and then came a faint rattling of dust down the gully, and the creaking of twigs.

Ugh-lomi gripped his axe, and went to the edge of the ledge, for the bulge of the chalk overhead had hidden the upper part of the gully. And forthwith, with a sudden contraction of the heart, he saw the cave bear halfway down from the brow, and making a gingerly backward step with his flat hind-foot. His hind-quarters were towards Ugh-lomi, and he clawed at the rock and bushes so that he seemed flattened against the cliff. He looked none the less for that. From his shining snout to his stumpy tail he was a lion and a half, the length of two tall men. He looked over his shoulder, and his huge mouth was open with the exertion of holding up his great carcase, and his tongue lay out. . . .

He got his footing, and came down slowly, a yard nearer. "Bear," said Ugh-lomi, looking round with his face white.

But Eudena, with terror in her eyes, was pointing down the cliff.

Ugh-lomi's mouth fell open. For down below, with her big

fore-feet against the rock, stood another big brown-grey bulk—the she-bear. She was not so big as Andoo, but she was big enough for all that.

Then suddenly Ugh-lomi gave a cry, and catching up a handful of the litter of ferns that lay scattered on the ledge, he thrust it into the pallid ash of the fire. "Brother Fire!" he cried. "Brother Fire!" And Eudena, starting into activity, did likewise. "Brother Fire! Help, help! Brother Fire!"

Brother Fire was still red in his heart, but he turned to grey as they scattered him. "Brother Fire!" they screamed. But he whispered and passed, and there was nothing but ashes. Then Ugh-lomi danced with anger and struck the ashes with his fist. But Eudena began to hammer the firestone against a flint. And the eyes of each were turning ever and again towards the gully by which Andoo was climbing down. Brother Fire!

Suddenly the huge furry hind-quarters of the bear came into view, beneath the bulge of the chalk that had hidden him. He was still clambering gingerly down the nearly vertical surface. His head was yet out of sight, but they could hear him talking to himself. "Pig and monkey," said the cave bear. "It ought to be good."

Eudena struck a spark and blew at it; it twinkled brighter and then—went out. At that she cast down flint and firestone and stared blankly. Then she sprang to her feet and scrambled a yard or so up the cliff above the ledge. How she hung on even for a moment I do not know, for the chalk was vertical and without grip for a monkey. In a couple of seconds she had slid back to the ledge again with bleeding hands.

Ugh-lomi was making frantic rushes about the ledge— now he would go to the edge, now to the gully. He did not know what to do, he could not think. The she-bear looked smaller than her mate—much. If they rushed down on her together, *one* might live. "Ugh?" said the cave bear, and Ugh-lomi turned again and saw his little eyes peering under the bulge of the chalk.

Eudena, cowering at the end of the ledge, began to scream like a gripped rabbit.

At that a sort of madness came upon Ugh-lomi. With a mighty cry, he caught up his axe and ran towards Andoo. The monster gave a grunt of surprise. In a moment Ugh-lomi was clinging to a bush right underneath the bear, and in another he was hanging to its back half buried in fur, with one fist clutched in the hair under its jaw. The bear was too astonished at this fantastic attack to do more than cling passive. And then the axe, the first of all axes, rang on its skull.

The bear's head twisted from side to side, and he began a petulant scolding growl. The axe bit within an inch of the left eye, and the hot blood blinded that side. At that the brute roared with surprise and anger, and his teeth gnashed six inches from Ugh-lomi's face. Then the axe, clubbed close, came down heavily on the corner of the jaw.

The next blow blinded the right side and called forth a roar, this time of pain. Eudena saw the huge, flat feet slipping and sliding, and suddenly the bear gave a clumsy leap sideways, as if for the ledge. Then everything vanished, and the hazels smashed, and a roar of pain and a tumult of shouts and growls came up from far below.

Eudena screamed and ran to the edge and peered over. For a moment, man and bears were a heap together, Ugh-lomi uppermost; and then he had sprung clear and was scaling the gully again, with the bears rolling and striking at one another among the hazels. But he had left his axe below, and three knob-ended streaks of carmine were shooting down his thigh. "Up!" he cried, and in a moment Eudena was leading the way to the top of the cliff.

In half a minute they were at the crest, their hearts pumping noisily, with Andoo and his wife far and safe below them. Andoo was sitting on his haunches, both paws at work, trying with quick, exasperated movements to wipe the blindness out of his eyes, and the she-bear stood on all-fours a little way off, ruffled in appearance and growling angrily. Ugh-lomi flung himself flat on the grass, and lay panting and bleeding with his face on his arms.

For a second Eudena regarded the bears, then she came and sat beside him, looking at him. . . .

Presently she put forth her hand timidly and touched him, and made the guttural sound that was his name. He turned over and raised himself on his arm. His face was pale, like the face of one who is afraid. He looked at her steadfastly for a moment, and then suddenly he laughed. "Waugh!" he said exultantly.

"Waugh!" she said—a simple but expressive conversation.

Then Ugh-lomi came and knelt beside her, and on hands and knees peered over the brow and examined the gorge. His breath was steady now, and the blood on his leg had ceased to flow, though the scratches the she-bear had made were open and wide. He squatted up and sat staring at the footmarks of the great bear as they came to the gully—they were as wide as his head and twice as long. Then he jumped up and went along the cliff face until the ledge was visible. Here he sat down for some time thinking, while Eudena watched him. Presently she saw the bears had gone.

At last Ugh-lomi rose, as one whose mind is made up. He returned towards the gully, Eudena keeping close by him, and together they clambered to the ledge. They took the firestone and a flint, and then Ugh-lomi went down to the foot of the cliff very cautiously, and found his axe. They returned to the cliff as quietly as they could, and set off at a brisk walk. The ledge was a home no longer, with such callers in the neighbourhood. Ugh-lomi carried the axe and Eudena the firestone. So simple was a Palæolithic removal.

They went up stream, although it might lead to the very lair of the cave bear, because there was no other way to go. Down the stream was the tribe, and had not Ugh-lomi killed Uya and Wau? By the stream they had to keep—because of drinking.

So they marched through beech-trees, with the gorge deepening until the river flowed, a frothing rapid, five hundred feet below them. Of all the changeful things in this world of change, the courses of rivers in deep valleys change least. It was the river Wey, the river we know to-day, and they marched over the very spots where nowadays stand little Guildford and Godalming—the first human beings to come into the land. Once a grey ape chattered and vanished, and all along the cliff edge, vast and even, ran the spoor of the great cave bear.

And then the spoor of the bear fell away from the cliff, showing, Ugh-lomi thought, that he came from some place to the left, and keeping to the cliff's edge, they presently came to an end. They found themselves looking down on a great semicircular space caused by the collapse of the cliff. It had smashed right across the gorge, banking the up-stream water back in a pool which overflowed in a rapid. The slip had happened long ago. It was grassed over, but the face of the cliffs that stood about the semicircle was still almost fresh-looking and white as on the day when the rock must have broken and slid down. Starkly exposed and black under the foot of these cliffs were the mouths of several caves. And as they stood there, looking at the space, and disinclined to skirt it, because they thought the bears' lair lay somewhere on the left in the direction they must needs take, they saw suddenly first one bear and then two coming up the grass slope to the right and going across the amphitheatre towards the caves. Andoo was first; he dropped a little on his fore-foot and his mien was despondent, and the she-bear came shuffling behind.

Eudena and Ugh-lomi stepped back from the cliff until they could just see the bears over the verge. Then Ugh-lomi stopped. Eudena pulled his arm, but he turned with a forbidding gesture, and her hand dropped. Ugh-lomi stood watching the bears, with his axe in his hand, until they had vanished into the cave. He growled softly, and shook the axe at the she-bear's receding quarters. Then to Eudena's terror, instead of creeping off with her, he lay flat down and crawled forward into such a position that he could just see the cave. It was bears—and he did it as calmly as if it had been rabbits he was watching!

He lay still, like a bared log, sun-dappled, in the shadow of the trees. He was thinking. And Eudena had learnt, even when a little girl, that when Ugh-lomi became still like that, jaw-bone on fist, novel things presently began to happen.

It was an hour before the thinking was over; it was noon when the two little savages had found their way to the cliff brow that overhung the bears' cave. And all the long afternoon they fought desperately with a great boulder of chalk; trundling it, with nothing but their unaided sturdy muscles, from the gully where it had hung like a loose tooth, towards the cliff top. It was full two yards about, it stood as high as Eudena's waist, it was obtuse-angled and toothed with flints. And when the sun set it was poised, three inches from the edge, above the cave of the great cave bear.

In the cave conversation languished during that afternoon. The she-bear snoozed sulkily in her corner—for she was fond of pig and monkey—and Andoo was busy licking the side of his paw and smearing his face to cool the smart and inflammation of his wounds. Afterwards he went and sat just within the mouth of the cave, blinking out at the afternoon sun with his uninjured eye, and thinking.

"I never was so startled in my life," he said at last. "They are the most extraordinary beasts. Attacking *me!*"

"I don't like them," said the she-bear, out of the darkness behind.

"A feebler sort of beast I *never* saw. I can't think what the world is coming to. Scraggy, weedy legs. . . . Wonder how they keep warm in winter?"

"Very likely they don't," said the she-bear.

"I suppose it's a sort of monkey gone wrong."

"It's a change," said the she-bear.

A pause.

"The advantage he had was merely accidental," said Andoo. "These things *will* happen at times."

"*I* can't understand why you let go," said the she-bear.

That matter had been discussed before, and settled. So Andoo, being a bear of experience, remained silent for a space. Then he resumed upon a different aspect of the matter. "He has a sort of claw—a long claw that he seemed to have first on one paw and then on the other. Just one claw. They're very odd things. The bright thing, too, they seemed to have—like that glare that comes in the sky in daytime—only it jumps about—it's really worth seeing. It's a thing with a root, too—like grass when it is windy."

"Does it bite?" asked the she-bear. "If it bites it can't be a plant."

"No—— I don't know," said Andoo. "But it's curious, anyhow."

"I wonder if they *are* good eating?" said the she-bear.

"They look it," said Andoo, with appetite—for the cave bear, like the polar bear, was an incurable carnivore—no roots or honey for *him*.

The two bears fell into a meditation for a space. Then Andoo resumed his simple attentions to his eye. The sunlight up the green slope before the cave mouth grew warmer in tone and warmer, until it was a ruddy amber.

"Curious sort of thing—day," said the cave bear. "Lot too much of it, I think. Quite unsuitable for hunting. Dazzles me always. I can't smell nearly so well by day."

The she-bear did not answer, but there came a measured crunching sound out of the darkness. She had turned up a bone. Andoo yawned. "Well," he said. He strolled to the cave mouth and stood with his head projecting, surveying the amphitheatre. He found he had to turn his head completely round to see objects on his right-hand side. No doubt that eye would be all right to-morrow.

He yawned again. There was a tap overhead, and a big mass of chalk flew out from the cliff face, dropped a yard in front of his nose, and starred into a dozen unequal fragments. It startled him extremely.

When he had recovered a little from his shock, he went and sniffed curiously at the representative pieces of the fallen projectile. They had a distinctive flavour, oddly reminiscent of the two drab animals of the ledge. He sat up and pawed the larger lump, and walked round it several times, trying to find a man about it somewhere. . . .

When night had come he went off down the river gorge to see if he could cut off either of the ledge's occupants. The ledge was empty, there were no signs of the red thing, but as he was rather hungry he did not loiter long that night, but pushed on to pick up a red deer fawn. He forgot about the drab animals. He found a fawn, but the doe was close by and made an ugly fight for her young. Andoo had to leave the fawn, but as her blood was up she stuck to the attack, and at last he got in a blow of his paw on her nose, and so got hold of her. More meat but less delicacy, and the she-bear, following, had her share. The next afternoon, curiously enough, the very fellow of the first white rock fell, and smashed precisely according to precedent.

The aim of the third, that fell the night after, however, was better. It hit Andoo's unspeculative skull with a crack that echoed up the cliff, and the white fragments went dancing to all the points of the compass. The she-bear, coming after him and sniffing curiously at him, found him lying in an odd sort of attitude, with his head wet and all out of shape. She was a young she-bear, and inexperienced, and having sniffed about him for some time and licked him a little, and so forth, she decided to leave him until the odd mood had passed, and went on her hunting alone.

She looked up the fawn of the red doe they had killed two nights ago, and found it. But it was lonely hunting without Andoo, and she returned caveward before dawn. The sky was grey and overcast, the trees up the gorge were black and unfamiliar, and into her ursine mind came a dim sense of strange and dreary happenings. She lifted up her voice and called Andoo by name. The sides of the gorge reechoed her.

As she approached the caves she saw in the half-light, and heard a couple of jackals scuttle off, and immediately after a hyæna howled and a dozen clumsy bulks went lumbering up the slope, and stopped and yelled derision. "Lord of the rocks and caves—ya-ha!" came down the wind. The dismal feeling in the she-bear's mind became suddenly acute. She shuffled across the anphitheatre.

"Ya-ha!" said the hyænas, retreating. "Ya-ha!"

The cave bear was not lying quite in the same attitude, because the hyænas had been busy, and in one place his ribs showed white. Dotted over the turf about him lay the smashed fragments of the three great lumps of chalk. And the air was full of the scent of death.

The she-bear stopped dead. Even now that the great and wonderful Andoo was killed was beyond her believing. Then she heard far overhead a sound, a queer sound, a little like the shout of a hyæna but fuller and lower in pitch. She looked up, her little dawn-blinded eyes seeing little, her nostrils quivering. And there, on the cliff edge, far above her against the bright pink of dawn, were two little shaggy round dark things, the heads of Eudena and Ugh-lomi, as they shouted derision at her. But though she could not see them very distinctly she could hear, and dimly she began to apprehend. A novel feeling as of imminent strange evils came into her heart.

She began to examine the smashed fragments of chalk that lay about Andoo. For a space she stood still, looking about her and making a low continuous sound that was almost a moan. Then she went back incredulously to Andoo to make one last effort to rouse him.

III.   The First Horseman

In the days before Ugh-lomi there was little trouble between the horses and men. They lived apart—the men in the river swamps and thickets, the horses on the wide grassy uplands between the chestnuts and the pines. Sometimes a pony would come straying into the clogging marshes to make a flint-hacked meal, and sometimes the tribe would find one, the kill of a lion, and drive off the jackals, and feast heartily while the sun was high. These horses of the old time were clumsy at the fetlock and dun-coloured, with a rough tail and big head. They came every spring-time north-westward into the country after the swallows and before the hippopotami, as the grass on the wide downland stretches grew long. They came only in small bodies thus far, each herd, a stallion and two or three mares and a foal or so, having its own stretch of country, and they went again when the chestnut-trees were yellow and the wolves came down the Wealden mountains.

It was their custom to graze right out in the open, going into cover only in the heat of the day. They avoided the long stretches of thorn and beech-wood, preferring an isolated group of trees void of ambuscade, so that it was hard to come upon them. They were never fighters; their heels and teeth were for one another, but in the clear country, once they were started, no living thing came near them, though perhaps the elephant might have done so had he felt the need. And in those days man seemed a harmless thing enough. No whisper of prophetic intelligence told the species of the terrible slavery that was to come, of the whip and spur and bearing-rein, the clumsy load and the slippery street, the insufficient food, and the knacker's yard, that was to replace the wide grass-land and the freedom of the earth.

Down in the Wey marshes Ugh-lomi and Eudena had never seen the horses closely, but now they saw them every day as the two of them raided out from their lair on the ledge in the gorge, raiding together in search of food. They had returned to the ledge after the killing of Andoo; for of the she-bear they were not afraid. The she-bear had become afraid of them, and when she winded them she went aside. The two went together everywhere; for since they had left the tribe Eudena was not so much Ugh-lomi's woman as his mate; she learnt to hunt even—as much, that is, as any woman could. She was indeed a marvellous woman. He would lie for hours watching a beast, or planning catches in that shock head of his, and she would stay beside him, with her bright eyes upon him, offering no irritating suggestions—as still as any man. A wonderful woman!

At the top of the cliff was an open grassy lawn and then beech-woods, and going through the beech-woods one came to the edge of the rolling grassy expanse, and in sight of the horses. Here, on the edge of the wood and bracken, were the rabbit-burrows, and here among the fronds Eudena and Ugh-lomi would lie with their throwing-stones ready, until the little people came out to nibble and play in the sunset. And while Eudena would sit, a silent figure of watchfulness, regarding the burrows, Ugh-lomi's eyes were ever away across the greensward at those wonderful grazing strangers.

In a dim way he appreciated their grace and their supple nimbleness. As the sun declined in the evening-time, and the heat of the day passed, they would become active, would start chasing one another, neighing, dodging, shaking their manes, coming round in great curves, sometimes so close that the pounding of the turf sounded like hurried thunder. It looked so fine that Ugh-lomi wanted to join in badly. And sometimes one would roll over on the turf, kicking four hoofs heavenward, which seemed formidable and was certainly much less alluring.

Dim imaginings ran through Ugh-lomi's mind as he watched —by virtue of which two rabbits lived the longer. And sleeping, his brains were clearer and bolder—for that was the way in those days. He came near the horses, he dreamt, and fought, smiting-stone against hoof, but then the horses changed to men, or, at least, to men with horses' heads, and he awoke in a cold sweat of terror.

Yet the next day in the morning, as the horses were grazing, one of the mares whinnied, and they saw Ugh-lomi coming up the wind. They all stopped their eating and watched him. Ugh-lomi was not coming towards them, but strolling obliquely across the open, looking at anything in the world but horses. He had stuck three fern-fronds into the mat of his hair, giving him a remarkable appearance, and he walked very slowly. "What's up now?" said the Master Horse, who was capable but inexperienced.

"It looks more like the first half of an animal than anything else in the world," he said. "Fore-legs and no hind."

"It's only one of those pink monkey things," said the Eldest Mare. "They're a sort of river monkey. They're quite common on the plains."

Ugh-lomi continued his oblique advance. The Eldest Mare was struck with the want of motive in his proceedings.

"Fool!" said the Eldest Mare, in a quick, conclusive way

she had. She resumed her grazing. The Master Horse and the Second Mare followed suit.

"Look! he's nearer," said the Foal with a stripe.

One of the younger foals made uneasy movements. Ugh-lomi squatted down, and sat regarding the horses fixedly. In a little while he was satisfied that they meant neither flight nor hostilities. He began to consider his next procedure. He did not feel anxious to kill, but he had his axe with him, and the spirit of sport was upon him. How would one kill one of these creatures?—these great beautiful creatures!

Eudena, watching him with a fearful admiration from the cover of the bracken, saw him presently go on all fours, and so proceed again. But the horses preferred him a biped to a quadruped, and the Master Horse threw up his head and gave the word to move. Ugh-lomi thought they were off for good, but after a minute's gallop they came round in a wide curve, and stood winding him. Then, as a rise in the ground hid him, they tailed out, the Master Horse leading, and approached him spirally.

He was as ignorant of the possibilities of a horse as they were of his. And at this stage it would seem he funked. He knew this kind of stalking would make red deer or buffalo charge, if it were persisted in. At any rate, Eudena saw him jump up and come walking towards her with the fern plumes held in his hand.

She stood up, and he grinned to show that the whole thing was an immense lark, and that what he had done was just what he had planned to do from the very beginning. So that incident ended. But he was very thoughtful all that day.

The next day this foolish drab creature with the leonine mane, instead of going about the grazing or hunting he was made for, was prowling round the horses again. The Eldest Mare was all for silent contempt. "I suppose he wants to learn something from us," she said, and "*Let* him." The next day he was at it again. The Master Horse decided he meant absolutely nothing. But as a matter of fact, Ugh-lomi, the first of men to feel that curious spell of the horse that binds us even to this day, meant a great deal. He admired them unreservedly. There was a rudiment of the snob in him, I am afraid, and he wanted to be near these beautifully-curved animals. Then there were vague conceptions of a kill. If only they would let him come near them! But they drew the line, he found, at fifty yards. If he came nearer than that they moved off—with dignity. I suppose it was the way he had blinded Andoo that made him think of leaping on the back of one of them. But though Eudena after a time came out in the open too, and they did some unobtrusive stalking, things stopped there.

Then one memorable day a new idea came to Ugh-lomi. The horse looks down and level, but he does not look up. No animals look up—they have too much common sense. It was only that fantastic creature, man, could waste his wits skyward. Ugh-lomi made no philosophical deductions, but he perceived the thing was so. So he spent a weary day in a beech that stood in the open, while Eudena stalked. Usually the horses went into the shade in the heat of the afternoon, but that day the sky was overcast, and they would not, in spite of Eudena's solicitude.

It was two days after that that Ugh-lomi had his desire. The day was blazing hot, and the multiplying flies asserted themselves. The horses stopped grazing before mid-day, and came into the shadow below him, and stood in couples nose to tail, flapping.

The Master Horse, by virtue of his heels, came closest to the tree. And suddenly there was a rustle and a creak, a *thud.* . . . Then a sharp chipped flint bit him on the cheek. The Master Horse stumbled, came on one knee, rose to his feet, and was off like the wind. The air was full of the whirl of limbs, the prance of hoofs, and snorts of alarm. Ugh-lomi was pitched a foot in the air, came down again, up again, his stomach was hit violently, and then his knees got a grip of something between them. He found himself clutching with knees, feet, and hands, careering violently with extraordinary oscillation through the air—his axe gone Heaven knows whither. "Hold tight," said Mother Instinct, and he did.

He was aware of a lot of coarse hair in his face, some of it between his teeth, and of green turf streaming past in front of his eyes. He saw the shoulder of the Master Horse, vast and sleek, with the muscles flowing swiftly under the skin. He perceived that his arms were round the neck, and that the violent jerkings he experienced had a sort of rhythm.

Then he was in the midst of a wild rush of tree-stems, and then there were fronds of bracken about, and then more open turf. Then a stream of pebbles rushing past, little pebbles flying sideways athwart the stream from the blow of the swift hoofs. Ugh-lomi began to feel frightfully sick and giddy, but he was not the stuff to leave go simply because he was uncomfortable.

He dared not leave his grip, but he tried to make himself more comfortable. He released his hug on the neck, gripping the mane instead. He slipped his knees forward, and pushing back, came into a sitting position where the quarters broaden. It was nervous work, but he managed it, and at last he was fairly seated astride, breathless indeed, and uncertain, but with that frightful pounding of his body at any rate relieved.

Slowly the fragments of Ugh-lomi's mind got into order again. The pace seemed to him terrific, but a kind of exultation was beginning to oust his first frantic terror. The air rushed by, sweet and wonderful, the rhythm of the hoofs changed and broke up and returned into itself again. They were on turf now, a wide glade—the beech-trees a hundred yards away on either side, and a succulent band of green starred with pink blossom and shot with silver water here and there, meandered down the middle. Far off was a glimpse of blue valley—far away. The exultation grew. It was man's first taste of pace.

Then came a wide space dappled with flying fallow deer scattering this way and that, and then a couple of jackals, mistaking Ugh-lomi for a lion, came hurrying after him. And when they saw it was not a lion they still came on out of curiosity. On galloped the horse, with his one idea of escape, and after him the jackals, with pricked ears and quickly barked remarks. "Which kills which?" said the first jackal. "It's the horse being killed," said the second. They gave the howl of following, and the horse answered to it as a horse answers nowadays to the spur.

On they rushed, a little tornado through the quiet day, putting up startled birds, sending a dozen unexpected things darting to cover, raising a myriad of indignant dung-flies, smashing little blossoms, flowering complacently, back into their parental turf. Trees again, and then splash, splash across a torrent; then a hare shot out of a tuft of grass under the very hoofs of the Master Horse, and the jackals left them incontinently. So presently they broke into the open again, a wide expanse of turfy hillside—the very grassy downs that fall northward nowadays from the Epsom Stand.

The first hot bolt of the Master Horse was long since over. He was falling into a measured trot, and Ugh-lomi, albeit bruised exceedingly and quite uncertain of the future, was in a state of glorious enjoyment. And now came a new development. The pace broke again, the Master Horse came round on a short curve, and stopped dead. . . .

Ugh-lomi became alert. He wished he had a flint, but the throwing flint he had carried in a thong about his waist was—like the axe—Heaven knows where. The Master Horse turned his head, and Ugh-lomi became aware of an eye and teeth. He whipped his leg into a position of security, and hit at the cheek with his fist. Then the head went down somewhere out of existence apparently, and the back he was sitting on flew up into a dome. Ugh-lomi became a thing of instinct again—strictly prehensile; he held by knees and feet, and his head seemed sliding towards the turf. His fingers were twisted into the shock of mane, and the rough hair of the horse saved him. The gradient he was on lowered again, and then—"Whup!" said Ugh-lomi, astonished, and the slant was the other way up. But Ugh-lomi was a thousand generations nearer the primordial than man: no monkey could have held on better. And the lion had been training the horse for countless generations against the tactics of rolling and rearing back. But he kicked like a master, and buck-jumped rather neatly. In five minutes Ugh-lomi lived a lifetime. If he came off the horse would kill him, he felt assured.

Then the Master Horse decided to stick to his old tactics again, and suddenly went off at a gallop. He headed down the slope, taking the steep places at a rush, swerving neither to the right nor to the left, and, as they rode down, the wide expanse of valley sank out of sight behind the approaching skirmishers of oak and hawthorn. They skirted a sudden hollow with the pool of a spring, rank weeds and silver bushes. The ground grew softer and the grass taller, and on the right-hand side and the left came scattered bushes of May—still splashed with belated blossom. Presently the bushes thickened until they lashed the passing rider, and little flashes and gouts of blood came out on horse and man. Then the way opened again.

And then came a wonderful adventure. A sudden squeal of unreasonable anger rose amidst the bushes, the squeal of some creature bitterly wronged. And crashing after them appeared a big, grey-blue shape. It was Yaaa, the big-horned rhinoceros, in one of those fits of fury of his, charging full tilt, after the manner of his kind. He had been startled at his feeding, and someone, it did not matter who, was to be ripped and trampled therefor. He was bearing down on them from the left, with his wicked little eye red, his great horn down, and his tail like a jury-mast behind him. For a minute Ugh-lomi was minded to slip off and dodge, and then behold! the staccato of the hoofs grew swifter, and the rhinoceros and his stumpy hurrying little legs seemed to slide out at the back corner of Ugh-lomi's eye. In two minutes they were through the bushes of May, and out in the open, going fast. For a space he could hear the ponderous paces in pursuit receding behind him, and then it was just as if Yaaa had not lost his temper, as if Yaaa had never existed.

The pace never faltered, on they rode and on.

Ugh-lomi was now all exultation. To exult in those days was to insult. "Ya-ha! big nose!" he said, trying to crane back and see some remote speck of a pursuer. "Why don't you carry your smiting-stone in your fist?" he ended with a frantic whoop.

But that whoop was unfortunate, for coming close to the ear

of the horse, and being quite unexpected, it startled the stallion extremely. He shied violently. Ugh-lomi suddenly found himself uncomfortable again. He was hanging on to the horse, he found, by one arm and one knee.

The rest of the ride was honourable but unpleasant. The view was chiefly of blue sky, and that was combined with the most unpleasant physical sensations. Finally, a bush of thorn lashed him and he let go.

He hit the ground with his cheek and shoulder, and then, after a complicated and extraordinarily rapid movement, hit it again with the end of his backbone. He saw splashes and sparks of light and colour. The ground seemed bouncing about just like the horse had done. Then he found he was sitting on turf, six yards beyond the bush. In front of him was a space of grass, growing greener and greener, and a number of human beings in the distance, and the horse was going round at a smart gallop quite a long way off to the right.

The human beings were on the opposite side of the river, some still in the water, but they were all running away as hard as they could go. The advent of a monster that took to pieces was not the sort of novelty they cared for. For quite a minute Ugh-lomi sat regarding them in a purely spectacular spirit. The bend of the river, the knoll among the reeds and royal ferns, the thin streams of smoke going up to Heaven, were all perfectly familiar to him. It was the squatting-place of the Sons of Uya, of Uya from whom he had fled with Eudena, and whom he had waylaid in the chestnut-woods and killed with the first axe.

He rose to his feet, still dazed from his fall, and as he did so the scattering fugitive turned and regarded him. Some pointed to the receding horse and chattered. He walked slowly towards them, staring. He forgot the horse, he forgot his own bruises, in the growing interest of this encounter. There were fewer of them than there had been—he supposed the others must have hid—the heap of fern for the night fire was not so high. By the flint heaps should have sat Wau—but then he remembered he had killed Wau. Suddenly brought back to this familiar scene, the gorge and the bears and Eudena seemed things remote, things dreamt of.

He stopped at the bank and stood regarding the tribe. His mathematical abilities were of the slightest, but it was certain there were fewer. The men might be away, but there were fewer women and children. He gave the shout of home-coming. His quarrel had been with Uya and Wau—not with the others. "Children of Uya!" he cried. They answered with his name, a little fearfully because of the strange way he had come.

For a space they spoke together. Then an old woman lifted a shrill voice and answered him, "Our Lord is a Lion."

Ugh-lomi did not understand that saying. They answered him again several together, "Uya comes again. He comes as a Lion. Our Lord is a Lion. He comes at night. He slays whom he will. But none other may slay us, Ugh-lomi, none other may slay us."

Still Ugh-lomi did not understand.

"Our Lord is a Lion. He speaks no more to men."

Ugh-lomi stood regarding them. He had had dreams—he knew that though he had killed Uya, Uya still existed. And now they told him Uya was a Lion.

The shrivelled old woman, the mistress of the fire-minders, suddenly turned and spoke softly to those next to her. She was a very old woman indeed, she had been the first of Uya's wives, and he had let her live beyond the age to which it is seemly a woman should be permitted to live. She had been cunning from the first, cunning to please Uya and to get food. And now she was great in counsel. She spoke softly, and Ugh-lomi watched her shrivelled form across the river with a curious distaste. Then she called aloud, "Come over to us, Ugh-Lomi."

A girl suddenly lifted up her voice. "Come over to us, Ugh-lomi," she said. And they all began crying, "Come over to us, Ugh-lomi."

It was strange how their manner changed after the old woman called.

He stood quite still watching them all. It was pleasant to be called, and the girl who had called first was a pretty one. But she made him think of Eudena.

"Come over to us, Ugh-lomi," they cried, and the voice of the shrivelled old woman rose above them all. At the sound of her voice his hesitation returned.

He stood on the river bank, Ugh-lomi—Ugh the Thinker—with his thoughts slowly taking shape. Presently one and then another paused to see what he would do. He was minded to go back, he was minded not to. Suddenly his fear or his caution got the upper hand. Without answering them he turned, and walked back towards the distant thorn-trees, the way he had come. Forthwith the whole tribe started crying to him again very eagerly. He hesitated and turned, then he went on, then he turned again, and then once again, regarding them with troubled eyes as they called. The last time he took two paces back, before his fear stopped him. They saw him stop once more, and suddenly shake his head and vanish among the hawthorn-trees.

Then all the women and children lifted up their voices together, and called to him in one last vain effort.

Far down the river the reeds were stirring in the breeze, where, convenient for his new sort of feeding, the old lion, who had taken to man-eating, had made his lair.

The old woman turned her face that way, and pointed to the hawthorn thickets. "Uya," she screamed, "there goes thine enemy! There goes thine enemy, Uya! Why do you devour us nightly? We have tried to snare him! There goes thine enemy, Uya!"

But the lion who preyed upon the tribe was taking his siesta. The cry went unheard. That day he had dined on one of the plumper girls, and his mood was a comfortable placidity. He really did not understand that he was Uya or that Ugh-lomi was his enemy.

So it was that Ugh-lomi rode the horse, and heard first of Uya the Lion, who had taken the place of Uya the Master, and was eating up the tribe. And as he hurried back to the gorge his mind was no longer full of the horse, but of the thought that Uya was still alive, to slay or be slain. Over and over again he saw the shrunken band of women and children crying that Uya was a lion. Uya was a lion!

And presently, fearing the twilight might come upon him, Ugh-lomi began running.

IV. Uya the Lion

The old lion was in luck. The tribe had a certain pride in their ruler, but that was all the satisfaction they got out of it. He came the very night that Ugh-lomi killed Uya the Cunning, and so it was they named him Uya. It was the old woman, the fire-minder, who first named him Uya. A shower had lowered the fires to a glow, and made the night dark. And as they conversed together, and peered at one another in the darkness, and wondered fearfully what Uya would do to them in their dreams now that he was dead, they heard the mounting reverberations of the lion's roar close at hand. Then everything was still.

They held their breath, so that almost the only sounds were the patter of the rain and the hiss of the raindrops in the ashes. And then, after an interminable time, a crash, and a shriek of fear, and a growling. They sprang to their feet, shouting, screaming, running this way and that, but brands would not burn, and in a minute the victim was being dragged away through the ferns. It was Irk, the brother of Wau.

So the lion came.

The ferns were still wet from the rain the next night, and he came and took Click with the red hair. That sufficed for two nights. And then in the dark between the moons he came three nights, night after night, and that though they had good fires. He was an old lion with stumpy teeth, but very silent and very cool; he knew of fires before; these were not the first of mankind that had ministered to his old age. The third night he came between the outer fire and the inner, and he leapt the flint heap, and pulled down Irm the son of Irk, who had seemed like to be the leader. That was a dreadful night, because they lit great flares of fern and ran screaming, and the lion missed his hold of Irm. By the glare of the fire they saw Irm struggle up, and run a little way towards them, and then the lion in two bounds had him down again. That was the last of Irm.

So fear came, and all the delight of spring passed out of their lives. Already there were five gone out of the tribe, and four nights added three more to the number. Food-seeking became spiritless, none knew who might go next, and all day the women toiled, even the favourite women, gathering litter and sticks for the night-fires. And the hunters hunted ill: in the warm spring-time hunger came again as though it was still winter. The tribe might have moved, had they had a leader, but they had no leader, and none knew where to go that the lion could not follow them. So the old lion waxed fat and thanked heaven for the kindly race of men. Two of the children and a youth died while the moon was still new, and then it was the shrivelled old fire-minder first bethought herself in a dream of Eudena and Ugh-lomi, and of the way Uya had been slain. She had lived in fear of Uya all her days, and now she lived in fear of the lion. That Ugh-lomi could kill Uya for good—Ugh-lomi whom she had seen born—was impossible. It was Uya still seeking his enemy!

And then came the strange return of Ugh-lomi, a wonderful animal seen galloping far across the river, that suddenly changed into two animals, a horse and a man. Following this portent, the vision of Ugh-lomi on the farther bank of the river. . . . Yes, it was all plain to her. Uya was punishing them, because they had not hunted down Ugh-lomi and Eudena.

The men came straggling back to the chances of the night while the sun was still golden in the sky. They were received with the story of Ugh-lomi. She went across the river with them and showed them his spoor hesitating on the farther bank. Siss the Tracker knew the feet for Ugh-lomi's. "Uya needs Ugh-lomi," cried the old woman, standing on the left of the bend, a gesticulating figure of flaring bronze in the sunset. Her cries were strange sounds, flitting to and fro on the borderland of speech, but this was the sense they carried: "The lion needs Eudena. He comes night after night seeking

Eudena and Ugh-lomi. When he cannot find Eudena and Ugh-lomi, he grows angry and he kills. Hunt Eudena and Ugh-lomi, Eudena whom he pursued, and Ugh-lomi for whom he gave the death-word! Hunt Eudena and Ugh-lomi!"

She turned to the distant reed-bed, as sometimes she had turned to Uya in his life. "Is it not so, my lord?" she cried. And, as if in answer, the tall reeds bowed before a breath of wind.

Far into the twilight the sound of hacking was heard from the squatting-places. It was the men sharpening their ashen spears against the hunting of the morrow. And in the night, early before the moon rose, the lion came and took the girl of Siss the Tracker.

In the morning before the sun had risen, Siss the Tracker, and the lad Wau-hau, who now chipped flints, and One Eye, and Bo, and the snail-eater, the two red-haired men, and Cat's-skin and Snake, all the men that were left alive of the Sons of Uya, taking their ash spears and their smiting-stones, and with throwing-stones in the beast-paw bags, started forth upon the trail of Ugh-lomi through the hawthorn thickets where Yaaa the Rhinoceros and his brothers were feeding, and up the bare downland towards the beech-woods.

That night the fires burnt high and fierce, as the waxing moon set, and the lion left the crouching women and children in peace.

And the next day, while the sun was still high, the hunters returned—all save One Eye, who lay dead with a smashed skull at the foot of the ledge. (When Ugh-lomi came back that evening from stalking the horses, he found the vultures already busy over him.) And with them the hunters brought Eudena, bruised and wounded, but alive. That had been the strange order of the shrivelled old woman, that she was to be brought alive—"She is no kill for us. She is for Uya the Lion." Her hands were tied with thongs, as though she had been a man, and she came weary and drooping—her hair over her eyes and matted with blood. They walked about her, and ever and again the Snail-Eater, whose name she had given, would laugh and strike her with his ashen spear. And after he had struck her with his spear, he would look over his shoulder like one who had done an over-bold deed. The others, too, looked over their shoulders ever and again, and all were in a hurry save Eudena. When the old woman saw them coming, she cried aloud with joy.

They made Eudena cross the river with her hands tied, although the current was strong and when she slipped the old woman screamed, first with joy and then for fear she might be drowned. And when they had dragged Eudena to shore, she could not stand for a time, albeit they beat her sore. So they let her sit with her feet touching the water, and her eyes staring before her, and her face set, whatever they might do or say. All the tribe came down to the squatting-place, even curly little Haha, who as yet could scarcely toddle and stood staring at Eudena and the old woman, as now we should stare at some strange wounded beast and its captor.

The old woman tore off the necklace of Uya that was about Eudena's neck, and put it on herself—she had been the first to wear it. Then she tore at Eudena's hair, and took a spear from Siss and beat her with all her might. And when she had vented the warmth of her heart on the girl she looked closely into her face. Eudena's eyes were closed and her features were set, and she lay so still that for a moment the old woman feared she was dead. And then her nostrils quivered. At that the old woman slapped her face and laughed and gave the spear to Siss again, and went a little way off from her and began to talk and jeer at her after her manner.

The old woman had more words than any in the tribe. And her talk was a terrible thing to hear. Sometimes she screamed and moaned incoherently, and sometimes the shape of her guttural cries was the mere phantom of thoughts. But she conveyed to Eudena, nevertheless, much of the things that were yet to come, of the Lion and of the torment he would do her. "And Ugh-lomi! Ha, ha! Ugh-lomi is slain?"

And suddenly Eudena's eyes opened and she sat up again, and her look met the old woman's fair and level. "No," she said slowly, like one trying to remember, "I did not see my Ugh-lomi slain. I did not see my Ugh-lomi slain."

"Tell her," cried the old woman. "Tell her—he that killed him. Tell her how Ugh-lomi was slain."

She looked, and all the women and children there looked, from man to man.

None answered her. They stood shamefaced.

"Tell her," said the old woman. The men looked at one another.

Eudena's face suddenly lit.

"Tell her," she said. "Tell her, mighty men! Tell her the killing of Ugh-lomi."

The old woman rose and struck her sharply across her mouth.

"We could not find Ugh-lomi," said Siss the Tracker, slowly. "Who hunts two, kills none."

Then Eudena's heart leapt, but she kept her face hard. It was as well, for the old woman looked at her sharply, with murder in her eyes.

Then the old woman turned her tongue upon the men because they had feared to go on after Ugh-lomi. She dreaded no one now Uya was slain. She scolded them as one scolds children. And they scowled at her, and began to accuse one another. Until suddenly Siss the Tracker raised his voice and bade her hold her peace.

And so when the sun was setting they took Eudena and went—though their hearts sank within them—along the trail the old lion had made in the reeds. All the men went together. At one place was a group of alders, and here they hastily bound Eudena where the lion might find her when he came abroad in the twilight, and having done so they hurried back until they were near the squatting-place. Then they stopped. Siss stopped first and looked back again at the alders. They could see her head even from the squatting-place, a little black shock under the limb of the larger tree. That was as well.

All the women and children stood watching upon the crest of the mound. And the old woman stood and screamed for the lion to take her whom he sought, and counselled him on the torments he might do her.

Eudena was very weary now, stunned by beatings and fatigue and sorrow, and only the fear of the thing that was still to come upheld her. The sun was broad and blood-red between the stems of the distant chestnuts, and the west was all on fire; the evening breeze had died to a warm tranquillity. The air was full of midge swarms, the fish in the river hard by would leap at times, and now and again a cockchafer would drone through the air. Out of the corner of her eye Eudena could see a part of the squatting-knoll, and little figures standing and staring at her. And—a very little sound but very clear—she could hear the beating of the firestone. Dark and near to her and still was the reed-fringed thicket of the lair.

Presently the firestone ceased. She looked for the sun and found he had gone, and overhead and growing brighter was the waxing moon. She looked towards the thicket of the lair, seeking shapes in the reeds, and then suddenly she began to wriggle and wriggle, weeping and calling upon Ugh-lomi.

But Ugh-lomi was far away. When they saw her head moving with her struggles, they shouted together on the knoll, and she desisted and was still. And then came the bats, and the star that was like Ugh-lomi crept out of its blue hiding place in the west. She called to it, but softly, because she feared the lion. And all through the coming of the twilight the thicket was still.

So the dark crept upon Eudena, and the moon grew bright, and the shadows of things that had fled up the hillside and vanished with the evening came back to them short and black. And the dark shapes in the thicket of reeds and alders where the lion lay, gathered, and a faint stir began there. But nothing came out therefrom all through the gathering of the darkness.

She looked at the squatting-place and saw the fires glowing smoky-red, and the men and women going to and fro. The other way, over the river, a white mist was rising. Then far away came the whimpering of young foxes and the yell of a hyæna.

There were long gaps of aching waiting. After a long time some animal splashed in the water, and seemed to cross the river at the ford beyond the lair, but what animal it was she could not see. From the distant drinking-pools she could hear the sound of splashing, and the noise of elephants—so still was the night.

The earth was now a colourless arrangement of white reflections and impenetrable shadows, under the blue sky. The silvery moon was already spotted with the filigree crests of the chestnut-woods, and over the shadowy eastward hills the stars were multiplying. The knoll fires were bright red now, and black figures stood waiting against them. They were waiting for a scream. . . . Surely it would be soon.

The night suddenly seemed full of movement. She held her breath. Things were passing—one, two, three—subtly sneaking shadows. . . . Jackals.

Then a long waiting again.

Then, asserting itself as real at once over all the sounds her mind had imagined, came a stir in the thicket, then a vigorous movement. There was a snap. The reeds crashed heavily, once, twice, thrice, and then everything was still save a measured swishing. She heard a low tremulous growl, and then everything was still again. The stillness lengthened—would it never end? She held her breath; she bit her lips to stop screaming. Then something scuttled through the undergrowth. Her scream was involuntary. She did not hear the answering yell from the mound.

Immediately the thicket woke up to vigorous movement again. She saw the grass stems waving in the light of the setting moon, the alders swaying. She struggled violently—her last struggle. But nothing came towards her. A dozen monsters seemed rushing about in that little place for a couple of minutes, and then again came silence. The moon sank behind the distant chestnuts and the night was dark.

Then an odd sound, a sobbing panting, that grew faster and fainter. Yet another silence, and then dim sounds and the grunting of some animal.

Everything was still again. Far away eastwards an elephant trumpeted, and from the woods came a snarling and yelping that died away.

In the long interval the moon shone out again, between the stems of the trees on the ridge, sending two great bars of light and a bar of darkness across the reedy waste. Then came a steady rustling, a splash, and the reeds swayed wider and wider apart. And at last they broke open, cleft from root to crest. . . . The end had come.

She looked to see the thing that had come out of the reeds. For a moment it seemed certainly the great head and jaw she expected, and then it dwindled and changed. It was a dark low thing, that remained silent, but it was not the lion. It became still—everything became still. She peered. It was like some gigantic frog, two limbs and a slanting body. Its head moved about searching the shadows. . . .

A rustle, and it moved clumsily, with a sort of hopping. And as it moved it gave a low groan.

The blood rushing through her veins was suddenly joy. "*Ugh-lomi!*" she whispered.

The thing stopped. "*Eudena*," he answered softly with pain in his voice, and peering into the alders.

He moved again, and came out of the shadow beyond the reeds into the moonlight. All his body was covered with dark smears. She saw he was dragging his leg, and that he gripped his axe, the first axe, in one hand. In another moment he had struggled into the position of all fours, and had staggered over to her. "The lion," he said in a strange mingling of exultation and anguish. "Wau!—I have slain a lion. With my own hand. Even as I slew the great bear." He moved to emphasise his words, and suddenly broke off with a faint cry. For a space he did not move.

"Let me free," whispered Eudena. . . .

He answered her no words but pulled himself up from his crawling attitude by means of the alder stem, and hacked at her thongs with the sharp edge of his axe. She heard him sob at each blow. He cut away the thongs about her chest and arms, and then his hand dropped. His chest struck against her shoulder and he slipped down beside her and lay still.

But the rest of her release was easy. Very hastily she freed herself. She made one step from the tree, and her head was spinning. Her last conscious movement was towards him. She reeled, and dropped. Her hand fell upon his thigh. It was soft and wet, and gave way under her pressure; he cried out at her touch, and writhed and lay still again.

Presently a dark dog-like shape came very softly through the reeds. Then stopped dead and stood sniffing, hesitated, and at last turned and slunk back into the shadows.

Long was the time they remained there motionless, with the light of the setting moon shining on their limbs. Very slowly, as slowly as the setting of the moon, did the shadow of the reeds towards the mound flow over them. Presently their legs were hidden, and Ugh-lomi was but a bust of silver. The shadow crept to his neck, crept over his face, and so at last the darkness of the night swallowed them up.

The shadow became full of instinctive stirrings. There was a patter of feet, and a faint snarling—the sound of a blow.

There was little sleep that night for the women and children at the squatting-place until they heard Eudena scream. But the men were weary and sat dozing. When Eudena screamed they felt assured of their safety, and hurried to get the nearest places to the fires. The old woman laughed at the scream, and laughed again because Si, the little friend of Eudena, whimpered. Directly the dawn came they were all alert and looking towards the alders. They could see that Eudena had been taken. They could not help feeling glad to think that Uya was appeased. But across the minds of the men the thought of Ugh-lomi fell like a shadow. They could understand revenge, for the world was old in revenge, but they did not think of rescue. Suddenly a hyæna fled out of the thicket, and came galloping across the reed space. His muzzle and paws were dark-stained. At that sight all the men shouted and clutched at throwing-stones and ran towards him, for no animal is so pitiful a coward as the hyæna by day. All men hated the hyæna because he preyed on children, and would come and bite when one was sleeping on the edge of the squatting-place. And Cat's-skin, throwing fair and straight, hit the brute shrewdly on the flank, whereat the whole tribe yelled with delight.

At the noise they made there came a flapping of wings from the lair of the lion, and three white-headed vultures rose slowly and circled and came to rest amidst the branches of an alder, overlooking the lair. "Our lord is abroad," said the old woman, pointing. "The vultures have their share of Eudena." For a space they remained there, and then first one and then another dropped back into the thicket.

Then over the eastern woods, and touching the whole world of life and colour, poured, with the exaltation of a trumpet blast, the light of the rising sun. At the sight of him the children shouted together, and clapped their hands and began to race off towards the water. Only little Si lagged behind and looked wonderingly at the alders where she had seen the head of Eudena overnight.

But Uya, the old lion, was not abroad, but at home, and he lay very still, and a little on one side. He was not in his lair, but a little way from it in a place of trampled grass. Under one eye was a little wound, the feeble little bite of the first axe. But all the ground beneath his chest was ruddy brown with a vivid streak, and in his chest was a little hole that had been made by Ugh-lomi's stabbing-spear. Along his side and at his neck the vultures had marked their claims. For so Ugh-lomi had slain him, lying stricken under his paw and thrusting haphazard at his chest. He had driven the spear in with all his strength and stabbed the giant to the heart. So it was the reign of the lion, of the second incarnation of Uya the Master, came to an end.

From the knoll the bustle of preparation grew, the hacking of spears and throwing-stones. None spake the name of Ugh-lomi for fear that it might bring him. The men were going to keep together, close together, in the hunting for a day or so. And their hunting was to be Ugh-lomi, lest instead he should come a-hunting them.

But Ugh-lomi was lying very still and silent, outside the lion's lair, and Eudena squatted beside him, with the ash spear, all smeared with lion's blood, gripped in her hand.

V. The Fight in the Lion's Thicket

Ugh-lomi lay still, his back against an alder, and his thigh was a red mass terrible to see. No civilised man could have lived who had been so sorely wounded, but Eudena got him thorns to close his wounds, and squatted beside him day and night, smiting the flies from him with a fan of reeds by day, and in the night threatening the hyænas with the first axe in her hand; and in a little while he began to heal. It was high summer, and there was no rain. Little food they had during the first two days his wounds were open. In the low place where they hid were no roots nor little beasts, and the stream, with its water-snails and fish, was in the open a hundred yards away. She could not go abroad by day for fear of the tribe, her brothers and sisters, nor by night for fear of the beasts, both on his account and hers. So they shared the lion with the vultures. But there was a trickle of water near by, and Eudena brought him plenty in her hands.

Where Ugh-lomi lay was well hidden from the tribe by a thicket of alders, and all fenced about with bulrushes and tall reeds. The dead lion he had killed lay near his old lair on a place of trampled reeds fifty yards away, in sight through the reed-stems, and the vultures fought each other for the choicest pieces and kept the jackals off him. Very soon a cloud of flies that looked like bees hung over him, and Ugh-lomi could hear their humming. And when Ugh-lomi's flesh was already healing—and it was not many days before that began—only a few bones of the lion remained scattered and shining white.

For the most part Ugh-lomi sat still during the day, looking before him at nothing; sometimes he would mutter of the horses and bears and lions, and sometimes he would beat the ground with the first axe and say the names of the tribe—he seemed to have no fear of bringing the tribe—for hours together. But chiefly he slept, dreaming little because of his loss of blood and the slightness of his food. During the short summer night both kept awake. All the while the darkness lasted things moved about them, things they never saw by day. For some nights the hyænas did not come, and then one moonless night near a dozen came and fought for what was left of the lion. The night was a tumult of growling, and Ugh-lomi and Eudena could hear the bones snap in their teeth. But they knew the hyæna dare not attack any creature alive and awake, and so they were not greatly afraid.

Of a daytime Eudena would go along the narrow path the old lion had made in the reeds until she was beyond the bend, and then she would creep into the thicket and watch the tribe. She would lie close by the alders where they had bound her to offer her up to the lion, and thence she could see them on the knoll by the fire, small and clear, as she had seen them that night. But she told Ugh-lomi little of what she saw, because she feared to bring them by their names. For so they believed in those days, that naming called.

She saw the men prepare stabbing-spears and throwing-stones on the morning after Ugh-lomi had slain the lion, and go out to hunt him, leaving the women and children on the knoll. Little they knew how near he was as they tracked off in single file towards the hills, with Siss the Tracker leading them. And she watched the women and children, after the men had gone, gathering fern-fronds and twigs for the night-fire, and the boys and girls running and playing together. But the very old woman made her feel afraid. Towards noon, when most of the others were down at the stream by the bend, she came and stood on the hither side of the knoll, a gnarled brown figure, and gesticulated so that Eudena could scarce believe she was not seen. Eudena lay like a hare in its form, with shining eyes fixed on the bent witch away there, and presently she dimly understood it was the lion the old woman was worshipping—the lion Ugh-lomi had slain.

And the next day the hunters came back weary, carrying a fawn, and Eudena watched the feast enviously. And then came a strange thing. She saw—distinctly she heard—the old woman shrieking and gesticulating and pointing towards her. She was afraid, and crept like a snake out of sight again. But presently curiosity overcame her and she was back at her spying-place, and as she peered her heart stopped, for there were all the men, with their weapons in their hands, walking together towards her from the knoll.

She dared not move lest her movement should be seen, but she pressed herself close to the ground. The sun was low and the golden light was in the faces of the men. She saw they carried a piece of rich red meat thrust through by an ashen stake. Presently they stopped. "Go on!" screamed the old woman. Cat's-skin grumbled, and they came on, searching the thicket with sun-dazzled eyes. "Here!" said Siss. And they took the ashen stake with the meat upon it and thrust it into the ground. "Uya!" cried Siss, "behold thy portion. And Ugh-lomi we have slain. Of a truth we have slain Ugh-lomi. This day we slew Ugh-lomi, and to-morrow we will bring his body to you." And the others repeated the words.

They looked at each other and behind them, and partly turned and began going back. At first they walked half-turned to the thicket, then, facing the mound, they walked faster, looking over their shoulders, then faster; soon they ran, it was a race at last, until they were near the knoll. Then Siss, who was hindmost, was first to slacken his pace.

The sunset passed and the twilight came, the fires glowed red against the hazy blue of the distant chestnut-trees, and the voices over the mound were merry. Eudena lay scarcely stirring, looking from the mound to the meat and then to the mound. She was hungry, but she was afraid. At last she crept back to Ugh-lomi.

He looked round at the little rustle of her approach. His face was in shadow. "Have you got me some food?" he said.

She said she could find nothing, but that she would seek farther, and went back along the lion's path until she could see the mound again, but she could not bring herself to take the meat; she had the brute's instinct of a snare. She felt very miserable.

She crept back at last towards Ugh-lomi and heard him stirring and moaning. She turned back to the mound again; then she saw something in the darkness near the stake, and peering distinguished a jackal. In a flash she was brave and angry; she sprang up, cried out, and ran towards the offering.

She stumbled and fell, and heard the growling of the jackal going off.

When she arose only the ashen stake lay on the ground, the meat was gone. So she went back, to fast through the night with Ugh-lomi; and Ugh-lomi was angry with her, because she had no food for him; but she told him nothing of the things she had seen.

Two days passed and they were near starving, when the tribe slew a horse. Then came the same ceremony, and a haunch was left on the ashen stake; but this time Eudena did not hesitate.

By acting and words she made Ugh-lomi understand, but he ate most of the food before he understood; and then as her meaning passed to him he grew merry with his food. "I am Uya," he said; "I am the Lion. I am the Great Cave Bear, I who was only Ugh-lomi. I am Wau the Cunning. It is well that they should feed me, for presently I will kill them all."

Then Eudena's heart was light, and she laughed with him; and afterwards she ate what he had left of the horseflesh with gladness.

After that it was he had a dream, and the next day he made Eudena bring him the lion's teeth and claws—so much of them as she could find—and hack him a club of alder. And he put the teeth and claws very cunningly into the wood so that the points were outward. Very long it took him, and he blunted two of the teeth hammering them in, and was very angry and threw the thing away; but afterwards he dragged himself to where he had thrown it and finished it—a club of a new sort set with teeth. That day there was more meat for them both, an offering to the lion from the tribe.

It was one day—more than a hand's fingers of days, more than anyone had skill to count—after Ugh-lomi had made the club, that Eudena while he was asleep was lying in the thicket watching the squatting-place. There had been no meat for three days. And the old woman came and worshipped after her manner. Now while she worshipped, Eudena's little friend Si and another, the child of the first girl Siss had loved, came over the knoll and stood regarding her skinny figure, and presently they began to mock her. Eudena found this entertaining, but suddenly the old woman turned on them quickly and saw them. For a moment she stood and they stood motionless, and then with a shriek of rage, she rushed towards them, and all three disappeared over the crest of the knoll.

Presently the children reappeared among the ferns beyond the shoulder of the hill. Little Si ran first, for she was an active girl, and the other child ran squealing with the old woman close upon her. And over the knoll came Siss with a bone in his hand, and Bo and Cat's-skin obsequiously behind him, each holding a piece of food, and they laughed aloud and shouted to see the old woman so angry. And with a shriek the child was caught and the old woman set to work slapping and the child screaming, and it was very good after-dinner fun for them. Little Si ran on a little way and stopped at last between fear and curiosity.

And suddenly came the mother of the child, with hair streaming, panting, and with a stone in her hand, and the old woman turned about like a wild cat. She was the equal of any woman, was the chief of the fire-minders, in spite of her years; but before she could do anything Siss shouted to her and the clamour rose loud. Other shock heads came into sight. It seemed the whole tribe was at home and feasting. But the old woman dared not go on wreaking herself on the child Siss befriended.

Everyone made noises and called names—even little Si. Abruptly the old woman let go of the child she had caught and made a swift run at Si, for Si had no friends; and Si, realising her danger when it was almost upon her, made off headlong, with a faint cry of terror, not heeding whither she ran, straight to the lair of the lion. She swerved aside into the reeds presently, realising now whither she went.

But the old woman was a wonderful old woman, as active as she was spiteful, and she caught Si by the streaming hair within thirty yards of Eudena. All the tribe now was running down the knoll and shouting and laughing, ready to see the fun.

Then something stirred in Eudena; something that had never stirred in her before; and, thinking all of little Si and nothing of her fear, she sprang up from her ambush and ran swiftly forward. The old woman did not see her, for she was busy beating little Si's face with her hand, beating with all her heart, and suddenly something hard and heavy struck her cheek. She went reeling, and saw Eudena with flaming eyes and cheeks between her and little Si. She shrieked with astonishment and terror, and little Si, not understanding, set off towards the gaping tribe. They were quite close now, for the sight of Eudena had driven their fading fear of the lion out of their heads.

In a moment Eudena had turned from the cowering old woman and overtaken Si. "Si!" she cried, "Si!" She caught the child up in her arms as it stopped, pressed the nail-lined face to hers, and turned about to run towards her lair, the lair of the old lion. The old woman stood waist-high in the reeds, and screamed foul things and inarticulate rage, but did not dare to intercept her; and at the bend of the path Eudena looked back and saw all the men of the tribe crying to one another and Siss coming at a trot along the lion's trail.

She ran straight along the narrow way through the reeds to the shady place where Ugh-lomi sat with his healing thigh, just awakened by the shouting and rubbing his eyes. She came to him, a woman, with little Si in her arms. Her heart throbbed in her throat. "Ugh-lomi!" she cried. "Ugh-lomi, the tribe comes!"

Ugh-lomi sat staring in stupid astonishment at her and Si.

She pointed with Si in one arm. She sought among her feeble store of words to explain. She could hear the men calling. Apparently they had stopped outside. She put down Si and caught up the new club with the lion's teeth, and put it into Ugh-lomi's hand, and ran three yards and picked up the first axe.

"Ah!" said Ugh-lomi, waving the new club, and suddenly he perceived the occasion and, rolling over, began to struggle to his feet.

He stood but clumsily. He supported himself by one hand against the tree, and just touched the ground gingerly with the toe of his wounded leg. In the other hand he gripped the new club. He looked at his healing thigh; and suddenly the reeds began whispering, and ceased and whispered again, and coming cautiously along the track, bending down and holding his fire-hardened stabbing-stick of ash in his hand, appeared Siss. He stopped dead, and his eyes met Ugh-lomi's.

Ugh-lomi forgot he had a wounded leg. He stood firmly on both feet. Something trickled. He glanced down and saw a little gout of blood had oozed out along the edge of the healing wound. He rubbed his hand there to give him the grip of his club, and fixed his eyes again on Siss.

"Wau!" he cried, and sprang forward, and Siss, still stooping and watchful, drove his stabbing-stick up very quickly in an ugly thrust. It ripped Ugh-lomi's guarding arm and the club came down in a counter that Siss was never to understand. He fell, as an ox falls to the pole-axe, at Ugh-lomi's feet.

To Bo it seemed the strangest thing. He had a comforting sense of tall reeds on either side, and an impregnable rampart, Siss, between him and any danger. Snail-eater was close behind and there was no danger there. He was prepared to shove behind and send Siss to death or victory. That was his place as second man. He saw the butt of the spear Siss carried leap away from him, and suddenly a dull whack and the broad back fell away forward, and he looked Ugh-lomi in the face over his prostrate leader. It felt to Bo as if his heart had fallen down a well. He had a throwing-stone in one hand and an ashen stabbing-stick in the other. He did not live to the end of his momentary hesitation which to use.

Snail-eater was a readier man, and besides Bo did not fall forward as Siss had done, but gave at his knees and hips, crumpling up with the toothed club upon his head. The Snail-eater drove his spear forward swift and straight, and took Ugh-lomi in the muscle of the shoulder, and then he drove him hard with the smiting-stone in his other hand, shouting out as he did so. The new club swished ineffectually through the reeds. Eudena saw Ugh-lomi come staggering back from the narrow path into the open space, tripping over Siss and with a foot of ashen stake sticking out of him over his arm. And then the Snail-eater, whose name she had given, had his final injury from her, as his exultant face came out of the reeds after his spear. For she swung the first axe swift and high, and hit him fair and square on the temple; and down he went on Siss at prostrate Ugh-lomi's feet.

But before Ugh-lomi could get up, the two red-haired men were tumbling out of the reeds, spears and smiting-stones ready, and Snake hard behind them. One she struck on the neck, but not to fell him, and he blundered aside and spoilt his brother's blow at Ugh-lomi's head. In a moment Ugh-lomi dropped his club and had his assailant by the waist, and had pitched him sideways sprawling. He snatched at his club again and recovered it. The man Eudena had hit stabbed at her with his spear as he stumbled from her blow, and involuntarily she gave ground to avoid him. He hesitated between her and Ugh-lomi, half-turned, gave a vague cry at finding Ugh-lomi so near, and in a moment Ugh-lomi had him by the throat, and the club had its third victim. As he went down Ugh-lomi shouted—no words, but an exultant cry.

The other red-haired man was six feet from her with his back to her, and a darker red streaking his head. He was struggling to his feet. She had an irrational impulse to stop his rising. She flung the axe at him, missed, saw his face in profile, and he had swerved beyond little Si, and was running through the reeds. She had a transitory vision of Snake standing in the throat of the path, half-turned away from her, and then she saw his back. She saw the club whirling through the air, and the shock head of Ugh-lomi, with blood in the hair and blood upon the shoulder, vanishing below the reeds in pursuit. Then she heard Snake scream like a woman.

She ran past Si to where the handle of the axe stuck out of a clump of fern, and turning, found herself panting and alone with three motionless bodies. The air was full of shouts and screams. For a space she was sick and giddy, and then it came into her head that Ugh-lomi was being killed along the reed-path, and with an inarticulate cry she leapt over the body of Bo and hurried after him. Snake's feet lay across the path, and his head was among the reeds. She followed the path until it bent round and opened out by the alders, and thence she saw all that was left of the tribe in the open, scattering like dead leaves before a gale, and going back over the knoll. Ugh-lomi was hard upon Cat's-skin.

But Cat's-skin was fleet of foot and got away, and so did young Wau-Hau when Ugh-lomi turned upon him, and Ugh-lomi pursued Wau-Hau far beyond the knoll before he desisted. He had the rage of battle on him now, and the wood thrust through his shoulder stung him like a spur. When she saw he was in no danger she stopped running and stood panting, watching the distant active figures run up and vanish one by one over the knoll. In a little time she was alone again. Everything had happened very swiftly. The smoke of Brother Fire rose straight and steady from the squatting-place, just as it had done ten minutes ago, when the old woman had stood yonder worshipping the lion.

And after a long time, as it seemed, Ugh-lomi reappeared over the knoll, and came back to Eudena, triumphant and breathing heavily. She stood, her hair about her eyes and hot-faced, with the blood-stained axe in her hand, at the place where the tribe had offered her as a sacrifice to the lion. "Wau!" cried Ugh-lomi at the sight of her, his face alight with the fellowship of battle, and he waved his new club, red now and hairy; and at the sight of his glowing face her tense pose relaxed somewhat, and she stood sobbing and rejoicing.

Ugh-lomi had a queer, unaccountable pang at the sight of her tears; but he only shouted "Wau!" the louder and shook the axe east and west. He called manfully to her to follow him and turned back, striding, with the club swinging in his hand, towards the squatting-place, as if he had never left the tribe; and she ceased her weeping and followed quickly as a woman should.

So Ugh-lomi and Eudena came back to the squatting-place from which they had fled many days before from the face of Uya; and by the squatting-place lay a deer half-eaten, just as there had been before Ugh-lomi was man or Eudena woman. So Ugh-lomi sat down to eat, and Eudena beside him like a man, and the rest of the tribe watched them from safe hiding places. And after a time one of the elder girls came back timorously, carrying little Si in her arms, and Eudena called to them by name, and offered them food. But the elder girl was afraid and would not come, though Si struggled to come to Eudena. Afterwards, when Ugh-lomi had eaten, he sat dozing, and at last he slept, and slowly the others came out of the hiding places and drew near. And when Ugh-lomi woke, save that there were no men to be seen, it seemed as though he had never left the tribe.

Now, there is a thing strange but true: that all through this fight Ugh-lomi forgot that he was lame, and was not lame, and after he had rested behold! he was a lame man; and he remained a lame man to the end of his days.

Cat's-skin and the second red-haired man and Wau-Hau, who chipped flints cunningly, as his father had done before him, fled from the face of Ugh-lomi, and none knew where they hid. But two days after they came and squatted a good way off from the knoll among the bracken under the chestnuts and watched. Ugh-lomi's rage had gone, he moved to go against them and did not, and at sundown they went away. That day, too, they found the old woman among the ferns, where Ugh-lomi had blundered upon her when he had pursued Wau-Hau. She was dead and more ugly than ever, but whole. The jackals and vultures had tried her and left her;—she was ever a wonderful old woman.

The next day the three men came again and squatted nearer, and Wau-Hau had two rabbits to hold up, and the red-haired man a wood-pigeon, and Ugh-lomi stood before the women and mocked them.

The next day they sat again nearer—without stones or sticks, and with the same offerings, and Cat's-skin had a trout. It was rare men caught fish in those days, but Cat's-skin would stand silently in the water for hours and catch them with his hand. And the fourth day Ugh-lomi suffered these three to come to the squatting-place in peace, with the food they had with them. Ugh-lomi ate the trout. Thereafter for many moons Ugh-lomi was master and had his will in peace. And on the fulness of time he was killed and eaten even as Uya had been slain.

ÆPYORNIS ISLAND

THE man with the scarred face leant over the table and looked at my bundle.

"Orchids?" he asked.

"A few," I said.

"Cypripediums," he said.

"Chiefly," said I.

"Anything new? I thought not. I did these islands twenty-five—twenty-seven years ago. If you find anything new here —well, it's brand new. I didn't leave much."

"I'm not a collector," said I.

"I was young then," he went on. "Lord! how I used to fly round." He seemed to take my measure. "I was in the East Indies two years and in Brazil seven. Then I went to Madagascar."

"I know a few explorers by name," I said, anticipating a yarn. "Whom did you collect for?"

"Dawsons'. I wonder if you've heard the name of Butcher ever?"

"Butcher—Butcher?" The name seemed vaguely present in my memory; then I recalled *Butcher* v. *Dawson*. "Why!" said I, "you are the man who sued them for four years' salary —got cast away on a desert island. . . ."

"Your servant," said the man with the scar, bowing. "Funny case, wasn't it? Here was me, making a little fortune on that island, doing nothing for it neither, and them quite unable to give me notice. It often used to amuse me thinking over it while I was there. I did calculations of it—big—all over the blessed atoll in ornamental figuring."

"How did it happen?" said I. "I don't rightly remember the case.".

"Well. . . . You've heard of the Æpyornis?"

"Rather. Andrews was telling me of a new species he was

418

working on only a month or so ago. Just before I sailed. They've got a thigh-bone, it seems, nearly a yard long. Monster the thing must have been!"

"I believe you," said the man with the scar. "It *was* a monster. Sindbad's roc was just a legend of 'em. But when did they find these bones?"

"Three or four years ago—'91, I fancy. Why?"

"Why? Because *I* found them—Lord!—it's nearly twenty years ago. If Dawsons' hadn't been silly about that salary they might have made a perfect ring in 'em. . . . I couldn't help the infernal boat going adrift."

He paused. "I suppose it's the same place. A kind of swamp about ninety miles north of Antananarivo. Do you happen to know? You have to go to it along the coast by boats. You don't happen to remember, perhaps?"

"I don't. I fancy Andrews said something about a swamp."

"It must be the same. It's on the east coast. And somehow there's something in the water that keeps things from decaying. Like creosote it smells. It reminded me of Trinidad. Did they get any more eggs? Some of the eggs I found were a foot and a half long. The swamp goes circling round, you know, and cuts off this bit. It's mostly salt, too. Well. . . . What a time I had of it! I found the things quite by accident. We went for eggs, me and two native chaps, in one of those rum canoes all tied together, and found the bones at the same time. We had a tent and provisions for four days, and we pitched on one of the firmer places. To think of it brings that odd tarry smell back even now. It's funny work. You go probing into the mud with iron rods, you know. Usually the egg gets smashed. I wonder how long it is since these Æpyornises really lived. The missionaries say the natives have legends about when they were alive, but I never heard any such stories myself.* But certainly those eggs we got were as fresh as if they had been new laid. Fresh! Carrying them down to the boat one of my nigger chaps dropped one on a rock and it smashed. How I lammed into the beggar! But sweet it was,

---

*No European is known to have seen a live Æpyornis, with the doubtful exception of Macer, who visited Madagascar in 1745.—H. G. W.

as if it was new laid, not even smelly, and its mother dead
these four hundred years, perhaps. Said a centipede had bit
him. However, I'm getting off the straight with the story.
It had taken us all day to dig into the slush and get these
eggs out unbroken, and we were all covered with beastly
black mud, and naturally I was cross. So far as I knew they
were the only eggs that have ever been got out not even
cracked. I went afterwards to see the ones they have at the
Natural History Museum in London; all of them were cracked
and just stuck together like a mosaic, and bits missing. Mine
were perfect, and I meant to blow them when I got back.
Naturally I was annoyed at the silly duffer dropping three
hours' work just on account of a centipede. I hit him about
rather."

The man with the scar took out a clay pipe. I placed my
pouch before him. He filled up absent-mindedly.

"How about the others? Did you get those home? I don't
remember——"

"That's the queer part of the story. I had three others.
Perfectly fresh eggs. Well, we put 'em in the boat, and then
I went up to the tent to make some coffee, leaving my two
heathens down by the beach—the one fooling about with his
sting and the other helping him. It never occurred to me that
the beggar would take advantage of the peculiar position I
was in to pick a quarrel. But I suppose the centipede poison
and the kicking I had given him had upset the one—he was
always a cantankerous sort—and he persuaded the other.

"I remember I was sitting and smoking and boiling up the
water over a spirit-lamp business I used to take on these expeditions. Incidentally I was admiring the swamp under the
sunset. All black and blood-red it was, in streaks—a beautiful
sight. And up beyond the land rose grey and hazy to the hills,
and the sky behind them red, like a furnace mouth. And fifty
yards behind the back of me was these blessed heathen—quite
regardless of the tranquil air of things—plotting to cut off
with the boat and leave me all alone with three days' provisions and a canvas tent, and nothing to drink whatsoever
beyond a little keg of water. I heard a kind of yelp behind me,

and there they were in this canoe affair—it wasn't properly a boat—and, perhaps, twenty yards from land. I realised what was up in a moment. My gun was in the tent, and, besides, I had no bullets—only duck shot. They knew that. But I had a little revolver in my pocket, and I pulled that out as I ran down to the beach.

"'Come back!' says I, flourishing it.

"They jabbered something at me, and the man that broke the egg jeered. I aimed at the other—because he was unwounded and had the paddle, and I missed. They laughed. However, I wasn't beat. I knew I had to keep cool, and I tried him again and made him jump with the whang of it. He didn't laugh that time. The third time I got his head, and over he went, and the paddle with him. It was a precious lucky shot for a revolver. I reckon it was fifty yards. He went right under. I don't know if he was shot, or simply stunned and drowned. Then I began to shout to the other chap to come back, but he huddled up in the canoe and refused to answer. So I fired out my revolver at him and never got near him.

"I felt a precious fool, I can tell you. There I was on this rotten black beach, flat swamp all behind me, and the flat sea, cold after the sun set, and just this black canoe drifting steadily out to sea. I tell you I damned Dawsons' and Jamrach's and Museums and all the rest of it just to rights. I bawled to this nigger to come back, until my voice went up into a scream.

"There was nothing for it but to swim after him and take my luck with the sharks. So I opened my clasp-knife and put it in my mouth, and took off my clothes and waded in. As soon as I was in the water I lost sight of the canoe, but I aimed, as I judged, to head it off. I hoped the man in it was too bad to navigate it, and that it would keep on drifting in the same direction. Presently it came up over the horizon again to the south-westward about. The afterglow of sunset was well over now and the dim of night creeping up. The stars were coming through the blue. I swum like a champion, though my legs and arms were soon aching.

"However, I came up to him by the time the stars were

fairly out. As it got darker I began to see all manner of glowing things in the water—phosphorescence, you know. At
times it made me giddy. I hardly knew which was stars and
which was phosphorescence, and whether I was swimming on
my head or my heels. The canoe was as black as sin, and the
ripple under the bows like liquid fire. I was naturally chary
of clambering up into it. I was anxious to see what he was up
to first. He seemed to be lying cuddled up in a lump in the
bows, and the stern was all out of water. The thing kept turning round slowly as it drifted—kind of waltzing, don't you
know. I went to the stern and pulled it down, expecting him
to wake up. Then I began to clamber in with my knife in
my hand, and ready for a rush. But he never stirred. So there
I sat in the stern of the little canoe, drifting away over the
calm phosphorescent sea and with all the host of the stars
above me, waiting for something to happen.

"After a long time I called him by name, but he never
answered. I was too tired to take any risks by going along to
him. So we sat there. I fancy I dozed once or twice. When
the dawn came I saw he was as dead as a door-nail and all
puffed up and purple. My three eggs and the bones were
lying in the middle of the canoe, and the keg of water and
some coffee and biscuits wrapped in a Cape *Argus* by his feet,
and a tin of methylated spirit underneath him. There was no
paddle, nor, in fact, anything except the spirit tin that I
could use as one, so I settled to drift until I was picked up.
I held an inquest on him, brought in a verdict against some
snake, scorpion, or centipede unknown, and sent him overboard.

"After that I had a drink of water and a few biscuits, and
took a look round. I suppose a man low down as I was don't
see very far; leastways, Madagascar was clean out of sight,
and any trace of land at all. I saw a sail going south-westward
—looked like a schooner but her hull never came up. Presently the sun got high in the sky and began to beat down
upon me. Lord! it pretty near made my brains boil. I tried
dipping my head in the sea, but after a while my eye fell on
the Cape *Argus*, and I lay down flat in the canoe and spread

this over me. Wonderful things these newspapers! I never read one through thoroughly before, but it's odd what you get up to when you're alone, as I was. I suppose I read that blessed old Cape *Argus* twenty times. The pitch in the canoe simply reeked with the heat and rose up into big blisters.

"I drifted ten days," said the man with the scar. "It's a little thing in the telling, isn't it? Every day was like the last. Except in the morning and the evening I never kept a lookout even—the blaze was so infernal. I didn't see a sail after the first three days, and those I saw took no notice of me. About the sixth night a ship went by scarcely half a mile away from me, with all its lights ablaze and its ports open, looking like a big firefly. There was music aboard. I stood up and shouted and screamed at it. The second day I broached one of the Æpyornis eggs, scraped the shell away at the end bit by bit, and tried it, and I was glad to find it was good enough to eat. A bit flavoury—not bad, I mean—but with something of the taste of a duck's egg. There was a kind of circular patch, about six inches across, on one side of the yolk, and with streaks of blood and a white mark like a ladder in it that I thought queer, but I did not understand what this meant at the time, and I wasn't inclined to be particular. The egg lasted me three days, with biscuits and a drink of water. I chewed coffee-berries, too—invigorating stuff. The second egg I opened about the eighth day, and it scared me."

The man with the scar paused. "Yes," he said, "developing.

"I dare say you find it hard to believe. I did, with the thing before me. There the egg had been, sunk in that cold black mud, perhaps three hundred years. But there was no mistaking it. There was the—what is it?—embryo, with its big head and curved back, and its heart beating under its throat, and the yolk shrivelled up and great membranes spreading inside of the shell and all over the yolk. Here was I hatching out the eggs of the biggest of all extinct birds, in a little canoe in the midst of the Indian Ocean. If old Dawson had known that! It was worth four years' salary. What do *you* think?

"However, I had to eat that precious thing up, every bit of

it, before I sighted the reef, and some of the mouthfuls were beastly unpleasant. I left the third one alone. I held it up to the light, but the shell was too thick for me to get any notion of what might be happening inside; and though I fancied I heard blood pulsing, it might have been the rustle in my own ears, like what you listen to in a seashell.

"Then came the atoll. Came out of the sunrise, as it were, suddenly, close up to me. I drifted straight towards it until I was about half a mile from shore, not more, and then the current took a turn, and I had to paddle as hard as I could with my hands and bits of the Æpyornis shell to make the place. However, I got there. It was just a common atoll about four miles round, with a few trees growing and a spring in one place, and the lagoon full of parrot-fish. I took the egg ashore and put it in a good place, well above the tide lines and in the sun, to give it all the chance I could, and pulled the canoe up safe, and loafed about prospecting. It's rum how dull an atoll is. As soon as I had found a spring all the interest seemed to vanish. When I was a kid I thought nothing could be finer or more adventurous than the Robinson Crusoe business, but that place was as monotonous as a book of sermons. I went round finding eatable things and generally thinking; but I tell you I was bored to death before the first day was out. It shows my luck—the very day I landed the weather changed. A thunderstorm went by to the north and flicked its wing over the island, and in the night there came a drencher and a howling wind slap over us. It wouldn't have taken much, you know, to upset that canoe.

"I was sleeping under the canoe, and the egg was luckily among the sand higher up the beach, and the first thing I remember was a sound like a hundred pebbles hitting the boat at once, and a rush of water over my body. I'd been dreaming of Antananarivo, and I sat up and halloaed to Intoshi to ask her what the devil was up, and clawed out at the chair where the matches used to be. Then I remembered where I was. There were phosphorescent waves rolling up as if they meant to eat me, and all the rest of the night as black as pitch. The air was simply yelling. The clouds seemed down on your head almost, and the rain fell as if heaven was sinking and they were baling out the waters above the firmament. One great roller came writhing at me, like a fiery serpent, and I bolted. Then I thought of the canoe, and ran down to it as the water went hissing back again; but the thing had gone. I wondered about the egg, then, and felt my way to it. It was all right and well out of reach of the maddest waves, so I sat down beside it and cuddled it for company. Lord! what a night that was!

"The storm was over before the morning. There wasn't a rag of cloud left in the sky when the dawn came, and all along the beach there were bits of plank scattered—which was the disarticulated skeleton, so to speak, of my canoe. However, that gave me something to do, for taking advantage of two of the trees being together, I rigged up a kind of storm-shelter with these vestiges. And that day the egg hatched.

"Hatched, sir, when my head was pillowed on it and I was asleep. I heard a whack and felt a jar and sat up, and there was the end of the egg pecked out and a rum little brown head looking out at me. 'Lord!' I said, 'you're welcome'; and with a little difficulty he came out.

"He was a nice friendly little chap at first, about the size of a small hen—very much like most other young birds, only bigger. His plumage was a dirty brown to begin with, with a sort of grey scab that fell off it very soon, and scarcely feathers—a kind of downy hair. I can hardly express how pleased I was to see him. I tell you, Robinson Crusoe don't make near enough of his loneliness. But here was interesting company. He looked at me and winked his eye from the front backward, like a hen, and gave a chirp and began to peck about at once, as though being hatched three hundred years too late was just nothing. 'Glad to see you, Man Friday!' says I, for I had naturally settled he was to be called Man Friday if ever he was hatched, as soon as ever I found the egg in the canoe had developed. I was a bit anxious about his feed, so I gave him a lump of raw parrot-fish at once. He took it, and opened his beak for more. I was glad of that, for, under the circumstances, if he'd been at all fanciful, I should have had to eat him, after all.

"You'd be surprised what an interesting bird that Æpyornis chick was. He followed me about from the very beginning. He used to stand by me and watch while I fished in the lagoon, and go shares in anything I caught. And he was sensible, too. There were nasty green warty things, like pickled gherkins, used to lie about on the beach, and he tried one of these and it upset him. He never even looked at any of them again.

"And he grew. You could almost see him grow. And as I was never much of a society man, his quiet, friendly ways suited me to a T. For nearly two years we were as happy as we could be on that island. I had no business worries, for I knew my salary was mounting up at Dawsons'. We would see a sail now and then, but nothing ever came near us. I amused myself, too, by decorating the island with designs worked in sea-urchins and fancy shells of various kinds. I put ÆPYORNIS ISLAND all around the place very nearly, in big letters, like what you see done with coloured stones at railway stations in the old country, and mathematical calculations and drawings of various sorts. And I used to lie watching the blessed bird stalking round and growing, growing; and think how I could make a living out of him by showing him about if I ever got taken off. After his first moult he began to get handsome, with a crest and a blue wattle, and a lot of green feathers at the behind of him. And then I used to puzzle whether Dawsons' had any right to claim him or not. Stormy weather and in the rainy season we lay snug under the shelter I had made out of the old canoe, and I used to tell him lies about my friends at home. And after a storm we would go round the island together to see if there was any drift. It was a kind of idyll, you might say. If only I had had some tobacco it would have been simply just like heaven.

"It was about the end of the second year our little paradise went wrong. Friday was then about fourteen feet high to the bill of him, with a big, broad head like the end of a pickaxe, and two huge brown eyes with yellow rims, set together like a man's—not out of sight of each other like a hen's. His plumage was fine—none of the half-mourning style of your ostrich

—more like a cassowary as far as colour and texture go. And then it was he began to cock his comb at me and give himself airs, and show signs of a nasty temper. . . .

"At last came a time when my fishing had been rather unlucky, and he began to hang about me in a queer, meditative way. I thought he might have been eating sea-cucumbers or something, but it was really just discontent on his part. I was hungry, too, and when at last I landed a fish I wanted it for myself. Tempers were short that morning on both sides. He pecked at it and grabbed it, and I gave him a whack on the head to make him leave go. And at that he went for me. Lord! . . .

"He gave me this in the face." The man indicated his scar. "Then he kicked me. It was like a carthorse. I got up, and seeing he hadn't finished, I started off full tilt with my arms doubled up over my face. But he ran on those gawky legs of his faster than a race-horse, and kept landing out at me with sledge-hammer kicks and bringing his pickaxe down on the back of my head. I made for the lagoon, and went in up to my neck. He stopped at the water, for he hated getting his feet wet, and began to make a shindy, something like a peacock's only hoarser. He started strutting up and down the beach. I'll admit I felt small to see this blessed fossil lording it there. And my head and face were all bleeding, and—well, my body just one jelly of bruises.

"I decided to swim across the lagoon and leave him alone for a bit, until the affair blew over. I shinned up the tallest palm-tree, and sat there thinking of it all. I don't suppose I ever felt so hurt by anything before or since. It was the brutal ingratitude of the creature. I'd been more than a brother to him. I'd hatched him, educated him. A great gawky, out-of-date bird! And me a human being—heir of the ages and all that.

"I thought after a time he'd begin to see things in that light himself, and feel a little sorry for his behaviour. I thought if I was to catch some nice little bits of fish, perhaps, and go to him presently in a casual kind of way, and offer them to him, he might do the sensible thing. It took me some time to learn how unforgiving and cantankerous an extinct bird can be. Malice!

"I won't tell you all the little devices I tried to get that bird round again. I simply can't. It makes my cheek burn with shame even now to think of the snubs and buffets I had from this infernal curiosity. I tried violence. I chucked lumps of coral at him from a safe distance, but he only swallowed them. I shied my open knife at him and almost lost it, though it was too big for him to swallow. I tried starving him out and struck fishing, but he took to picking along the beach at low water after worms, and rubbed along on that. Half my time I spent up to my neck in the lagoon, and the rest up the palm-trees. One of them was scarcely high enough, and when he caught me up it he had a regular Bank Holiday with the calves of my legs. It got unbearable. I don't know if you have ever tried sleeping up a palm-tree. It gave me the most horrible nightmares. Think of the shame of it, too! Here was this extinct animal mooning about my island like a sulky duke, and me not allowed to rest the sole of my foot on the place. I used to cry with weariness and vexation. I told him straight that I didn't mean to be chased about a desert island by any damned anachronisms. I told him to go and peck a navigator of his own age. But he only snapped his beak at me. Great ugly bird, all legs and neck!

"I shouldn't like to say how long that went on altogether. I'd have killed him sooner if I'd known how. However, I hit on a way of settling him at last. It is a South American dodge. I joined all my fishing lines together with stems of seaweed and things, and made a stoutish string, perhaps twelve yards in length or more, and I fastened two lumps of coral rock to the ends of this. It took me some time to do, because every now and then I had to go into the lagoon or up a tree as the fancy took me. This I whirled rapidly round my head, and then let it go at him. The first time I missed, but the next time the string caught his legs beautifully, and wrapped round them again and again. Over he went. I threw it standing waist-deep in the lagoon, and as soon as he went down I was out of the water and sawing at his neck with my knife. . . .

"I don't like to think of that even now. I felt like a mur-

derer while I did it, though my anger was hot against him
When I stood over him and saw him bleeding on the white
sand, and his beautiful great legs and neck writhing in his
last agony . . . Pah!

"With that tragedy loneliness came upon me like a curse.
Good Lord! you can't imagine how I missed that bird. I sat
by his corpse and sorrowed over him, and shivered as I looked
round the desolate, silent reef. I thought of what a jolly little
bird he had been when he was hatched, and of a thousand
pleasant tricks he had played before he went wrong. I thought
if I'd only wounded him I might have nursed him round
into a better understanding. If I'd had any means of digging
into the coral rock I'd have buried him. I felt exactly as if he
was human. As it was, I couldn't think of eating him, so I
put him in the lagoon, and the little fishes picked him clean.
I didn't even save the feathers. Then one day a chap cruising
about in a yacht had a fancy to see if my atoll still existed.

"He didn't come a moment too soon, for I was about sick
enough of the desolation of it, and only hesitating whether I
should walk out into the sea and finish up the business that
way, or fall back on the green things. . . .

"I sold the bones to a man named Winslow—a dealer near
the British Museum, and he says he sold them to old Havers.
It seems Havers didn't understand they were extra large, and
it was only after his death they attracted attention. They
called 'em Æpyornis—what was it?"

"*Æpyornis vastus*," said I. "It's funny, the very thing was
mentioned to me by a friend of mine. When they found an
Æpyornis with a thigh a yard long, they thought they had
reached the top of the scale, and called him *Æpyornis maximus*. Then someone turned up another thigh-bone four feet
six or more, and that they called *Æpyornis titan*. Then your
vastus was found after old Havers died, in his collection, and
then a *vastissimus* turned up."

"Winslow was telling me as much," said the man with the
scar. "If they get any more Æpyornises, he reckons some
scientific swell will go and burst a blood-vessel. But it was a
queer thing to happen to a man; wasn't it—altogether?"

THE REMARKABLE CASE OF
DAVIDSON'S EYES

THE transitory mental aberration of Sidney Davidson, remarkable enough in itself, is still more remarkable if Wade's
explanation is to be credited. It sets one dreaming of the
oddest possibilities of intercommunication in the future, of
spending an intercalary five minutes on the other side of the
world, or being watched in our most secret operations by
unsuspected eyes. It happened that I was the immediate
witness of Davidson's seizure, and so it falls naturally to me
to put the story upon paper.

When I say that I was the immediate witness of this seizure,
I mean that I was the first on the scene. The thing happened
at the Harlow Technical College, just beyond the Highgate
Archway. He was alone in the larger laboratory when the
thing happened. I was in a smaller room, where the balances
are, writing up some notes. The thunderstorm had completely
upset my work, of course. It was just after one of the louder
peals that I thought I heard some glass smash in the other
room. I stopped writing, and turned round to listen. For a
moment I heard nothing; the hail was playing the devil's
tattoo on the corrugated zinc of the roof. Then came another
sound, a smash—no doubt of it this time. Something heavy
had been knocked off the bench. I jumped up at once and
went and opened the door leading into the big laboratory.

I was surprised to hear a queer sort of laugh, and saw
Davidson standing unsteadily in the middle of the room,
with a dazzled look on his face. My first impression was that
he was drunk. He did not notice me. He was clawing out at
something invisible a yard in front of his face. He put out
his hand slowly, rather hesitatingly, and then clutched nothing. "What's come to it?" he said. He held up his hands to
his face, fingers spread out. "Great Scott!" he said. The

430

thing happened three or four years ago, when everyone swore by that personage. Then he began raising his feet clumsily, as though he had expected to find them glued to the floor.

"Davidson!" cried I. "What's the matter with you?" He turned round in my direction and looked about for me. He looked over me and at me and on either side of me, without the slightest sign of seeing me. "Waves," he said; "and a remarkably neat schooner. I'd swear that was Bellows' voice. *Hullo!*" He shouted suddenly at the top of his voice.

I thought he was up to some foolery. Then I saw littered about his feet the shattered remains of the best of our electrometers. "What's up, man?" said I. "You've smashed the electrometer!"

"Bellows again!" said he. "Friends left, if my hands are gone. Something about electrometers. Which way *are* you, Bellows?" He suddenly came staggering towards me. "The damned stuff cuts like butter," he said. He walked straight into the bench and recoiled. "None so buttery that!" he said, and stood swaying.

I felt scared. "Davidson," said I, "what on earth's come over you?"

He looked round him in every direction. "I could swear that was Bellows. Why don't you show yourself like a man, Bellows?"

It occurred to me that he must be suddenly struck blind. I walked round the table and laid my hand upon his arm. I never saw a man more startled in my life. He jumped away from me, and came round into an attitude of self-defence, his face fairly distorted with terror. "Good God!" he cried. "What was that?"

"It's I—Bellows. Confound it, Davidson!"

He jumped when I answered him and stared—how can I express it?—right through me. He began talking, not to me, but to himself. "Here in broad daylight on a clear beach. Not a place to hide in." He looked about him wildly. "Here! I'm *off*." He suddenly turned and ran headlong into the big electromagnet—so violently that, as we found afterwards, he bruised his shoulder and jawbone cruelly. At that he stepped back a pace, and cried out with almost a whimper: "What, in Heaven's name, has come over me?" He stood, blanched with terror and trembling violently, with his right arm clutching his left, where that had collided with the magnet.

By that time I was excited and fairly scared. "Davidson," said I, "don't be afraid."

He was startled at my voice, but not so excessively as before. I repeated my words in as clear and as firm a tone as I could assume. "Bellows," he said, "is that you?"

"Can't you see it's me?"

He laughed. "I can't even see it's myself. Where the devil are we?"

"Here," said I, "in the laboratory."

"The laboratory!" he answered in a puzzled tone, and put his hand to his forehead. "I *was* in the laboratory—till that flash came, but I'm hanged if I'm there now. What ship is that?"

"There's no ship," said I. "Do be sensible, old chap."

"No ship!" he repeated, and seemed to forget my denial forthwith. "I suppose," said he slowly, "we're both dead. But the rummy part is I feel just as though I still had a body. Don't get used to it all at once, I suppose. The old ship was struck by lighting, I suppose. Jolly quick thing, Bellows—eigh?"

"Don't talk nonsense. You're very much alive. You are in the laboratory, blundering about. You've just smashed a new electrometer. I don't envy you when Boyce arrives."

He stared away from me towards the diagrams of cryohydrates. "I must be deaf," said he. "They've fired a gun, for there goes the puff of smoke, and I never heard a sound."

I put my hand on his arm again, and this time he was less alarmed. "We seem to have a sort of invisible bodies," said he. "By jove! there's a boat coming round the headland. It's very much like the old life, after all—in a different climate."

I shook his arm. "Davidson," I cried, "wake up!"

It was just then that Boyce came in. So soon as he spoke Davidson exclaimed: "Old Boyce! Dead, too! What a lark!"

I hastened to explain that Davidson was in a kind of somnambulistic trance. Boyce was interested at once. We both did all we could to rouse the fellow out of his extraordinary state. He answered our questions, and asked us some of his own, but his attention seemed distracted by his hallucination about a beach and a ship. He kept interpolating observations concerning some boat and the davits, and sails filling with the wind. It made one feel queer, in the dusky laboratory, to hear him saying such things.

He was blind and helpless. We had to walk him down the passage, one at each elbow, to Boyce's private room, and while Boyce talked to him there, and humoured him about this ship idea, I went along the corridor and asked old Wade to come and look at him. The voice of our Dean sobered him a little, but not very much. He asked where his hands were, and why he had to walk about up to his waist in the ground. Wade thought over him a long time—you know how he knits his brows—and then made him feel the couch, guiding his hands to it. "That's a couch," said Wade. "The couch in the private room of Prof. Boyce. Horsehair stuffing."

Davidson felt about, and puzzled over it, and answered presently that he could feel it all right, but he couldn't see it.

"What do you see?" asked Wade. Davidson said he could see nothing but a lot of sand and broken-up shells. Wade gave him some other things to feel, telling him what they were, and watching him keenly.

"The ship is almost hull down," said Davidson presently, apropos of nothing.

"Never mind the ship," said Wade. "Listen to me, Davidson. Do you know what hallucination means?"

"Rather," said Davidson.

"Well, everything you see is hallucinatory."

"Bishop Berkeley," said Davidson.

"Don't mistake me," said Wade. "You are alive and in this room of Boyce's. But something has happened to your eyes. You cannot see; you can feel and hear, but not see. Do you follow me?"

"It seems to me that I see too much." Davidson rubbed his knuckles into his eyes. "Well?" he said.

"That's all. Don't let it perplex you. Bellows here and I will take you home in a cab."

"Wait a bit," Davidson thought. "Help me to sit down," said he presently; "and now—I'm sorry to trouble you—but will you tell me all that over again?"

Wade repeated it very patiently. Davidson shut his eyes, and pressed his hands upon his forehead. "Yes," said he. "It's quite right. Now my eyes are shut I know you're right. That's you, Bellows, sitting by me on the couch. I'm in England again. And we're in the dark."

Then he opened his eyes. "And there," said he, "is the sun just rising, and the yards of the ship, and a tumbled sea, and a couple of birds flying. I never saw anything so real. And I'm sitting up to my neck in a bank of sand."

He bent forward and covered his face with his hands. Then he opened his eyes again. "Dark sea and sunrise! And yet I'm sitting on a sofa in old Boyce's room! . . . God help me!"

That was the beginning. For three weeks this strange affection of Davidson's eyes continued unabated. It was far worse than being blind. He was absolutely helpless, and had to be fed like a newly hatched bird, and led about and undressed. If he attempted to move, he fell over things or struck himself against walls or doors. After a day or so he got used to hearing our voices without seeing us, and willingly admitted he was at home, and that Wade was right in what he told him. My sister, to whom he was engaged, insisted on coming to see him, and would sit for hours every day while he talked about this beach of his. Holding her hand seemed to comfort him immensely. He explained that when we left the College and drove home—he lived in Hampstead village—it appeared to him as if we drove right through a sandhill—it was perfectly black until he emerged again—and through rocks and trees and solid obstacles, and when he was taken to his own room it made him giddy and almost frantic with the fear of falling, because going upstairs seemed to lift him thirty or forty feet above the rocks of his imaginary island. He kept saying he should smash all the eggs. The end was that he had to be taken down into his father's consulting-room and laid upon a couch that stood there.

He described the island as being a bleak kind of place on the whole, with very little vegetation, except some peaty stuff, and a lot of bare rock. There were multitudes of penguins, and they made the rocks white and disagreeable to see. The sea was often rough, and once there was a thunderstorm, and he lay and shouted at the silent flashes. Once or twice seals pulled up on the beach, but only on the first two or three days. He said it was very funny the way in which the penguins used to waddle right through him, and how he seemed to lie among them without disturbing them.

I remember one odd thing, and that was when he wanted very badly to smoke. We put a pipe in his hands—he almost poked his eye out with it—and lit it. But he couldn't taste anything. I've since found it's the same with me—I don't know if it's the usual case—that I cannot enjoy tobacco at all unless I can see the smoke.

But the queerest part of his vision came when Wade sent him out in a Bath-chair to get fresh air. The Davidsons hired a chair, and got that deaf and obstinate dependant of theirs, Widgery, to attend to it. Widgery's ideas of healthy expeditions were peculiar. My sister, who had been to the Dogs' Home, met them in Camden Town, towards King's Cross, Widgery trotting along complacently, and Davidson, evidently most distressed, trying in his feeble, blind way to attract Widgery's attention.

He positively wept when my sister spoke to him. "Oh, get me out of this horrible darkness!" he said, feeling for her hand. "I must get out of it, or I shall die." He was quite incapable of explaining what was the matter, but my sister decided he must go home, and presently, as they went uphill towards Hampstead, the horror seemed to drop from him. He said it was good to see the stars again, though it was then about noon and a blazing day.

"It seemed," he told me afterwards, "as if I was being

carried irresistibly towards the water. I was not very much alarmed at first. Of course it was night there—a lovely night."

"Of course?" I asked, for that struck me as odd.

"Of course," said he. "It's always night there when it is day here. . . . Well, we went right into the water, which was calm and shining under the moonlight—just a broad swell that seemed to grow broader and flatter as I came down into it. The surface glistened just like a skin—it might have been empty space underneath for all I could tell to the contrary. Very slowly, for I rode slanting into it, the water crept up to my eyes. Then I went under and the skin seemed to break and heal again about my eyes. The moon gave a jump up in the sky and grew green and dim, and fish, faintly glowing, came darting round me—and things that seemed made of luminous glass; and I passed through a tangle of seaweeds that shone with an oily lustre. And so I drove down into the sea, and the stars went out one by one, and the moon grew greener and darker, and the seaweed became a luminous purple-red. It was all very faint and mysterious, and everything seemed to quiver. And all the while I could hear the wheels of the Bath-chair creaking, and the footsteps of people going by, and a man in the distance selling the special *Pall Mall*.

"I kept sinking down deeper and deeper into the water. It became inky black about me, not a ray from above came down into that darkness, and the phosphorescent things grew brighter and brighter. The snaky branches of the deeper weeds flickered like the flames of spirit-lamps; but, after a time, there were no more weeds. The fishes came staring and gaping towards me, and into me and through me. I never imagined such fishes before. They had lines of fire along the sides of them as though they had been outlined with a luminous pencil. And there was a ghastly thing swimming backward with a lot of twining arms. And then I saw, coming very slowly towards me through the gloom, a hazy mass of light that resolved itself as it drew nearer into multitudes of fishes, struggling and darting round something that drifted.

I drove on straight towards it, and presently I saw in the midst of the tumult, and by the light of the fish, a bit of splintered spar looming over me, and a dark hull tilting over, and some glowing phosphorescent forms that were shaken and writhed as the fish bit at them. Then it was I began to try to attract Widgery's attention. A horror came upon me. Ugh! I should have driven right into those half-eaten —— things. If your sister had not come! They had great holes in them, Bellows, and . . . Never mind. But it was ghastly!"

For three weeks Davidson remained in this singular state, seeing what at the time we imagined was an altogether phantasmal world, and stone blind to the world around him. Then, one Tuesday, when I called I met old Davidson in the passage. "He can see his thumb!" the old gentleman said, in a perfect transport. He was struggling into his overcoat. "He can see his thumb, Bellows!" he said, with the tears in his eyes. "The lad will be all right yet."

I rushed in to Davidson. He was holding up a little book before his face, and looking at it and laughing in a weak kind of way.

"It's amazing," said he. "There's a kind of patch come there." He pointed with his finger. "I'm on the rocks as usual, and the penguins are staggering and flapping about as usual, and there's been a whale showing every now and then, but it's got too dark now to make him out. But put something *there*, and I see it—I do see it. It's very dim and broken in places, but I see it all the same, like a faint spectre of itself. I found it out this morning while they were dressing me. It's like a hole in this infernal phantom world. Just put your hand by mine. No—not there. Ah! Yes! I see it. The base of your thumb and a bit of cuff! It looks like the ghost of a bit of your hand sticking out of the darkling sky. Just by it there's a group of stars like a cross coming out."

From that time Davidson began to mend. His account of the change, like his account of the vision, was oddly convincing. Over patches of his field of vision, the phantom world grew fainter, grew transparent, as it were, and through these translucent gaps he began to see dimly the real world about him. The patches grew in size and number, ran together and spread until only here and there were blind spots left upon his eyes. He was able to get up and steer himself about, feed himself once more, read, smoke, and behave like an ordinary citizen again. At first it was very confusing to him to have these two pictures overlapping each other like the changing views of a lantern, but in a little while he began to distinguish the real from the illusory.

At first he was unfeignedly glad, and seemed only too anxious to complete his cure by taking exercise and tonics. But as that odd island of his began to fade away from him, he became queerly interested in it. He wanted particularly to go down into the deep sea again, and would spend half his time wandering about the low-lying parts of London, trying to find the water-logged wreck he had seen drifting. The glare of real daylight very soon impressed him so vividly as to blot out everything of his shadowy world, but of a night time, in a darkened room, he could still see the white-splashed rocks of the island, and the clumsy penguins staggering to and fro. But even these grew fainter and fainter, and, at last, soon after he married my sister, he saw them for the last time.

And now to tell of the queerest thing of all. About two years after his cure I dined with the Davidsons, and after dinner a man named Atkins called in. He is a lieutenant in the Royal Navy, and a pleasant, talkative man. He was on friendly terms with my brother-in-law, and was soon on friendly terms with me. It came out that he was engaged to Davidson's cousin, and incidentally he took out a kind of pocket photograph case to show us a new rendering of his *fiancée*. "And, by the bye," said he, "here's the old *Fulmar*."

Davidson looked at it casually. Then suddenly his face lit up. "Good heavens!" said he. "I could almost swear——"

"What?" said Atkins.

"That I had seen that ship before."

"Don't see how you can have. She hasn't been out of the South Seas for six years, and before then——"

"But," began Davidson, and then: "Yes—that's the ship

I dreamt of; I'm sure that's the ship I dreamt of. She was standing off an island that swarmed with penguins, and she fired a gun."

"Good Lord!" said Atkins, who had now heard the particulars of the seizure. "How the deuce could you dream that?"

And then, bit by bit, it came out that on the very day Davidson was seized, H. M. S. *Fulmar* had actually been off a little rock to the south of Antipodes Island. A boat had landed overnight to get penguins' eggs, had been delayed, and a thunderstorm drifting up, the boat's crew had waited until the morning before rejoining the ship. Atkins had been one of them, and he corroborated, word for word, the descriptions Davidson had given of the island and the boat. There is not the slightest doubt in any of our minds that Davidson has really seen the place. In some unaccountable way, while he moved hither and thither in London, his sight moved hither and thither, in a manner that corresponded, about this distant island. *How* is absolutely a mystery.

That completes the remarkable story of Davidson's eyes. It's perhaps the best authenticated case in existence of real vision at a distance. Explanation there is none forthcoming, except what Prof. Wade has thrown out. But his explanation involves the Fourth Dimension, and a dissertation on theoretical kinds of space. To talk of there being a "kink in space" seems mere nonsense to me; it may be because I am no mathematician. When I said that nothing would alter the fact that the place is eight thousand miles away, he answered that two points might be a yard away on a sheet of paper, and yet be brought together by bending the paper round. The reader may grasp his argument, but I certainly do not. His idea seems to be that Davidson, stooping between the poles of the big electromagnet, had some extraordinary twist given to his retinal elements through the sudden change in the field of force due to the lightning.

He thinks, as a consequence of this, that it may be possible to live visually in one part of the world, while one lives bodily in another. He has even made some experiments in support

of his views; but, so far, he has simply succeeded in blinding
a few dogs. I believe that is the net result of his work, though
I have not seen him for some weeks. Latterly I have been so
busy with my work in connection with the Saint Pancras
installation that I have had little opportunity of calling to see
him. But the whole of his theory seems fantastic to me. The
facts concerning Davidson stand on an altogether different
footing, and I can testify personally to the accuracy of every
detail I have given.

THE PLATTNER STORY

WHETHER the story of Gottfried Plattner is to be credited or not is a pretty question in the value of evidence. On the one hand, we have seven witnesses—to be perfectly exact, we have six and a half pairs of eyes, and one undeniable fact; and on the other we have—what is it?—prejudice, common sense, the inertia of opinion. Never were there seven more honest-seeming witnesses; never was there a more undeniable fact than the inversion of Gottfried Plattner's anatomical structure, and—never was there a more preposterous story than the one they have to tell! The most preposterous part of the story is the worthy Gottfried's contribution (for I count him as one of the seven). Heaven forbid that I should be led into giving countenance to superstition by a passion for impartiality, and so come to share the fate of Eusapia's patrons! Frankly, I believe there is something crooked about this business of Gottfried Plattner; but what that crooked factor is, I will admit as frankly, I do not know. I have been surprised at the credit accorded to the story in the most unexpected and authoritative quarters. The fairest way to the reader, however, will be for me to tell it without further comment.

Gottfried Plattner is, in spite of his name, a free-born Englishman. His father was an Alsatian who came to England in the Sixties, married a respectable English girl of unexceptionable antecedents, and died, after a wholesome and uneventful life (devoted, I understand, chiefly to the laying of parquet flooring), in 1887. Gottfried's age is seven-and-twenty. He is, by virtue of his heritage of three languages, Modern Languages Master in a small private school in the South of England. To the casual observer he is singularly like any other Modern Languages Master in any other small private school. His costume is neither very costly nor very fashionable, but, on the other hand, it is not markedly cheap or shabby; his complexion, like his height and his bearing, is inconspicuous. You would notice perhaps that, like the majority of people, his face was not absolutely symmetrical, his right eye a little larger than the left, and his jaw a trifle heavier on the right side. If you, as an ordinary careless person, were to bare his chest and feel his heart beating, you would probably find it quite like the heart of anyone else. But here you and the trained observer would part company. If you found his heart quite ordinary, the trained observer would find it quite otherwise. And once the thing was pointed out to you, you, too, would perceive the peculiarity easily enough. It is that Gottfried's heart beats on the right side of his body.

Now that is not the only singularity of Gottfried's structure, although it is the only one that would appeal to the untrained mind. Careful sounding of Gottfried's internal arrangements, by a well-known surgeon, seems to point to the fact that all the other unsymmetrical parts of his body are similarly misplaced. The right lobe of his liver is on the left side, the left on his right; while his lungs, too, are similarly contraposed. What is still more singular, unless Gottfried is a consummate actor we must believe that his right hand has recently become his left. Since the occurrences we are about to consider (as impartially as possible), he has found the utmost difficulty in writing except from right to left across the paper with his left hand. He cannot throw with his right hand, he is perplexed at meal times between knife and fork, and his ideas of the rule of the road—he is a cyclist—are still a dangerous confusion. And there is not a scrap of evidence to show that before these occurrences Gottfried was at all left-handed.

There is yet another wonderful fact in this preposterous business. Gottfried produces three photographs of himself. You have him at the age of five or six, thrusting fat legs at you from under a plaid frock, and scowling. In that photograph his left eye is a little larger than his right, and his jaw is a trifle heavier on the left side. This is the reverse of his present living conditions. The photograph of Gottfried at fourteen seems to contradict these facts, but that is because it is one of those cheap "Gem" photographs that were then in vogue, taken direct upon metal, and therefore reversing things just as a looking-glass would. The third photograph represents him at one-and-twenty, and confirms the record of the others. There seems here evidence of the strongest confirmatory character that Gottfried has exchanged his left side for his right. Yet how a human being can be so changed, short of a fantastic and pointless miracle, it is exceedingly hard to suggest.

In one way, of course, these facts might be explicable on the supposition that Plattner has undertaken an elaborate mystification on the strength of his heart's displacement. Photographs may be fudged, and left-handedness imitated. But the character of the man does not lend itself to any such theory. He is quiet, practical, unobtrusive, and thoroughly sane from the Nordau standpoint. He likes beer and smokes moderately, takes walking exercise daily, and has a healthily high estimate of the value of his teaching. He has a good but untrained tenor voice, and takes a pleasure in singing airs of a popular and cheerful character. He is fond, but not morbidly fond, of reading—chiefly fiction pervaded with a vaguely pious optimism—sleeps well, and rarely dreams. He is, in fact, the very last person to evolve a fantastic fable. Indeed, so far from forcing this story upon the world, he has been singularly reticent on the matter. He meets inquirers with a certain engaging—bashfulness is almost the word, that disarms the most suspicious. He seems genuinely ashamed that anything so unusual has occurred to him.

It is to be regretted that Plattner's aversion to the idea of post-mortem dissection may postpone, perhaps for ever, the positive proof that his entire body has had its left and right sides transposed. Upon that fact mainly the credibility of his story hangs. There is no way of taking a man and moving him about *in space*, as ordinary people understand space, that will result in our changing his sides. Whatever you do, his right is still his right, his left his left. You can do that with a perfectly thin and flat thing, of course. If you were to cut a figure out of paper, any figure with a right and left side, you could change its sides simply by lifting it up and turning it over. But with a solid it is different. Mathematical theorists tell us that the only way in which the right and left sides of a solid body can be changed is by taking that body clean out of space as we know it—taking it out of ordinary existence, that is, and turning it somewhere outside space. This is a little abstruse, no doubt, but anyone with a slight knowledge of mathematical theory will assure the reader of its truth. To put the thing in technical language, the curious inversion of Plattner's right and left sides is proof that he has moved out of our space into what is called the Fourth Dimension, and that he has returned again to our world. Unless we choose to consider ourselves the victims of an elaborate and motiveless fabrication, we are almost bound to believe that this has occurred.

So much for the tangible facts. We come now to the account of the phenomena that attended his temporary disappearance from the world. It appears that in the Sussexville Proprietary School, Plattner not only discharged the duties of Modern Languages Master, but also taught chemistry, commercial geography, bookkeeping, shorthand, drawing, and any other additional subject to which the changing fancies of the boy's parents might direct attention. He knew little or nothing of these various subjects, but in secondary as distinguished from Board or elementary schools, knowledge in the teacher is, very properly, by no means so necessary as high moral character and gentlemanly tone. In chemistry he was particularly deficient, knowing, he says, nothing beyond the Three Gases (whatever the three gases may be). As, however, his pupils began by knowing nothing, and derived all their information from him, this caused him (or anyone) but little inconvenience for several terms. Then a little boy named Whibble joined the school, who had been educated, it seems, by some mischievous relative into an inquiring habit of mind. This little boy followed Plattner's lessons with marked and sustained interest, and in order to exhibit his zeal on the subject, brought at various times substances for Plattner to analyse. Plattner, flattered by this evidence of his power to awaken interest and trusting to the boy's ignorance, analysed these and even made general statements as to their composition. Indeed he was so far stimulated by his pupil as to obtain a work upon analytical chemistry, and study it during his supervision of the evening's preparation. He was surprised to find chemistry quite an interesting subject.

So far the story is absolutely commonplace. But now the greenish powder comes upon the scene. The source of that greenish powder seems, unfortunately, lost. Master Whibble tells a tortuous story of finding it done up in a packet in a disused limekiln near the Downs. It would have been an excellent thing for Plattner, and possibly for Master Whibble's family, if a match could have been applied to that powder there and then. The young gentleman certainly did not bring it to school in a packet, but in a common eight-ounce graduated medicine bottle, plugged with masticated newspaper. He gave it to Plattner at the end of the afternoon school. Four boys had been detained after school prayers in order to complete some neglected tasks, and Plattner was supervising these in the small classroom in which the chemical teaching was conducted. The appliances for the practical teaching of chemistry in the Sussexville Proprietary School, as in most private schools in this country, are characterised by a severe simplicity. They are kept in a cupboard standing in a recess and having about the same capacity as a common travelling trunk. Plattner, being bored with his passive superintendence, seems to have welcomed the intervention of Whibble with his green powder as an agreeable diversion, and, unlocking this cupboard, proceeded at once with his analytical experiments. Whibble sat, luckily for himself, at a safe distance, regarding him. The four malefactors, feigning a profound absorption in their work, watched him furtively with the keenest interest. For even within the limits of the Three Gases, Plattner's practical chemistry was, I understand, temerarious.

They are practically unanimous in their account of Plattner's proceedings. He poured a little of the green powder into a test-tube, and tried the substance with water, hydrochloric acid, nitric acid, and sulphuric acid in succession. Getting no result, he emptied out a little heap—nearly half the bottleful, in fact—upon a slate and tried a match. He held the medicine bottle in his left hand. The stuff began to smoke and melt, and then—exploded with deafening violence and a blinding flash.

The five boys, seeing the flash and being prepared for catastrophes, ducked below their desks, and were none of them seriously hurt. The window was blown out into the playground, and the blackboard on its easel was upset. The slate was smashed to atoms. Some plaster fell from the ceiling. No other damage was done to the school edifice or appliances, and the boys at first, seeing nothing of Plattner, fancied he was knocked down and lying out of their sight below the desks. They jumped out of their places to go to his assistance, and were amazed to find the space empty. Being still confused by the sudden violence of the report, they hurried to the open door, under the impression that he must have been hurt, and have rushed out of the room. But Carson, the foremost, nearly collided in the doorway with the principal, Mr. Lidgett.

Mr. Lidgett is a corpulent, excitable man with one eye. The boys describe him as stumbling into the room mouthing some of those tempered expletives irritable schoolmasters accustom themselves to use—lest worse befall. "Wretched mumchancer!" he said. "Where's Mr. Plattner?" The boys are agreed on the very words. ("Wobbler," "snivelling puppy," and "mumchancer" are, it seems, among the ordinary small change of Mr. Lidgett's scholastic commerce.)

Where's Mr. Plattner? That was a question that was to be repeated many times in the next few days. It really seemed as though that frantic hyperbole, "blown to atoms," had for once realised itself. There was not a visible particle of Plattner to be seen; not a drop of blood nor a stitch of clothing to be found. Apparently he had been blown clean out of existence and left not a wrack behind. Not so much as would cover a sixpenny piece, to quote a proverbial expression! The evidence of his absolute disappearance, as a consequence of that explosion, is indubitable.

It is not necessary to enlarge here upon the commotion excited in the Sussexville Proprietary School, and in Sussexville and elsewhere, by this event. It is quite possible, indeed, that some of the readers of these pages may recall the hearing of some remote and dying version of that excitement during the last summer holidays. Lidgett, it would seem, did everything in his power to suppress and minimise the story. He instituted a penalty of twenty-five lines for any mention of Plattner's name among the boys, and stated in the schoolroom that he was clearly aware of his assistant's whereabouts. He was afraid, he explains, that the possibility of an explosion happening, in spite of the elaborate precautions taken to minimise the practical teaching of chemistry, might injure the reputation of the school; and so might any mysterious quality in Plattner's departure. Indeed, he did everything in his power to make the occurrence seem as ordinary as possible. In particular, he cross-examined the five eye-witnesses of the occurrence so searchingly that they began to doubt the plain evidence of their senses. But, in spite of these efforts, the tale, in a magnified and distorted state, made a nine days' wonder in the district, and several parents withdrew their sons on colourable pretexts. Not the least remarkable point in the matter is the fact that a large number of people in the neighbourhood dreamed singularly vivid dreams of Plattner during the period of excitement before his return, and that these dreams had a curious uniformity. In almost all of them Plattner was seen, sometimes singly, sometimes in company, wandering about through a coruscating iridescence. In all cases his face was pale and distressed, and in some he gesticulated towards the dreamer. One or two of the boys, evidently under the influence of nightmare, fancied that Plattner approached them with remarkable swiftness, and seemed to look closely into their very eyes. Others fled with Plattner from the pursuit of vague and extraordinary creatures of a globular shape. But all these fancies were forgotten in inquiries and speculations when, on the Wednesday next but one after the Monday of the explosion, Plattner returned.

The circumstances of his return were as singular as those of his departure. So far as Mr. Lidgett's somewhat choleric outline can be filled in from Plattner's hesitating statements, it would appear that on Wednesday evening, towards the hour of sunset, the former gentleman, having dismissed evening preparation, was engaged in his garden, picking and eating strawberries, a fruit of which he is inordinately fond. It is a large old-fashioned garden, secured from observation, fortunately, by a high and ivy-covered red-brick wall. Just as he was stooping over a particularly prolific plant, there was a flash in the air and a heavy thud, and before he could look round, some heavy body struck him violently from behind. He was pitched forward, crushing the strawberries he held in his hand, and with such force that his silk hat—Mr. Lidgett adheres to the older ideas of scholastic costume—was driven violently down upon his forehead, and almost over one eye. This heavy missile, which slid over him sideways and collapsed into a sitting posture among the strawberry plants, proved to be our long-lost Mr. Gottfried Plattner, in an extremely dishevelled condition. He was collarless and hatless, his linen was dirty, and there was blood upon his hands. Mr. Lidgett was so indignant and surprised that he remained on all-fours, and with his hat jammed down on his eye, while he expostulated vehemently with Plattner for his disrespectful and unaccountable conduct.

This scarcely idyllic scene completes what I may call the exterior version of the Plattner story—its exoteric aspect. It is quite unnecessary to enter here into all the details of his dismissal by Mr. Lidgett. Such details, with the full names and dates and references, will be found in the larger report of these occurrences that was laid before the Society for the Investigation of Abnormal Phenomena. The singular transposition of Plattner's right and left sides was scarcely observed for the first day or so, and then first in connection with his disposition to write from right to left across the blackboard. He concealed rather than ostended this curious confirmatory circumstance, as he considered it would unfavourably affect his prospects in a new situation. The displacement of his heart was discovered some months after, when he was having a tooth extracted under anæsthetics. He then, very unwillingly, allowed a cursory surgical examination to be made of himself, with a view to a brief account in the *Journal of Anatomy*. That exhausts the statement of the material facts; and we may now go on to consider Plattner's account of the matter.

But first let us clearly differentiate between the preceding portion of this story and what is to follow. All I have told thus far is established by such evidence as even a criminal lawyer would approve. Every one of the witnesses is still alive; the reader, if he have the leisure, may hunt the lads out tomorrow, or even brave the terrors of the redoubtable Lidgett, and cross-examine and trap and test to his heart's content; Gottfried Plattner, himself, and his twisted heart and his three photographs are producible. It may be taken as proved that he did disappear for nine days as the consequence of an explosion; that he returned almost as violently, under circumstances in their nature annoying to Mr. Lidgett, whatever the details of those circumstances may be; and that he returned inverted, just as a reflection returns from a mirror. From the last fact, as I have already stated, it follows almost inevitably that Plattner, during those nine days, must have been in some state of existence altogether out of space. The evidence to these statements is, indeed, far stronger than that upon which most murderers are hanged. But for his own particular account of where he had been, with its confused explanations and well-nigh self-contradictory details, we have only Mr. Gottfried Plattner's word. I do not wish to discredit that, but I must point out—what so many writers upon obscure psychic phenomena fail to do—that we are passing here from the practically undeniable to that kind of matter which any reasonable man is entitled to believe or reject as he thinks proper. The previous statements render it plausible; its discordance with common experience tilts it towards the incredible. I would prefer not to sway the beam of the reader's judgment either way, but simply to tell the story as Plattner told it me.

He gave me his narrative, I may state, at my house at Chislehurst; and so soon as he had left me that evening, I went into my study and wrote down everything as I remembered it. Subsequently he was good enough to read over a type-written copy, so that its substantial correctness is undeniable.

He states that at the moment of the explosion he distinctly thought he was killed. He felt lifted off his feet and driven forcibly backward. It is a curious fact for psychologists that he thought clearly during his backward flight, and wondered whether he should hit the chemistry cupboard or the blackboard easel. His heels struck ground, and he staggered and fell heavily into a sitting position on something soft and firm. For a moment the concussion stunned him. He became aware at once of a vivid scent of singed hair, and he seemed to hear the voice of Lidgett asking for him. You will understand that for a time his mind was greatly confused.

At first he was distinctly under the impression that he was still in the classroom. He perceived quite distinctly the surprise of the boys and the entry of Mr. Lidgett. He is quite positive upon that score. He did not hear their remarks, but that he ascribed to the deafening effect of the experiment. Things about him seemed curiously dark and faint, but his mind explained that on the obvious but mistaken idea that the explosion had engendered a huge volume of dark smoke. Through the dimness the figures of Lidgett and the boys moved, as faint and silent as ghosts. Plattner's face still tingled with the stinging heat of the flash. He was, he says, "all muddled." His first definite thoughts seem to have been of his personal safety. He thought he was perhaps blinded and deafened. He felt his limbs and face in a gingerly manner. Then his perceptions grew clearer, and he was astonished to miss the old familiar desks and other schoolroom furniture about him. Only dim, uncertain, grey shapes stood in the place of these. Then came a thing that made him shout aloud, and awoke his stunned faculties to instant activity. *Two of the boys, gesticulating, walked one after the other clean through him!* Neither manifested the slightest consciousness of his presence. It is difficult to imagine the sensation he felt. They came against him, he says, with no more force than a wisp of mist.

Plattner's first thought after that was that he was dead. Having been brought up with thoroughly sound views in these matters, however, he was a little surprised to find his body still about him. His second conclusion was that he was not dead, but that the others were: that the explosion had destroyed the Sussexville Proprietary School and every soul in it except himself. But that, too, was scarcely satisfactory. He was thrown back upon astonished observation.

Everything about him was extraordinarily dark: at first it seemed to have an altogether ebony blackness. Overhead was a black firmament. The only touch of light in the scene was a faint greenish glow at the edge of the sky in one direction, which threw into prominence a horizon of undulating black hills. This, I say, was his impression at first. As his eye grew accustomed to the darkness, he began to distinguish a faint quality of differentiating greenish colour in the circumambient night. Against this background the furniture and occupants of the classroom, it seems, stood out like phosphorescent spectres, faint and impalpable. He extended his hand, and thrust it without an effort through the wall of the room by the fireplace.

He describes himself as making a strenuous effort to attract attention. He shouted to Lidgett, and tried to seize the boys as they went to and fro. He only desisted from these attempts when Mrs. Lidgett, whom he as an Assistant Master naturally disliked, entered the room. He says the sensation of being in the world, and yet not a part of it, was an extraordinarily disagreeable one. He compared his feelings not inaptly to those of a cat watching a mouse through a window.

Whenever he made a motion to communicate with the dim, familiar world about him, he found an invisible, incomprehensible barrier preventing intercourse.

He then turned his attention to his solid environment. He found the medicine bottle still unbroken in his hand, with the remainder of the green powder therein. He put this in his pocket, and began to feel about him. Apparently, he was sitting on a boulder of rock covered with a velvety moss. The dark country about him he was unable to see, the faint, misty picture of the schoolroom blotting it out, but he had a feeling (due perhaps to a cold wind) that he was near the crest of a hill, and that a steep valley fell away beneath his feet. The green glow along the edge of the sky seemed to be growing in extent and intensity. He stood up, rubbing his eyes.

It would seem that he made a few steps, going steeply downhill, and then stumbled, nearly fell, and sat down again upon a jagged mass of rock to watch the dawn. He became aware that the world about him was absolutely silent. It was as still as it was dark, and though there was a cold wind blowing up the hill-face, the rustle of grass, the soughing of the boughs that should have accompanied it, were absent. He could hear, therefore, if he could not see, that the hillside upon which he stood was rocky and desolate. The green grew brighter every moment, and as it did so a faint, transparent blood-red mingled with, but did not mitigate, the blackness of the sky overhead and the rocky desolations about him. Having regard to what follows, I am inclined to think that that redness may have been an optical effect due to contrast. Something black fluttered momentarily against the livid yellow-green of the lower sky, and then the thin and penetrating voice of a bell rose out of the black gulf below him. An oppressive expectation grew with the growing light.

It is probable that an hour or more elapsed while he sat there, the strange green light growing brighter every moment, and spreading slowly, in flamboyant fingers, upward towards the zenith. As it grew, the spectral vision of *our* world became relatively or absolutely fainter. Probably both, for the time must have been about that of our earthly sunset. So far as his vision of our world went, Plattner, by his few steps down-hill, had passed through the floor of the classroom, and was now, it seemed, sitting in mid-air in the larger schoolroom downstairs. He saw the boarders distinctly, but much more faintly than he had seen Lidgett. They were preparing their evening tasks, and he noticed with interest that several were cheating with their Euclid riders by means of a crib, a compilation whose existence he had hitherto never sus-pected. As the time passed they faded steadily, as steadily as the light of the green dawn increased.

Looking down into the valley, he saw that the light had crept far down its rocky sides, and that the profound black-ness of the abyss was now broken by a minute green glow, like the light of a glow-worm. And almost immediately the limb of a huge heavenly body of blazing green rose over the basaltic undulations of the distant hills, and the monstrous hill-masses about him came out gaunt and desolate, in green light and deep, ruddy black shadows. He became aware of a vast number of ball-shaped objects drifting as thistledown drifts over the high ground. There were none of these nearer to him than the opposite side of the gorge. The bell below twanged quicker and quicker, with something like impatient insistence, and several lights moved hither and thither. The boys at work at their desks were now almost impercep-tibly faint.

This extinction of our world, when the green sun of this other universe rose, is a curious point upon which Plattner insists. During the Other-World night it is difficult to move about, on account of the vividness with which the things of this world are visible. It becomes a riddle to explain why, if this is the case, we in this world catch no glimpse of the Other-World. It is due, perhaps, to the comparatively vivid illumination of this world of ours. Plattner describes the mid-day of the Other-World, at its brightest, as not being nearly so bright as this world at full moon, while its night is pro-foundly black. Consequently, the amount of light, even in an ordinary dark room, is sufficient to render the things of the

Other-World invisible, on the same principle that faint phosphorescence is only visible in the profoundest darkness. I have tried, since he told me his story, to see something of the Other-World by sitting for a long space in a photographer's dark room at night. I have certainly seen indistinctly the form of greenish slopes and rocks, but only, I must admit, very indistinctly indeed. The reader may possibly be more successful. Plattner tells me that since his return he has seen and recognised places in the Other-World in his dreams, but this is probably due to his memory of these scenes. It seems quite possible that people with unusually keen eyesight may occasionally catch a glimpse of this strange Other-World about us.

However, this is digression. As the green sun rose, a long street of black buildings became perceptible, though only darkly and indistinctly, in the gorge, and, after some hesitation, Plattner began to clamber down the precipitous descent towards them. The descent was long and exceedingly tedious, being so not only by the extraordinary steepness, but also by reason of the looseness of the boulders with which the whole face of the hill was strewn. The noise of his descent—now and then his heels struck fire from the rocks—seemed now the only sound in the universe, for the beating of the bell had ceased. As he drew nearer he perceived that the various edifices had a singular resemblance to tombs and mausoleums and monuments, saving only that they were all uniformly black instead of being white as most sepulchres are. And then he saw, crowding out of the largest building very much as people disperse from church, a number of pallid, rounded, pale-green figures. These scattered in several directions about the broad street of the place, some going through side alleys and reappearing upon the steepness of the hill, others entering some of the small black buildings which lined the way.

At the sight of these things drifting up towards him, Plattner stopped, staring. They were not walking, they were indeed limbless; and they had the appearance of human heads beneath which a tadpole-like body swung. He was too astonished at their strangeness, too full indeed of strangeness, to be seriously alarmed by them. They drove towards him, in front of the chill wind that was blowing uphill, much as soap-bubbles drive before a draught. And as he looked at the nearest of those approaching, he saw it was indeed a human head, albeit with singularly large eyes, and wearing such an expression of distress and anguish as he had never seen before upon mortal countenance. He was surprised to find that it did not turn to regard him, but seemed to be watching and following some unseen moving thing. For a moment he was puzzled, and then it occurred to him that this creature was watching with its enormous eyes something that was happening in the world he had just left. Nearer it came, and nearer, and he was too astonished to cry out. It made a very faint fretting sound as it came close to him. Then it struck his face with a gentle pat—its touch was very cold—and drove past him, and upward towards the crest of the hill.

An extraordinary conviction flashed across Plattner's mind that this head had a strong likeness to Lidgett. Then he turned his attention to the other heads that were now swarming thickly up the hillside. None made the slightest sign of recognition. One or two, indeed, came close to his head and almost followed the example of the first, but he dodged convulsively out of the way. Upon most of them he saw the same expression of unavailing regret he had seen upon the first, and heard the same faint sounds of wretchedness from them. One or two wept, and one rolling swiftly uphill wore an expression of diabolical rage. But others were cold, and several had a look of gratified interest in their eyes. One, at least, was almost in an ecstasy of happiness. Plattner does not remember that he recognised any more likenesses in those he saw at this time.

For several hours, perhaps, Plattner watched these strange things dispersing themselves over the hills, and not till long after they had ceased to issue from the clustering black buildings in the gorge did he resume his downward climb. The darkness about him increased so much that he had a difficulty in stepping true. Overhead the sky was now a bright pale green. He felt neither hunger nor thirst. Later, when he did, he found a chilly stream running down the centre of the gorge, and the rare moss upon the boulders, when he tried it at last in desperation, was good to eat.

He groped about among the tombs that ran down the gorge, seeking vaguely for some clue to these inexplicable things. After a long time he came to the entrance of the big mausoleum-like building from which the heads had issued. In this he found a group of green lights burning upon a kind of basaltic altar, and a bell-rope from a belfry overhead hanging down into the centre of the place. Round the wall ran a lettering of fire in a character unknown to him. While he was still wondering at the purport of these things, he heard the receding tramp of heavy feet echoing far down the street. He ran out into the darkness again, but he could see nothing. He had a mind to pull the bell-rope, and finally decided to follow the footsteps. But although he ran far, he never overtook them; and his shouting was of no avail. The gorge seemed to extend an interminable distance. It was as dark as earthly starlight throughout its length, while the ghastly green day lay along the upper edge of its precipices. There were none of the heads, now, below. They were all, it seemed, busily occupied along the upper slopes. Looking up, he saw them drifting hither and thither, some hovering stationary, some flying swiftly through the air. It reminded him, he said, of "big snowflakes"; only these were black and pale green.

In pursuing the firm, undeviating footsteps that he never overtook, in groping into new regions of this endless devil's dyke, in clambering up and down the pitiless heights, in wandering about the summits, and in watching the drifting faces, Plattner states that he spent the better part of seven or eight days. He did not keep count, he says. Though once or twice he found eyes watching him, he had word with no living soul. He slept among the rocks on the hillside. In the gorge things earthly were. invisible, because, from the earthly standpoint, it was far underground. On the altitudes, so soon as the earthly day began, the world became visible to him. He found himself sometimes stumbling over the dark green rocks, or arresting himself on a precipitous brink, while all about him the green branches of the Sussexville lanes were swaying; or, again, he seemed to be walking through the Sussexville streets, or watching unseen the private business of some household. And then it was he discovered that to almost every human being in our world there pertained some of these drifting heads; that everyone in the world is watched intermittently by these helpless disembodiments.

What are they—these Watchers of the Living? Plattner never learned. But two that presently found and followed him were like his childhood's memory of his father and mother. Now and then other faces turned their eyes upon him: eyes like those of dead people who had swayed him, or injured him, or helped him in his youth and manhood. Whenever they looked at him, Plattner was overcome with a strange sense of responsibility. To his mother he ventured to speak; but she made no answer. She looked sadly, steadfastly, and tenderly—a little reproachfully, too, it seemed—into his eyes.

He simply tells this story: he does not endeavour to explain. We are left to surmise who these Watchers of the Living may be, or if they are indeed the Dead, why they should so closely and passionately watch a world they have left for ever. It may be—indeed to my mind it seems just—that, when our life has closed, when evil or good is no longer a choice for us, we may still have to witness the working out of the train of consequences we have laid. If human souls continue after death, then surely human interests continue after death. But that is merely my own guess at the meaning of the things seen. Plattner offers no interpretation, for none was given him. It is well the reader should understand this clearly. Day after day, with his head reeling, he wandered about this green-lit world outside the world, weary and, towards the end, weak and hungry. By day—by our earthly day, that is—the ghostly vision of the old familiar scenery of Sussexville, all about him, irked and worried him. He could not see where to put his feet, and ever and again with a chilly touch one of these Watching Souls would come against his face. And after dark the multitude of these Watchers about him, and their intent distress, confused his mind beyond

describing. A great longing to return to the earthly life that
was so near and yet so remote consumed him. The unearthliness of things about him produced a positively painful mental
distress. He was worried beyond describing by his own particular followers. He would shout at them to desist from staring
at him, scold at them, hurry away from them. They were
always mute and intent. Run as he might over the uneven
ground, they followed his destinies.

On the ninth day, towards evening, Plattner heard the
invisible footsteps approaching, far away down the gorge.
He was then wandering over the broad crest of the same hill
upon which he had fallen in his entry into this strange Other-
World of his. He turned to hurry down into the gorge, feeling
his way hastily, and was arrested by the sight of the thing
that was happening in a room in a back street near the
school. Both of the people in the room he knew by sight.
The windows were open, the blinds up, and the setting sun
shone clearly into it. so that it came out quite brightly at
first, a vivid oblong of room, lying like a magic-lantern picture upon the black landscape and the livid green dawn. In
addition to the sunlight, a candle had just been lit in the
room.

On the bed lay a lank man, his ghastly white face terrible
upon the tumbled pillow. His clenched hands were raised
above his head. A little table beside the bed carried a few
medicine bottles, some toast and water, and an empty glass.
Every now and then the lank man's lips fell apart, to indicate
a word he could not articulate. But the woman did not notice
that he wanted anything, because she was busy turning out
papers from an old-fashioned bureau in the opposite corner
of the room. At first the picture was very vivid indeed, but
as the green dawn behind it grew brighter and brighter, so it
became fainter and more and more transparent.

As the echoing footsteps paced nearer and nearer, those
footsteps that sound so loud in that Other-World and come so
silently in this, Plattner perceived about him a great multitude of dim faces gathering together out of the darkness and
watching the two people in the room. Never before had he

seen so many of the Watchers of the Living. A multitude had eyes only for the sufferer in the room, another multitude, in infinite anguish, watched the woman as she hunted with greedy eyes for something she could not find. They crowded about Plattner, they came across his sight and buffeted his face, the noise of their unavailing regrets was all about him. He saw clearly only now and then. At other times the pictures quivered dimly, through the veil of green reflections upon their movements. In the room it must have been very still, and Plattner says the candle flame streamed up into a perfectly vertical line of smoke, but in his ears each footfall and its echoes beat like a clap of thunder. And the faces! Two more particularly, near the woman's: one a woman's also, white and clear-featured, a face which might have once been cold and hard but which was now softened by the touch of a wisdom strange to earth. The other might have been the woman's father. Both were evidently absorbed in the contemplation of some act of hateful meanness, so it seemed, which they could no longer guard against and prevent. Behind were others, teachers it may be who had taught ill, friends whose influence had failed. And over the man, too—a multitude, but none that seemed to be parents or teachers! Faces that might once have been coarse, now purged to strength by sorrow! And in the forefront one face, a girlish one, neither angry nor remorseful but merely patient and weary, and, as it seemed to Plattner, waiting for relief. His powers of description fail him at the memory of this multitude of ghastly countenances. They gathered on the stroke of the bell. He saw them all in the space of a second. It would seem that he was so worked upon by his excitement that quite involuntarily his restless fingers took the bottle of green powder out of his pocket and held it before him. But he does not remember that.

Abruptly the footsteps ceased. He waited for the next and there was silence, and then suddenly, cutting through the unexpected stillness like a keen, thin blade, came the first stroke of the bell. At that the multitudinous faces swayed to and fro, and a louder crying began all about him. The woman did not hear; she was burning something now in the candle flame. At the second stroke everything grew dim, and a breath of wind, icy cold, blew through the host of watchers. They swirled about him like an eddy of dead leaves in the spring, and at the third stroke something was extended through them to the bed. You have heard of a beam of light. This was like a beam of darkness, and looking again at it, Plattner saw that it was a shadowy arm and hand.

The green sun was now topping the black desolations of the horizon, and the vision of the room was very faint. Plattner could see that the white of the bed struggled, and was convulsed; and that the woman looked round over her shoulder at it, startled.

The cloud of watchers lifted high like a puff of green dust before the wind, and swept swiftly downward towards the temple in the gorge. Then suddenly Plattner understood the meaning of the shadowy black arm that stretched across his shoulder and clutched its prey. He did not dare turn his head to see the Shadow behind the arm. With a violent effort, and covering his eyes, he set himself to run, made perhaps twenty strides, then slipped on a boulder and fell. He fell forward on his hands, and the bottle smashed and exploded as he touched the ground.

In another moment he found himself, stunned and bleeding, sitting face to face with Lidgett in the old walled garden behind the school.

There the story of Plattner's experiences ends. I have resisted, I believe successfully, the natural disposition of a writer of fiction to dress up incidents of this sort. I have told the thing as far as possible in the order in which Plattner told it to me. I have carefully avoided any attempt at style, effect, or construction. It would have been easy, for instance, to have worked the scene of the death-bed into a kind of plot in which Plattner might have been involved. But quite apart from the objectionableness of falsifying a most extraordinary true story, any such trite devices would spoil, to my mind, the peculiar effect of this dark world, with its livid green illumina-

tion and its drifting Watchers of the Living, which, unseen
and unapproachable to us, is yet lying all about us.

It remains to add, that a death did actually occur in Vin-
cent Terrace, just beyond the school garden, and, so far as can
be proved, at the moment of Plattner's return. Deceased was
a rate-collector and insurance agent. His widow, who was
much younger than himself, married last month a Mr.
Whymper, a veterinary surgeon of Allbeeding. As the portion
of this story given here has in various forms circulated orally
in Sussexville, she has consented to my use of her name, on
condition that I make it distinctly known that she emphati-
cally contradicts every detail of Plattner's account of her
husband's last moments. She burnt no will, she says, although
Plattner never accused her of doing so: her husband made
but one will, and that just after their marriage. Certainly,
from a man who had never seen it, Plattner's account of the
furniture of the room was curiously accurate.

One other thing, even at the risk of an irksome repetition,
I must insist upon lest I seem to favour the credulous superstitious view. Plattner's absence from the world for nine days
is, I think, proved. But that does not prove his story. It is
quite conceivable that even outside space hallucinations may
be possible. That, at least, the reader must bear distinctly in
mind.

THE ARGONAUTS OF THE AIR

ONE saw Monson's Flying Machine from the windows of the trains passing either along the South-Western main line or along the line between Wimbledon and Worcester Park—to be more exact, one saw the huge scaffoldings which limited the flight of the apparatus. They rose over the tree-tops, a massive alley of interlacing iron and timber, and an enormous web of ropes and tackle, extending the best part of two miles. From the Leatherhead branch this alley was foreshortened and in part hidden by a hill with villas; but from the main line one had it in profile, a complex tangle of girders and curving bars, very impressive to the excursionist from Portsmouth and Southampton and the West. Monson had taken up the work where Maxim had left it, had gone on at first with an utter contempt for the journalistic wit and ignorance that had irritated and hampered his predecessor, and had spent (it was said) rather more than half his immense fortune upon his experiments. The results, to an impatient generation, seemed inconsiderable. When some five years had passed after the growth of the colossal iron groves at Worcester Park, and Monson still failed to put in a fluttering appearance over Trafalgar Square, even the Isle of Wight trippers felt their liberty to smile. And such intelligent people as did not consider Monson a fool stricken with the mania for invention, denounced him as being (for no particular reason) a self-advertising quack.

Yet now and again a morning trainload of season-ticket holders would see a white monster rush headlong through the airy tracery of guides and bars, and hear the further stays, nettings, and buffers snap, creak, and groan with the impact of the blow. Then there would be an efflorescence of black-set white-rimmed faces along the sides of the train, and the morning papers would be neglected for a vigorous discussion of the possibility of flying (in which nothing new was

462

ever said by any chance), until the train reached Waterloo, and its cargo of season-ticket holders dispersed themselves over London. Or the fathers and mothers in some multitudinous train of weary excursionists returning. exhausted from a day of rest by the sea, would find the dark fabric, standing out against the evening sky, useful in diverting some bilious child from its introspection, and be suddenly startled by the swift transit of a huge black flapping shape that strained upward against the guides. It was a great and forcible thing beyond dispute, and excellent for conversation; yet, all the same, it was but flying in leading-strings, and most of those who witnessed it scarcely counted its flight as flying. More of a switchback it seemed to the run of the folk.

Monson, I say, did not trouble himself very keenly about the opinions of the press at first. But possibly he, even, had formed but a poor idea of the time it would take before the tactics of flying were mastered, the swift assured adjustment of the big soaring shape to every gust and chance movement of the air; nor had he clearly reckoned the money this prolonged struggle against gravitation would cost him. And he was not so pachydermatous as he seemed. Secretly he had his periodical bundles of cuttings sent him by Romeike, he had his periodical reminders from his banker; and if he did not mind the initial ridicule and scepticism, he felt the growing neglect as the months went by and the money dribbled away. Time was when Monson had sent the enterprising journalist, keen after readable matter, empty from his gates. But when the enterprising journalist ceased from troubling, Monson was anything but satisfied in his heart of hearts. Still day by day the work went on, and the multitudinous subtle difficulties of the steering diminished in number. Day by day, too, the money trickled away, until his balance was no longer a matter of hundreds of thousands, but of tens. And at last came an anniversary.

Monson, sitting in the little drawing-shed, suddenly noticed the date on Woodhouse's calendar.

"It was five years ago to-day that we began," he said to Woodhouse suddenly.

"Is it?" said Woodhouse.

"It's the alterations play the devil with us," said Monson, biting a paper-fastener.

The drawings for the new vans to the hinder screw lay on the table before him as he spoke. He pitched the mutilated brass paper-fastener into the waste-paper basket and drummed with his fingers. "These alterations! Will the mathematicians ever be clever enough to save us all this patching and experimenting? Five years—learning by rule of thumb, when one might think that it was possible to calculate the whole thing out beforehand. The cost of it! I might have hired three senior wranglers for life. But they'd only have developed some beautifully useless theorems in pneumatics. What a time it has been, Woodhouse!"

"These mouldings will take three weeks," said Woodhouse. "At special prices."

"Three weeks!" said Monson, and sat drumming.

"Three weeks certain," said Woodhouse, an excellent engineer, but no good as a comforter. He drew the sheets towards him and began shading a bar.

Monson stopped drumming, and began to bite his fingernails, staring the while at Woodhouse's head.

"How long have they been calling this Monson's Folly?" he said suddenly.

"*Oh!* Year or so," said Woodhouse carelessly, without looking up.

Monson sucked the air in between his teeth, and went to the window. The stout iron columns carrying the elevated rails upon which the start of the machine was made rose up close by, and the machine was hidden by the upper edge of the window. Through the grove of iron pillars, red painted and ornate with rows of bolts, one had a glimpse of the pretty scenery towards Esher. A train went gliding noiselessly across the middle distance, its rattle drowned by the hammering of the workmen overhead. Monson could imagine the grinning faces at the windows of the carriages. He swore savagely under his breath, and dabbed viciously at a blowfly that suddenly became noisy on the window-pane.

"What's up?" said Woodhouse, staring in surprise at his employer.

"I'm about sick of this."

Woodhouse scratched his cheek. "Oh!" he said, after an assimilating pause. He pushed the drawing away from him.

"Here these fools . . . I'm trying to conquer a new element —trying to do a thing that will revolutionise life. And instead of taking an intelligent interest, they grin and make their stupid jokes, and call me and my appliances names."

"Asses!" said Woodhouse, letting his eye fall again on the drawing.

The epithet, curiously enough, made Monson wince. "I'm about sick of it, Woodhouse, anyhow," he said, after a pause.

Woodhouse shrugged his shoulders.

"There's nothing for it but patience, I suppose," said Monson, sticking his hands in his pockets. "I've started. I've made my bed, and I've got to lie on it. I can't go back. I'll see it through, and spend every penny I have and every penny I can borrow. But I tell you, Woodhouse, I'm infernally sick of it, all the same. If I'd paid a tenth part of the money towards some political greaser's expenses—I'd have been a baronet before this."

Monson paused. Woodhouse stared in front of him with a blank expression he always employed to indicate sympathy, and tapped his pencil-case on the table. Monson stared at him for a minute.

"Oh, *damn!*" said Monson suddenly, and abruptly rushed out of the room.

Woodhouse continued his sympathetic rigour for perhaps half a minute. Then he sighed and resumed the shading of the drawings. Something had evidently upset Monson. Nice chap, and generous, but difficult to get on with. It was the way with every amateur who had anything to do with engineering—wanted everything finished at once. But Monson had usually the patience of the expert. Odd he was so irritable. Nice and round that aluminium rod did look now! Woodhouse threw back his head, and put it, first this side and then that, to appreciate his bit of shading better.

"Mr. Woodhouse," said Hooper, the foreman of the labourers, putting his head in at the door.

"Hullo!" said Woodhouse, without turning round.

"Nothing happened, sir?" said Hooper.

"Happened?" said Woodhouse.

"The governor just been up the rails swearing like a tornader."

"*Oh!*" said Woodhouse.

"It ain't like him, sir."

"No?"

"And I was thinking perhaps——"

"Don't think," said Woodhouse, still admiring the drawings.

Hooper knew Woodhouse, and he shut the door suddenly with a vicious slam. Woodhouse stared stonily before him for some further minutes, and then made an ineffectual effort to pick his teeth with his pencil. Abruptly he desisted, pitched that old, tried, and stumpy servitor across the room, got up, stretched himself, and followed Hooper.

He looked ruffled—it was visible to every workman he met. When a millionaire who has been spending thousands on experiments that employ quite a little army of people suddenly indicates that he is sick of the undertaking, there is almost invariably a certain amount of mental friction in the ranks of the little army he employs. And even before he indicates his intentions there are speculations and murmurs, a watching of faces and a study of straws. Hundreds of people knew before the day was out that Monson was ruffled, Woodhouse ruffled, Hooper ruffled. A workman's wife, for instance (whom Monson had never seen), decided to keep her money in the savings-bank instead of buying a velveteen dress. So far-reaching are even the casual curses of a millionaire.

Monson found a certain satisfaction in going on the works and behaving disagreeably to as many people as possible. After a time even that palled upon him, and he rode off the grounds, to everyone's relief there, and through the lanes south-eastward, to the infinite tribulation of his house steward at Cheam.

And the immediate cause of it all, the little grain of annoyance that had suddenly precipitated all this discontent with his life-work was—these trivial things that direct all our great decisions!—half-a-dozen ill-considered remarks made by a pretty girl, prettily dressed, with a beautiful voice and something more than prettiness in her soft grey eyes. And of these half-dozen remarks, two words especially—"Monson's Folly." She had felt she was behaving charmingly to Monson; she reflected the next day how exceptionally effective she had been, and no one would have been more amazed than she, had she learned the effect she had left on Monson's mind. I hope, considering everything, that she never knew.

"How are you getting on with your flying machine?" she asked. ("I wonder if I shall ever meet anyone with the sense not to ask that," thought Monson.) "It will be very dangerous at first, will it not?" ("Thinks I'm afraid.") "Jorgon is going to play presently; have you heard him before?" ("My mania being attended to, we turn to rational conversation.") Gush about Jorgon; gradual decline of conversation, ending with—"You must let me know when your flying machine is finished, Mr. Monson, and then I will consider the advisability of taking a ticket," ("One would think I was still playing inventions in the nursery.") But the bitterest thing she said was not meant for Monson's ears. To Phlox, the novelist, she was always conscientiously brilliant. "I have been talking to Mr. Monson, and he can think of nothing, positively nothing, but that flying machine of his. Do you know, all his workmen call that place of his 'Monson's Folly'? He is quite impossible. It is really very, very sad. I always regard him myself in the light of sunken treasure—the Lost Millionaire, you know."

She was pretty and well educated—indeed, she had written an epigrammatic novelette; but the bitterness was that she was typical. She summarised what the world thought of the man who was working sanely, steadily, and surely towards a more tremendous revolution in the appliances of civilisation, a more far-reaching alteration in the ways of humanity than has ever been effected since history began. They did not even take him seriously. In a little while he would be proverbial. "I *must* fly now," he said on his way home, smarting with a sense of absolute social failure. "I must fly soon. If it doesn't come off soon, by God! I shall run amuck."

He said that before he had gone through his passbook and his litter of papers. Inadequate as the cause seems, it was that girl's voice and the expression of her eyes that precipitated his discontent. But certainly the discovery that he had no longer even one hundred thousand pounds' worth of realisable property behind him was the poison that made the wound deadly.

It was the next day after this that he exploded upon Woodhouse and his workmen, and thereafter his bearing was consistently grim for three weeks, and anxiety dwelt in Cheam and Ewell, Malden, Morden, and Worcester Park, places that had thriven mightily on his experiments.

Four weeks after that first swearing of his, he stood with Woodhouse by the reconstructed machine as it lay across the elevated railway, by means of which it gained its initial impetus. The new propeller glittered a brighter white than the rest of the machine, and a gilder, obedient to a whim of Monson's, was picking out the aluminium bars with gold. And looking down the long avenue between the ropes (gilded now with the sunset), one saw red signals, and two miles away an ant-hill of workmen busy altering the last falls of the run into a rising slope.

"I'll *come*," said Woodhouse. "I'll come right enough. But I tell you it's infernally foolhardy. If only you would give another year———"

"I tell you I won't. I tell you the thing works. I've given years enough———"

"It's not that," said Woodhouse. "We're all right with the machine. But it's the steering———"

"Haven't I been rushing, night and morning, backwards and forwards, through this squirrel's cage? If the thing steers true here, it will steer true all across England. It's just funk,

I tell you, Woodhouse. We could have gone a year ago. And besides——"

"Well?" said Woodhouse.

"The money!" snapped Monson over his shoulder.

"Hang it! I never thought of the money," said Woodhouse, and then, speaking now in a very different tone from that in which he had said the words before, he repeated, "I'll come. Trust me."

Monson turned suddenly, and saw all that Woodhouse had not the dexterity to say shining on his sunset-lit face. He looked for a moment, then impulsively extended his hand. "Thanks," he said.

"All right," said Woodhouse, gripping the hand, and with a queer softening of his features. "Trust me."

Then both men turned to the big apparatus that lay with its flat wings extended upon the carrier, and stared at it meditatively. Monson, guided perhaps by a photographic study of the flight of birds, and by Lilienthal's methods, had gradually drifted from Maxim's shapes towards the bird form again. The thing, however, was driven by a huge screw behind in the place of the tail; and so hovering, which needs an almost vertical adjustment of a flat tail, was rendered impossible. The body of the machine was small, almost cylindrical, and pointed. Forward and aft on the pointed ends were two small petroleum engines for the screw, and the navigators sat deep in a canoe-like recess, the foremost one steering, and being protected by a low screen, with two plate-glass windows, from the blinding rush of air. On either side a monstrous flat framework with a curved front border could be adjusted so as either to lie horizontally, or to be tilted upward or down. These wings worked rigidly together, or, by releasing a pin, one could be tilted through a small angle independently of its fellow. The front edge of either wing could also be shifted back so as to diminish the wing-area about one-sixth. The machine was not only not designed to hover, but it was also incapable of fluttering. Monson's idea was to get into the air with the initial rush of the apparatus, and then to skim, much as a playing-card may be skimmed, keeping up the rush by means of the screw at the stern. Rooks and gulls fly enormous distances in that way with scarcely a perceptible movement of the wings. The bird really drives along on an aërial switchback. It glides slanting downward for a space, until it has gained considerable momentum, and then altering the inclination of its wings, glides up again almost to its original altitude. Even a Londoner who has watched the birds in the aviary in Regent's Park knows that.

But the bird is practising this art from the moment it leaves its nest. It has not only the perfect apparatus, but the perfect instinct to use it. A man off his feet has the poorest skill in balancing. Even the simple trick of the bicycle costs him some hours of labour. The instantaneous adjustments of the wings, the quick response to a passing breeze, the swift recovery of equilibrium, the giddy, eddying movements that require such absolute precision—all that he must learn, learn with infinite labour and infinite danger, if ever he is to conquer flying. The flying machine that will start off some fine day, driven by neat "little levers," with a nice open deck like a liner, and all loaded up with bomb-shells and guns, is the easy dreaming of a literary man. In lives and in treasure the cost of the conquest of the empire of the air may even exceed all that has been spent in man's great conquest of the sea. Certainly it will be costlier than the greatest war that has ever devastated the world.

No one knew these things better than these two practical men. And they knew they were in the front rank of the coming army. Yet there is hope even in a forlorn hope. Men are killed outright in the reserves sometimes, while others who have been left for dead in the thickest corner crawl out and survive.

"If we miss these meadows——" said Woodhouse presently in his slow way.

"My dear chap," said Monson, whose spirits had been rising fitfully during the last few days, "we mustn't miss these meadows. There's a quarter of a square mile for us to hit, fences removed, ditches levelled. We shall come down all right—rest assured. And if we don't——"

"Ah!" said Woodhouse. "If we don't!"

Before the day of the start, the newspaper people got wind of the alterations at the northward end of the framework, and Monson was cheered by a decided change in the comments Romeike forwarded him. "He will be off some day," said the papers. "He will be off some day," said the South-Western season-ticket holders one to another; the seaside excursionists, the Saturday-to-Monday trippers from Sussex and Hampshire and Dorset and Devon, the eminent literary people from Haslemere, all remarked eagerly one to another, "He will be off some day," as the familiar scaffolding came in sight. And actually, one bright morning, in full view of the ten-past-ten train from Basingstoke, Monson's flying-machine started on its journey.

They saw the carrier running swiftly along its rail, and the white-and-gold screw spinning in the air. They heard the rapid rumble of wheels, and a thud as the carrier reached the buffers at the end of its run. Then a whirr as the Flying Machine was shot forward into the networks. All that the majority of them had seen and heard before. The thing went with a drooping flight through the framework and rose again, and then every beholder shouted, or screamed, or yelled, or shrieked after his kind. For instead of the customary concussion and stoppage, the Flying Machine flew out of its five years' cage like a bolt from a crossbow, and drove slantingly upward into the air, curved round a little, so as to cross the line, and soared in the direction of Wimbledon Common.

It seemed to hang momentarily in the air and grow smaller, then it ducked and vanished over the clustering blue tree-tops to the east of Coombe Hill, and no one stopped staring and gasping until long after it had disappeared.

That was what the people in the train from Basingstoke saw. If you had drawn a line down the middle of that train, from engine to guard's van, you would not have found a living soul on the opposite side to the Flying Machine. It was a mad rush from window to window as the thing crossed the line. And the engine-driver and stoker never took their eyes off the low hills about Wimbledon, and never noticed that they had run clean through Coombe and Malden and Raynes Park, until, with returning animation, they found themselves pelting, at the most indecent pace, into Wimbledon station.

From the moment when Monson had started the carrier with a "*Now!*" neither he nor Woodhouse said a word. Both men sat with clenched teeth. Monson had crossed the line with a curve that was too sharp, and Woodhouse had opened and shut his white lips; but neither spoke. Woodhouse simply gripped his seat, and breathed sharply through his teeth, watching the blue country to the west rushing past, and down, and away from him. Monson knelt at his post forward, and his hands trembled on the spoked wheel that moved the wings. He could see nothing before him but a mass of white clouds in the sky.

The machine went slanting upward, travelling with an enormous speed still, but losing momentum every moment. The land ran away underneath with diminishing speed.

"*Now!*" said Woodhouse at last, and with a violent effort Monson wrenched over the wheel and altered the angle of the wings. The machine seemed to hang for half a minute motionless in mid-air, and then he saw the hazy blue-house-covered hills of Kilburn and Hampstead jump up before his eyes and rise steadily, until the little sunlit dome of the Albert Hall appeared through his windows. For a moment he scarcely understood the meaning of this upward rush of the horizon, but as the nearer and nearer houses came into view, he realised what he had done. He had turned the wings over too far, and they were swooping steeply downward towards the Thames.

The thought, the question, the realisation were all the business of a second of time. "Too much!" gasped Woodhouse. Monson brought the wheel halfway back with a jerk, and forthwith the Kilburn and Hampstead ridge dropped again to the lower edge of his windows. They had been a thousand feet above Coombe and Malden station; fifty seconds after they whizzed, at a frightful pace, not eighty feet above the East Putney station, on the Metropolitan District line, to the screaming astonishment of a platformful of people. Monson flung up the vans against the air, and over Fulham they rushed up their atmospheric switchback again, steeply—too steeply. The 'buses went floundering across the Fulham Road, the people yelled.

Then down again, too steeply still, and the distant trees and houses about Primrose Hill leapt up across Monson's window, and then suddenly he saw straight before him the greenery of Kensington Gardens and the towers of the Imperial Institute. They were driving straight down upon South Kensington. The pinnacles of the Natural History Museum rushed up into view. There came one fatal second of swift thought, a moment of hesitation. Should he try and clear the towers, or swerve eastward?

He made a hesitating attempt to release the right wing, left the catch half released, and gave a frantic clutch at the wheel.

The nose of the machine seemed to leap up before him. The wheel pressed his hand with irresistible force, and jerked itself out of his control.

Woodhouse, sitting crouched together, gave a hoarse cry, and sprang up towards Monson. "Too far!" he cried, and then he was clinging to the gunwale for dear life, and Monson had been jerked clean overhead, and was falling backwards upon him.

So swiftly had the thing happened that barely a quarter of the people going to and fro in Hyde Park, and Brompton Road, and the Exhibition Road saw anything of the aerial catastrophe. A distant winged shape had appeared above the clustering houses to the south, had fallen and risen, growing larger as it did so; had swooped swiftly down towards the Imperial Institute, a broad spread of flying wings, had swept round in a quarter circle, dashed eastward, and then suddenly sprang vertically into the air. A black object shot out of it, and came spinning downward. A man! Two men clutching each other! They came whirling down, separated as they struck the roof of the Students' Club, and bounded off into the green bushes on its southward side.

For perhaps half a minute, the pointed stem of the big machine still pierced vertically upward, the screw spinning desperately. For one brief instant, that yet seemed an age to all who watched, it had hung motionless in mid-air. Then a spout of yellow flame licked up its length from the stern engine, and swift, swifter, swifter, and flaring like a rocket, it rushed down upon the solid mass of masonry which was formerly the Royal College of Science. The big screw of white and gold touched the parapet, and crumpled up like wet linen. Then the blazing spindle-shaped body smashed and splintered, smashing and splintering in its fall, upon the north-westward angle of the building.

But the crash, the flame of blazing paraffin that shot heavenward from the shattered engines of the machine, the crushed horrors that were found in the garden beyond the Students' Club, the masses of yellow parapet and red brick that fell headlong into the roadway, the running to and fro of people like ants in a broken ant-hill, the galloping of fire-engines, the gathering of crowds—all these things do not belong to this story, which was written only to tell how the first of all successful flying machines was launched and flew. Though he failed, and failed disastrously, the record of Monson's work remains—a sufficient monument—to guide the next of that band of gallant experimentalists who will sooner or later master this great problem of flying. And between Worcester Park and Malden there still stands that portentous avenue of iron-work, rusting now, and dangerous here and there, to witness to the first desperate struggle for man's right of way through the air.

THE STORY OF THE LATE
MR. ELVESHAM

I SET this story down, not expecting it will be believed, but, if possible, to prepare a way of escape for the next victim. He perhaps may profit by my misfortune. My own case, I know, is hopeless, and I am now in some measure prepared to meet my fate.

My name is Edward George Eden. I was born at Trentham, in Staffordshire, my father being employed in the gardens there. I lost my mother when I was three years old and my father when I was five, my uncle, George Eden, then adopting me as his own son. He was a single man, self-educated, and well-known in Birmingham as an enterprising journalist; he educated me generously, fired my ambition to succeed in the world, and at his death, which happened four years ago, left me his entire fortune, a matter of about five hundred pounds after all outgoing charges were paid. I was then eighteen. He advised me in his will to expend the money in completing my education. I had already chosen the profession of medicine, and through his posthumous generosity, and my good fortune in a scholarship competition, I became a medical student at University College, London. At the time of the beginning of my story I lodged at 11A University Street, in a little upper room, very shabbily furnished, and draughty, overlooking the back of Shoolbred's premises. I used this little room both to live in and sleep in, because I was anxious to eke out my means to the very last shillingsworth.

I was taking a pair of shoes to be mended at a shop in the Tottenham Court Road when I first encountered the little old man with the yellow face, with whom my life has now become so inextricably entangled. He was standing on the kerb, and staring at the number on the door in a doubtful way, as I opened it. His eyes—they were dull grey eyes, and reddish under the rims—fell to my face, and his countenance immediately assumed an expression of corrugated amiability.

"You come," he said, "apt to the moment. I had forgotten the number of your house. How do you do, Mr. Eden?"

I was a little astonished at his familiar address, for I had never set eyes on the man before. I was annoyed, too, at his catching me with my boots under my arm. He noticed my lack of cordiality.

"Wonder who the deuce I am, eh? A friend, let me assure you. I have seen you before, though you haven't seen me. Is there anywhere where I can talk to you?"

I hesitated. The shabbiness of my room upstairs was not a matter for every stranger. "Perhaps," said I, "we might walk down the street. I'm unfortunately prevented——" My gesture explained the sentence before I had spoken it.

"The very thing," he said, and faced this way and then that. "The street? Which way shall we go?" I slipped my boots down in the passage. "Look here!" he said abruptly; "this business of mine is a rigmarole. Come and lunch with me, Mr. Eden. I'm an old man, a very old man, and not good at explanations, and what with my piping voice and the clatter of the traffic——"

He laid a persuasive skinny hand that trembled a little upon my arm.

I was not so old that an old man might not treat me to a lunch. Yet at the same time I was not altogether pleased by this abrupt invitation. "I had rather——" I began. "But *I* had rather," he said, catching me up, "and a certain civility is surely due to my grey hairs," and so I consented, and went away with him.

He took me to Blavitski's; I had to walk slowly to accommodate myself to his paces; and over such a lunch as I had never tasted before, he fended off my leading questions, and I took a better note of his appearance. His clean-shaven face was lean and wrinkled, his shrivelled lips fell over a set of false teeth, and his white hair was thin and rather long; he seemed small to me—though, indeed, most people seemed small to me—and his shoulders were rounded and bent. And, watching him, I could not help but observe that he, too, was taking note of me, running his eyes, with a curious touch of greed in them, over me from my broad shoulders to my sun-tanned hands and up to my freckled face again. "And now," said he, as we lit our cigarettes, "I must tell you of the business in hand.

"I must tell you, then, that I am an old man, a very old man." He paused momentarily. "And it happens that I have money that I must presently be leaving, and never a child have I to leave it to." I thought of the confidence trick, and resolved I would be on the alert for the vestiges of my five hundred pounds. He proceeded to enlarge on his loneliness, and the trouble he had to find a proper disposition of his money. "I have weighed this plan and that plan, charities, institutions, and scholarships, and libraries, and I have come to this conclusion at last,"—he fixed his eyes on my face,— "that I will find some young fellow, ambitious, pure-minded, and poor, healthy in body and healthy in mind, and, in short, make him my heir, give him all that I have." He repeated, "Give him all that I have. So that he will suddenly be lifted out of all the trouble and struggle in which his sympathies have been educated, to freedom and influence."

I tried to seem disinterested. With a transparent hypocrisy, I said, "And you want my help, my professional services maybe, to find that person."

He smiled and looked at me over his cigarette, and I laughed at his quiet exposure of my modest pretence.

"What a career such a man might have!" he said. "It fills me with envy to think how I have accumulated that another man may spend——

"But there are conditions, of course, burdens to be imposed. He must, for instance, take my name. You cannot expect everything without some return. And I must go into all the circumstances of his life before I can accept him. He *must* be sound. I must know his heredity, how his parents and grandparents died, have the strictest inquiries made into his private morals——"

This modified my secret congratulations a little. "And do I understand," said I, "that I——?"

"Yes," he said, almost fiercely. "You. *You.*"

I answered never a word. My imagination was dancing wildly, my innate scepticism was useless to modify its transports. There was not a particle of gratitude in my .mind—I did not know what to say nor how to say it. "But why me in particular?" I said at last.

He had chanced to hear of me from Professor Haslar, he said, as a typically sound and sane young man, and he wished, as far as possible, to leave his money where health and integrity were assured.

That was my first meeting with the little old man. He was mysterious about himself; he would not give his name yet, he said, and after I had answered some questions of his, he left me at the Blavitski portal. I noticed that he drew a handful of gold coins from his pocket when it came to paying for the lunch. His insistence upon bodily health was curious. In accordance with an arrangement we had made I applied that day for a life policy in the Loyal Insurance Company for a large sum, and I was exhaustively overhauled by the medical advisers of that company in the subsequent week. Even that did not satisfy him, and he insisted I must be reëxamined by the great Doctor Henderson. It was Friday in Whitsun week before he came to a decision. He called me down quite late in the evening,—nearly nine it was,—from cramming chemical equations for my Preliminary Scientific examination. He was standing in the passage under the feeble gas-lamp, and his face was a grotesque interplay of shadows. He seemed more bowed than when I had first seen him, and his cheeks had sunk in a little.

His voice shook with emotion. "Everything is satisfactory, Mr. Eden," he said. "Everything is quite, quite satisfactory. And this night of all nights, you must dine with me and celebrate your—accession." He was interrupted by a cough. "You won't have long to wait, either," he said, wiping his handkerchief across his lips, and gripping my hand with his long bony claw that was disengaged. "Certainly not very long to wait."

We went into the street and called a cab. I remember every

incident of that drive vividly, the swift, easy motion, the contrast of gas and oil and electric light, the crowds of people in the streets, the place in Regent Street to which we went, and the sumptuous dinner we were served with there. I was disconcerted at first by the well-dressed waiter's glances at my rough clothes, bothered by the stones of the olives, but as the champagne warmed my blood, my confidence revived. At first the old man talked of himself. He had already told me his name in the cab; he was Egbert Elvesham, the great philosopher, whose name I had known since I was a lad at school. It seemed incredible to me that this man, whose intelligence had so early dominated mine, this great abstraction should suddenly realise itself as this decrepit, familiar figure. I dare say every young fellow who has suddenly fallen among celebrities has felt something of my disappointment. He told me now of the future that the feeble streams of his life would presently leave dry for me, houses, copyrights, investments; I had never suspected that philosophers were so rich. He watched me drink and eat with a touch of envy. "What a capacity for living you have!" he said; and then, with a sigh, a sigh of relief I could have thought it, "It will not be long."

"Ay," said I, my head swimming now with champagne; "I have a future perhaps—of a fairly agreeable sort, thanks to you. I shall now have the honour of your name. But you have a past. Such a past as is worth all my future."

He shook his head and smiled, as I thought with half-sad appreciation of my flattering admiration. "That future," he said; "would you in truth change it?" The waiter came with liqueurs. "You will not perhaps mind taking my name, taking my position, but would you indeed—willingly—take my years?"

"With your achievements," said I gallantly.

He smiled again. "Kümmel—both," he said to the waiter, and turned his attention to a little paper packet he had taken from his pocket. "This hour," said he, "this after-dinner hour is the hour of small things. Here is a scrap of my unpublished wisdom." He opened the packet with his shaking yellow fingers, and showed a little pinkish powder on the paper. "This," said he—"well, you must guess what it is, But Kümmel—put but a dash of this powder in it—is Himmel." His large greyish eyes watched mine with an inscrutable expression.

It was a bit of a shock to me to find this great teacher gave his mind to the flavour of liqueurs. However, I feigned a great interest in his weakness, for I was drunk enough for such small sycophancy.

He parted the powder between the little glasses, and rising suddenly with a strange unexpected dignity, held out his hand towards me. I imitated his action, and the glasses rang. "To a quick succession," said he, and raised his glass towards his lips.

"Not that," I said hastily. "Not that."

He paused, with the liqueur at the level of his chin, and his eyes blazing into mine.

"To a long life," said I.

He hesitated. "To a long life," said he, with a sudden bark of laughter, and with eyes fixed on one another we tilted the little glasses. His eyes looked straight into mine, and as I drained the stuff off, I felt a curiously intense sensation. The first touch of it set my brain in a furious tumult; I seemed to feel an actual physical stirring in my skull, and a seething humming filled my ears. I did not notice the flavour in my mouth, the aroma that filled my throat; I saw only the grey intensity of his gaze that burnt into mine. The draught, the mental confusion, the noise and stirring in my head, seemed to last an interminable time. Curious vague impressions of half-forgotten things danced and vanished on the edge of my consciousness. At last he broke the spell. With a sudden explosive sigh he put down his glass.

"Well?" he said.

"It's glorious," said I, though I had not tasted the stuff.

My head was spinning. I sat down. My brain was chaos. Then my perception grew clear and minute as though I saw things in a concave mirror. His manner seemed to have changed into something nervous and hasty. He pulled out his watch and grimaced at it. "Eleven-seven! And to-night I

must—Seven—twenty-five. Waterloo! I must go at once."
He called for the bill, and struggled with his coat. Officious
waiters came to our assistance. In another moment I was wishing him good-bye, over the apron of a cab, and still with an
absurd feeling of minute distinctness, as though—how can I
express it?—I not only saw but *felt* through an inverted opera-
glass.

"That stuff," he said. He put his hand to his forehead. "I
ought not to have given it to you. It will make your head
split to-morrow. Wait a minute. Here." He handed me out a
little flat thing like a seidlitz-powder. "Take that in water
as you are going to bed. The other thing was a drug. Not till
you're ready to go to bed, mind. It will clear your head.
That's all. One more shake—Futurus!"

I gripped his shrivelled claw. "Good-bye," he said, and by
the droop of his eyelids I judged he, too, was a little under the
influence of that brain-twisting cordial.

He recollected something else with a start, felt in his breast-
pocket, and produced another packet, this time a cylinder
the size and shape of a shaving-stick. "Here," said he. "I'd
almost forgotten. Don't open this until I come to-morrow—
but take it now."

It was so heavy that I well-nigh dropped it. "All ri'!"
said I, and he grinned at me through the cab window, as the
cabman flicked his horse into wakefulness. It was a white
packet he had given me, with red seals at either end and along
its edge. "If this isn't money," said I, "it's platinum or lead."

I stuck it with elaborate care into my pocket, and with a
whirling brain walked home through the Regent Street
loiterers and the dark back streets beyond Portland Road.
I remember the sensations of that walk very vividly, strange
as they were. I was still so far myself that I could notice my
strange mental state, and wonder whether this stuff I had had
was opium—a drug beyond my experience. It is hard now to
describe the peculiarity of my mental strangeness—mental
doubling vaguely expresses it. As I was walking up Regent
Street I found in my mind a queer persuasion that it was
Waterloo station, and had an odd impulse to get into the

Polytechnic as a man might get into a train. I put a knuckle
in my eye, and it was Regent Street. How can I express it?
You see a skilful actor looking quietly at you, he pulls a
grimace, and lo!—another person. Is it too extravagant if I
tell you that it seemed to me as if Regent Street had, for the
moment, done that? Then, being persuaded it was Regent
Street again, I was oddly muddled about some fantastic
reminiscences that cropped up. "Thirty years ago," thought I,
"it was here that I quarrelled with my brother." Then I
burst out laughing, to the astonishment and encouragement
of a group of night prowlers. Thirty years ago I did not exist,
and never in my life had I boasted a brother. The stuff was
surely liquid folly, for the poignant regret for that lost brother
still clung to me. Along Portland Road the madness took
another turn. I began to recall vanished shops, and to compare the street with what it used to be. Confused, troubled
thinking was comprehensible enough after the drink I had
taken, but what puzzled me were these curiously vivid phantasmal memories that had crept into my mind; and not only
the memories that had crept in, but also the memories that
had slipped out. I stopped opposite Stevens', the natural
history dealer's, and cudgelled my brains to think what he had
to do with me. A 'bus went by, and sounded exactly like the
rumbling of a train. I seemed to be dipped into some dark,
remote pit for the recollection. "Of course," said I, at last,
"he has promised me three frogs to-morrow. Odd I should
have forgotten."

Do they still show children dissolving views? In those I
remember one view would begin like a faint ghost, and grow
and oust another. In just that way it seemed to me that a
ghostly set of new sensations was struggling with those of my
ordinary self.

I went on through Euston Road to Tottenham Court
Road, puzzled, and a little frightened, and scarcely noticed
the unusual way I was taking, for commonly I used to cut
through the intervening network of back streets. I turned
into University Street, to discover that I had forgotten my
number. Only by a strong effort did I recall 11A, and even

then it seemed to me that it was a thing some forgotten person had told me. I tried to steady my mind by recalling the incidents of the dinner, and for the life of me I could conjure up no picture of my host's face; I saw him only as a shadowy outline, as one might see oneself reflected in a window through which one was looking. In his place, however, I had a curious exterior vision of myself sitting at a table, flushed, bright-eyed, and talkative.

"I must take this other powder," said I. "This is getting impossible."

I tried the wrong side of the hall for my candle and the matches, and had a doubt of which landing my room might be on. "I'm drunk," I said, "that's certain," and blundered needlessly on the staircase to sustain the proposition.

At the first glance my room seemed unfamiliar. "What rot!" I said, and stared about me. I seemed to bring myself back by the effort and the odd phantasmal quality passed into the concrete familiar. There was the old looking-glass, with my notes on the albumens stuck in the corner of the frame, my old everyday suit of clothes pitched about the floor. And yet it was not so real, after all. I felt an idiotic persuasion trying to creep into my mind, as it were, that I was in a railway carriage in a train just stopping, that I was peering out of the window at some unknown station. I gripped the bed-rail firmly to reassure myself. "It's clairvoyance, perhaps," I said. "I must write to the Psychical Research Society."

I put the rouleau on my dressing-table, sat on my bed and began to take off my boots. It was as if the picture of my present sensations was painted over some other picture that was trying to show through. "Curse it!" said I; "my wits are going, or am I in two places at once?" Half-undressed, I tossed the powder into a glass and drank it off. It effervesced, and became a fluorescent amber colour. Before I was in bed my mind was already tranquillised. I felt the pillow at my cheek, and thereupon I must have fallen asleep.

I awoke abruptly out of a dream of strange beasts, and found myself lying on my back. Probably everyone knows that dismal emotional dream from which one escapes, awake indeed but strangely cowed. There was a curious taste in my mouth, a tired feeling in my limbs, a sense of cutaneous discomfort. I lay with my head motionless on my pillow, expecting that my feeling of strangeness and terror would probably pass away, and that I should then doze off again to sleep. But instead of that, my uncanny sensations increased. At first I could perceive nothing wrong about me. There was a faint light in the room, so faint that it was the very next thing to darkness, and the furniture stood out in it as vague blots of absolute darkness. I stared with my eyes just over the bedclothes.

It came into my mind that someone had entered the room to rob me of my rouleau of money, but after lying for some moments, breathing regularly to simulate sleep, I realised this was mere fancy. Nevertheless, the uneasy assurance of something wrong kept fast hold of me. With an effort I raised my head from the pillow, and peered about me at the dark. What it was I could not conceive. I looked at the dim shapes around me, the greater and lesser darknesses that indicated curtains, table, fireplace, bookshelves, and so forth. Then I began to perceive something unfamiliar in the forms of the darkness. Had the bed turned round? Yonder should be the bookshelves, and something shrouded and pallid rose there, something that would not answer to the bookshelves, however I looked at it. It was far too big to be my shirt thrown on a chair.

Overcoming a childish terror, I threw back the bedclothes and thrust my leg out of bed. Instead of coming out of my truckle-bed upon the floor, I found my foot scarcely reached the edge of the mattress. I made another step, as it were, and sat up on the edge of the bed. By the side of my bed should be the candle, and the matches upon the broken chair. I put out my hand and touched—nothing. I waved my hand in the darkness, and it came against some heavy hanging, soft and thick in texture, which gave a rustling noise at my touch. I grasped this and pulled it; it appeared to be a curtain suspended over the head of my bed.

I was now thoroughly awake, and beginning to realise

that I was in a strange room. I was puzzled. I tried to recall the overnight circumstances, and I found them now, curiously enough, vivid in my memory: the supper, my reception of the little packages, my wonder whether I was intoxicated, my slow undressing, the coolness to my flushed face of my pillow. I felt a sudden distrust. Was that last night, or the night before? At any rate, this room was strange to me, and I could not imagine how I had got into it. The dim, pallid outline was growing paler, and I perceived it was a window, with the dark shape of an oval toilet-glass against the weak intimation of the dawn that filtered through the blind. I stood up, and was surprised by a curious feeling of weakness and unsteadiness. With trembling hands outstretched, I walked slowly towards the window, getting, nevertheless, a bruise on the knee from a chair by the way. I fumbled round the glass, which was large, with handsome brass sconces, to find the blind-cord. I could not find any. By chance I took hold of the tassel, and with the click of a spring the blind ran up.

I found myself looking out upon a scene that was altogether strange to me. The night was overcast, and through the flocculent grey of the heaped clouds there filtered a faint half-light of dawn. Just at the edge of the sky, the cloud-canopy had a blood-red rim. Below, everything was dark and indistinct, dim hills in the distance, a vague mass of buildings running up into pinnacles, trees like spilt ink, and below the window a tracery of black bushes and pale grey paths. It was so unfamiliar that for the moment I thought myself still dreaming. I felt the toilet-table; it appeared to be made of some polished wood, and was rather elaborately furnished—there were little cut-glass bottles and a brush upon it. There was also a queer little object, horseshoe-shaped it felt, with smooth, hard projections, lying in a saucer. I could find no matches nor candle-stick.

I turned my eyes to the room again. Now the blind was up, faint spectres of its furnishing came out of the darkness. There was a huge curtained bed, and the fireplace at its foot had a large white mantel with something of the shimmer of marble.

I leant against the toilet-table, shut my eyes and opened

them again, and tried to think. The whole thing was far too real for dreaming. I was inclined to imagine there was still some hiatus in my memory as a consequence of my draught of that strange liqueur; that I had come into my inheritance, perhaps, and suddenly lost my recollection of everything since my good fortune had been announced. Perhaps if I waited a little, things would be clearer to me again. Yet my dinner with old Elvesham was now singularly vivid and recent. The champagne, the observant waiters, the powder, and the liqueurs—I could have staked my soul it all happened a few hours ago.

And then occurred a thing so trivial and yet so terrible to me that I shiver now to think of that moment. I spoke aloud. I said, "How the devil did I get here?" . . . *And the voice was not my own.*

It was not my own, it was thin, the articulation was slurred, the resonance of my facial bones was different. Then to reassure myself I ran one hand over the other, and felt loose folds of skin, the bony laxity of age. "Surely," I said in that horrible voice that had somehow established itself in my throat, "surely this thing is a dream!" Almost as quickly as if I did it involuntarily, I thrust my fingers into my mouth. My teeth had gone. My finger-tips ran on the flaccid surface of an even row of shrivelled gums. I was sick with dismay and disgust.

I felt then a passionate desire to see myself, to realise at once in its full horror the ghastly change that had come upon me. I tottered to the mantel, and felt along it for matches. As I did so, a barking cough sprang up in my throat, and I clutched the thick flannel nightdress I found about me. There were no matches there, and I suddenly realised that my extremities were cold. Sniffing and coughing, whimpering a little perhaps, I fumbled back to bed. "It is surely a dream," I whimpered to myself as I clambered back, "surely a dream." It was a senile repetition. I pulled the bedclothes over my shoulders, over my ears, I thrust my withered hand under the pillow, and determined to compose myself to sleep. Of course it was a dream. In the morning the dream would be over, and

I should wake up strong and vigorous again to my youth and studies. I shut my eyes, breathed regularly, and, finding myself wakeful, began to count slowly through the powers of three.

But the thing I desired would not come. I could not get to sleep. And the persuasion of the inexorable reality of the change that had happened to me grew steadily. Presently I found myself with my eyes wide open, the powers of three forgotten, and my skinny fingers upon my shrivelled gums. I was indeed, suddenly and abruptly, an old man. I had in some unaccountable manner fallen through my life and come to old age, in some way I had been cheated of all the best of my life, of love, of struggle, of strength and hope. I grovelled into the pillow and tried to persuade myself that such hallucination was possible. Imperceptibly, steadily, the dawn grew clearer.

At last, despairing of further sleep, I sat up in bed and looked about me. A chill twilight rendered the whole chamber visible. It was spacious and well-furnished, better furnished than any room I had ever slept in before. A candle and matches became dimly visible upon a little pedestal in a recess. I threw back the bedclothes, and shivering with the rawness of the early morning, albeit it was summer-time, I got out and lit the candle. Then, trembling horribly so that the extinguisher rattled on its spike, I tottered to the glass and saw —*Elvesham's face!* It was none the less horrible because I had already dimly feared as much. He had already seemed physically weak and pitiful to me, but seen now, dressed only in a coarse flannel nightdress that fell apart and showed the stringy neck, seen now as my own body, I cannot describe its desolate decrepitude. The hollow cheeks, the straggling tail of dirty grey hair, the rheumy bleared eyes, the quivering, shrivelled lips, the lower displaying a gleam of the pink interior lining, and those horrible dark gums showing. You who are mind and body together at your natural years, cannot imagine what this fiendish imprisonment meant to me. To be young and full of the desire and energy of youth, and to be caught, and presently to be crushed in this tottering ruin of a body. . . .

But I wander from the course of my story. For some time I must have been stunned at this change that had come upon me. It was daylight when I did so far gather myself together as to think. In some inexplicable way I had been changed, though how, short of magic, the thing had been done, I could not say. And as I thought, the diabolical ingenuity of Elvesham came home to me. It seemed plain to me that as I found myself in his, so he must be in possession of *my* body, of my strength that is, and my future. But how to prove it? Then as I thought, the thing became so incredible even to me that my mind reeled, and I had to pinch myself, to feel my toothless gums, to see myself in the glass, and touch the things about me before I could steady myself to face the facts again. Was all life hallucination? Was I indeed Elvesham, and he me? Had I been dreaming of Eden overnight? Was there any Eden? But if I was Elvesham, I should remember where I was on the previous morning, the name of the town in which I lived, what happened before the dream began. I struggled with my thoughts. I recalled the queer doubleness of my memories overnight. But now my mind was clear. Not the ghost of any memories but those proper to Eden could I raise.

"This way lies insanity!" I cried in my piping voice. I staggered to my feet, dragged my feeble, heavy limbs to the washhand-stand, and plunged my grey head into a basin of cold water. Then, towelling myself, I tried again. It was no good. I felt beyond all question that I was indeed Eden, not Elvesham. But Eden in Elvesham's body!

Had I been a man of any other age, I might have given myself up to my fate as one enchanted. But in these sceptical days miracles do not pass current. Here was some trick of psychology. What a drug and a steady stare could do, a drug and a steady stare, or some similar treatment, could surely undo. Men have lost their memories before. But to exchange memories as one does umbrellas! I laughed. Alas! not a healthy laugh, but a wheezing, senile titter. I could have fancied old Elvesham laughing at my plight, and a gust of petulant anger, unusual to me, swept across my feelings. I began dressing eagerly in the clothes I found lying about on the floor, and only realised when I was dressed that it was an evening suit I had assumed. I opened the wardrobe and found some ordinary clothes, a pair of plaid trousers, and an old-fashioned dressing-gown. I put a venerable smoking-cap on my venerable head, and, coughing a little from my exertions, tottered out upon the landing.

It was then perhaps a quarter to six, and the blinds were closely drawn and the house quite silent. The landing was a spacious one, a broad, richly-carpeted staircase went down into the darkness of the hall below, and before me a door ajar showed me a writing-desk, a revolving bookcase, the back of a study chair, and a fine array of bound books, shelf upon shelf.

"My study," I mumbled, and walked across the landing. Then at the sound of my voice a thought struck me, and I went back to the bedroom and put in the set of false teeth. They slipped in with the ease of old habit. "That's better," said I, gnashing them, and so returned to the study.

The drawers of the writing-desk were locked. Its revolving top was also locked. I could see no indications of the keys, and there were none in the pockets of my trousers. I shuffled back at once to the bedroom, and went through the dress suit, and afterwards the pockets of all the garments I could find. I was very eager; and one might have imagined that burglars had been at work, to see my room when I had done. Not only were there no keys to be found, but not a coin, nor a scrap of paper —save only the receipted bill of the overnight dinner.

A curious weariness asserted itself. I sat down and stared at the garments flung here and there, their pockets turned inside out. My first frenzy had already flickered out. Every moment I was beginning to realise the immense intelligence of the plans of my enemy, to see more and more clearly the hopelessness of my position. With an effort I rose and hurried into the study again. On the staircase was a housemaid pulling up the blinds. She stared, I think, at the expression of my face. I shut the door of the study behind me, and, seizing a poker, began an attack upon the desk. That is how they found me. The cover of the desk was split, the lock smashed, the

letters torn out of the pigeon-holes and tossed about the
room. In my senile rage I had flung about the pens and other
such light stationery, and overturned the ink. Moreover, a
large vase upon the mantel had got broken—I do not know
how. I could find no cheque-book, no money, no indications
of the slightest use for the recovery of my body. I was battering madly at the drawers, when the butler, backed by two
women-servants, intruded upon me.

That simply is the story of my change. No one will believe my frantic assertions. I am treated as one demented,
and even at this moment I am under restraint. But I am sane,
absolutely sane, and to prove it I have sat down to write this
story minutely as the thing happened to me. I appeal to the
reader, whether there is any trace of insanity in the style or
method of the story he has been reading. I am a young man
locked away in an old man's body. But the clear fact is incredible to everyone. Naturally I appear demented to those
who will not believe this, naturally I do not know the names of
my secretaries, of the doctors who come to see me, of my
servants and neighbours, of this town (wherever it is) where I
find myself. Naturally I lose myself in my own house, and
suffer inconveniences of every sort. Naturally I ask the oddest
questions. Naturally I weep and cry out, and have paroxysms
of despair. I have no money and no cheque-book. The bank
will not recognise my signature, for I suppose that, allowing
for the feeble muscles I now have, my handwriting is still
Eden's. These people about me will not let me go to the bank
personally. It seems, indeed, that there is no bank in this
town, and that I have taken an account in some part of London. It seems that Elvesham kept the name of his solicitor
secret from all his household—I can ascertain nothing.
Elvesham was, of course, a profound student of mental
science, and all my declarations of the facts of the case merely
confirm the theory that my insanity is the outcome of over-
much brooding upon psychology. Dreams of the personal
identity indeed! Two days ago I was a healthy youngster, with
all life before me; now I am a furious old man, unkempt and

desperate and miserable, prowling about a great luxurious strange house, watched, feared, and avoided as a lunatic by everyone about me. And in London is Elvesham beginning life again in a vigorous body, and with all the accumulated knowledge and wisdom of threescore and ten. He has stolen my life.

What has happened I do not clearly know. In the study are volumes of manuscript notes referring chiefly to the psychology of memory, and parts of what may be either calculations or ciphers in symbols absolutely strange to me. In some passages there are indications that he was also occupied with the philosophy of mathematics. I take it he has transferred the whole of his memories, the accumulation that makes up his personality, from this old withered brain of his to mine, and, similarly, that he has transferred mine to his discarded tenement. Practically, that is, he has changed bodies. But how such a change may be possible is without the range of my philosophy. I have been a materialist for all my thinking life, but here, suddenly, is a clear case of man's detachability from matter.

One desperate experiment I am about to try. I sit writing here before putting the matter to issue. This morning, with the help of a table-knife that I had secreted at breakfast, I succeeded in breaking open a fairly obvious secret drawer in this wrecked writing-desk. I discovered nothing save a little green glass phial containing a white powder. Round the neck of the phial was a label, and thereon was written this one word, "*Release.*" This may be—is most probably, poison. I can understand Elvesham placing poison in my way, and I should be sure that it was his intention so to get rid of the only living witness against him were it not for this careful concealment. The man has practically solved the problem of immortality. Save for the spite of chance, he will live in my body until it has aged, and then, again, throwing that aside, he will assume some other victim's youth and strength. When one remembers his heartlessness, it is terrible to think of the ever-growing experience, that . . . How long has he been leaping from body to body? . . . But I tire of writing. The powder appears to be soluble in water. The taste is not un-pleasant.

There the narrative found upon Mr. Elvesham's desk ends. His dead body lay between the desk and the chair. The latter had been pushed back, probably by his last convulsions. The story was written in pencil, and in a crazy hand quite unlike his usual minute characters. There remain only two curious facts to record. Indisputably there was some connection be-tween Eden and Elvesham, since the whole of Elvesham's property was bequeathed to the young man. But he never inherited. When Elvesham committed suicide, Eden was, strangely enough, already dead. Twenty-four hours before, he had been knocked down by a cab and killed instantly, at the crowded crossing at the intersection of Gower Street and Euston Road. So that the only human being who could have thrown light upon this fantastic narrative is beyond the reach of questions.

IN THE ABYSS

THE lieutenant stood in front of the steel sphere and gnawed a piece of pine splinter. "What do you think of it, Steevens?" he asked.

"It's an idea," said Steevens, in the tone of one who keeps an open mind.

"I believe it will smash—flat," said the lieutenant.

"He seems to have calculated it all out pretty well," said Steevens, still impartial.

"But think of the pressure," said the lieutenant. "At the surface of the water it's fourteen pounds to the inch, thirty feet down it's double that; sixty, treble; ninety, four times; nine hundred, forty times; five thousand, three hundred—that's a mile—it's two hundred and forty times fourteen pounds; that's—let's see—thirty hundredweight—a ton and a half, Steevens; *a ton and a half* to the square inch. And the ocean where he's going is five miles deep. That's seven and a half——"

"Sounds a lot," said Steevens, "but it's jolly thick steel."

The lieutenant made no answer, but resumed his pine splinter. The object of their conversation was a huge ball of steel, having an exterior diameter of perhaps nine feet. It looked like the shot for some Titanic piece of artillery. It was elaborately nested in a monstrous scaffolding built into the framework of the vessel, and the gigantic spars that were presently to sling it overboard gave the stern of the ship an appearance that had raised the curiosity of every decent sailor who had sighted it, from the Pool of London to the Tropic of Capricorn. In two places, one above the other, the steel gave place to a couple of circular windows of enormously thick glass, and one of these, set in a steel frame of great solidity, was now partially unscrewed. Both the men had seen the interior of this globe for the first time that morning. It was elaborately padded with air cushions, with little studs sunk between bulging pillows to work the simple mechanism of the affair. Everything was elaborately padded, even the Myers apparatus which was to absorb carbonic acid and replace the oxygen inspired by its tenant, when he had crept in by the glass manhole, and had been screwed in. It was so elaborately padded that a man might have been fired from a gun in it with perfect safety. And it had need to be, for presently a man was to crawl in through that glass manhole, to be screwed up tightly, and to be flung overboard, and to sink down— down—down, for five miles, even as the lieutenant said. It had taken the strongest hold of his imagination; it made him a bore at mess; and he found Steevens, the new arrival aboard, a godsend to talk to about it, over and over again.

"It's my opinion," said the lieutenant, "that that glass will simply bend in and bulge and smash, under a pressure of that sort. Daubrée has made rocks run like water under big pressures—and, you mark my words——"

"If the glass did break in," said Steevens, "what then?"

"The water would shoot in like a jet of iron. Have you ever felt a straight jet of high-pressure water? It would hit as hard as a bullet. It would simply smash him and flatten him. It would tear down his throat, and into his lungs; it would blow in his ears——"

"What a detailed imagination you have!" protested Steevens, who saw things vividly.

"It's a simple statement of the inevitable," said the lieutenant.

"And the globe?"

"Would just give out a few little bubbles, and it would settle down comfortably against the day of judgment, among the oozes and the bottom clay—with poor Elstead spread over his own smashed cushions like butter over bread."

He repeated this sentence as though he liked it very much. "Like butter over bread," he said.

"Having a look at the jigger?" said a voice, and Elstead stood behind them, spick and span in white, with a cigarette between his teeth, and his eyes smiling out of the shadow of his ample hat-brim. "What's that about bread and butter, Weybridge? Grumbling as usual about the insufficient pay of naval officers? It won't be more than a day now before I start. We are to get the slings ready to-day. This clean sky and gentle swell is just the kind of thing for swinging off a dozen tons of lead and iron, isn't it?"

"It won't affect you much," said Weybridge.

"No. Seventy or eighty feet down, and I shall be there in a dozen seconds, there's not a particle moving, though the wind shriek itself hoarse up above, and the water lifts half-way to the clouds. No. Down there——" He moved to the side of the ship and the other two followed him. All three leant forward on their elbows and stared down into the yellow-green water.

"*Peace*," said Elstead, finishing his thought aloud.

"Are you dead certain that clockwork will act?" asked Weybridge presently.

"It has worked thirty-five times," said Elstead. "It's bound to work."

"But if it doesn't?"

"Why shouldn't it?"

"I wouldn't go down in that confounded thing," said Weybridge, "for twenty thousand pounds."

"Cheerful chap you are," said Elstead, and spat sociably at a bubble below.

"I don't understand yet how you mean to work the thing," said Steevens.

"In the first place, I'm screwed into the sphere," said Elstead, "and when I've turned the electric light off and on three times to show I'm cheerful, I'm swung out over the stern by that crane, with all those big lead sinkers slung below me. The top lead weight has a roller carrying a hundred fathoms of strong cord rolled up, and that's all that joins the sinkers to the sphere, except the slings that will be cut when the affair is dropped. We use cord rather than wire rope because it's easier to cut and more buoyant—necessary points, as you will see.

"Through each of these lead weights you notice there

is a hole, and an iron rod will be run through that and will project six feet on the lower side. If that rod is rammed up from below, it knocks up a lever and sets the clockwork in motion at the side of the cylinder on which the cord winds.

"Very well. The whole affair is lowered gently into the water, and the slings are cut. The sphere floats,—with the air in it, it's lighter than water,—but the lead weights go down straight and the cord runs out. When the cord is all paid out, the sphere will go down, too, pulled down by the cord."

"But why the cord?" asked Steevens. "Why not fasten the weights directly to the sphere?"

"Because of the smash down below. The whole affair will go rushing down, mile after mile, at a headlong pace at last. It would be knocked to pieces on the bottom if it wasn't for that cord. But the weights will hit the bottom, and directly they do, the buoyancy of the sphere will come into play. It will go on sinking slower and slower; come to a stop at last, and then begin to float upward again.

"That's where the clockwork comes in. Directly the weights smash against the sea bottom, the rod will be knocked through and will kick up the clockwork, and the cord will be rewound on the reel. I shall be lugged down to the sea bottom. There I shall stay for half an hour, with the electric light on, looking about me. Then the clockwork will release a spring knife, the cord will be cut, and up I shall rush again, like a soda-water bubble. The cord itself will help the flotation."

"And if you should chance to hit a ship?" said Weybridge.

"I should come up at such a pace, I should go clean through it," said Elstead, "like a cannon ball. You needn't worry about that."

"And suppose some nimble crustacean should wriggle into your clockwork———"

"It would be a pressing sort of invitation for me to stop," said Elstead, turning his back on the water and staring at the sphere.

They had swung Elstead overboard by eleven o'clock. The day was serenely bright and calm, with the horizon lost in haze. The electric glare in the little upper compartment beamed cheerfully three times. Then they let him down slowly to the surface of the water, and a sailor in the stern chains hung ready to cut the tackle that held the lead weights and the sphere together. The globe, which had looked so large on deck, looked the smallest thing conceivable under the stern of the ship. It rolled a little, and its two dark windows, which floated uppermost, seemed like eyes turned up in round wonderment at the people who crowded the rail. A voice wondered how Elstead liked the rolling. "Are you ready?" sang out the commander. "Ay, ay, sir!" "Then let her go!"

The rope of the tackle tightened against the blade and was cut, and an eddy rolled over the globe in a grotesquely helpless fashion. Someone waved a handkerchief, someone else tried an ineffectual cheer, a middy was counting slowly: "Eight, nine, ten!" Another roll, then with a jerk and a splash the thing righted itself.

It seemed to be stationary for a moment, to grow rapidly smaller, and then the water closed over it, and it became visible, enlarged by refraction and dimmer, below the surface. Before one could count three it had disappeared. There was a flicker of white light far down in the water, that diminished to a speck and vanished. Then there was nothing but a depth of water going down into blackness, through which a shark was swimming.

Then suddenly the screw of the cruiser began to rotate, the water was crickled, the shark disappeared in a wrinkled confusion, and a torrent of foam rushed across the crystalline clearness that had swallowed up Elstead. "What's the idee?" said one A. B. to another.

"We're going to lay off about a couple of miles, 'fear he should hit us when he comes up," said his mate.

The ship steamed slowly to her new position. Aboard her almost everyone who was unoccupied remained watching the breathing swell into which the sphere had sunk. For the next half-hour it is doubtful if a word was spoken that did not bear directly or indirectly on Elstead. The December sun was now high in the sky, and the heat very considerable.

"He'll be cold enough down there," said Weybridge. "They say that below a certain depth sea water's always just about freezing."

"Where'll he come up?" asked Steevens. "I've lost my bearings."

"That's the spot," said the commander, who prided himself on his omniscience. He extended a precise finger southeastward. "And this, I reckon, is pretty nearly the moment," he said. "He's been thirty-five minutes."

"How long does it take to reach the bottom of the ocean?" asked Steevens.

"For a depth of five miles, and reckoning—as we did—an acceleration of two feet per second, both ways, is just about three-quarters of a minute."

"Then he's overdue," said Weybridge.

"Pretty nearly," said the commander. "I suppose it takes a few minutes for that cord of his to wind in."

"I forgot that," said Weybridge, evidently relieved.

And then began the suspense. A minute slowly dragged itself out, and no sphere shot out of the water. Another followed, and nothing broke the low oily swell. The sailors explained to one another that little point about the winding-in of the cord. The rigging was dotted with expectant faces. "Come up, Elstead!" called one hairy-chested salt impatiently, and the others caught it up, and shouted as though they were waiting for the curtain of a theatre to rise.

The commander glanced irritably at them.

"Of course, if the acceleration's less than two," he said, "he'll be all the longer. We aren't absolutely certain that was the proper figure. I'm no slavish believer in calculations."

Steevens agreed concisely. No one on the quarter-deck spoke for a couple of minutes. Then Steevens' watchcase clicked.

When, twenty-one minutes after, the sun reached the zenith, they were still wating for the globe to reappear, and not a man aboard had dared to whisper that hope was dead. It was Weybridge who first gave expression to that realisation.

He spoke while the sound of eight bells still hung in the air. "I always distrusted that window," he said quite suddenly to Steevens.

"Good God!" said Steevens; "you don't think——?"

"Well!" said Weybridge, and left the rest to his imagination.

"I'm no great believer in calculations myself," said the commander dubiously, "so that I'm not altogether hopeless yet." And at midnight the gunboat was steaming slowly in a spiral round the spot where the globe had sunk, and the white beam of the electric light fled and halted and swept discontentedly onward again over the waste of phosphorescent waters under the little stars.

"If his window hasn't burst and smashed him," said Weybridge, "then it's a cursed sight worse, for his clockwork has gone wrong, and he's alive now, five miles under our feet, down there in the cold and dark, anchored in that little bubble of his, where never a ray of light has shone or a human being lived, since the waters were gathered together. He's there without food, feeling hungry and thirsty and scared, wondering whether he'll starve or stifle. Which will it be? The Myers apparatus is running out, I suppose. How long do they last?"

"Good heavens!" he exclaimed; "what little things we are! What daring little devils! Down there, miles and miles of water—all water, and all this empty water about us and this sky. Gulfs!" He threw his hands out, and as he did so, a little white streak swept noiselessly up the sky, travelled more slowly, stopped, became a motionless dot, as though a new star had fallen up into the sky. Then it went sliding back again and lost itself amidst the reflections of the stars and the white haze of the sea's phosphorescence.

At the sight he stopped, arm extended and mouth open. He shut his mouth, opened it again, and waved his arms with an impatient gesture. Then he turned, shouted "El-stead ahoy!" to the first watch, and went at a run to Lindley and the search-light. "I saw him," he said. "Starboard there! His light's on, and he's just shot out of the water. Bring the

light round. We ought to see him drifting, when he lifts on
the swell."

But they never picked up the explorer until dawn. Then
they almost ran him down The crane was swung out and a
boat's crew hooked the chain to the sphere. When they had
shipped the sphere, they unscrewed the manhole and peered
into the darkness of the interior (for the electric-light chamber
was intended to illuminate the water about the sphere, and
was shut off entirely from its general cavity).

The air was very hot within the cavity, and the indiarubber
at the lip of the manhole was soft. There was no answer to
their eager questions and no sound of movement within.
Elstead seemed to be lying motionless, crumpled up in the
bottom of the globe. The ship's doctor crawled in and lifted
him out to the men outside. For a moment or so they did not
know whether Elstead was alive or dead. His face, in the yellow light of the ship's lamps, glistened with perspiration.
They carried him down to his own cabin.

He was not dead, they found, but in a state of absolute
nervous collapse, and besides cruelly bruised. For some days
he had to lie perfectly still. It was a week before he could tell
his experiences.

Almost his first words were that he was going down again.
The sphere would have to be altered, he said, in order to
allow him to throw off the cord if need be, and that was all.
He had had the most marvellous experience. "You thought
I should find nothing but ooze," he said. "You laughed at
my explorations, and I've discovered a new world!" He told
his story in disconnected fragments, and chiefly from the
wrong end, so that it is impossible to re-tell it in his words.
But what follows is the narrative of his experience.

It began atrociously, he said. Before the cord ran out, the
thing kept rolling over. He felt like a frog in a football. He
could see nothing but the crane and the sky overhead, with an
occasional glimpse of the people on the ship's rail. He couldn't
tell a bit which way the thing would roll next. Suddenly he
would find his feet going up, and try to step, and over he went
rolling, head over heels, and just anyhow, on the padding.

Any other shape would have been more comfortable, but no other shape was to be relied upon under the huge pressure of the nethermost abyss.

Suddenly the swaying ceased; the globe righted, and when he had picked himself up, he saw the water all about him greeny-blue, with an attenuated light filtering down from above, and a shoal of little floating things went rushing up past him, as it seemed to him, towards the light. And even as he looked, it grew darker and darker, until the water above was as dark as the midnight sky, albeit of a greener shade, and the water below black. And little transparent things in the water developed a faint glint of luminosity, and shot past him in faint greenish streaks.

And the feeling of falling! It was just like the start of a lift. he said, only it kept on. One has to imagine what that means, that keeping on. It was then of all times that Elstead repented of his adventure. He saw the chances against him in an altogether new light. He thought of the big cuttle-fish people knew to exist in the middle waters, the kind of things they find half digested in whales at times, or floating dead and rotten and half eaten by fish. Suppose one caught hold and wouldn't let go. And had the clockwork really been sufficiently tested? But whether he wanted to go on or to go back mattered not the slightest now.

In fifty seconds everything was as black as night outside, except where the beam from his light struck through the waters, and picked out every now and then some fish or scrap of sinking matter. They flashed by too fast for him to see what they were. Once he thinks he passed a shark. And then the sphere began to get hot by friction against the water. They had under-estimated this, it seems.

The first thing he noticed was that he was perspiring, and then he heard a hissing growing louder under his feet, and saw a lot of little bubbles—very little bubbles they were—rushing upward like a fan through the water outside. Steam! He felt the window, and it was hot. He turned on the minute glow-lamp that lit his own cavity, looked at the padded watch by the studs, and saw he had been travelling now for two minutes. It came into his head that the window would crack through the conflict of temperatures, for he knew the bottom water is very near freezing.

Then suddenly the floor of the sphere seemed to press against his feet, the rush of bubbles outside grew slower and slower, and the hissing diminished. The sphere rolled a little. The window had not cracked, nothing had given, and he knew that the dangers of sinking, at any rate, were over.

In another minute or so he would be on the floor of the abyss. He thought, he said, of Steevens and Weybridge and the rest of them five miles overhead, higher to him than the very highest clouds that ever floated over land are to us, steaming slowly and staring down and wondering what had happened to him.

He peered out of the window. There were no more bubbles now, and the hissing had stopped. Outside there was a heavy blackness—as black as black velvet—except where the electric light pierced the empty water and showed the colour of it—a yellow-green. Then three things like shapes of fire swam into sight, following each other through the water. Whether they were little and near or big and far off he could not tell.

Each was outlined in a bluish light almost as bright as the lights of a fishing smack, a light which seemed to be smoking greatly, and all along the sides of them were specks of this, like the lighter portholes of a ship. Their phosphorescence seemed to go out as they came into the radiance of his lamp, and he saw then that they were little fish of some strange sort, with huge heads, vast eyes, and dwindling bodies and tails. Their eyes were turned towards him, and he judged they were following him down. He supposed they were attracted by his glare.

Presently others of the same sort joined them. As he went on down, he noticed that the water became of a pallid colour, and that little specks twinkled in his ray like motes in a sunbeam. This was probably due to the clouds of ooze and mud that the impact of his leaden sinkers had disturbed.

By the time he was drawn down to the lead weights he was in a dense fog of white that his electric light failed altogether to pierce for more than a few yards, and many minutes elapsed before the hanging sheets of sediment subsided to any extent. Then, lit by his light and by the transient phosphorescence of a distant shoal of fishes, he was able to see under the huge blackness of the super-incumbent water an undulating expanse of greyish-white ooze, broken here and there by tangled thickets of a growth of sea lilies, waving hungry tentacles in the air.

Farther away were the graceful, translucent outlines of a group of gigantic sponges. About this floor there were scattered a number of bristling flattish tufts of rich purple and black, which he decided must be some sort of sea-urchin, and small, large-eyed or blind things having a curious resemblance, some to woodlice, and others to lobsters, crawled sluggishly across the track of the light and vanished into the obscurity again, leaving furrowed trails behind them.

Then suddenly the hovering swarm of little fishes veered about and came towards him as a flight of starlings might do. They passed over him like a phosphorescent snow, and then he saw behind them some larger creature advancing towards the sphere.

At first he could see it only dimly, a faintly moving figure remotely suggestive of a walking man, and then it came into the spray of light that the lamp shot out. As the glare struck it, it shut its eyes, dazzled. He stared in rigid astonishment.

It was a strange vertebrated animal. Its dark purple head was dimly suggestive of a chameleon, but it had such a high forehead and such a braincase as no reptile ever displayed before; the vertical pitch of its face gave it a most extraordinary resemblance to a human being.

Two large and protruding eyes projected from sockets in chameleon fashion, and it had a broad reptilian mouth with horny lips beneath its little nostrils. In the position of the ears were two huge gill-covers, and out of these floated a branching tree of coralline filaments, almost like the tree-like gills that very young rays and sharks possess.

But the humanity of the face was not the most extraordinary thing about the creature. It was a biped; its almost glob-

ular body was poised on a tripod of two frog-like legs and a
long thick tail, and its fore limbs, which grotesquely caricatured the human hand, much as a frog's do, carried a long
shaft of bone, tipped with copper. The colour of the creature
was variegated; its head, hands, and legs were purple; but its
skin, which hung loosely upon it, even as clothes might do,
was a phosphorescent grey. And it stood there blinded by the
light.

At last this unknown creature of the abyss blinked its eyes
open, and, shading them with its disengaged hand, opened
its mouth and gave vent to a shouting noise, articulate almost
as speech might be, that penetrated even the steel case and
padded jacket of the sphere. How a shouting may be accomplished without lungs Elstead does not profess to explain.
It then moved sideways out of the glare into the mystery of
shadow that bordered it on either side, and Elstead felt rather
than saw that it was coming towards him. Fancying the light
had attracted it, he turned the switch that cut off the current.
In another moment something soft dabbed upon the steel,
and the globe swayed.

Then the shouting was repeated, and it seemed to him that
a distant echo answered it. The dabbing recurred, and the
globe swayed and ground against the spindle over which the
wire was rolled. He stood in the blackness and peered out into
the everlasting night of the abyss. And presently he saw, very
faint and remote, other phosphorescent quasi-human forms
hurrying towards him.

Hardly knowing what he did, he felt about in his swaying
prison for the stud of the exterior electric light, and came by
accident against his own small glow-lamp in its padded recess.
The sphere twisted, and then threw him down; he heard
shouts like shouts of surprise, and when he rose to his feet,
he saw two pairs of stalked eyes peering into the lower window and reflecting his light.

In another moment hands were dabbing vigorously at his
steel casing, and there was a sound, horrible enough in his
position, of the metal protection of the clockwork being
vigorously hammered. That, indeed, sent his heart into his

mouth, for if these strange creatures succeeded in stopping that, his release would never occur. Scarcely had he thought as much when he felt the sphere sway violently, and the floor of it press hard against his feet. He turned off the small glow-lamp that lit the interior, and sent the ray of the large light in the separate compartment out into the water. The sea-floor and the man-like creatures had disappeared, and a couple of fish chasing each other dropped suddenly by the window.

He thought at once that these strange denizens of the deep sea had broken the rope, and that he had escaped. He drove up faster and faster, and then stopped with a jerk that sent him flying against the padded roof of his prison. For half a minute, perhaps, he was too astonished to think.

Then he felt that the sphere was spinning slowly, and rocking, and it seemed to him that it was also being drawn through the water. By crouching close to the window, he managed to make his weight effective and roll that part of the sphere downward, but he could see nothing save the pale ray of his light striking down ineffectively into the darkness. It occurred to him that he would see more if he turned the lamp off, and allowed his eyes to grow accustomed to the profound obscurity.

In this he was wise. After some minutes the velvety blackness became a translucent blackness, and then, far away, and as faint as the zodiacal light of an English summer evening, he saw shapes moving below. He judged these creatures had detached his cable, and were towing him along the sea bottom.

And then he saw something faint and remote across the undulations of the submarine plain, a broad horizon of pale luminosity that extended this way and that way as far as the range of his little window permitted him to see. To this he was being towed, as a balloon might be towed by men out of the open country into a town. He approached it very slowly, and very slowly the dim irradiation was gathered together into more definite shapes.

It was nearly five o'clock before he came over this luminous area, and by that time he could make out an arrangement suggestive of streets and houses grouped about a vast roofless erection that was grotesquely suggestive of a ruined abbey. It was spread out like a map below him. The houses were all roofless enclosures of walls, and their substance being, as he afterwards saw, of phosphorescent bones, gave the place an appearance as if it were built of drowned moonshine.

Among the inner caves of the place waving trees of crinoid stretched their tentacles, and tall, slender, glassy sponges shot like shining minarets and lilies of filmy light out of the general glow of the city. In the open spaces of the place he could see a stirring movement as of crowds of people, but he was too many fathoms above them to distinguish the individuals in those crowds.

Then slowly they pulled him down, and as they did so, the details of the place crept slowly upon his apprehension. He saw that the courses of the cloudy buildings were marked out with beaded lines of round objects, and then he perceived that at several points below him, in broad open spaces, were forms like the encrusted shapes of ships.

Slowly and surely he was drawn down, and the forms below him became brighter, clearer, more distinct. He was being pulled down, he perceived, towards the large building in the centre of the town, and he could catch a glimpse ever and again of the multitudinous forms that were lugging at his cord. He was astonished to see that the rigging of one of the ships, which formed such a prominent feature of the place, was crowded with a host of gesticulating figures regarding him, and then the walls of the great building rose about him silently, and hid the city from his eyes.

And such walls they were, of water-logged wood, and twisted wire-rope, and iron spars, and copper, and the bones and skulls of dead men. The skulls ran in zigzag lines and spirals and fantastic curves over the building; and in and out of their eye-sockets, and over the whole surface of the place, lurked and played a multitude of silvery little fishes.

Suddenly his ears were filled with a low shouting and a noise like the violent blowing of horns, and this gave place to a fantastic chant. Down the sphere sank, past the huge pointed windows, through which he saw vaguely a great number of these strange, ghostlike people regarding him, and at last he came to rest, as it seemed, on a kind of altar that stood in the centre of the place.

And now he was at such a level that he could see these strange people of the abyss plainly once more. To his astonishment, he perceived that they were prostrating themselves before him, all save one, dressed as it seemed in a robe of placoid scales, and crowned with a luminous diadem, who stood with his reptilian mouth opening and shutting, as though he led the chanting of the worshippers.

A curious impulse made Elstead turn on his small glow-lamp again, so that he became visible to these creatures of the abyss, albeit the glare made them disappear forthwith into night. At this sudden sight of him, the chanting gave place to a tumult of exultant shouts; and Elstead, being anxious to watch them, turned his light off again, and vanished from before their eyes. But for a time he was too blind to make out what they were doing, and when at last he could distinguish them, they were kneeling again. And thus they continued worshipping him, without rest or intermission, for a space of three hours.

Most circumstantial was Elstead's account of this astounding city and its people, these people of perpetual night, who have never seen sun or moon or stars, green vegetation, nor any living, air-breathing creatures, who know nothing of fire, nor any light but the phosphorescent light of living things.

Startling as is his story, it is yet more startling to find that scientific men, of such eminence as Adams and Jenkins, find nothing incredible in it. They tell me they see no reason why intelligent, water-breathing, vertebrated creatures, inured to a low temperature and enormous pressure, and of such a heavy structure, that neither alive nor dead would they float, might not live upon the bottom of the deep sea, and quite unsuspected by us, descendants like ourselves of the great Theriomorpha of the New Red Sandstone age.

We should be known to them, however, as strange, meteoric creatures, wont to fall catastrophically dead out of the mys-

terious blackness of their watery sky. And not only we ourselves, but our ships, our metals, our appliances, would come
raining down out of the night. Sometimes sinking things
would smite down and crush them, as if it were the judgment
of some unseen power above, and sometimes would come
things of the utmost rarity or utility, or shapes of inspiring
suggestion. One can understand, perhaps, something of their
behaviour at the descent of a living man, if one thinks what
a barbaric people might do, to whom an enhaloed, shining
creature came suddenly out of the sky.

At one time or another Elstead probably told the officers
of the *Ptarmigan* every detail of his strange twelve hours in
the abyss. That he also intended to write them down is certain, but he never did, and so unhappily we have to piece
together the discrepant fragments of his story from the reminiscences of Commander Simmons, Weybridge, Steevens,
Lindley, and the others.

We see the thing darkly in fragmentary glimpses—the huge
ghostly building, the bowing, chanting people, with their dark
chameleon-like heads and faintly luminous clothing, and
Elstead, with his light turned on again, vainly trying to convey to their minds that the cord by which the sphere was
held was to be severed. Minute after minute slipped away, and
Elstead, looking at his watch, was horrified to find that he had
oxygen only for four hours more. But the chant in his honour
kept on as remorselessly as if it was the marching song of his
approaching death.

The manner of his release he does not understand, but to
judge by the end of cord that hung from the sphere, it had
been cut through by rubbing against the edge of the altar.
Abruptly the sphere rolled over, and he swept up, out of their
world, as an ethereal creature clothed in a vacuum would
sweep through our own atmosphere back to its native ether
again. He must have torn out of their sight as a hydrogen
bubble hastens upward from our air. A strange ascension it
must have seemed to them.

The sphere rushed up with even greater velocity than, when
weighted with the lead sinkers, it had rushed down. It became

exceedingly hot. It drove up with the windows uppermost, and he remembers the torrent of bubbles frothing against the glass. Every moment he expected this to fly. Then suddenly something like a huge wheel seemed to be released in his head, the padded compartment began spinning about him, and he fainted. His next recollection was of his cabin, and of the doctor's voice.

But that is the substance of the extraordinary story that Elstead related in fragments to the officers of the *Ptarmigan*. He promised to write it all down at a later date. His mind was chiefly occupied with the improvement of his apparatus, which was effected at Rio.

It remains only to tell that on February 2, 1896, he made his second descent into the ocean abyss, with the improvements his first experience suggested. What happened we shall probably never know. He never returned. The *Ptarmigan* beat about over the point of his submersion, seeking him in vain for thirteen days. Then she returned to Rio, and the news was telegraphed to his friends. So the matter remains for the present. But it is hardly probable that no further attempt will be made to verify his strange story of these hitherto unsuspected cities of the deep sea.

STAR BEGOTTEN

CHAPTER ONE

THE MIND OF MR. JOSEPH DAVIS IS GREATLY TROUBLED

§ 1

THIS is the story of an idea and how it played about in the minds of a number of intelligent people.

Whether there was any reality behind this idea it is not the business of the storyteller to say. The reader must judge for himself. One man believed it without the shadow of a doubt and he shall be the principal figure in the story.

Maybe we have not heard the last of this idea. It spread from the talk of a few people into the magazines and the popular press. It had a vogue. You certainly heard of it at the time though perhaps you have forgotten. Popular attention waned. Now the thing flickers about in people's minds, not quite dead and not quite alive, disconnected and ineffective. It is a queer and almost incredible idea, but yet not absolutely incredible. It is a bare possibility that this thing is really going on.

This idea arose in the mind of Mr. Joseph Davis, a man of letters, a sensitive, intelligent, and cultivated man. It came to him when he was in a state of neurasthenia, when the strangest ideas may invade and find a lodgment in the mind.

§ 2

The idea was born, so to speak, one morning in November at the Planetarium Club.

Yet perhaps before we describe its impact upon Mr. Joseph

Davis in the club smoking-room after lunch, it may be well to tell the reader a few things about him.

We will begin right at the beginning. He was born just at the turn of the century and about the vernal equinox. He had come into the world with a lively and precocious intelligence and his "quickness" had been the joy of his mother and his nurses. And, after the manner of our kind, he had clutched at the world, squinted at it, and then looked straight at it, got hold of things and put them in his mouth, begun to imitate, begun to make and then interpret sounds, and so developed his picture of this strange world in which we live.

His nurse told him things and sang to him; his mother sang to him and told him things; a nursery governess arrived in due course to tell him things, and then a governess and a school and a lot of people and pictures and little books in words of one syllable and then normal polysyllabic books and a large mellifluous parson and various husky small boys and indeed a great miscellany of people went on telling him things. And so continually, his picture of this world, and his conception of himself and what he would have to do, and ought to do and wanted to do, grew clearer.

But it was only very gradually that he began to realize that there was something about his picture of the universe that perhaps wasn't in the pictures of the universe of all the people about him. On the whole the universe they gave him had an air of being real and true and just there and nothing else. There were, they intimated, good things that were simply good and bad things that were awful and rude things that you must never even *think* of, and there were good people and bad people and simply splendid people, people you had to like and admire and obey and people you were against, people who were rich and prosecuted you if if you trespassed and ran over you with motor cars if you did not look out, and people who were poor and did things for you for small sums, and it was all quite nice and clear and definite and you went your way amidst it all circumspectly and happily, laughing not infrequently.

Only—and this was a thing that came to him by such imperceptible degrees that at no time was he able to get it in such a way that he could ask questions about it—ever and again there was an effect as though this sure and certain established world was just in some elusive manner at this point or that point translucent, translucent and a little threadbare, and as though something else quite different lay behind it. It was never transparent. It was commonly, nine days out of ten, a full, complete universe and then for a moment, for a phase, for a perplexing interval, it was as if it was a painted screen that hid—What did it hide?

They told him that a God of Eastern Levantine origin, the God of Abraham (who evidently had a stupendous bosom) and Isaac and Jacob, had made the whole universe, stars and atoms, from start to finish in six days and made it wonderfully and perfect, and had set it all going and, after some necessary ennuis called the Fall and the Flood, had developed arrangements that were to culminate in the earthly happiness and security and eternal bliss of our Joseph, which had seemed to him a very agreeable state of affairs. And further they had shown him the most convincing pictures of Adam and Eve and Cain and Abel and had given him a Noah's Ark to play with and told him simple Bible stories about the patriarchs and the infant Samuel and Solomon and David and their remarkable lessons for us, the promise of salvation spreading out from the Eastern Levant until it covered the world, and he had taken it all in without flinching because at the time he had no standards of comparison. Anything might be as true as anything else. Except for the difference in colour they put him into the world of *Green Pastures* and there they trained him to be a simply believing little Anglican.

And yet the same time he found a book in the house with pictures of animals that were quite unlike any of the animals that frequented the Garden of Eden or entered the Ark. And pictures of men of a pithecoid unpleasant type who had lived, it seemed, long before Adam and Eve were created. It seemed all sorts of things had been going on before Adam and Eve were created, but when he began to develop a curiosity about this pre-scriptual world and to ask questions about it his current governess snapped his head off and hid that disconcerting book away. They were "just antediluvian animals," she said, and Noah had not troubled to save them. And when he had remarked that a lot of them could swim, she told him not to try to be a Mr. Cleverkins.

He did his best not to be Mr. Cleverkins. He did his best to love this God of Abraham, Isaac, and Jacob as well as fear him (which he did horribly, more even than he did the gorilla in Wood's *Natural History)* and to be overcome with gratitude for the wisdom and beauty of a scheme of things which first of all damned him to hell-fire before he was born and then went to what he couldn't help thinking were totally unnecessary pains on the part of omnipotence to save him. Why should omnipotence do that? Why need He do that? All He had to do was just to say it. He had made the whole world just by saying it.

Master Joseph did his very best to get his feelings properly adjusted to the established conception of the universe. And since most of the scriptures concerned events that were now happily out of date, and since his mother, his governess, the mellifluous parson, the scripture teacher at school, and everybody set in authority over him converged in assuring him that now, at the price of a little faith and conformity, things were absolutely all right here and hereafter so far as he was concerned, he did get through some years pretty comfortably. He did not think about it too much. He put it all away from him—until the subtle alchemy of growth as he became ado-lescent sent queer winds of inquiry and correlation banging open again unsorted cupboards of his brain.

He went to St. Hobart's school and then to Camborne Hall, Oxford. There is much unreasonable criticism of the English public schools, but it is indisputable that they do give a sort of education to an elect percentage of their boys. There was quite a lot of lively discussion at St. Hobart's in those days, it wasn't one of your mere games-and-cram schools, and the reaction against the dogmatic materialism of the later nineteenth century was in full swing there. The head in his sermons and the staff generally faced up to the fact that there had been Doubt, and that the boys ought to know about it.

The science master was in a minority of one on the staff and he came up to St. Hobart's by way of a technical school; the public school spirit cowed him. St. Hobart's did not ignore science but it despised the stuff, and all the boys were given some science so that they could see just what it was like.

Davis because of his mental quickness had specialized in the classical side; nevertheless he did his minimum of public school science. He burnt his fingers with hot glass and smashed a number of beakers during a brief interlude of chemistry, and he thought biology the worst of stinks. He found the outside of a rabbit delightful but the inside made him sick; it made him physically sick. He acquired a great contempt for "mere size" and that kept astronomy in its place. And when he came to grips with doubt, in prep aration for confirmation, he realized that he had been much too crude in feeling uncomfortable about that early Bible narrative and the scheme of salvation and all the rest of it.

As a matter-of-fact statement it was not perhaps in the coarser sense true, but that was because of the infirmities of language and the peculiar low state of Eastern Levantine intelligence and Eastern Levantine moral ideas when the hour to "reveal" religion had struck. Great resort had had to be made for purposes of illustration to symbols, parables, and inaccurate but edifying stories. People like David and Jacob had been poor material for demonstration purposes, but that was a point better disregarded.

The story of creation was symbolical and its failure to correspond with the succession of life on earth did not matter in the least, the Fall was symbolical of things too mysterious to explain, and why there had to be an historical redemption when the historical fall had vanished into thin air was the sort of thing no competent theologian would dream of dis- cussing. There it was. Through such matters of faith and doctrine Joseph Davis was taken at a considerable speed, which left him hustled and baffled rather than convinced.

But the curious thing about these initiatory explanations was that all the time another set of ideas at an entirely different level was being put before him as a complete justifi- cation for the uncritical acceptance of Bible, Church, and Creed. It was being conveyed to him that it really did not matter what foundations of myth or fantasy the existing system of Western civilization was built upon; the fact that mattered was that it was built upon that foundation and that a great ritual of ceremonial and observance, which might be logically unmeaning, and an elaborate code of morality, which might ultimately prove to be arbitrary, nevertheless constituted the co-ordinating fabric of current social life and that social life could not now go on without them. So that all this freethinker and rationalist stuff became irrelevant and indeed contemptibly crude. Reasonable men didn't assert. They didn't deny. They were thinking and living at a different level. You could no more reconstruct religion, social usage, political tradition, than you could replan the human skeleton—which also was open to considerable criticism.

That put Joseph Davis in his place. Arguments about the Garden of Eden and Jonah's Whale passed out of discussion. He was left face to face with history and society. Christianity and its churches, the monarchy and political institutions, the social hierarchy, seemed to be regarding him blandly. It is no good inquiring into our credentials now, they seemed to say. Here we are. We work. (They seemed to be working then.) And what other reality is there?

By this time he was at Oxford, talking and thinking occasionally, pretending to think a lot and believing that he was thinking a lot. The dualism that had dawned upon him in childhood looked less like being resolved than ever. The world-that-is no longer contested his fundamental criticisms, but it challenged him to produce any alternative world-that-might-be. There it was, the ostensible world, definite, fundamentally inconsistent maybe, but consistent in texture. An immense accumulation of falsity and yet a going concern. So things are.

It looked so enduring. He wavered for a time. On one hand was the brightly lit story of current things, the front-window story, a mother's-knee story of a world made all for his reception, a world of guidance, safe government, a plausible social order, institutions beyond effective challenge, a sure triumph for good behaviour and a clear definition of right and wrong, of what was done and what was not done, and against it was no more than a shadowy story which was told less by positive statement than by hints, discords that stirred beneath the brightness, murmurs from beneath, and vague threats from incidental jars. That shadow world, that mere criticism of accepted things, had no place for him, offered him nothing. No shapes appeared there but only interrogations. The brightly lit story seemed safest, brightest, and best to his ripening imagination; he did his best to thrust that other tale down among all sorts of other things, improper and indecent thoughts for example, that have to be kept under hatches in the mind.

Momentous decisions have to be made by all of us in those three or four undergraduate years; we take our road, and afterwards there is small opportunity for a return. Mr. Joseph Davis had a quick mind and a facile pen and he was already writing, and writing rather well, before he came down. He chose to write anyhow. His father had left him with a comfortable income and there was no mercenary urgency upon him. He elected to write about the braver, more confident aspects of life. He was for the show. He began to write heartening and stalwart books and to gird remorselessly at dissidence and doubt. What I write, he said, shall have banners in it and trumpets and drums. No carping, nothing subversive. Sociology is going out of fashion. So he committed himself. He began first with some success-ful, brave historical romances and followed up with short histories of this or that gallant interlude in the record.

King Richard and Saladin was his first book and then he wrote *The Singing Seamen*. Then came *Smite with Hammer, Smite with Sword,* and after that he ran up and down the human tree, telling of the jolly adventures of Alexander and Cæsar and Jenghiz Khan *(The Mighty Riders)* and the Elizabethan pirates and explorers and so on. But as he had a sound instinct for good writing and an exceptionally sensi-tive nature, the more he wrote, the more he read and learned and—which was the devil of it—thought.

He should not have thought. When he took his side he should, like a sensible man, have stopped thinking.

Besides which some people criticized him rather penetratingly, and for an out-and-out champion he was much too attentive to criticism.

He became infected with a certain hesitation about what he was doing. Perhaps he was undergoing that first subtle deterioration from that assurance of youth which is called "growing up," a phase that may occur at any age. He wrote with diminishing ease and confidence and let qualifying shadows creep into his heroic portraits. He would sometimes admit quite damaging things, and then apologize. He found this enhanced the solidity of some of his figures, but it cast a shadow on his forthright style. He told no one of this loss of inner elasticity, but he worried secretly about it.

Then, courageously but perhaps unwisely, he resolved to make a grand culminating frontal attack upon the doubt, materialism, and pessimism of shadowland, in the form of a deliberately romanticized history of mankind. It was to be a world history justifying the ways of God to man. It was also to justify his own ways to himself. It was to be a great parade—a cavalcade of humanity.

For some reason he never made clear to himself, he did not begin at the creation of the world but on the plain of Shinar. He put the earlier history into the mouths of retro-spective wise old men. From the Tower of Babel man dispersed about the world.

History regarded with a right-minded instinct has often a superficial appearance of being only a complicated tangle still awaiting analysis, and it was not always easy to show Man winning all the time and Right for ever triumphant against the odds—in the long run, that is. *The Heritage of Mankind, the Promise and the Struggle*—that was one of the titles he was considering—implies a struggle with, among other things, malignant fact. Fact sometimes can be very obstinate and malignant.

He had got himself into a tangle with the Black Death.

He had started—rashly, he was beginning to realize—upon a chapter dealing with the ennobling effect of disease, one of three to be called respectively, *Flood, Fire,* and *Pestilence;* and that had led him into a considerable amount of special reading. He had always been for taking his own where he found it, and he had been inspired by Paul de Kruif's *Microbe Hunters* to annex some of that writer's material, infuse it with religious devotion, and then extend his discourse to show how throughout the ages these black visitations, properly regarded, had been glorious stimulants (happily no longer urgently needed) for the human soul. But he found the records of exemplary human behaviour during the Black Death period disconcertingly meagre. The stress was all on the horror of the time, and when everything was said and done, our species emerged hardly better in its reactions than a stampede of poisoned rats. That at any rate was how the confounded records showed things. And this in spite of his heroic efforts to read between the lines and in spite of his poetic disposition to supplement research with a little in-vention—intuition, let us say, rather than invention. That he knew was a dangerous disposition. Too much intuition might bring down the disparagement of some scholarly but unsympathetic pedant upon him, and all the other fellows would be only too glad to pick it up and repeat it.

And then suddenly his mind began to slip and slide. He had, he realized, been overworking and, what is so common an aspect of overwork, he could not leave off. Overwork had brought worry and sleeplessness in its train. He would lie awake thinking of the Black Death and the pitiful be-haviour to which tormented humanity can sink. Vivid de-scriptive phrases in the old records it would have been healthier to forget, recurred to him. At first it was only the Black Death that distressed him and then his faith in human splendour began to collapse more widely. A cracked handbell heralded an open cart through the streets of plague-stricken London and once more the people were called upon to bring out the dead. Something revived his memory of the horror pictures of Goya in the Prado, and that dragged up the sinister paintings in the Wiertz Museum in Brussels. That again carried him to the underside of Napoleon's career and the heaped dead of the Great War. Why write a *Grand Parade of Humanity,* asked doubt, when Winwood Reade has already written *The Martyrdom of Man?* He found himself criticizing his early book about Alexander the Great, *Youth the Conqueror.*

He had told that story triumphantly. Now in the black morning hours, it came back upon him in reverse. Something in his own brain confronted him and challenged him. Your Alexander, it said, your great Alexander, the pupil of Aristotle, who was, as you say, the master mind of the world, was in truth, as you know, just an ill-educated spendthrift. Why do you try to pervert the facts? By sheer accident— and most history is still a tale of accidents—he found him- self in a rotten, nerveless, self-indulgent world that had no grown men in it able to hold him out and give him the spanking he deserved, and as luck would have it, he had the only up-to-date and seasoned army in existence completely at his disposal. *He* hadn't made it. It came to him. The fools went where he told them to go. When you wrote all that stuff about his taking Greek civilization to Persia and Egypt and India, you were merely giving him credit for what had happened already. Why? Greek civilization owed nothing to him. He took advantage of it. He picked it up and smashed it over the head of poor old Darius. Smashed it—just as these plunging dictators of today seem likely to smash your poor civilization—nobody able to gainsay them. He left the Glory that was Greece in fragments, for the Romans to pick up in their turn. He wasted the Macedonian cavalry and phalanx, just as our fools today are going to waste aviation. For no good at all; for no plain result. Alexander was just a witless accident in an aimless world. And think of his massacres and lootings and how it fared with the women and children, the common life of the world. Why did you write this florid stuff about Alexander the Great? And about Cæsar—and about all these other pitiful heroes of mankind? Why do you keep it up, Joseph? If you did not know better then, you know better now. Your newspapers should be teaching you. Why do you pretend that a sort of destiny was unrolling? That it was all leading up to Anglicanism, cricket, the British Empire, and what not? Why do you go on with these pretences? These great men of yours never existed. The human affair is more intricate than that. More touching. Saints are sinners and philoso' phers are fools. Religions are rigmaroles. If there is gold it is still in the quartz. Look reality in the face. *Then* maybe something might be done about it.

He got up. He walked about his room.

"But I thought I had settled all this years ago," he said. "How can I get on with *Grand Parade of Humanity* if I give way to this sort of thing? Already I have spent nearly a year on this over-whelming book."

He felt like some ancient hermit assailed by diabolical questionings. But that ancient hermit would at least have prayed and made the sign of the cross and got over it.

In his solitude Mr. Joseph Davis tried that. But on his knees he had a frightful sense of play-acting. He didn't believe there was a hearer. He didn't believe that any one believes nowadays—not Cantuar, not Ebor, not the Pope. These old boys eased down on their knees out of habit and let their minds wander along a neglected familiar lane to nothing in particular.

He got up again with his prayer half said and sat staring

at the situation. *Defensor Fidei!* He couldn't pray.

§ 3

But this peculiar feeling of—mental duplicity shall we call it?—this doubt of himself; this struggle to sustain the clear bright assurance of his chosen convictions, was not the only strain upon Mr. Davis's serenity. Several other matters not directly connected with his literary work were also conspiring his abnormally sensitive mind.

As he walked down Lower Regent Street from Piccadilly Station towards his club, various discontents, new ones and old ones, threaded their way round and about each other, each rasping against him and eluding him, dodging down into the subconscious and giving place to another whenever he tried to challenge it. The day was grey and overcast and it gave him no help—was indeed definitely against him. He was inclined to think he would have been wiser to have put on his medium coat rather than his thin Burberry, and at the same time he found the air moist and stuffy.

Chief among these accessory troubles was this, that for the first time in his life he was to become a father. It is an occasion few men face with absolute calm; it stirs up all sorts of neglected or unexplored regions of possibility in the mind. No psycho-analyst as yet has investigated the imaginative undercurrents in the mind of the expectant father. No one has attempted a review of the onset of parentage in the male. Here we must confine our attention strictly to the case of Mr. Joseph Davis. For some time he had been developing a curious vague perplexity about this wife of his, who was so soon to add the responsibilities and anxieties of fatherhood to his already febrile mental activities, and that expectation had greatly intensified this perplexity.

Here again the subtle sensitiveness of the imaginative temperament came in. A literary man carries about with him in his head a collection of edged tools known as his Vocabulary. And sometimes he cuts himself. Two or three years ago "enigmatical" had, so to speak, stuck up suddenly and caught him when he was thinking about his wife. And "fey." She was fifteen years younger than he was, he had married her when she was scarcely more than a girl, and yet, he had been compelled to realize, she was enigmatical, extremely enigmatical.

To begin with he had loved her in a simple, straightforward, acquisitive way and she had seemed to love him. He had not thought about her very much; he had just loved her as a man loves a woman. Their early married life, subject to the obvious discretions of our time, had been natural and happy; she had learned to type for him and they had been inseparable and all that sort of thing. Then by imperceptible degrees things had seemed to change. His satisfaction in her clouded over. She had seemed to disentangle herself from him and draw herself together. More and more was he aware of a lack of response in her.

And then came the memorable evening when she had remarked: "I don't know whether I care for very much more of this sort of thing unless I am going to have a child."

This sort of thing! Roses, raptures, whispers, dusk, moonlight, nightingales, all the love poetry that ever was— *this sort of thing!*

So that was it!

"You are quite well off," she said.

As though that mattered. . . .

There had been a certain amount of argument, in which delicacy had prevailed over explicitness, and then she had carried her point. He had made it plain to her that whatever reluctance he might have displayed at first was solely on her account and that now they were embarked together on a shining adventure. They were to make life "more abundant." Once the proposal was accepted his imagination seemed to bubble offspring. He buried "this sort of thing" as deeply as he could under high-piled flower-beds of philo-progenitive sentiment; he tried his utmost to forget her strangely inhuman phrase.

Yet after everything was settled, still his uneasiness deepened, still her detachment seemed to increase.

It *seemed* to increase. But that was where another queer worry came now into his mind. Had she always had some or all of this disposition towards detachment, and had he failed to observe it hitherto? In the first bright months or so of their married life, when he had looked at her and she had looked at him their eyes had met upon a common purpose as if they were smacking hands together. But now it was as if her hand had become a phantom hand that his own hand went right through, and his gaze seemed always just to miss meeting her deep regard. Her dark eyes had become inaccessible. "Unfathomable" the vocabulary threw up. She scrutinized him and revealed nothing. Husbands and wives ought to become more easy with each other, more familiar, as life goes on, but she was increasingly aloof.

The majority of discontented husbands, the burden of comic literature, proverbial wisdom, testify to the terrors of a talkative wife, but indeed these terrors are nothing to those of a silent woman, a silent thoughtful woman. A scolding wife can say endless disconcerting things and she hits or misses, but a silent woman says everything.

Always nowadays she seemed to be thinking him over. And his morbidly sensitive self-consciousness filled her silences with criticisms against which he had no defence.

When he had married her, a young, dark, shy girl, he had radiated protective possession all over her. It would have seemed impossible then that he should ever feel—it is a strange word to use about a wife and as we use it here we use it in its most sublimated and attenuated sense, but the word is— *fear*. Latterly his uneasiness with his wife and about his wife had increased almost to the quality of that emotion.

Of course he had always realized that there was something subtly unusual about her, even about her appearance. But at first he had found that simply attractive. She was neither big nor clumsy but she was broadly built; her brow was broad and her dark grey eyes were unusually wide apart; the corners of her full mouth drooped gravely and at times she had a way of moving that was, so to speak, absentminded, preoccupied. At first he had valued all this as "distinction," but later he had come rather to think of her as "unusual." She was far more unusual than the slow deliberation of her speech justified her in being.

He had never liked her people, which was odd because he had hardly seen anything of them. She had come into his world, as it seemed at first, romantically. He had met her at a publisher's cocktail party, she had been invited there rather for her ambitions than her performance, and she had told him then that her people lived in the Outer Hebrides and that they opposed her wish to study and write. She had just spoken of them as "people." She had won scholar-ships at a Glasgow high school, she had got to the university and so worked her way to London in defiance of them. She had written poetry, she told him, and she wanted to see it printed.

But London, she said, wasn't quite what she had expected it to be. London astonished, frightened, and stimulated her, and kept on seeming stranger and stranger. She was not growing accustomed to it. People were always saying and doing the most unaccountable things.

"At times," she said, "I feel like a stray from another world. But then, you know, I felt very much the same when

I was at home in the islands where I was born. Have you ever had that feeling? All you people here seem so sure of your world and yourselves."

It was when she said this that the idea of guiding this quiet, unsure, and lovely young stranger to all the braveries of life entered the head of Mr. Joseph Davis. It was so exceptional to meet an intelligent young woman who seemed unsure of herself and who was willing to be taught and hadn't already, in an irrational hurry to begin, taken the braveries of life to herself in her own fashion. It was not so much a candid inviting white virginity as an elusive elfin one she had. Here, he thought, was something fine and un-formed to mould and shape and write flourishes upon.

He went about thinking of her more and more, with all those exploratory impulses aroused in him which constitute falling in love. He was soon completely in love with her.

When he offered to read some of her verse, she said she didn't want it read, she just wanted to see it in print and read it herself. When at last he saw it he liked it. It was like a missionary's translations from the Chinese; mostly vivid little word pictures. From the point of view of publication and running the gauntlet of all these modern poets and reviewers who cut you up with one hand and cut you out with the other, he did not think it likely to be successful. But it had nevertheless a curious simplicity, a curious di-rectness and a faint wistful flavour.

He learnt that she was living in a students' hostel in Bloomsbury, he established contacts with her and he was able to take her about very freely. Perhaps at one time he had thought simply of becoming her first lover, but she had an unobtrusive defensiveness that made marriage the only way to her.

Two rawboned fishermen in bonnets and broadcloth suddenly appeared in London to "take a look at him" when the marriage was mooted. They were the most astonishing and unexpected "people" for her to produce. They had her dark colouring and dark grey eyes like hers, but otherwise they were singularly unlike her. Brawny they were. They had none of her manifest fineness and restraint.

"You'll have to take care of her," they told him, "for she's been the treasure of our eyes. She's better than we and we know it. Why we ever let her persuade us that she had to come on to London is more than we can explain, but the mischief's been done and you've got her."

"She's lovely. You're telling me that?" said Davis, and the elder brother, darkly reproachful, said: "Aye. We're telling you."

They stayed in London until the wedding, and entertaining them was a little like making hay with seaweed. They seemed to keep on looking at him and passing Hebridean judgments on him. They were full of unspoken things.

He would say things to them and they would say: "Eh" —just "Eh." Not an interrogative "Eh?" but an ambiguous acknowledgment.

They got drunk in a dutiful, dubious, and melancholy way for the registry office, and the last he saw of them was on the platform at Victoria when he carried her off to show her the wonders of Paris. They were standing together grave and distrustful, not gesticulating nor waving good-bye but each holding up a great red hand as who should say: "We're here."

And when at last the curve hid them and he pulled up the carriage window and turned to her to meet the love-light in her eyes she said to him: "And now you are going to show me the real world and all those cities and lakes and mountains where at last we shall feel at home."

Only she never did seem to feel at home.

She never talked about this family of hers to him, after

the transit of these two samples, and she corresponded with them with an infrequent regularity. She never gave him any reason to suppose she cared very much for them. But the fact which presently became apparent, that, unlike him, she was a good sailor and loved wind and rough seas, seemed to link her to them rather than to him. Many husbands have objected to their wives' relations because they were too near, but he found he objected to hers because they were too remote. And also she loved mountains and crags and precipitous places. He didn't. They climbed the Matterhorn at great expense, he gave more trouble to the guides than she did, and at the summit she seemed to be pleased but still gravely looking for more.

Once on holiday in Cornwall they had been basking together on the beach after lunch and suddenly her pose, as she sat thinking, reminded him of a picture he had seen somewhere of Undine, La Motte Fouque's Undine, sweet and detached, looking across the far levels of the sea, lost in some unimaginable reverie. Undine too had had some uncouth and menacing brothers. That was when the fancy of her as a sort of changeling, as something ultra-terrestrial and not quite human, first came to him. That was when "fey" came out of the vocabulary.

This Undine suggestion hung about for months. First he let this exaggeration of her faint unearthliness play mischievously in his mind, and then he tried to restrain and banish it. Sometimes he tried to persuade himself that every man's wife is really an Undine, but he could never make really convincing observations in that matter. Maybe, he thought, you never get near enough to any woman but your own wife to appreciate her remoteness.

A multitude of possibly quite accidental divergences grouped themselves about that "fey."

He spun the thread of that word's suggestion into a web

about her. It swept aside the one worse alternative that conceivably she was just simple and lacking in æsthetic enterprise. At first that "fey" was a fantastic exaggeration and then it became more and more an observation, an explanation for her undeniable detachment from so much that excited and stirred him, and from so much that he believed ought to excite and stir anybody. That struggle of his ideals with a dark underworld of doubts, which made it urgent for him to keep thinking, feeling, appreciating—like an urgent skater over thin ice and a cold abyss of disbelief—had no counterpart. She could keep still and remain content in her convictions, in something deep—whatever it was that she knew and did not communicate.

There was no malice in her detachment from him. He could have understood malice better. He had seen mutual jealousy and mutual detraction often enough among his married friends. The better the artists the worse the lovers. He understood that fight for individual assertion which makes love a legendary unreality, a blend of fantasy and grossness, in the world of the intelligentsia. But this was not the assertion of an individuality; it was a complete indifference to his values. It was a foreignness—to the whole world.

Whenever Mr. Davis had a slump in his vitality he realized this widening estrangement from his wife more acutely. The lower the ebb the intenser the realization. And this day his realization was exceptionally vivid. . . .

This very morning she had made a remark that stirred him to a protest he abandoned in despair. There was to be a big concert at the Pantechnicon Hall with Rodhammer conducting. He was enthusiastic for going. She did not want to go.

He argued against her disinclination. "You used to like music."

"But I have *heard* music, dearest."

"Heard music! My dear, what a queer way to put things!"

She shook her head from side to side without speaking. There was a time when the self-assurance of her faint smile had seemed very lovely to him. Mona Lisa and all that, but now it irritated him with a sense of invincible and unapproachable opposition.

"But you've only heard Rodhammer once before!"

"Why should I want to hear Rodhammer again—a little better or not so good?"

"But music!"

"There's a limit to music," she said.

"A limit!"

"I've a feeling that I've done with music. It was wonderful, charming, sustaining, all that music we went to hear—to begin with. I loved that as much as I've loved anything. But if one has taken music in—hasn't one taken it in?"

"Taken it in! You mean—?" he tried.

"I mean you don't always want to be sitting down to attend to it after you've heard —what there is of it. We aren't—professional."

Professional! When she did use words she used them in a very deadly fashion. *"I* never tire of music," he said.

"But does the sort of music there is say anything—does it say anything fresh?"

"It's eternally fresh."

"How?"

He made a hopeless gesture. "But why have you become indifferent?"

"But why are you still so enthusiastic?"

"But don't you get—something wonderful? An exaltation? A world of absolute sensuous emotion?"

"No—I did at first. A sort of exaltation. I agree. And still I like—rhythm. It's pleasant to hear music going on, but it's no longer something I want to listen to *specially.*

Going to hear music in concerts seems to me like going to see pictures in galleries. . . . Or reading anthologies. . . . Or looking over a collection of butterflies in a museum. . . . A time comes . . ."

"Then, in short, you won't go to the concert?"

"I feel a little tired but I will go if you like."

"Oh! not like *that*," he said and ended their talk.

But he went over it again in his own mind and now he was going over it once more. He knew people to whom music meant much and people to whom music meant little, but to take up music as Mary had, in a spirit of glad discovery, and then put it down again as one might put down an un-important novel, distressed his mind. But that was how she seemed to deal with everything in life. Even with friendship, even with love, she had that same flash of interest, that rapid appreciation, and then she turned away. To what?

He spoke aloud, addressing Lower Regent Street: "You can't *afford* to give up music like that. You can't *afford* to give up art."

And what he did not say because he could not bring him-self to say it, was: "And how can you afford to give up love?"

When the child comes, will she give up that?

Or will she go on loving the child. Leaving me behind? My part played?

This eternal going on! This complete instability of values! . . .

Could it fail to distress a man who was in effect a pro-fessor of stable values?

§ 4

And here we must note another rather unusual element in the *melange* of Mr. Davis's troubles, a queer little thing that would have mattered nothing to a less imaginative man, but which was to thread through all the train of thought upon which he was presently to embark. It was a very slender thread indeed, a matter so irrational and ridiculous that it seems almost unfair to him to mention it. And yet it certainly played a slight deflecting role in guiding him to the strange idea. It cannot therefore be ignored altogether.

Since his school days he had had a secret detestation of his own Christian name. Facetious upper-school boys had made it plain that there was a shadow on it. Neither in the Old Testament nor in the New, is the name of Joseph adorned with that halo of triumphant virility which is the desire of every young male. He had struggled to insist that he should always be called "Jo." But the mortifying realization that he was a "Joseph" damped his private meditations.

There was not the faintest circumstance to justify any marital uneasiness on his part. No one sane could have entertained a suspicion of his Mary's integrity—nor did he, in the foreground of his mind. And yet, he would have been happier under a different name.

So it was.

§ 5

Such were the ruling factors in the weak hotch-potch of thoughts and half-thoughts, fancies, suggestions, dream scraps, and almost completely unsymbolized feelings that circled in his mind on his way to the pillared portals of the Planetarium Club and his first encounter with this strange idea that was destined to stab through his imagination like a dagger and work a revolution in his life.

CHAPTER TWO

MR. JOSEPH DAVIS LEARNS ABOUT COSMIC RAYS

§ 1

THE Planetarium Club abounds in unexpected conversations. It has a core of scientific men who are mostly devotees of the exact sciences, grave, shy, precise men, but wrapped round them are layers of biologists, engineers, explorers, civil servants, patent lawyers, criminologists, writers, even an artist or so. Almost any subject may be started in the smoking-room where most of the talk goes on, but the feeling against chewed newspaper is strong. Mr. Davis, as he ascended the club steps, made an effort to throw off those vague shadows that oppressed his mind, and to brighten his bearing to the quality that may be reasonably expected of a temperamental optimist.

But as he recrossed the hall from the vestiary to the dining-room he was still undecided whether he should sit at one of the small tables and go on with his state of uneasy deterioration, or take a place at one of the sociable boards. He elected for solitude, but repented as soon as his decision was made, and after his solitary lunch he made a real effort at sociability and joined a talking circle of a dozen men or more between the window and the fire, sitting down next to Foxfield, that hairy, untidy biologist, for whom he had a slightly condescending liking. The talk was rather under the stress of a new member, a parliamentary barrister, who might be almost anything in a few years' time and manifestly felt as much. This man had been elected before it was realized that he was slightly larger than any one else in the club and disposed to behave accordingly, and his conversational method was rather an elucidatory cross-examination than an original contribution to the interchanges.

"Tell me," he would say and even point a finger. "I don't know anything about these things. Tell me——"

"Tell me," except in the case of monarchs, heirs apparent, and presidents of the United States, is by the standards of the Planetarium atrocious conversational manners. But so far no one in the club had been able to get this point of view over to the new-comer. It would happen sooner or later but so far it had not happened. He was talking now with an air of making out some sort of case against modern physics and demonstrating how entirely more sensible and practical a mind which had passed through the ennobling exercises of Greats and a straightforward legal and political training could be.

"Atoms and force were good enough for Lucretius and they were good enough for my stinks master when I was a boy. Then suddenly you have to disturb all that. There's wonderful discoveries, and the air is full of electrons and neutrons and positons."

"Positrons," a voice corrected.

"It's all the same to us. Positrons. And photons and protons and deutrons. Alpha rays and Beta rays and Gamma rays and X rays and Y rays. And they fly about like solar systems and all the rest of it. And the dear old Universe that used to be fixed and stable begins to expand and contract —like God playing a concertina. Tell me—frankly. I suggest to you—it's a Bluff. It's something out of nothing. It's just a way of selling us mystery bottles with scientific labels. I ask you."

He paused with the air of a man who has put a poser.

A small, elderly, but still acutely acid old gentleman was sitting deep in one of the armchairs. The finger had not challenged him, but now he put out a lean hand and spoke with a thin penetrating voice, like a rapier, with the faint glint of a Scotch accent along the edge.

"You say Tell me—and Tell me. Will you have the grace to listen while I tell ye? And not interrupt?"

And when the slightly outsize member made as if he had something further to say, the old gentleman just raised his hand and said: *"No.* Listen, I tell ye, and told you shall be."

The rising man, just faintly abashed, assumed an attitude of sceptical and slightly impatient intelligence, looking round the group for support in what he evidently imagined was going to be a duel of wits. Just for a moment he imagined that. And then suddenly he felt like facing twelve implacably hostile jurymen and the first lesson of the Planetarium Club entered into his soul. Not to bounce.

Quietly and unobtrusively he allowed himself to lapse into the pose of the modest best boy in the class who knows that he still has much to learn and who cannot command any one to tell him but is glad to be told.

"These things boil down," said the old gentleman. "I've lectured about them for years. And followed the changes. When one gets old one has to be concise and it's fortunate I've had some practice in packing my statements. Still I'll have to take five minutes. I'll do all I can for you. Those Oxford teachers of yours—for it's Oxford you come from— probably left your mathematical philosophy in a worse state than they found it when you came up from your English public school—if indeed your formula-dodging school-masters gave you any mathematical understanding at all even there— so I may not be able to *explain* everything to you. Some bits I'll just have to *tell* you—*as* you put it. But it's really quite simple and credible stuff they've made of it in the last twenty-five years, Rutherford and Bragg and Niels Bohr and the rest of those fellows, and the younger people find no difficulty about it at all."

And with that and a galling air of careful simplification he proceeded to unfold a compact modern view of space and time and the movements of things therein. "Don't ask me what electricity is," he said, "and I'll tell you everything else as we have it up to date. It's none so complicated as you think and there's never a contradiction."

And very neatly he took his nucleus, twisted up his atoms with electrons and neutrons round the central proton, and sent them eddying into a world of throbbing photons. Then he ran his hand along the sixty-odd octaves of the spectrum from the hundred-yard electro-magnetic undulations beyond the longest radio length through heat rays and light rays to X rays and Gamma rays, smacked a few atoms together, shot them through with helium atoms, and described the results, and by way of epilogue gave a lucid word to those flying sub-atomies, the cosmic rays.

"After all, it's none so confused," he said, and indeed the pictures that arose as one listened to his slightly remonstrating, very persuasive Scotch intonation had the music of ripples and wavelets, of dancing reflections upon the side of a ship, of the concentric colour rings of films on water, of every sort of pleasant patterning and logical ornamentation. He made dead matter dance and circle, set to partners, interfere, shimmer, glow, become iridescent and mysteriously endowed with energy. The atoms of our fathers seemed by contrast like a game of marbles abandoned in a corner of a muddy playground on a wet day. He even had a cautious word for the young neutrinos, the latest aspirants to this dance in the atomic assembly-rooms. The one or two men who were experts in the subject listened, pleased to hear the A B C of their subject so lucidly delivered, and the rest were glad to check up their vague impressions of these fluctuating modern conceptions.

"And where do we come in?" asked someone. "Where is thought and the soul in all this?"

"Just a film, just a thin zone of reflection halfway in the scale of size between those electrons and the stars."

§ 2

Davis followed that compact discourse in a mood of unusual self-forgetfulness. It was, he found, as refreshing as good drink, and as little likely to linger in the system. And even the new member betrayed a certain humility in his attention.

But he still felt it was his duty to himself to talk.

"Those cosmic rays of yours," he said. "They are the most difficult part of your story. They aren't radiations. They aren't protons. What are they? They go sleeting through the universe incessantly, day and night, going from nowhere to nowhere. For the life of me I find that hard to imagine."

"They must come from *somewhere*," said a quiet little man with an air of producing a very special contribution to the discussion.

"We note their existence," said the old gentleman. "We watch them but we draw no premature conclusions. They are infinitesimal particles flying at an inconceivable velocity. They come from all directions of outer space. And that's as much as we know about them. If I put out my finger like that for a second or so, there's only just a dozen or so gone through it in a second. And no harm done. Which is just as well. There's more up above us in the outer atmosphere. But fortunately they get reflected and absorbed. You know we have a sort of filtering halo about the earth, a sort of cloak of electrons, which keeps off any excess of these radiations."

"That Heaviside layer," a stout rufous man, who had apparently been asleep, interpolated.

"And what may that be?" asked the barrister.

"It's a beautiful sample of scientific terminology," said the stout rufous man still somnolently. "This Heaviside layer, so far as I can understand it, is called so, because firstly it isn't heavy, secondly it hasn't any side, and thirdly it is almost as much a layer as—as a rheumatic chill or glow of indignation. Go on, Professor."

His eyes, which had been partly open, closed again.

"You said," said the examining barrister, "that *fortunately* they are kept off. *Why*—fortunately? May I ask?"

"My thankfulness may have been a little unwarranted," said the old gentleman. "But these cosmic rays have a lot of energy, considering their size. They knock atoms about when they hit them. And we and our belongings are made of atoms. A lot of them, a great lot of them, a real douche of cosmic rays, might cause all sorts of tissue diseases, blow up mines, strike the matches in our pockets. But as it is they don't often hit even *one* atom—quantitatively they're more ineffective even than that infinitesimal quantity of radiation that is always coming up from the radium in the earth; and so Nature is able to clean up any little speck of mess that occurs."

"Not always," said Foxfield suddenly.

"I've heard of that idea you're alluding to, Mr. Foxfield," said the old gentleman. "You mean that idea about the chromosomes."

"Now tell me," said the barrister, relapsing for a moment. "I've heard somewhere before of this idea you're speaking of. I'm told these cosmic rays affect—what is it you call them?—mutations."

"I have no doubt of it," said Foxfield.

"You'll find no physicist to encourage you," said the old gentleman.

"Or contradict me," said Foxfield.

"Aye, aye," said the old gentleman cheerfully. "It's a case of not proven."

"But what is this?" asked Davis. "Do you mean that these—these cosmic rays may affect heredity—inheritance?"

"I should be inclined to say they must," said Foxfield.

"But why them in particular?" asked the barrister.

"Because we have eliminated almost every other possible cause for changes in the chromosomes."

"It's a most extraordinary thing," said the rufous man, slowly waking up and passing by swift stages from sleepiness to a bright alertness.

"The chromosomes," said Foxfield, "the germinal elements, have very complicated and enormous molecules. They are rather elaborately protected from most types of disturbance. They have a sort of independence of the parent body. They go their way alone."

"Transmission of acquired characteristics strictly forbidden," someone interjected.

"It seems to be. But the X rays, the Gamma rays, and particularly these cosmic rays *can* get through, and so, I reason, they must get through—to start something fresh. Since something fresh is always being started."

And now it was Foxfield's turn to answer intelligent questions and give a brief lecture.

He summarized the new realizations of the past twenty-five years about mutations and survival almost as expertly as the old professor had elucidated his atoms. He showed how the changing of species bit by bit, by imperceptible gradations, which the early Darwinians had stressed, had given place in modern evolutionary theory to a realization of the frequency of extensive simultaneous sports and mutations. And there was nothing in the circumstances of an animal species which could explain these sports and mutations. And so it was that Foxfield was compelled to think they were produced by some penetrating exterior force.

"But why not Providence?" asked the quiet man.

"Because the vast majority of these mutations are aimless and useless," said Foxfield.

"And so, having eliminated everything else," said the barrister, "you lay the burden of change and mutation—and in fact all the responsibility for evolution—on those little cosmic rays! Countless myriads fly by and miss. Then one hits—Ping! Ping!—and we get a double-headed calf or a superman."

"What an *unsettled* universe it is!" said someone.

§ 3

And then suddenly the rufous man was touched by fantasy. His sleepiness had fallen from him altogether. He sat up brightly now. "Look here!" he said. "I've got an idea! Suppose——"

He paused. He produced that "suppose" like a juicy fruit and hovered with his hand in the air for a voluptuous moment before he squeezed the juice from it.

"Suppose these cosmic rays come from Mars!"

"They come, I tell ye, from every direction," said the old professor.

"Including Mars. Yes, Mars, that wizened elder brother of the planet Earth. Mars, where intelligent life has gone on far beyond anything this planet has ever known. Mars, the planet which is being frozen out, exhausted, done for. Some of you may have read a book called *The War of the Worlds*— I forget who wrote it—Jules Verne, Conan Doyle, one of those fellows. But it told how the Martians invaded the world, wanted to colonize it, and exterminate mankind. Hopeless attempt! They couldn't stand the different atmospheric pressure, they couldn't stand the difference in gravitation; bacteria finished them up. Hopeless from the start.

The only impossible thing in the story was to imagine that the Martians would be fools enough to try anything of the sort. *But——"*

He held up his hand and waggled his fingers with pleasure at his idea.

"Suppose they say up there: 'Let's start varying and modify-ing life on the earth. Let's change it. Let's get at the human character and the human brain and make it Martian-minded. Let's stop having children on this rusty little old planet of ours, and let's change men until they become in effect *our* children. Let's get spiritual children there.' D'you see? Martian minds in seasoned terrestrial bodies."

"And so they start firing away at us with these cosmic rays!"

"And presently," said the rufous man, almost gobbling with the excitement of his idea, "presently when they have got the world Martianized——"

"I never heard such nonsense," said the old professor and got up to go away. "I tell ye these cosmic rays come from every direction."

"And why shouldn't they use a sort of shrapnel?" said the rufous man to his retreating back. "Shells full of these cosmic rays, so to speak, with a back-lash. Nothing impossible in that, is there?"

The old professor's back made no reply. And yet it had a certain eloquence.

"They'd probably begin with wild mutations," somebody suggested after a pause; "and then get more accurate."

"It may have been going on for a long time," said the quiet man, helpful as ever.

"You're assuming of course that they know a lot more about us than we know about them," said the rising barrister.

"And isn't that easily possible?" the rufous man countered "Mars is the older planet. Far beyond us along the line of evolution. What we know is nothing to what *they* must know. They may be as able to look through us as we are to take a microscope and look through an amœba. And when they have got the world Martianized, when they've started a race here with minds like their own and yet with bodies fit for earth, when they have practically incerbred with us and ousted our strain, *then* they'll begin to send along their treasures, their apparatus—*grafting* their life on ours. Making men into their heirs and their continuation. Eh? Am I talking nonsense?"

"The jokes of today may become the facts of tomorrow," said Foxfield. "Nonsense *pro tem,* let us say."

"I'm beginning to believe my own story," said the rufous man. "With your endorsement. It's wonderful."

"But tell me," said the lawyer, also a little excited by this strange idea, "is there any evidence in confirmation? Any evidence at all? For example—has there been any increase of freaks and monsters in the world in the last few years?"

"It's only recently that there has been any attempt to give a statistical account of abnormalities and mutations," said Foxfield. "Monstrosities are hushed up—human monstrosities particularly. Even animal-breeders have a sort of shame about them, and wild creatures kill strange offspring instinctively. Every living creature seems to want to breed *true*. But from the fruit fly and plants and so on we know there is an amount of variation going on—much larger than everyday people imagine."

"Mostly unfavourable variation though?" asked the barrister.

"Ninety-nine and nine-tenths per cent," said Foxfield. "With no survival value at all. Chance. Like the wildest experimenting. . . ."

§ 4

Now this was the last kind of stuff to which an anxious prospective parent on the verge of neurasthenia ought to have listened.

And yet is it not out of accidents and disasters and fantastic twists of the mind that the greatest discoveries of science and the profoundest revelation of nature's processes have come? Things long unsuspected may be laid bare by a jest. The jokes of today may become the facts of tomorrow, even as Foxfield had said.

As Mr. Joseph Davis walked home from the Planetarium Club he seemed to hear and see those cosmic rays, flashing like tracer bullets, singing like arrows, gleaming and vanishing like falling stars, through the world about him. You might wrap yourself from them, the old professor had remarked, in solid lead, and still they got through to you.

CHAPTER THREE

MR. JOSEPH DAVIS WRESTLES WITH AN INCREDIBLE IDEA

§ 1

IT is an open question how freely an obstetrician should talk to the husband of his patient. Dr. Holdman Stedding erred perhaps on the communicative side. It may be he should have realized more promptly that Mr. Joseph Davis was troubled in his imagination, and he should have exercised more care than he did in avoiding topics that might intensify his imaginative disturbance. Yet it may be pleaded in extenuation that it was Mr. Davis who started the subject of these mysterious extra-terrestrial radiations and that it was Dr. Holdman Stedding who was taken by surprise with a novel idea. He too had his imaginative side. He liked novel ideas and there was just that streak of scientific curiosity and communicativeness in him which impairs discretion.

He was a stout, large-faced, warmish-blond man, always a little out of breath and always with a faint flavour of surprise in his expression. And he liked to be made to laugh. His mouth was always just a little open, as if ready to laugh. But he knew his work marvellously well; he had strong and skilful hands and he never got flurried.

Davis had called on him before. He had wanted to have an exact account of the health of his wife. Was she strong enough to bear a child? She was as strong, said Dr. Holdman Stedding, "as a young pony."

The way in which Davis beat about that idea that things were not quite right with his wife gave the good doctor a queer feeling that a less reassuring reply would have been more acceptable. For obscure reasons—sub-reasons rather—it seemed that Davis did not want this child.

Like every practising obstetrician Dr. Holdman Stedding knew all the faint intimations of a tentative to abortion, and knew how to nip any such suggestion in the bud. Panic before fatherhood is a more frequent thing than the lay mind realizes. It is constantly peeping out in these consultations. Davis, if such had been his disposition, had departed unsatisfied. But here he was again.

"I suppose everything is going all right with Mary?" he asked, advancing uneasily into the consulting-room.

"Couldn't be better."

"You made a second examination?"

"At your request. It was unnecessary."

"There is nothing unusual . . . ?" Mr. Davis rephrased his question. "The child, the embryo, so far as you can ascertain, is not different in any way from any other child at the same stage?"

"It is coming on well. There is absolutely no ground for worry."

"And the mother—physically and mentally. You are sure she can stand this? Because, you know, say what you like, she is not a normal woman."

"Do sit down," said the doctor, recapturing the hearth-rug by putting his visitor into a chair, and then standing over him. "Don't you think, Mr. Davis, that you are—just a trifle *fanciful* about your wife?"

"Well," said Davis, sticking to his point, "**is** she normal?"

"Few women in her condition remain as sane and healthy as she is. If that is abnormal. Her mind like her body is as sound as a bell."

"You don't think a woman can be too sane? I confess, Dr. Stedding, I don't always understand my wife. There is a sort of hard scepticism in her mind. . . . You don't think a woman can be *too* intelligent to make a good mother?"

"Really, Mr. Davis! What's fretting your mind? With her clearheadedness and your literary genius your child may be something quite outstanding."

"And that is what bothers me. The fact of it is, Doctor, I've been hearing talk lately. . . . I don't know if you know Foxfield and his work. . . . I take a scientific interest in this as well as a personal one. . . . The point is——"

§ 2

He kept the doctor waiting for a moment.

"The point is, do you, with your experience, think that latterly—how shall I put it?—exceptional children have become rather more *frequent* than they used to be?"

"Exceptional? Gifted?"

"Yes, gifted. In some cases perhaps. And also—what shall I say?—abnormalities?"

"H'm!" said the doctor. He was interested. He attempted a brief survey of his experience. "There *are* some rather surprising children and youngsters about. But I suppose something of that sort has always been going on."

"To the same extent?" pressed Davis. "To the same extent."

"Possibly not. It is very hard to say. Naturally in this part of London and with a clientele like mine, we have exceptional parents. My impression, my unchecked and uncontrolled impression, is that, in the world I know, maternal mortality is extremely low and the infants are—*bright* is the word. Some with biggish heads. But anything in the way—of out-of-the-way novelties, no. If you are worrying about monstrosities—you need not worry. And exceptionally bright children are nothing to worry about. The Cæsarean operation is probably more frequent nowadays. . . . That may be due rather to improved gynæcology than to any increase in mutations. . . ."

Pause.

"I would like to talk to you rather fantastically," said Davis abruptly. "It's not only my wife I am thinking about. Don't think I'm mad in what I am saying to you, but just think I am letting my imagination out for a romp."

"Nothing better," said Dr. Holdman Stedding, who like most medical practitioners nowadays had a disposition towards a rather amateurish psycho-analysis. "Say what you like. Let it rip."

"Well," said Mr. Davis, and hesitated at the strangeness and difficulty of the ideas he had to explain. "Biologists—I was talking to Foxfield the other day—biologists say that when a species comes to a difficult phase in its struggle for existence—and I suppose no one can say that is not fairly true of the human situation nowadays—there is an increased disposition to vary. There is—how did Foxfield put it?— for one thing, there is less insistence on the normal. Less insistence on the normal. It is as if the species began to try round and feel for new possibilities."

"Ye-es," said the doctor, with non-committal encouragement in his tone.

"And as if it became more capable of accepting abnormalities and weaving them into its destinies."

"Yes," said the doctor, weighing the proposition. "That is in accordance with current ideas."

"As an industrious student of history," began Mr. Davis. "You know I have written one or two books?"

"Who does not? My two nephews got your *Alexander, or Youth the Conqueror* and your *Story of the Spanish Main* as prizes last term, and I can assure you I read them myself with great delight."

"Well. It seems to me that for ages human life has been playing much the same tune with variations—but much the same tune. What we call human nature. The general behaviour, the normal system of reactions, has been the same. The old, old story. Abnormal people have been kept in their places. You don't think, Doctor, that that uniformity of human experience is going to be disturbed?"

"I wish you would explain a little more."

"Suppose there are—*Martians.*"

"Well?"

"Suppose there are beings, real material beings like our-selves, in another planet, but far wiser, more intelligent, much more highly developed. Suppose they are able to see us and know about us—as we know about the creatures under a microscope, which have no suspicion of us. . . . Mind you, this isn't my idea. I'm only repeating something I heard in the club. But suppose that in some way these older, wiser, greater, and better organized intelligences are able to influence human life."

"How?"

"They may have tried all sorts of ways. They may have been experimenting for ages. Much as we might run a reagent into a microscope slide. The amœbæ and so on would have no idea. . . ."

"If you are thinking of anything like inter-planetary te-lepathy, anything of that sort, I'm not with you. Even between closely similar minds, between identical twins for example, I doubt if such a thing is possible. . . . I *detest* telepathy."

"This is quite a different idea."

"Well?"

"Suppose that for the last few thousand years they have been experimenting in human genetics. Suppose they have been trying to alter mankind in some way, through the hu-man genes."

"But how?"

"You have heard of cosmic rays, Doctor?"

The doctor took it in with some deliberation. "It is a *quite* fantastic idea," he said after a pause.

"But neither impossible nor incredible."

"Some things one puts outside the range of practical possibility."

"And some things refuse to be put outside the range of practical possibility."

"But you don't mean to tell me you believe—?"

"No. But I face a possibility with an open mind."

"Which is?"

"That these Martians——"

"But we don't know there **are** any Martians!"

"We don't know that there aren't"

"No."

"Quite possibly these rays do not come from Mars—more probably than not. But—let us call the senders——"

"Senders?"

"Well, whatever originates them. Let us call them Martians—just to avoid inventing a new name——"

"Very well. And your suggestion is—?"

"That these Martians have been firing away with increasing accuracy and effectiveness at our chromosomes—perhaps for long ages. That is the story, the fancy, if you like, that I want in some way to put to the test. Every now and then in history, strange exceptional figures have appeared, Confucius, Buddha; men with strange memories, men with uncanny mathematical gifts, men with unaccountable intuitions. Mostly they have been persons in advance of their times, as we say, and out of step with their times. . . . Do you see what I am driving at, Doctor?"

"But this is the purest fantasy!"

"Or the realization of a fantastic fact."

"But!"

§ 3

Dr. Holdman Stedding wavered in his mind. Ought he to let this talk run on or close down on it forthwith?

At least half the disordered minds of the present time, he reflected, develop delusions about radiations. That kind of fancy has largely replaced those spiritual visions and inner voices which supplied the demented with crazy interpretations of their perplexities in the past. It was *dangerous* stuff, and the mind of Davis, to say the least of it, was very delicately poised. And yet there was something faintly plausible—a sort of fairy-tale plausibility—about this idea that caught the unprofessional elements of the doctor's imagination. He went on taking the idea seriously.

"What sort of confirmation is possible?" he considered.

"That is where the puzzle comes in. That is why I am consulting you."

"You think that if one attempted some sort of examination of human births, past and present—it would of course be very hard to get any adequate records about this sort of thing—one might be able to detect—?"

"That we are being played upon."

"But you don't *believe*—?"

"Not a bit of it. Oh, no! I didn't come here to be certified. I am advancing a certain hypothesis. I am being purely scientific in my method. I advance a provisional theory that a certain thing is going on. And, mind you, if anything of the sort is going on, it is of great—of supreme importance to our race. And having made our trial assumption, we try and work out what would be some of the logical consequences of this process of extra-terrestrial influence, if my theory proves to hold good. Is it possible to detect non-human characteristics, superhuman characteristics perhaps, in some of the children born nowadays, and are these non-human characteristics on the increase? Are there people—what shall

I call them?—*fey* people about? People as sane as you and
I and yet strange? We can try them with special intelligence
tests perhaps. We can go into the reports of educational
institutions. So far I have not planned the lay-out of this
investigation. It is all quite new in my mind. But isn't
it a legitimate inquiry? I ask you."

"You will need genius for that lay-out."

"Every original research needs that. But my theory I
think is plain. My theory is that new influences are being
brought to bear on human reproduction. For the purposes
of our research I call the source of these influences—
Martians. If my suspicions are confirmed, these Martians—
for purposes at which we can only guess—are thrusting
mutations upon us. They are experimenting with human
mutations. So that presently our very children may not
prove to be our own!"

As Mr. Davis said these last words, a full realization of
the indiscretion of this talk dawned upon Dr. Holdman
Stedding.

"But that is going too far!" he cried. "That is going
much too far. We are talking—we are amusing ourselves—
with pseudo-scientific nonsense."

Mr. Davis perceived quite clearly what was in his interlocutor's mind. "It is too late, Doctor, to say that to me.
This notion has bitten me. I mean to devote myself to this
investigation; I feel called to it; and I want you to interest
yourself in it also. If there is one chance in a million of
this suspicion being true, then it demands attention. Even
on a chance so bare as that we ought to get watchers and
searchers, planetary coast-guards, so to speak, at work. We
have to specify and measure and determine the nature of
this inflow and herd it back upon itself before it is too late."

"H'm," said Dr. Holdman Stedding, regarding his queer
visitor with an expression of infinite perplexity.

"I am under no delusions," said Mr. Davis. "I agree I am talking about something almost absolutely improbable. Let me make it clear to you that I am perfectly clear upon that. I am skirting the giddy edge of utter impossibility. Well and good. But sometimes there are intuitions. How many discoveries have flashed forth at first as the wildest of surmises? It may be circumstances have conspired to point my mind in a certain direction. Never mind about that. I myself do not feel that this is an impossibility. Just simply that—not an absolute impossibility. No more. That is where I stand."

CHAPTER FOUR

DR. HOLDMAN STEDDING IS INFECTED WITH THE IDEA

§ 1

DR. Holdman Stedding lay awake that night thinking about the state of mind of Mr. Davis and about the queer idea of a genetic invasion of Martian qualities that he had pro-pounded. There was something provocative about the idea; something that made his intelligence bristle defensively. "Pure balderdash!" he said aloud, but as a matter of fact what made it so irritating was that it was not pure balderdash. There was an attenuated but unbreakable thread of silly plausibility about the suggestion that prevented him from throwing it altogether out of his mind. He threw words like "balderdash" at it as one might throw stones at a dog that persists in following one, and presently there was the damned thing back again.

"If it *should* chance that something of the sort was going on . . ."

He found himself asking himself whether there was any sort of evidence that some new type or perhaps even new types of human being were appearing in the world. Can there be such things as Martianized minds? "Silly phrase," he said. "But somehow a contagious phrase."

He ran his mind over its collection of facts about the subject. He knew most of what was known and he realized that, for the purpose of getting a conclusive answer, it amounted to hardly anything at all. He reviewed the question methodically. The most confident statements, he reflected, are made that man has not changed since Neolithic times, that he has degenerated since the days of Pericles, that he is larger or smaller, healthier, less healthy, than his ancestors, that he has become finer and subtler or anything else that suits the private convictions, stated or implicit, of the "authority" who flings out this sort of stuff to the public. When you came to think it over as he was doing, it was all without exception opinionated rubbish. No one has yet devised the means of getting the confused and irregular records available into any sort of order. No one has been able to do that work. People like J. B. S. Haldane and suchlike pioneer biologists were trying to form a research society now. Even the men most in contact with the facts have nothing better than "impressions" and "persuasions," and some, thought Dr. Holdman Stedding with righteous self-applause, know that that is so, and some do not and let their prejudices rip. Dr. Holdman Stedding's private and unproven "impression" was just the impression most favourable to Mr. Davis's wild surmise. His unproven belief was that a considerable change in the human mind was going on. He thought that heavy and clumsy types were not so abundant in the population as they were on the increase.

"But what has that to do with Martians and cosmic rays?" his common sense protested, and his common sense answered: "Nothing."

After which he continued to pursue the subject.

§ 2

Such discursive nocturnal meditations as Dr. Holdman Stedding was now committed to, combine the advantage that they cover a wide ground and find the most diverse evidence in their excursions, with the disadvantage that they sometimes lose their way altogether and never return to the main issue. For a time the doctor's train of thought was in danger of the latter fate. He wandered into a labyrinth of possibility about the peculiar scepticism of the contemporary mind and the perplexing obduracies and wilfulnesses of so many of the rising generation. He knew more about the ideas of his hospital students than most of his colleagues, and sometimes they filled him with hope and sometimes they terrified him. Like all youth since our race began, most of them were sheep and went whither they were told or led, but for all that it was quite conceivable that the proportion of independent and wilful minds was higher than it had ever been before.

The stiff troublesome fellows were the interesting ones.

He passed to the marked increase of effective medical research and from that to the general inventiveness of our age. Inventiveness had never been so manifest as it was today. For more than a century it had been increasing. Directly you said a thing could not possibly be done, there it was—done. Yet so far no one had suggested that this must be due to the release of new mental types. It might be.

He felt that he would like to have another talk with Davis about the whole matter. Where had Davis got his evidently very strong belief that there were new and strange types appearing in the world? Could he know of anything that a leading obstetrician of wide scientific reading was not likely to know? The trouble about talking to Davis was the doctor's persuasion—possibly an exaggerated one—that mentally he was not too safely balanced. It would be unwise to "encourage" him, if he was in fact drifting towards a delusion. And then abruptly Dr. Holdman Stedding remembered something.

"His wife!"

Several times Davis had practically asserted that his wife was strange, odd, exceptional. Dr. Holdman Stedding tried to recall the exact words but he found he could not do so. But that manifest disturbance at the advent of a child was bound up with that.

"If he's beginning to think his wife is one of these Mar-tianized people . . . ! I wonder what a fellow of that sort might not do. . . . What was it he said? Something about our very children not proving to be our own?"

Dr. Holdman Stedding spent some time that night trying to recall every particular he could of both these people. She was very quiet in her manner, observant, sane. If she was exceptional mentally it was because she was exceptionally sane. She moved easily and gracefully, as one does who has no conflicting nervous impulses. She did so even in her present condition; she was being one of the calmest and most competent patients he had ever known. "If *she's* Martianized," reflected the doctor, "then the sooner we all get Martianized the better."

But then, he considered, he had not seen her a dozen times altogether and there might be qualities in her of which he knew nothing, to account for her husband's attitude, for that faintly distrustful insecurity about her.

The doctor speculated about the relations of the Davis couple for a while. He liked her and he found something slightly antipathetic about her husband. The man's quick, incalculable, and ill-adjusted mental movements made him uncomfortable. No doubt his literary gifts were considerable, but like so many of these literary people he had much more control over himself upon paper than in real life. He must be a great trial to her and she ought to be protected, now at any rate, from his possible eccentricities. The doctor felt that something ought to be done about it, and began think-ing of possible things that might or might not be done, until it occurred to him that it was through this sort of breach in impartiality that unprofessional conduct may enter into the life of a practitioner.

§ 3

In the morning he wrote a very carefully considered letter to Davis which he marked "Private" and addressed to the Planetarium Club.

It was a long and repetitious letter. It beat about the bush too much to be quoted in full here, but the gist of it was a warning not to give way to a "fantasy-suggestion." "These little imaginative ideas one takes into one's mind are like those insidious creatures the medieval doctors used to talk about, little things that seem nothing at all, that leap into your mouth before you know where you are and grow into monsters inside your brain and devour your sanity." No human mind, the doctor declared, was sufficiently balanced as yet to resist the disturbance of a too persistently cherished idea. That was why nearly everyone who investigated "psychic phenomena" or "telepathy" or "astrology" or "chiromancy" or the tarot cards presently began to find there was "something in it." Mr. Davis was to think no more about it, distract his mind, take up chess, play golf on new courses, before this obsession really gripped his mind. "You are standing on the brink of a long mental slide at the bottom of which is delusional insanity. I write plainly to you, because you are still a perfectly sane man."

§ 4

"He knows—he knows as well as I do," said Mr. Joseph Davis. "But he's afraid to go on with it. . . .

"I *want* to go on with it. But how I am to do that I don't know. Watch. . . . And meanwhile these cosmic rays fly noiselessly about me—the arrows of the Martians— and by a birth here and a birth there—humanity undergoes —dehumanization."

CHAPTER FIVE

PROFESSOR ERNEST KEPPEL TAKES UP THE IDEA IN HIS OWN PECULIAR FASHION

§ 1

NOW Dr. Holdman Stedding had a great friend and crony, a bachelor like himself and a queer imaginative talker, Professor Ernest Keppel. He was nominally professor of philosophy, but latterly he had engaged more and more in psycho-therapy. He was accused of psychologizing his philosophy away into a descriptive science and he was a frequent and formidable controversialist, more often in hot water than not.

He was a dark, scarred, halting man. He had been scarred by the explosion of a hidden mine in the German trenches during the September advances in 1918. The scar ran as a dark red suture from the middle of his forehead across the left brow, where an overhanging exostosis thrust his eye into a deep and sinister cavern. Moreover, the explosion had stiffened the joint of his forearm, injured his pelvis, and left him lame. Before that he must have been very animated and attractive indeed. But this mutilation had left a curious bitterness in his nature. He understood why he was bitter; he did his best not to be bitter, but taking thought about it could not make him sweet. He was over-sensitive to the effect of his scar when he met new people; his incurable delusion that he was repulsive made him abrupt and rude, more particularly with women, and perhaps he exaggerated the delights of the normal experiences from which he felt he was shut off. He was prosperous and he lived well, and his energy and persistence in research and speculation were making a great reputation for him.

The doctor found his company extremely stimulating. He was accustomed to bring new ideas to him and toast them, so to speak, in front of his glowing mind. Indeed he hardly ever took an idea to himself and assimilated it until he had warmed it up first before Professor Keppel. And now accordingly he took advantage of a lunch engagement to bring up the matter of the Martians. They often arranged by telephone to lunch together, because Keppel's place was so much nearer than clubland.

"I was talking to a lunatic yesterday," said the doctor, "and he broached a most remarkable idea."

He sketched Mr. Davis's alleged discovery in a tone of appreciative scepticism as lunch went on.

"It's nonsense," he concluded.

"It's nonsense," Professor Keppel agreed. "But——"

"Exactly! But——"

"But—" repeated Keppel and waved the hand of his inferior arm stiffly, while his trim parlour-maid stood at his elbow with the savoury.

A certain brightness appeared in his overhung eye. His expression became profound.

Dr. Holdman Stedding waited.

"The interesting point," said Professor Keppel, helping himself to his Gruyere a la Roi Alphonse, "the interesting point is, as you say, that we do in fact know nothing about what human modification may be going on at the present time. Nothing. Demographic science has hardly begun to be a precise science—much less an exact science. Our social statistics are extravagantly clumsy. (A) We don't know what to count or measure and (B) we haven't an idea how to measure it. It **is** quite possible that new human types may be appearing in the world, or that once rare types may be

increasing in number relatively.   More geniuses—more ab-
errant gifts.   And the queer thing is that, when this lunatic
comes to you and starts this idea in your head, you don't
say Pish or Tush and just turn it down; you begin to have
a vague sense that somehow you have felt something—you
hardly know what."

"That's it."

"And when you bring it to me (Do try this savoury.
Don't pass it. I got the recipe from Martinez at that Spanish
restaurant in Swallow Street) I begin to have the same
feeling."

§ 2

"One's imagination wants to play with it.   It's as attractive
as a hare's foot to a kitten.   Suppose, Keppel, suppose—for
the sake of a talk—there *are* Martians."

"Let's suppose it.   I'm more than willing."

"What sort of minds would they have and what would
they think of our minds and what might they not try to
make of them?"

"Regarded as an exercise in speculative general psychology?
That's attractive."

"As a speculative exercise then."

"Exactly.   You know that man Olaf Stapledon has already
tried something of the sort in a book called *Last and First
Men*.   Some day we shall certainly have to come to a general
psychology independent of the human type, just as now these
young men in the Society of Experimental Biology are getting
away from the highly specialized peculiarities of human physiology towards a general physiological science.   Now away
there in Mars, as any astronomer will tell you, there are
all the conditions necessary for a sort of life similar, if not
identically similar, to life upon earth, the same elements—air,
water, a temperature range not widely different.   The proba-

bilities are in favour of there having been a parallel—a roughly parallel evolution. Parallel but in some ways different. The gravitational energy, atmospheric pressure, and suchlike things are different and that would mean differences in lightness, vigour, and size. Martian plants and animals would probably run much bigger. *Much* bigger."

"I forget the relative masses of the two planets," said the doctor.

"I forget too. Roughly it's something like eight to one— perhaps a bit more. So the Martian if he had a human form would be twice as tall and eight times our weight. A bigger, longer-lived creature. Assuming——"

"What *don't* we assume!"

"No. It's not *wild* assumption. The odds are in favour that there are or have been growths, detachments, moving feeling things, in existence on that planet. This is bold speculation, Holdman Stedding, I admit, but it isn't extravaganza."

"Go on. But you wouldn't dare to talk to your students like this."

"Possibly not. How far would the evolution of life, if it had an independent start elsewhere under slightly but not essentially different conditions, run parallel to the evolution of life on earth?"

"The same tune, I suppose, with variations."

"It is difficult to imagine anything else. There would be plants—I think green plants—and animals. The animals would run about as individuals and have senses, something like ours—perhaps very like ours. They might see more colours than we do, for example, have a longer or shorter range of sound, subtler feelers in the place of our hands. Probably Nature has tried out all the possible senses on earth here. But not all the possible shapes and patterns. Anyhow these Martians would respond to stimuli; they would have reflexes; they would condition their reflexes. I believe if we could call up the spirit of dear old Pavlov, we should find him agreeing with us, that the chances are heavily in favour of any possible minds there being minds fundamentally like ours."

"But with a longer past."

"Yes, Mars was cool long before earth was. A longer past, a hotter summer and a harder winter—the year of Mars is twice the length of ours—a larger body and a larger brain. With more room for memories—more and better memories—and more space for ideas, more and better ideas. And so the problem comes down to this. What sort of mind would a man have if he had a longer ancestry, an ampler memory, a less hurried life?"

"I accept all that as just possible," said the doctor.

"It is certainly where the weight of probability lies. Now all these pseudo-scientific story-writers who write about Mars make their Martians monsters and horrors, inhuman in the bad sense, cruel. Why should they be anything of the sort? Why," repeated Professor Keppel, taking coffee, "why should they be anything of the sort?"

"Quite nice monsters?"

"Why not?"

"Well, the German professor evolved his idea of a camel from is inner consciousness; why shouldn't we do the same with our Martians?"

"Having regard to the facts. Why not?"

Dr. Holdman Stedding looked at his watch.

"Not till you've smoked one of those pennant-shaped Coronas you like," said Keppel, "and just a whiff of brandy. Because, confound it! you started this talk, you've interested me, and you've got to hear it out. If there is such a thing as a Martian, rest assured, Holdman Stedding, he's humanity's big brother."

"Big in every way you think. A super-superman."

"Good anyhow."

"Beyond good and evil?"

"Everything alive must have its good and evil. Beyond *our* good and evil anyhow. None the worse for that perhaps. No; if you talk to your lunatic again, you can at least dispel any fear he has of his Martians. The odds are they are not so much invading us as acting as a sort of interplanetary tutor. Bless my heart! At the mere thought I feel a sort of benevolent influence."

"No," said Dr. Holdman Stedding, emitting a smoke jet with the appreciative expression of a cigar advertisement in *Punch* and weighing the possibilities of the case with luxurious deliberation. "It's your cook."

§ 3

"She's a very goo cook," Professor Keppel admitted. "But about these Martians. We are letting our fancy play too wildly about them. Let's leave them for a bit. There's another point your patient has raised that's quite available for separate treatment. Practically another question. There may or may not be these sane and mature watchers over human destiny, these Celestial Uncles, these friends in the midnight sky, but what does seem to be possible and even within our reach is this idea, that the species *Homo sapiens,* because of some possible increase or change in direction of the cosmic rays, or from some other unknown cause, is starting to mutate, and mutate along some such line as that larger wisdom indicates."

"Some *sort* of large wisdom," said Dr. Holdman Stedding, "a purely hypothetical wisdom."

"You are very precise," said Professor Keppel. "But anyhow that is what we want to know. Is there such a biological movement going on? Is there any means of tracing it if it is going on? The real feeling at the back of both our minds is that, if there is not something of the sort going on, then this breed of pretentious, self-protective imbeciles——"

"Poor *Homo sapiens!*" murmured the doctor. *"How* he catches it nowadays!"

"Is very near the end of its tether. It's no good pretending you disagree with that. Haven't all reasonable civilized men nowadays this feeling of being dilettantes on a sinking ship? We all want a break towards something better in the way of living. Hopes and our wishes speak together. And it may be—as we half hope. But how are we to test this idea? How are we to set about the investigation?"

"Without making everyone think we have gone crazy?"

"Precisely."

"Nietzsche?" hazarded the doctor. "Are these his super-men we are thinking about?"

"He brings in too much Oriental bric-a-brac for my taste," said Keppel. "And so far as I can make out, he has at least two different meanings for that Ubermensch of his. On the one hand is a biologically better sort of man and on the other a sort of aggregate synthetic being like Hobbes's Leviathan. You never know how to take him. Let's rule Nietzche out. Let us follow up this question whether there is an increase in—what shall I call them?—high-grade intellectual types."

The doctor helped himself with infinite restraint and discretion to just the merest splash more brandy. "I think, Keppel, there may be a possible way to set this note of interrogation working."

"We have our reputations to consider."

"We have our reputations to consider, but quite possibly this fellow—well, to commit a very slight indiscretion—it is Mr. Joseph Davis, the man who writes those extremely popular, those *florid* —shall I say?—those almost too glorifying *glosses,* so to speak, on history—might do something for us in this respect. His writings, his association with what one might call the more romantic aspects of the human record, his almost strained belief in the faith, hope, and glory of our species, put him, I think, in a position to ask questions . . ."

"Joseph Davis," considered Keppel. "The man who wrote *From Agincourt to Trafalgar?* Him! You got this idea about the Martians from *him!*"

"I told him to think no more about it."

"But he will?"

"He will. He wants to think about it. He wants to follow this up. He—something has shaken him up, I can't make up my mind whether he is going mad or going sane. But if I give him a hint, he'll be off on the scent of these Martians now like a dog after a rabbit."

CHAPTER SIX

OPENING PHASES OF THE GREAT EUGENIC RESEARCH

§ 1

"NOW here, now there," whispered Mr. Davis to himself as he stood on the doorstep of the headmaster of Gorpel School and looked at the headmaster's trim but beautiful garden.

It was six months later and high summer and he was the father of an extremely healthy but extremely intelligent-looking child. And the belief that he had discovered that the most wonderful event in the history of our planet was now happening had entered into and become part of his being.

Ostensibly he had come to Gorpel to lecture on "The Grandeur That Was Rome," but really he had come to look that interesting collection of boys over and talk to the headmaster about any mentally (or even physically) exceptional lads who might have attracted his attention. Nothing was to be said about Martians, cosmic rays, or anything of that sort. It was to be put before the headmaster as a mild little inquiry into the prospects of the "odd" type of boy.

It was Dr. Holdman Stedding who had suggested this line of inquiry to him. Really the excellent doctor wanted this material collected to feed the -whimsical and- nine-tenths sceptical curiosity of Keppel and himself, but he had succeeded in persuading himself that it was absolutely the best treatment for Davis's mental worries that his imaginative vagaries should be steadied and assuaged by a methodical exploration of what might quite possibly prove to be illuminating facts. This brought with it a certain sense of benevolence, because Davis was not his patient under treatment, paid no fees. It was indeed simply helping the man as one man helps another.

Davis at this stage was looking for mental abnormalities— on the upward side. He was getting whatever could be got from prison governors, educational authorities, schools of every sort where there was close contact between teachers and pupils, even from army instructors, institutions for de- fectives, lunatic asylums—and making a general report and a digest of his results. A number of facts not generally known was emerging from these inquiries. The proportion of children of the calculating-boy and musical-prodigy type seemed to be increasing quite markedly; finer muscular ad- justment was in a very conspicuous way ousting mere beef from athleticism; critical obduracy at quite an early age was far more in evidence than it had ever been before.

Possibly Davis, like many investigators, was disposed to find what he looked for. Dr. Holdman Stedding fancied he could allow for that.

What Dr. Holdman Stedding did not allow for were the practical effects of these preoccupations upon an author's normal activities. Like most men of sound professional stand- ing he thought authors did their work outside time and space occupied their normal hours in the pursuit of royalties and publicity and in making speeches on irrelevent topics to un- necessary societies. But Joseph Davis had been engaged upon a great constellation of books, which were to give history, ennobled and illuminated, to the common man. He had schemed that as what he called his "life task." That task was now beginning to look like a modern cathedral under construction when some new heresy breaks out among the more opulent faithful and funds run short. Sometimes for six or seven days not a line was added.

Meanwhile every day it grew plainer to Davis that this theory, which at first seemed even to him a fantastic hypothesis, was real and true. A new quality of human being was being inserted into the fabric of human life, "one here, one there."

It was hard not to talk about it. It was hard to have to keep up the pretence of making a mere respectable inquiry as trivial and pointless as—let us say—a research thesis in pedagogics for an American University. He went about the world to social gatherings, to assemblies and theatres and restaurants; he mingled in crowds, he watched people's unsuspecting faces, and now the thought was always in his mind: *If only they knew!*

If only they knew what the Martians were doing to them!

At first his attitude had been one of stark antagonism to this Martian intrusion. He had something more than an ordinary man's instinctive loyalty to race and kind. He had superimposed a mental habit. He had made himself a champion of that ancient and venerable normal life of humanity, unaltered through the ages—except now and then through the providential punishment of some transitory heresy—the simple, old, beautiful story of childhood, learning, love, industry, parentage, honour, and the easy passage to a venerable old age and a brightly hopeful death. It was a story at once earthly, in the best, the honest pious peasant sense, and profoundly spiritual. This life, age after age, had been set in a stimulating round of seedtime and harvest, cold and heat, thirst and hunger, reasonable desires and modest satisfactions. Of such stuff was history woven, and across this sound, enduring fabric were embroidered the great historical figures, in a bright operadrama as glad in quality as an illuminated missal. History told of their conquests, triumphs, glories, heroisms, of heartstirring tragedies and lovely sacrifices. They were all far greater than lifesize— like the monarchs and gods in an Assyrian relief—the common people ran about beneath their feet according to the best historical traditions. So it had been. So it would go on until at last the Almighty commanded the curtain to ring down and called the actors forward from their various retiring-rooms, to receive appropriate rewards.

Such was the picture of the world and its promise that he had been working to realize, overworking to realize, when this fantastic and distracting suspicion of a Martian intervention first came to him. It was as if the vast canvas on which he had been working with such resolution had suddenly cracked across·and betrayed his light and shade, his heights and depths, as the completest unreality.

Now—and here there seems to have been some gap in his logical process—he felt that the Martians would certainly be against all these fine things for which he struggled. Why, one may ask, should the Martians be against them? Why should they be by necessity spoilers of so rich and noble a fabric? But he had his full share of that infirmity of our impatient minds which makes us leap naturally to the conclusion that what is not uncritically on our side and subject to our ideas is against us. At the onset of a strange way of living we bristle like dogs at the sight of a strange animal. He hated these Martians as soon as he thought of them. He could not imagine their interference with our nice world could be anything but devastating.

His motive to begin with, therefore, was an altogether uncomplicated desire to detect, expose, and repel an insidious and dreadful attack upon this dear and happy human life we all enjoy so greatly and relinquish so reluctantly. These Martians presented themselves to him as the blackest of threats to all those convictions that make life worth living upon earth. Indisputably they must be *inhuman,* whatever else they are. That went without saying. To be inhuman implied to him, as to most of us, malignant cruelty; it seemed impossible that it could mean anything else. (And yet this is a world where lots of us live upon terms of sentimental indulgence towards cats, dogs, monkeys, horses, cows, and suchlike unhuman creatures, help them in a myriad simple troubles, and attribute the most charming reactions to them!)

Among other things it seemed to him unquestionable that the drive of these so elaborately aimed cosmic missiles among our chromosomes would be to increase the intellectual power of the Martianized individuals very greatly. There seemed to be no alternative to that conclusion. And for some very deep-seated reason in his make-up, it was an intolerable thought for him that there should appear any class of creatures on earth intellectually above his own, unless they were profoundly inferior to him morally, and so repulsive and ugly as practically to reverse the handicap against him. They *had* to be ugly in appearance, they *had* to be ugly in motive and action. There had to be that compensation at least. This idea of their ugliness followed the idea of their intelligence with such an air of necessity that it was some weeks before he began even to suspect that the two ideas might be separated.

At first he pictured a Martian as something hunched together, like an octopus, tentacular, saturated with evil poisons, oozing unpleasant juices, a gigantic leathery bladder of hate. The smell, he thought, would be terrible. And those indirect offspring who were to be so foully disseminated upon earth, were bound, he imagined, to be not simply intelligent in a hard unsympathetic way but in some manner disfigured and disgusting. They would be bound to have turnip heads, bladder-of-lard crania, shortsighted eyes, horrible little faces, long detestable hands, unathletic and possibly crippled bodies. . . .

Yet struggling desperately against this trend were certain vague apprehensions about his wife and child.

§ 2

There was an extraordinary division in his mind at this time. Two cognate currents of suspicion ran side by side and would not mingle.

His wife was at once associated with and separated from his general line of thought. If, for instance, Dr. Holdman Stedding had asked him outright: "Do you think your wife is one of these people who have been touched in their natal phase by the magic of the cosmic vibrations?" he would have answered at once with almost perfect honesty that these Martian speculations of his had absolutely nothing to do with her. But he would not have answered the question calmly; he would have had a touch of defensive indignation in his voice. And it was not a question he would have asked himself. It was a question he could not have asked himself; there was some barrier against that.

He was resisting a very obvious impulse to complete the link of association and fear that linked his long-standing sense of some strangeness about his wife, with this Martian idea. The two lines of suggestion were in reality connected and consecutive, but by some self-protective necessity he would not see that his extreme readiness to accept the suggestion of a Martian influx had any direct relation to his long-incubated sense of the elfin quality of his wife. They were groups of ideas in different spheres.

But these spheres, of which the Martian one was now spinning so busily, were drawing closer and closer together in his mind. Within a measurable time they were bound to collide, to coalesce into one common whirlpool, which might be a very tumbled whirlpool indeed. Then he would be bound to face the realization that had already projected itself in his words to the doctor: "So that presently our very children may not prove to be our own."

This intimation, breaking through his resistances, evoked

first the dread of an abnormal child, prematurely wise, macrocephalic, with dreadful tentacular hands. . . . So his essential humanity presented the thing. If the thing was a monster, what should he do?

He thought of doing some very dreadful things.

Such nightmare ideas haunted him more and more distressingly until the birth of his child. The immediate advent of that event filled him with almost uncontrollable terror. By an immense effort he concealed it and behaved himself.

He was amazed—even Dr. Holdman Stedding was amazed —to have the young man brought into the world after a labour of less than an hour. No monstrous struggle. No frightful crisis. No Cæsarean operation.

"Is he—is he *all right*," he asked incredulous.

"Fit as a fiddle," said Dr. Holdman Stedding almost boisterously. Because he had found something contagious in the father's uneasiness.

"No malformations? No strangeness?"

"On my honour, Mr. Davis, you don't deserve such a child! You don't. When they've done a little washing you shall see it. I'm not often enthusiastic. I've seen too many of 'em."

And it looked indeed a perfect little creature. When they put it into his parental arms a great wave of instinctive tenderness surged up in the heart of Joseph Davis. Like endless fathers in his position before him, he was overcome by the wonderful fact that the creature's little hands had perfect nails and fingers.

Why had he ever been afraid?

"I feel I'd like to see her," he said.

"Not just yet. A little while yet. Though she's doing splendidly." Whereupon Dr. Holdman Stedding said a slightly unfortunate thing: "There's not a painted Madonna in all the world with a lovelier bambino than hers."

Mr. Joseph Davis's expression became thoughtful.

Silently he handed back his precious burden to the hovering nurse.

He was minded to go out and not see Mary for a time. Then by a great effort he overcame this impulse and stayed indoors in his study downstairs, and presently he was taken in to her, and when he saw her, tired but flushed and triumphant, with the child laid close to her, some long-standing restraint seemed to break between them and he called her his darling and knelt down beside her, weeping.

"Dear Joe!" she said, and her hand crept out and ruffled his hair gently. "Queer Joe!"

§ 3

After that his ideas about the quality of the Martians' influences and purposes began to change. After all, the two streams of realization came together in his mind gently and naturally, and he felt with the completest assurance and with no lingering trace of horror that both his wife and his child belonged to this new order of human beings that was appearing upon the planet.

After that it was his researches, which at the beginning had been directed mainly to Poor Law institutions for defective and malformed children, asylums, wonder children, and the more grotesque arcana of gynæcology, turned rather to schools and universities and the ascertainable characteristics of exceptional and gifted people. He passed from a hunt for monsters to an investigation of outstanding endowment, to the detection and analysis of what is called genius in every field of human activity. He brooded over the pictured riddles of Durer, he read the notebooks of Leonardo. He found a new interest in symbolic art and in whatever moody and inexplicable decoration from remote times and places came to his attention. Were these enigmas like cries in the dark, the struggling intimations of novel reactions and novel attitudes on the part of Martian pioneers towards the customs and traditions of our world?

He had never told any one, least of all would he have told Dr. Holdman Stedding, that dreams about Martians were becoming rather frequent with him. They were extremely consistent dreams or at least they were pervaded with a sense of consistency. These dream-Martians were no longer repulsive creatures, grotesques and caricatures, and yet their visible appearance was not human. They had steadfast, dark eyes, very widely separated, and their mouths were still and resolute. Their broad brows and round heads made him think of the smooth wise-looking heads of seals and cats, and he could not distinguish clearly whether they had shadowy hands and arms or tentacles. There was always a lens-like effect about his vision, as though he saw them through the eyepiece of some huge optical instrument. Ripples passed across the lens and increased the indistinctness, and ever and again flickering bunches of what he assumed were cosmic rays exploded from nothingness across the picture and flashed out radiating to the periphery and vanished. He felt that his dreams were taking him into a world where our ideas of form and process, of space and time, are no longer valid. In his dreams it was not as if he went across space to Mars, it was as if a veil became translucent.

Once or twice in the daytime he had tried to make sketches of these watchers, but their physical forms had always eluded his pencil. He had never been able to draw very well, but also he had a feeling that even for a skilled artist there would have been difficulties about the planes and dimensions of these beings.

Moreover, not only was he finding this difficulty in determining a Martian form but he was finding a parallel difficulty in fixing any common characteristics for the earthly types he was beginning to distinguish as "Martianized." All that they had in common was that they were "different" and that this difference involved a certain detachment from common reactions. They lived apart. They thought after their own fashion. He was not sure whether they were actually insusceptible to mass emotions; he may have expected them to be, and that with him would have been half-way to thinking them so.

§ 4

On this visit to Gorpel he pursued what was becoming his usual technique. It was at once subtle and a trifle crazy. There was a streak of masochism about it. He had written all his books so far to appeal to the heroic common humanity in all of us. And now he was using the same stuff to eliminate, so to speak, common humanity. He was looking for minds that did not respond.

He had brought down a lecture that had always proved extremely successful with ordinary schoolboys, "The Grandeur That Was Rome." In this he unfolded his tale of the heroic patriots who stud the Latin tradition, from Horatius defend-ing the Bridge, to Cæsar crowning the great task of the Republic by annexing it to British history, Octavius creating the Empire and Justinian giving us Roman law. It was a procession of statuesque figures, more or less clean-shaven and for the most part in togas, evoking as they passed a fungoid growth of unnecessary aqueducts, corpulent amphi-theatres, and Corinthian columns, and conferring on the whole world the blessings of the Pax Romana. The Punic Wars, with a faint flavouring of Anti-Semitism, too faint to be disagreeable, he presented as a gigantic necessary struggle between noble north-side soldiers and revengeful, obdurate, but extremely competent south-side loanmongers. He ignored every reality of hate, suspicion, greed, panic, and brutish

cruelty that characterized that monstrous mutual destruction
of the Mediterranean civilizations, the Punic Wars, and still
less did he let those essential features of the mighty Pax,
the omnipresent cross for rebels and the omnipresent tax-
collector for every one, peep out from behind those glorious
Roman arches. As he orated this familiar discourse he
watched the boys. A few, incapable of attention, were
inattentive, but the discipline of the school was good and
their inattention was passive. The majority were responsive.
They drank in the mighty fable. Their eyes betrayed their
imaginative excitement. Their faces became nobler, stern.
They became conquering generals subduing barbarians, pro-
consuls assuaging the bickerings of subject races.

It was an answer to trumpets that stirred in them. It was
what he had heard someone call the "Onward, Christian
Soldiers" reaction.

With all that Davis was familiar. But now he was looking
for scepticism and intelligent dissent.

There was one little fellow sitting up near the corner who
from the start he felt assured was Martianized. He had
untidy hair and a shrewd faintly humorous white face, and
he listened throughout, cheek on hand, very attentively and
with a questioning expression. He heard, untouched. The
real Martian quality.

"That's my boy *here,*" said Davis and inquired about him
afterwards.

"A queer little chap," said the headmaster. "A queer little
chap. Behaves pretty well, but he's somehow disappointing.
Doesn't *throw* himself **into** things. A streak of something
very nearly amounting to—well, scepticism. Yet his people
are quite decent people and the Dean of Clumps is his
uncle. He asks questions no other boy would think of. The
other day he asked, what is *spiritual?*"

"Well," said Mr. Davis after a thoughtful pause, "what

is spiritual?"

"But need I tell *you* of all people?"

"What did you tell him? I'm finding a sort of difficulty in putting this in a chapter I am writing about the saintly life."

The headmaster of Gorpel did not answer the question immediately. Instead he went on to say in a slightly offended voice: "I find all my normal boys understand the word without discussion, take it for granted. Spiritual-Material, a natural opposition. One ascends, the other gravitates. There it is, plain as a pikestaff. No need to discuss it."

"Unless some little—toad, like that, asks the question point-blank."

"He refuses to see. Why, he said, should we make a sort of extract of reality and call it spirituality and pretend the two things are primary opposites?"

"He said that! Rather—subtle."

"Too subtle for a boy of his age. Unwholesome."

"But spirit isn't an extract, is it?"

"So I said to him. 'Life,' he said, seems to me just one, Sir. I can't think of it in any other way. Sorry, Sir, I've tried.' "

"He said that—that he couldn't think in any other way? That's very interesting. How did you meet that?"

"In this particular case I explained by means of illustrations."

"And he was satisfied?"

"Not in the least. He criticized my illustrations. Rather penetratingly, I admit. He wanted me to define. But you see, Mr. Davis, the fundamental things of life cannot be defined. He made me realize that more clearly than I have ever done before. *All* the great fundamentals, Deity, Eternity—Faith in What?—it is as if there was a sort of holy of holies beyond the reach of exact definitions. So it seems

to me. It is useless, I find, to argue about them. It robs
our attitudes of dignity . . . robs *them* of dignity. . . .
We are reduced to logic-chopping. Quibbles. . . . We
understand by intuition what we mean and what other people
mean. Best to leave it at that."

"And you told him if he didn't understand what spiritual
meant, not to go on thinking about it yet but wait."

"And pray," said the headmaster of Gorpel. "In effect
I said that. In effect. Not exactly. Not too definitely.
One must go carefully. Afterwards I made him learn
Corinthians One Thirteen by heart—not as if it was exactly
an answer but as if it threw a light—and I hope it did him
good."

"You don't know?"

"I don't know. These are elusive matters, Mr. Davis. A
boy who wants to argue must not be indulged too far. There
are limits."

"I wonder," said Mr. Davis, feeling his way carefully,
"if perhaps *types*—types like this youngster may really be
something more than merely obstinate. Whether by some
instinctive necessity, by some difference in themselves, they
may not find something—some inacceptable lack of fineness,
some lack of clearness, in various distinctions we assume,
distinctions we *have* assumed and which we make by
habit. . . ."

"I can't entertain thoughts like that," said the headmaster
abruptly. "I cannot conduct the work of this great school
and prepare my regiment of youngsters year by year for their
attack on life and responsibility, if I am also to carry on an
examination of the fundamental values we set on things."

"But if presently instead of one inassimilable boy you find
half a dozen of him turning up—or a score?"

The headmaster looked at his visitor. "I devoutly hope
not, Mr. Davis," he said. "I devoutly hope not. You are

giving me food—not for thought—no!—for nightmares. . . ."

"Now here, now here," said Mr. Davis as he stood on the headmaster's doorstep. "Certainly that boy is one of them. They don't see life as we see it. They can't think of it in our way. And they make us begin to doubt that we see it ourselves as we have always imagined we did."

CHAPTER SEVEN

THE WORLD BEGINS TO HEAR ABOUT THE MARTIANS

§ 1

IT is almost impossible to trace how this realization that mankind, under the spur of the cosmic rays, was launched upon a career of genetic change, seeped from the minds of the first discoveries, Laidlaw, that rufous man in the Planet-arium Club (to whom it seemed no more than a passing freak of fancy), Mr. Davis (who was first to take it seriously), Dr. Holdman Stedding, and Professor Ernest Keppel, into the general consciousness. But a few weeks after the birth of Mary's child, an article appeared in the *Weekly Refresher* from the pen of that admirable scientific popularizer, Harold Rigamey, in which, as Professor Keppel rather inelegantly put it, he "completely spilt the beans."

It is possible that Rigamey got the thing at second or third hand from Dr. Holdman Stedding, who oddly enough seems to have been the least discreet of all that primary group. Dr. Stedding may have described it to one or two fellow-practitioners as an example of the extreme intellectual elaboration that may appear in a case of delusional insanity. There is no evidence that Laidlaw, after his first imaginative outbreak, ever gave the matter a second thought until he got the echo in the newspapers. But he may very well have repeated his fantasy on some after-dinner occasion. He was the last survivor of the old Bob Stevenson, York Powell, school of talk, a gorgeous talker.

Harold Rigamey was a peculiarly constituted being, he had a mind that did not so much act as react. He was born ultra-heretic. He disbelieved everything and then doubled back on his disbelief. From a sound historical and literary training he had recoiled in a state of unsympathetic curiosity to science and had achieved a very respectable position on the literary side of journalism by writing about science in a manner that caused the greatest discomfort and perplexity to men of science. He found wonders for them when they saw nothing wonderful and incredible triumphs of paradox in their simplest statements. He mated them to the strangest associates.

He had an infuriating openmindedness to every unorthodox extravagance. He hated dogma and he was full of faith. He was always reconciling science and religion, spiritualism and behaviourism, medicine and Christian Science, and this reconciling disposition won him quite a large following of readers eager to keep their mental peace amidst the vast, the incongruous, alarming, and sometimes far too urgent suggestions of our modern world.

They were all a little uneasy with him and that was a part of his charm. There were stimulants in all his sedatives. When he asked his readers to come and meet spiritual worth, they were never quite sure whether that meant the dear Archbishop of Canterbury, all clean and scented with his pretty purple-and-red evening clothes, his pretty lace cuffs, his pretty episcopal ring, and his general vacuous urbanity, or whether it meant a rather repellent, though no doubt equally edifying, encounter with some unsanitarily pure and indecently stark fakir on a bed of nails; and when he remarked upon the stern veracities of science, whether it would be a fresh explosion in the mathematical engine-room, a vitamin of incredible potency, or a breathing exercise from America that at once confirmed and completed the remarkable inhalations of ancient Tibet, he had in mind. For some time Harold Rigamey had been working out in his own mind some

sort of linkage of interplanetary communications with the all
too neglected science of astrology; he thought he might make
something quite exciting out of it, and this weird idea of
Laidlaw's came to him like the voice of the Lord to a
Hebrew prophet.

For some time he had been feeling that his characteristic
methods of popularizing science were no longer growing in
popular favour. Men of science are a peculiar, an almost
ungracious, class, and very often the more you popularize
them the less they like it. Maybe it was a public realization
of their lack of appreciation for Harold Rigamey's services,
or maybe it was just a surfeit of subtle but occasionally very
incomprehensible wonders, that was affecting the first
abundant public response to Harold Rigamey; at any rate he
felt that his popularity was dimmer than it used to be. A
really new and exciting topic. that only needed a little care
and thought in the handling to go far and wide, was just
the tonic he had been requiring.

Mindful of the faint elements of insecurity in his own
credit he set about the subject with considerable skill and
discretion. He first informed his public through a couple of
articles, called "The Voice of the Stars," of a "growing
realization" that "extra-terrestrial forces of some unknown
kind" were "indubitably" attempting to establish communication with our planet. He invoked almost every known
authority upon extra-terrestrial radiations, produced in a
skilfully clipped form some rare unguarded statements by
eminent professors, promoted one or two rash speculations
by obscure people in remote parts of the earth to a distinguished scientific standing, and invented a few anonymous
scientists of his own. (Some day *Nature* will have to publish
a list of otherwise non-existent scientists, available for public
controversy.)

"Scientists tell us" was a very favourite phrase with Harold

Rigamey. He wrote of "numerous efforts" which he said had been made to "discover codes" in these extra-terrestrial radiations and of the growing conviction of "scientists" of all sorts and shades and sizes of the existence of these persistent attempts to attract our attention from outside our world.

"This present century," wrote Harold Rigamey, "already goes far beyond its predecessor, the Century of Invention. This is the Century of Discovery. The sixteenth century was a Century of Terrestrial Discovery; but this is the Century of Extra-Terrestrial Discovery. Already the immortality of the soul, or at any rate persistence after death, seems to be experimentally established, and now we realize upon the most convincing evidence that man is not alone on his planet; he is a citizen in what may prove to be an abundantly populated universe."

Eminent men of science read Harold Rigamey's latest revelation of what science is doing in a mood of apoplectic fury. "What are we to do about this sort of thing?" they said to their wives at breakfast, and their wives said: "My dear, *what* can you do?" And there the matter ended. The mystical mathematicians with their expanding and contracting universes, relativity-exponents, and the like retired from the arena of popular attention like a small group of concertina players on the entry of a large brass band. An unprecedented mail informed Harold Rigamey of the successful opening of his campaign. His next stage was to go on to "The Fantastic Connexion of Cosmic Rays and Human Mutations" and then straightaway to "The Martian Genes" and "The Martian Type" and so told the whole story as we have already seen it unfolding in the mind of Mr. Joseph Davis, but with a richness of confirmatory detail altogether beyond our modest record of actualities.

§ 2

The reception of the astounding revelation was ample and inconclusive, and it afforded Professor Keppel considerable scope for his gift for bitter comment. Popular intelligence, the professor pointed out to the acquiescent Dr. Holdman Stedding, has long since ceased to attach any real importance to concrete statements except in so far as they concern football and cricket results, the winners of races, and (with caution and reservations) stock-exchange quotations. Outside this definite range of immediate rational interests it has achieved an almost complete toleration, an inactive indifference, to any statement whatever. "You may tell the public anything you like nowadays," said Keppel, "and it will not care a rap. It is not that it disbelieves; it is not that it believes; but that its belief apparatus has been overstrained and misused beyond any sort of reaction, positive or negative, to the things that it is told.

"Consider," he expatiated, "the—we will not say *contents* —of the average human mind today; but consider the things that are lying about side by side upon that flaccid expanse of mentality." (Dr. Holdman Stedding repeated these precious words silently: flaccid expanse of mentality.) "It has been told a beautiful story of Creation, the Garden of Eden and the Fall. It does not know whether that story is a fable, a parable, or a statement of fact, and manifestly it does not care. If Sir Leonard Woolley and Mr. H. V. Morton announced a joint discovery of Eden, raised a restoration fund, and provided tourist facilities at reasonable rates, the public would go in a state of inscrutable acquiescence and enormous numbers, to visit the ancestral garden-plot. And at the same time in the same brain, so to speak, this public has accepted a great mass of statement to the effect that it is descended, through something called Evolution, from gorilla-like ancestors. It would be quite capable of visiting in the morning the veritable scene where six or seven thousand years ago Eve, surrounded by all the latest novelties of Creation, her wedding presents, so to speak, accepted the apple from the serpent, and then of inspecting a caveful of fifty-thousand-year-old Neanderthaler remains in the afternoon. It has lost all sense of incongruity. It has lost all sense of relevance. It neither rejects nor assimilates nor correlates anything. It believes everything and it believes nothing.

"In effect," said Professor Keppel, "it does nothing about anything at all. There is no conceivable issue now upon which it can be roused to spontaneous action. If it opened its newspaper one morning and read that Christianity has been abolished, it would wonder what sort of pensions the bishops would get—'pretty fat, I expect'—and then turn over to see if the cross-word puzzle was an easy one. If it read that the queer noises it had heard in the night were the trumpets announcing the Resurrection of the Dead and the end of the world for tomorrow afternoon, it would probably remark that the buses and tubes were full enough as it was without all these Dead coming up, and that a thing of that sort ought to be held somewhere abroad where there was more room. . . ."

In America the disclosure of the Martian intervention was received with bright incredulity. Rigamey's articles were syndicated everywhere and credited nowhere. It is a popular error Keppel insisted, that Americans are more accessible to ideas than the British. Notions indeed they are never averse to. Notions are different. A notion is something you can handle. But an idea, a general idea, has a way of getting all over you and subjugating you, and no free spirit submits to that. Confronted with an idea the American says: "Oh, yeah!" or "Sez you," and the Englishman says: "I *don't* fink," or at a higher social level: "Piffle—piffle before the wind." These simple expressions are as good against ideas as the sign of the cross used to be against the medieval devil. The pressure is at once relieved.

But your American has none of the Englishman's ability to ignore. After having said his "Sez you" or "Oh, yeah" and killed an idea, your American is only too ready to make light of the corpse. His joy in caricature and extravaganza is as vast as his sense of reality is deficient. So that Harold Rigamey's revelations, relieved of all terror of actuality and being vigorously syndicated, went widely and swiftly through the thought and phraseology of those quick-witted millions. "Are you a Martian?" was on the cars within a week of the syndication of Harold's last article and "Don't appeal to my Martian side" had become a conversational counter in circulation from coast to coast. A new caricaturist started a series of Martian cartoons in the *New Yorker* that caught on at once and were very widely imitated. The vaudeville stage was brisk rather than clever in taking up the idea. Along a thousand divergent channels flowed the fertilizing suggestion and evoked a weedy jungle of responses. "Dry Martians" became the dominant cocktail. Hundreds of deep-ly preoccupied Negroes pranced and flung themselves about in the Southern sunshine in search of a real Martian Newstep. Thousands of industrious advertisement designers spent sleepless nights subduing the new idea in this way and that way to the varied uses of their calling.

And Harold Rigamey turned his pen to other things.

§ 3

The only real attempt to deal with the coming of the Martians upon a serious scale was made on the British side, and it was made by no less a person than Lord Thunderclap, that great synthetic press peer. It was made against the advice of his most trusted associates and it failed.

Lord Thunderclap was one of the supreme successes of the journalistic and business world; he had become enormously rich and influential in a gigantic inaccurate way all out of nasty little periodicals, and he was quite intelligent enough to understand there must be something wrong about his headlong, unchallenged prominence. Both he and his slightly derisive rival and associate Lord Bendigo, deep down in their very bright minds, had that same sense of haphazard expansion and unjustifiable eminence; they could not believe, however much they tried, that in the long run the world would not call them to account; they had none of the innate assurance of royal personages and born aristocrats, and they were both haunted by the feeling that sooner or later, something hard, stern, and powerful, a Sphinx, a Nemesis, would come round a corner upon them and unfold an indictment for immediate attention, asking them what they thought they were and what in the last resort they thought they were up to.

The mercurial Bendigo regarded that possibility with unaffected facetiousness but Thunderclap was made of less mobile stuff. He liked being the large massive thing he was; the longer he lived the more he wanted to believe in his own importance and feel that he was really true. The longer he lived the more he liked himself and the less could he bear that sense of a delayed but pursuing judgment. He could ill endure the unprotesting acquiescence of this world in him; the accumulated menace of its uncritical disregard; but even less now could he endure the thought that this toleration might end.

The dark other-world of insomnia added itself to his daylight existence. That awful Court of Inquiry without any definite charges, just asking what he was and why, sat there in perpetual unprogressive session, waiting—waiting for something. There was no hurry. Most terrifyingly there was no hurry. But what could they be saving up for him? Day after day he went about his large abundant life, being the great Lord Thunderclap—because what else on earth could he be? What else on earth could he do? The day passed into evening, evening to night, and so at last to bed. And then that insatiable question. . . . What net were they weaving?

The faces about him were polite masks. You challenged them: "You were saying about me—?"

"I said nothing, my lord."

He told nobody of this increasing obsession, but the existence of his profound uneasiness was more or less manifest to most of his associates and subordinates. Was there something that had never been found out? They tried to guess at that. But nothing definite appeared, it was a dread at large. Evidently he feared men of science and knowledge, especially men who were reputed to be profoundly and exceptionally versed in political and and social and economic affairs. What must they really think of his jouranalistic influence, his activities in party matters, his financial affairs? Were they just quietly letting him have rope, sewing him up unobtrusively? And he suspected the civil service profoundly. The civil servants, he thought, knew more than was good for them already and they were always trying to know more. The word "inspector" moved him to a pallid rage. "More Inspectors!" was one of the shrillest screams in his multifarious publications. Nasty mean men, he insisted, these inspectors were, with sharp noses like foxes', needy dependants, and a passion for petty bribes; always peeping through keyholes they were, looking into windows, creeping up pipes, getting through gratings, weaving a net about all wholesome business enterprise. They had to be fought off. They had to be frustrated, denounced, caricatured at every turn. And all these Trade Union and Labour people wanting to know, perpetually wanting to know, and then, I suppose, interfere. And this London School of Economics! What were they putting together and plotting and planning there? What did they want to have a school of economics for anyhow? It was like marking the cards.

In Lord Thunderclap's mind socialism was another name for malignant investigation. He had no idea what harmless, disconnected, doctrinaire little creatures socialists are, and how limited an area of the social problem they have ever explored. He really thought they had a strong, clear plan for a workable human society all ready for use, a hard competent society, ready to thrust him and his like out of existence. At any time now they might spring it upon him. He fought wildly in the darkness against that persuasion, but it held him. He was probably the only man alive in England who believed in socialism to that extent.

In his perpetual attempt to materialize his terror he mixed up all these professors, civil servants, inspectors, socialists, sociologists (whom he regarded as a nastier variety of social-ist), liberals—every sort of interrogator and critic—in a great jumble of hateful menace, the "Intelligentsia," the "Lefts," the "Reds." He imagined a world-wide, hostile, incredibly subtle, incredibly farsighted net closing about him. And he never really got them plain for a straight fight to a finish and have done with it. Never could he drag them into the light of open day. He knew that they were at it, at it all the time, conspiring, scheming, taking their orders, passing their messages, nodding, winking, giving their signals, work-ing their mischiefs. They ramified everywhere. You never knew who was with them. They were Jesuits today and Freemasons tomorrow. Even judges and lawyers might be scheming. Hard to do a deal with them. You were safe with no one.

All his partners and secretaries and editors knew those odd

moments of his, when he would affect to look out of the window idly, and then spin round upon you with incredible nimbleness to scrutinize your face.

Or when he would lead you through a long rambling talk about Russia, about Germany, about China, to jump upon you suddenly with a handful of carefully premeditated posers, designed to wring the very plotting soul out of you.

Such was the large fear-obsessed mentality to which the disclosures of Harold Rigamey came like a torch to a hayrick.

Never for a moment when he heard it did Lord Thunderclap doubt the story. Not until he read about it in his own papers had he a twinge of doubt. It came as the embodiment and confirmation of his worst fears. He felt he had really known all about it from the very beginning. He carried Harold Rigamey off for dinner and the night to his suburban headquarters at Castle Windrow, Bunting Hayland, and thither he assembled by wire and telephone all his most trusted henchmen, tools, stooges, subordinates, intimates, Watsons, yes-girls, medical advisers, soothsayers, astrologists, stenographers, masseurs, soothers, and family connexions.

"The thing's out at last," he said. "Listen to him! Listen to what Rigamey has to tell us. We've been barking up the wrong tree. These Reds—Moscow—Bernard Shaw—New Dealers—Atheists—Protocols of Zion, all of that—mere agents. It's *Mars* that is after us. Listen to him. Mars! What are we to do about it? What are we to do?

"Everything we value in life. Cross and crown. Nation and loyalty. Morals. Christmas. Family life. The Reds are just their front line. While we stand about here and stare at each other and do nothing, there they are working away, getting born, growing up, plotting, planning—one after another—these monsters. I ask you: Is nothing to be done?"

"Well, Chief," said Cotton-Jones, the arch-soother. "Everything has to be done. But it's got to be done in the right way. No need to tell *you* that."

"The whole world is in danger. Hideous danger."

"That's too big for stop-press news. Chief, we've got to go into conference right away. Here and now. We've got to just hold the whole thing in silence, until we've organized a plan of campaign and a general staff. You said it, Chief, yourself, years ago. 'The more urgent the crisis,' you said, 'the more danger there is in hurry.' "

"I said that?" said Lord Thunderclap.

"Yes, Sir. You said that. . . ."

It was daylight before that assembly at Castle Windrow dispersed and Lord Thunderclap was safely put to bed. His sedatives were furtively doubled. And throughout all the offices and organizations which owed him allegiance, grave and weary men plotted guardedly with each other—no double-crossing mind!—against the call for action that would come to them when he awoke.

Cotton-Jones, toiling wearily up to his suite under the roof at headquarters, realized suddenly the mysterious sensitiveness of the Thunderclap system. Two small lift attendants stopped upon the second landing to exchange news, unaware of his presence in the middle elevator. The youngest and shrillest spoke without emotion.

"Jimmy, you heard? The Chief's nuts at last."

"Clean off it?"

"Clean."

"Bound to happen sooner or later. What dislodged him?"

"Them Martians. . . ."

Now how had the little devils got hold of that? . . .

Throughout the most difficult ten days in their lives the entourage of Lord Thunderclap struggled to mitigate the impact of his full excitement upon the public. What he had in mind seemed to be some sort of world-wide witch-smelling for Martians everywhere. He swept aside every difficulty there might be in distinguishing them. You could tell them by the things they said and the way they behaved. You could tell them because *instinctively* you disliked them. . . . Not a massacre. Massacres were out of date. What was needed was a vast sanitary concentration of all these people to save our race (Lord Thunderclap) alive.

Rigamey had brought some entirely irrelevant facts about what are called Mongoloid children into the discussion, and Thunderclap seized upon them as data for the first selection of victims in this world drive against the Martians. Individuals of this type should be at once arrested and secluded in protective isolation. There ought to be a human race-purity conference set up in permanent session. All the leading obstetricians in the world ought to be in it, with stimulating fees and unlimited powers.

Like to like. It was natural for the turbid stream of Anti-Semitism to contribute some richly helpful ideas to this fresh flow of anti-Martian animosity. . . .

Cotton-Jones took his courage in both hands and withstood his master. "We can't do this," he said, with the Chief's programme in his hand.

"We can't do this? Then what on earth *are* we to do?"

"The public mind is not prepared for anything of the sort."

His lordship raged up and down the room but Cotton-Jones felled him with the deadliest, most arresting assertion than an editorial assistant can use.

"It will fall *flat*," said Cotton-Jones.

"This!?"

"It will fall *flat*."

"We can't go on with this on our own responsibility," he insisted, and Thunderclap knew that he was right. "We must have authority. We must quote. We ourselves cannot seem to be bringing this out from the office. Merely from the office. Journalistic stunt, they will say. Yes, Sir. They will say that. Newspapers may lead but they should not appear to lead. We must seem to be responding to 'publicly responsible, unquestionable appeals.' *Your* words, Chief. Someone not ourselves, someone else, must make for righteousness."

He shook the programme in his hand. He added a still more difficult assertion.

"And really—for a thing of this size—we must bring in other groups of papers."

"I have had something of that sort in mind throughout," said Thunderclap, after a stupendous pause.

He walked across the room. "Perhaps I have been precipitate. I see things too quickly."

He sat down to his desk and began to write down, strike out, and tick off names. There were one or two great physicians on the verge of advertisement; they ought to give him something. After all he had done for them. No. Damn them, they wouldn't. One or two of the more pushful young bishops were still in the toady stage, still rather anxious to prove how serviceable and friendly they could be to any lord of publicity. They surely might be called upon to denounce this diabolical threat to mankind. He sent them urgent and embarrassing communications, held them up himself on the telephone, and found them as blandly evasive as they knew how. They knew very well how. He cast about for this great public figure and then that to shoulder the new burden. Gradually, as he sought, with diminishing success, among these great instruments of public stimulation, the pressure of his own initiative dispersed itself. Fatigue supervened. Violence deferred maketh the heart grow sick. Four, five, six days passed and nothing stupendous was done. In the life of Lord Thunderclap two days are as a thousand years. The bright surface of his great disclosure was dulled by familiarity. The preparatory articles, announcements, and so forth became less and less a preparation and more and more like the wailing and booming of a receding school of ichthyosauri heard through the twilight of the past.

It came to him abruptly one night that he didn't care a damn now if nothing was done. The affair had evaporated. If nobody cared to stir a finger, the whole silly business might slide. The Martians might *eat* the world now so far as he was concerned. It would last his time—anyhow. What was the sense of being the one earnest energetic man in a world of unresponsive fools?

He called Cotton-Jones into his presence. "You've been going too strong on this Martian stuff," he said, and Cotton-Jones knew at once that the brainstorm was over. "You've made it a bit too loud and brassy. The public doesn't want to hear about them in this serious way you've been putting it. They want it guyed. What the public won't hear about can't exist really. Circulation dies down and then where are you? Ease off on it. Guy it."

"After all we have said!" reflected Cotton-Jones.

"Ease off on it. Make it kind of semi-symbolical—humorous and all that."

"I get you," said Cotton-Jones, trying not to look too glad. "I think I can manage to ease it off. Yes, it's a damned good political nickname, Chief, whatever you like to say. You've never thought of anything better   Give 'Highbrow' and 'Brain Trust' a holiday for the next ten years. Let the Reds fade out. *Martians!* People will hate them from the word Go!"

§ 4

Mr. Joseph Davis stood at the upper corner of Trafalgar Square watching the westward flow of buses below.   A number of them were carrying huge starry advertisement boards with a new inscription.   He could make out three capital M's but he had to look hard before he could read the intervening letters. They spelled out "Musical Martian Midgets."

"That's how they see it," said Mr. Davis. "H'm."

His eyes were lifted sharply by a challenging flash across the twilight blue. A sky sign took up the words in letters of raw red fire, "Musical Martian Midgets." . . .

"And all the same," whispered Mr. Davis after some moments of silent reflection, *"they are here."*

CHAPTER EIGHT

HOW THESE STAR-BEGOTTEN PEOPLE MAY PRESENTL. GET TOGETHER

§ 1

"SO your Martians are coming after all, Davis," said Dr. Holdman Stedding.

"I've given you my facts," said Mr. Davis, "a new sort of human being is appearing. Of that I am convinced. . . . I never said they were Martians."

"The name's got into the story. And after all, you know —they may be."

"Why not the star-men?" said Keppel. *"Homo sideralis?"* How would one say *Star-Begotten* as a specific adjective?"

"One name seems to be as good as another," said Davis, affecting indifference. "Until we know better what they are, why trouble about the name? Let us stick to Martians."

"The newspapers have no doubt about it. Either there are Martians, they insist, or there is nothing."

Davis shrugged his shoulders.

"On the whole I wish this hadn't leaked out to the press," said Keppel, crouching upon his arms over his mahogany and looking malignantly intelligent. "Marvellous how the press can make almost anything—unbelievable. What has the press made of it? First this Thunderclap boom. Then general derision. Then general disregard. Nothing stales so rapidly as a new popular idea. What have we now? General indifference. A few pathetic believers run about, half ashamed of themselves, and assert their faith by starting silly-looking little special periodicals and societies. I am told there are at least two pro-Martian societies in London, and three against. The people who produce that pink-covered journal called *Welcome* seem to be the chief. In America there are quite a lot of associations, I'm told, but all small. Most of them have a tendency to amalgamate with occultists and mix up Mars with Tibet. Then a new type of delusional insanity has appeared. God Almighty, it seems, is out of fashion among our lunatics. They are all Martians nowadays and most of them are Kings or Emperors of Mars. What else has come out of your great disclosure? Ourselves—we *toughs*, who knew all along just how much there was in it, and were too wise to shout."

He looked sideways at Davis from under his overhanging brow.

"You believe really—?" asked Davis.

Keppel would neither assent nor deny.

"No one would believe what we in our bones feel to be the reality. We're not quite sure—but we feel it. We're not quite definite but a reality is there. It *is* unbelievable. So why incur suspicion and contempt by talking about it? Nothing is to be done. We cannot control what is happening. We cannot avert it. Here they come. Here we are."

§ 2

"I want to talk about it," said Keppel. "I want badly to talk about it."

"I find myself thinking about it a lot," said Dr. Holdman Stedding.

"I think now of nothing else," said Davis.

It seemed to him that Keppel had got this Martian fever now almost as badly as himself. That grotesque, distorted dark face was flushed, and every gesture suggested the repression of a profound excitement. But Keppel's resolve to control the stir in his imagination and to keep things as matter-of-fact as possible was very evident.

The three men were dining at Keppel's house for the express purpose of receiving and discussing the first results of Davis's investigations.

"Let's see how far we have got," said Keppel. "Let us try to disentangle as far as we can the pure guess-fantasy of an extra-terrestrial intervention, from the established realities that Davis has been elucidating. A new sort of mind **is** coming into the world, with a new, simpler, clearer, and more powerful way of thinking. That I think is manifest. It has already got into operation individually here and there and produced a sort of disorder of innovation in human affairs. But so far these new minds haven't got together for any sort of associated living. So far. They are hardly aware of themselves, much less of each other. They are scattered about anyhow. . . . All that, I think, seems to be established? . . ."

Mr. Davis nodded assent.

"These new types have made their presence felt, as yet, chiefly through discoveries in material science and mechanical invention. At this present stage they are too scattered and isolated for novel social inventions. That sort of thing requires extensive co-operations. It is on a different plane. These new-comers are dispersed; they are not appearing in bunches; they do not even know that they are a peculiar people; each one of them has been deeply embedded, so to speak, in the circumstances of his or her own birth. From birth they have all been presented with established views of the world and compelled to adjust their social behaviour to established institutions. Many no doubt have been completely baffled by the dogmatic unreason of the normal human arrangements in which they found themselves *set*. In—what shall I say?—in human affairs, they've never had a chance so far. But in regard to *things*, mere things, bits of glass, scraps of metal, springs and balances, they have not been encumbered to the same extent. There they have been able to think freely almost from the outset. . . .

"That has been the opening phase. Nobody has ever tried to explain the immense advance in scientific knowledge in the past century and a half—but this does explain it. There has been a great outbreak of precise mechanical discovery and invention. That meant—that means—a necessary discordance in human affairs—scattered inventions everywhere, a great forward drive, a revolutionary drive in mechanical science and a relative lag in social understanding. There is an almost complete inability to make new ideas in the latter field *real*. That is a tougher proposition altogether. I think it is easy to explain why that should be so. But there is the reason why every one nowadays is contrasting our material progress with what is called—how do the bishops put it?—our ethical and social backwardness. A temporary phase."

"But a damned unpleasant one," said Dr. Holdman Sted-ding, "when the superman makes an aeroplane and the ape gets hold of it."

"Nevertheless—a *temporary* phase," continued Keppel, holding to his argument with resolute tenacity. "Because, as I say, to begin with, these Martians have been rare and scattered. But as they become more numerous—and I assume that there is no reason whatever why they should not become more and more numerous—they will necessarily become aware of one another, and get into touch with one another. Such minds, following the line of least resistance, will gravitate to scientific work. They will note and classify mental types. This must lead almost directly to self-discovery. They will observe how they resemble each other and how they differ from the wimble-wamble of the common world. They will begin to know themselves for what they are."

"A new chapter in history," said Mr. Davis, contemplating

it. "And then?"

"Let us think this out for a bit," said Keppel. "I believe a considerable amount of analysis of what is coming is possible. I think myself we can already make a rough forecast, but I shall feel much more certain about that when I have put what I have in mind before you two. If I get away with it. It does seem worth while to ask a few fairly obvious questions. What is going to be the next phase in this invasion? As these Martians multiply among us, they will, I assume, tend to crystallize out in some such way as I have indicated. They will begin to realize themselves for what they are, look for their own sort, feel their way towards a common understanding. They will emerge to social action in some fashion. . . . In what fashion?"

§ 3

"But first of all," he said, "I want to clear up a preliminary matter—of some practical importance."

He concentrated on his hands spread out on the table before him. "I'd like to put it to Davis. Here we have, he says, a new kind of mind appearing in the world, a hard, clear, insistent mind. It used to appear at uncertain intervals. Rarely. It said: 'Why not?' and it made discoveries. Now apparently it is becoming—frequent. Not abundant as yet but frequent. Well, what I want to know is, is this new kind of mind when it appears *complete?* Let me be perfectly plain about that. Certain genes making up the human mentality, we agree, have been altered in this new type. These new minds are harder, clearer, more essentially honest —yes. But are they completely detached from the old stuff or are they in many cases a sort of half-breed and all mixed up with it?

"I want to stress that half-breed idea. Are they so much human, human of the old pattern still, and so much—and only so much—clean Martians? So that one side of them is just the old system of self-regarding complexes, vanities, dear delusions—while the other side is like a crystal growing in mud? You see what I am after? It may not be true to talk as though we were dealing with human clay *vis-a-vis* with Martians. We are talking about human mud and against it we have to pit these partially liberated intelligences, still largely mixed with the old mud. All three of us have been in our various ways trying to get something like a real sense of what these new beings are. These new creatures——"

Keppel paused and looked at his hands. "They are going to be very tragic creatures. . . . In many cases. . . . What do you make of it, Davis? Of the half-breed idea?"

"I haven't seen it like that yet. You see, I have been going about trying to find certain lucid, intractable types. That was your suggestion, Doctor. I've certainly found them. I've been looking for a sort of difference. . . ."

"You haven't thought of any other aspect?"

"No. . . . I haven't looked for resemblances, so to speak, in the difference," he added after a pause. "I've been looking for uncommon humanity; not for common humanity."

"Well," Keppel went on, talking chiefly to his intelligent-looking fingers, "that half-breed idea opens up a whole new world of considerations. It banishes Thunderclap's nightmare of a lot of little active hobgoblins swarming and multiplying and desecrating our homes and everything that has made human life et cetera. In the place of that sort of thing we have to suppose an increasing number of individuals scattered about the world, who, so far at any rate, never seem to have had a suspicion that they are not just ordinary human stuff, but who find life tremendously puzzling, much more puzzling than other people do. . . . Now perhaps—it will be different. . . .

"As children, like any other children, they will have begun

by taking the world as they found it and believing everything they were told. Then as they grew up they will have found themselves mentally out of key. They will have found a disconcerting inconsistency about things in general. They will have thought at first that the abnormality was on the side of particular people about them and not on their own. They will have found themselves doubting whether their parents and teachers could possibly believe what they were saying. I think that among these Martians, that odd doubt—which many children nowadays certainly have—whether the whole world isn't some queer sort of put-up job and that it will all turn out quite differently presently—I think that streak of doubt would be an almost inevitable characteristic of them all."

"That doubt about the reality of what they are told?" considered Davis. "Children certainly have it. Even I . . ."

Keppel glanced at him for one half-instant.

"Now," said Keppel, still addressing his hands, "before I go on with these problems of what these Martians are going to do to our world, I would like to put some rather penetrating questions to myself and—both of you. You don't mind if I sort of lecture you? Or retail the obvious? I'm a professor in grain, you must remember."

Dr. Holdman Stedding made assenting gestures and Davis remained obviously attentive.

"Let us try and make this room an apartment in the palace of truth for the time being. About ourselves . . . We are sane respectable citizens in a social order that gives us a fairly good return for the services we render it. We have adjusted ourselves—and pretty comfortably—to life as we know it. . . . Well . . .

"I will ask a question and answer for myself first. Am I at ease about the validity of my mental processes? As I was when I was rising twenty? No. Since then we have had our minds washed out by a real drench of psycho-analysis. We are beginning to realize the complex system of self-deception in which we live, our wilful blindness to humiliating and restraining things, our conscious acceptance of flattering and exalting things, our tortuous subconscious or half-conscious evasions and conformities to social pressures and menaces. We take everything ready-made that we can possibly find ready-made, and there are a thousand moral issues, public issues, customary imperatives, about which—it isn't so much that we conceal our thoughts and are hypocritical, as that we *will not* think about them at all. We *will not* have thoughts to conceal. We are shifty even with ourselves. Am I overstating our subservience to the world about us?"

"I don't think so," said Dr. Holdman Stedding. "No."

Davis said nothing.

"We have been born and brought up in a social order that is now obviously a failure in quite primary respects. Our social order is bankrupt. It is not delivering the goods. It is defaulting and breaking up. War, pervading and increasing brutality, lack of any real liberty, economic mismanagement, frightful insufficiency in the midst of possible super-abundance—am I overstating the indictment?"

"No," said Dr. Holdman Stedding with a sigh. "No."

"Quite a lot of highly intelligent people seem to be persuaded that we are heading for a world-wide war-smash—a smash-up of civilization they call it, and all that. You have denounced all that as blank pessimism, Mr. Davis."

"Never mind what I have written," said Davis. "Sufficient for the present discussion—is the present discussion."

"Well, then, I may say the outlook for our world is, to put it mildly, menacing and disappointing."

Dr. Holdman Stedding put both his elbows on the table. "For any farsighted people the outlook for humanity has always been menacing."

"And not particularly now? Air warfare, germs in warfare, the entire aimlessness of the unemployed, dissolving social cohesion, the rapid disappearance of mental freedom?"

"Yes," said Dr. Holdman Stedding. "Yes. Perhaps—particularly now. For the things we value it is an exceptionally bad outlook."

"And a general effect of things going to pieces—of large lumps falling down. Subsidences. And what I find most terrifying of all—and that is where the grim outlook for these Martians of ours comes in—the increasing *ineffectiveness* of any fine, clear thinking in the world. I don't know if things have shown themselves to you in the same light, but what impresses me most about the present state of the world is the entire dominance of the violent, common mind, the base mind. It brutalizes. It brutalizes everything new and fine. Inventions. Our children. Either it expresses itself in stampeding mob action, revolutionary or reactionary—it is all the same in the long run—or else it embodies itself in some Hero—like this fellow Hitler—identifies itself with him and so achieves its vehement releases. Assertive patriotism, mass fear, and the impulse to persecute—particularly the impulse to persecute—seem to me to be more dreadfully in evidence today than ever before in human affairs. Dreadfully and hideously. That's a question in your line, Davis. A question of historical estimates. Anyhow it is glaringly in evidence.

"We three sit here—lucky ones—we've got a sort of foothold. We seem comparatively safe. We've fixed up things for ourselves apparently. We may not feel quite so secure as we might have felt in Harley Street twenty-five years ago, but still we feel pretty secure. We are part of the intellectual cream of the world. And how much, I ask you, is it our world? How far dare we go out of this room and speak our minds about the things that are happening in the world now? How far dare we go even into the back corners of our own minds—with a bright light, with ruthless questions? Even you and I, Holdman Stedding, have been extremely discreet—and we are going on being extremely discreet—about this Martian business. We have our reputations to consider. We musn't be extravagant. And so on. We are discreet even with ourselves. Do we let out what we really think about politics now, about all this bawling patriotism, about all this clammy, stale, canting religiosity, about such institutions as the monarchy? Although we live here in a free country! A free country! So we are told. No concentration camps here, no inquisition, no exile, no martyrs. No visible means of restraint—and yet we are restrained. How far is our intellectual freedom here still ours, only because, as a matter of fact, we are too discreet to exercise it? Have we intellectuals here or anywhere any influence, any voice to arrest, divert, or guide this stampeding of crowds which we call the course of history—?"

"Eh?" said Davis.

"Suppose we went out, to as public a position as possible, and said plainly what we think of human affairs today?"

"I suppose," said Dr. Holdman Stedding, "they'd begin by smashing our windows."

He reflected. "The British Broadcasting Company would probably let a leash of babbling bishops loose at you. And then your students would make trouble. Your back-bench students. . . . I'm rather in a different position. My professional gifts give me a kind of Rasputin hold on one or two exalted families."

§ 4

"I have been thinking lately," began Davis, and halted. He had the phraseological unreadiness of the habitual writer. "You spoke just now of *stale* religion," he went on. "Such a lot of things in life now are stale. Out of date. . . . I agree. . . ."

He felt his way forward with his argument. "I suppose—I suppose all the main working ideas that have held people together in communities have been getting out of date pretty rapidly in the last hundred years. Strange new influences have been at work—as we three at least are beginning to understand. But because human society is a going concern, the main working ideas have never been replaced. There never came a definite time to replace them. They have been used in new senses, made ambiguous, expanded, attenu-ated. Replacement was something too heroic altogether. But each time there was a patch-up there had to be fresh strains and fresh distortions. Old things got used for new purposes and they did not stand the wear. So that—what shall I call it?—the social ideology—the social ideology has become a terrific accumulation of old clutter which now, simply through the wear and tear of terms misused, has come to mean any-thing or nothing. And to work less and less surely and safely. . . . Do I make myself plain, Keppel?"

"You put what I think better than I could myself."

"I'm in entire agreement," said the doctor. "Go on."

Mr. Davis pushed back his plate and folded his arms on the table, after the manner of Keppel. He spoke with care. He held on carefully to his argument and both men watched him.

"And you see, there is a vast number of reasonable practical people who—the more they realize the unsoundness, the rottenness, to put it brutally, of their ideological framework—the more they are, as one says, disillusioned, the more they are terrified at what may happen if this vast complex col-lapses. . . .

"*I* have been," he added after a momentary pause.

"Practically," he amplified, "my life work so far has been

bolstering up what I thought were still sound working ideas. I begin to see clearly through my own motives—for the first time. . . ."

Keppel sat back and put his hands in his pockets. It was plain he liked what Davis had said. "Here we are," he said, "in the palace of truth. And we find ourselves in virtual agreement that this world is as it were floating on a raft of rotting ideas, no longer firmly bound together, an accumulation of once sustaining institutions, customs, moral codes, loyalties, sapping one another, all so badly decayed and eaten away that in the aggregate they no longer amount to anything much better than a vast accumulation of driftwood—floating debris.

"We all seem to be agreed on that. And now these new creatures from outside, these creatures we call Martians, are coming aboard our drifting system. With their hard, clear minds and their penetrating, unrelenting questions stinging our darkness as the stars sting the sky. Are they going to salvage us? Shall we let them even if they can? And if not what is going to happen to them and this mental raft of a world?"

§ 5

"Mental raft of a world," said Dr. Holdman Stedding, trying over the doubtful phrase. "Mental raft of a world!"

Keppel looked at his friend with an expression in his twisted dissimilar eyes, half defensive and half affectionate. "Well, isn't it?" he said.

"What's wrong with it?" said the doctor. "Don't answer me: 'Everything.' Be specific. What's wrong with the raft? What's your case, Keppel? I'd like to have it clearer."

"Well," said Keppel, and gathered his forces. "It's a half-born mind as yet. Yes—your, mine, and everybody's. Half-born like a very young foal, encumbered by the fœtal membranes it can't shake off yet. It is blundering about, half blinded and squinting. All our philosophies, the best, are no better than that. Especially——"

"Especially?"

"There is this secondary world which has worked its way into language everywhere, a sort of fold in the membrane that has established itself in a thousand metaphors, got itself most unwarrantably taken for granted by nearly everybody. Otherworldliness, the idea of a ghost world, a spirit world, side by side with actuality. It overlaps and lies beside reality, like it and yet different; a parody of it done in phantoms; a sort of fuddled overlap; a universe of imaginary emanations, the consequence of a congenital squint. Beside every man we see his spirit—which is not really there—beside the universe we imagine a Great Spirit. Whenever the mental going is a bit hard, whenever our intellectual eyes feel the glare of truth, we lose focus and slither off into Ghostland. Ghostland is half-way to dreamland, where *all* rational checks are lost. In Ghostland, that world of the spirit, you can find unlimited justifications for your impulses; unlimited evasions from rational obligation. That's my main charge against the human mind; this persistent confusing dualism. The last achievement of the human mind is to see life simply and see it whole."

("That boy at Gorpel," reflected Davis.)

"But we're getting it straighter now," said the doctor.

"We've got new influences coming in," said Davis.

"But that isn't all," said Keppel, ignoring those new influences. "There are other things wrong with the silly creature."

"Homo sapiens," whispered the doctor.

"Let's have the full indictment."

"The creature hardly ever becomes adult. Hardly any of *Homo superbus,* I suggest."

us grow up fully. Particularly do we dread and shirk complete personal responsibility—which is what being adult means. Man is the boy who won't grow up, but he grows monstrous clumsy and heavy at times all the same, a Goering monster, a Mussolini—the bouncing boys of Europe. Most of us to the very end of our lives are obsessed by infantile cravings for protection and direction, and out of these cravings come all these impulses towards slavish subjection to gods, kings, leaders, heroes, bosses, mystical personifications like the People, My Country Right or Wrong, the Church, the Party, the Masses, the Proletariat. Our imaginations hang on to some such Big Brother idea almost to the end. We will accept almost any self-abasement rather than step out of the crowd and be full-grown individuals. And like all cubs and puppies and larval things, we are full of fear. What is the Sense of Sin but the instinctive fear of an immature animal? Oh, we are doing wrong! We are going to be punished for it! We are full of fears, fears of primal curses and mystical sin, masochistic impulses to sacrifice and propitiate and kneel and crawl. It paralyses our happiest impulses. It fills our world with mean, cruel, and crazy acts.

"And what isn't purely infantile in us is at best early adolescent. Our excess of egotism! We all have it. It is a commonplace to say man is as over-sexed as a cageful of monkeys, but sex is only one manifestation of his stupendous egotism. In every respect he is insanely self-centred—beyond any biological need. No animal, not even a dog, has the acute self-consciousness, the incessant, sore, personal jealousy of a human being. Fear is linked to this—there is no clear boundary here—and so is the hoarding instinct. The love of property for its own sake comes straight out of fear. This terrified, immature thing wants to be safe, invincibly safe, and so, by the most natural transition, fear develops into the craving for possessions and the craving for power. From the escape defensive to the aggressive defensive is a step. He not only fears other beings, he hates them, he flies at them. He fights needlessly. He is cruel. He loves to conquer. He loves to persecute. . . . Man! What was it Swift said? *That such a creature should deal in pride!"*

"*Homo superbus,* eh?" said the doctor. "But listen, Keppel. Is he really so bad as all this? Just a scared, self-defensive, immature beast squinting at the world because he has never yet learned to look straight? And hopeless at that? You experimental psychologists have been cleaning up our ideas about the human mind very fast in the past thirty or forty years. Very fast. You have been making this damaging— well, this salutary—analysis of our motives and errors—our queer little ways. Yes. . . . You couldn't have said a word of this forty years ago. . . . In my profession we say a sound diagnosis is half-way to a cure. Indicting the human mind is like sending a patient to bed for treatment. Maybe the treatment begins at that."

"Well?" said Keppel.

"Isn't the time almost ripe for a new education that would clear the stuff from the creature's eyes, stiffen his backbone, teach him to think straight and grow up? Make a man of him at last?"

Davis shook his head. He spoke rather to himself than to the others. "Man is what we've got. Humanity is humanity. Starry souls are born not made."

§ 6

"In guessing about these coming people," said Keppel, "there is one thing we have to keep in mind. A hard, clear mind does not mean what we call a hard individual. What we call a hard man is a stupid man, who specializes in inflexibility to escape perplexity. But a hard, clear mind is a clear crystalline mind; it turns about like a lens, revealing and scrutinizing one aspect after another, one possibility after another, and this and that necessary correlation. But anyhow, let us do our best to imagine how this—this infiltration of intelligence is going to work. No mighty revolutionary con-spiracy—no. They will begin to say things, question things, point things out. How will people respond?"

"Dislike, certainly," said the doctor.

"At first, I think, they will encounter what one might call hostile neglect. They will be said to be indecisive and inef-fective. They will, you see, be up against the Common Fool, the Natural Man in either of his chief forms, either dispersed in mob form as the Masses, or concentrated as a Boss. But the new kind of man will be neither, as the phrase goes, leftish nor rightish. Then, to be colloquial, where the hell *are* they? They won't be available for either side in the storm of silly wars and civil wars, the new Thirty Years' War, massacres, revenges, and so on, Pro-Red, Anti-Red, into which we are plainly drifting. They won't count."

"That should give them a spell for getting together," said Dr. Holdman Stedding.

"Not perhaps for very long. People will realize that these neutral things they say, these impartial suggestions they make, have a certain intrinsic power. They will be producing not fighting ideas but working ideas. Next, especially when the Boss side of the Common Man is in the ascendant, will come an attempt to annex their prestige and abilities in the interests of partisan governments. They will be asked to label their ideas *for* the Boss or *against*. If they refuse to be annexed, and they *will* refuse to be annexed, they will be said to be purely destructive, contented with nothing; accused of critical treachery. There are bad times ahead for uncompliant sane men. They will be hated by the right and by the left with an equal intensity."

"Then how," asked Dr. Holdman Stedding, "will they ever

gain any sort of control of the world?"

"How will sanity ever gain any sort of control of the world?"

"Yes. If you think that is an identical question."

"I am not a prophet," said Keppel. "I am discussing probabilities. But given this constant seeping of clearer intelligences into our world, may not this sort of thing happen? May not all these clearer intelligences, confronted with the same world, confronted with the same problems; may they not, without any sort of political or religious organization, arrive at practically identical judgments about them—put similar values on the same things? Without much confabulation among themselves. I cling to the belief that for the human brain, properly working, there is one wisdom and not many. And if it is true, as Davis thinks, that one characteristic of this new type of mind is its resistance to crowd suggestions, crowd loyalties, instinctive mass prejudices, and mere phrases, then, without any political organization or party or movement or anything of the sort, may not these strong-minded individualists everywhere begin doing sensible things and refusing to do cruel, monstrous, and foolish things—*on their own?*

"We assume they are going to be very capable, self-reliant people, able to do all sorts of things. Quite a large proportion of the scientific, medical, mechanical, administrative positions in the world are likely therefore to fall into their hands as they spread and increase, and their ways of thinking and acting are likely to infect all sorts of subordinates, workers and so on, associated with them. Yes. You have suggested already, Doctor, that one might possibly Martianize even ordinary people by a saner education. . . .

"Well, then suppose presently you find an aviator in a bomber to whom it occurs to ask: 'Why in the name of blood and brains am I doing this cruel and idiotic task? Why don't I go off home again and drop this on those solemn homicides at G. H. Q.? And then without further hesitation suiting the action to the thought. And when he comes down, suppose one or two men on the ground agree with him and are not in the least indignant? And in fact stand by him. Even the Roman gladiators had the wit to revolt. The Christian name of the new fighting experts we are training for the air in such quantities may prove to be Spartacus.

"Suppose again you have a skilled worker doing some very delicate work upon a big gun and it comes quite clearly into his head that it will be better for the world if that gun does not shoot. Will it shoot? Or it is a chemist manufacturing explosives. That sort of thing will certainly become quite a problem as the Martians multiply. Your blustering demagogue or your blustering dictator feels ill and needs an operation, and there is either a disastrous patriotic quack who will make a mess of him anyhow, or some quiet, self-reliant, but incalculable man with knowledge and a needle or scalpel, able to kill or cure. Why should he cure?

"The dictator will glare his cheap overpowering personality at him as far as his illness permits. Much a Martian will care. He for his part will be entirely unmelodramatic. It is your world against mine, he will say, and he will do what he thinks best for the world, and keep his own counsel. Power would be with the experts already, if only they had enough lucidity to take it. And it needs such a small step forward in lucidity."

"But this is—sabotage!" said Dr. Holdman Stedding.

"The only reasonable reply to unreasonable compulsion is sabotage."

"And you hint even at assassination."

"I don't hint. *Hint* indeed! I speak plainly of assassination —if shooting mad dogs or rogue elephants is assassination.

Assassination is the legitimate assertion of personal dignity in the face of dictatorship. It is not merely a right; it is a duty. A sacred duty. A dictator is an outlaw. He has outlawed himself. He exists and he degrades you by his mere existence. He imposes filthy tasks upon you. He can conscript you. He confronts you with a choice of evils. It is surely better to kill your dictator than let him make you kill other people—directly or indirectly. You can tell him: 'You be damned' if you are strong enough; if that stops him, you can be merciful to him; but if you are not strong enough, you must kill. What else can you do? As a law-abiding man?"

"Awful," said the doctor.

"Plain common sense."

"No end of your Martians will get shot—if this is to be their line."

"They will be shot to good purpose," said Davis.

"Shooting them will do the old order no good," said Keppel. "There will always be more of these cool-brained gentlemen now. Trust those cosmic rays now they have begun. Trust the undying intelligence behind our minds. In a fools world sane men will have a bad time anyhow; but they can help wind up the world of fools even if they cannot hope to see it out. One sane man will follow another; one sane man will understand another, more and more clearly. A sort of etiquette of the sane will come into operation. They will stand by each other. In spite of bad laws, in spite of foolish authority."

"A revolution—without even a revolutionary organization?"

"No revolution. Something better than a revolution. A revolution is just a social turnover. A revolution changes nothing essential. What is a revolution really? There is an increasing disequilibrium of classes or groups, the centre of gravity shifts, the clumsy raft turns over, and a different side of the old stuff comes uppermost. That is all there is in a revolution. What I am talking about is not a revolution; it is a new kind of behaviour; it is daybreak."

"The Enlightenment," said Davis, trying a phrase.

"Which is coming," said Keppel with a sudden access of emphasis, "Martians or no Martians. . . ."

"But, my dear Keppel," said the doctor, "isn't this stuff you are talking just anarchism?"

"It would be anarchism, I suppose; it would mean 'back to chaos,' if it were not true that all sane minds released from individual motives and individual obsessions move in the same direction towards practically the same conclusions. Human minds just as much as Martians'. Rational minds don't disagree so much as people pretend. They have to follow quite definite laws. We misunderstand. We don't pause to understand. We let life hustle us along. Every tyranny in the world lives—and such systems have always lived—in a perpetual struggle against plain knowledge and illuminating discussion. We are living—let us face the facts—in a lunatic asylum crowded with patients prevented from knowledge and afraid to go sane."

He paused and pushed the cigar-boxes towards his guests.

"A world gone sane," said Davis.

"Planetary psycho-therapeutics," said the doctor. "A sane world, my masters—and then?"

CHAPTER NINE

PROFESSOR KEPPEL IS INSPIRED TO FORETELL THE END OF HUMANITY

§ 1

"I wish, Keppel," said Dr. Holdman Stedding, after a reflective pause, "I wish you would say something about the world these starry folk of yours—of ours—are likely to make here. In my way, as you know, I'm an amateur of Utopias and Future Worlds—and, God, how unpleasant they are! They come tumbling into my collection now, a score or so every year. I sometimes wish I hadn't begun it. But if these starmen of yours do gradually spread a network of sanity about the world and stop what you call the Common Fool—Demos, *Homo pseudo-sapiens* —from ravening, grabbing, and destroying—just by barring his way, refusing to implement his silly impulses, and telling him plainly not to, then—can we, even in general terms, imagine the sort of world they are likely to make of it? What *would* a world of human beings that had, as Davis has put it, *gone sane* be like?"

"Let us admit," said Keppel, "that this is attempting the most impossible of tasks. The hypothesis is that these coming supermen are strongerwitted, betterbalanced, and altogether wiser than we are. How can we begin to put our imaginations into their minds and figure out what they will think or do? If our intelligences were as tall as theirs, we should be making their world now."

"In general terms," persuaded Dr. Holdman Stedding, gently obstetric as ever. "Try."

616

"Well, perhaps, *in general terms,* we may be able to say a few things at least about what their world will **not** be. You—what do you find in all these Utopias and Visions of the Future of yours? I suppose you get the same stuff over and over again, first of all caricatures of current novelties—skyscrapers five thousand feet high, aeroplanes at two thousand miles an hour, radio receivers on your wrist-watch; secondly, discursive minor novelties along the lines of current research; thirdly, attempts to be startling in artistic matters by putting it all in an insanely unusual and extravagant *decor;* and, finally, odd little fancies about sex relations and a scornfully critical attitude towards the present time. But these people of the future are invariably represented as being—I put it mildly—prigs and damned fools. World peace is assumed, but the atmosphere of security simply makes them seem rather aimless, fattish, and out of training. They are collectively up to nothing—or they are off in a storm of collective hysteria to conquer the moon or some remote nonsense of that sort. Imaginative starvation. They have apparently made no advances whatever in subtlety, delicacy, simplicity. Rather the reverse. They never say a witty thing; they never do a charming act. The general effect is of very pink, rather absurdly dressed celluloid dolls living on tabloids in a glass lavatory. That's about true, isn't it?"

"Lamentably so," smiled the doctor. "Nobody seems able to do much better. Some of 'em try to put it over portentously. Some make faces as they do it. But whether you preach about the Future or sneer about the Future, it remains, all the same, an empty sack that won't stand up."

"Alternatively to these progressive Utopias," said Keppel, carefully not looking at Davis, "the future world relapses into the romantic stench of a not very carefully preserved past? . . . You don't believe either story of course; none of us do; but the trouble is that we have no material in our minds out of which we can build a concrete vision of things to come. How can we see or feel the future until we have made the future and are actually there? All the same——"

"Yes?"

Dr. Holdman Stedding was amused to see his friend descending into the pit in which so many a prophet had preceded him and perished.

§ 2

"If we stick to general terms. *Some* things we may be sure of. At least—so far as my intelligence goes. This new starry race into which our own is passing is going to be clearer in every way—clearer—less moved, that is, by herd influences. Apart from their natural aptitudes they will have escaped all the mis-education and mental contagion that today nobody escapes completely. They will not only be abler people in themselves but they will be better educated. They will co-operate to make the world a world of peace. About that all sane minds must think alike. They will keep the peace. That Pax Mundi will not be any sort of repressive peace. Why should it be? At a certain stage in the—in the *mental treatment* of our world, there may have to be a certain amount of fighting and killing, police hunts for would-be dictators and gangsters and so forth, but I doubt if intelligences more and more able to control the genes will need to eliminate undesirable types by force. Sanity will ride this planet with fine hands. No spurs. No sawing at the bit.

"Certainly there will be a World Pax. That is to say, except for the obstacles of Nature and the vagaries of climate, a man will be free to go anywhere he pleases and exercise the rights and duties of a citizen wherever he goes. An abundance system of economics and not a want system of pressures and exactions. Everywhere your needs will be satisfied. You will take no thought for the morrow so far as food, comfort, and dignity go. No burden of toil in that saner world, and very little work that is not pleasant and in-teresting. All that is possible even today. To suppose the world saner is to suppose such things will be brought about. One is merely expanding the word 'sanity.'

"But when it comes to visualizing the new world the diffi-culties increase. To attempt that is in fact trying to antici-pate all that will happen generation after generation in millions of brains, each one of them not only better than my own but better equipped. They will make a sort of garden of the planet. That seems reasonable. Probably they will leave some of it a wild garden. They will readjust the balance of life, which swings about nowadays with some ugly variations. Who wants to see locusts swarming over cornfields, or weed-choked rivers flooding and rotting a forest district, or a plague of brown rats, or a lagoon crawling with croco-diles, or pastures smothered acre by acre, mile by mile, under blown sand? Making a garden of the world doesn't mean bandstands, fountains, marble terraces, promenades; it doesn't even mean the abolition of danger, but does mean a firm control of old Nature in her filthier moods. And it does mean intelligence in economic life. No sane enterprise would give us ugly factories, hopeless industrial regions, intolerable noises, slag-heaps, overcrowding here and desolation there. Sanity is the antithesis of all that. It's the ape has made this mess with our machinery. Today we are still such fools that none of us can solve the complicated but surely quite finite riddle of private property and money. That beats us—just as the common cold beats us—or cancer. It tangles up on us and chokes economic life. It inflames our instinct of self-preservation to an incessant acquisitive warfare. A little matter of distributing our products and we are defeated.

"Serenity. Certitude means serenity. You may say what

you like about this world to come, but rest assured that it will be not only a richer but a more beautiful world, as various as it is today and with all the beauty of land that is intelligently loved and cared for. Green slopes under trees. Glimpses of a proud and happy river. Mountains and the clear distances of great plains. I can see it all like that. Do you realize that in this world today there is hardly such a thing as an altogether healthy full-grown tree?

"And then about the way they will live, while still sticking to general terms, we *can* say something. We can be sure of certain things. The universe is rhythm. Throughout. There is a music of the atoms as well as a music of the spheres. Every living creature is an intricately rhythmic thing. It rejoices in rhythms corresponding to the complexity of its sensibilities. These masterful people with their control over materials, over all forces of the world and over their own nervous reactions, are not going to starve their æsthetic impulses. It is impossible that they should not have music and dancing in the normal course of their lives; that they should not have vigorous and beautiful bodies and that they should not be richly and variously clad. The variations will be subtle; you will have none of the clamorous grotesqueness of a fancy-dress ball. It is ridiculous even to try and picture that sort of thing now. Their music may not be our raucous bang, bang, bump stuff, their decorations may not be many repetitions of noughts and crosses, whirls and twiddles, but trust them nevertheless for music, architecture, and decoration.

"And their social life? They are likely to be highly individualized, personally more varied, and so they are likely to find much more interest even than we do in assemblies, parties, and personal encounters. People who don't find other people exciting will go into retirement and their sort will die out. Savages like gatherings; people like them just as much today; there are no intimations of any decline in social pleasure. I suppose these inheritors of our world will be what we call lovers, with a keen appreciation of the beauties both of character and body. I suppose that, being born of women and living interdependently in a large society, they will want and find satisfactions in companionship, friendship, partnership, and caresses. Maybe they will pass through an emotional adolescence and have their storms of individual possessiveness, inflamed egotism, intense physical desire. The individual will repeat something of the romantic experiences of the race. That's still sound developmental theory; isn't it, Doctor? Why anticipate a bleak rationalism in these things? Blood that does not circulate festers; imaginations that are not stirred decay. But these people will be going through these experiences in an atmosphere of understanding and freedom, with a better morale about them, a lovelier poetry to guide them, a pervasive, penetrating contempt for ugliness, vanity, and mere mean competitiveness and self-assertion. How can we, who live in a whirl of sexual catch-as-catch-can—I score off you and you score off me—bounded on the north by what frightened people call 'purity,' on the south by the *tout nu* ballet, on the east by a fear of offspring, and on the west by a sewer of envious ridicule, how can we imagine what the sexual life of sane men and women can be like?"

"Phew!" said the doctor.

"You disagree with that description?"

"I wish I could. But you draw with a heavy line, Keppel."

"Everybody wants to love," said Davis suddenly, "and everybody makes a mess of it. Every one. Suspicion. Misunderstanding. . . ."

It was one of those sayings that leave nothing to be said.

§ 3

"You do give us," said the doctor, with the air of opening a new chapter, "some idea of these starry ladies and gentlemen, fine-living and full-living, who may inherit our earth. We don't see them directly, I admit, but when you talk, Keppel, it is as if we saw and heard the grace and colour of their brightly lit movements, dimly reflected on a distant wall. But they go about their business out of sight of us. Their business? Business today is mainly getting the better of each other and getting things away from each other. All that apparently is to end. No Wall Street, no Exchange, no City, no Turf, no Casino. What will their business be, Keppel? What will occupy them? What will they be doing? Can you say anything of that?"

"You make me feel like the sculptor's dog trying to explain his master's life to the musician's cat."

"But—in general terms."

"Yes. I think one can even say something about that. Every living organ has in it an urge to exercise, and the greatest pleasure of a living thing comes through a satisfactory use of its powers. Our successors will have incessant minds. Even we poor creatures of today use our minds and bodies in games and exercises and all sorts of rather feeble amateur-isms, as much as we can. We hate being unemployed.

"But men who are keenly interested in scientific or creative work are very little addicted to games. Your games-player is a pervert who fiddles about with his mind because he is unable to use it, good and hard, for a definable natural end. Hunting was a great game in the past; and war, when you get down to it, is only a monstrously expensive and destructive hunting. For want of better imaginations. War will go when boredom goes. . . .

"But you need not worry to find jobs for the new-comers now. These heirs of ours will have their impulses to exercise skill, to discover and impose new patterns upon life, much more powerfully developed and much more intelligently adjusted. They will be enormously interested by research and by making and controlling things. They will—it seems to me to go without saying—be much more *alive to things*. Immensely—I really *mean* immensely—amused. Research and artistic exploration are full of surprises. They will be constantly coming on unexpected things. They will be busy, laughing people. Nobody can know the extent of the unknown, but the interest we find in life is only limited by our physical and mental limitations. . . . The saner the merrier."

Keppel paused and screwed up his face. "It is curious," he said, "that what I am saying now would arouse an intense antagonism in a great number of people if they could hear me. Here tonight we three are more or less in accord, because we have been travelling the same road together. Insensibly we have trained ourselves and each other. But bringing a human mind up against the living idea of progress is like bringing a badly trained dog into a house; its first impulse is to defile the furniture.

"Stupid people are offended by anything they do not understand or cannot master. They become spiteful and want to destroy it and banish it from their thoughts. I suppose if there were no guardians and watchers in our picture galleries, there is not a masterpiece that would not be defaced maliciously within a year. And probably defaced —filthily.

"But even contemporary man is emerging from that jealousy of what he cannot subdue. I am bound to believe our heirs will always find plenty to do and that this world community will be growing in knowledge, power, beauty, interest, steadily and delightfully. They will be capable of knowledge I cannot even dream about; they will gain powers over space,

time, existence, such as we cannot conceive. Not even in
general terms. There you are. In general terms—that is
what I see before us. Like a great door beginning to open.
Sanity coming, sanity growing, broadening power, quickening
tempo, and such a great life ahead as will make the whole
course of history up 'to the present day seem like a crazy,
incredible nightmare before the dawn. That is what I believe in my bones."

§ 4

"And that greater world," said the doctor, "really exists
for you, Keppel? In such general terms as you use. But
it exists?"

"Practically."

"Away ahead—not so hopelessly far perhaps?"

"Integral to this scheme of space and time."

"One might even, in certain moods, Keppel, feel a kind
of nostalgia—?"

"One might," agreed Keppel compactly. And then: "My
God! one does."

"And that music of theirs we shall never hear, that perfect
health they will have we shall never enjoy, those enhanced
senses—they are not for us; the whole world cared for
lovingly, the very beasts subdued and trained by kindliness
and every living man and woman with an intelligible purpose
in life. That distant world. Have you *never* had a glimpse
of that sane world of yours—in anything more than general
terms? Nothing concrete with colour and substance, Keppel
—not even in a dream?"

"Yes. I do dream. I dream that I dream about it. I
confess it. Often. And when I awake it escapes me, it
vanishes. . . . Dissolves into the turbid current of present
things and is lost altogether."

For a moment Keppel spoke without restraint. "Lost altogether," he said. "Leaving not a wrack behind. . . . Well, something **is** left. A sense of life frustrated. A sense of irreparable loss. Oh! The life that might be—the life that may be—the life that will be! This life that is not for us! This life we *might* have had, instead of these mere compromises and consolations which make up life today."

"Keppel," said the doctor, "let us be plain about this— you are foretelling now the end of common humanity. No less. This would not be human life. This new world is something beyond all ordinary experience, something alien."

"Yes," said Keppel.

And then he said something that startled Davis.

"That is where **my** hate goes," he said. "I hate common humanity. This oafish crowd which tramples the ground whence my cloud-capped pinnacles might rise. I am tired of humanity—beyond measure. Take it away. This gaping, stinking, bombing, shooting, throat-slitting, cringing brawl of gawky, under-nourished riff-raff. Clear the earth of them!"

"You do not even pity poor humanity?"

"I pity it *in* myself and everywhere. But I hate it none the less. I hate it. . . ."

§ 5

Davis sat deep in thought.

"Keppel," he said abruptly. "Do you *believe* all this— about these coming people? Or are you just talking? Tell me that clearly. Are you sure the world, after a few more troubled decades, a troubled age or so at most, will go sane?"

Keppel hung fire for a moment. Then he said: *"No."*

"H'm," said Davis, and then with a flash of intuition: "But do you *disbelieve* it?"

Keppel smiled the smile of a friendly and yet mischievous

gnome. *"No,"* he repeated with equal conviction.

"And that also," said Dr. Holdman Stedding, after a moment's deliberation, "is my position."

CHAPTER TEN

MR. JOSEPH DAVIS TEARS UP A MANUSCRIPT

§ 1

ONE day in October while that table talk of Keppel's was still very vivid in the mind of Mr. Joseph Davis, G. B. Query, his Literary Agent, called to see him and discuss his prospects for the coming year. How was the great work getting on about which Davis had spoken a year ago? Was it sufficiently in shape to negotiate? What had he called it after all? *The Glorious Succession? Sword and Cross? The Undying Past? Our Mighty Heritage? Grand Parade of Humanity?*

G. B. Q. couldn't remember. G. B. Q. had heard nothing about Davis for months. He was quite out of touch.

Davis stood defiantly in front of his study fire. "I've not looked at it for half a year," he said. "I've decided at last —I'm not going to finish it. Ever. It's on the wrong lines."

"But you had done a lot of work upon it. You even let me see some passages. They seemed to me quite a splendid beginning."

"It got more and more splendid. It became like an altar screen of saints and heroes. It became like a cathedral. It became like the great grotto at Han. It became a sort of compendium of all the epics and sagas and all the patriotic history and all the romance and all the brave stuff human beings have told themselves about themselves since the very beginning of things. It took on more colour and more. It blew out like a magnificent bubble. And it burst. There's heaps of it in these drawers."

"*But—*" protested Mr. Query. "*The Pageant of Mankind.*"

627

"The bankruptcy," said Davis compactly.

"You of all people! *You're* not joining the pessimists!?"

"Have you never heard of the Martians?"

"But that I thought was just a pseudo-scientific mystification."

"It's a fact. Our world is in liquidation. We are played out. And they are coming, they are coming now, to succeed us and make a new world."

Mr. Query considered this announcement. It was not his business to measure the mental balance of his clients. Davis was not joking. He believed what he was saying, simply and entirely.

"Maybe you will write something about that?" said Mr. Query.

"I belong to the bankrupt system," said Davis, "one of the inconvertibles—one of the encumbrances. Gradually as our agreements fall in I mean all my books to go out of print."

Mr. Query opened out his hand helplessly. On the spur of the moment he could summon no argument against this immense withdrawal.

"A new world is coming," said Davis, "and I have tied myself to the old. I know better now, but there it is."

Query roused himself to say something more, but he knew the case was hopeless even while he spoke. He didn't argue now. He lamented.

"Just now," he said. "When people need encouragement. They feel so doubtful. Where they are going? What is happening? Even about the Coronation? Perplexing issues everywhere. Armament? After the Peace Ballot! America too. Profoundly unsettled. And now *you* too! Your book would have been a great success—a heartening success. A certainty. It would have sold like hot cakes. Even H. V. Morton would have had to look to his laurels. . . ."

He stood up. He shrugged his shoulders helplessly. "It is a very great pity."

§ 2

Davis showed his visitor out and returned to his study. For a time he stood on his hearth-rug staring at nothing. Then with a certain deliberation he unlocked various drawers and took out a number of folders. He arranged these carefully on his writing-desk and contemplated the accumulation. He opened one or two and read passages. He grimaced, pushed his chair back a foot or so, turned aside from his work, and fell into a profound meditation.

The great book was dead.

It was stillborn—an abortion. He would never publish any of it.

"And I wrote that stuff," he reflected. "I *wrote* that. Only a few months ago. . . .

"I've done with it."

He repeated Query's words aloud. He mimicked his manner. "It would have sold like hot cakes. . . . A great success. A certainty. . . ."

He discovered a new streak in his own composition. What was it in him that had turned now against successfulness? he asked himself. What was it in him that was making him thrust himself contrariwise to his own reasonable disposition to go with the swim? What had divided him against himself? He realized quite vividly that people were eager beyond measure to be told that all was right with the world. Never had the market for reassurance, for brave optimism, been so promising as in these frightened years. It was true as Query had said that the piled MSS before him represented a sure success. His phrase-making mind struck out: "I've done with lullabies. Let them wake up as I am doing. . . .

"Wake up to what?" he asked and started another train

of thought.

Suddenly he felt very small and feeble and lonely, and it seemed to him that his universe, his immense bare modern universe, said to him: *"Well?"*

He felt that for a moment he must leave that challenge unanswered. A desire to go to his wife and talk to her arose in him.

He found her waiting to give him his tea. She smiled a silent welcome. "So you saw Query?" she said.

"I told him the great book was off."

"I thought you might do that."

"I haven't touched it for ages."

"I know."

He sat down on the sofa and found there a book she had put down on his entry. He picked up the slender volume. It was one of his earliest successes in the heroic style, *Alexander, or Youth the Conqueror.*

"You don't often read me, Mary," he said.

"I've been reading a lot of you lately."

"Why?"

"Because—I'm no good at talking, dear, and I want more and more to understand you."

"Latterly I've been trying to understand myself."

"I know that," she said, and poured out his tea.

He turned over the pages of the book. "I wonder what you make of this. . . .

"If you were a properly cultivated woman, Mary, instead of being a wild, natural, poetic thing out of Lewis and Glasgow, you'd reel off a yard of trite criticism straightaway. But you, being you, sit there, too wise to chatter. Because for you, you of all people, it would be an incredibly difficult thing to say, truly and gently, what you think of me. But that book puzzles you. Well, it puzzles me too now. . . .

"Mary, I want to talk to you. I'm frightfully troubled—

in my mind."

"I've known that. I know. It is something about these Martians. I don't understand. But I feel it there."

"Tremendous things, Mary, are happening to the world— incredible things. It is time I said something. These so-called Martians—you have seen foolish and inexact things in the papers. You do not realize how close it comes to us, how nearly it touches us. It means something new in the world, a dreadful and terrifying newness. The world is being born again, Mary. And strangely. . . . I cannot tell you everything. But I have been drifting all my life, and all the time I have drifted, this tremendous thing I speak of has been happening to the world. The world has swung round with a sort of smooth swiftness into a new course. How can I tell you? I was deaf and blind. . . . Now I see. . . ."

He felt his great explanation was impossible, for the present at any rate.

"I want to rest for a time. I want to think."

"I have known your work was worrying you," she said. "Dear, I've known that. I have felt you wanted a rest. . . . Whatever I can do to help you . . ."

"Bear with me," he whispered and felt he could tell no more.

"I must rest, dear," he repeated. "I must think things over. I must get things clearer in my head. I must make new plans."

§ 3

He walked to the door of his study and she followed him. He stared at the files of the abandoned opus and with her at his side went across the landing to the nursery.

He surveyed his sleeping son for a while and then let his eyes wander about the neat, bright room.

"That's a fine big rubbish basket," he said abruptly.

She thought that a queer thing for him to say.

"It's a good basket to bundle things into when they get too much in the way," she admitted. "I bought it yesterday."

"It's a great basket," he agreed and seemed to forget about it.

He returned to his study and sat down there among the piled manuscripts. Mary after a thoughtful moment went downstairs. When she came upstairs again she went to look at him in his study but she found he had gone back to the nursery. There she discovered him seated in the nurse's arm-chair with that fine big rubbish basket he had admired before his knees. On a chair at his side was a large pile of manu-script and this he was taking twenty or thirty sheets at a time and tearing, tearing into little fragments. He was facing the cot. It was as if he was tearing the paper at the sleeping child.

"What are you doing?" she asked.

"Tearing it up. Tearing it all up."

"The Pageant of Mankind?"

"Yes."

"But there was such good writing in it."

"No matter. Nothing to the writing that will come."

He pointed to his son. "He will do better," he said. "He will do better. I'm tearing up the past to make way for him. Him and *his* kind—in their turn."

"No one can tear up the past," she said.

"You can tear up every lie that has ever been told about it. And mostly we have lied about it. Mythology, fantasy, elaborated misconceptions. Some of the truth is coming out now. But it is only beginning to be told. Let the new race begin clean."

"The new race?" she questioned.

He went on tearing and thinking while he tore.

Should he tell her what he knew she was? Should he tell her what their child was? No. The creatures must find themselves out in their own time. They must realize in their own fashion the reason for their instinctive detachment from this old played-out world. Maybe she was on the verge of that awakening. But it must come by degrees.

He glanced up for a moment and then averted his eyes from her grave scrutiny. He took up another handful of sheets and began to tear them.

"Every generation," he quibbled, "is a new race. Every generation begins again."

"But *every one,*" she said, "is always beginning."

"No. It has taken me half a lifetime to free even myself —even to begin to free myself—from religious falsehoods and from historical lies and from tradition and a slavish carrying on with the patterns of past things. Even now am I sure that I am free?"

"But you have begun!"

"I doubt," he said, "whether I and my sort are made for fresh beginnings."

"But what else are you made for?" she asked. "You of all people! Look even at this that you are doing and saying now!"

And then she did a wonderful thing for him. She could have done nothing better. She came across the room to him and bent down over him and brought her face very close to his. "If I could help you . . ." she whispered.

"You see, dear," she said, in a low, hurried voice, with both hands on his shoulders, "I know you are terribly troubled in your mind—bothered with new ideas that crowd and crowd upon one another. I know you are worried—even about these Martians in the papers. I know that. I wish I understood better. I'm slow. I don't keep pace with you. If I could—! If only I could! I feel very often I don't get what

you are driving at until it is too late. I make some flat reply.
And then you are hurt. Darling, you are so easily hurt.
That imagination of yours dances about like quicksilver.
Sometimes I think—you seem hardly to belong to this
world. . . ."

She had a freakish idea.

"*Is it that?*" she said.

She moved round to look him in the face. Joe! Joe,
dear! Tell me. . . ."

Would the jest offend him? No. She stood away from
him and put out a finger at him. "Joe! *You* aren't by any
chance a sort of fairy changeling? Not—not one of these
Martians?"

He stopped tearing the scraps of paper in his hand. A
sort of fairy changeling? Not one of these Martians? He
stared at this new, this tremendous idea, for a time. "*Me!*"
he said at last. "*You think that of me!*"

The miracle happened in an instant.

A great light seemed to irradiate and in a moment to
tranquillize the troubled ocean of his disordered mind. The
final phase of his mental pacification was very swift indeed.
At a stroke everything became coherent and plain to him.
Everything fell into place. He had, he realized, completed
his great disclosure with this culminating discovery. His
mind swung round full compass and clicked into place. He
too was starborn! He too was one of these invaders and
strangers and innovators to our fantastic planet, who were
crowding into life and making it over anew! Throwing the
torn scraps into a basket and beginning again in the nursery.
Fantastic how long it had taken him to realize this!

"*Of course!*" he whispered.

His mind had gone all round the world indeed, but only
to discover himself and his home again in a new orientation.
He stood up abruptly, stared at Mary as though he had that

moment realized her existence, and then slowly and silently took her in his arms and put his cheek to hers.

"You were star-begotten," he said, "and so was I."

She nodded agreement. If he wished it, so be it.

"Starry changelings both," he said presently. "And not afraid—even of the uttermost change."

"Why should one fear change?" she asked, trying hard to follow these flickering thoughts of his. "Why should one be afraid of change? All life is change. Why should we fear it?"

The child lay on its side in its cot in a dreamless sleep. It scarcely seemed to breathe. The expression of that flushed little face with its closed eyes was one of veiled determination. One small clenched fist peeped over the coverlet. Afraid of change? Afraid of the renascence to come?

Never, he thought, had anything in the world looked so calmly and steadfastly resolved to assert its right to think and act in its own way in its own time.

UNDER THE KNIFE

"WHAT if I die under it?" The thought recurred again and again as I walked home from Haddon's. It was a purely personal question. I was spared the deep anxieties of a married man, and I knew there were few of my intimate friends but would find my death troublesome chiefly on account of their duty of regret. I was surprised indeed and perhaps a little humiliated, as I turned the matter over, to think how few could possibly exceed the conventional requirement. Things came before me stripped of glamour, in a clear dry light, during that walk from Haddon's house over Primrose Hill. There were the friends of my youth; I perceived now that our affection was a tradition which we foregathered rather laboriously to maintain. There were the rivals and helpers of my later career: I suppose I had been cold-blooded or undemonstrative—one perhaps implies the other. It may be that even the capacity for friendship is a question of physique. There had been a time in my own life when I had grieved bitterly enough at the loss of a friend; but as I walked home that afternoon the emotional side of my imagination was dormant. I could not pity myself, nor feel sorry for my friends, nor conceive of them as grieving for me.

I was interested in this deadness of my emotional nature—no doubt a concomitant of my stagnating physiology; and my thoughts wandered off along the line it suggested. Once before, in my hot youth, I had suffered a sudden loss of blood and had been within an ace of death. I remembered now that my affections as well as my passions had drained out of me, leaving scarcely anything but a tranquil resignation, a dreg of self-pity. It had been weeks before the old ambitions, and tendernesses, and all the complex moral interplay of a man, had reasserted themselves. Now again I was bloodless; I had been feeding down for a week or more. I was not even hungry. It occurred to me that the real meaning of this numbness might be a gradual slipping away from the pleasure-pain guidance of the animal man. It has been proven, I take it, as thoroughly as anything can be proven in this world, that the higher emotions, the moral feelings, even the subtle tendernesses of love, are evolved from the elemental desires and fears of the simple animal: they are the harness in which man's mental freedom goes. And it may be that, as death overshadows us, as our possibility of acting diminishes, this complex growth of balanced impulse, propensity, and aversion whose interplay inspires our acts, goes with it. Leaving what?

I was suddenly brought back to reality by an imminent collision with a butcher-boy's tray. I found that I was crossing the bridge over the Regent's Park Canal which runs parallel with that in the Zoölogical Gardens. The boy in blue had been looking over his shoulder at a black barge advancing slowly, towed by a gaunt white horse. In the Gardens a nurse was leading three happy little children over the bridge. The trees were bright green; the spring hopefulness was still unstained by the dusts of summer; the sky in the water was bright and clear, but broken by long waves, by quivering bands of black, as the barge drove through. The breeze was stirring; but it did not stir me as the spring breeze used to do.

Was this dulness of feeling in itself an anticipation? It was curious that I could reason and follow out a network of suggestion as clearly as ever: so, at least, it seemed to me. It was calmness rather than dulness that was coming upon me. Was there any ground for the belief in the presentiment of death? Did a man near to death begin instinctively to withdraw himself from the meshes of matter and sense, even before the cold hand was laid upon his? I felt strangely isolated—isolated without regret—from the life and existence about me. The children playing in the sun and gathering strength and experience for the business of life, the park-keeper gossiping with a nursemaid, the nursing mother, the young couple intent upon each other as they passed me, the trees by the wayside spreading new pleading leaves to the sunlight, the stir in their branches—I had been part of it all, but I had nearly done with it now.

Some way down the Broad Walk I perceived that I was tired, and that my feet were heavy. It was hot that afternoon, and I turned aside and sat down on one of the green chairs that line the way. In a minute I had dozed into a dream, and the tide of my thoughts washed up a vision of the resurrection. I was still sitting in the chair, but I thought myself actually dead, withered, tattered, dried, one eye (I saw) pecked out by birds. "Awake!" cried a voice; and incontinently the dust of the path and the mould under the grass became insurgent. I had never before thought of Regent's Park as a cemetery, but now through the trees, stretching as far as eye could see, I beheld a flat plain of writhing graves and heeling tombstones. There seemed to be some trouble: the rising dead appeared to stifle as they struggled upward, they bled in their struggles, the red flesh was tattered away from the white bones. "Awake!" cried a voice; but I determined I would not rise to such horrors. "Awake!" They would not let me alone. "Wike up!" said an angry voice. A cockney angel! The man who sells the tickets was shaking me, demanding my penny.

I paid my penny, pocketed my ticket, yawned, stretched my legs, and, feeling now rather less torpid, got up and walked on towards Langham Place. I speedily lost myself again in a shifting maze of thoughts about death. Going across Marylebone Road into that crescent at the end of Langham Place, I had the narrowest escape from the shaft of a cab, and went on my way with a palpitating heart and a bruised shoulder. It struck me that it would have been curious if my meditations on my death on the morrow had led to my death that day.

But I will not weary you with more of my experiences that day and the next. I knew more and more certainly that I should die under the operation; at times I think I was inclined to pose to myself. At home I found everything prepared; my room cleared of needless objects and hung with white sheets; a nurse installed and already at loggerheads with my housekeeper. They wanted me to go to bed early, and after a little resistance I obeyed.

In the morning I was very indolent, and though I read my newspapers and the letters that came by the first post, I did not find them very interesting. There was a friendly note from Addison, my old school friend, calling my attention to two discrepancies and a printer's error in my new book, with one from Langridge venting some vexation over Minton. The rest were business communications. I had a cup of tea but nothing to eat. The glow of pain at my side seemed more massive. I knew it was pain, and yet, if you can understand, I did not find it very painful. I had been awake and hot and thirsty in the night, but in the morning bed felt comfortable. In the night-time I had lain thinking of things that were past; in the morning I dozed over the question of immortality. Haddon came, punctual to the minute, with a neat black bag; and Mowbray soon followed. Their arrival stirred me up a little. I began to take a more personal interest in the proceedings. Haddon moved the little octagonal table close to the bedside, and, with his broad black back to me, began taking things out of his bag. I heard the light click of steel upon steel. My imagination, I found, was not altogether stagnant. "Will you hurt me much?" I said in an off-hand tone.

"Not a bit," Haddon answered over his shoulder. "We shall chloroform you. Your heart's as sound as a bell." And as he spoke I had a whiff of the pungent sweetness of the anæsthetic.

They stretched me out, with a convenient exposure of my side, and, almost before I realised what was happening, the chloroform was being administered. It stings the nostrils, and there is a suffocating sensation, at first. I knew I should die—that this was the end of consciousness for me. And suddenly I felt that I was not prepared for death: I had a vague sense of a duty overlooked—I knew not what. What was it I had not done? I could think of nothing more to do, nothing desirable left in life; and yet I had the strangest disinclination for death. And the physical sensation was painfully oppressive. Of course the doctors did not know they were going to kill me. Possibly I struggled. Then I fell motionless, and a great silence, a monstrous silence, and an impenetrable blackness came upon me.

There must have been an interval of absolute unconsciousness, seconds or minutes. Then, with a chilly, unemotional clearness, I perceived that I was not yet dead. I was still in my body; but all the multitudinous sensations that come sweeping from it to make up the background of consciousness had gone, leaving me free of it all. No, not free of it all; for as yet something still held me to the poor stark flesh upon the bed—held me, yet not so closely that I did not feel myself external to it, independent of it, straining away from it. I do not think I saw, I do not think I heard; but I perceived all that was going on, and it was as if I both heard and saw. Haddon was bending over me, Mowbray behind me; the scalpel—it was a large scalpel—was cutting my flesh at the side under the flying ribs. It was interesting to see myself cut like cheese, without a pang, without even a qualm. The interest was much of a quality with that one might feel in a game of chess between strangers. Haddon's face was firm and his hand steady; but I was surprised to perceive (*how* I know not) that he was feeling the gravest doubt as to his own wisdom in the conduct of the operation.

Mowbray's thoughts, too, I could see. He was thinking that Haddon's manner showed too much of the specialist. New suggestions came up like bubbles through a stream of frothing meditation; and burst one after another in the little bright spot of his consciousness. He could not help noticing and admiring Haddon's swift dexterity, in spite of his envious quality and his disposition to detract. I saw my liver exposed. I was puzzled at my own condition. I did not feel that I was dead, but I was different in some way from my living self. The grey depression that had weighed on me for a year or more and coloured all my thoughts, was gone. I perceived and thought without any emotional tint at all. I wondered if everyone perceived things in this way under chloroform, and forgot it again when he came out of it. It would be inconvenient to look into some heads, and not forget.

Although I did not think that I was dead, I still perceived quite clearly that I was soon to die. This brought me back to the consideration of Haddon's proceedings. I looked into his mind, and saw that he was afraid of cutting a branch of the portal vein. My attention was distracted from details by the curious changes going on in his mind. His consciousness was like the quivering little spot of light which is thrown by the mirror of a galvanometer. His thoughts ran under it like a stream, some through the focus bright and distinct, some shadowy in the half-light of the edge. Just now the little glow was steady; but the least movement on Mowbray's part, the slightest sound from outside, even a faint difference in the slow movement of the living flesh he was cutting, set the light-spot shivering and spinning. A new sense-impression came rushing up through the flow of thoughts, and lo! the light-spot jerked away towards it, swifter than a frightened fish. It was wonderful to think that upon that unstable, fitful thing depended all the complex motions of the man; that for the next five minutes, therefore, my life hung upon its movements. And he was growing more and more nervous in his work. It was as if a little picture of a cut vein grew brighter, and struggled to oust from his brain another picture of a cut falling short of the mark. He was afraid: his dread of cutting too little was battling with his dread of cutting too far.

Then, suddenly, like an escape of water from under a lock-gate, a great uprush of horrible realisation set all his thoughts swirling, and simultaneously I perceived that the vein was cut. He started back with a hoarse exclamation, and I saw the brown-purple blood gather in a swift bead, and run trickling. He was horrified. He pitched the red stained scalpel on to the octagonal table; and instantly both doctors flung themselves upon me, making hasty and ill-conceived efforts to remedy the disaster. "Ice!" said Mowbray, gasping. But I knew that I was killed, though my body still clung to me.

I will not describe their belated endeavours to save me, though I perceived every detail. My perceptions were sharper and swifter than they had ever been in life; my thoughts rushed through my mind with incredible swiftness, but with perfect definition. I can only compare their crowded clarity to the effects of a reasonable dose of opium. In a moment it would all be over, and I should be free. I knew I was immortal, but what would happen I did not know. Should I drift off presently, like a puff of smoke from a gun, in some kind of half-material body, an attenuated version of my material self? Should I find myself suddenly among the innumerable hosts of the dead, and know the world about me for the phantasmagoria it had always seemed? Should I drift to some spiritualistic *séance*, and there make foolish, incomprehensible attempts to affect a purblind medium? It was a state of unemotional curiosity, of colourless expectation. And then I realised a growing stress upon me, a feeling as though some huge human magnet was drawing me upward out of my body. The stress grew and grew. I seemed an atom for which monstrous forces were fighting. For one brief, terrible. moment sensation came back to me. That feeling of falling headlong which comes in nightmares, that feeling a thousand times intensified, that and a black horror swept across my thoughts in a torrent. Then the two doctors, the naked body with its cut side, the little room, swept away from under me and vanished as a speck of foam vanishes down an eddy.

I was in mid-air. Far below was the West End of London, receding rapidly,—for I seemed to be flying swiftly upward, —and, as it receded, passing westward, like a panorama. I could see, through the faint haze of smoke, the innumerable roofs chimney-set, the narrow roadways stippled with people and conveyances, the little specks of squares, and the church steeples like thorns sticking out of the fabric. But it spun away as the earth rotated on its axis, and in a few seconds (as it seemed) I was over the scattered clumps of town about Ealing, the little Thames a thread of blue to the south, and the Chiltern Hills and the North Downs coming up like the rim of a basin, far away and faint with haze. Up I rushed. And at first I had not the faintest conception what this headlong rush upward could mean.

Every moment the circle of scenery beneath me grew wider and wider, and the details of town and field, of hill and valley, got more and more hazy and pale and indistinct, a luminous grey was mingled more and more with the blue of the hills and the green of the open meadows; and a little patch of cloud, low and far to the west, shone ever more dazzlingly white. Above, as the veil of atmosphere between myself and outer space grew thinner, the sky, which had been a fair springtime blue at first, grew deeper and richer in colour, passing steadily through the intervening shades until presently it was as dark as the blue sky of midnight, and presently as black as the blackness of a frosty starlight, and at last as black as no blackness I had ever beheld. And first one star and then many, and at last an innumerable host broke out upon the sky: more stars than anyone has ever seen from the face of the earth. For the blueness of the sky is the light of the sun and stars sifted and spread abroad blindingly: there is diffused light even in the darkest skies of winter, and we do not see the stars by day only because of the dazzling irradiation of the sun. But now I saw things —I know not how; assuredly with no mortal eyes—and that defect of bedazzlement blinded me no longer. The sun was incredibly strange and wonderful. The body of it was a disc of blinding white light: not yellowish as it seems to those who live upon the earth, but livid white, all streaked with scarlet streaks and rimmed about with a fringe of writhing tongues of red fire. And, shooting halfway across the heavens from either side of it, and brighter than the Milky Way, were two pinions of silver-white, making it look more like those winged globes I have seen in Egyptian sculpture than anything else I can remember upon earth. These I knew for the solar corona, though I had never seen anything of it but a picture during the days of my earthly life.

When my attention came back to the earth again, I saw that it had fallen very far away from me. Field and town were long since indistinguishable, and all the varied hues of the country were merging into a uniform bright grey, broken only by the brilliant white of the clouds that lay scattered in flocculent masses over Ireland and the west of England. For now I could see the outlines of the north of France and Ireland, and all this island of Britain save where Scotland passed over the horizon to the north, or where the coast was blurred or obliterated by cloud. The sea was a dull grey, and darker than the land; and the whole panorama was rotating slowly towards the east.

All this had happened so swiftly that, until I was some thousand miles or so from the earth, I had no thought for myself. But now I perceived I had neither hands nor feet, neither parts nor organs, and that I felt neither alarm nor pain. All about me I perceived that the vacancy (for I had already left the air behind) was cold beyond the imagination of man; but it troubled me not. The sun's rays shot through the void, powerless to light or heat until they should strike on matter in their course. I saw things with a serene self-forgetfulness, even as if I were God. And down below there, rushing away from me,—countless miles in a second,—where a little dark spot on the grey marked the position of London, two doctors were struggling to restore life to the poor hacked and outworn shell I had abandoned. I felt then such release, such serenity as I can compare to no mortal delight I have ever known.

It was only after I had perceived all these things that the meaning of that headlong rush of the earth grew into comprehension. Yet it was so simple, so obvious, that I was amazed at my never anticipating the thing that was happening to me. I had suddenly been cut adrift from matter: all that was material of me was there upon earth, whirling away through space, held to the earth by gravitation, partaking of the earth's inertia, moving in its wreath of epicycles round the sun, and with the sun and the planets on their vast march through space. But the immaterial has no inertia, feels nothing of the pull of matter for matter: where it parts from its garments of flesh, there it remains (so far as space concerns it any longer) immovable in space. *I* was not leaving the earth: the earth was leaving *me*, and not only the earth, but the whole solar system was streaming past. And about me in space, invisible to me, scattered in the wake of the earth upon its journey, there must be an innumerable multitude of souls, stripped like myself of the material, stripped like myself of the passions of the individual and the generous emotions of the gregarious brute, naked intelligences, things of newborn wonder and thought, marvelling at the strange release that had suddenly come on them!

As I receded faster and faster from the strange white sun in the black heavens, and from the broad and shining earth upon which my being had begun, I seemed to grow, in some incredible manner, vast: vast as regards this world I had left, vast as regards the moments and periods of a human life. Very soon I saw the full circle of the earth, slightly gibbous, like the moon when she nears her full, but very large; and the silvery shape of America was now in the noonday blaze wherein (as it seemed) little England had been basking but minutes ago. At first the earth was large and shone in the heavens, filling a great part of them; but every moment she grew smaller and more distant. As she shrank, the broad moon in its third quarter crept into view over the rim of her disc. I looked for the constellations. Only that part of Aries directly behind the sun, and the Lion, which the earth covered, were hidden. I recognised the tortuous, tattered band of the Milky Way, with Vega very bright between sun and earth; and Sirius and Orion shone splendid against the unfathomable blackness in the opposite quarter of the heavens. The Pole Star was overhead, and the Great Bear hung over the circle of the earth. And away beneath and beyond the shining corona of the sun were strange groupings of stars I had never seen in my life—notably, a dagger-shaped group that I knew for the Southern Cross. All these were no larger than when they had shone on earth; but the little stars that one scarcely sees shone now against the setting of black vacancy as brightly as the first-magnitudes had done, while the larger worlds were points of indescribable glory and colour. Aldebaran was a spot of blood-red fire, and Sirius condensed to one point the light of a world of sapphires. And they shone steadily: they did not scintillate, they were calmly glorious.

My impressions had an adamantine hardness and brightness: there was no blurring softness, no atmosphere, nothing
but infinite darkness set with the myriads of these acute and
brilliant points and specks of light. Presently, when I looked
again, the little earth seemed no bigger than the sun, and it
dwindled and turned as I looked until, in a second's space
(as it seemed to me), it was halved; and so it went on swiftly
dwindling. Far away in the opposite direction, a little pinkish pin's head of light, shining steadily, was the planet Mars.
I swam motionless in vacancy, and, without a trace of terror
or astonishment, watched the speck of cosmic dust we call
the world fall away from me.

Presently it dawned upon me that my sense of duration
had changed: that my mind was moving not faster but infinitely slower, that between each separate impression there
was a period of many days. The moon spun once round the
earth as I noted this; and I perceived clearly the motion of
Mars in his orbit. Moreover, it appeared as if the time between thought and thought grew steadily greater, until at
last, a thousand years was but a moment in my perception.

At first the constellations had shone motionless against the
black background of infinite space; but presently it seemed as
though the group of stars about Hercules and the Scorpion
was contracting, while Orion and Aldebaran and their neighbours were scattering apart. Flashing suddenly out of the
darkness there came a flying multitude of particles of rock,
glittering like dust specks in a sunbeam, and encompassed
in a faintly luminous haze. They swirled all about me, and
vanished again in a twinkling far behind. And then I saw that
a bright spot of light, that shone a little to one side of my
path, was growing very rapidly larger, and perceived that it
was the planet Saturn rushing towards me. Larger and larger
it grew, swallowing up the heavens behind it, and hiding
every moment a fresh multitude of stars. I perceived its
flattened, whirling body, its disc-like belt, and seven of its
little satellites. It grew and grew, till it towered enormous;
and then I plunged amid a streaming multitude of clashing
stones and dancing dust-particles and gas-eddies, and saw

for a moment the mighty triple belt like three concentric arches of moonlight above me, its shadow black on the boiling tumult below. These things happened in one-tenth of the time it takes to tell of them. The planet went by like a flash of lightning; for a few seconds it blotted out the sun, and there and then became a mere black, dwindling, winged patch against the light. The earth, the mother mote of my being, I could no longer see.

So with a stately swiftness, in the profoundest silence, the solar system fell from me, as it had been a garment, until the sun was a mere star amid the multitude of stars, with its eddy of planet-specks, lost in the confused glittering of the remoter light. I was no longer a denizen of the solar system: I had come to the Outer Universe, I seemed to grasp and comprehend the whole world of matter. Ever more swiftly the stars closed in about the spot where Antares and Vega had vanished in a luminous haze, until that part of the sky had the semblance of a whirling mass of nebulæ, and ever before me yawned vaster gaps of vacant blackness and the stars shone fewer and fewer. It seemed as if I moved towards a point between Orion's belt and sword: and the void about that region opened vaster and vaster every second, an incredible gulf of nothingness, into which I was falling. Faster and ever faster the universe rushed by, a hurry of whirling motes at last, speeding silently into the void. Stars glowing brighter and brighter, with their circling planets catching the light in a ghostly fashion as I neared them, shone out and vanished again into inexistence; faint comets, clusters of meteorites, winking specks of matter, eddying light-points, whizzed past, some perhaps a hundred millions of miles or so from me at most, few nearer, travelling with unimaginable rapidity, shooting constellations, momentary darts of fire, through that black, enormous night. More than anything else it was like a dusty draught, sunbeam-lit. Broader, and wider, and deeper grew the starless space, the vacant Beyond, into which I was being drawn. At last a quarter of the heavens was black and blank, and the whole headlong rush of stellar universe closed in behind me like a veil of light that is gathered together. It drove away from me like a monstrous jack-o'-lantern driven by the wind. I had come out into the wilderness of space. Ever the vacant blackness grew broader, until the hosts of the stars seemed only like a swarm of fiery specks hurrying away from me, inconceivably remote, and the darkness, the nothingness and emptiness, was about me on every side. Soon the little universe of matter, the cage of points in which I had begun to be, was dwindling, now to a whirling disc of luminous glittering, and now to one minute disc of hazy light. In a little while it would shrink to a point, and at last would vanish altogether.

Suddenly feeling came back to me—feeling in the shape of overwhelming terror: such a dread of those dark vastitudes as no words can describe, a passionate resurgence of sympathy and social desire. Were there other souls, invisible to me as I to them, about me in the blackness? or was I indeed, even as I felt, alone? Had I passed out of being into something that was neither being nor not-being? The covering of the body, the covering of matter, had been torn from me, and the hallucinations of companionship and security. Everything was black and silent. I had ceased to be. I was nothing. There was nothing, save only that infinitesimal dot of light that dwindled in the gulf. I strained myself to hear and see, and for a while there was naught but infinite silence, intolerable darkness, horror, and despair.

Then I saw that about the spot of light into which the whole world of matter had shrunk there was a faint glow. And in a band on either side of that the darkness was not absolute. I watched it for ages, as it seemed to me, and through the long waiting the haze grew imperceptibly more distinct. And then about the band appeared an irregular cloud of the faintest, palest brown. I felt a passionate impatience; but the things grew brighter so slowly that they scarcely seemed to change. What was unfolding itself? What was this strange reddish dawn in the interminable night of space?

The cloud's shape was grotesque. It seemed to be looped along its lower side into four projecting masses, and, above,

it ended in a straight line. What phantom was it? I felt assured I had seen that figure before; but I could not think
what, nor where, nor when it was. Then the realisation rushed
upon me. *It was a clenched Hand.* I was alone in space, alone
with this huge, shadowy Hand, upon which the whole Universe of Matter lay like an unconsidered speck of dust. It
seemed as though I watched it through vast periods of time.
On the forefinger glittered a ring; and the universe from which
I had come was but a spot of light upon the ring's curvature.
And the thing that the hand gripped had the likeness of a
black rod. Through a long eternity I watched this Hand, with
the ring and the rod, marvelling and fearing and waiting
helplessly on what might follow. It seemed as though nothing
could follow: that I should watch for ever, seeing only the
Hand and the thing it held, and understanding nothing of
its import. Was the whole universe but a refracting speck
upon some greater Being? Were our worlds but the atoms of
another universe, and those again of another, and so on
through an endless progression? And what was I? Was I indeed immaterial? A vague persuasion of a body gathering
about me came into my suspense. The abysmal darkness
about the Hand filled with impalpable suggestions, with
uncertain, fluctuating shapes.

Came a sound, like the sound of a tolling bell; faint, as if
infinitely far, muffled as though heard through thick swath-
ings of darkness: a deep, vibrating resonance, with vast gulfs
of silence between each stroke. And the Hand appeared to
tighten on the rod. And I saw far above the Hand, towards
the apex of the darkness, a circle of dim phosphorescence, a
ghostly sphere whence these sounds came throbbing; and at
the last stroke the Hand vanished, for the hour had come,
and I heard a noise of many waters. But the black rod remained as a great band across the sky. And then a voice,
which seemed to run to the uttermost parts of space, spoke,
saying, "There will be no more pain."

At that an almost intolerable gladness and radiance rushed
upon me, and I saw the circle shining white and bright, and
the rod black and shining, and many things else distinct and

clear. And the circle was the face of the clock, and the rod the rail of my bed. Haddon was standing at the foot, against the rail, with a small pair of scissors on his fingers; and the hands of my clock on the mantel over his shoulder were clasped together over the hour of twelve. Mowbray was washing something in a basin at the octagonal table, and at my side I felt a subdued feeling that could scarce be spoken of as pain.

The operation had not killed me. And I perceived, suddenly, that the dull melancholy of half a year was lifted from my mind.

THE SEA RAIDERS

UNTIL the extraordinary affair at Sidmouth, the peculiar species *Haploteuthis ferox* was known to science only generically, on the strength of a half-digested tentacle obtained near the Azores, and a decaying body pecked by birds and nibbled by fish, found early in 1896 by Mr. Jennings, near Land's End.

In no department of zoölogical science, indeed, are we quite so much in the dark as with regard to the deep-sea cephalopods. A mere accident, for instance, it was that led to the Prince of Monaco's discovery of nearly a dozen new forms in the summer of 1895; a discovery in which the before-mentioned tentacle was included. It chanced that a cachalot was killed off Terceira by some sperm whalers, and in its last struggles charged almost to the Prince's yacht, missed it, rolled under, and died within twenty yards of his rudder. And in its agony it threw up a number of large objects, which the Prince, dimly perceiving they were strange and important, was, by a happy expedient, able to secure before they sank. He set his screws in motion, and kept them circling in the vortices thus created until a boat could be lowered. And these specimens were whole cephalopods and fragments of cephalopods, some of gigantic proportions, and almost all of them unknown to science!

It would seem, indeed, that these large and agile creatures, living in the middle depths of the sea, must, to a large extent, for ever remain unknown to us, since under water they are too nimble for nets, and it is only by such rare unlooked-for accidents that specimens can be obtained. In the case of *Haploteuthis ferox*, for instance, we are still altogether ignorant of its habitat, as ignorant as we are of the breeding-ground of the herring or the sea-ways of the salmon. And zoölogists are altogether at a loss to account for its sudden appearance on our coast. Possibly it was the stress of a hunger migration that drove it hither out of the deep. But it will be, perhaps, better to avoid necessarily inconclusive discussion, and to proceed at once with our narrative.

The first human being to set eyes upon a living *Haplo-teuthis*—the first human being to survive, that is, for there can be little doubt now that the wave of bathing fatalities and boating accidents that travelled along the coast of Cornwall and Devon in early May was due to this cause—was a retired tea-dealer of the name of Fison, who was stopping at a Sidmouth boarding-house. It was in the afternoon, and he was walking along the cliff path between Sidmouth and Ladram Bay. The cliffs in this direction are very high, but down the red face of them in one place a kind of ladder staircase has been made. He was near this when his attention was attracted by what at first he thought to be a cluster of birds struggling over a fragment of food that caught the sunlight and glistened pinkish-white. The tide was right out, and this object was not only far below him, but remote across a broad waste of rock reefs covered with dark seaweed and interspersed with silvery shining tidal pools. And he was, moreover, dazzled by the brightness of the further water.

In a minute, regarding this again, he perceived that his judgment was in fault, for over this struggle circled a number of birds, jackdaws and gulls for the most part, the latter gleaming blindingly when the sunlight smote their wings, and they seemed minute in comparison with it. And his curiosity was, perhaps, aroused all the more strongly because of his first insufficient explanations.

As he had nothing better to do than amuse himself, he decided to make this object, whatever it was, the goal of his afternoon walk, instead of Ladram Bay, conceiving it might perhaps be a great fish of some sort, stranded by some chance, and flapping about in its distress. And so he hurried down the long steep ladder, stopping at intervals of thirty feet or so to take breath and scan the mysterious movement.

At the foot of the cliff he was, of course, nearer his object than he had been; but, on the other hand, it now came up against the incandescent sky, beneath the sun, so as to seem dark and indistinct. Whatever was pinkish of it was now hidden by a skerry of weedy boulders. But he perceived that it was made up of seven rounded bodies, distinct or connected, and that the birds kept up a constant croaking and screaming, but seemed afraid to approach it too closely.

Mr. Fison, torn by curiosity, began picking his way across the wave-worn rocks, and, finding the wet seaweed that covered them thickly rendered them extremely slippery, he stopped, removed his shoes and socks, and coiled his trousers above his knees. His object was, of course, merely to avoid stumbling into the rocky pools about him, and perhaps he was rather glad, as all men are, of an excuse to resume, even for a moment, the sensations of his boyhood. At any rate, it is to this, no doubt, that he owes his life.

He approached his mark with all the assurance which the absolute security of this country against all forms of animal life gives its inhabitants. The round bodies moved to and fro, but it was only when he surmounted the skerry of boulders I have mentioned that he realised the horrible nature of the discovery. It came upon him with some suddenness.

The rounded bodies fell apart as he came into sight over the ridge, and displayed the pinkish object to be the partially devoured body of a human being, but whether of a man or woman he was unable to say. And the rounded bodies were new and ghastly-looking creatures, in shape somewhat resembling an octopus, and with huge and very long and flexible tentacles, coiled copiously on the ground. The skin had a glistening texture, unpleasant to see, like shiny leather. The downward bend of the tentacle-surrounded mouth, the curious excrescence at the bend, the tentacles, and the large intelligent eyes, gave the creatures a grotesque suggestion of a face. They were the size of a fair-sized swine about the body, and the tentacles seemed to him to be many feet in length. There were, he thinks, seven or eight at least of the creatures. Twenty yards beyond them, amid the surf of the now returning tide, two others were emerging from the sea.

Their bodies lay flatly on the rocks, and their eyes regarded him with evil interest: but it does not appear that Mr. Fison was afraid, or that he realized that he was in any danger. Possibly his confidence is to be ascribed to the limpness of their attitudes. But he was horrified, of course, and intensely excited and indignant at such revolting creatures preying upon human flesh. He thought they had chanced upon a drowned body. He shouted to them, with the idea of driving them off, and, finding they did not budge, cast about him, picked up a big rounded lump of rock, and flung it at one.

And then, slowly uncoiling their tentacles, they all began moving towards him—creeping at first deliberately, and making a soft purring sound to each other.

In a moment Mr. Fison realised that he was in danger. He shouted again, threw both his boots and started off, with a leap, forthwith. Twenty yards off he stopped and faced about, judging them slow, and behold! the tentacles of their leader were already pouring over the rocky ridge on which he had just been standing!

At that he shouted again, but this time not threatening, but a cry of dismay, and began jumping, striding, slipping, wading across the uneven expanse between him and the beach. The tall red cliffs seemed suddenly at a vast distance, and he saw, as though they were creatures in another world, two minute workmen engaged in the repair of the ladder-way, and little suspecting the race for life that was beginning below them. At one time he could hear the creatures splashing in the pools not a dozen feet behind him, and once he slipped and almost fell.

They chased him to the very foot of the cliffs, and desisted only when he had been joined by the workmen at the foot of the ladder-way up the cliff. All three of the men pelted them with stones for a time, and then hurried to the cliff top and along the path towards Sidmouth, to secure assistance and a boat, and to rescue the desecrated body from the clutches of these abominable creatures.

§ 2

And, as if he had not already been in sufficient peril that day, Mr. Fison went with the boat to point out the exact spot of his adventure.

As the tide was down, it required a considerable détour to reach the spot, and when at last they came off the ladder-way, the mangled body had disappeared. The water was now running in, submerging first one slab of slimy rock and then another, and the four men in the boat—the workmen, that is, the boatman, and Mr. Fison—now turned their attention from the bearings off shore to the water beneath the keel.

At first they could see little below them save a dark jungle of laminaria, with an occasional darting fish. Their minds were set on adventure, and they expressed their disappointment freely. But presently they saw one of the monsters swimming through the water seaward, with a curious rolling motion that suggested to Mr. Fison the spinning roll of a captive balloon. Almost immediately after, the waving streamers of laminaria were extraordinarily perturbed, parted for a moment, and three of these beasts became darkly visible, struggling for what was probably some fragment of the drowned man. In a moment the copious olive-green ribbons had poured again over this writhing group.

At that all four men, greatly excited, began beating the water with oars and shouting, and immediately they saw a tumultuous movement among the weeds. They desisted to see more clearly, and as soon as the water was smooth, they saw, as it seemed to them, the whole sea bottom among the weeds set with eyes.

"Ugly swine!" cried one of the men. "Why, there's dozens!"

And forthwith the things began to rise through the water about them. Mr. Fison has since described to the writer this startling eruption out of the waving laminaria meadows. To him it seemed to occupy a considerable time, but it is probable that really it was an affair of a few seconds only. For a time nothing but eyes, and then he speaks of tentacles streaming out and parting the weed fronds this way and that. Then these things, growing larger, until at last the bottom was hidden by their intercoiling forms, and the tips of tentacles rose darkly here and there into the air above the swell of the waters.

One came up boldly to the side of the boat, and, clinging to this with three of its sucker-set tentacles, threw four others over the gunwale, as if with an intention either of oversetting the boat or of clambering into it. Mr. Fison at once caught up the boathook, and, jabbing furiously at the soft tentacles, forced it to desist. He was struck in the back and almost pitched overboard by the boatman, who was using his oar to resist a similar attack on the other side of the boat. But the tentacles on either side at once relaxed their hold at this, slid out of sight, and splashed into the water.

"We'd better get out of this," said Mr. Fison, who was trembling violently. He went to the tiller, while the boatman and one of the workmen seated themselves and began rowing. The other workman stood up in the fore part of the boat, with the boathook, ready to strike any more tentacles that might appear. Nothing else seems to have been said. Mr. Fison had expressed the common feeling beyond amendment. In a hushed, scared mood, with faces white and drawn, they set about escaping from the position into which they had so recklessly blundered.

But the oars had scarcely dropped into the water before dark, tapering, serpentine ropes had bound them, and were about the rudder; and creeping up the sides of the boat with a looping motion came the suckers again. The men gripped their oars and pulled, but it was like trying to move a boat in a floating raft of weeds. "Help here!" cried the boatman, and Mr. Fison and the second workman rushed to help lug at the oar.

Then the man with the boathook—his name was Ewan, or Ewen—sprang up with a curse, and began striking downward over the side, as far as he could reach, at the bank of tentacles that now clustered along the boat's bottom. And, at the same time, the two rowers stood up to get a better purchase for the recovery of their oars. The boatman handed his to Mr. Fison, who lugged desperately, and, meanwhile, the boatman opened a big clasp-knife, and, leaning over the side of the boat, began hacking at the spiring arms upon the oar shaft.

Mr. Fison, staggering with the quivering rocking of the boat, his teeth set, his breath coming short, and the veins starting on his hands as he pulled at his oar, suddenly cast his eyes seaward. And there, not fifty yards off, across the long rollers of the incoming tide, was a large boat standing in towards them, with three women and a little child in it. A boatman was rowing, and a little man in a pink-ribboned straw hat and whites stood in the stern, hailing them. For a moment, of course, Mr. Fison thought of help, and then he thought of the child. He abandoned his oar forthwith, threw up his arms in a frantic gesture, and screamed to the party in the boat to keep away "for God's sake!" It says much for the modesty and courage of Mr. Fison that he does not seem to be aware that there was any quality of heroism in his action at this juncture. The oar he had abandoned was at once drawn under, and presently reappeared floating about twenty yards away.

At the same moment Mr. Fison felt the boat under him lurch violently, and a hoarse scream, a prolonged cry of terror from Hill, the boatman, caused him to forget the party of excursionists altogether. He turned, and saw Hill crouching by the forward rowlock, his face convulsed with terror, and his right arm over the side and drawn tightly down. He gave now a succession of short, sharp cries, "Oh! oh! oh!—oh!" Mr. Fison believes that he must have been hacking at the tentacles below the water-line, and have been grasped by them, but, of course, it is quite impossible to say now certainly what had happened. The boat was heeling over, so that the gunwale was within ten inches of the water, and both Ewan and the other labourer were striking down into the water, with oar and boathook, on either side of Hill's arm. Mr. Fison instinctively placed himself to counterpoise them.

Then Hill, who was a burly, powerful man, made a strenuous effort, and rose almost to a standing position. He lifted his arm, indeed, clean out of the water. Hanging to it was a complicated tangle of brown ropes; and the eyes of one of the brutes that had hold of him, glaring straight and resolute, showed momentarily above the surface. The boat heeled more and more, and the green-brown water came pouring in a cascade over the side. Then Hill slipped and fell with his ribs across the side, and his arm and the mass of tentacles about it splashed back into the water. He rolled over; his boot kicked Mr. Fison's knee as that gentleman rushed forward to seize him, and in another moment fresh tentacles had whipped about his waist and neck, and after a brief, convulsive struggle, in which the boat was nearly capsized, Hill was lugged overboard. The boat righted with a violent jerk that all but sent Mr. Fison over the other side, and hid the struggle in the water from his eyes.

He stood staggering to recover his balance for a moment, and as he did so, he became aware that the struggle and the inflowing tide had carried them close upon the weedy rocks again. Not four yards off a table of rock still rose in rhythmic movements above the inwash of the tide. In a moment Mr. Fison seized the oar from Ewan, gave one vigorous stroke, then, dropping it, ran to the bows and leapt. He felt his feet slide over the rock, and, by a frantic effort, leapt again towards a further mass. He stumbled over this, came to his knees, and rose again.

"Look out!" cried someone, and a large drab body struck him. He was knocked flat into a tidal pool by one of the workmen, and as he went down he heard smothered, choking cries, that he believed at the time came from Hill. Then he found himself marvelling at the shrillness and variety of Hill's voice. Someone jumped over him, and a curving rush of foamy water poured over him, and passed. He scrambled to his feet dripping, and, without looking seaward, ran as fast as his terror would let him shoreward. Before him, over the flat space of scattered rocks, stumbled the two workmen— one a dozen yards in front of the other.

He looked over his shoulder at last, and, seeing that he was not pursued, faced about. He was astonished. From the moment of the rising of the cephalopods out of the water, he had been acting too swiftly to fully comprehend his actions. Now it seemed to him as if he had suddenly jumped out of an evil dream.

For there were the sky, cloudless and blazing with the afternoon sun, the sea weltering under its pitiless brightness, the soft creamy foam of the breaking water, and the low, long, dark ridges of rock. The righted boat floated, rising and falling gently on the swell about a dozen yards from shore. Hill and the monsters, all the stress and tumult of that fierce fight for life, had vanished as though they had never been.

Mr. Fison's heart was beating violently; he was throbbing to the finger-tips, and his breath came deep.

There was something missing. For some seconds he could not think clearly enough what this might be. Sun, sky, sea, rocks—what was it? Then he remembered the boatload of excursionists. It had vanished. He wondered whether he had imagined it. He turned, and saw the two workmen standing side by side under the projecting masses of the tall pink cliffs. He hesitated whether he should make one last attempt to save the man Hill. His physical excitement seemed to desert him suddenly, and leave him aimless and helpless. He turned shoreward, stumbling and wading towards his two companions.

He looked back again, and there were now two boats floating, and the one farthest out at sea pitched clumsily, bottom upward.

§ 3

So it was *Haploteuthis ferox* made its appearance upon the Devonshire coast. So far, this has been its most serious aggression. Mr. Fison's account, taken together with the wave of boating and bathing casualties to which I have already alluded, and the absence of fish from the Cornish coasts that year, points clearly to a shoal of these voracious deep-sea monsters prowling slowly along the sub-tidal coastline. Hunger migration has, I know, been suggested as the force that drove them hither; but, for my own part, I prefer to believe the alternative theory of Hemsley. Hemsley holds that a pack or shoal of these creatures may have become enamoured of human flesh by the accident of a foundered ship sinking among them, and have wandered in search of it out of their accustomed zone; first waylaying and following ships, and so coming to our shores in the wake of the Atlantic traffic. But to discuss Hemsley's cogent and admirably-stated arguments would be out of place here.

It would seem that the appetites of the shoal were satisfied by the catch of eleven people—for so far as can be ascertained, there were ten people in the second boat, and certainly these creatures gave no further signs of their presence off Sidmouth that day. The coast between Seaton and Budleigh Salterton was patrolled all that evening and night by four Preventive Service boats, the men in which were armed with harpoons and cutlasses, and as the evening advanced, a number of more or less similarly equipped expeditions, organised by private individuals, joined them. Mr. Fison took no part in any of these expeditions.

About midnight excited hails were heard from a boat about a couple of miles out at sea to the southeast of Sidmouth, and a lantern was seen waving in a strange manner to and fro and up and down. The nearer boats at once hurried towards the alarm. The venturesome occupants of the boat, a seaman, a curate, and two schoolboys, had actually seen the monsters passing under their boat. The creatures, it seems, like most deep-sea organisms, were phosphorescent, and they had been floating, five fathoms deep or so, like creatures of moonshine through the blackness of the water, their tentacles retracted and ·as if asleep, rolling over and over, and moving slowly in a wedge-like formation towards the south-east.

These people told their story in gesticulated fragments, as first one boat drew alongside and then another. At last there was a little fleet of eight or nine boats collected together, and from them a tumult, like the chatter of a marketplace, rose into the stillness of the night. There was little or no disposition to pursue the shoal, the people had neither weapons nor experience for such a dubious chase, and presently —even with a certain relief, it may be—the boats turned shoreward.

And now to tell what is perhaps the most astonishing fact in this whole astonishing raid. We have not the slightest knowledge of the subsequent movements of the shoal, although the whole south-west coast was now alert for it. But it may, perhaps, be significant that a cachalot was stranded off Sark on June 3rd. Two weeks and three days after this Sidmouth affair, a living *Haploteuthis* came ashore on Calais sands. It was alive, because several witnesses saw its tentacles moving in a convulsive way. But it is probable that it was dying. A gentleman named Pouchet obtained a rifle and shot it.

That was the last appearance of a living *Haploteuthis*. No others were seen on the French coast. On the 15th of June a dead body, almost complete, was washed ashore near Torquay, and a few days later a boat from the Marine Biological station, engaged in dredging off Plymouth, picked up a rotting specimen, slashed deeply with a cutlass wound. How the former specimen had come by its death it is impossible to say. And on the last day of June, Mr. Egbert Caine, an artist, bathing near Newlyn, threw up his arms, shrieked, and was drawn under. A friend bathing with him made no attempt to save him, but swam at once for the shore. This is the last fact to tell of this extraordinary raid from the deeper sea. Whether it is really the last of these horrible creatures it is, as yet, premature to say. But it is believed, and certainly it is to be hoped, that they have returned now, and returned for good, to the sunless depths of the middle seas, out of which they have so strangely and so mysteriously arisen.

THE CRYSTAL EGG

THERE was, until a year ago, a little and very grimy-looking shop near Seven Dials, over which, in weatherworn yellow lettering, the name of "C. Cave, Naturalist and Dealer in Antiquities," was inscribed. The contents of its window were curiously varied. They comprised some elephant tusks and an imperfect set of chessmen, beads and weapons, a box of eyes, two skulls of tigers and one human, several moth-eaten stuffed monkeys (one holding a lamp), an old-fashioned cabinet, a fly-blown ostrich egg or so, some fishing-tackle, and an extraordinarily dirty, empty glass fish-tank. There was also, at the moment the story begins, a mass of crystal, worked into the shape of an egg and brilliantly polished. And at that two people, who stood outside the window, were looking, one of them a tall, thin clergyman, the other a black-bearded young man of dusky complexion and unobtrusive costume. The dusky young man spoke with eager gesticulation, and seemed anxious for his companion to purchase the article.

While they were there, Mr. Cave came into his shop, his beard still wagging with the bread and butter of his tea. When he saw these men and the object of their regard, his countenance fell. He glanced guiltily over his shoulder, and softly shut the door. He was a little old man, with pale face and peculiar watery blue eyes; his hair was a dirty grey, and he wore a shabby blue frock-coat, an ancient silk hat, and carpet slippers very much down at heel. He remained watching the two men as they talked. The clergyman went deep into his trouser pocket, examined a handful of money, and showed his teeth in an agreeable smile. Mr. Cave seemed still more depressed when they came into the shop.

The clergyman, without any ceremony, asked the price of the crystal egg. Mr. Cave glanced nervously towards the door leading into the parlour, and said five pounds. The clergyman protested that the price was high, to his companion as well as to Mr. Cave—it was, indeed, very much more than Mr. Cave had intended to ask, when he had stocked the article— and an attempt at bargaining ensued. Mr. Cave stepped to the shop door, and held it open. "Five pounds is my price," he said, as though he wished to save himself the trouble of unprofitable discussion. As he did so, the upper portion of a woman's face appeared above the blind in the glass upper panel of the door leading into the parlour, and stared curiously at the two customers. "Five pounds is my price," said Mr. Cave, with a quiver in his voice.

The swarthy young man had so far remained a spectator, watching Cave keenly. Now he spoke. "Give him five pounds," he said. The clergyman glanced at him to see if he were in earnest, and, when he looked at Mr. Cave again, he saw that the latter's face was white. "It's a lot of money," said the clergyman, and, diving into his pocket, began counting his resources. He had little more than thirty shillings, and he appealed to his companion, with whom he seemed to be on terms of considerable intimacy. This gave Mr. Cave an opportunity of collecting his thoughts, and he began to explain in an agitated manner that the crystal was not, as a matter of fact, entirely free for sale. His two customers were naturally surprised at this, and inquired why he had not thought of that before he began to bargain. Mr. Cave became confused, but he stuck to his story, that the crystal was not in the market that afternoon, that a probable purchaser of it had already appeared. The two, treating this as an attempt to raise the price still further, made as if they would leave the shop. But at this point the parlour door opened, and the owner of the dark fringe and the little eyes appeared.

She was a coarse-featured, corpulent woman, younger and very much larger than Mr. Cave; she walked heavily, and her face was flushed. "That crystal *is* for sale," she said. "And five pounds is a good enough price for it. I can't think what you're about, Cave, not to take the gentleman's offer!"

Mr. Cave, greatly perturbed by the irruption, looked angrily at her over the rims of his spectacles, and, without excessive assurance, asserted his right to manage his business in his own way. An altercation began. The two customers watched the scene with interest and some amusement, occasionally assisting Mrs. Cave with suggestions. Mr. Cave, hard driven, persisted in a confused and impossible story of an inquiry for the crystal that morning, and his agitation became painful. But he stuck to his point with extraordinary persistence. It was the young Oriental who ended this curious controversy. He proposed that they should call again in the course of two days—so as to give the alleged inquirer a fair chance. "And then we must insist," said the clergyman. "Five pounds." Mrs. Cave took it on herself to apologise for her husband, explaining that he was sometimes "a little odd," and as the two customers left, the couple prepared for a free discussion of the incident in all its bearings.

Mrs. Cave talked to her husband with singular directness. The poor little man, quivering with emotion, muddled himself between his stories, maintaining on the one hand that he had another customer in view, and on the other asserting that the crystal was honestly worth ten guineas. "Why did you ask five pounds?" said his wife. "*Do* let me manage my business my own way!" said Mr. Cave.

Mr. Cave had living with him a step-daughter and a step-son, and at supper that night the transaction was rediscussed. None of them had a high opinion of Mr. Cave's business methods, and this action seemed a culminating folly.

"It's my opinion he's refused that crystal before," said the step-son, a loose-limbed lout of eighteen.

"But *Five Pounds!*" said the step-daughter, an argumentative young woman of six-and-twenty.

Mr. Cave's answers were wretched; he could only mumble weak assertions that he knew his own business best. They drove him from his half-eaten supper into the shop, to close it for the night, his ears aflame and tears of vexation behind his spectacles. "Why had he left the crystal in the window so long? The folly of it!" That was the trouble closest in his mind. For a time he could see no way of evading sale.

After supper his step-daughter and step-son smartened

themselves up and went out and his wife retired upstairs to reflect upon the business aspects of the crystal, over a little sugar and lemon and so forth in hot water. Mr. Cave went into the shop, and stayed there until late, ostensibly to make ornamental rockeries for goldfish cases but really for a private purpose that will be better explained later. The next day Mrs. Cave found that the crystal had been removed from the window, and was lying behind some second-hand books on angling. She replaced it in a conspicuous position. But she did not argue further about it, as a nervous headache disinclined her from debate. Mr. Cave was always disinclined. The day passed disagreeably. Mr. Cave was, if anything, more absent-minded than usual, and uncommonly irritable withal. In the afternoon, when his wife was taking her customary sleep, he removed the crystal from the window again.

The next day Mr. Cave had to deliver a consignment of dog-fish at one of the hospital schools, where they were needed for dissection. In his absence Mrs. Cave's mind reverted to the topic of the crystal, and the methods of expenditure suitable to a windfall of five pounds. She had already devised some very agreeable expedients, among others a dress of green silk for herself and a trip to Richmond, when a jangling of the front door bell summoned her into the shop. The customer was an examination coach who came to complain of the non-delivery of certain frogs asked for the previous day. Mrs. Cave did not approve of this particular branch of Mr. Cave's business, and the gentleman, who had called in a somewhat aggressive mood, retired after a brief exchange of words— entirely civil so far as he was concerned. Mrs. Cave's eye then naturally turned to the window; for the sight of the crystal was an assurance of the five pounds and of her dreams. What was her surprise to find it gone!

She went to the place behind the locker on the counter, where she had discovered it the day before. It was not there; and she immediately began an eager search about the shop.

When Mr. Cave returned from his business with the dog-fish, about a quarter to two in the afternoon, he found the shop in some confusion, and his wife, extremely exasperated and on her knees behind the counter, routing among his taxidermic material. Her face came up hot and angry over the counter, as the gangling bell announced his return, and she forthwith accused him of "hiding it."

"Hid *what?*" asked Mr. Cave.

"The crystal!"

At that Mr. Cave, apparently much surprised, rushed to the window. "Isn't it here?" he said. "Great Heavens! what has become of it?"

Just then, Mr. Cave's step-son reëntered the shop from the inner room—he had come home a minute or so before Mr. Cave—and he was blaspheming freely. He was apprenticed to a second-hand furniture dealer down the road, but he had his meals at home, and he was naturally annoyed to find no dinner ready.

But, when he heard of the loss of the crystal, he forgot his meal, and his anger was diverted from his mother to his step-father. Their first idea, of course, was that he had hidden it. But Mr. Cave stoutly denied all knowledge of its fate— freely offering his bedabbled affidavit in the matter—and at last was worked up to the point of accusing, first, his wife and then his step-son of having taken it with a view to a private sale. So began an exceedingly acrimonious and emotional discussion, which ended for Mrs. Cave in a peculiar nervous condition midway between hysterics and amuck, and caused the step-son to be half-an-hour late at the furniture establishment in the afternoon. Mr. Cave took refuge from his wife's emotions in the shop.

In the evening the matter was resumed, with less passion and in a judicial spirit, under the presidency of the step-daughter. The supper passed unhappily and culminated in a painful scene. Mr. Cave gave way at last to extreme exasperation, and went out banging the front door violently. The rest of the family, having discussed him with the freedom his absence warranted, hunted the house from garret to cellar, hoping to light upon the crystal.

The next day the two customers called again. They were received by Mrs. Cave almost in tears. It transpired that no one *could* imagine all that she had stood from Cave at various times in her married pilgrimage. . . . She also gave a garbled account of the disappearance. The clergyman and the Oriental laughed silently at one another, and said it was very extraordinary. As Mrs. Cave seemed disposed to give them the complete history of her life they made to leave the shop. Thereupon Mrs. Cave, still clinging to hope, asked for the clergyman's address, so that, if she could get anything out of Cave, she might communicate it. The address was duly given, but apparently was afterwards mislaid. Mrs. Cave can remember nothing about it.

In the evening of that day, the Caves seem to have exhausted their emotions, and Mr. Cave, who had been out in the afternoon, supped in a gloomy isolation that contrasted pleasantly with the impassioned controversy of the previous days. For some time matters were very badly strained in the Cave household, but neither crystal nor customer reappeared.

Now, without mincing the matter, we must admit that Mr. Cave was a liar. He knew perfectly well where the crystal was. It was in the rooms of Mr. Jacoby Wace, Assistant Demonstrator at St. Catherine's Hospital, Westbourne Street. It stood on the sideboard partially covered by a black velvet cloth, and beside a decanter of American whisky. It is from Mr. Wace, indeed, that the particulars upon which this narrative is based were derived. Cave had taken off the thing to the hospital hidden in the dog-fish sack, and there had pressed the young investigator to keep it for him. Mr. Wace was a little dubious at first. His relationship to Cave was peculiar. He had a taste for singular characters, and he had more than once invited the old man to smoke and drink in his rooms, and to unfold his rather amusing views of life in general and of his wife in particular. Mr. Wace had encountered Mrs. Cave, too, on occasions when Mr. Cave was not at home to attend to him. He knew the constant interference to which Cave was subjected, and having weighed the story judicially, he decided to give the crystal a refuge. Mr. Cave promised to explain the reasons for his remarkable affection for the crystal more fully on a later occasion, but he spoke distinctly of seeing visions therein. He called on Mr. Wace the same evening.

He told a complicated story. The crystal he said had come into his possession with other oddments at the forced sale of another curiosity dealer's effects, and not knowing what its value might be, he had ticketed it at ten shillings. It had hung upon his hands at that price for some months, and he was thinking of "reducing the figure," when he made a singular discovery.

At that time his health was very bad—and it must be borne in mind that, throughout all this experience, his physical condition was one of ebb—and he was in considerable distress by reason of the negligence, the positive ill-treatment even, he received from his wife and step-children. His wife was vain, extravagant, unfeeling, and had a growing taste for private drinking; his step-daughter was mean and over-reaching; and his step-son had conceived a violent dislike for him, and lost no chance of showing it. The requirements of his business pressed heavily upon him, and Mr. Wace does not think that he was altogether free from occasional intemperance. He had begun life in a comfortable position, he was a man of fair education, and he suffered, for weeks at a stretch, from melancholia and insomnia. Afraid to disturb his family, he would slip quietly from his wife's side, when his thoughts became intolerable, and wander about the house. And about three o'clock one morning, late in August, chance directed him into the shop.

The dirty little place was impenetrably black except in one spot, where he perceived an unusual glow of light. Approaching this, he discovered it to be the crystal egg, which was standing on the corner of the counter towards the window. A thin ray smote through a crack in the shutters, impinged upon the object, and seemed as it were to fill its entire interior.

It occurred to Mr. Cave that this was not in accordance with the laws of optics as he had known them in his younger days. He could understand the rays being refracted by the crystal and coming to a focus in its interior, but this diffusion jarred with his physical conceptions. He approached the crystal nearly, peering into it and round it, with a transient revival of the scientific curiosity that in his youth had determined his choice of a calling. He was surprised to find the light not steady, but writhing within the substance of the egg, as though that object was a hollow sphere of some luminous vapour. In moving about to get different points of view, he suddenly found that he had come between it and the ray, and that the crystal none the less remained luminous. Greatly astonished, he lifted it out of the light ray and carried it to the darkest part of the shop. It remained bright for some four or five minutes, when it slowly faded and went out. He placed it in the thin streak of daylight, and its luminousness was almost immediately restored.

So far, at least, Mr. Wace was able to verify the remarkable story of Mr. Cave. He has himself repeatedly held this crystal in a ray of light (which had to be of a less diameter than one millimetre). And in a perfect darkness, such as could be produced by velvet wrapping, the crystal did undoubtedly appear very faintly phosphorescent. It would seem, however, that the luminousness was of some exceptional sort, and not equally visible to all eyes; for Mr. Harbinger—whose name will be familiar to the scientific reader in connection with the Pasteur Institute—was quite unable to see any light whatever. And Mr. Wace's own capacity for its appreciation was out of comparison inferior to that of Mr. Cave's. Even with Mr. Cave the power varied very considerably: his vision was most vivid during states of extreme weakness and fatigue.

Now from the outset this light in the crystal exercised an irresistible fascination upon Mr. Cave. And it says more for his loneliness of soul than a volume of pathetic writing could do, that he told no human being of his curious observations. He seems to have been living in such an atmosphere of petty spite that to admit the existence of a pleasure would have been to risk the loss of it. He found that as the dawn advanced, and the amount of diffused light increased, the crystal became to all appearance non-luminous. And for some time he was unable to see anything in it, except at night-time. in dark corners of the shop.

But the use of an old velvet cloth, which he used as a background for a collection of minerals, occurred to him, and by doubling this, and putting it over his head and hands, he was able to get a sight of the luminous movement within the crystal even in the day-time. He was very cautious lest he should be thus discovered by his wife, and he practised this occupation only in the afternoons, while she was asleep upstairs, and then circumspectly in a hollow under the counter. And one day, turning the crystal about in his hands, he saw something. It came and went like a flash, but it gave him the impression that the object had for a moment opened to him the view of a wide and spacious and strange country, and turning it about, he did, just as the light faded, see the same vision again.

Now, it would be tedious and unnecessary to state all the phases of Mr. Cave's discovery from this point. Suffice that the effect was this: the crystal, being peered into at an angle of about 137 degrees from the direction of the illuminating ray, gave a clear and consistent picture of a wide and peculiar country-side. It was not dream-like at all; it produced a definite impression of reality, and the better the light the more real and solid it seemed. It was a moving picture: that is to say, certain objects moved in it, but slowly in an orderly manner like real things, and according as the direction of the lighting and vision changed, the picture changed also. It must, indeed, have been like looking through an oval glass at a view, and turning the glass about to get at different aspects.

Mr. Cave's statements, Mr. Wace assures me, were extremely circumstantial, and entirely free from any of that emotional quality that taints hallucinatory impressions. But it must be remembered that all the efforts of Mr. Wace to see any similar clarity in the faint opalescence of the crystal were wholly unsuccessful, try as he would. The difference in intensity of the impressions received by the two men was very great, and it is quite conceivable that what was a view to Mr. Cave was a mere blurred nebulosity to Mr. Wace.

The view, as Mr. Cave described it, was invariably of an extensive plain, and he seemed always to be looking at it from a considerable height, as if from a tower or a mast. To the east and to the west the plain was bounded at a remote distance by vast reddish cliffs, which reminded him of those he had seen in some picture; but what the picture was Mr. Wace was unable to ascertain. These cliffs passed north and south—he could tell the points of the compass by the stars that were visible of a night—receding in an almost illimitable perspective and fading into the mists of the distance before they met. He was nearer the eastern set of cliffs, on the occasion of his first vision the sun was rising over them, and black against the sunlight and pale against their shadow appeared a multitude of soaring forms that Mr. Cave regarded as birds. A vast range of buildings spread below him; he seemed to be looking down upon them; and, as they approached the blurred and refracted edge of the picture, they became indistinct. There were also trees curious in shape, and in colouring, a deep mossy green and an exquisite grey, beside a wide and shining canal. And something great and brilliantly coloured flew across the picture. But the first time Mr. Cave saw these pictures he saw only in flashes, his hands shook, his head moved, the vision came and went, and grew foggy and indistinct. And at first he had the greatest difficulty in finding the picture again once the direction of it was lost.

His next clear vision, which came about a week after the first, the interval having yielded nothing but tantalising glimpses and some useful experience, showed him the view down the length of the valley. The view was different, but he had a curious persuasion, which his subsequent observations abundantly confirmed, that he was regarding this strange world from exactly the same spot, although he was looking in a different direction. The long façade of the great building, whose roof he had looked down upon before, was now receding in perspective. He recognised the roof. In the front of the façade was a terrace of massive proportions and extraordinary length, and down the middle of the terrace, at certain intervals, stood huge but very graceful masts, bearing small shiny objects which reflected the setting sun. The import of these small objects did not occur to Mr. Cave until some time after, as he was describing the scene to Mr. Wace. The terrace overhung a thicket of the most luxuriant and graceful vegetation, and beyond this was a wide grassy lawn on which certain broad creatures, in form like beetles but enormously larger, reposed. Beyond this again was a richly decorated causeway of pinkish stone; and beyond that, and lined with dense *red* weeds, and passing up the valley exactly parallel with the distant cliffs, was a broad and mirror-like expanse of water. The air seemed full of squadrons of great birds, manœuvring in stately curves; and across the river was a multitude of splendid buildings, richly coloured and glittering with metallic tracery and facets, among a forest of moss-like and lichenous trees. And suddenly something flapped repeatedly across the vision, like the fluttering of a jewelled fan or the beating of a wing, and a face, or rather the upper part of a face with very large eyes, came as it were close to his own and as if on the other side of the crystal. Mr. Cave was so startled and so impressed by the absolute reality of these eyes, that he drew his head back from the crystal to look behind it. He had become so absorbed in watching that he was quite surprised to find himself in the cool darkness of his little shop, with its familiar odour of methyl, mustiness, and decay. And, as he blinked about him, the glowing crystal faded, and went out.

Such were the first general impressions of Mr. Cave. The story is curiously direct and circumstantial. From the outset, when the valley first flashed momentarily on his senses, his imagination was strangely affected, and, as he began to appreciate the details of the scene he saw, his wonder rose to the point of a passion. He went about his business listless and distraught, thinking only of the time when he should be able to return to his watching. And then a few weeks after his first sight of the valley came the two customers, the stress and excitement of their offer, and the narrow escape of the crystal from sale, as I have already told.

Now while the thing was Mr. Cave's secret, it remained a mere wonder, a thing to creep to covertly and peep at, as a child might peep upon a forbidden garden. But Mr. Wace has, for a young scientific investigator, a particularly lucid and consecutive habit of mind. Directly the crystal and its story came to him, and he had satisfied himself, by seeing the phosphorescence with his own eyes, that there really was a certain evidence for Mr. Cave's statements, he proceeded to develop the matter systematically. Mr. Cave was only too eager to come and feast his eyes on this wonderland he saw, and he came every night from half-past eight until half-past ten, and sometimes, in Mr. Wace's absence, during the day. On Sunday afternoons, also, he came. From the outset, Mr. Wace made copious notes, and it was due to his scientific method that the relation between the direction from which the initiating ray entered the crystal and the orientation of the picture was proved. And, by covering the crystal in a box perforated only with a small aperture to admit the exciting ray, and by substituting black holland for his buff blinds, he greatly improved the conditions of the observations; so that in a little while they were able to survey the valley in any direction they desired.

So having cleared the way, we may give a brief account of this visionary world within the crystal. The things were in all cases seen by Mr. Cave, and the method of working was invariably for him to watch the crystal and report what he saw, while Mr. Wace (who as a science student had learnt the trick of writing in the dark) wrote a brief note of his report. When the crystal faded, it was put into its box in the proper position and the electric light turned on. Mr. Wace asked questions, and suggested observations to clear up difficult points. Nothing, indeed, could have been less visionary and more matter-of-fact.

The attention of Mr. Cave had been speedily directed to the bird-like creatures he had seen so abundantly present in each of his earlier visions. His first impression was soon corrected, and he considered for a time that they might represent a diurnal species of bat. Then he thought, grotesquely enough, that they might be cherubs. Their heads were round, and curiously human, and it was the eyes of one of them that had so startled him on his second observation. They had broad, silvery wings not feathered, but glistening almost as brilliantly as new-killed fish and with the same subtle play of colour, and these wings were not built on the plan of bird-wing or bat, Mr. Wace learned, but supported by curved ribs radiating from the body. (A sort of butterfly wing with curved ribs seems best to express their appearance.) The body was small, but fitted with two bunches of prehensile organs, like long tentacles, immediately under the mouth. Incredible as it appeared to Mr. Wace, the persuasion at last became irresistible, that it was these creatures which owned the great quasi-human buildings and the magnificent garden that made the broad valley so splendid. And Mr. Cave perceived that the buildings, with other peculiarities, had no doors, but that the great circular windows, which opened freely, gave the creatures egress and entrance. They would alight upon their tentacles, fold their wings to a smallness almost rod-like, and hop into the interior. But among them was a multitude of smaller-winged creatures, like great dragon-flies and moths and flying beetles, and across the greensward brilliantly coloured gigantic ground-beetles crawled lazily to and fro. Moreover, on the causeways and terraces, large-headed creatures similar to the greater winged flies, but wingless, were visible, hopping busily upon their hand-like tangle of tentacles.

Allusion has already been made to the glittering objects upon masts that stood upon the terrace of the nearer building. It dawned upon Mr. Cave, after regarding one of these masts very fixedly on one particularly vivid day, that the glittering object there was a crystal exactly like that into which he peered. And a still more careful scrutiny convinced him that each one in a vista of nearly twenty carried a similar object.

Occasionally one of the large flying creatures would flutter up to one, and, folding its wings and coiling a number of its tentacles about the mast, would regard the crystal fixedly for a space—sometimes for as long as fifteen minutes. And a series of observations, made at the suggestion of Mr. Wace, convinced both watchers that, so far as this visionary world was concerned, the crystal into which they peered actually stood at the summit of the end-most mast on the terrace, and that on one occasion at least one of these inhabitants of this other world had looked into Mr. Cave's face while he was making these observations.

So much for the essential facts of this very singular story. Unless we dismiss it all as the ingenious fabrication of Mr. Wace, we have to believe one of two things: either that Mr. Cave's crystal was in two worlds at once, and that, while it was carried about in one, it remained stationary in the other, which seems altogether absurd; or else that it had some peculiar relation of sympathy with another and exactly similar crystal in this other world, so that what was seen in the interior of the one in this world was, under suitable conditions, visible to an observer in the corresponding crystal in the other world; and *vice versa*. At present, indeed, we do not know of any way in which two crystals could so come *en rapport*, but nowadays we know enough to understand that the thing is not altogether impossible. This view of the crystals as *en rapport* was the supposition that occurred to Mr. Wace, and to me at least it seems extremely plausible. . . .

And where was this other world? On this, also, the alert intelligence of Mr. Wace speedily threw light. After sunset, the sky darkened rapidly—there was a very brief twilight interval indeed—and the stars shone out. They were recognisably the same as those we see, arranged in the same constellations. Mr. Cave recognised the Bear, the Pleiades, Aldebaran, and Sirius: so that the other world must be somewhere in the solar system, and, at the utmost, only a few hundreds of millions of miles from our own. Following up this clue, Mr. Wace learned that the midnight sky was a darker blue even than our midwinter sky, and that the sun seemed a little smaller. *And there were two small moons!* "like our moon but smaller, and quite differently marked," one of which moved so rapidly that its motion was clearly visible as one regarded it. These moons were never high in the sky, but vanished as they rose: that is, every time they revolved they were eclipsed because they were so near their primary planet. And all this answers quite completely, although Mr. Cave did not know it, to what must be the condition of things on Mars.

Indeed, it seems an exceedingly plausible conclusion that peering into this crystal Mr. Cave did actually see the planet Mars and its inhabitants. And, if that be the case, then the evening star that shone so brilliantly in the sky of that distant vision was neither more nor less than our own familiar earth.

For a time the Martians—if they were Martians—do not seem to have known of Mr. Cave's inspection. Once or twice one would come to peer, and go away very shortly to some other mast, as though the vision was unsatisfactory. During this time Mr. Cave was able to watch the proceedings of these winged people without being disturbed by their attentions, and, although his report is necessarily vague and fragmentary, it is nevertheless very suggestive. Imagine the impression of humanity a Martian observer would get who, after a difficult process of preparation and with considerable fatigue to the eyes, was able to peer at London from the steeple of St. Martin's Church for stretches, at longest, of four minutes at a time. Mr. Cave was unable to ascertain if the winged Martians were the same as the Martians who hopped about the causeways and terraces, and if the latter could put on wings at will. He several times saw certain clumsy bipeds, dimly suggestive of apes, white and partially translucent, feeding among certain of the lichenous trees, and once some of these fled before one of the hopping, round-headed Martians. The latter caught one in its tentacles, and then the picture faded suddenly and left Mr. Cave most tantalisingly in the dark. On another occasion a vast thing, that Mr. Cave thought at first was some gigantic insect, appeared advancing along the causeway beside the canal with extraordinary rapidity. As this drew nearer Mr. Cave perceived that it was a mechanism of shining metals and of extraordinary complexity. And then, when he looked again, it had passed out of sight.

After a time Mr. Wace aspired to attract the attention of the Martians, and the next time that the strange eyes of one of them appeared close to the crystal Mr. Cave cried out and sprang away, and they immediatley turned on the light and began to gesticulate in a manner suggestive of signalling. But when at last Mr. Cave examined the crystal again the Martian had departed.

Thus far these observations had progressed in early November, and then Mr. Cave, feeling that the suspicions of his family about the crystal were allayed, began to take it to and fro with him in order that, as occasion arose in the daytime or night, he might comfort himself with what was fast becoming the most real thing in his existence.

In December Mr. Wace's work in connection with a forthcoming examination became heavy, the sittings were reluctantly suspended for a week, and for ten or eleven days—he is not quite sure which—he saw nothing of Cave. He then grew anxious to resume these investigations, and, the stress of his seasonal labours being abated, he went down to Seven Dials. At the corner he noticed a shutter before a bird fancier's window, and then another at a cobbler's. Mr. Cave's shop was closed.

He rapped and tne door was opened by the step-son in black. He at once called Mrs. Cave, who was, Mr. Wace could not but observe, in cheap but ample widow's weeds of the most imposing pattern. Without any very great surprise Mr. Wace learnt that Cave was dead and already buried. She was in tears, and her voice was a little thick. She had just returned from Highgate. Her mind seemed occupied with her own prospects and the honourable details of the obsequies, but Mr. Wace was at last able to learn the particulars of Cave's death. He had been found dead in his shop in the early morning, the day after his last visit to Mr. Wace, and the crystal had been clasped in his stone-cold hands. His face was smiling, said Mrs. Cave, and the yelvet cloth from the minerals lay on the floor at his feet. He must have been dead five or six hours when he was found.

This came as a great shock to Wace, and he began to reproach himself bitterly for having neglected the plain symptoms of the old man's ill-health. But his chief thought was of the crystal. He approached that topic in a gingerly manner, because he knew Mrs. Cave's peculiarities. He was dumbfounded to learn that it was sold.

Mrs. Cave's first impulse, directly Cave's body had been taken upstairs, had been to write to the mad clergyman who had offered five pounds for the crystal, informing him of its recovery; but after a violent hunt in which her daughter joined her, they were convinced of the loss of his address. As they were without the means required to mourn and bury Cave in the elaborate style the dignity of an old Seven Dials inhabitant demands, they had appealed to a friendly fellow-tradesman in Great Portland Street. He had very kindly taken over a portion of the stock at a valuation. The valuation was his own and the crystal egg was included in one of the lots. Mr. Wace, after a few suitable consolatory observations, a little off-handedly proffered perhaps, hurried at once to Great Portland Street. But there he learned that the crystal egg had already been sold to a tall, dark man in grey. And there the material facts in this curious, and to me at least very suggestive, story come abruptly to an end. The Great Portland Street dealer did not know who the tall dark man in grey was, nor had he observed him with sufficient attention to describe him minutely. He did not even know which way this person had gone after leaving the shop. For a time Mr. Wace remained in the shop, trying the dealer's patience with hopeless questions, venting his own exasperation. And at last, realising abruptly that the whole thing had passed out of his hands, had vanished like a vision of the night, he returned to his own rooms, a little astonished to find the notes he had made still tangible and visible upon his untidy table.

His annoyance and disappointment were naturally very great. He made a second call (equally ineffectual) upon the Great Portland Street dealer, and he resorted to advertisements in such periodicals as were likely to come into the hands of a bric-à-brac collector. He also wrote letters to *The Daily Chronicle* and *Nature*, but both those periodicals, suspecting a hoax, asked him to reconsider his action before they printed, and he was advised that such a strange story, unfortunately so bare of supporting evidence, might imperil his reputation as an investigator. Moreover, the calls of his proper work were urgent. So that after a month or so, save for an occasional reminder to certain dealers, he had reluctantly to abandon the quest of the crystal egg, and from that day to this it remains undiscovered. Occasionally, however, he tells me, and I can quite believe him, he has bursts of zeal in which he abandons his more urgent occupation and resumes the search.

Whether or not it will remain lost for ever, with the material and origin of it, are things equally speculative at the present time. If the present purchaser is a collector, one would have expected the inquiries of Mr. Wace to have reached him through the dealers. He has been able to discover Mr. Cave's clergyman and "Oriental"—no other than the Rev. James Parker and the young Prince of Bosso-Kuni in Java. I am obliged to them for certain particulars. The object of the Prince was simply curiosity—and extravagance. He was so eager to buy, because Cave was so oddly reluctant to sell. It is just as possible that the buyer in the second instance was simply a casual purchaser and not a collector at all, and the crystal egg, for all I know, may at the present moment be within a mile of me, decorating a drawing-room or serving as a paper-weight—its remarkable functions all unknown. Indeed, it is partly with the idea of such a possibility that I have thrown this narrative into a form that will give it a chance of being read by the ordinary consumer of fiction.

My own ideas in the matter are practically identical with those of Mr. Wace. I believe the crystal on the mast in Mars and the crystal egg of Mr. Cave's to be in some physical, but at present quite inexplicable, way *en rapport*, and we both believe further that the terrestrial crystal must have been—possibly at some remote date—sent hither from that planet, in order to give the Martians a near view of our affairs. Possibly fellows to the crystals in the other masts are also on our globe. No theory of hallucination suffices for the facts.

THE STAR

IT WAS on the first day of the new year that the announcement was made, almost simultaneously from three observatories, that the motion of the planet Neptune, the outermost of all the planets that wheel about the sun, had become very erratic. Ogilvy had already called attention to a suspected retardation in its velocity in December. Such a piece of news was scarcely calculated to interest a world the greater portion of whose inhabitants were unaware of the existence of the planet Neptune, nor outside the astronomical profession did the subsequent discovery of a faint, remote speck of light in the region of the perturbed planet cause any very great excitement. Scientific people, however, found the intelligence remarkable enough, even before it became known that the new body was rapidly growing larger and brighter, that its motion was quite different from the orderly progress of the planets, and that the deflection of Neptune and its satellite was becoming now of an unprecedented kind.

Few people without a training in science can realise the huge isolation of the solar system. The sun with its specks of planets, its dust of planetoids, and its impalpable comets, swims in a vacant immensity that almost defeats the imagination. Beyond the orbit of Neptune there is space, vacant so far as human observation has penetrated, without warmth or light or sound, blank emptiness, for twenty million times a million miles. That is the smallest estimate of the distance to be traversed before the very nearest of the stars is attained. And, saving a few comets more unsubstantial than the thinnest flame, no matter had ever to human knowledge crossed this gulf of space, until early in the twentieth century this strange wanderer appeared. A vast mass of matter it was, bulky, heavy, rushing without warning out of the black mystery of the sky into the radiance of the sun. By the second day it was clearly visible to any decent instrument, as a speck with a barely sensible diameter, in the constellation Leo near Regulus. In a little while an opera glass could attain it.

On the third day of the new year the newspaper readers of two hemispheres were made aware for the first time of the real importance of this unusual apparition in the heavens. "A Planetary Collision," one London paper headed the news, and proclaimed Duchaine's opinion that this strange new planet would probably collide with Neptune. The leader writers enlarged upon the topic. So that in most of the capitals of the world, on January 3rd, there was an expectation, however vague, of some imminent phenomenon in the sky; and as the night followed the sunset round the globe, thousands of men turned their eyes skyward to see—the old familiar stars just as they had always been.

Until it was dawn in London and Pollux setting and the stars overhead grown pale. The winter's dawn it was, a sickly filtering accumulation of daylight, and the light of gas and candles shone yellow in the windows to show where people were astir. But the yawning policeman saw the thing, the busy crowds in the markets stopped agape, workmen going to their work betimes, milkmen, the drivers of news-carts, dissipation going home jaded and pale, homeless wanderers, sentinels on their beats, and in the country, labourers trudging afield, poachers slinking home, all over the dusky quickening country it could be seen—and out at sea by seamen watching for the day—a great white star, come suddenly into the westward sky!

Brighter it was than any star in our skies; brighter than the evening star at its brightest. It still glowed out white and large, no mere twinkling spot of light, but a small round clear shining disc, an hour after the day had come. And where science has not reached, men stared and feared, telling one another of the wars and pestilences that are foreshadowed by these fiery signs in the Heavens. Sturdy Boers, dusky Hottentots, Gold Coast negroes, Frenchmen, Spaniards, Portuguese, stood in the warmth of the sunrise watching the setting of this strange new star.

And in a hundred observatories there had been suppressed
excitement, rising almost to shouting pitch, as the two remote
bodies had rushed together, and a hurrying to and fro to
gather photographic apparatus and spectroscope, and this
appliance and that, to record this novel astonishing sight, the
destruction of a world. For it was a world, a sister planet of
our earth, far greater than our earth indeed, that had so
suddenly flashed into flaming death. Neptune it was had been
struck, fairly and squarely, by the strange planet from outer
space and the heat of the concussion had incontinently turned
two solid globes into one vast mass of incandescence. Round
the world that day, two hours before the dawn, went the pallid
great white star, fading only as it sank westward and the sun
mounted above it. Everywhere men marvelled at it, but of all
those who saw it none could have marvelled more than those
sailors, habitual watchers of the stars, who far away at sea
had heard nothing of its advent and saw it now rise like a
pigmy moon and climb zenithward and hang overhead and
sink westward with the passing of the night.

And when next it rose over Europe everywhere were crowds
of watchers on hilly slopes, on house-roofs, in open spaces,
staring eastward for the rising of the great new star. It rose
with a white glow in front of it, like the glare of a white fire,
and those who had seen it come into existence the night before
cried out at the sight of it. "It is larger," they cried. "It is
brighter!" And, indeed the moon a quarter full and sinking in
the west was in its apparent size beyond comparison, but
scarcely in all its breadth had it as much brightness now as
the little circle of the strange new star.

"It is brighter!" cried the people clustering in the streets.
But in the dim observatories the watchers held their breath
and peered at one another. "*It is nearer*," they said. "*Nearer!*"

And voice after voice repeated, "It is nearer," and the
clicking telegraph took that up, and it trembled along telephone wires, and in a thousand cities grimy compositors
fingered the type. "It is nearer." Men writing in offices,
struck with a strange realisation, flung down their pens; men
talking in a thousand places suddenly came upon a grotesque

possibility in those words, "It is nearer." It hurried along awakening streets, it was shouted down the frost-stilled ways of quiet villages, men who had read these things from the throbbing tape stood in yellow-lit doorways shouting the news to the passers-by. "It is nearer." Pretty women, flushed and glittering, heard the news told jestingly between the dances, and feigned an intelligent interest they did not feel. "Nearer! Indeed. How curious! How very, very clever people must be to find out things like that!"

Lonely tramps faring through the wintry night murmured those words to comfort themselves—looking skyward. "It has need to be nearer, for the night's as cold as charity. Don't seem much warmth from it if it *is* nearer, all the same."

"What is a new star to me?" cried the weeping woman kneeling beside her dead.

The schoolboy, rising early for his examination work, puzzled it out for himself—with the great white star, shining broad and bright through the frost-flowers of his window. "Centrifugal, centripetal," he said, with his chin on his fist. "Stop a planet in its flight, rob it of its centrifugal force, what then? Centripetal has it, and down it falls into the sun! And this——!"

"Do *we* come in the way? I wonder——"

The light of that day went the way of its brethren, and with the later watches of the frosty darkness rose the strange star again. And it was now so bright that the waxing moon seemed but a pale yellow ghost of itself, hanging huge in the sunset. In a South African city a great man had married, and the streets were alight to welcome his return with his bride. "Even the skies have illuminated," said the flatterer. Under Capricorn, two negro lovers, daring the wild beasts and evil spirits, for love of one another, crouched together in a cane brake where the fire-flies hovered. "That is our star," they whispered, and felt strangely comforted by the sweet brilliance of its light.

The master mathematician sat in his private room and pushed the papers from him. His calculations were already finished. In a small white phial there still remained a little of the drug that had kept him awake and active for four long nights. Each day, serene, explicit, patient as ever, he had given his lecture to his students, and then had come back at once to this momentous calculation. His face was grave, a little drawn and hectic from his drugged activity. For some time he seemed lost in thought. Then he went to the window, and the blind went up with a click. Halfway up the sky, over the clustering roofs, chimneys, and steeples of the city, hung the star.

He looked at it as one might look into the eyes of a brave enemy. "You may kill me," he said after a silence. "But I can hold you—and all the universe for that matter—in the grip of this little brain. I would not change. Even now."

He looked at the little phial. "There will be no need of sleep again," he said. The next day at noon, punctual to the minute, he entered his lecture theatre, put his hat on the end of the table as his habit was, and carefully selected a large piece of chalk. It was a joke among his students that he could not lecture without that piece of chalk to fumble in his fingers, and once he had been stricken to impotence by their hiding his supply. He came and looked under his grey eyebrows at the rising tiers of young fresh faces, and spoke with his accustomed studied commonness of phrasing. "Circumstances have risen—circumstances beyond my control," he said and paused, "which will debar me from completing the course I had designed. It would seem, gentlemen, if I may put the thing clearly and briefly, that—Man has lived in vain."

The students glanced at one another. Had they heard aright? Mad? Raised eyebrows and grinning lips there were, but one or two faces remained intent upon his calm grey-fringed face. "It will be interesting," he was saying, "to devote this morning to an exposition, so far as I can make it clear to you, of the calculations that have led me to this conclusion. Let us assume——"

He turned towards the blackboard, meditating a diagram

in the way that was usual to him. "What was that about 'lived in vain'?" whispered one student to another. "Listen," said the other, nodding towards the lecturer.

And presently they began to understand.

That night the star rose later, for its proper eastward motion had carried it some way across Leo towards Virgo, and its brightness was so great that the sky became a luminous blue as it rose, and every star was hidden in its turn, save only Jupiter near the zenith, Capella, Aldebaran, Sirius, and the pointers of the Bear. It was very white and beautiful. In many parts of the world that night a pallid halo encircled it about. It was perceptibly larger; in the clear refractive sky of the tropics it seemed as if it were nearly a quarter the size of the moon. The frost was still on the ground in England, but the world was as brightly lit as if it were midsummer moonlight. One could see to read quite ordinary print by that cold clear light, and in the cities the lamps burnt yellow and wan.

And everywhere the world was awake that night, and throughout Christendom a sombre murmur hung in the keen air over the countryside like the belling of bees in the heather, and this murmurous tumult grew to a clangour in the cities. It was the tolling of the bells in a million belfry towers and steeples, summoning the people to sleep no more, to sin no more, but to gather in their churches and pray. And overhead, growing larger and brighter as the earth rolled on its way and the night passed, rose the dazzling star.

And the streets and houses were alight in all the cities, the shipyards glared, and whatever roads led to high country were lit and crowded all night along. And in all the seas about the civilised lands, ships with throbbing engines, and ships with belling sails, crowded with men and living creatures, were standing out to ocean and the north. For already the warning of the master mathematician had been telegraphed all over the world, and translated into a hundred tongues. The new planet and Neptune, locked in a fiery embrace, were whirling headlong, ever faster and faster towards the sun. Already every second this blazing mass flew a hundred miles, and every second its terrific velocity increased. As it flew now, indeed, it must pass a hundred million of miles wide of the earth and scarcely affect it. But near its destined path, as yet only slightly perturbed, spun the mighty planet Jupiter and his moons sweeping splendid round the sun. Every moment now the attraction between the fiery star and the greatest of the planets grew stronger. And the result of that attraction? Inevitably Jupiter would be deflected from his orbit into an elliptical path, and the burning star, swung by his attraction wide of its sunward rush, would "describe a curved path" and perhaps collide with, and certainly pass very close to, our earth. "Earthquakes, volcanic outbreaks, cyclones, sea waves, floods, and a steady rise in temperature to I know not what limit"—so prophesied the master mathematician.

And overhead, to carry out his words, lonely and cold and livid, blazed the star of the coming doom.

To many who stared at it that night until their eyes ached, it seemed that it was visibly approaching. And that night, too, the weather changed, and the frost that had gripped all Central Europe and France and England softened towards a thaw.

But you must not imagine because I have spoken of people praying through the night and people going aboard ships and people fleeing towards mountainous country that the whole world was already in a terror because of the star. As a matter of fact, use and wont still rulled the world, and save for the talk of idle moments and the splendour of the night, nine human beings out of ten were still busy at their common occupations. In all the cities the shops, save one here and there, opened and closed at their proper hours, the doctor and the undertaker plied their trades, the workers gathered in the factories, soldiers drilled, scholars studied, lovers sought one another, thieves lurked and fled, politicians planned their schemes. The presses of the newspapers roared through the nights, and many a priest of this church and that would not open his holy building to further what he considered a foolish panic. The newsapapers insisted on the lesson of the year 1000—for then, too, people had anticipated the end. The star was no star—mere gas—a comet; and were it a star it could not possibly strike the earth. There was no precedent for such a thing. Common sense was sturdy everywhere, scornful, jesting, a little inclined to persecute the obdurate fearful. That night, at seven-fifteen by Greenwich time, the star would be at its nearest to Jupiter. Then the world would see the turn things would take. The master mathematician's grim warnings were treated by many as so much mere elaborate self-advertisement. Common sense at last, a little heated by argument, signified its unalterable convictions by going to bed. So, too, barbarism and savagery, already tired of the novelty, went about their mighty business, and save for a howling dog here and there, the beast world left the star unheeded.

And yet, when at last the watchers in the European States saw the star rise, an hour later it is true, but no larger than it had been the night before, there were still plenty awake to laugh at the master mathematician—to take the danger as if it had passed.

But hereafter the laughter ceased. The star grew—it grew with a terrible steadiness hour after hour, a little larger each hour, a little nearer the midnight zenith, and brighter and brighter, until it had turned night into a second day. Had it come straight to the earth instead of in a curved path, had it lost no velocity to Jupiter, it must have leapt the intervening gulf in a day, but as it was it took five days altogether to come by our planet. The next night it had become a third the size of the moon before it set to English eyes, and the thaw was assured. It rose over America near the size of the moon, but blinding white to look at, and *hot;* and a breath of hot wind blew now with its rising and gathering strength, and in Virginia, and Brazil, and down the St. Lawrence valley, it shone intermittently through a driving reek of thunder-clouds, flickering violet lightning and hail unprecedented. In Manitoba was a thaw and devastating floods. And upon all the mountains of the earth the snow and ice began to melt that night, and all the rivers coming out of high country flowed thick and turbid, and soon—in their upper reaches—with swirling trees and the bodies of beasts and men. They rose steadily, steadily in the ghostly brilliance, and came trickling over their banks at last, behind the flying population of their valleys.

And along the coast of Argentina and up the South Atlantic the tides were higher than had ever been in the memory of man, and the storms drove the waters in many cases scores of miles inland, drowning whole cities. And so great grew the heat during the night that the rising of the sun was like the coming of a shadow. The earthquakes began and grew until all down America from the Arctic Circle to Cape Horn, hillsides were sliding, fissures were opening, and houses and walls crumbling to destruction. The whole side of Cotopaxi slipped out in one vast convulsion, and a tumult of lava poured out so high and broad and swift and liquid that in one day it reached the sea.

So the star, with the wan moon in its wake, marched across the Pacific, trailed the thunderstorms like the hem of a robe, and the growing tidal wave that toiled behind it, frothing and eager, poured over island and island and swept them clear of men. Until that wave came at last—in a blinding light and with the breath of a furnace, swift and terrible it came—a wall of water, fifty feet high, roaring hungrily, upon the long coasts of Asia, and swept inland across the plains of China. For a space the star, hotter now and larger and brighter than the sun in its strength, showed with pitiless brilliance the wide and populous country; towns and villages with their pagodas and trees, roads, wide, cultivated fields, millions of sleepless people staring in helpless terror at the incandescent sky; and then, low and growing, came the murmur of the flood. And thus it was with millions of men that night—a flight nowhither, with limbs heavy with heat and breath fierce and scant, and the flood like a wall swift and white behind. And then death.

China was lit glowing white, but over Japan and Java and all the islands of Eastern Asia the great star was a ball of dull red fire because of the steam and smoke and ashes the volcanoes were spouting forth to salute its coming. Above was the lava, hot gases and ash, and below the seething floods, and the whole earth swayed and rumbled with the earthquake shocks. Soon the immemorial snows of Thibet and the Himalaya were melting and pouring down by ten million deepening converging channels upon the plains of Burmah and Hindostan. The tangled summits of the Indian jungles were aflame in a thousand places, and below the hurrying waters around the stems were dark objects that still struggled feebly and reflected the blood-red tongues of fire. And in a rudderless confusion a multitude of men and women fled down the broad riverways to that one last hope of men—the open sea.

Larger grew the star, and larger, hotter, and brighter with a terrible swiftness now. The tropical ocean had lost its phosphorescence, and the whirling steam rose in ghostly wreaths from the black waves that plunged incessantly, speckled with storm-tossed ships.

And then came a wonder. It seemed to those who in Europe watched for the rising of the star that the world must have ceased its rotation. In a thousand open spaces of down and upland the people who had fled thither from the floods and the falling houses and sliding slopes of hill watched for that rising in vain. Hour followed hour through a terrible suspense, and the star rose not. Once again men set their eyes upon the old constellations they had counted lost to them for ever. In England it was hot and clear overhead, though the ground quivered perpetually, but in the tropics, Sirius and Capella and Aldebaran showed through a veil of steam. And when at last the great star rose near ten hours late, the sun rose close upon it, and in the centre of its white heart was a disc of black.

Over Asia it was the star had begun to fall behind the movement of the sky, and then suddenly, as it hung over India, its light had been veiled. All the plain of India from the mouth of the Indus to the mouths of the Ganges was a shallow waste of shining water that night, out of which rose temples and palaces, mounds and hills, black with people. Every minaret was a clustering mass of people, who fell one by one into the turbid waters, as heat and terror overcame them. The whole land seemed a-wailing, and suddenly there swept a shadow across that furnace of despair, and a breath of cold wind, and a gathering of clouds, out of the cooling air. Men looking up, near blinded, at the star, saw that a black disc was creeping across the light. It was the moon, coming between the star and the earth. And even as men cried to God at this respite, out of the East with a strange inexplicable swiftness sprang the sun. And then star, sun, and moon rushed together across the heavens.

So it was that presently, to the European watchers, star and sun rose close upon each other, drove headlong for a space and then slower, and at last came to rest, star and sun merged into one glare of flame at the zenith of the sky. The moon no longer eclipsed the star but was lost to sight in the brilliance of the sky. And though those who were still alive regarded it for the most part with that dull stupidity that hunger, fatigue, heat, and despair engender, there were still men who could perceive the meaning of these signs. Star and earth had been at their nearest, had swung about one another, and the star had passed. Already it was receding, swifter and swifter, in the last stage of its headlong journey downward into the sun.

And then the clouds gathered, blotting out the vision of the sky, the thunder and lightning wove a garment round the world; all over the earth was such a downpour of rain as men had never before seen, and where the volcanoes flared red against the cloud canopy there descended torrents of mud. Everywhere the waters were pouring off the land, leaving mud-silted ruins, and the earth littered like a storm-worn beach with all that had floated, and the dead bodies of the men and brutes, its children. For days the water streamed off the land, sweeping away soil and trees and houses in the way, and piling huge dykes and scooping out Titanic gullies over the countryside. Those were the days of darkness that followed the star and the heat. All through them, and for many weeks and months, the earthquakes continued.

But the star had passed, and men, hunger-driven and gathering courage only slowly, might creep back to their ruined cities, buried granaries, and sodden fields. Such few ships as had escaped the storms of that time came stunned and shattered and sounding their way cautiously through the new marks and shoals of once-familiar ports. And as the storms subsided men perceived that everywhere the days were hotter than of yore, and the sun larger, and the moon, shrunk to a third of its former size, took now fourscore days between its new and new.

But of the new brotherhood that grew presently among men, of the saving of laws and books and machines, of the strange change that had come over Iceland and Greenland and the shores of Baffin's Bay, so that the sailors coming there presently found them green and gracious, and could scarce believe their eyes, this story does not tell. Nor of the movement of mankind now that the earth was hotter, northward and southward towards the poles of the earth. It concerns itself only with the coming and the passing of the star.

The Martian astronomers—for there are astronomers on Mars, although they are very different beings from men—were naturally profoundly interested by these things. They saw them from their own standpoint, of course. "Considering the mass and temperature of the missile that was flung through our solar system into the sun," one wrote, "it is astonishing what a little damage the earth, which it missed so narrowly, has sustained. All the familiar continental markings and the masses of the seas remain intact, and indeed the only difference seems to be a shrinkage of the white discoloration (supposed to be frozen water) round either pole." Which only shows how small the vastest of human catastrophes may seem, at a distance of a few million miles.

THE MAN WHO COULD WORK MIRACLES

A Pantoum in Prose

IT IS doubtful whether the gift was innate. For my own part, I think it came to him suddenly. Indeed, until he was thirty he was a sceptic, and did not believe in miraculous powers. And here, since it is the most convenient place, I must mention that he was a little man, and had eyes of a hot brown, very erect red hair, a moustache with ends that he twisted up, and freckles. His name was George McWhirter Fotheringay—not the sort of name by any means to lead to any expectation of miracles—and he was clerk at Gomshott's. He was greatly addicted to assertive argument. It was while he was asserting the impossibility of miracles that he had his first intimation of his extraordinary powers. This particular argument was being held in the bar of the Long Dragon, and Toddy Beamish was conducting the opposition by a monotonous but effective "So *you* say," that drove Mr. Fotheringay to the very limit of his patience.

There were present, besides these two, a very dusty cyclist, landlord Cox, and Miss Maybridge, the perfectly respectable and rather portly barmaid of the Dragon. Miss Maybridge was standing with her back to Mr. Fotheringay, washing glasses; the others were watching him, more or less amused by the present ineffectiveness of the assertive method. Goaded by the Torres Vedras tactics of Mr. Beamish, Mr. Fotheringay determined to make an unusual rhetorical effort. "Looky here, Mr. Beamish," said Mr. Fotheringay. "Let us clearly understand what a miracle is. It's something contrariwise to the course of nature done by power of Will, something what couldn't happen without being specially willed."

"So *you* say," said Mr. Beamish, repulsing him.

Mr. Fotheringay appealed to the cyclist, who had hitherto been a silent auditor, and received his assent—given with a hesitating cough and a glance at Mr. Beamish. The landlord would express no opinion, and Mr. Fotheringay, returning to Mr. Beamish, received the unexpected concession of a qualified assent to his definition of a miracle.

"For instance," said Mr. Fotheringay, greatly encouraged. "Here would be a miracle. That lamp, in the natural course of nature, couldn't burn like that upsy-down, could it, Beamish?"

"*You* say it couldn't," said Beamish.

"And you?" said Fotheringay. "You don't mean to say—eh?"

"No," said Beamish reluctantly. "No, it couldn't."

"Very well," said Mr. Fotheringay. "Then here comes someone, as it might be me, along here, and stands as it might be here, and says to that lamp, as I might do, collecting all my will—'Turn upsy-down without breaking, and go on burning steady,' and—— Hullo!"

It was enough to make anyone say "Hullo!" The impossible, the incredible, was visible to them all. The lamp hung inverted in the air, burning quietly with its flame pointing down. It was as solid, as indisputable as ever a lamp was, the prosaic common lamp of the Long Dragon bar.

Mr. Fotheringay stood with an extended forefinger and the knitted brows of one anticipating a catastrophic smash. The cyclist, who was sitting next the lamp, ducked and jumped across the bar. Everybody jumped, more or less. Miss Maybridge turned and screamed. For nearly three seconds the lamp remained still. A faint cry of mental distress came from Mr. Fotheringay. "I can't keep it up," he said, "any longer." He staggered back, and the inverted lamp suddenly flared, fell against the corner of the bar, bounced aside, smashed upon the floor, and went out.

It was lucky it had a metal receiver, or the whole place would have been in a blaze. Mr. Cox was the first to speak, and his remark, shorn of needless excrescences, was to the effect that Fotheringay was a fool. Fotheringay was beyond disputing even so fundamental a proposition as that! He was astonished beyond measure at the thing that had occurred. The subsequent conversation threw absolutely no light on the matter so far as Fotheringay was concerned; the general opinion not only followed Mr. Cox very closely but very vehemently. Everyone accused Fotheringay of a silly trick, and presented him to himself as a foolish destroyer of comfort and security. His mind was in a tornado of perplexity, he was himself inclined to agree with them, and he made a remarkably ineffectual opposition to the proposal of his departure.

He went home flushed and heated, coat-collar crumpled, eyes smarting, and ears red. He watched each of the ten street lamps nervously as he passed it. It was only when he found himself alone in his little bedroom in Church Row that he was able to grapple seriously with his memories of the occurrence, and ask, "What on earth happened?"

He had removed his coat and boots, and was sitting on the bed with his hands in his pockets repeating the text of his defence for the seventeenth time, "*I* didn't want the confounded thing to upset," when it occurred to him that at the precise moment he had said the commanding words he had inadvertently willed the thing he said, and that when he had seen the lamp in the air he had felt that it depended on him to maintain it there without being clear how this was to be done. He had not a particularly complex mind, or he might have stuck for a time at that "inadvertently willed," embracing, as it does, the abstrusest problems of voluntary action; but as it was, the idea came to him with a quite acceptable haziness. And from that, following, as I must admit, no clear logical path, he came to the test of experiment.

He pointed resolutely to his candle and collected his mind, though he felt he did a foolish thing. "Be raised up," he said. But in a second that feeling vanished. The candle was raised, hung in the air one giddy moment, and as Mr. Fotheringay gasped, fell with a smash on his toilet-table, leaving him in darkness save for the expiring glow of its wick.

For a time Mr. Fotheringay sat in the darkness, perfectly still. "It did happen, after all," he said. "And 'ow I'm to explain it I *don't* know." He sighed heavily, and began feeling in his pockets for a match. He could find none, and he rose and groped about the toilet-table. "I wish I had a match," he said. He resorted to his coat, and there were none there, and then it dawned upon him that miracles were possible even with matches. He extended a hand and scowled at it in the dark. "Let there be a match in that hand," he said. He felt some light object fall across his palm, and his fingers closed upon a match.

After several ineffectual attempts to light this, he discovered it was a safety-match. He threw it down, and then it occurred to him that he might have willed it lit. He did, and perceived it burning in the midst of his toilet-table mat. He caught it up hastily, and it went out. His perception of possibilities enlarged, and he felt for and replaced the candle in its candlestick. "Here! *you* be lit," said Mr. Fotheringay, and forthwith the candle was flaring, and he saw a little black hole in the toilet-cover, with a wisp of smoke rising from it. For a time he stared from this to the little flame and back, and then looked up and met his own gaze in the looking-glass. By this help he communed with himself in silence for a time.

"How about miracles now?" said Mr. Fotheringay at last, addressing his reflection.

The subsequent meditations of Mr. Fotheringay were of a severe but confused description. So far as he could see, it was a case of pure willing with him. The nature of his first experiences disinclined him for any further experiments except of the most cautious type. But he lifted a sheet of paper, and turned a glass of water pink and then green, and he created a snail, which he miraculously annihilated, and got himself a miraculous new toothbrush. Somewhen in the small hours he had reached the fact that his will-power must be of a particularly rare and pungent quality, a fact of which he had certainly had inklings before, but no certain assurance. The scare and perplexity of his first discovery were now qualified by pride in this evidence of singularity and by vague intimations of advantage. He became aware that the church clock was striking one, and as it did not occur to him that his daily duties at Gomshott's might be miraculously dispensed with, he resumed undressing, in order to get to bed without further delay. As he struggled to get his shirt over his head he was struck with a brilliant idea. "Let me be in bed," he said, and found himself so. "Undressed," he stipulated; and, finding the sheets cold, added hastily, "and in my nightshirt— no, in a nice soft woollen nightshirt. Ah!" he said with immense enjoyment. "And now let me be comfortably asleep. . . ."

He awoke at his usual hour and was pensive all through breakfast-time, wondering whether his overnight experience might not be a particularly vivid dream. At length his mind turned again to cautious experiments. For instance, he had three eggs for breakfast; two his landlady had supplied, good, but shoppy, and one was a delicious fresh goose-egg, laid, cooked, and served by his extraordinary will. He hurried off to Gomshott's in a state of profound but carefully concealed excitement, and only remembered the shell of the third egg when his landlady spoke of it that night. All day he could do no work because of this astonishingly new self-knowledge, but this caused him no inconvenience, because he made up for it miraculously in his last ten minutes.

As the day wore on his state of mind passed from wonder to elation, albeit the circumstances of his dismissal from the Long Dragon were still disagreeable to recall, and a garbled account of the matter that had reached his colleagues led to some badinage. It was evident he must be careful how he lifted frangible articles, but in other ways his gift promised more and more as he turned it over in his mind. He intended among other things to increase his personal property by unostentatious acts of creation. He called into existence a pair of very splendid diamond studs, and hastily annihilated them again as young Gomshott came across the counting-house to his desk. He was afraid young Gomshott might wonder how he had come by them. He saw quite clearly the gift required caution and watchfulness in its exercise, but so far as he could judge the difficulties attending its mastery would be no greater than those he had already faced in the study of cycling. It was that analogy, perhaps, quite as much as the feeling that he would be unwelcome in the Long Dragon, that drove him out after supper into the lane beyond the gas-works, to rehearse a few miracles in private.

There was possibly a certain want of originality in his attempts, for apart from his will-power Mr. Fotheringay was not a very exceptional man. The miracle of Moses' rod came to his mind, but the night was dark and unfavourable to the proper control of large miraculous snakes. Then he recollected the story of "Tannhäuser" that he had read on the back of the Philharmonic programme. That seemed to him singularly attractive and harmless. He stuck his walking-stick—a very nice Poona-Penang lawyer—into the turf that edged the footpath, and commanded the dry wood to blossom. The air was immediately full of the scent of roses, and by means of a match he saw for himself that this beautiful miracle was indeed accomplished. His satisfaction was ended by advancing footsteps. Afraid of a premature discovery of his powers, he addressed the blossoming stick hastily: "Go back." What he meant was "Change back"; but of course he was confused. The stick receded at a considerable velocity, and incontinently came a cry of anger and a bad word from the approaching person. "Who are you throwing brambles at, you fool?" cried a voice. "That got me on the shin."

"I'm sorry, old chap," said Mr. Fotheringay, and then, realising the awkward nature of the explanation, caught nervously at his moustache. He saw Winch, one of the three Immering constables, advancing.

"What d'yer mean by it?" asked the constable. "Hullo! It's you, is it? The gent that broke the lamp at the Long Dragon!"

"I don't mean anything by it," said Mr. Fotheringay. "Nothing at all."

"What d'yer do it for then?"

"Oh, bother!" said Mr. Fotheringay.

"Bother, indeed? D'yer know that stick hurt? What d'yer do it for, eh?"

For the moment Mr. Fotheringay could not think what he had done it for. His silence seemed to irritate Mr. Winch. "You've been assaulting the police, young man, this time. That's what *you* done."

"Look here, Mr. Winch," said Mr. Fotheringay, annoyed and confused, "I'm very sorry. The fact is——"

"Well?"

He could think of no way but the truth. "I was working a miracle." He tried to speak in an off-hand way, but try as he would he couldn't.

"Working a——! 'Ere, don't you talk rot. Working a miracle, indeed! Miracle! Well, that's downright funny! Why, you's the chap that don't believe in miracles. . . . Fact is, this is another of your silly conjuring tricks—that's what this is. Now, I tell you——"

But Mr. Fotheringay never heard what Mr. Winch was going to tell him. He realised he had given himself away, flung his valuable secret to all the winds of heaven. A violent gust of irritation swept him to action. He turned on the constable swiftly and fiercely. "Here," he said, "I've had enough of this, I have! I'll show you a silly conjuring trick, I will! Go to Hades! Go, now!"

He was alone!

Mr. Fotheringay performed no more miracles that night nor did he trouble to see what had become of his flowering stick. He returned to the town, scared and very quiet, and went to his bedroom. "Lord!" he said, "it's a powerful gift— an extremely powerful gift. I didn't hardly mean as much as that. Not really. . . . I wonder what Hades is like!"

He sat on the bed taking off his boots. Struck by a happy thought he transferred the constable to San Francisco, and without any more interference with normal causation went soberly to bed. In the night he dreamt of the anger of Winch.

The next day Mr. Fotheringay heard two interesting items of news. Someone had planted a most beautiful climbing rose

against the elder Mr. Gomshott's private house in the Lulla-
borough Road, and the river as far as Rawling's Mill was to
be dragged for Constable Winch.

Mr. Fotheringay was abstracted and thoughtful all that
day, and performed no miracles except certain provisions for
Winch, and the miracle of completing his day's work with
punctual perfection in spite of all the bee-swarm of thoughts
that hummed through his mind. And the extraordinary
abstraction and meekness of his manner was remarked by
several people, and made a matter for jesting. For the most
part he was thinking of Winch.

On Sunday evening he went to chapel, and oddly enough,
Mr. Maydig, who took a certain interest in occult matters,
preached about "things that are not lawful." Mr. Fotheringay was not a regular chapel goer, but the system of assertive
scepticism, to which I have already alluded, was now very
much shaken. The tenor of the sermon threw an entirely
new light on these novel gifts, and he suddenly decided to
consult Mr. Maydig immediately after the service. So soon
as that was determined, he found himself wondering why he
had not done so before.

Mr. Maydig, a lean, excitable man with quite remarkably
long wrists and neck, was gratified at a request for a private
conversation from a young man whose carelessness in religious matters was a subject for general remark in the town.
After a few necessary delays, he conducted him to the study of
the Manse, which was contiguous to the chapel, seated him
comfortably, and, standing in front of a cheerful fire—his legs
threw a Rhodian arch of shadow on the opposite wall—re-
quested Mr. Fotheringay to state his business.

At first Mr. Fotheringay was a little abashed, and found
some difficulty in opening the matter. "You will scarcely
believe me, Mr. Maydig, I am afraid"—and so forth for some
time. He tried a question at last, and asked Mr. Maydig his
opinion of miracles.

Mr. Maydig was still saying "Well" in an extremely
judicial tone, when Mr. Fotheringay interrupted again: "You
don't believe, I suppose, that some common sort of person—

like myself, for instance—as it might be sitting here now, might have some sort of twist inside him that made him able to do things by his will."

"It's possible," said Mr. Maydig. "Something of the sort, perhaps, is possible."

"If I might make free with something here, I think I might show you by a sort of experiment," said Mr. Fotheringay. "Now, take that tobacco-jar on the table, for instance. What I want to know is whether what I am going to do with it is a miracle or not. Just half a minute, Mr. Maydig, please."

He knitted his brows, pointed to the tobacco-jar and said: "Be a bowl of vi'lets."

The tobacco-jar did as it was ordered.

Mr. Maydig started violently at the change, and stood looking from the thaumaturgist to the bowl of flowers. He said nothing. Presently he ventured to lean over the table and smell the violets; they were fresh-picked and very fine ones. Then he stared at Mr. Fotheringay again.

"How did you do that?" he asked.

Mr. Fotheringay pulled his moustache. "Just told it—and there you are. Is that a miracle, or is it black art, or what is it? And what do you think's the matter with me? That's what I want to ask."

"It's a most extraordinary occurrence."

"And this day last week I knew no more that I could do things like that than you did. It came quite sudden. It's something odd about my will, I suppose, and that's as far as I can see."

"Is *that*—the only thing? Could you do other things besides that?"

"Lord, yes!" said Mr. Fotheringay. "Just anything." He thought, and suddenly recalled a conjuring entertainment he had seen. "Here!" He pointed. "Change into a bowl of fish—no, not that—change into a glass bowl full of water with goldfish swimming in it. That's better! You see that, Mr. Maydig?"

"It's astonishing. It's incredible. You are either a most extraordinary . . . But no——"

"I could change it into anything," said Mr. Fotheringay. "Just anything. Here! be a pigeon, will you?"

In another moment a blue pigeon was fluttering round the room and making Mr. Maydig duck every time it came near him. "Stop there, will you," said Mr. Fotheringay; and the pigeon hung motionless in the air. "I could change it back to a bowl of flowers," he said, and after replacing the pigeon on the table worked that miracle. "I expect you will want your pipe in a bit," he said, and restored the tobacco-jar.

Mr. Maydig had followed all these later changes in a sort of ejaculatory silence. He stared at Mr. Fotheringay and, in a very gingerly manner, picked up the tobacco-jar, examined it, replaced it on the table. "*Well!*" was the only expression of his feelings.

"Now, after that it's easier to explain what I came about," said Mr. Fotheringay; and proceeded to a lengthy and involved narrative of his strange experiences, beginning with the affair of the lamp in the Long Dragon and complicated by persistent allusions to Winch. As he went on, the transient pride Mr. Maydig's consternation had caused passed away; he became the very ordinary Mr. Fotheringay of everyday intercourse again. Mr. Maydig listened intently, the tobacco-jar in his hand, and his bearing changed also with the course of the narrative. Presently, while Mr. Fotheringay was dealing with the miracle of the third egg, the minister interrupted with a fluttering extended hand—

"It is possible," he said. "It is credible. It is amazing, of course, but it reconciles a number of difficulties. The power to work miracles is a gift—a peculiar quality like genius or second sight—hitherto it has come vary rarely and to exceptional people. But in this case . . . I have always wondered at the miracles of Mahomet, and at Yogi's miracles, and the miracles of Madame Blavatsky. But, of course! Yes, it is simply a gift! It carries out so beautifully the arguments of that great thinker"—Mr. Maydig's voice sank—"his Grace the Duke of Argyll. Here we plumb some profounder law—deeper than the ordinary laws of nature. Yes—yes. Go on. Go on!"

Mr. Fotheringay proceeded to tell of his misadventure with Winch, and Mr. Maydig, no longer overawed or scared, began to jerk his limbs about and interject astonishment. "It's this what troubled me most," proceeded Mr. Fotheringay; "it's this I'm most mijitly in want of advice for; of course he's at San Francisco—wherever San Francisco may be—but of course it's awkward for both of us, as you'll see, Mr. Maydig. I don't see how he can understand what has happened, and I dare say he's scared and exasperated something tremendous, and trying to get at me. I dare say he keeps on starting off to come here. I send him back, by a miracle, every few hours, when I think of it. And of course, that's a thing he won't be able to understand, and it's bound to annoy him; and, of course, if he takes a ticket every time it will cost him a lot of money. I done the best I could for him, but of course it's difficult for him to put himself in my place. I thought afterwards that his clothes might have got scorched, you know—if Hades is all it's supposed to be—before I shifted him. In that case I suppose they'd have locked him up in San Francisco. Of course I willed him a new suit of clothes on him directly I thought of it. But, you see, I'm already in a deuce of a tangle——"

Mr. Maydig looked serious. "I see you are in a tangle. Yes, it's a difficult position. How you are to end it . . ." He became diffuse and inconclusive.

"However, we'll leave Winch for a little and discuss the larger question. I don't think this is a case of the black art or anything of the sort. I don't think there is any taint of criminality about it at all, Mr. Fotheringay—none whatever, unless you are suppressing material facts. No, it's miracles—pure miracles—miracles, if I may say so, of the very highest class."

He began to pace the hearthrug and gesticulate, while Mr. Fotheringay sat with his arm on the table and his head on his arm, looking worried. "I don't see how I'm to manage about Winch," he said.

"A gift of working miracles—apparently a very powerful gift," said Mr. Maydig, "will find a way about Winch—never 'ear. My dear sir, you are a most important man—a man of the most astonishing possibilities. As evidence, for example! And in other ways, the things you may do. . . ."

"Yes, I've thought of a thing or two," said Mr. Fotheringay. "But—some of the things came a bit twisty. You saw that fish at first? Wrong sort of bowl and wrong sort of fish. And I thought I'd ask someone."

"A proper course," said Mr. Maydig, "a very proper course—altogether the proper course." He stopped and looked at Mr. Fotheringay. "It's practically an unlimited gift. Let us test your powers, for instance. If they really are . . . If they really are all they seem to be."

And so, incredible as it may seem, in the study of the little house behind the Congregational Chapel, on the evening of Sunday, Nov. 10, 1896, Mr. Fotheringay, egged on and inspired by Mr. Maydig, began to work miracles. The reader's attention is specially and definitely called to the date. He will object, probably has already objected, that certain points in this story are improbable, that if any things of the sort already described had indeed occurred, they would have been in all the papers a year ago. The details immediately following he will find particularly hard to accept, because among other things they involve the conclusion that he or she, the reader in question, must have been killed in a violent and unprecedented manner more than a year ago. Now a miracle is nothing if not improbable, and as a matter of fact the reader *was* killed in a violent and unprecedented manner a year ago. In the subsequent course of this story that will become perfectly clear and credible, as every right-minded and reasonable reader will admit. But this is not the place for the end of the story, being but little beyond the hither side of the middle. And at first the miracles worked by Mr. Fotheringay were timid little miracles—little things with the cups and parlour fitments, as feeble as the miracles of Theosophists, and, feeble as they were, they were received with awe by his collaborator. He would have preferred to settle the Winch business out of hand, but Mr. Maydig would not let him. But after they had worked a dozen of these domestic trivialities, their sense of power grew, their imagination began to show signs of stimulation, and their ambition enlarged. Their first larger enterprise was due to hunger and the negligence of Mrs. Minchin, Mr. Maydig's housekeeper. The meal to which the minister conducted Mr. Fotheringay was certainly ill-laid and uninviting as refreshment for two industrious miracle-workers; but they were seated, and Mr. Maydig was descanting in sorrow rather than in anger upon his housekeeper's shortcomings, before it occurred to Mr. Fotheringay that an opportunity lay before him. "Don't you think, Mr. Maydig," he said, "if it isn't a liberty, I——"

"My dear Mr. Fotheringay! Of course! No—I didn't think."

Mr. Fotheringay waved his hand. "What shall we have?" he said, in a large, inclusive spirit, and, at Mr. Maydig's order, revised the supper very thoroughly. "As for me," he said, eyeing Mr. Maydig's selection, "I am always particularly fond of a tankard of stout and a nice Welsh rarebit, and I'll order that. I ain't much given to Burgundy," and forthwith stout and Welsh rarebit promptly appeared at his command. They sat long at their supper, talking like equals, as Mr. Fotheringay presently perceived with a glow of surprise and gratification, of all the miracles they would presently do. "And, by the bye, Mr. Maydig," said Mr. Fotheringay, "I might perhaps be able to help you—in a domestic way."

"Don't quite follow," said Mr. Maydig, pouring out a glass of miraculous old Burgundy.

Mr. Fotheringay helped himself to a second Welsh rarebit out of vacancy, and took a mouthful. "I was thinking," he said, "I might be able (*chum, chum*) to work (*chum, chum*) a miracle with Mrs. Minchin (*chum, chum*)—make her a better woman."

Mr. Maydig put down the glass and looked doubtful. "She's—— She strongly objects to interference, you know, Mr. Fotheringay. And—as a matter of fact—it's well past eleven and she's probably in bed and asleep. Do you think, on the whole——"

Mr. Fotheringay considered these objections. "I don't see that it shouldn't be done in her sleep."

For a time Mr. Maydig opposed the idea, and then he yielded. Mr. Fotheringay issued his orders, and a little less at their ease, perhaps, the two gentlemen proceeded with their repast. Mr. Maydig was enlarging on the changes he might expect in his housekeeper next day, with an optimism that seemed even to Mr. Fotheringay's supper senses a little forced and hectic, when a series of confused noises from upstairs began. Their eyes exchanged interrogations, and Mr. Maydig left the room hastily. Mr. Fotheringay heard him calling up to his housekeeper and then his footsteps going softly up to her.

In a minute or so the minister returned, his step light, his face radiant. "Wonderful!" he said, "and touching! Most touching!"

He began pacing the hearthrug. "A repentance—a most touching repentance—through the crack of the door. Poor woman! A most wonderful change! She had got up. She must have got up at once. She had got up out of her sleep to smash a private bottle of brandy in her box. And to confess it, too! . . . But this gives us—it opens—a most amazing vista of possibilities. If we can work this miraculous change in *her* . . ."

"The thing's unlimited seemingly," said Mr. Fotheringay. "And about Mr. Winch——"

"Altogether unlimited." And from the hearthrug Mr. Maydig, waving the Winch difficulty aside, unfolded a series of wonderful proposals—proposals he invented as he went along.

Now what those proposals were does not concern the essentials of this story. Suffice it that they were designed in a spirit of infinite benevolence, the sort of benevolence that used to be called post-prandial. Suffice it, too, that the problem of Winch remained unsolved. Nor is it necessary to describe how far that series got to its fulfilment. There were astonishing changes. The small hours found Mr. Maydig and Mr. Fotheringay careering across the chilly market-square under the still moon, in a sort of ecstasy of thaumaturgy, Mr. Maydig all flap and gesture, Mr. Fotheringay short and bristling, and no longer abashed at his greatness. They had reformed every drunkard in the Parliamentary division, changed all the beer and alcohol to water (Mr. Maydig had overruled Mr. Fotheringay on this point), they had, further, greatly improved the railway communication of the place, drained Flinder's swamp, improved the soil of One Tree Hill, and cured the Vicar's wart. And they were going to see what could be done with the injured pier at South Bridge. "The place," gasped Mr. Maydig, "won't be the same place to-morrow. How surprised and thankful everyone will be!" And just at that moment the church clock struck three.

"I say," said Mr. Fotheringay, "that's three o'clock! I must be getting back. I've got to be at business by eight. And besides, Mrs. Wimms——"

"We're only beginning," said Mr. Maydig, full of the sweetness of unlimited power. "We're only beginning. Think of all the good we're doing. When people wake——"

"But——," said Mr. Fotheringay.

Mr. Maydig gripped his arm suddenly. His eyes were bright and wild. "My dear chap," he said, "there's no hurry. Look"—he pointed to the moon at the zenith—"Joshua!"

"Joshua?" said Mr. Fotheringay.

"Joshua," said Mr. Maydig. "Why not? Stop it."

Mr. Fotheringay looked at the moon.

"That's a bit tall," he said after a pause.

"Why not?" said Mr. Maydig. "Of course it doesn't stop. You stop the rotation of the earth, you know. Time stops. It isn't as if we were doing harm."

"H'm!" said Mr. Fotheringay. "Well." He sighed. "I'll try. Here——"

He buttoned up his jacket and addressed himself to the habitable globe, with as good an assumption of confidence as lay in his power. "Jest stop rotating, will you?" said Mr. Fotheringay.

Incontinently he was flying head over heels through the air at the rate of dozens of miles a minute. In spite of the innumerable circles he was describing per second, he thought; for thought is wonderful—sometimes as sluggish as flowing pitch, sometimes as instantaneous as light. He thought in a second, and willed. "Let me come down safe and sound. Whatever else happens, let me down safe and sound."

He willed it only just in time, for his clothes, heated by his rapid flight through the air, were already beginning to singe. He came down with a forcible but by no means injurious bump in what appeared to be a mound of fresh-turned earth. A large mass of metal and masonry, extraordinarily like the clock-tower in the middle of the market-square, hit the earth near him, ricochetted over him, and flew into stonework, bricks, and masonry, like a bursting bomb. A hurtling cow hit one of the larger blocks and smashed like an egg. There was a crash that made all the most violent crashes of his past life seem like the sound of falling dust, and this was followed by a descending series of lesser crashes. A vast wind roared throughout earth and heaven, so that he could scarcely lift his head to look. For a while he was too breathless and astonished even to see where he was or what had happened. And his first movement was to feel his head and reassure himself that his streaming hair was still his own.

"Lord!" gasped Mr. Fotheringay, scarce able to speak for the gale, "I've had a squeak! What's gone wrong? Storms and thunder. And only a minute ago a fine night. It's Maydig set me on to this sort of thing. *What* a wind! If I go on fooling in this way I'm bound to have a thundering accident! . . .

"Where's Maydig?

"What a confounded mess everything's in!"

He looked about him so far as his flapping jacket would permit. The appearance of things was really extremely strange. "The sky's all right anyhow," said Mr. Fotheringay. "And that's about all that is all right. And even there it looks like a terrific gale coming up. But there's the moon overhead. Just as it was just now. Bright as midday. But as for the rest —— Where's the village? Where's—where's anything? And what on earth set this wind a-blowing? *I* didn't order no wind."

Mr. Fotheringay struggled to get to his feet in vain, and after one failure, remained on all fours, holding on. He surveyed the moonlit world to leeward, with the tails of his jacket streaming over his head. "There's something seriously wrong," said Mr. Fotheringay. "And what it is—goodness knows."

Far and wide nothing was visible in the white glare through the haze of dust that drove before a screaming gale but tumbled masses of earth and heaps of inchoate ruins, no trees, no houses, no familiar shapes, only a wilderness of disorder vanishing at last into the darkness beneath the whirling columns and streamers, the lightnings and thunderings of a swiftly rising storm. Near him in the livid glare was something that might once have been an elm-tree, a smashed mass of splinters, shivered from boughs to base, and further a twisted mass of iron girders—only too evidently the viaduct—rose out of the piled confusion.

You see, when Mr. Fotheringay had arrested the rotation of the solid globe, he had made no stipulation concerning the trifling movables upon its surface. And the earth spins so fast that the surface at its equator is travelling at rather more than a thousand miles an hour, and in these latitudes at more than half that pace. So that the village, and Mr. Maydig, and Mr. Fotheringay, and everybody and everything had been jerked violently forward at about nine miles per second—that is to say, much more violently than if they had been fired out of a cannon. And every human being, every living creature, every house, and every tree—all the world as we know it—had been so jerked and smashed and utterly destroyed. That was all.

These things Mr. Fotheringay did not, of course, fully appreciate. But he perceived that his miracle had miscarried, and with that a great disgust of miracles came upon him. He was in darkness now, for the clouds had swept together and blotted out his momentary glimpse of the moon, and the air was full of fitful struggling tortured wraiths of hail. A great roaring of wind and waters filled earth and sky, and, peering under his hand through the dust and sleet to windward, he saw by the play of the lightnings a vast wall of water pouring towards him.

"Maydig!" screamed Mr. Fotheringay's feeble voice amid the elemental uproar. "Here!—Maydig!"

"Stop!" cried Mr. Fotheringay to the advancing water. "Oh, for goodness' sake, stop!

"Just a moment," said Mr. Fotheringay to the lightnings and thunder. "Stop jest a moment while I collect my thoughts . . . And now what shall I do?" he said. "What *shall* I do? Lord! I wish Maydig was about.

"I know," said Mr. Fotheringay. "And for goodness' sake let's have it right *this* time."

He remained on all fours, leaning against the wind, very intent to have everything right.

"Ah!" he said. "Let nothing what I'm going to order happen until I say 'Off!' . . . Lord! I wish I'd thought of that before!"

He lifted his little voice against the whirlwind, shouting louder and louder in the vain desire to hear himself speak. "Now then!—here goes! Mind about that what I said just now. In the first place, when all I've got to say is done, let me lose my miraculous power, let my will become just like anybody else's will, and all these dangerous miracles be stopped. I don't like them. I'd rather I didn't work 'em. Ever so much. That's the first thing. And the second is—let me be back just before the miracles begin; let everything be just as it was before that blessed lamp turned up. It's a big job, but it's the last. Have you got it? No more miracles, everything as it was —me back in the Long Dragon just before I drank my half-pint. That's it! Yes."

He dug his fingers into the mould, closed his eyes, and said "Off!"

Everything became perfectly still. He perceived that he was standing erect.

"So *you* say," said a voice.

He opened his eyes. He was in the bar of the Long Dragon, arguing about miracles with Toddy Beamish. He had a vague sense of some great thing forgotten that instantaneously passed. You see, except for the loss of his miraculous powers, everything was back as it had been; his mind and memory therefore were now just as they had been at the time when this story began. So that he knew absolutely nothing of all that is told here, knows nothing of all that is told here to this day. And among other things, of course, he still did not believe in miracles.

"I tell you that miracles, properly speaking, can't possibly happen," he said, "whatever you like to hold. And I'm prepared to prove it up to the hilt."

"That's what *you* think," said Toddy Beamish, and "Prove it if you can."

"Looky here, Mr. Beamish," said Mr. Fotheringay. "Let us clearly understand what a miracle is. It's something contrariwise to the course of nature done by power of Will. . . ."

FILMER

IN TRUTH the mastery of flying was the work of thousands of men—this man a suggestion and that an experiment, until at last only one vigorous intellectual effort was needed to finish the work. But the inexorable injustice of the popular mind has decided that of all these thousands, one man, and that a man who never flew, should be chosen as the discoverer, just as it has chosen to honour Watt as the discoverer of steam and Stephenson of the steam-engine. And surely of all honoured names none is so grotesquely and tragically honoured as poor Filmer's, the timid, intellectual creature who solved the problem over which the world had hung perplexed and a little fearful for so many generations, the man who pressed the button that has changed peace and warfare and wellnigh every condition of human life and happiness. Never has that recurring wonder of the littleness of the scientific man in the face of the greatness of his science found such an amazing exemplification. Much concerning Filmer is, and must remain, profoundly obscure—Filmers attract no Boswells—but the essential facts and the concluding scene are clear enough, and there are letters, and notes, and casual allusions to piece the whole together. And this is the story one makes, putting this thing with that, of Filmer's life and death.

The first authentic trace of Filmer on the page of history is a document in which he applies for admission as a paid student in physics to the Government laboratories at South Kensington, and therein he describes himself as the son of a "military bootmaker" ("cobbler" in the vulgar tongue) of Dover, and lists his various examination proofs of a high proficiency in chemistry and mathematics. With a certain want of dignity he seeks to enhance these attainments by a profession of poverty and disadvantages, and he writes of the laboratory as the "goal" of his ambitious, a slip which re-inforces his claim to have devoted himself exclusively to the exact sciences. The document is endorsed in a manner that shows Filmer was admitted to this coveted opportunity; but until quite recently no traces of his success in the Government institution could be found.

It has now, however, been shown that in spite of his pro-fessed zeal for research, Filmer, before he had held this scholarship a year, was tempted by the possibility of a small increase in his immediate income to abandon it in order to become one of the nine-pence-an-hour computers employed by a well-known Professor in his vicarious conduct of those extensive researches of his insolar physics—researches which are still a matter of perplexity to astronomers. Afterwards, for the space of seven years, save for the pass lists of the London University, in which he is seen to climb slowly to a double first-class B. Sc., in mathematics and chemistry, there is no evidence of how Filmer passed his life. No one knows how or where he lived, though it seems highly probable that he continued to support himself by teaching while he prose-cuted the studies necessary for this distinction. And then, oddly enough, one finds him mentioned in the correspondence of Arthur Hicks, the poet.

"You remember Filmer," Hicks writes to his friend Vance; "well *he* hasn't altered a bit, the same hostile mumble and the nasty chin—how *can* a man contrive to be always three days from shaving?—and a sort of furtive air of being engaged in sneaking in front of one; even his coat and that frayed collar of his show no further signs of the passing of years. He was writing in the library and I sat down beside him in the name of God's charity, whereupon he deliberately insulted me by covering up his memoranda. It seems he has some brilliant research on hand that he suspects me of all people—with a Bodley Booklet a-printing—of stealing. He has taken re-markable honours at the University—he went through them with a sort of hasty slobber, as though he feared I might inter-rupt him before he had told me all—and he spoke of taking his D. Sc. as one might speak of taking a cab. And he asked what I was doing—with a sort of comparative accent, and his arm was spread nervously, positively a protecting arm, over the paper that hid the precious idea—his one hopeful idea.

"'Poetry,' he said, 'poetry. And what do you profess to teach in it, Hicks?'

"The thing's a provincial professorling in the very act of budding, and I thank the Lord devoutly that but for the precious gift of indolence I also might have gone this way to D. Sc. and destruction . . ."

A curious little vignette that I am inclined to think caught Filmer in or near the very birth of his discovery.

Hicks was wrong in anticipating a provincial professorship for Filmer. Our next glimpse of him is lecturing on "rubber and rubber substitutes," to the Society of Arts—he had become manager to a great plastic-substance manufactory—and at that time, it is now known, he was a member of the Aëronautical Society, albeit he contributed nothing to the discussions of that body, preferring no doubt to mature his great conception without external assistance. And within two years of that paper before the Society of Arts he was hastily taking out a number of patents and proclaiming in various undignified ways the completion of the divergent inquiries which made his flying-machine possible. The first definite statement to that effect appeared in a halfpenny evening paper through the agency of a man who lodged in the same house with Filmer. His final haste after his long laborious secret patience seems to have been due to a needless panic, Bootle, the notorious American scientific quack, having made an announcement that Filmer interpreted wrongly as an anticipation of his idea.

Now what precisely was Filmer's idea? Really a very simple one. Before his time the pursuit of aëronautics had taken two divergent lines, and had developed on the one hand balloons—large apparatus lighter than air, easy in ascent, and comparatively safe in descent, but floating helplessly before any breeze that took them; and on the other, flying-machines that flew only in theory—vast flat structures heavier than air, propelled and kept up by heavy engines and for the most part smashing at the first descent. But, neglecting the fact that the inevitable final collapse rendered them impossible, the weight of the flying-machines gave them this theoretical advantage, that they could go through the air against a wind, a necessary condition if aërial navigation was to have any practical value. It is Filmer's particular merit that he perceived the way in which the contrasted and hitherto incompatible merits of balloon and heavy flying-machine might be combined in one apparatus, which should be at choice either heavier or lighter than air. He took hints from the contractile bladders of fish and the pneumatic cavities of birds. He devised an arrangement of contractile and absolutely closed balloons which when expanded could lift the actual flying apparatus with ease, and when retracted by the complicated "musculature" he wove about them, were withdrawn almost completely into the frame; and he built the large framework which these balloons sustained, of hollow, rigid tubes, the air in which, by an ingenious contrivance, was automatically pumped out as the apparatus fell, and which then remained exhausted so long as the aëronaut desired. There were no wings or propellers to his machine, such as there had been to all previous aëroplanes, and the only engine required was the compact and powerful little appliance needed to contract the balloons. He perceived that such an apparatus as he had devised might rise with frame exhausted and balloons expanded to a considerable height, might then contract its balloons and let the air into its frame, and by an adjustment of its weights slide down the air in any desired direction. As it fell it would accumulate velocity and at the same time lose weight, and the momentum accumulated by its down-rush could be utilised by means of a shifting of its weights to drive it up in the air again as the balloons expanded. This conception, which is still the structural conception of all successful flying-machines, needed, however, a vast amount of toil upon its details before it could actually be realised, and such toil Filmer—as he was accustomed to tell the numerous interviewers who crowded upon him in the heyday of his fame—"ungrudgingly and unsparingly gave." His particular difficulty was the elastic lining of the contractile balloon. He found he needed a new substance, and in the discovery and manufacture of that new substance he had, as he never failed to impress upon the interviewers, "performed a far more arduous work than even in the actual achievement of my seemingly greater discovery."

But it must not be imagined that these interviews followed hard upon Filmer's proclamation of his invention. An interval of nearly five years elapsed during which he timidly remained at his rubber factory—he seems to have been entirely dependent on his small income from this source—making misdirected attempts to assure a quite indifferent public that he really *had* invented what he had invented. He occupied the greater part of his leisure in the composition of letters to the scientific and daily press, and so forth, stating precisely the net result of his contrivances, and demanding financial aid. That alone would have sufficed for the suppression of his letters. He spent such holidays as he could arrange in unsatisfactory interviews with the door-keepers of leading London papers—he was singularly not adapted for inspiring hall-porters with confidence—and he positively attempted to induce the War Office to take up his work with him. There remains a confidential letter from Major-General Volleyfire to the Earl of Frogs. "The man's a crank and a bounder to boot," says the Major-General in his bluff, sensible, army way, and so left it open for the Japanese to secure, as they subsequently did, the priority in this side of warfare—a priority they still to our great discomfort retain.

And then by a stroke of luck the membrane Filmer had invented for his contractile balloon was discovered to be useful for the valves of a new oil-engine, and he obtained the means for making a trial model of his invention. He threw up his rubber factory appointment, desisted from all further writing, and, with a certain secrecy that seems to have been an inseparable characteristic of all his proceedings, set to work upon the apparatus. He seems to have directed the making of its parts and collected most of it in a room in Shoreditch, but its final putting together was done at Dymchurch, in

Kent. He did not make the affair large enough to carry a man, but he made an extremely ingenious use of what were then called the Marconi rays to control its flight. The first flight of this first practicable flying-machine took place over some fields, near Burford Bridge, near Hythe, in Kent, and Filmer followed and controlled its flight upon a specially constructed motor tricycle.

The flight was, considering all things, an amazing success. The apparatus was brought in a cart from Dymchurch to Burford Bridge, ascended there to a height of nearly three hundred feet, swooped thence very nearly back to Dymchurch, came about in its sweep, rose again, circled, and finally sank uninjured in a field behind the Burford Bridge Inn. At its descent a curious thing happened. Filmer got off his tricycle, scrambled over the intervening dyke, advanced perhaps twenty yards towards his triumph, threw out his arms in a strange gesticulation, and fell down in a dead faint. Everyone could then recall the ghastliness of his features and all the evidences of extreme excitement they had observed throughout the trial, things they might otherwise have forgotten. Afterwards in the inn he had an unaccountable gust of hysterical weeping.

Altogether there were not twenty witnesses of this affair, and those for the most part uneducated men. The New Romney doctor saw the ascent but not the descent, his horse being frightened by the electrical apparatus in Filmer's tricycle and giving him a nasty spill. Two members of the Kent constabulary watched the affair from a cart in an unofficial spirit, and a grocer calling round the Marsh for orders and two lady cyclists seem almost to complete the list of educated people. There were two reporters present, one representing a Folkestone paper and the other being a fourth-class interviewer and "symposium" journalist, whose expenses down, Filmer, anxious as ever for adequate advertisement—and now quite realising the way in which adequate advertisement may be obtained—had paid. The latter was one of those writers who can throw a convincing air of unreality over the most credible events, and his half-facetious account of the affair appeared in the magazine page of a popular journal. But, happily for Filmer, this person's colloquial methods were more convincing. He went to offer some further screed upon the subject to Banghurst, the proprietor of the *New Paper*, and one of the ablest and most unscrupulous men in London journalism, and Banghurst instantly seized upon the situation. The interviewer vanishes from the narrative, no doubt very doubtfully remunerated, and Banghurst, Banghurst himself, double chin, grey twill suit, abdomen, voice, gestures and all, appears at Dymchurch, following his large, unrivalled journalistic nose. He had seen the whole thing at a glance, just what it was and what it might be.

At his touch, as it were, Filmer's long-pent investigations exploded into fame. He instantly and most magnificently was a Boom. One turns over the files of the journals of the year 1907 with a quite incredulous recognition of how swift and flaming the boom of those days could be. The July papers know nothing of flying, see nothing in flying, state by a most effective silence that men never would, could, or should fly. In August flying and Filmer and flying and parachutes and aërial tactics and the Japanese Government and Filmer and again flying, shouldered the war in Yunnan and the gold mines of Upper Greenland off the leading page. And Banghurst had given ten thousand pounds, and, further, Banghurst was giving five thousand pounds, and Banghurst had devoted his well-known, magnificent (but hitherto sterile) private laboratories and several acres of land near his private residence on the Surrey hills to the strenuous and violent completion—Banghurst fashion—of the life-size practicable flying-machine. Meanwhile, in the sight of privileged multitudes in the walled-garden of the Banghurst town residence in Fulham, Filmer was exhibited at weekly garden parties putting the working model through its paces. At enormous initial cost, but with a final profit, the *New Paper* presented its readers with a beautiful photographic souvenir of the first of these occasions.

Here again the correspondence of Arthur Hicks and his friend Vance comes to our aid.

"I saw Filmer in his glory," he writes, with just the touch of envy natural to his position as a poet *passé*. "The man is brushed and shaved, dressed in the fashion of a Royal-Institution-Afternoon Lecturer, the very newest shape in frock-coats and long patent shoes, and altogether in a state of extraordinary streakiness between an owlish great man and a scared, abashed, self-conscious bounder cruelly exposed. He hasn't a touch of colour in the skin of his face, his head juts forward, and those queer little dark amber eyes of his watch furtively round him for his fame. His clothes fit perfectly and yet sit upon him as though he had bought them ready-made. He speaks in a mumble still, but he says, you perceive indistinctly, enormous self-assertive things, he backs into the rear of groups by instinct if Banghurst drops the line for a minute, and when he walks across Banghurst's lawn one perceives him a little out of breath and going jerky, and that his weak white hands are clenched. His is a state of tension—horrible tension. And he is the Greatest Discoverer of This or Any Age—the Greatest Discoverer of This or Any Age! What strikes one so forcibly about him is that he didn't somehow quite expect it ever, at any rate, not at all like this. Banghurst is about everywhere, the energetic M.C. of his great little catch, and I swear he will have everyone down on his lawn there before he has finished with the engine; he had bagged the prime minister yesterday, and he, bless his heart! didn't look particularly outsize, on the very first occasion. Conceive it! Filmer! Our obscure unwashed Filmer, the Glory of British science! Duchesses crowd upon him, beautiful, bold peeresses say in their beautiful, clear loud voices—have you noticed how penetrating the great lady is becoming nowadays?—'Oh, Mr. Filmer, how *did* you do it?'

"Common men on the edge of things are too remote for the answer. One imagines something in the way of that interview, 'toil ungrudgingly and unsparingly given, Madam, and, perhaps—I don't know—but perhaps a little special aptitude.'"

So far Hicks and the photographic supplement to the *New Paper* are in sufficient harmony with the description. In one picture the machine swings down towards the river, and the tower of Fulham church appears below it through a gap in the elms, and in another, Filmer sits at his guiding batteries, and the great and beautiful of the earth stand around him, with Banghurst massed modestly but resolutely in the rear. The grouping is oddly apposite. Occluding much of Banghurst, and looking with a pensive, speculative expression at Filmer, stands the Lady Mary Elkinghorn, still beautiful, in spite of the breath of scandal and her eight-and-thirty years, the only person whose face does not admit a perception of the camera that was in the act of snapping them all.

So much for the exterior facts of the story, but, after all, they are very exterior facts. About the real interest of the business one is necessarily very much in the dark. How was Filmer feeling at the time? How much was a certain unpleasant anticipation present inside that very new and fashionable frock-coat? He was in the halfpenny, penny, sixpenny, and more expensive papers alike, and acknowledged by the whole world as "the Greatest Discoverer of This or Any Age." He had invented a practicable flying-machine, and every day down among the Surrey hills the life-sized model was getting ready. And when it was ready, it followed as a clear inevitable consequence of his having invented and made it—everybody in the world, indeed, seemed to take it for granted; there wasn't a gap anywhere in that serried front of anticipation—that he would proudly and cheerfully get aboard it, ascend with it, and fly.

But we know now pretty clearly that simple pride and cheerfulness in such an act were singularly out of harmony with Filmer's private constitution. It occurred to no one at the time, but there the fact is. We can guess with some confidence now that it must have been drifting about in his mind a great deal during the day, and, from a little note to his physician complaining of persistent insomnia, we have the soundest reason for supposing it dominated his nights—the idea that it would be after all, in spite of his theoretical security, an abominably sickening, uncomfortable, and dangerous thing for him to flap about in nothingness a thousand feet or so in the air. It must have dawned upon him quite early in the period of being the Greatest Discoverer of This or Any Age, the vision of doing this and that with an extensive void below. Perhaps somewhen in his youth he had looked down a great height or fallen down in some excessively uncomfortable way; perhaps some habit of sleeping on the wrong side had resulted in that disagreeable falling nightmare one knows, and given him his horror; of the strength of that horror there remains now not a particle of doubt.

Apparently he had never weighed this duty of flying in his earlier days of research; the machine had been his end, but now things were opening out beyond his end, and particularly this giddy whirl up above there. He was a Discoverer and he had Discovered. But he was not a Flying Man, and it was only now that he was beginning to perceive clearly that he was expected to fly. Yet, however much the thing was present in his mind he gave no expression to it until the very end, and meanwhile he went to and fro from Banghurst's magnificent laboratories, and was interviewed and lionised, and wore good clothes, and ate good food, and lived in an elegant flat, enjoying a very abundant feast of such good, coarse, wholesome Fame and Success as a man, starved for all his years as he had been starved, might be reasonably expected to enjoy.

After a time, the weekly gatherings in Fulham ceased. The model had failed one day just for a moment to respond to Filmer's guidance, or he had been distracted by the compliments of an archbishop. At any rate, it suddenly dug its nose into the air just a little too steeply as the archbishop was sailing through a Latin quotation for all the world like an archbishop in a book, and it came down in the Fulham Road within three yards of a 'bus horse. It stood for a second, perhaps, astonishing and in its attitude astonished, then it crumpled, shivered into pieces, and the 'bus horse was incidentally killed.

Filmer lost the end of the archiepiscopal compliment. He stood up and stared as his invention swooped out of sight and reach of him. His long white hands still gripped his useless apparatus. The archbishop followed his skyward stare with an apprehension unbecoming in an archbishop.

Then came the crash and the shouts and uproar from the road to relieve Filmer's tension. "My God!" he whispered, and sat down.

Everyone else almost was staring to see where the machine had vanished, or rushing into the house.

The making of the big machine progressed all the more rapidly for this. Over its making presided Filmer, always a little slow and very careful in his manner, always with a growing preoccupation in his mind. His care over the strength and soundness of the apparatus was prodigious. The slightest doubt, and he delayed everything until the doubtful part could be replaced. Wilkinson, his senior assistant, fumed at some of these delays, which, he insisted, were for the most part unnecessary. Banghurst magnified the patient certitude of Filmer in the *New Paper*, and reviled it bitterly to his wife, and MacAndrew, the second assistant, approved Filmer's wisdom. "We're not wanting a *fiasco*, man," said Mac-Andrew. "He's perfectly well advised."

And whenever an opportunity arose Filmer would expound to Wilkinson and MacAndrew just exactly how every part of the flying-machine was to be controlled and worked, so that in effect they would be just as capable, and even more capable when at last the time came, of guiding it through the skies.

Now I should imagine that if Filmer had seen fit at this stage to define just what he was feeling, and to take a definite line in the matter of his ascent, he might have escaped that painful ordeal quite easily. If he had had it clearly in his mind he could have done endless things. He would surely have found no difficulty with a specialist to demonstrate a weak heart, or something gastric or pulmonary, to stand in his way—that is the line I am astonished he did not take—or he might, had he been man enough, have declared simply and finally that he did not intend to do the thing. But the fact is, though the dread was hugely present in his mind, the thing was by no means sharp and clear. I fancy that all through this period he kept telling himself that when the occasion came he would find himself equal to it. He was like a man just gripped by a great illness, who says he feels a little out of sorts, and expects to be better presently. Meanwhile he delayed the completion of the machine, and let the assumption that he was going to fly it take root and flourish exceedingly about him. He even accepted anticipatory compliments on his courage. And, barring this secret squeamishness, there can be no doubt he found all the praise and distinction and fuss he got a delightful and even intoxicating draught.

The Lady Mary Elkinghorn made things a little more complicated for him.

How *that* began was a subject of inexhaustible speculation to Hicks. Probably in the beginning she was just a little "nice" to him with that impartial partiality of hers, and it may be that to her eyes, standing out conspicuously as he did ruling his monster in the upper air, he had a distinction that Hicks was not disposed to find. And somehow they must have had a moment of sufficient isolation, and the great Discoverer a moment of sufficient courage for something just a little personal to be mumbled or blurted. However it began, there is no doubt that it did begin, and presently became quite perceptible to a world accustomed to find in the proceedings of the Lady Mary Elkinghorn a matter of entertainment. It complicated things, because the state of love in such a virgin mind as Filmer's would brace his resolution, if not sufficiently, at any rate considerably, towards facing a danger he feared, and hampered him in such attempts at evasion as would otherwise be natural and congenial.

It remains a matter for speculation just how the Lady Mary felt for Filmer and just what she thought of him. At thirty-eight one may have gathered much wisdom and still be not altogether wise, and the imagination still functions actively enough in creating glamours and effecting the impossible. He came before her eyes as a very central man, and that always counts, and he had powers, unique powers as it seemed, at any rate in the air. The performance with the model had just a touch of the quality of a potent incantation, and women have ever displayed an unreasonable disposition to imagine that when a man has powers he must necessarily have Power. Given so much, and what was not good in Filmer's manner and appearance became an added merit. He was modest, he hated display, but given an occasion where *true* qualities are needed, then—then one would see!

The late Mrs. Bampton thought it wise to convey to Lady Mary her opinion that Filmer, all things considered, was rather a "grub." "He's certainly not a sort of man I have ever met before," said the Lady Mary, with a quite unruffled serenity. And Mrs. Bampton, after a swift, imperceptible glance at that serenity, decided that so far as saying anything to Lady Mary went, she had done as much as could be expected of her. But she said a great deal to other people.

And at last, without any undue haste or unseemliness, the day dawned, the great day, when Banghurst had promised his public—the world, in fact—that flying should be finally attained and overcome. Filmer saw it dawn, watched even in the darkness before it dawned, watched its stars fade and the grey and pearly pinks give place at last to the clear blue sky of a sunny, cloudless day. He watched it from the window of his bedroom in the new-built wing of Banghurst's Tudor house. And as the stars were overwhelmed and the shapes and substances of things grew into being out of the amorphous dark, he must have seen more and more distinctly the festive preparations beyond the beech clumps near the green pavilion in the outer park, the three stands for the privileged spectators, the raw new fencing of the enclosure, the sheds and workshops, the Venetian masts and fluttering flags that Banghurst had considered essential, black and limp in the breezeless dawn, and amidst all these things a great shape covered with tarpaulin. A strange and terrible portent for humanity was that shape, a beginning that must surely spread and widen and change and dominate all the affairs of men, but to Filmer it is very doubtful whether it appeared in anything but a narrow and personal light. Several people heard him pacing in the small hours—for the vast place was packed with guests by a proprietor editor who, before all things, understood compression. And about five o'clock, if not before, Filmer left his room and wandered out of the sleeping house into the park, alive by that time with sunlight and birds and squirrels and the fallow deer. MacAndrew, who was also an early riser, met him near the machine, and they went and had a look at it together.

It is doubtful if Filmer took any breakfast, in spite of the urgency of Banghurst. So soon as the guests began to be about in some number he seems to have retreated to his room. Thence about ten he went into the shrubbery, very probably because he had seen the Lady Mary Elkinghorn there. She was walking up and down, engaged in conversation with her old school friend, Mrs. Brewis-Craven, and although Filmer had never met the latter lady before, he joined them and walked beside them for some time. There were several silences in spite of the Lady Mary's brilliance. The situation was a difficult one, and Mrs. Brewis-Craven did not master its difficulty. "He struck me," she said afterwards with a luminous self-contradiction, "as a very unhappy person who had something to say, and wanted before all things to be helped to say it. But how was one to help him when one didn't know what it was?"

At half-past eleven the enclosures for the public in the outer park were crammed, there was an intermittent stream of equipages along the belt which circles the outer park, and the house party was dotted over the lawn and shrubbery and the corner of the inner park, in a series of brilliantly attired knots, all making for the flying-machine. Filmer walked in a group of three with Banghurst, who was supremely and conspicuously happy, and Sir Theodore Hickle, the president of the Aëronautical Society. Mrs. Banghurst was close behind with the Lady Mary Elkinghorn, Georgina Hickle, and the Dean of Stays. Banghurst was large and copious in speech and such interstices as he left were filled in by Hickle with complimentary remarks to Filmer. And Filmer walked between them saying not a word except by way of unavoidable reply. Behind, Mrs. Banghurst listened to the admirably suitable and shapely conversation of the Dean with that fluttered attention to the ampler clergy ten years of social ascent and ascendency had not cured in her; and the Lady Mary watched, no doubt with an entire confidence in the world's disillusionment, the drooping shoulders of the sort of man she had never met before.

There was some cheering as the central party came into view of the enclosures, but it was not very unanimous nor invigorating cheering. They were within fifty yards of the apparatus when Filmer took a hasty glance over his shoulder to measure the distance of the ladies behind them, and decided to make the first remark he had initiated since the house had been left. His voice was just a little hoarse, and he cut in on Banghurst in mid-sentence on Progress.

"I say, Banghurst," he said, and stopped.

"Yes," said Banghurst.

"I wish——" He moistened his lips. "I'm not feeling well."

Banghurst stopped dead. "Eh?" he shouted.

"A queer feeling." Filmer made to move on, but Banghurst was immovable. "I don't know. I may be better in a minute. If not—perhaps. . . . MacAndrew——"

"You're not feeling *well?*" said Banghurst, and stared at his white face.

"My dear!" he said, as Mrs. Banghurst came up with them, "Filmer says he isn't feeling *well.*"

"A little queer," exclaimed Filmer, avoiding the Lady Mary's eyes. "It may pass off——"

There was a pause.

It came to Filmer that he was the most isolated person in the world.

"In any case," said Banghurst, "the ascent must be made. Perhaps if you were to sit down somewhere for a moment——"

"It's the crowd, I think," said Filmer.

There was a second pause. Banghurst's eye rested in scrutiny on Filmer, and then swept the sample of public in the enclosure.

"It's unfortunate," said Sir Theodore Hickle; "but still— I suppose—— Your assistants—— Of course, if you feel out of condition and disinclined——"

"I don't think Mr. Filmer would permit *that* for a moment," said the Lady Mary.

"But if Mr. Filmer's nerve is run—— It might even be dangerous for him to attempt——" Hickle coughed.

"It's just because it's dangerous," began the Lady Mary, and felt she had made her point of view and Filmer's plain enough.

Conflicting motives struggled for Filmer.

"I feel I ought to go up," he said, regarding the ground. He looked up and met the Lady Mary's eyes. "I want to go up," he said, and smiled whitely at her. He turned towards Banghurst. "If I could just sit down somewhere for a moment out of the crowd and sun——"

Banghurst, at least, was beginning to understand the case. "Come into my little room in the green pavilion," he said. "It's quite cool there." He took Filmer by the arm.

Filmer turned his face to the Lady Mary Elkinghorn again. "I shall be all right in five minutes," he said. "I'm tremendously sorry——"

The Lady Mary Elkinghorn smiled at him. "I couldn't think," he said to Hickle, and obeyed the compulsion of Banghurst's pull.

The rest remained watching the two recede.

"He is so fragile," said the Lady Mary.

"He's certainly a highly nervous type," said the Dean, whose weakness it was to regard the whole world, except married clergymen with enormous families, as "neurotic."

"Of course," said Hickle, "it isn't absolutely necessary for him to go up because he has invented——"

"How *could* he avoid it?" asked the Lady Mary, with the faintest shadow of scorn.

"It's certainly most unfortunate if he's going to be ill now," said Mrs. Banghurst a little severely.

"He's not going to be ill," said the Lady Mary, and certainly she had met Filmer's eye.

"*You'll* be all right," said Banghurst, as they went towards the pavilion. "All you want is a nip of brandy. It ought to be you, you know. You'll be—you'd get it rough, you know, if you let another man——"

"Oh, I want to go," said Filmer. "I shall be all right. As a matter of fact, I'm almost inclined *now*—— No—— I think I'll have that nip of brandy first."

Banghurst took him into the little room and routed out an empty decanter. He departed in search of a supply. He was gone perhaps five minutes.

The history of those five minutes cannot be written. At intervals Filmer's face could be seen by the people on the easternmost of the stands erected for spectators, against the window pane peering out, and then it would recede and fade. Banghurst vanished shouting behind the grandstand, and presently the butler appeared going pavilionward with a tray.

The apartment·in which Filmer came to his last solution was a pleasant little room very simply furnished with green furniture and an old bureau—for Banghurst was simple in all his private ways. It was hung with little engravings after Morland and it had a shelf of books. But as it happened, Banghurst had left a rook rifle he sometimes played with on the top of the desk, and on the corner of the mantelshelf was a tin with three or four cartridges remaining in it. As Filmer went up and down that room wrestling with his intolerable dilemma he went first towards the neat little rifle athwart the blotting-pad and then towards the neat little red label

"**.22 LONG.**"

The thing must have jumped into his mind in a moment. Nobody seems to have connected the report with him, though the gun, being fired in a confined space, must have sounded loud, and there were several people in the billiard-room, separated from him only by a lath-and-plaster partition. But directly Banghurst's butler opened the door and smelt the sour smell of the smoke, he knew, he says, what had happened. For the servants at least of Banghurst's household had guessed something of what was going on in Filmer's mind.

All through that trying afternoon Banghurst behaved as

he held a man should behave in the presence of hopeless disaster, and his guests for the most part succeeded in not insisting upon the fact—though to conceal their perception of
it altogether was impossible—that Banghurst had been
pretty elaborately and completely swindled by the deceased.
The public in the enclosure, Hicks told me, dispersed "like
a party that has been ducking a welsher," and there wasn't
a soul in the train to London, it seems, who hadn't known all
along that flying was a quite impossible thing for man. "But
he might have tried it," said many, "after carrying the thing
so far."

In the evening, when he was comparatively alone, Banghurst broke down and went on like a man of clay. I have been
told he wept, which must have made an imposing scene, and
he certainly said Filmer had ruined his life, and offered and
sold the whole apparatus to MacAndrew for half-a-crown.
"I've been thinking——" said MacAndrew at the conclusion
of the bargain, and stopped.

The next morning the name of Filmer was, for the first time,
less conspicuous in the *New Paper* than in any other daily
paper in the world. The rest of the world's instructors, with
varying emphasis, according to their dignity and the degree
of competition between themselves and the *New Paper*, proclaimed the "Entire Failure of the New Flying-Machine,"
and "Suicide of the Impostor." But in the district of north
Surrey the reception of the news was tempered by a perception of unusual aërial phenomena.

Overnight Wilkinson and MacAndrew had fallen into
violent argument on the exact motives of their principal's
rash act.

"The man was certainly a poor, cowardly body, but so far
as his science went he was *no* impostor," said MacAndrew,
"and I'm prepared to give that proposition a very practical
demonstration, Mr. Wilkinson, so soon as we've got the place
a little more to ourselves. For I've no faith in all this publicity
for experimental trials."

And to that end, while all the world was reading of the
certain failure of the new flying-machine, MacAndrew was

soaring and curvetting with great amplitude and dignity over the Epsom and Wimbledon divisions; and Banghurst, restored once more to hope and energy, and regardless of public security and the Board of Trade, was pursuing his gyrations and trying to attract his attention, on a motor car and in his pyjamas—he had caught sight of the ascent when pulling up the blind of his bedroom window—equipped, among other things, with a film camera that was subsequently discovered to be jammed.

And Filmer was lying on the billiard table in the green pavilion with a sheet about his body.

A STORY OF THE DAYS TO COME

I. The Cure for Love

THE excellent Mr. Morris was an Englishman, and he lived in the days of Queen Victoria the Good. He was a prosperous and very sensible man; he read *The Times* and went to church, and as he grew towards middle age an expression of quiet contented contempt for all who were not as himself settled on his face. He was one of those people who do everything that is right and proper and sensible with inevitable regularity. He always wore just the right and proper clothes, steering the narrow way between the smart and the shabby, always subscribed to the right charities, just the judicious compromise between ostentation and meanness, and never failed to have his hair cut to exactly the proper length.

Everything that it was right and proper for a man in his position to possess, he possessed; and everything that it was not right and proper for a man in his position to possess, he did not possess.

And among other right and proper possessions, this Mr. Morris had a wife and children. They were the right sort of wife, and the right sort and number of children, of course; nothing imaginative or highty-flighty about any of them, so far as Mr. Morris could see; they wore perfectly correct clothing, neither smart nor hygienic nor faddy in any way, but just sensible; and they lived in a nice sensible house in the later Victorian sham Queen Anne style of architecture, with sham half-timbering of chocolate-painted plaster in the gables, Lincrusta Walton sham carved oak panels, a terrace of terra cotta to imitate stone, and cathedral glass in the front door. His boys went to good solid schools, and were put to respectable professions; his girls, in spite of a fantastic protest or so, were all married to suitable, steady, oldish young men with good prospects. And when it was a fit and proper thing for him to do so, Mr. Morris died. His tomb was of marble, and, without any art nonsense or laudatory inscription, quietly imposing—such being the fashion of his time.

He underwent various changes according to the accepted custom in these cases, and long before this story begins his bones even had become dust, and were scattered to the four quarters of heaven. And his sons and his grandsons and his great-grandsons and his great-great-grandsons, they too were dust and ashes, and were scattered likewise. It was a thing he could not have imagined, that a day would come when even his great-great-grandsons would be scattered to the four winds of heaven. If anyone had suggested it to him he would have resented it. He was one of those worthy people who take no interest in the future of mankind at all. He had grave doubts, indeed, if there was any future for mankind after he was dead.

It seemed quite impossible and quite uninteresting to imagine anything happening after he was dead. Yet the thing was so, and when even his great-great-grandson was dead and decayed and forgotten, when the sham half-timbered house had gone the way of all shams, and *The Times* was extinct, and the silk hat a ridiculous antiquity, and the modestly imposing stone that had been sacred to Mr. Morris had been burnt to make lime for mortar, and all that Mr. Morris had found real and important was sere and dead, the world was still going on, and people were still going about it, just as heedless and impatient of the Future, or, indeed, of anything but their own selves and property, as Mr. Morris had been.

And, strange to tell, and much as Mr. Morris would have been angered if anyone had foreshadowed it to him, all over the world there were scattered a multitude of people, filled with the breath of life, in whose veins the blood of Mr. Morris flowed. Just as some day the life which is gathered now in the reader of this very story may also be scattered far and wide about this world, and mingled with a thousand alien strains, beyond all thought and tracing.

And among the descendants of this Mr. Morris was one almost as sensible and clear-headed as his ancestor. He had just the same stout, short frame as that ancient man of the nineteenth century, from whom his name of Morris—he spelt it Mwres—came; he had the same half-contemptuous expression of face. He was a prosperous person, too, as times went, and he disliked the "new-fangled," and bothers about the future and the lower classes, just as much as the ancestral Morris had done. He did not read *The Times:* indeed, he did not know there ever had been a *Times*—that institution had foundered somewhere in the intervening gulf of years; but the phonograph machine, that talked to him as he made his toilet of a morning, might have been the voice of a reincarnated Blowitz when it dealt with the world's affairs. This phonographic machine was the size and shape of a Dutch clock, and down the front of it were electric barometric indicators, and an electric clock and calendar, and automatic engagement reminders, and where the clock would have been was the mouth of a trumpet. When it had news the trumpet gobbled like a turkey, "Galloop, galloop," and then brayed out its message as, let us say, a trumpet might bray. It would tell Mwres in full, rich, throaty tones about the overnight accidents to the omnibus flying-machines that plied around the world, the latest arrivals at the fashionable resorts in Tibet, and of all the great monopolist company meetings of the day before, while he was dressing. If Mwres did not like hearing what it said, he had only to touch a stud, and it would choke a little and talk about something else.

Of course his toilet differed very much from that of his ancestor. It is doubtful which would have been the more shocked and pained to find himself in the clothing of the other. Mwres would certainly have sooner gone forth to the world stark naked than in the silk hat, frock-coat, grey trousers, and watch-chain that had filled Mr. Morris with sombre self-respect in the past. For Mwres there was no shaving to do: a skilful operator had long ago removed every hair-root from his face. His legs he encased in pleasant pink and amber garments of an air-tight material, which with the help of an ingenious little pump he distended so as to suggest enormous muscles. Above this he also wore pneumatic garments beneath an amber silk tunic, so that he was clothed in air and admirably protected against sudden extremes of heat or cold. Over this he flung a scarlet cloak with its edge fantastically curved. On his head, which had been skilfully deprived of every scrap of hair, he adjusted a pleasant little cap of bright scarlet, held on by suction and inflated with hydrogen, and curiously like the comb of a cock. So his toilet was complete; and, conscious of being soberly and becomingly attired, he was ready to face his fellow-beings with a tranquil eye.

This Mwres—the civility of "Mr." had vanished ages ago—was one of the officials under the Wind Vane and Waterfall Trust, the great company that owned every wind wheel and waterfall in the world, and which pumped all the water and supplied all the electric energy that people in these latter days required. He lived in a vast hotel near that part of London called Seventh Way, and had very large and comfortable apartments on the seventeenth floor. Households and family life had long since disappeared with the progressive refinement of manners; and indeed the steady rise in rents and land values, the disappearance of domestic servants, the elaboration of cookery, had rendered the separate domicile of Victorian times impossible, even had anyone desired such a savage seclusion. When his toilet was completed he went towards one of the two doors of his apartment—there were doors at opposite ends, each marked with a huge arrow pointing one one way and one the other—touched a stud to open it, and emerged on a wide passage, the centre of which bore chairs and was moving at a steady pace to the left. On some of these chairs were seated gaily-dressed men and women. He nodded to an acquaintance—it was not in those days etiquette to talk before breakfast—and seated himself on one of these chairs, and in a few seconds he had been carried to the doors of a lift, by which he descended to the great and splendid hall in which his breakfast would be automatically served.

It was a very different meal from a Victorian breakfast. The rude masses of bread needing to be car ed and smeared over with animal fat before they could be made palatable, the still recognisable fragments of recently killed animals, hideously charred and hacked, the eggs torn ruthlessly from beneath some protesting hen,—such things as these, though they constituted the ordinary fare of Victorian times, would have awakened only horror and disgust in the refined minds of the people of these latter days. Instead were pastes and cakes of agreeable and variegated design, without any suggestion in colour or form of the unfortunate animals from which their substance and juices were derived. They appeared on little dishes sliding out upon a rail from a little box at one side of the table. The surface of the table, to judge by touch and eye, would have appeared to a nineteenth-century person to be covered with fine white damask, but this was really an oxidised metallic surface, and could be cleaned instantly after a meal. There were hundreds of such little tables in the hall, and at most of them were other latter-day citizens singly or in groups. And as Mwres seated himself before his elegant repast, the invisible orchestra, which had been resting during an interval, resumed and filled the air with music.

But Mwres did not display any great interest either in his breakfast or the music; his eye wandered incessantly about the hall, as though he expected a belated guest. At last he rose eagerly and waved his hand, and simultaneously across the hall appeared a tall dark figure in a costume of yellow and olive green. As this person, walking amidst the tables with measured steps, drew near, the pallid earnestness of his face and the unusual intensity of his eyes became apparent. Mwres reseated himself and pointed to a chair beside him.

"I feared you would never come," he said. In spite of the intervening space of time, the English language was still almost exactly the same as it had been in England under Victoria the Good. The invention of the phonograph and suchlike means of recording sound, and the gradual replacement of books by such contrivances, had not only saved the human eyesight from decay, but had also by the establishment of a sure standard arrested the process of change in accent that had hitherto been so inevitable.

"I was delayed by an interesting case," said the man in green and yellow. "A prominent politician—ahem!—suffering from overwork." He glanced at the breakfast and seated himself. "I have been awake for forty hours."

"Eh dear!" said Mwres: "fancy that! You hypnotists have your work to do."

The hypnotist helped himself to some attractive amber-coloured jelly. "I happen to be a good deal in request," he said modestly.

"Heaven knows what we should do without you."

"Oh! we're not so indispensable as all that," said the hypnotist, ruminating the flavour of the jelly. "The world did very well without us for some thousands of years. Two hundred years ago even—not one! In practice, that is. Physicians by the thousand, of course—frightfully clumsy brutes for the most part, and following one another like sheep —but doctors of the mind, except a few empirical flounderers, there were none."

He concentrated his mind on the jelly.

"But were people so sane——?" began Mwres.

The hypnotist shook his head. "It didn't matter then if they were a bit silly or faddy. Life was so easy-going then. No competition worth speaking of—no pressure. A human being had to be very lopsided before anything happened. Then, you know, they clapped 'em away in what they called a lunatic asylum."

"I know," said Mwres. "In these confounded historical romances that everyone is listening to, they always rescue a beautiful girl from an asylum or something of the sort. I don't know if you attend to that rubbish."

"I must confess I do," said the hypnotist. "It carries one out of oneself to hear of those quaint, adventurous, half-civilised days of the nineteenth century, when men were stout and women simple. I like a good swaggering story before all things. Curious times they were, with their smutty railways and puffing old iron trains, their rum little houses and their horse vehicles. I suppose you don't read books?"

"Dear, no!" said Mwres. "I went to a modern school and we had none of that old-fashioned nonsense. Phonographs are good enough for me."

"Of course," said the hypnotist, "of course"; and surveyed the table for his next choice. "You know," he said, helping himself to a dark blue confection that promised well, "in those days our business was scarcely thought of. I daresay if anyone had told them that in two hundred years' time a class of men would be entirely occupied in impressing things upon the memory, effacing unpleasant ideas, controlling and overcoming instinctive but undesirable impulses, and so forth, by means of hypnotism, they would have refused to believe the thing possible. Few people knew that an order made during a mesmeric trance, even an order to forget or an order to desire, could be given so as to be obeyed after the trance was over. Yet there were men alive then who could have told them the thing was as absolutely certain to come about as—well, the transit of Venus."

"They knew of hypnotism then?"

"Oh, dear, yes! They used it—for painless dentistry and things like that! This blue stuff is confoundedly good: what is it?"

"Haven't the faintest idea," said Mwres, "but I admit it's very good. Take some more."

The hypnotist repeated his praises, and there was an appreciative pause.

"Speaking of these historical romances," said Mwres, with an attempt at an easy, off-hand manner, "brings me—ah—to the matter I—ah—had in mind when I asked you—when I expressed a wish to see you." He paused and took a deep breath.

The hypnotist turned an attentive eye upon him, and continued eating.

"The fact is," said Mwres, "I have a—in fact a—daughter. Well, you know I have given her—ah—every educational advantage. Lectures—not a solitary lecturer of ability in the

world but she has had a telephone direct, dancing, deport-
ment, conversation, philosophy, art criticism. . . ." He indicated catholic culture by a gesture of his hand. "I l ad
intended her to marry a very good friend of mine—Bindon
of the Lighting Commission—plain little man, you know, and
a bit unpleasant in some of his ways, but an excellent fellow
really—an excellent fellow."

"Yes," said the hypnotist, "go on. How old is she?"

"Eighteen."

"A dangerous age. Well?"

"Well: it seems that she has been indulging in these historical romances—excessively. Excessively. Even to the
neglect of her philosophy. Filled her mind with unutterable
nonsense about soldiers who fight—what is it?—Etruscans?"

"Egyptians."

"Egyptians—very probably. Hack about with swords and
revolvers and things—bloodshed galore—horrible!—and
about young men on torpedo catchers who blow up—Spaniards, I fancy—and all sorts of irregular adventurers. And
she has got it into her head that she must marry for Love,
and that poor little Bindon——"

"I've met similar cases," said the hypnotist. "Who is the
other young man?"

Mwres maintained an appearance of resigned calm. "You
may well ask," he said. "He is"—and his voice sank with
shame—"a mere attendant upon the stage on which the
flying-machines from Paris alight. He has—as they say in the
romances—good looks. He is quite young and very eccentric.
Affects the antique—he can read and write! So can she.
And instead of communicating by telephone, like sensible
people, they write and deliver—what is it?"

"Notes?"

"No—not notes. . . . Ah—poems."

The hypnotist raised his eyebrows. "How did she meet
him?"

"Tripped coming down from the flying-machine from Paris
—and fell into his arms. The mischief was done in a moment!"

"Yes?"

"Well—that's all. Things must be stopped. That is what I want to consult you about. What must be done? What *can* be done? Of course I'm not a hypnotist; my knowledge is limited. But you——?"

"Hypnotism is not magic," said the man in green, putting both arms on the table.

"Oh, precisely! But still——!"

"People cannot be hypnotised without their consent. If she is able to stand out against marrying Bindon, she will probably stand out against being hypnotised. But if once she can be hypnotised—even by somebody else—the thing is done."

"You can——?"

"Oh, certainly! Once we get her amenable, then we can suggest that she *must* marry Bindon—that that is her fate; or that the young man is repulsive, and that when she sees him she will be giddy and faint, or any little thing of that sort. Or if we can get her into a sufficiently profound trance we can suggest that she should forget him altogether——"

"Precisely."

"But the problem is to get her hypnotised. Of course no sort of proposal or suggestion must come from you—because no doubt she already distrusts you in the matter."

The hypnotist leant his head upon his arm and thought.

"It's hard a man cannot dispose of his own daughter," said Mwres irrelevantly.

"You must give me the name and address of the young lady," said the hypnotist, "and any information bearing upon the matter. And, by the bye, is there any money in the affair?"

Mwres hesitated.

"There's a sum—in fact, a considerable sum—invested in the Patent Road Company. From her mother. That's what makes the thing so exasperating."

"Exactly," said the hypnotist. And he proceeded to cross-examine Mwres on the entire affair.

It was a lengthy interview.

And meanwhile "Elizabeθ Mwres," as she spelt her name,

or "Elizabeth Morris," as a nineteenth-century person would have put it, was sitting in a quiet waiting place beneath the great stage upon which the flying-machine from Paris descended. And beside her sat her slender, handsome lover reading her the poem he had written that morning while on duty upon the stage. When he had finished they sat for a time in silence; and then, as if for their special entertainment, the great machine that had come flying through the air from America that morning rushed down out of the sky.

At first it was a little oblong, faint and blue amidst the distant fleecy clouds; and then it grew swiftly large and white, and larger and whiter, until they could see the separate tiers of sails, each hundreds of feet wide, and the lank body they supported, and at last even the swinging seats of the passengers in a dotted row. Although it was falling it seemed to them to be rushing up the sky, and over the roof-spaces of the city below its shadow leapt towards them. They heard the whistling rush of the air about it and its yelling siren, shrill and swelling, to warn those who were on its landing-stage of its arrival. And abruptly the note fell down a couple of octaves, and it had passed, and the sky was clear and void, and she could turn her sweet eyes again to Denton at her side.

Their silence ended; and Denton, speaking in a little language of broken English that was, they fancied, their private possession—though lovers have used such little languages since the world began—told her how they, too, would leap into the air one morning out of all the obstacles and difficulties about them, and fly to a sunlit city of delight he knew of in Japan, halfway about the world.

She loved the dream, but she feared the leap; and she put him off with "Some day, dearest one, some day," to all his pleading that it might be soon; and at last came a shrilling of whistles, and it was time for him to go back to his duties on the stage. They parted—as lovers have been wont to part for thousands of years. She walked down a passage to a lift, and so came to one of the streets of that latter-day London, all glazed in with glass from the weather, and with incessant moving platforms that went to all parts of the city. And by one of these she returned to her apartments in the Hotel for Women where she lived, the apartments that were in telephonic communication with all the best lecturers in the world. But the sunlight of the flying-stage was in her heart, and the wisdom of all the best lecturers in the world seemed folly in that light.

She spent the middle part of the day in the gymnasium, and took her midday meal with two other girls and their common chaperon—for it was still the custom to have a chaperon in the case of motherless girls of the more prosperous classes. The chaperon had a visitor that day, a man in green and yellow, with a white face and vivid eyes, who talked amazingly. Among other things, he fell to praising a new historical romance that one of the great popular story-tellers of the day had just put forth. It was, of course, about the spacious times of Queen Victoria; and the author, among other pleasing novelties, made a little argument before each section of the story, in imitation of the chapter headings of the old-fashioned books: as for example, "How the Cabmen of Pimlico Stopped the Victoria Omnibuses, and of the Great Fight in Palace Yard," and "How the Piccadilly Policeman Was Slain in the Midst of His Duty." The man in green and yellow praised this innovation. "These pithy sentences," he said, "are admirable. They show at a glance those headlong, tumultuous times, when men and animals jostled in the filthy streets, and death might wait for one at every corner. Life was life then! How great the world must have seemed then! How marvellous! There were still parts of the world absolutely unexplored. Nowadays we have almost abolished wonder, we lead lives so trim and orderly that courage, endurance, faith, all the noble virtues seem fading from mankind."

And so on, taking the girls' thoughts with him, until the life they led, life in the vast and intricate London of the twenty-second century, a life interspersed with soaring excursions to every part of the globe, seemed to them a monotonous misery compared with the dædal past.

At first Elizabeth did not join in the conversation, but after a time the subject became so interesting that she made a few shy interpolations. But he scarcely seemed to notice her as he talked. He went on to describe a new method of entertaining people. They were hypnotised, and then suggestions were made to them so skilfully that they seemed to be living in ancient times again. They played out a little romance in the past as vivid as reality, and when at last they awakened they remembered all they had been through as though it were a real thing.

"It is a thing we have sought to do for years and years," said the hypnotist. "It is practically an artificial dream. And we know the way at last. Think of all it opens out to us—the enrichment of our experience, the recovery of adventure, the refuge it offers from this sordid, competitive life in which we live! Think!"

"And you can do that!" said the chaperon eagerly.

"The thing is possible at last," the hypnotist said. "You may order a dream as you wish."

The chaperon was the first to be hypnotised, and the dream, she said, was wonderful, when she came to again.

The other two girls, encouraged by her enthusiasm, also placed themselves in the hands of the hypnotist and had plunges into the romantic past. No one suggested that Elizabeth should try this novel entertainment; it was at her own request at last that she was taken into the land of dreams where there is neither any freedom of choice nor will. . . .

And so the mischief was done.

One day, when Denton went down to that quiet seat beneath the flying-stage, Elizabeth was not in her wonted place. He was disappointed, and a little angry. The next day she did not come, and the next also. He was afraid. To hide his fear from himself, he set to work to write sonnets for her when she should come again. . . .

For three days he fought against his dread by such distraction, and then the truth was before him clear and cold, and would not be denied. She might be ill, she might be dead; but he would not believe that he had been betrayed. There followed a week of misery. And then he knew she was the only thing on earth worth having, and that he must seek her, however hopeless the search, until she was found once more.

He had some small private means of his own, and so he threw over his appointment on the flying-stage, and set himself to find this girl who had become at last all the world to him. He did not know where she lived, and little of her circumstances; for it had been part of the delight of her girlish romance that he should know nothing of her, nothing of the difference of their station. The ways of the city opened before him east and west, north and south. Even in Victorian days London was a maze, that little London with its poor four millions of people; but the London he explored, the London of the twenty-second century, was a London of thirty million souls. At first he was energetic and headlong, taking time neither to eat nor sleep. He sought for weeks and months, he went through every imaginable phase of fatigue and despair, over-excitement and anger. Long after hope was dead, by the sheer inertia of his desire he still went to and fro, peering into faces and looking this way and that, in the incessant ways and lifts and passages of that interminable hive of men.

At last chance was kind to him, and he saw her.

It was in a time of festivity. He was hungry; he had paid the inclusive fee and had gone into one of the gigantic dining-places of the city; he was pushing his way among the tables and scrutinising by mere force of habit every group he passed.

He stood still, robbed of all power of motion, his eyes wide, his lips apart. Elizabeth sat scarcely twenty yards away from him, looking straight at him. Her eyes were as hard to him, as hard and expressionless and void of recognition, as the eyes of a statue.

She looked at him for a moment, and then her gaze passed beyond him.

Had he had only her eyes to judge by he might have doubted if it was indeed Elizabeth, but he knew her by the gesture of her hand, by the grace of a wanton little curl that floated over her ear as she moved her head. Something was said to her, and she turned smiling tolerantly to the man beside her, a little man in foolish raiment knobbed and spiked like some odd reptile with pneumatic horns—the Bindon of her father's choice.

For a moment Denton stood white and wild-eyed; then came a terrible faintness, and he sat before one of the little tables. He sat down with his back to her, and for a time he did not dare to look at her again. When at last he did, she and Bindon and two other people were standing up to go. The others were her father and her chaperon.

He sat as if incapable of action until the four figures were remote and small, and then he rose up possessed with the one idea of pursuit. For a space he feared he had lost them, and then he came upon Elizabeth and her chaperon again in one of the streets of moving platforms that intersected the city. Bindon and Mwres had disappeared.

He could not control himself to patience. He felt he must speak to her forthwith, or die. He pushed forward to where they were seated, and sat down beside them. His white face was convulsed with half-hysterical excitement.

He laid his hand on her wrist. "Elizabeth?" he said.

She turned in unfeigned astonishment. Nothing but the fear of a strange man showed in her face.

"Elizabeth," he cried, and his voice was strange to him: "dearest—you *know* me?"

Elizabeth's face showed nothing but alarm and perplexity. She drew herself away from him. The chaperon, a little grey-headed woman with mobile features, leant forward to intervene. Her resolute bright eyes examined Denton. "*What* do you say?" she asked.

"This young lady," said Denton,—"she knows me."

"Do you know him, dear?"

"No," said Elizabeth in a strange voice, and with a hand to her forehead, speaking almost as one who repeats a lesson. "No, I do not know him. I *know* I do not know him."

"But—but . . . Not know me! It is I—Denton. Denton! To whom you used to talk. Don't you remember the flying-stages? The little seat in the open air? The verses——"

"No," cried Elizabeth,—"no. I do not know him. I do not know him. There is something . . . But I don't know. All I know is that I do not know him." Her face was a face of infinite distress.

The sharp eyes of the chaperon flitted to and fro from the girl to the man. "You see?" she said, with the faint shadow of a smile. "She does not know you."

"I do not know you," said Elizabeth. "Of that I am sure."

"But, dear—the songs—the little verses——"

"She does not know you," said the chaperon. "You must not . . . You have made a mistake. You must not go on talking to us after that. You must not annoy us on the public ways."

"But——" said Denton, and for a moment his miserably haggard face appealed against fate.

"You must not persist, young man," protested the chaperon.

"*Elizabeth!*" he cried.

Her face was the face of one who is tormented. "I do not know you," she cried, hand to brow. "Oh, I do not know you!"

For an instant Denton sat stunned. Then he stood up and groaned aloud.

He made a strange gesture of appeal towards the remote glass roof of the public way, then turned and went plunging recklessly from one moving platform to another, and vanished amidst the swarms of people going to and fro thereon. The chaperon's eyes followed him, and then she looked at the curious faces about her.

"Dear," asked Elizabeth, clasping her hand, and too deeply moved to heed observation, "who was that man? Who *was* that man?"

The chaperon raised her eyebrows. She spoke in a clear, audible voice. "Some half-witted creature. I have never set eyes on him before."

"Never?"

"Never, dear. Do not trouble your mind about a thing like this."

And soon after this the celebrated hypnotist who dressed in

green and yellow had another client. The young man paced his consulting-room, pale and disordered. "I want to forget," he cried. "I *must* forget."

The hypnotist watched him with quiet eyes, studied his face and clothes and bearing. "To forget anything—pleasure or pain—is to be, by so much—*less*. However, you know your own concern. My fee is high."

"If only I can forget——"

"That's easy enough with you. You wish it. I've done much harder things. Quite recently. I hardly expected to do it: the thing was done against the will of the hypnotised person. A love affair, too—like yours. A girl. So rest assured."

The young man came and sat beside the hypnotist. His manner was a forced calm. He looked into the hypnotist's eyes. "I will tell you. Of course you will want to know what it is. There was a girl. Her name was Elizabeth Mwres. Well . . ."

He stopped. He had seen the instant surprise on the hypnotist's face. In that instant he knew. He stood up. He seemed to dominate the seated figure by his side. He gripped the shoulder of green and gold. For a time he could not find words.

"*Give her me back !*" he said at last. "Give her me back!"

"What do you mean?" gasped the hypnotist.

"Give her me back."

"Give whom?"

"Elizabeth Mwres—the girl——"

The hypnotist tried to free himself; he rose to his feet. Denton's grip tightened.

"Let go!" cried the hypnotist, thrusting an arm against Denton's chest.

In a moment the two men were locked in a clumsy wrestle. Neither had the slightest training—for athleticism, except for exhibition and to afford opportunity for betting, had faded out of the earth—but Denton was not only the younger but the stronger of the two. They swayed across the room, and then the hypnotist had gone down under his antagonist. They fell together. . . .

Denton leaped to his feet, dismayed at his own fury; but the hypnotist lay still, and suddenly from a little white mark where his forehead had struck a stool shot a hurrying band of red. For a space Denton stood over him irresolute, trembling.

A fear of the consequences entered his gently nurtured mind. He turned towards the door. "No," he said aloud, and came back to the middle of the room. Overcoming the instinctive repugnance of one who had seen no act of violence in all his life before, he knelt down beside his antagonist and felt his heart. Then he peered at the wound. He rose quietly and looked about him. He began to see more of the situation.

When presently the hypnotist recovered his senses, his head ached severely, his back was against Denton's knees, and Denton was sponging his face.

The hypnotist did not speak. But presently he indicated by a gesture that in his opinion he had been sponged enough. "Let me get up," he said.

"Not yet," said Denton.

"You have assaulted me, you scoundrel!"

"We are alone," said Denton, "and the door is secure."

There was an interval of thought.

"Unless I sponge," said Denton, "your forehead will develop a tremendous bruise."

"You can go on sponging," said the hypnotist sulkily.

There was another pause.

"We might be in the Stone Age," said the hypnotist. "Violence! Struggle!"

"In the Stone Age no man dared to come between man and woman," said Denton.

The hypnotist thought again.

"What are you going to do?" he asked.

"While you were insensible I found the girl's address on your tablets. I did not know it before. I telephoned. She will be here soon. Then——"

"She will bring her chaperon."

"That is all right."

"But what——"? I don't see. What do you mean to do?"

"I looked about for a weapon also. It is an astonishing thing how few weapons there are nowadays. If you consider that in the Stone Age men owned scarcely anything *but* weapons. I hit at last upon this lamp. I have wrenched off the wires and things, and I hold it so." He extended it over the hypnotist's shoulders. "With that I can quite easily smash your skull. I *will*—unless you do as I tell you."

"Violence is no remedy," said the hypnotist, quoting from the *Modern Man's Book of Moral Maxims*.

"It's an undesirable disease," said Denton.

"Well?"

"You will tell that chaperon you are going to order the girl to marry that knobby little brute with the red hair and ferrety eyes. I believe that's how things stand?"

"Yes—that's how things stand."

"And, pretending to do that, you will restore her memory of me."

"It's unprofessional."

"Look here! If I cannot have that girl I would rather die than not. I don't propose to respect your little fancies. If anything goes wrong you shall not live five minutes. This is a rude makeshift of a weapon, and it may quite conceivably be painful to kill you. But I will. It is unusual, I know, nowadays, to do things like this—mainly because there is so little in life that is worth being violent about."

"The chaperon will see you directly she comes——"

"I shall stand in that recess. Behind you."

The hypnotist thought. "You are a determined young man," he said, "and only half-civilised. I have tried to do my duty to my client, but in this affair you seem likely to get your own way. . . ."

"You mean to deal straightly."

"I'm not going to risk having my brains scattered in a petty affair like this."

"And afterwards?"

"There is nothing a hypnotist or doctor hates so much as a scandal. I at least am no savage. I am annoyed. . . . But in a day or so I shall bear no malice. . . ."

"Thank you. And now that we understand each other, there is no necessity to keep you sitting any longer on the floor."

II.   The Vacant Country

The world, they say, changed more between the year 1800 and the year 1900 than it had done in the previous five hundred years. That century, the nineteenth century, was the dawn of a new epoch in the history of mankind—the epoch of the great cities, the end of the old order of country life.

In the beginning of the nineteenth century the majority of mankind still lived upon the countryside, as their way of life had been for countless generations. All over the world they dwelt in little towns and villages then, and engaged either directly in agriculture, or in occupations that were of service to the agriculturist. They travelled rarely, and dwelt close to their work, because swift means of transit had not yet come. The few who travelled went either on foot, or in slow sailing-ships, or by means of jogging horses incapble of more than sixty miles a day. Think of it!—sixty miles a day. Here and there, in those sluggish times, a town grew a little larger than its neighbours, as a port or as a centre of government; but all the towns in the world with more than a hundred thousand inhabitants could be counted on a man's fingers. So it was in the beginning of the nineteenth century. By the end, the invention of railways, telegraphs, steamships, and complex agricultural machinery, had changed all these things: changed them beyond all hope of return. The vast shops, the varied pleasures, the countless conveniences of the larger towns were suddenly possible, and no sooner existed than they were brought into competition with the homely resources of the rural centres. Mankind were drawn to the cities by an overwhelming attraction. The demand for labour fell with the increase of machinery, the local markets were entirely superseded, and there was a rapid growth of the larger centres at the expense of the open country.

The flow of population townward was the constant pre-occupation of Victorian writers. In Great Britain and New

England, in India and China, the same thing was remarked: everywhere a few swollen towns were visibly .replacing the ancient order. That this was an inevitable result of improved means of travel and transport—that, given swift means of transit, these things must be—was realised by few; and the most puerile schemes were devised to overcome the mysterious magnetism of the urban centres, and keep the people on the land.

Yet the developments of the nineteenth century were only the dawning of the new order. The first great cities of the new time were horribly inconvenient, darkened by smoky fogs, insanitary and noisy; but the discovery of new methods of building, new methods of heating, changed all this. Between 1900 and 2000 the march of change was still more rapid; and between 2000 and 2100 the continually accelerated progress of human invention made the reign of Victoria the Good seem at last an almost incredible vision of idyllic tranquil days.

The introduction of railways was only the first step in that development of those means of locomotion which finally revolutionised human life. By the year 2000 railways and roads had vanished together. The railways, robbed of their rails, had become weedy ridges and ditches upon the face of the world; the old roads, strange barbaric tracks of flint and soil, hammered by hand or rolled by rough iron rollers, strewn with miscellaneous filth, and cut by iron hoofs and wheels into ruts and puddles often many inches deep, had been replaced by patent tracks made of a substance called Eadhamite. This Eadhamite—it was named after its patentee —ranks with the invention of printing and steam as one of the epoch-making discoveries of the world's history.

When Eadham discovered the substance, he probably thought of it as a mere cheap substitute for indiarubber; it cost a few shillings a ton. But you can never tell all an invention will do. It was the genius of a man named Warming that pointed to the possibility of using it, not only for the tires of wheels, but as a road substance, and who organised the enormous network of public ways that speedily covered the world.

These public ways were made with longitudinal divisions. On the outer on either side went foot cyclists and conveyances travelling at a less speed than twenty-five miles an hour; in the middle, motors capable of speed up to a hundred; and the inner, Warming (in the face of enormous ridicule) reserved for vehicles travelling at speeds of a hundred miles an hour and upward.

For ten years his inner ways were vacant. Before he died they were the most crowded of all, and vast light frame-works with wheels of twenty and thirty feet in diameter hurled along them at paces that year after year rose steadily towards two hundred miles an hour. And by the time this revolution was accomplished, a parallel revolution had transformed the ever-growing cities. Before the development of practical science the fogs and filth of Victorian times vanished. Electric heating replaced fires (in 2013 the lighting of a fire that did not absolutely consume its own smoke was made an indictable nuisance), and all the city ways, all public squares and places, were covered in with a recently invented glass-like substance. The roofing of London became practically continuous. Certain short-sighted and foolish legislation against tall buildings was abolished, and London, from a squat expanse of petty houses—feebly archaic in design—rose steadily towards the sky. To the municipal responsibility for water, light, and drainage, was added another, and that was ventilation.

But to tell of all the changes in human convenience that these two hundred years brought about, to tell of the long foreseen invention of flying, to describe how life in households was steadily supplanted by life in interminable hotels, how at last even those who were still concerned in agricultural work came to live in the towns and to go to and fro to their work every day, to describe how at last in all England only four towns remained, each with many millions of people, and how there were left no inhabited houses in all the countryside: to tell all this would take us far from our story of Denton and his Elizabeth. They had been separated and reunited, and still they could not marry. For Denton—it was his only fault—had no money. Neither had Elizabeth until she was twenty-one, and as yet she was only eighteen. At twenty-one all the property of her mother would come to her, for that was the custom of the time. She did not know that it was possible to anticipate her fortune, and Denton was far too delicate a lover to suggest such a thing. So things stuck hopelessly between them. Elizabeth said that she was very unhappy, and that nobody understood her but Denton, and that when she was away from him she was wretched; and Denton said that his heart longed for her day and night. And they met as often as they could to enjoy the discussion of their sorrows.

They met one day at their little seat upon the flying-stage. The precise site of this meeting was where in Victorian times the road from Wimbledon came out upon the common. They were, however, five hundred feet above that point. Their seat looked far over London. To convey the appearance of it all to a nineteenth-century reader would have been difficult. One would have had to tell him to think of the Crystal Palace, of the newly-built "mammoth" hotels—as those little affairs were called—of the larger railway stations of his time, and to imagine such buildings enlarged to vast proportions and run together and continuous over the whole metropolitan area. If then he was told that this continuous roof-space bore a huge forest of rotating wind-wheels, he would have begun very dimly to appreciate what to these young people was the commonest sight in their lives.

To their eyes it had something of the quality of a prison, and they were talking, as they had talked a hundred times before, of how they might escape from it and be at last happy together: escape from it, that is, before the appointed three years were at an end. It was, they both agreed, not only impossible but almost wicked, to wait three years. "Before that," said Denton—and the notes of his voice told of a splendid chest—"*we might both be dead!*"

Their vigorous young hands had to grip at this, and then Elizabeth had a still more poignant thought that brought the tears from her wholesome eyes and down her healthy cheeks. "*One* of us," she said, "*one* of us might be——"

She choked; she could not say the word that is so terrible to the young and happy.

Yet to marry and be very poor in the cities of that time was—for anyone who had lived pleasantly—a very dreadful thing. In the old agricultural days that had drawn to an end in the eighteenth century there had been a pretty proverb of love in a cottage; and indeed in those days the poor of the countryside had dwelt in flower-covered, diamond-windowed cottages of thatch and plaster, with the sweet air and earth about them, amidst tangled hedges and the song of birds, and with the ever-changing sky overhead. But all this had changed (the change was already beginning in the nineteenth century), and a new sort of life was opening for the poor—in the lower quarters of the city.

In the nineteenth century the lower quarters were still beneath the sky; they were areas of land on clay or other unsuitable soil, liable to floods or exposed to the smoke of more fortunate districts, insufficiently supplied with water, and as insanitary as the great fear of infectious diseases felt by the wealthier classes permitted. In the twenty-second century, however, the growth of the city storey above storey, and the coalescence of buildings, had led to a different arrangement. The prosperous people lived in a vast series of sumptuous hotels in the upper storeys and halls of the city fabric; the industrial population dwelt beneath in the tremendous ground-floor and basement, so to speak, of the place.

In the refinement of life and manners these lower classes differed little from their ancestors, the East-enders of Queer Victoria's time; but they had developed a distinct dialect of their own. In these under ways they lived and died, rarely ascending to the surface except when work took them there. Since for most of them this was the sort of life to which they had been born, they found no great misery in such circumstances; but for people like Denton and Elizabeth, such a plunge would have seemed more terrible than death.

"And yet what else is there?" asked Elizabeth.

Denton professed not to know. Apart from his own feeling

of delicacy, he was not sure how Elizabeth would like the idea of borrowing on the strength of her expectations.

The passage from London to Paris even, said Elizabeth, was beyond their means; and in Paris, as in any other city in the world, life would be just as costly and impossible as in London.

Well might Denton cry aloud: "If only we had lived in those days, dearest! If only we had lived in the past!" For to their eyes even nineteenth-century Whitechapel was seen through a mist of romance.

"Is there *nothing?*" cried Elizabeth, suddenly weeping. "Must we really wait for those three long years? Fancy *three* years—six-and-thirty months!" The human capacity for patience had not grown with the ages.

Then suddenly Denton was moved to speak of something that had already flickered across his mind. He had hit upon it at last. It seemed to him so wild a suggestion that he made it only half-seriously. But to put a thing into words has ever a way of making it seem more real and possible than it seemed before. And so it was with him.

"Suppose," he said, "we went into the country?"

She looked at him to see if he was serious in proposing such an adventure.

"The country?"

"Yes—beyond there. Beyond the hills."

"How could we live?" she said. "*Where* could we live?"

"It is not impossible," he said. "People used to live in the country."

"But then there were houses."

"There are the ruins of villages and towns now. On the clay lands they are gone, of course. But they are still left on the grazing land, because it does not pay the Food Company to remove them. I know that—for certain. Besides, one sees them from the flying-machines, you know. Well, we might shelter in some one of these, and repair it with our hands. Do you know, the thing is not so wild as it seems. Some of the men who go out every day to look after the crops and herds might be paid to bring us food. . . ."

She stood in front of him. "How strange it would be if one really could. . . ."

"Why not?"

"But no one dares."

"That is no reason."

"It would be—oh! it would be so romantic and strange. If only it were possible."

"Why not possible?"

"There are so many things. Think of all the things we have, things that we should miss."

"Should we miss them? After all, the life we lead is very unreal—very artificial." He began to expand his idea, and as he warmed to his exposition the fantastic quality of his first proposal faded away.

She thought. "But I have heard of prowlers—escaped criminals."

He nodded, He hesitated over his answer because he thought it sounded boyish. He blushed. "I could get someone I know to make me a sword."

She looked at him with enthusiasm growing in her eyes. She had heard of swords, had seen one in a museum; she thought of those ancient days when men wore them as a common thing. His suggestion seemed an impossible dream to her, and perhaps for that reason she was eager for more detail. And inventing for the most part as he went along, he told her how they might live in the country as the old-world people had done. With every detail her interest grew, for she was one of those girls for whom romance and adventure have a fascination.

His suggestion seemed, I say, an impossible dream to her on that day, but the next day they talked about it again, and it was strangely less impossible.

"At first we should take food," said Denton. "We could carry food for ten or twelve days." It was an age of compact artificial nourishment, and such a provision had none of the unwieldy suggestion it would have had in the nineteenth century.

"But—until our house," she asked—"until it was ready, where should we sleep?"

"It is summer."

"But. . . . What do you mean?"

"There was a time when there were no houses in the world; when all mankind slept always in the open air."

"But for us! The emptiness! No walls—no ceiling!"

"Dear," he said, "in London you have many beautiful ceilings. Artists paint them and stud them with lights. But I have seen a ceiling more beautiful than any in London. . . ."

"But where?"

"It is the ceiling under which we two would be alone. . . ."

"You mean. . . .?"

"Dear," he said, "it is something the world has forgotten. It is Heaven and all the host of stars."

Each time they talked the thing seemed more possible and more desirable to them. In a week or so it was quite possible. Another week, and it was the inevitable thing they had to do. A great enthusiasm for the country seized hold of them and possessed them. The sordid tumult of the town, they said, overwhelmed them. They marvelled that this simple way out of their troubles had never come upon them before.

One morning near Midsummer-day, there was a new minor official upon the flying-stage, and Denton's place was to know him no more.

Our two young people had secretly married, and were going forth manfully out of the city in which they and their ancestors before them had lived all their days. She wore a new dress of white cut in an old-fashioned pattern, and he had a bundle of provisions strapped athwart his back, and in his hand he carried—rather shamefacedly, it is true, and under his purple cloak—an implement of archaic form, a cross-hilted thing of tempered steel.

Imagine that going forth! In their days the sprawling suburbs of Victorian times with their vile roads, petty houses, foolish little gardens of shrub and geranium, and all their futile, pretentious privacies, had disappeared: the towering buildings of the new age, the mechanical ways, the electric and water mains, all came to an end together, like a wall, like a cliff, near four hundred feet in height, abrupt and sheer. All about the city spread the carrot, swede, and turnip fields of the Food Company, vegetables that were the basis of a thousand varied foods, and weeds and hedgerow tangles had been utterly extirpated. The incessant expense of weeding that went on year after year in the petty, wasteful, and barbaric farming of the ancient days, the Food Company had economised for ever more by a campaign of extermination. Here and there, however, neat rows of bramble standards and apple trees with whitewashed stems, intersected the fields, and at places groups of gigantic teazles reared their favoured spikes. Here and there huge agricultural machines hunched under waterproof covers. The mingled waters of the Wey and Mole and Wandle ran in rectangular channels; and wherever a gentle elevation of the ground permitted a fountain of deodorised sewage distributed its benefits athwart the land and made a rainbow of the sunlight.

By a great archway in that enormous city wall emerged the Eadhamite road to Portsmouth, swarming in the morning sunshine with an enormous traffic bearing the blue-clad servants of the Food Company to their toil. A rushing traffic, beside which they seemed two scarce-moving dots. Along the outer tracks hummed and rattled the tardy little old-fashioned motors of such as had duties within twenty miles or so of the city; the inner ways were filled with vaster mechanisms— swift monocycles bearing a score of men, lank multicycles, quadricycles sagging with heavy loads, empty gigantic produce carts that would come back again filled before the sun was setting, all with throbbing engines and noiseless wheels and a perpetual wild melody of horns and gongs.

Along the very verge of the outermost way our young people went in silence, newly wed and oddly shy of one another's company. Many were the things shouted to them as they tramped along, for in 2100 a foot-passenger on an English road was almost as strange a sight as a motor car would have been in 1800. But they went on with steadfast eyes into the country, paying no heed to such cries.

Before them in the south rose the Downs, blue at first, and as they came nearer changing to green, surmounted by the row of gigantic wind-wheels that supplemented the wind-wheels upon the roof-spaces of the city, and broken and restless with the long morning shadows of those whirling vanes. By midday they had come so near that they could see here and there little patches of pallid dots—the sheep the Meat Department of the Food Company owned. In another hour they had passed the clay and the root crops and the single fence that hedged them in, and the prohibition against trespass no longer held: the levelled roadway plunged into a cutting with all its traffic, and they could leave it and walk over the greensward and up the open hillside.

Never had these children of the latter days been together in such a lonely place.

They were both very hungry and footsore—for walking was a rare exercise—and presently they sat down on the weedless, close-cropped grass, and looked back for the first time at the city from which they had come, shining wide and splendid in the blue haze of the valley of the Thames. Elizabeth was a little afraid of the unenclosed sheep away up the slope—she had never been near big unrestrained animals before—but Denton reassured her. And overhead a white-winged bird circled in the blue.

They talked but little until they had eaten, and then their tongues were loosened. He spoke of the happiness that was now certainly theirs, of the folly of not breaking sooner out of that magnificent prison of latter-day life, of the old romantic days that had passed from the world for ever. And then he became boastful. He took up the sword that lay on the ground beside him, and she took it from his hand and ran a tremulous finger along the blade.

"And you could," she said, "*you*—could raise this and strike a man?"

"Why not? If there were need."

"But," she said, "it seems so horrible. It would slash. . . . There would be"—her voice sank—"*blood*."

"In the old romances you have read often enough. . . .

"Oh, I know: in those—yes. But that is different. One

knows it is not blood, but just a sort of red ink. . . . And *you*
—killing!"

She looked at him doubtfully, and then handed him back
the sword.

After they had rested and eaten, they rose up and went on
their way towards the hills. They passed quite close to a huge
flock of sheep, who stared and bleated at their unaccustomed
figures. She had never seen sheep before, and she shivered to
think such gentle things must needs be slain for food. A sheep
dog barked from a distance, and then a shepherd appeared
amidst the supports of the wind-wheels, and came down
towards them.

When he drew near he called out asking whither they were
going.

Denton hesitated, and told him briefly that they sought
some ruined house among the Downs, in which they might
live together. He tried to speak in an off-hand manner, as
though it was a usual thing to do. The man stared incredulously.

"Have you *done* anything?" he asked.

"Nothing," said Denton. "Only we don't want to live in
a city any longer. Why should we live in cities?"

The shepherd stared more incredulously than ever. "You
can't live here," he said.

"We mean to try."

The shepherd stared from one to the other. "You'll go
back to-morrow," he said. "It looks pleasant enough in the
sunlight. . . . Are you sure you've done nothing? We shepherds
are not such *great* friends of the police."

Denton looked at him steadfastly. "No," he said. "But we
are too poor to live in the city, and we can't bear the thought
of wearing clothes of blue canvas and doing drudgery. We
are going to live a simple life here, like the people of old."

The shepherd was a bearded man with a thoughtful face.
He glanced at Elizabeth's fragile beauty.

"*They* had simple minds," he said.

"So have we," said Denton.

The shepherd smiled.

"If you go along here," he said, "along the crest beneath the wind-wheels, you will see a heap of mounds and ruins on your right-hand side. That was once a town called Epsom. There are no houses there, and the bricks have been used for a sheep pen. Go on, and another heap on the edge of the root-land is Leatherhead; and then the hill turns away along the border of a valley, and there are woods of beech. Keep along the crest. You will come to quite wild places. In some parts, in spite of all the weeding that is done, ferns and bluebells and other such useless plants are growing still. And through it all underneath the wind-wheels runs a straight lane paved with stones, a roadway of the Romans two thousand years old. Go to the right of that, down into the valley and follow it along by the banks of the river. You come presently to a street of houses, many with the roofs still sound upon them. There you may find shelter."

They thanked him.

"But it's a quiet place. There is no light after dark there. and I have heard tell of robbers. It is lonely. Nothing happens there. The phonographs of the story-tellers, the kinematograph entertainments, the news machines—none of them are to be found there. If you are hungry there is no food, if you are ill no doctor. . . ." He stopped.

"We shall try it," said Denton, moving to go on. Then a thought struck him, and he made an agreement with the shepherd, and learnt where they might find him, to buy and bring them anything of which they stood in need, out of the city.

And in the evening they came to the deserted village, with its houses that seemed so small and odd to them: they found it golden in the glory of the sunset, and desolate and still. They went from one deserted house to another, marvelling at their quaint simplicity, and debating which they should choose. And at last, in a sunlit corner of a room that had lost its outer wall, they came upon a wild flower, a little flower of blue that the weeders of the Food Company had overlooked.

That house they decided upon; but they did not remain

in it long that night, because they were resolved to feast upon nature. And moreover the houses became very gaunt and shadowy after the sunlight had faded out of the sky. So after they had rested a little time they went to the crest of the hill again to see with their own eyes the silence of heaven set with stars, about which the old poets had had so many things to tell. It was a wonderful sight, and Denton talked like the stars, and when they went down the hill at last the sky was pale with dawn. They slept but little, and in the morning when they woke a thrush was singing in a tree.

So these young people of the twenty-second century began their exile. That morning they were very busy exploring the resources of this new home in which they were going to live the simple life. They did not explore very fast or very far, because they went everywhere hand-in-hand; but they found the beginnings of some furniture. Beyond the village was a store of winter fodder for the sheep of the Food Company, and Denton dragged great armfuls to the house to make a bed; and in several of the houses were old fungus-eaten chairs and tables—rough, barbaric, clumsy furniture, it seemed to them, and made of wood. They repeated many of the things they had said on the previous day, and towards evening they found another flower, a harebell. In the late afternoon some Company shepherds went down the river valley riding on a big multicycle; but they hid from them, because their presence, Elizabeth said, seemed to spoil the romance of this old-world place altogether.

In this fashion they lived a week. For all that week the days were cloudless, and the nights, nights of starry glory, that were invaded each a little more by a crescent moon.

Yet something of the first splendour of their coming faded —faded imperceptibly day after day; Denton's eloquence became fitful, and lacked fresh topics of inspiration; the fatigue of their long march from London told in a certain stiffness of the limbs, and each suffered from a slight unaccountable cold. Moreover, Denton became aware of unoccupied time. In one place among the carelessly heaped lumber of the old times he found a rust-eaten spade, and with this

he made a fitful attack on the razed and grass-grown garden
—though he had nothing to plant or sow. He returned to
Elizabeth with a sweat-streaming face, after half an hour of
such work.

"There were giants in those days," he said, not understanding what wont and training will do. And their walk that day
led them along the hills until they could see the city shimmer-
ing far away in the valley. "I wonder how things are going
on there," he said.

And then came a change in the weather. "Come out and
see the clouds," she cried; and behold! they were a sombre
purple in the north and east, streaming up to ragged edges
at the zenith. And as they went up the hill these hurrying
streamers blotted out the sunset. Suddenly the wind set the
beech-trees swaying and whispering, and Elizabeth shivered.
And then far away the lightning flashed, flashed like a sword
that is drawn suddenly, and the distant thunder marched
about the sky, and even as they stood astonished, pattering
upon them came the first headlong raindrops of the storm. In
an instant the last streak of sunset was hidden by a falling
curtain of hail, and the lightning flashed again, and the voice
of the thunder roared louder, and all about them the world
scowled dark and strange.

Seizing hands, these children of the city ran down the hill
to their home, in infinite astonishment. And ere they reached
it, Elizabeth was weeping with dismay, and the darkling
ground about them was white and brittle and active with the
pelting hail.

Then began a strange and terrible night for them. For the
first time in their civilised lives they were in absolute darkness; they were wet and cold and shivering, all about them
hissed the hail, and through the long-neglected ceilings of the
derelict home came noisy spouts of water and formed pools
and rivulets on the creaking floors. As the gusts of the storm
struck the worn-out building, it groaned and shuddered, and
now a mass of plaster from the wall would slide and smash, and
now some loosened tile would rattle down the roof and
crash into the empty greenhouse below. Elizabeth shuddered,

and was still; Denton wrapped his gay and flimsy city cloak about her, and so they crouched in the darkness. And ever the thunder broke louder and nearer, and ever more lurid flashed the lightning, jerking into a momentary gaunt clearness the steaming, dripping room in which they sheltered.

Never before had they been in the open air save when the sun was shining. All their time had been spent in the warm and airy ways and halls and rooms of the latter-day city. It was to them that night as if they were in some other world, some disordered chaos of stress and tumult, and almost beyond hoping that they should ever see the city ways again.

The storm seemed to last interminably, until at last they dozed between the thunderclaps, and then very swiftly it fell and ceased. And as the last patter of the rain died away they heard an unfamiliar sound.

"What is that?" cried Elizabeth.

It came again. It was the barking of dogs. It drove down the desert lane and passed; and through the window, whitening the wall before them and throwing upon it the shadow of the window-frame and of a tree in black silhouette, shone the light of the waxing moon. . . .

Just as the pale dawn was drawing the things about them into sight, the fitful barking of dogs came near again, and stopped. They listened. After a pause they heard the quick pattering of feet seeking round the house, and short, half-smothered barks. Then again everything was still.

"Ssh!" whispered Elizabeth, and pointed to the door of their room.

Denton went halfway towards the door, and stood listening. He came back with a face of affected unconcern. "They must be the sheep-dogs of the Food Company," he said. "They will do us no harm."

He sat down again beside her. "What a night it has been!" he said, to hide how keenly he was listening.

"I don't like dogs," answered Elizabeth, after a long silence.

"Dogs never hurt anyone," said Denton. "In the old days —in the nineteenth century—everybody had a dog."

"There was a romance I heard once. A dog killed a man."

"Not this sort of dog," said Denton confidently. "Some of those romances—are exaggerated."

Suddenly a half-bark and a pattering up the staircase; the sound of panting. Denton sprang to his feet and drew the sword out of the damp straw upon which they had been lying. Then in the doorway appeared a gaunt sheep-dog, and halted there. Behind it stared another. For an instant man and brute faced each other, hesitating.

Then Denton, being ignorant of dogs, made a sharp step forward. "Go away," he said, with a clumsy motion of his sword.

The dog started and growled. Denton stopped sharply. "Good dog!" he said.

The growling jerked into a bark.

"Good dog!" said Denton. The second dog growled and barked. A third out of sight down the staircase took up the barking also. Outside others gave tongue—a large number it seemed to Denton.

"This is annoying," said Denton, without taking his eye off the brutes before him. "Of course the shepherds won't come out of the city for hours yet. Naturally these dogs don't quite make us out."

"I can't hear,'" shouted Elizabeth. She stood up and came to him.

Denton tried again, but the barking still drowned his voice. The sound had a curious effect upon his blood. Odd disused emotions began to stir; his face changed as he shouted. He tried again; the barking seemed to mock him, and one dog danced a pace forward, bristling. Suddenly he turned, and uttering certain words in the dialect of the underways, words incomprehensible to Elizabeth, he made for the dogs. There was a sudden cessation of the barking, a growl and a snapping. Elizabeth saw the snarling head of the foremost dog, its white teeth and retracted ears, and the flash of the thrust blade. The brute leapt into the air and was flung back.

Then Denton, with a shout, was driving the dogs before him. The sword flashed above his head with a sudden new freedom of gesture, and then he vanished down the staircase. She made six steps to follow him, and on the landing there was blood. She stopped, and hearing the tumult of dogs and Denton's shouts pass out of the house, ran to the window.

Nine wolfish sheep-dogs were scattering, one writhed before the porch; and Denton, tasting that strange delight of combat that slumbers still in the blood of even the most civilised man, was shouting and running across the garden space. And then she saw something that for a moment he did not see. The dogs circled round this way and that, and came again. They had him in the open.

In an instant she divined the situation. She would have called to him. For a moment she felt sick and helpless, and then, obeying a strange impulse, she gathered up her white skirt and ran downstairs. In the hall was the rusting spade. That was it! She seized it and ran out.

She came none too soon. One dog rolled before him, wellnigh slashed in half; but a second had him by the thigh, a third gripped his collar behind, and a fourth had the blade of the sword between its teeth, tasting its own blood. He parried the leap of a fifth with his left arm.

It might have been the first century instead of the twenty-second, so far as she was concerned. All the gentleness of her eighteen years of city life vanished before this primordial need. The spade smote hard and sure, and cleft a dog's skull. Another, crouching for a spring, yelped with dismay at this unexpected antagonist, and rushed aside. Two wasted precious moments on the binding of a feminine skirt.

The collar of Denton's cloak tore and parted as he staggered back; and that dog, too, felt the spade, and ceased to trouble him. He sheathed his sword in the brute at his thigh.

"To the wall!" cried Elizabeth; and in three seconds the fight was at an end, and our young people stood side by side, while a remnant of five dogs, with ears and tails of disaster, fled shamefully from the stricken field.

For a moment they stood panting and victorious, and then Elizabeth, dropping her spade, covered her face, and sank to the ground in a paroxysm of weeping. Denton looked about him, thrust the point of his sword into the ground so that it was at hand, and stooped to comfort her.

At last their more tumultuous emotions subsided and they could talk again. She leant upon the wall, and he sat upon it so that he could keep an eye open for any returning dogs. Two, at any rate, were up on the hillside and keeping up a vexatious barking.

She was tear-stained, but not very wretched now, because for half an hour he had been repeating that she was brave and had saved his life. But a new fear was growing in her mind.

"They are the dogs of the Food Company," she said. "There will be trouble."

"I am afraid so. Very likely they will prosecute us for trespass."

A pause.

"In the old times," he said, "this sort of thing happened day after day."

"Last night!" she said. "I could not live through another such night."

He looked at her. Her face was pale for want of sleep, and drawn and haggard. He came to a sudden resolution. "We must go back," he said.

She looked at the dead dogs, and shivered. "We cannot stay here," she said.

"We must go back," he repeated, glancing over his shoulder to see if the enemy kept their distance. "We have been happy for a time. . . . But the world is too civilised. Ours is the age of cities. More of this will kill us."

"But what are we to do? How can we live there?"

Denton hesitated. His heel kicked against the wall on which he sat. "It's a thing I haven't mentioned before," he said, and coughed; "but . . ."

"Yes?"

"You could raise money on your expectations," he said.

"Could I?" she said eagerly.

"Of course you could. What a child you are!"

She stood up, and her face was bright. "Why did you not tell me before?" she asked. "And all this time we have been here!"

He looked at her for a moment, and smiled. Then the smile vanished. "I thought it ought to come from you," he said. "I didn't like to ask for your money. And besides—at first I thought this would be rather fine."

There was a pause.

"It *has* been fine," he said; and glanced once more over his shoulder. "Until all this began."

"Yes," she said, "those first days. The first three days."

They looked for a space into one another's faces, and then Denton slid down from the wall and took her hand.

"To each generation," he said, "the life of its time, I see it all plainly now. In the city—that is the life to which we were born. To live in any other fashion . . . Coming here was a dream, and this—is the awakening."

"It was a pleasant dream," she said, "in the beginning."

For a long space neither spoke.

"If we would reach the city before the shepherds come here, we must start," said Denton. "We must get our food out of the house and eat as we go."

Denton glanced about him again, and, giving the dead dogs a wide berth, they walked across the garden space and into the house together. They found the wallet with their food, and descended the blood-stained stairs again. In the hall Elizabeth stopped. "One minute," she said. "There is something here."

She led the way into the room in which that one little blue flower was blooming. She stooped to it, she touched it with her hand.

"I want it," she said; and then, "I cannot take it. . . ."

Impulsively she stooped and kissed its petals.

Then silently, side by side, they went across the empty garden-space into the old high road, and set their faces resolutely towards the distant city—towards the complex mechanical city of those latter days, the city that had swallowed up mankind.

III.   The Ways of the City

Prominent if not paramount among world-changing inventions in the history of man is that series of contrivances in
locomotion that began with the railway and ended for a century or more with the motor and the patent road. That these
contrivances, together with the device of limited liability joint
stock companies and the supersession of agricultural labourers
by skilled men with ingenious machinery would necessarily
concentrate mankind in cities of unparalleled magnitude
and work an entire revolution in human life, became, after the
event, a thing so obvious that it is a matter of astonishment
it was not more clearly anticipated. Yet that any steps should
be taken to anticipate the miseries such a revolution might
entail does not appear even to have been suggested; and the
idea that the moral prohibitions and sanctions, the privileges
and concessions, the conception of property, and responsibility
of comfort and beauty, that had rendered the mainly agricultural states of the past prosperous and happy, would fail in
the rising torrent of novel opportunities and novel stimula-
tions, never seems to have entered the nineteenth-century
mind. That a citizen, kindly and fair in his ordinary life, could
as a shareholder become almost murderously greedy; that
commercial methods that were reasonable and honourable on
the old-fashioned countryside should on an enlarged scale
be deadly and overwhelming; that ancient charity was modern
pauperisation, and ancient employment modern sweating;
that, in fact, a revision and enlargement of the duties and
rights of man had become urgently necessary, were things
could not entertain, nourished as it was on an archaic system of education and profoundly retrospective and legal in
all its habits of thought. It was known that the accumulation
of men in cities involved unprecedented dangers of pestilence;
there was an energetic development of sanitation; but that
the diseases of gambling and usury, of luxury and tyranny
should become endemic, and produce horrible consequences,
was beyond the scope of nineteenth-century thought. And

so, as if it were some inorganic process, practically unhindered
by the creative will of man, the growth of the swarming un
happy cities that mark the twenty-first century accomplished
itself.

The new society was divided into three main classes. A
the summit slumbered the property owner, enormously rich
by accident rather than design, potent save for the will an
aim, the last *avatar* of Hamlet in the world. Below was th
enormous multitude of workers employed by the giganti
companies that monopolised control; and between these tw
the dwindling middle class, officials of innumerable sorts
foremen, managers, the medical, legal, artistic, and scholasti
classes, and the minor rich, a middle class whose member
led a life of insecure luxury and precarious speculation amids
the movements of the great managers.

Already the love story and the marrying of two person
of this middle class have been told: how they overcame th
obstacles between them, and how they tried the simple, old
fashioned way of living on the countryside and came bac
speedily enough into the city of London. Denton had n
means, so Elizabeth borrowed money on the securities that he
father Mwres held in trust for her until she was one-and
twenty.

The rate of interest she paid was of course high, becaus
of the uncertainty of her security, and the arithmetic of lover
is often sketchy and optimistic. Yet they had very gloriou
times after that return. They determined they would not g
to a Pleasure city nor waste their days rushing through the a
from one part of the world to the other, for in spite of on
disillusionment, their tastes were still old-fashioned. The
furnished their little room with quaint old Victorian furnitur
and found a shop on the forty-second floor in Seventh Wa
where printed books of the old sort were still to be bought. I
was their pet affectation to read print instead of hearin
phonographs. And when presently there came a sweet littl
girl, to unite them further if it were possible, Elizabeth woul
not send it to a *crèche*, as the custom was, but insisted o

nursing it at home. The rent of their apartments was raised on account of this singular proceeding, but that they did not mind. It only meant borrowing a little more.

Presently Elizabeth was of age, and Denton had a business interview with her father that was not agreeable. An exceedingly disagreeable interview with their money-lender followed, from which he brought home a white face. On his return Elizabeth had to tell him of a new and marvellous intonation of "Goo" that their daughter had devised, but Denton was inattentive. In the midst, just as she was at the cream of her description, he interrupted. "How much money do you think we have left, now that everything is settled?"

She stared and stopped her appreciative swaying of the Goo genius that had accompanied her description.

"You don't mean . . .?"

"Yes," he answered. "Ever so much. We have been wild. It's the interest. Or something. And the shares you had, slumped. Your father did not mind. Said it was not his business, after what had happened. He's going to marry again. . . . Well—we have scarcely a thousand left!"

"Only a thousand?"

"Only a thousand."

And Elizabeth sat down. For a moment she regarded him with a white face, then her eyes went about the quaint, old-fashioned room, with its middle Victorian furniture and genuine oleographs, and rested at last on the little lump of humanity within her arms.

Denton glanced at her and stood downcast. Then he swung round on his heel and walked up and down very rapidly.

"I must get something to do," he broke out presently. "I am an idle scoundrel. I ought to have thought of this before. I have been a selfish fool. I wanted to be with you all day. . . ."

He stopped, looking at her white face. Suddenly he came and kissed her and the little face that nestled against her breast.

"It's all right, dear," he said, standing over her; "you won't be lonely now—now Dings is beginning to talk to you.

And I can soon get something to do, you know. Soon . . .
Easily . . . It's only a shock at first. But it will come all right.
It's sure to come right. I will go out again as soon as I have
rested, and find what can be done. For the present it's hard
to think of anything . . ."

"It would be hard to leave these rooms," said Elizabeth;
"but——"

"There won't be any need of that—trust me."

"They are expensive."

Denton waved that aside. He began talking of the work he
could do. He was not very explicit what it would be; but
he was quite sure that there was something to keep them
comfortably in the happy middle class, whose way of life
was the only one they knew.

"There are three-and-thirty million people in London," he
said: "some of them *must* have need of me."

"Some *must*."

"The trouble is . . . Well—Bindon, that brown little old
man your father wanted you to marry. He's an important
person. . . . I can't go back to my flying-stage work, because
he is now a Commissioner of the Flying-Stage Clerks."

"I didn't know that," said Elizabeth.

"He was made that in the last few weeks . . . or things
would be easy enough, for they liked me on the flying-stage.
But there's dozens of other things to be done—dozens. Don't
you worry, dear. I'll rest a little while, and then we'll dine
and then I'll start on my rounds. I know lots of people—
lots."

So they rested, and then they went to the public dining
room and dined, and then he started on his search for employment. But they soon realised that in the matter of one
convenience the world was just as badly off as it had ever
been, and that was a nice, secure, honourable, remunerative
employment, leaving ample leisure for the private life, and
demanding no special ability, no violent exertion nor risk,
and no sacrifice of any sort for its attainment. He evolved a
number of brilliant projects, and spent many days hurrying
from one part of the enormous city to another in search of

influential friends; and all his influential friends were glad to see him, and very sanguine until it came to definite proposals, and then they became guarded and vague. He would part with them coldly, and think over their behaviour, and get irritated on his way back, and stop at some telephone office and spend money on an animated but unprofitable quarrel. And as the days passed, he got so worried and irritated that even to seem kind and careless before Elizabeth cost him an effort—as she, being a loving woman, perceived very clearly.

After an extremely complex preface one day, she helped him out with a painful suggestion. He had expected her to weep and give way to despair when it came to selling all their joyfully bought early Victorian treasures, their quaint objects of art, their antimacassars, bead mats, repp curtains, veneered furniture, gold-framed steel engravings and pencil drawings, wax flowers under shades, stuffed birds, and all sorts of choice old things; but it was she who made the proposal. The sacrifice seemed to fill her with pleasure, and so did the idea of shifting to apartments ten or twelve floors lower in another hotel. "So long as Dings is with us, nothing matters," she said. "It's all experience." So he kissed her, said she was braver than when she fought the sheep-dogs, called her Boadicea, and abstained very carefully from reminding her that they would have to pay a considerably higher rent on account of the little voice with which Dings greeted the perpetual uproar of the city.

His idea had been to get Elizabeth out of the way when it came to selling the absurd furniture about which their affections were twined and tangled; but when it came to the sale it was Elizabeth who haggled with the dealer while Denton went about the running ways of the city, white and sick with sorrow and the fear of what was still to come. When they moved into their sparsely-furnished pink-and-white apartments in a cheap hotel, there came an outbreak of furious energy on his part, and then nearly a week of lethargy during which he sulked at home. Through those days Elizabeth shone like a star, and at the end Denton's misery found a vent in tears. And then he went out into the city ways again, and —to his utter amazement—found some work to do.

His standard of employment had fallen steadily until at last it had reached the lowest level of independent workers. At first he had aspired to some high official position in the great Flying or Windvane or Water Companies, or to an appointment on one of the General Intelligence Organisations that had replaced newspapers, or to some professional partnership, but those were the dreams of the beginning. From that he had passed to speculation, and three hundred gold "lions" out of Elizabeth's thousand had vanished one evening in the share market. Now he was glad his good looks secured him a trial in the position of salesman to the Suzannah Hat Syndicate, a Syndicate dealing in ladies' caps, hair decorations, and hats—for though the city was completely covered in, ladies still wore extremely elaborate and beautiful hats at the theatres and places of public worship.

It would have been amusing if one could have confronted a Regent Street shopkeeper of the nineteenth century with the development of his establishment in which Denton's duties lay. Nineteenth Way was still sometimes called Regent Street, but it was now a street of moving platforms and nearly eight hundred feet wide. The middle space was immovable and gave access by staircases descending into subterranean ways to the houses on either side. Right and left were an ascending series of continuous platforms each of which travelled about five miles an hour faster than the one internal to it, so that one could step from platform to platform until one reached the swiftest outer way and so go about the city. The establishment of the Suzannah Hat Syndicate projected a vast *façade* upon the outer way, sending out overhead at either end an overlapping series of huge white glass screens, on which gigantic animated pictures of the faces of well-known beautiful living women wearing novelties in hats were thrown. A dense crowd was always collected in the stationary central way watching a vast kinematograph which displayed the changing fashion. The whole front of the building was in perpetual chromatic change, and all down the *façade*—four

hundred feet it measured—and all across the street of moving
ways, laced and winked and glittered in a thousand varieties
of colour and lettering the inscription—

SUZANNA! 'ETS! SUZANNA! 'ETS!

A broadside of gigantic phonographs drowned all conversation in the moving way and roared "*hats*" at the passer-by,
while far down the street and up, other batteries counselled
the public to "walk down for Suzannah," and queried, "Why
don't you buy the girl a hat?"

For the benefit of those who chanced to be deaf—and deaf-
ness was not uncommon in the London of that age—inscrip-
tions of all sizes were thrown from the roof above upon the
moving platforms themselves, and on one's hand or on the
bald head of the man before one, or on a lady's shoulders, or in
a sudden jet of flame before one's feet, the moving finger wrote
in unanticipated letters of fire "'*ets r chip t'de*," or simply
"'*ets*." And spite of all these efforts so high was the pitch at
which the city lived, so trained became one's eyes and ears to
ignore all sorts of advertisement, that many a citizen had
passed that place thousands of times and was still unaware
of the existence of the Suzannah Hat Syndicate.

To enter the building one descended the staircase in the
middle way and walked through a public passage in which
pretty girls promenaded, girls who were willing to wear a
ticketed hat for a small fee. The entrance chamber was a large
hall in which wax heads fashionably adorned rotated gracefully upon pedestals, and from this one passed through a cash
office to an interminable series of little rooms, each room with
its salesman, its three or four hats and pins, its mirrors, its
kinematographs, telephones, and hat slides in communication
with the central dépôt, its comfortable lounge and tempting
refreshments. A salesman in such an apartment did Denton
now become. It was his business to attend to any of the incessant stream of ladies who chose to stop with him, to behave as
winningly as possible, to offer refreshment, to converse on
any topic the possible customer chose, and to guide the con-

versation dexterously but not insistently towards hats. He was to suggest trying on various types of hat and to show by his manner and bearing, but without any coarse flattery, the enhanced impression made by the hats he wished to sell. He had several mirrors, adapted by various subtleties of curvature and tint to different types of face and complexion, and much depended on the proper use of these.

Denton flung himself at these curious and not very congenial duties with a good will and energy that would have amazed him a year before; but all to no purpose. The Senior Manageress, who had selected him for appointment and conferred various small marks of favour upon him, suddenly changed in her manner, declared for no assignable cause that he was stupid, and dismissed him at the end of six weeks of salesmanship. So Denton had to resume his ineffectual search for employment.

This second search did not last very long. Their money was at the ebb. To eke it out a little longer they resolved to part with their darling Dings, and took that small person to one of the public *crèches* that abounded in the city. That was the common use of the time. The industrial emancipation of women, the correlated disorganisation of the secluded "home," had rendered *crèches* a necessity for all but very rich and exceptionally-minded people. Therein children encountered hygienic and educational advantages impossible without such organisation. *Crèches* were of all classes and types of luxury, down to those of the Labour Company, where children were taken on credit, to be redeemed in labour as they grew up.

But both Denton and Elizabeth being, as I have explained, strange old-fashioned young people, full of nineteenth-century ideas, hated these convenient *crèches* exceedingly and at last took their little daughter to one with extreme reluctance. They were received by a motherly person in a uniform who was very brisk and prompt in her manner until Elizabeth wept at the mention of parting from her child. The motherly person, after a brief astonishment at this unusual emotion, changed suddenly into a creature of hope and comfort, and so won Elizabeth's gratitude for life. They were conducted into a vast room presided over by several nurses and with hundreds of two-year-old girls grouped about the toy-covered floor. This was the Two-year-old Room. Two nurses came forward, and Elizabeth watched their bearing towards Dings with jealous eyes. They were kind—it was clear they felt kind, and yet . . .

Presently it was time to go. By that time Dings was happily established in a corner, sitting on the floor with her arms filled, and herself, indeed, for the most part hidden by an unaccustomed wealth of toys. She seemed careless of all human relationships as her parents receded.

They were forbidden to upset her by saying good-bye.

At the door Elizabeth glanced back for the last time, and behold! Dings had dropped her new wealth and was standing with a dubious face. Suddenly Elizabeth gasped, and the motherly nurse pushed her forward and closed the door.

"You can come again soon, dear," she said, with unexpected tenderness in her eyes. For a moment Elizabeth stared at her with a blank face. "You can come again soon," repeated the nurse. Then with a swift transition Elizabeth was weeping in the nurse's arms. So it was that Denton's heart was won also.

And three weeks after our young people were absolutely penniless, and only one way lay open. They must go to the Labour Company. So soon as the rent was a week overdue their few remaining possessions were seized, and with scant courtesy they were shown the way out of the hotel. Elizabeth walked along the passage towards the staircase that ascended to the motionless middle way, too dulled by misery to think. Denton stopped behind to finish a stinging and unsatisfactory argument with the hotel porter, and then came hurrying after her, flushed and hot. He slackened his pace as he overtook her, and together they ascended to the middle way in silence. There they found two seats vacant and sat down.

"We need not go there—*yet?*" said Elizabeth.

"No—not till we are hungry," said Denton.

They said no more.

Elizabeth's eyes sought a resting-place and found none. To the right roared the eastward ways, to the left the ways in the opposite direction, swarming with people. Backwards and forwards along a cable overhead rushed a string of gesticulating men, dressed like clowns, each marked on back and chest with one gigantic letter, so that altogether they spelt out:

"PURKINJE'S DIGESTIVE PILLS."

An anæmic little woman in horrible coarse blue canvas pointed a little girl to one of this string of hurrying advertisements.

"Look!" said the anæmic woman: "there's yer father."

"Which?" said the little girl.

"'Im wiv his nose coloured red," said the anæmic woman.

The little girl began to cry, and Elizabeth could have cried, too.

"Ain't 'e kickin' 'is legs!—*just !*" said the anæmic woman in blue, trying to make things bright again. "Looky—*now !*"

On the *façade* to the right a huge intensely bright disc of weird colour span incessantly, and letters of fire that came and went spelt out—

"DOES THIS MAKE YOU GIDDY?"

Then a pause, followed by

"TAKE A PURKINJE'S DIGESTIVE PILL."

A vast and desolating braying began. "If you love Swagger Literature, put your telephone on to Bruggles, the Greatest Author of all Time. The Greatest Thinker of all Time. Teaches you Morals up to your Scalp! The very image of Socrates, except the back of his head, which is like Shakespeare. He has six toes, dresses in red, and never cleans his teeth. Hear HIM!"

Denton's voice became audible in a gap in the uproar. "I never ought to have married you," he was saying. "I have wasted your money, ruined you, brought you to misery. I am a scoundrel! . . . Oh, this accursed world!"

She tried to speak, and for some moments could not. She grasped his hand. "No," she said at last.

A half-formed desire suddenly became determination. She stood up. "Will you come?"

He rose also.—"We need not go there yet."

"Not that. But I want you to come to the flying-stages— where we met. You know? The little seat."

He hesitated. "*Can* you?" he said, doubtfully.

"Must," she answered.

He hesitated still for a moment, then moved to obey her will.

And so it was they spent their last half-day of freedom out under the open air in the little seat under the flying-stages where they had been wont to meet five short years ago. There she told him, what she could not tell him in the tumultuous public ways, that she did not repent even now of their marriage—that whatever discomfort and misery life still had for them, she was content with the things that had been. The weather was kind to them, the seat was sunlit and warm, and overhead the shining aëroplanes went and came.

At last towards sunsetting their time was at an end, and they made their vows to one another and clasped hands, and then rose up and went back into the ways of the city, a shabby-looking, heavy-hearted pair, tired and hungry. Soon they came to one of the pale blue signs that marked a Labour Company Bureau. For a space they stood in the middle way regarding this and at last descended, and entered the waiting-room.

The Labour Company had originally been a charitable organisation; its aim was to supply food, shelter, and work to all comers. This it was bound to do by the conditions of its incorporation, and it was also bound to supply food and shelter and medical attendance to all incapable of work who chose to demand its aid. In exchange these incapables paid làbour notes, which they had to redeem upon recovery. They signed these labour notes with thumb-marks, which were photographed and indexed in such a way that this world-wide

Labour Company could identifiy any one of its two or three hundred million clients at the cost of an hour's inquiry. The day's labour was defined as two spells in a treadmill used in generating electrical force, or its equivalent, and its due performance could be enforced by law. In practice the Labour Company found it advisable to add to its statutory obligations of food and shelter a few pence a day as an inducement to effort; and its enterprise had not only abolished pauperisation altogether, but supplied practically all but the very highest and most responsible labour throughout the world. Nearly a third of the population of the world were its serfs and debtors from the cradle to the grave.

In this practical, unsentimental way the problem of the unemployed had been most satisfactorily met and overcome. No one starved in the public ways, and no rags, no costume less sanitary and sufficient than the Labour Company's hygienic but inelegant blue canvas, pained the eye throughout the whole world. It was the constant theme of the phonographic newspapers how much the world had progressed since nineteenth-century days, when the bodies of those killed by the vehicular traffic or dead of starvation were, they alleged, a common feature in all the busier streets.

Denton and Elizabeth sat apart in the waiting-room until their turn came. Most of the others collected there seemed limp and taciturn, but three or four young people gaudily dressed made up for the quietude of their companions. They were life clients of the Company, born in the Company's *crèche* and destined to die in its hospital, and they had been out for a spree with some shillings or so of extra pay. They talked vociferously in a later development of the Cockney dialect, manifestly very proud of themselves.

Elizabeth's eyes went from these to the less-assertive figures. One seemed exceptionally pitiful to her. It was a woman of perhaps forty-five, with gold-stained hair and a painted face, down which abundant tears had trickled; she had a pinched nose, hungry eyes, lean hands and shoulders, and her dusty worn-out finery told the story of her life. Another was a grey-bearded old man in the costume of a bishop of one of the high episcopal sects—for religion was now also a business, and had its ups and downs. And beside him a sickly, dissipated-looking boy of perhaps two-and-twenty glared at Fate.

Presently Elizabeth and then Denton interviewed the manageress—for the Company preferred women in this capacity—and found she possessed an energetic face, a contemptuous manner, and a particularly unpleasant voice. They were given various cheques, including one to certify that they need not have their heads cropped; and when they had given their thumb-marks, learnt the number corresponding thereunto, and exchanged their shabby middle-class clothes for duly-numbered blue canvas suits, they repaired to the huge plain dining-room for their first meal under these new conditions. Afterwards they were to return to her for instructions about their work.

When they had made the exchange of their clothing Elizabeth did not seem able to look at Denton at first; but he looked at her, and saw with astonishment that even in blue canvas she was still beautiful. And then their soup and bread came sliding on its little rail down the long table towards them and stopped with a jerk, and he forgot the matter. For they had had no proper meal for three days.

After they had dined they rested for a time. Neither talked —there was nothing to say; and presently they got up and went back to the manageress to learn what they had to do.

The manageress referred to a tablet. "Y'r rooms won't be here; it'll be in the Highbury Ward, Ninety-seventh way, number two thousand and seventeen. Better make a note of it on y'r card. *You*, nought nought nought, type seven, sixty-four, b.c.d., *gamma* forty-one, female; you 'ave to go to the Metal-beating Company and try that for a day—fourpence bonus if ye're satisfactory; and *you*, nought seven one, type four, seven hundred and nine, g.f.b., *pi* five and ninety male; you 'ave to go to the Photographic Company on Eighty-first way, and learn something or other—*I* don't know —thrippence. 'Ere's y'r cards. That's all. Next! *What?* Didn't catch it all? Lor! So suppose I must go over it all again. Why don't you listen? Keerless, unprovident people! One'd think these things didn't matter."

Their ways to their work lay together for a time. And now they found they could talk. Curiously enough, the worst of their depression seemed over now that they had actually donned the blue. Denton could talk with interest even of the work that lay before them. "Whatever it is," he said, "it can't be so hateful as that hat shop. And after we have paid for Dings, we shall still have a whole penny a day between us even now. Afterwards—we may improve—get more money."

Elizabeth was less inclined to speech. "I wonder why work should seem so hateful," she said.

"It's odd," said Denton. "I suppose it wouldn't be if it were not the thought of being ordered about. . . . I hope we shall have decent managers."

Elizabeth did not answer. She was not thinking of that. She was tracing out some thoughts of her own.

"Of course," she said presently, "we have been using up work all our lives. It's only fair——"

She stopped. It was too intricate.

"We paid for it," said Denton, for at that time he had not troubled himself about these complicated things.

"We did nothing—and yet we paid for it. That's what I cannot understand."

"Perhaps we are paying," said Elizabeth presently—for her theology was old-fashioned and simple.

Presently it was time for them to part, and each went to the appointed work. Denton's was to mind a complicated hydraulic press that seemed almost an intelligent thing. This press worked by the sea-water that was destined finally to flush the city drains—for the world had long since abandoned the folly of pouring drinkable water into its sewers. This water was brought close to the eastward edge of the city by a huge canal, and then raised by an enormous battery of pumps into reservoirs at a level of four hundred feet above the sea, from which it spread by a billion arterial branches over the city. Thence it poured down, cleansing, sluicing, working machinery of all sorts, through an infinite variety of capillary channels into the great drains, the *cloacae maximae*, and so carried the sewage out to the agricultural areas that surrounded London on every side.

The press was employed in one of the processes of the photographic manufacture, but the nature of the process it did not concern Denton to understand. The most salient fact to his mind was that it had to be conducted in ruby light, and as a consequence the room in which he worked was lit by one coloured globe that poured a lurid and painful illumination about the room. In the darkest corner stood the press whose servant Denton had now become: it was a huge, dim, glittering thing with a projecting hood that had a remote resemblance to a bowed head, and, squatting like some metal Buddha in this weird light that ministered to its needs, it seemed to Denton in certain moods almost as if this must needs be the obscure idol to which humanity in some strange aberration had offered up his life. His duties had a varied monotony. Such items as the following will convey an idea of the service of the press. The thing worked with a busy clicking so long as things went well; but if the paste that came pouring through a feeder from another room and which it was perpetually compressing into thin plates, changed in quality, the rhythm of its click altered and Denton hastened to make certain adjustments. The slightest delay involved a waste of paste and the docking of one or more of his daily pence. If the supply of paste waned—there were hand processes of a peculiar sort involved in its preparation, and sometimes the workers had convulsions which deranged their output— Denton had to throw the press out of gear. In the painful vigilance a multitude of such trivial attentions entailed, painful because of the incessant effort its absence of natural interest required, Denton had now to pass one-third of his days. Save for an occasional visit from the manager, a kindly but singularly foul-mouthed man, Denton passed his working hours in solitude.

Elizabeth's work was of a more social sort. There was a fashion for covering the private apartments of the very wealthy with metal plates beautifully embossed with repeated patterns. The taste of the time demanded, however, that the repetition of the patterns should not be exact—not mechanical, but "natural"—and it was found that the most pleasing arrangement of pattern irregularity was obtained by employing women of refinement and natural taste to punch out the patterns with small dites. So many square feet of plates was exacted from Elizabeth as a minimum, and for whatever square feet she did in excess she received a small payment. The room, like most rooms of women workers, was under a manageress: men had been found by the Labour Company not only less exacting but extremely liable to excuse favoured ladies from a proper share of their duties. The manageress was a not unkindly, taciturn person, with the hardened remains of beauty of the brunette type; and the other women workers, who of course hated her, associated her name scandalously with one of the metal-work directors in order to explain her position.

Only two or three of Elizabeth's fellow-workers were born labour serfs; plain, morose girls, but most of them corresponded to what the nineteenth century would have called a "reduced" gentlewoman. But the ideal of what constituted a gentlewoman had altered: the faint, faded, negative virtue, the modulated voice and restrained gesture of the old-fashioned gentlewoman had vanished from the earth. Most of her companions showed in discoloured hair, ruined complexions, and the texture of their reminiscent conversations, the vanished glories of a conquering youth. All of these artistic workers were much older than Elizabeth, and two openly expressed their surprise that anyone so young and pleasant should come to share their toil. But Elizabeth did not trouble them with her old-world moral conceptions.

They were permitted, and even encouraged to converse with each other, for the directors very properly judged that anything that conduced to variations of mood made for pleasing fluctuations in their patterning; and Elizabeth was almost forced to hear the stories of these lives with which her own interwove: garbled and distorted they were by vanity indeed and yet comprehensible enough. And soon she began

o appreciate the small spites and cliques, the little misun-
derstandings and alliances that enmeshed about her. One
woman was excessively garrulous and descriptive about a
wonderful son of hers; another had cultivated a foolish coarseness of speech, that she seemed to regard as the wittiest
expression of originality conceivable; a third mused for ever
on dress, and whispered to Elizabeth how she saved her pence
day after day, and would presently have a glorious day of
freedom, wearing . . . and then followed hours of description;
two others sat always together, and called one another pet
names, until one day some little thing happened, and they sat
apart, blind and deaf as it seemed to one another's being. And
always from them all came an incessant tap, tap, tap, tap, and
the manageress listened always to the rhythm to mark if
one fell away. Tap, tap, tap, tap: so their days passed, so their
lives must pass. Elizabeth sat among them, kindly and quiet,
grey-hearted, marvelling at Fate: tap, tap, tap; tap, tap,
tap; tap, tap, tap.

So there came to Denton and Elizabeth a long succession
of laborious days, that hardened their hands, wove strange
threads of some new and sterner substance into the soft
prettiness of their lives, and drew grave lines and shadows on
their faces. The bright, convenient ways of the former life
had receded to an inaccessible distance; slowly they learnt the
lesson of the under-world—sombre and laborious, vast and
pregnant. There were many little things happened: things
that would be tedious and miserable to tell, things that were
bitter and grievous to bear—indignities, tyrannies, such as
must ever season the bread of the poor in cities; and one thing
that was not little, but seemed like the utter blackening of
life to them, which was that the child they had given life to
sickened and died. But that story, that ancient, perpetually
recurring story, has been told so often, has been told so beautifully, that there is no need to tell it over again here. There
was the same sharp fear, the same long anxiety, the deferred
inevitable blow, and the black silence. It has always been the
same; it will always be the same. It is one of the things that
must be.

And it was Elizabeth who was the first to speak, after an aching, dull interspace of days: not, indeed, of the foolish little name that was a name no longer, but of the darkness that brooded over her soul. They had come through the shrieking, tumultuous ways of the city together; the clamour of trade, of yelling competitive religions, of political appeal, had beat upon deaf ears; the glare of focussed lights, of dancing letters, and fiery advertisements, had fallen upon the set, miserable faces unheeded. They took their dinner in the dining-hall at a place apart. "I want," said Elizabeth clumsily, "to go out to the flying-stages—to that seat. Here, one can say nothing. . . ."

Denton looked at her. "It will be night," he said.

"I have asked,—it is a fine night." She stopped.

He perceived she could find no words to explain herself. Suddenly he understood that she wished to see the stars once more, the stars they had watched together from the open downland in that wild honeymoon of theirs five years ago. Something caught at his throat. He looked away from her.

"There will be plenty of time to go," he said, in a matter-of-fact tone.

And at last they came out to their little seat on the flying-stage, and sat there for a long time in silence. The little seat was in shadow, but the zenith was pale blue with the effulgence of the stage overhead, and all the city spread below them, squares and circles and patches of brilliance caught in a mesh-work of light. The little stars seemed very faint and small: near as they had been to the old-world watcher, they had become now infinitely remote. Yet one could see them in the darkened patches amidst the glare, and especially in the northward sky, the ancient constellations gliding steadfast and patient about the pole.

Long our two people sat in silence, and at last Elizabeth sighed.

"If I understood," she said, "if I could understand. When one is down there the city seems everything—the noise, the hurry, the voices—you must live, you must scramble. Here

—it is nothing; a thing that passes. One can think in peace."

"Yes," said Denton. "How flimsy it all is! From here more than half of it is swallowed by the night. . . . It will pass."

"We shall pass first," said Elizabeth.

"I know," said Denton. "If life were not a moment, the whole of history would seem like the happening of a day. . . . Yes—we shall pass. And the city will pass, and all the things that are to come. Man and the Overman and wonders unspeakable. And yet . . ."

He paused, and then began afresh. "I know what you feel. At least I fancy. . . . Down there one thinks of one's work, one's little vexations and pleasures, one's eating and drinking and ease and pain. One lives, and one must die. Down there and every day—our sorrow seemed the end of life. . . .

"Up here it is different. For instance, down there it would seem impossible almost to go on living if one were horribly disfigured, horribly crippled, disgraced. Up here—under these stars—none of those things would matter. They don't matter. . . . They are a part of something. One seems just to touch that something—under the stars. . . ."

He stopped. The vague, impalpable things in his mind, cloudy emotions half-shaped towards ideas, vanished before the rough grasp of words. "It is hard to express," he said lamely.

They sat through a long stillness.

"It is well to come here," he said at last. "We stop—our minds are very finite. After all, we are just poor animals rising out of the brute, each with a mind, the poor beginning of a mind. We are so stupid. So much hurts. And yet . . ."

"I know, I know—and some day we shall *see*.

"All this frightful stress, all this discord will resolve to harmony, and we shall know it. Nothing is but it makes for that. Nothing. All the failures—every little thing makes for that harmony. Everything is necessary to it, we shall find. We shall find. Nothing, not even the most dreadful thing, could be left out. Not even the most trivial. Every tap of your hammer on the brass, every moment of work, my idleness even. . . . Dear one! every movement of our poor little one. . . .

All these things go on for ever.—And the faint, impalpable things. We, sitting here together.—Everything. . . .

"The passion that joined us, and what has come since. It is not passion now. More than anything else it is sorrow. *Dear*. . . ."

He could say no more, could follow his thoughts no further.

Elizabeth made no answer—she was very still; but presently her hand sought his and found it.

IV. Underneath

Under the stars one may reach upward and touch resignation, whatever the evil thing may be, but in the heat and stress of the day's work we lapse again, come disgust and anger and intolerable moods. How little is all our magnanimity—an accident! a phase! The very Saints of old had first to flee the world. And Denton and his Elizabeth could not flee their world, no longer were there open roads to unclaimed lands where men might live freely—however hardly—and keep their souls in peace. The city had swallowed up mankind.

For a time these two Labour Serfs were kept at their original occupations, she at her brass stamping and Denton at his press; and then came a move for him that brought with it fresh and still bitterer experiences of life in the underways of the great city. He was transferred to the care of a rather more elaborate press in the central factory of the London Tile Trust.

In this new situation he had to work in a long vaulted room with a number of other men, for the most part born Labour Serfs. He came to this intercourse reluctantly. His upbringing had been refined, and, until his ill fortune had brought him to that costume, he had never spoken in his life, except by way of command or some immediate necessity, to the white-faced wearers of the blue canvas. Now at last came contact; he had to work beside them, share their tools, eat with them. To both Elizabeth and himself this seemed a further degradation.

His taste would have seemed extreme to a man of the nineteenth century. But slowly and inevitably in the intervening years a gulf had opened between the wearers of the blue canvas and the classes above, a difference not simply of circumstances and habits of life, but of habits of thought—even of language. The underways had developed a dialect of their own: above, too, had arisen a dialect, a code of thought, a language of "culture," which aimed by a sedulous search after fresh distinction to widen perpetually the space between itself and "vulgarity." The bond of a common faith, moreover, no longer held the race together. The last years of the nineteenth century were distinguished by the rapid development among the prosperous idle of esoteric perversions of the popular religion: glosses and interpretations that reduced the broad teachings of the carpenter of Nazareth to the exquisite narrowness of their lives. And, spite of their inclination towards the ancient fashion of living, neither Elizabeth nor Denton had been sufficiently original to escape the suggestion of their surroundings. In matters of common behaviour they had followed the ways of their class, and so when they fell at last to be Labour Serfs it seemed to them almost as though they were falling among offensive inferior animals; they felt as a nineteenth-century duke and duchess might have felt who were forced to take rooms in the Jago.

Their natural impulse was to maintain a "distance." But Denton's first idea of a dignified isolation from his new surroundings was soon rudely dispelled. He had imagined that his fall to the position of a Labour Serf was the end of his lesson, that when their little daughter had died he had plumbed the deeps of life; but indeed these things were only the beginning. Life demands something more from us than acquiescence. And now in a roomful of machine minders he was to learn a wider lesson, to make the acquaintance of another factor in life, a factor as elemental as the loss of things dear to us, more elemental even than toil.

His quiet discouragement of conversation was an immediate cause of offence—was interpreted, rightly enough I fear, as disdain. His ignorance of the vulgar dialect, a thing upon which he had hitherto prided himself, suddenly took upon itself a new aspect. He failed to perceive at once that his reception of the coarse and stupid but genially intended remarks that greeted his appearance must have stung the makers of these advances like blows in their faces. "Don't understand," he said rather coldly, and at hazard, "No, thank you."

The man who had addressed him stared, scowled, and turned away.

A second, who also failed at Denton's unaccustomed ear, took the trouble to repeat his remark, and Denton discovered he was being offered the use of an oil can. He expressed polite thanks, and this second man embarked upon a penetrating conversation. Denton, he remarked, had been a swell, and he wanted to know how he had come to wear the blue. He clearly expected an interesting record of vice and extravagance. Had Denton ever been at a Pleasure City? Denton was speedily to discover how the existence of these wonderful places of delight permeated and defiled the thought and honour of these unwilling, hopeless workers of the underworld.

His aristocratic temperament resented these questions. He answered "No" curtly. The man persisted with a still more personal question, and this time it was Denton who turned away.

"Gorblimey!" said his interlocutor, much astonished.

It presently forced itself upon Denton's mind that this remarkable conversation was being repeated in indignant tones to more sympathetic hearers, and that it gave rise to astonishment and ironical laughter. They looked at Denton with manifestly enhanced interest. A curious perception of isolation dawned upon him. He tried to think of his press and its unfamiliar peculiarities. . . .

The machines kept everybody pretty busy during the first spell, and then came a recess. It was only an interval for refreshment, too brief for anyone to go out to a Labour

Company dining-room. Denton followed his fellow-workers into a short gallery, in which were a number of bins and refuse from the presses.

Each man produced a packet of food. Denton had no packet. The manager, a careless young man who held his position by influence, had omitted to warn Denton that it was necessary to apply for this provision. He stood apart, feeling hungry. The others drew together in a group and talked in undertones, glancing at him ever and again. He became uneasy. His appearance of disregard cost him an increasing effort. He tried to think of the levers of his new press.

Presently one, a man shorter but much broader and stouter than Denton, came forward to him. Denton turned to him as unconcernedly as possible. "Here!" said the delegate—as Denton judged him to be—extending a cube of bread in a not too clean hand. He had a swart, broad-nosed face, and his mouth hung down towards one corner.

Denton felt doubtful for the instant whether this was meant for civility or insult. His impulse was to decline. "No, thanks," he said; and, at the man's change of expression, "I'm not hungry."

There came a laugh from the group behind. "Told you so," said the man who had offered Denton the loan of an oil can. "He's top side, he is. You ain't good enough for 'im."

The swart face grew a shade darker.

"Here," said its owner, still extending the bread and speaking in a lower tone; "you got to eat this. See?"

Denton looked into the threatening face before him, and odd little currents of energy seemed to be running through his limbs and body.

"I don't want it," he said, trying a pleasant smile that twitched and failed.

The thickset man advanced his face, and the bread became a physical threat in his hand. Denton's mind rushed together to the one problem of his antagonist's eyes.

"Eat it," said the swart man.

There came a pause, and then they both moved quickly.

The cube of bread described a complicated path, a curve
that would have ended in Denton's face; and then his fist
hit the wrist of the hand that gripped it, and it flew upward
and out of the conflict—its part played.

He stepped back quickly, fists clenched and arms tense. The
hot, dark countenance receded, became an alert hostility
watching its chance. Denton for one instant felt confident
and strangely buoyant and serene. His heart beat quickly.
He felt his body alive, and glowing to the tips.

"Scrap, boys!" shouted someone, and then the dark figure
had leapt forward, ducked back and sideways, and come in
again. Denton struck out, and was hit. One of his eyes seemed
to him to be demolished, and he felt a soft lip under his fist
just before he was hit again—this time under the chin. A
huge fan of fiery needles shot open. He had a momentary
persuasion that his head was knocked to pieces, and then
something hit his head and back from behind, and the fight
became an uninteresting, an impersonal thing.

He was aware that time—seconds or minutes—had passed,
abstract, uneventful time. He was lying with his head in a
heap of ashes, and something wet and warm ran swiftly into
his neck. The first shock broke up into discrete sensations.
All his head throbbed; his eye and his chin throbbed exceedingly, and the taste of blood was in his mouth.

"He's all right," said a voice. "He's opening his eyes."

"Serve him —— well right," said a second.

His mates were standing about him. He made an effort and
sat up. He put his hand to the back of his head, and his hair
was wet and full of cinders. A laugh greeted the gesture. His
eye was partially closed. He perceived what had happened.
His momentary anticipation of a final victory had vanished.

"Looks surprised," said someone.

"'Ave any more?" said a wit; and then, imitating Denton's refined accent: "No, thank you."

Denton perceived the swart man with a blood-stained
handkerchief before his face, and somewhat in the background.

"Where's that bit of bread he's got to eat?" said a little

ferret-faced creature; and sought with his foot in the ashes of the adjacent bin.

Denton had a moment of internal debate. He knew the code of honour requires a man to pursue a fight he has begun to the bitter end; but this was his first taste of the bitterness. He was resolved to rise again, but he felt no passionate impulse. It occurred to him—and the thought was no very violent spur—that he was perhaps after all a coward. For a moment his will was heavy, a lump of lead.

"'Ere it is," said the little ferret-faced man, and stooped to pick up a cindery cube. He looked at Denton, then at the others.

Slowly, unwillingly, Denton stood up.

A dirty-faced albino extended a hand to the ferret-faced man.

"Gimme that toke," he said. He advanced threateningly, bread in hand, to Denton. "So you ain't 'ad your bellyful yet," he said. "Eh?"

Now it was coming. "No, I haven't," said Denton, with a catching of the breath, and resolved to try this brute behind the ear before he himself got stunned again. He knew he would be stunned again. He was astonished how ill he had judged himself beforehand. A few ridiculous lunges, and down he would go again. He watched the albino's eyes. The albino was grinning confidently, like a man who plans an agreeable trick. A sudden perception of impending indignities stung Denton.

"You leave 'im alone, Jim," said the swart man suddenly over the blood-stained rag. "He ain't done nothing to you."

The albino's grin vanished. He stopped. He looked from one to the other. It seemed to Denton that the swart man demanded the privilege of his destruction. The albino would have been better.

"You leave 'im alone," said the swart man. "See? 'E's 'ad 'is licks."

A clattering bell lifted up its voice and solved the situation. The albino hesitated. "Lucky for you," he said, adding a foul metaphor, and turned with the others towards the press-room again. "Wait for the end of the spell, mate," said the albino over his shoulder—an afterthought. The swart man waited for the albino to precede him. Denton realised that he had a reprieve.

The men passed towards an open door. Denton became aware of his duties, and hurried to join the tail of the queue. At the doorway of the vaulted gallery of presses a yellow-uniformed labour policeman stood ticking a card. He had ignored the swart man's hæmorrhage.

"Hurry up there!" he said to Denton.

"Hello!" he said, at the sight of his facial disarray. "Who's been hitting *you?*"

"That's my affair," said Denton.

"Not if it spiles your work, it ain't," said the man in yellow. "You mind that."

Denton made no answer. He was a rough—a labourer. He wore the blue canvas. The laws of assault and battery, he knew, were not for the likes of him. He went to his press.

He could feel the skin of his brow and chin and head lifting themselves to noble bruises, felt the throb and pain of each aspiring contusion. His nervous system slid down to lethargy; at each movement in his press adjustment he felt he lifted a weight. And as for his honour—that, too, throbbed and puffed. How did he stand? What precisely had happened in the last ten minutes? What would happen next? He knew that there was enormous matter for thought, and he could not think save in disordered snatches.

His mood was a sort of stagnant astonishment. All his conceptions were overthrown. He had regarded his security from physical violence as inherent, as one of the conditions of life. So, indeed, it had been while he wore his middle-class costume, had his middle-class property to serve for his defence. But who would interfere among Labour roughs fighting together? And indeed in those days no man would. In the Underworld there was no law between man and man; the law and machinery of the state had become for them something that held men down, fended them off from much desirable property and pleasure, and that was all. Violence, that ocean in which the brutes live for ever, and from which a thousand dykes and contrivances have won our hazardous civilised life, had flowed in again upon the sinking under-ways and submerged them. The fist ruled. Denton had come right down at last to the elemental—fist and trick and the stubborn heart and fellowship—even as it was in the begin-ning.

The rhythm of his machine changed, and his thoughts were interrupted.

Presently he could think again. Strange how quickly things had happened! He bore these men who had thrashed him no very vivid ill-will. He was bruised and enlightened. He saw with absolute fairness now the reasonableness of his un-popularity. He had behaved like a fool. Disdain, seclusion, are the privilege of the strong. The fallen aristocrat still clinging to his pointless distinction is surely the most pitiful creature of pretence in all this clamant universe. Good heavens! what was there for him to despise in these men?

What a pity he had not appreciated all this better five hours ago!

What would happen at the end of the spell? He could not tell. He could not imagine. He could not imagine the thoughts of these men. He was sensible only of their hostility and utter want of sympathy. Vague possibilities of shame and violence chased one another across his mind. Could he devise some weapon? He recalled his assault upon the hypnotist, but there were no detachable lamps here. He could see noth-ing that he could catch up in his defence.

For a space he thought of a headlong bolt for the security of the public ways directly the spell was over. Apart from the trivial consideration of his self-respect, he perceived that this would be only a foolish postponement and aggravation of his trouble. He perceived the ferret-faced man and the albino talking together with their eyes towards him. Presently they were talking to the swart man, who stood with his broad back studiously towards Denton.

At last came the end of the second spell. The lender of oil cans stopped his press sharply and turned round, wiping his

mouth with the back of his hand. His eyes had the quiet
expectation of one who seats himself in a theatre.

Now was the crisis, and all the little nerves of Denton'
being seemed leaping and dancing. He had decided to show
fight if any fresh indignity was offered him. He stopped his
press and turned. With an enormous affectation of ease he
walked down the vault and entered the passage of the ash
pits, only to discover he had left his jacket—which he had
taken off because of the heat of the vault—beside his press
He walked back. He met the albino eye to eye.

He heard the ferret-faced man in expostulation. " 'E reely
ought eat it," said the ferret-faced man. " 'E did reely."

"No—you leave 'im alone," said the swart man.

Apparently nothing further was to happen to him that day
He passed out to the passage and staircase that led up to the
moving platforms of the city.

He emerged on the livid brilliance and streaming move
ment of the public street. He became acutely aware of his
disfigured face, and felt his swelling bruises with a limp, in
vestigatory hand. He went up to the swiftest platform, and
seated himself on a Labour Company bench.

He lapsed into a pensive torpor. The immediate dangers
and stresses of his position he saw with a sort of static clear
ness. What would they do to-morrow? He could not tell
What would Elizabeth think of his brutalisation? He could
not tell. He was exhausted. He was aroused presently by a
hand upon his arm.

He looked up, and saw the swart man seated beside him
He started. Surely he was safe from violence in the public
way!

The swart man's face retained no traces of his share in the
light; his expression was free from hostility—seemed almost
deferential. " 'Scuse me," he said, with a total absence of
truculence. Denton realised that no assault was intended
He stared, awaiting the next development.

It was evident the next sentence was premeditated. "Wha
—I—was—going—to say—was this," said the swart man
and sought through a silence for further words.

"Whad—I—was—going—to say—was this," he repeated.

Finally he abandoned that gambit. "*You're* aw right," he cried, laying a grimy hand on Denton's grimy sleeve. "*You're* aw right. You're a ge'man. Sorry—very sorry. Wanted to tell you that."

Denton realised that there must exist motives beyond a mere impulse to abominable proceedings in the man. He meditated, and swallowed an unworthy pride.

"I did not mean to be offensive to you," he said, "in refusing that bit of bread."

"Meant it friendly," said the swart man, recalling the scene; "but—in front of that blarsted Whitey and his snigger—well—I '*ad* to scrap."

"Yes," said Denton with sudden fervour: "I was a fool."

"Ah," said the swart man, with great satisfaction. "*That's* aw right. Shake!"

And Denton shook.

The moving platform was rushing by the establishment of a face moulder, and its lower front was a huge display of mirror, designed to stimulate the thirst for more symmetrical features. Denton caught the reflection of himself and his new friend, enormously twisted and broadened. His own face was puffed, one-sided, and blood-stained; a grin of idiotic and insincere amiability distorted its latitude. A wisp of hair occluded one eye. The trick of the mirror presented the swart man as a gross expansion of lip and nostril. They were linked by shaking hands. Then abruptly this vision passed—to return to memory in the anæmic meditations of a waking dawn.

As he shook, the swart man made some muddled remark, to the effect that he had always known he could get on with a gentleman if one came his way. He prolonged the shaking until Denton, under the influence of the mirror, withdrew his hand. The swart man became pensive, spat impressively on the platform, and resumed his theme.

"Whad I was going to say was this," he said; was gravelled, and shook his head at his foot.

Denton became curious. "Go on," he said, attentive.

The swart man took the plunge. He grasped Denton's arm, became intimate in his attitude. "'Scuse me," he said. "Fact is, you done know '*ow* to scrap. Done know '*ow* to. Why— you done know 'ow to *begin*. You'll get killed if you don't mind. 'Ouldin' your 'ands—— *There!*"

He reinforced his statement by objurgation, watching the effect of each oath with a wary eye.

"F'r instance. You're tall. Long arms. You got a longer reach than anyone in the brasted vault. Gorblimey, but I thought I'd got a Tough on. 'Stead of which . . . 'Scuse me. I wouldn't have '*it* you if I'd known. It's like fighting sacks. 'Tisn' right. Y'r arms seemed 'ung on 'ooks. Reg'lar—'ung on 'ooks. There!"

Denton stared, and then surprised and hurt his battered chin by a sudden laugh. Bitter tears came into his eyes.

"Go on," he said.

The swart man reverted to his formula. He was good enough to say he liked the look of Denton, thought he had stood up "amazing plucky. On'y pluck ain't no good—ain't no brasted good—if you don't 'old your 'ands.

"Whad I was going to say was this," he said. "Lemme show you 'ow to scrap. Jest lemme. You're ig'nant, you ain't no class; but you might be a very decent scrapper—very decent. Shown. That's what I meant to say."

Denton hesitated. "But," he said, "I can't give you anything——"

"That's the ge'man all over," said the swart man. "Who arst you to?"

"But your time?"

"If you don't get learnt scrapping you'll get killed,—don't you make no bones of that."

Denton thought. "I don't know," he said.

He looked at the face beside him, and all its native coarseness shouted at him. He felt a quick revulsion from his transient friendliness. It seemed to him incredible that it should be necessary for him to be indebted to such a creature.

"The chaps are always scrapping," said the swart man. "Always. And, of course—if one gets waxy and 'its you vital . . ."

"By God!" said Denton; "I wish one would."

"Of course, if you feel like that——"

"You don't understand."

"P'raps I don't," said the swart man; and lapsed into a fuming silence.

When he spoke again his voice was less friendly, and he prodded Denton by way of address. "Look see!" he said; "are you going to let me show you 'ow to scrap?"

"It's tremendously kind of you," said Denton; "but——"

There was a pause. The swart man rose and bent over Denton.

"Too much ge'man," he said—"eh? I got a red face. . . . By gosh! you are—you *are* a brasted fool!"

He turned away, and instantly Denton realised the truth of this remark.

The swart man descended with dignity to a cross way, and Denton, after a momentary impulse to pursuit, remained on the platform. For a time the things that had happened filled his mind. In one day his graceful system of resignation had been shattered beyond hope. Brute force, the final, the fundamental, had thrust its face through all his explanations and glosses and consolations and grinned enigmatically. Though he was hungry and tired, he did not go on directly to the Labour Hotel, where he would meet Elizabeth. He found he was beginning to think, he wanted very greatly to think; and so, wrapped in a monstrous cloud of meditation, he went the circuit of the city on his moving platform twice. You figure him, tearing through the glaring, thunder-voiced city at a pace of fifty miles an hour, the city upon the planet that spins along its chartless path through space many thousands of miles an hour, funking most terribly, and trying to understand why the heart and will in him should suffer and keep alive.

When at last he came to Elizabeth, she was white and anxious. He might have noted she was in trouble had it not been for his own preoccupation. He feared most that she would desire to know every detail of his indignities, that she would be sympathetic or indignant. He saw her eyebrows rise at the sight of him.

"I've had rough handling," he said, and gasped. "It's too fresh—too hot. I don't want to talk about it." He sat down with an unavoidable air of sullenness.

She stared at him in astonishment, and as she read something of the significant hieroglyphic of his battered face, her lips whitened. Her hand—it was thinner now than in the days of their prosperity, and her first finger was a little altered by the metal punching she did—clenched convulsively. "This horrible world!" she said, and said no more.

In these latter days they had become a very silent couple; they said scarcely a word to each other that night, but each followed a private train of thought. In the small hours, as Elizabeth lay awake, Denton started up beside her suddenly —he had been lying as still as a dead man.

"I cannot stand it!" cried Denton. "I *will* not stand it!"

She saw him dimly, sitting up; saw his arm lunge as if in a furious blow at the enshrouding night. Then for a space he was still.

"It is too much—it is more than one can bear!"

She could say nothing. To her, also, it seemed that this was as far as one could go. She waited through a long stillness. She could see that Denton sat with his arms about his knees, his chin almost touching them.

Then he laughed.

"No," he said at last, "I'm going to stand it. That's the peculiar thing. There isn't a grain of suicide in us—not a grain. I suppose all the people with a turn that way have gone. We're going through with it—to the end."

Elizabeth thought gravely, and realised that this also was true.

"We're going through with it. To think of all who have gone through with it: all the generations—endless—endless. Little beasts that snapped and snarled, snapping and snarling, snapping and snarling, generation after generation."

His monotone, ended abruptly, resumed after a vast inter-
al.

"There were ninety thousand years of stone age. A Denton
omewhere in all those years. Apostolic succession. The grace
f going through. Let me see! Ninety—nine hundred—three
ines, twenty-seven—*three thousand* generations of men!—
en more or less. And each fought, and was bruised, and
amed, and somehow held his own—going through with it
—passing it on. . . . And thousands more to come perhaps—
housands!

"Passing it on. I wonder if they will thank us."

His voice assumed an argumentative note. "If one could
nd something definite. . . . If one could say, 'This is why—
his is why it goes on. . . .'"

He became still, and Elizabeth's eyes slowly separated him
om the darkness until at last she could see how he sat with
is head resting on his hand. A sense of the enormous remote-
ess of their minds came to her; that dim suggestion of another
eing seemed to her a figure of their mutual understanding.
Vhat could he be thinking now? What might he not say next?
nother age seemed to elapse before he sighed and whispered:
No. I don't understand it. No!" Then a long interval, and
e repeated this. But the second time it had the tone almost
f a solution.

She became aware that he was preparing to lie down. She
arked his movements, perceived with astonishment how he
djusted his pillow with a careful regard to comfort. He lay
own with a sigh of contentment almost. His passion had
assed. He lay still, and presently his breathing became
egular and deep.

But Elizabeth remained with eyes wide open in the dark-
ess, until the clamour of a bell and the sudden brilliance of
he electric light warned them that the Labour Company
ad need of them for yet another day.

That day came a scuffle with the albino Whitey and the
ttle ferret-faced man. Blunt, the swart artist in scrapping,
aving first let Denton grasp the bearing of his lesson, inter-
ened, not without a certain quality of patronage. "Drop' is

'air, Whitey, and let the man be," said his gross voice throug▌
a shower of indignities. "Can't you see 'e don't know 'o▐
to scrap?" And Denton, lying shamefully in the dust, realise▐
that he must accept that course of instruction, after all.

He made his apology straight and clean. He scrambled u▐
and walked to Blunt. "I was a fool, and you are right," h▐
said. "If it isn't too late . . ."

That night, after the second spell, Denton went with Blun▐
to certain waste and slime-soaked vaults under the Port o▐
London, to learn the first beginnings of the high art o▐
scrapping as it had been perfected in the great world of th▐
underways: how to hit or kick a man so as to hurt hin▐
excruciatingly or make him violently sick, how to hit or kic▌
"vital," how to use glass in one's garments as a club and t▐
spread red ruin with various domestic implements, how t▐
anticipate and demolish your adversary's intentions in othe▐
directions; all the pleasant devices, in fact, that had grow▌
up among the disinherited of the great cities of the twentiet▌
and twenty-first centuries, were spread out by a gifted exponent for Denton's learning. Blunt's bashfulness fell from hin▌
as the instruction proceeded, and he developed a certain expert dignity, a quality of fatherly consideration. He treated
Denton with the utmost consideration, only "flicking him▐
up a bit" now and then, to keep the interest hot, and roaring
with laughter at a happy fluke of Denton's that covered his▐
mouth with blood.

"I'm always keerless of my mouth," said Blunt, admitting a▌
weakness. "Always. It don't seem to matter, like, just getting
bashed in the mouth—not if your chin's all right. Tastin'
blood does me good. Always. But I better not 'it you again."▐

Denton went home, to fall asleep exhausted and wake in▌
the small hours with aching limbs and all his bruises tin-
gling. Was it worth while that he should go on living? He▐
listened to Elizabeth's breathing, and remembering that
he must have awaked her the previous night, he lay very
still. He was sick with infinite disgust at the new conditions▌
of his life. He hated it all, hated even the genial savage who▐
had protected him so generously. The monstrous fraud of

civilisation glared stark before his eyes; he saw it as a vast lunatic growth, producing a deepening torrent of savagery below, and above ever more flimsy gentility and silly wastefulness. He could see no redeeming reason, no touch of honour, either in the life he had led or in this life to which he had fallen. Civilisation presented itself as some catastrophic product as little concerned with men—save as victims—as a cyclone or a planetary collision. He, and therefore all mankind, seemed living utterly in vain. His mind sought some strange expedients of escape, if not for himself then at least for Elizabeth. But he meant them for himself. What if he hunted up Mwres and told him of their disaster? It came to him as an astonishing thing how utterly Mwres and Bindon had passed out of his range. Where were they? What were they doing? From that he passed to thoughts of utter dishonour. And finally, not arising in any way out of this mental tumult, but ending it as dawn ends the night, came the clear and obvious conclusion of the night before: the conviction that he had to go through with things; that, apart from any remoter view and quite sufficient for all his thought and energy, he had to stand up and fight among his fellows and quit himself like a man.

The second night's instruction was perhaps less dreadful than the first; and the third was even endurable, for Blunt dealt out some praise. The fourth day Denton chanced upon the fact that the ferret-faced man was a coward. There passed a fortnight of smouldering days and feverish instruction at night; Blunt, with many blasphemies, testified that never had he met so apt a pupil; and all night long Denton dreamt of kicks and counters and gouges and cunning tricks. For all that time no further outrages were attempted, for fear of Blunt; and then came the second crisis. Blunt did not come one day—afterwards he admitted his deliberate intention—and through the tedious morning Whitey awaited the interval between the spells with an ostentatious impatience. He knew nothing of the scrapping lessons, and he spent the time in telling Denton and the vault generally of certain disagreeable proceedings he had in mind.

Whitey was not popular, and the vault disgorged to see him haze the new man with only a languid interest. But matters changed when Whitey's attempt to open the proceedings by kicking Denton in the face was met by an excellently executed duck, catch, and throw, that completed the flight of Whitey's foot in its orbit and brought Whitey's head into the ash heap that had once received Denton's. Whitey arose a shade whiter, and now blasphemously bent upon vital injuries. There were indecisive passages, foiled enterprises that deepened Whitey's evidently growing perplexity; and then things developed into a grouping of Denton uppermost with Whitey's throat in his hand, his knee on Whitey's chest, and a tearful Whitey with a black face, protruding tongue, and broken finger endeavouring to explain the misunderstanding by means of hoarse sounds. Moreover, it was evident that among the bystanders there had never been a more popular person than Denton.

Denton, with proper precaution, released his antagonist and stood up. His blood seemed changed to some sort of fluid fire, his limbs felt light and supernaturally strong. The idea that he was a martyr in the civilisation machine had vanished from his mind. He was a man in a world of men.

The little ferret-faced man was the first in the competition to pat him on the back. The lender of oil cans was a radiant sun of genial congratulation. . . . It seemed incredible to Denton that he had ever thought of despair.

Denton was convinced that not only had he to go through with things, but that he could. He sat on the canvas pellet expounding this new aspect to Elizabeth. One side of his face was bruised. She had not recently fought, she had not been patted on the back, there were no hot bruises upon her face, only a pallor and a new line or so about the mouth. She was taking the woman's share. She looked steadfastly at Denton in his new mood of prophecy. "I feel that there is something," he was saying, "something that goes on, a Being of Life in which we live and move and have our being, something that began fifty—a hundred million years ago, perhaps, that goes on—on: growing, spreading, to things beyond us—things that will justify us all. . . . That will explain and justify my fighting—these bruises, and all the pain of it. It's the chisel —yes, the chisel of the Maker. If only I could make you feel as I feel, if I could make you! You *will*, dear, I know you will."

"No," she said in a low voice. "No, I shall not."

"So I might have thought——"

She shook her head. "No," she said, "I have thought as well. What you say—doesn't convince me."

She looked at his face resolutely. "I hate it," she said, and caught at her breath. "You do not understand, you do not think. There was a time when you said things and I believed them. I am growing wiser. You are a man, you can fight, force your way. You do not mind bruises. You can be coarse and ugly, and still a man. Yes—it makes you. It makes you. You are right. Only a woman is not like that. We are different. We have let ourselves get civilised too soon. This under-world is not for us."

She paused and began again.

"I hate it! I hate this horrible canvas! I hate it more than —more than the worst that can happen. It hurts my fingers to touch it. It is horrible to the skin. And the women I work with day after day! I lie awake at nights and think how I may be growing like them. . . ."

She stopped. "I *am* growing like them," she cried passionately.

Denton stared at her distress. "But——" he said and stopped.

"You don't understand. What have I? What have I to save me? *You* can fight. Fighting is man's work. But women— women are different. . . . I have thought it all out, I have done nothing but think night and day. Look at the colour of my face! I cannot go on. I cannot endure this life. . . . I cannot endure it."

She stopped. She hesitated.

"You do not know all," she said abruptly, and for an instant her lips had a bitter smile. "I have been asked to leave you."

"Leave me!"

She made no answer save an affirmative movement of the head.

Denton stood up sharply. They stared at one another through a long silence.

Suddenly she turned herself about, and flung face downward upon their canvas bed. She did not sob, she made no sound. She lay still upon her face. After a vast, distressful void her shoulders heaved and she began to weep silently.

"Elizabeth!" he whispered—"Elizabeth!"

Very softly he sat down beside her, bent down, put his arm across her in a doubtful caress, seeking vainly for some clue to this intolerable situation.

"Elizabeth," he whispered in her ear.

She thrust him from her with her hand. "I cannot bear a child to be a slave!" and broke out into loud and bitter weeping.

Denton's face changed—became blank dismay. Presently he slipped from the bed and stood on his feet. All the complacency had vanished from his face, had given place to impotent rage. He began to rave and curse at the intolerable forces which pressed upon him, at all the accidents and hot desires and heedlessness that mock the life of man. His little voice rose in that little room, and he shook his fist, this animalcule of the earth, at all that environed him about, at the millions about him, at his past and future and all the insensate vastness of the overwhelming city.

V. Bindon Intervenes

In Bindon's younger days he had dabbled in speculation and made three brilliant flukes. For the rest of his life he had the wisdom to let gambling alone, and the conceit to believe himself a very clever man. A certain desire for influence and reputation interested him in the business intrigues of the giant city in which his flukes were made. He became at last one of the most influential shareholders in the company that owned the London flying-stages to which the aëroplanes came from all parts of the world. This much for his public activities. In his private life he was a man of pleasure. And this is the story of his heart.

But before proceeding to such depths, one must devote a little time to the exterior of this person. Its physical basis was slender, and short, and dark; and the face, which was fine-featured and assisted by pigments, varied from an insecure self-complacency to an intelligent uneasiness. His face and head had been depilated, according to the cleanly and hygienic fashion of the time, so that the colour and contour of his hair varied with his costume. This he was constantly changing.

At times he would distend himself with pneumatic vestments in the rococo vein. From among the billowy developments of this style, and beneath a translucent and illuminated head-dress, his eye watched jealously for the respect of the less fashionable world. At other times he emphasised his elegant slenderness in close-fitting garments of black satin. For effects of dignity he would assume broad pneumatic shoulders, from which hung a robe of carefully arranged folds of China silk, and a classical Bindon in pink tights was also a transient phenomenon in the eternal pageant of Destiny. In the days when he hoped to marry Elizabeth, he sought to impress and charm her, and at the same time to take off something of his burthen of forty years, by wearing the last fancy of the contemporary buck, a costume of elastic material with distensible warts and horns, changing in colour as he walked, by an ingenious arrangement of versatile chromatophores. And no doubt, if Elizabeth's affection had not been already engaged by the worthless Denton, and if her tastes had not had that odd bias for old-fashioned ways, this extremely *chic* conception would have ravished her. Bindon had consulted Elizabeth's father before presenting himself in this garb—he was one of those men who always invite criticism of their costume —and Mwres had pronounced him all that the heart of woman could desire. But the affair of the hypnotist proved that his knowledge of the heart of woman was incomplete.

Bindon's idea of marrying had been formed some little time

before Mwres threw Elizabeth's budding womanhood in his way. It was one of Bindon's most cherished secrets that he had a considerable capacity for a pure and simple life of a grossly sentimental type. The thought imparted a sort of pathetic seriousness to the offensive and quite inconsequent and unmeaning excesses, which he was pleased to regard as dashing wickedness, and which a number of good people also were so unwise as to treat in that desirable manner. As a consequence of these excesses, and perhaps by reason also of an inherited tendency to early decay, his liver became seriously affected, and he suffered increasing inconvenience when travelling by aëroplane. It was during his convalescence from a protracted bilious attack that it occurred to him that in spite of all the terrible fascinations of Vice, if he found a beautiful, gentle, good young woman of a not too violently intellectual type to devote her life to him, he might yet be saved to Goodness, and even rear a spirited family in his likeness to solace his declining years. But like so many experienced men of the world, he doubted if there were any good women. Of such as he had heard tell he was outwardly sceptical and privately much afraid.

When the aspiring Mwres effected his introduction to Elizabeth, it seemed to him that his good fortune was complete. He fell in love with her at once. Of course, he had always been falling in love since he was sixteen, in accordance with the extremely varied recipes to be found in the accumulated literature of many centuries. But this was different. This was real love. It seemed to him to call forth all the lurking goodness in his nature. He felt that for her sake he could give up a way of life that had already produced the gravest lesions on his liver and nervous system. His imagination presented him with idyllic pictures of the life of the reformed rake. He would never be sentimental with her, or silly; but always a little cynical and bitter, as became the past. Yet he was sure she would have an intuition of his real greatness and goodness. And in due course he would confess things to her, pour his version of what he regarded as his wickedness—showing what a complex of Goethe, and Benvenuto Cellini, and Shelley, and all those other chaps he really was—into her shocked, very beautiful, and no doubt sympathetic ear. And preparatory to these things he wooed her with infinite subtlety and respect. And the reserve with which Elizabeth treated him seemed nothing more nor less than an exquisite modesty touched and enhanced by an equally exquisite lack of ideas.

Bindon knew nothing of her wandering affections, nor of the attempt made by Mwres to utilise hypnotism as a corrective to this digression of her heart; he conceived he was on the best of terms with Elizabeth, and had made her quite successfully various significant presents of jewellery and the more virtuous cosmetics, when her elopement with Denton threw the world out of gear for him. His first aspect of the matter was rage begotten of wounded vanity, and as Mwres was the most convenient person, he vented the first brunt of it upon him.

He went immediately and insulted the desolate father grossly, and then spent an active and determined day going to and fro about the city and interviewing people in a consistent and partly-successful attempt to ruin that matrimonial speculator. The effectual nature of these activities gave him a temporary exhilaration, and he went to the dining-place he had frequented in his wicked days in a devil-may-care frame of mind, and dined altogether too amply and cheerfully with two other golden youths in the early forties. He threw up the game; no woman was worth being good for, and he astonished even himself by the strain of witty cynicism he developed. One of the other desperate blades, warmed with wine, made a facetious allusion to his disappointment, but at the time this did not seem unpleasant.

The next morning found his liver and temper inflamed. He kicked his phonographic-news machine to pieces, dismissed his valet, and resolved that he would perpetrate a terrible revenge upon Elizabeth. Or Denton. Or somebody. But anyhow, it was to be a terrible revenge; and the friend who had made fun at him should no longer see him in the light of a foolish girl's victim. He knew something of the little property that was due to her, and that this would be the only support of the young couple until Mwres should relent. If Mwres did not relent, and if unpropitious things should happen to the affair in which Elizabeth's expectations lay, they would come upon evil times and be sufficiently amenable to temptation of a sinister sort. Bindon's imagination, abandoning its beautiful idealism altogether, expanded the idea of temptation of a sinister sort. He figured himself as the implacable, the intricate and powerful man of wealth pursuing this maiden who had scorned him. And suddenly her image came upon his mind vivid and dominant, and for the first time in his life Bindon realised something of the real power of passion.

His imagination stood aside like a respectful footman who has done his work in ushering in the emotion.

"My God!" cried Bindon: "I will have her! If I have to kill myself to get her! And that other fellow——!"

After an interview with his medical man and a penance for his overnight excesses in the form of bitter drugs, a mitigated but absolutely resolute Bindon sought out Mwres. Mwres he found properly smashed, and impoverished and humble, in a mood of frantic self-preservation, ready to sell himself body and soul, much more any interest in a disobedient daughter, to recover his lost position in the world. In the reasonable discussion that followed, it was agreed that these misguided young people should be left to sink into distress, or possibly even assisted towards that improving discipline by Bindon's financial influence.

"And then?" said Mwres.

"They will come to the Labour Company," said Bindon. "They will wear the blue canvas."

"And then?"

"She will divorce him," he said, and sat for a moment intent upon that prospect. For in those days the austere limitations of divorce of Victorian times were extraordinarily relaxed, and a couple might separate on a hundred different scores.

Then suddenly Bindon astonished himself and Mwres by

jumping to his feet. "She *shall* divorce him!" he cried. "I will have it so—I will work it so. By God! it shall be so. He shall be disgraced, so that she must. He shall be smashed and pulverised."

The idea of smashing and pulverising inflamed him further. He began a Jovian pacing up and down the little office. "I will have her," he cried. "I *will* have her! Heaven and Hell shall not save her from me!" His passion evaporated in its expression, and left him at the end simply histrionic. He struck an attitude and ignored with heroic determination a sharp twinge of pain about the diaphragm. And Mwres sat with his pneumatic cap deflated and himself very visibly impressed.

And so, with a fair persistency, Bindon set himself to the work of being Elizabeth's malignant providence, using with ingenious dexterity every particle of advantage wealth in those days gave a man over his fellow-creatures. A resort to the consolations of religion hindered these operations not at all. He would go and talk with an interesting, experienced, and sympathetic Father of the Huysmanite sect of the Isis cult, about all the irrational little proceedings he was pleased to regard as his Heaven-dismaying wickedness, and the interesting, experienced, and sympathetic Father representing Heaven dismayed, would with a pleasing affectation of horror suggest simple and easy penances, and recommend a monastic foundation that was airy, cool, hygienic, and not vulgarised, for viscerally disordered penitent sinners of the refined and wealthy type. And after these excursions, Bindon would come back to London quite active and passionate again. He would machinate with really considerable energy, and repair to a certain gallery high above the street of moving ways, from which he could view the entrance to the barrack of the Labour Company in the ward which sheltered Denton and Elizabeth. And at last one day he saw Elizabeth go in, and thereby his passion was renewed.

So in the fullness of time the complicated devices of Bindon ripened, and he could go to Mwres and tell him that the young people were near despair.

"It's time for you," he said, "to let your parental affections have play. She's been in blue canvas some months, and they've been cooped together in one of those Labour dens, and the little girl is dead. She knows now what his manhood is worth to her, by way of protection, poor girl. She'll see things now in a clearer light. You go to her—I don't want to appear in this affair yet—and point out to her how necessary it is that she should get a divorce from him. . . ."

"She's obstinate," said Mwres doubtfully.

"Spirit!" said Bindon. "She's a wonderful girl—a wonderful girl!"

"She'll refuse."

"Of course she will. But leave it open to her. Leave it open to her. And some day—in that stuffy den, in that irksome, toilsome life they can't help it—*they'll have a quarrel*. And then——"

Mwres meditated over the matter, and did as he was told.

Then Bindon, as he had arranged with his spiritual adviser, went into retreat. The retreat of the Huysmanite sect was a beautiful place, with the sweetest air in London, lit by natural sunlight, and with restful quadrangles of real grass open to the sky, where at the same time the penitent man of pleasure might enjoy all the pleasures of loafing and all the satisfaction of distinguished austerity. And, save for participation in the simple and wholesome dietary of the place and in certain magnificent chants, Bindon spent all his time in meditation upon the theme of Elizabeth, and the extreme purification his soul had undergone since he first saw her, and whether he would be able to get a dispensation to marry her from the experienced and sympathetic Father in spite of the approaching "sin" of her divorce; and then . . . Bindon would lean against a pillar of the quadrangle and lapse into reveries on the superiority of virtuous love to any other form of indulgence. A curious feeling in his back and chest that was trying to attract his attention, a disposition to be hot or shiver, a general sense of ill-health and cutaneous discomfort he did his best to ignore. All that of course belonged to the old life that he was shaking off.

When he came out of retreat he went at once to Mwres to ask for news of Elizabeth. Mwres was clearly under the impression that he was an exemplary father, profoundly touched about the heart by his child's unhappiness. "She was pale," he said, greatly moved. "She was pale. When I asked her to come away and leave him—and be happy—she put her head down upon the table"—Mwres sniffed—"and cried."

His agitation was so great that he could say no more.

"Ah!" said Bindon, respecting this manly grief. "Oh!" said Bindon quite suddenly, with his hand to his side.

Mwres looked up sharply out of the pit of his sorrows, startled. "What's the matter?" he asked, visibly concerned.

"A most violent pain. Excuse me! You were telling me about Elizabeth."

And Mwres, after a decent solicitude for Bindon's pain, proceeded with his report. It was even unexpectedly hopeful. Elizabeth, in her first emotion at discovering that her father had not absolutely deserted her, had been frank with him about her sorrows and disgusts.

"Yes," said Bindon, magnificently, "I shall have her yet." And then that novel pain twitched him for the second time.

For these lower pains the priest was comparatively ineffectual, inclining rather to regard the body and them as mental illusions amenable to contemplation; so Bindon took it to a man of a class he loathed, a medical man of extraordinary repute and incivility. "We must go all over you," said the medical man, and did so with the most disgusting frankness. "Did you ever bring any children into the world?" asked this gross materialist among other impertinent questions.

"Not that I know of," said Bindon, too amazed to stand upon his dignity.

"Ah!" said the medical man, and proceeded with his punching and sounding. Medical science in those days was just reaching the beginnings of precision. "You'd better go right away," said the medical man, "and make the Euthanasia. The sooner the better."

Bindon gasped. He had been trying not to understand the technical explanations and anticipations in which the medical man had indulged.

"I say!" he said. "But do you mean to say . . . Your science . . ."

"Nothing," said the medical man. "A few opiates. The thing is your own doing, you know, to a certain extent."

"I was sorely tempted in my youth."

"It's not that so much. But you come of a bad stock. Even if you'd have taken precautions you'd have had bad times to wind up with. The mistake was getting born. The indiscretions of the parents. And you've shirked exercise, and so forth."

"I had no one to advise me."

"Medical men are always willing."

"I was a spirited young fellow."

"We won't argue; the mischief's done now. You've lived. We can't start you again. You ought never to have started at all. Frankly—the Euthanasia!"

Bindon hated him in silence for a space. Every word of this brutal expert jarred upon his refinements. He was so gross, so impermeable to all the subtler issues of being. But it is no good picking a quarrel with a doctor. "My religious beliefs," he said. "I don't approve of suicide."

"You've been doing it all your life."

"Well, anyhow, I've come to take a serious view of life now."

"You're bound to, if you go on living. You'll hurt. But for practical purposes it's late. However, if you mean to do that—perhaps I'd better mix you a little something. You'll hurt a great deal. These little twinges . . ."

"Twinges!"

"Mere preliminary notices."

"How long can I go on? I mean, before I hurt—really."

"You'll get it hot soon. Perhaps three days."

Bindon tried to argue for an extension of time, and in the midst of his pleading gasped, put his hand to his side. Suddenly the extraordinary pathos of his life came to him clear and vivid. "It's hard," he said. "It's infernally hard! I've been no man's enemy but my own. I've always treated everybody quite fairly."

The medical man stared at him without any sympathy for some seconds. He was reflecting how excellent it was that there were no more Bindons to carry on that line of pathos. He felt quite optimistic. Then he turned to his telephone and ordered up a prescription from the Central Pharmacy.

He was interrupted by a voice behind him. "By God!" cried Bindon; "I'll have her yet."

The physician stared over his shoulder at Bindon's expression, and then altered the prescription.

So soon as this painful interview was over, Bindon gave way to rage. He settled that the medical man was not only an unsympathetic brute and wanting in the first beginnings of a gentleman, but also highly incompetent; and he went off to four other practitioners in succession, with a view to the establishment of this intuition. But to guard against surprises he kept that little prescription in his pocket. With each he began by expressing his grave doubts of the first doctor's intelligence, honesty, and professional knowledge, and then stated his symptoms, suppressing only a few more material facts in each case. These were always subsequently elicited by the doctor. In spite of the welcome depreciation of another practitioner, none of these eminent specialists would give Bindon any hope of eluding the anguish and helplessness that loomed now close upon him. To the last of them he unburthened his mind of an accumulated disgust with medical science. "After centuries and centuries," he exclaimed hotly; "and you can do nothing—except admit your helplessness. I say, 'save me'—and what do you do?"

"No doubt it's hard on you," said the doctor. "But you should have taken precautions."

"How was I to know?"

"It wasn't our place to run after you," said the medical man, picking a thread of cotton from his purple sleeve. "Why should we save you in particular? You see—from one point of view—people with imaginations and passions like yours have to go—they have to go."

"Go?"

"Die out. It's an eddy."

He was a young man with a serene face. He smiled at Bindon. "We get on with research, you know; we give advice when people have the sense to ask for it. And we bide our time."

"Bide your time?"

"We hardly know enough yet to take over the management, you know."

"The management?"

"You needn't be anxious. Science is young yet. It's got to keep on growing for a few generations. We know enough now to know we don't know enough yet. . . . But the time is coming, all the same. *You* won't see the time. But, between ourselves, you rich men and party bosses, with your natural play of the passions and patriotism and religion and so forth, have made rather a mess of things, haven't you? These Underways! And all that sort of thing. Some of us have a sort of fancy that in time we may know enough to take over a little more than the ventilation and drains. Knowledge keeps on piling up, you know. It keeps on growing. And there's not the slightest hurry for a generation or so. Some day—some day, men will live in a different way." He looked at Bindon and meditated. "There'll be a lot of dying out before that day can come."

Bindon attempted to point out to this young man how silly and irrelevant such talk was to a sick man like himself, how impertinent and uncivil it was to him, an older man occupying a position in the official world of extraordinary power and influence. He insisted that a doctor was paid to cure people—he laid great stress on "*paid*"—and had no business to glance even for a moment at "those other questions." "But we do," said the young man, insisting upon facts, and Bindon lost his temper.

His indignation carried him home. That these incompetent

mpostors, who were unable to save the life of a really influential man like himself, should dream of some day robbing
he legitimate property owners of social control, of inflicting
one knew not what tyranny upon the world. Curse science!
He fumed over the intolerable prospect for some time, and
hen the pain returned, and he recalled the made-up prescrip-
ion of the first doctor, still happily in his pocket. He took a
dose forthwith.

It calmed and soothed him greatly, and he could sit down
in his most comfortable chair beside his library (of phonographic records), and think over the altered aspect of af-
airs. His indignation passed, his anger and his passion
crumbled under the subtle attack of that prescription, pathos
became his sole ruler. He stared about him, at his magnificent
and voluptuously appointed apartment, at his statuary and
discreetly veiled pictures, and all the evidences of a cultivated
and elegant wickedness; he touched a stud and the sad pipings
of Tristan's shepherd filled the air. His eye wandered from
one object to another. They were costly and gross and   id—
but they were his. They presented in concrete form his ideals,
his conceptions of beauty and desire, his idea of all that is
precious in life. And now—he must leave it all like a common
man. He was, he felt, a slender and delicate flame, burning
out. So must all life flame up and pass, he thought. His eyes
filled with tears.

Then it came into his head that he was alone. Nobody
cared for him, nobody needed him! at any moment he
might begin to hurt vividly. He might even howl. Nobody
would mind. According to all the doctors he would have
excellent reason for howling in a day or so. It recalled what
his spiritual adviser had said of the decline of faith and
fidelity, the degeneration of the age. He beheld himself as a
pathetic proof of this; he, the subtle, able, important, volup-
uous, cynical, complex Bindon, possibly howling, and not one
faithful simple creature in all the world to howl in sympathy.
Not one faithful simple soul was there—no shepherd to pipe
to him! Had all such faithful simple creatures vanished from
his harsh and urgent earth? He wondered whether the

horrid vulgar crowd that perpetually went about the city could possibly know what he thought of them. If they did he felt sure *some* would try to earn a better opinion. Surely the world went from bad to worse. It was becoming impossible for Bindons. Perhaps some day . . . He was quite sure that the one thing he had needed in life was sympathy. For a time he regretted that he left no sonnets—no enigmatical pictures or something of that sort behind him to carry on his being until at last the sympathetic mind should come. . . .

It seemed incredible to him that this that came was extinction. Yet his sympathetic spiritual guide was in this matter annoyingly figurative and vague. Curse science! It had undermined all faith—all hope. To go out, to vanish from theatre and street, from office and dining-place, from the dear eyes of womankind. And not to be missed! On the whole, to leave the world happier!

He reflected that he had never worn his heart upon his sleeve. Had he after all been *too* unsympathetic? Few people could suspect how subtly profound he really was beneath the mask of that cynical gaiety of his. They would not understand the loss they had suffered. Elizabeth, for example, had not suspected. . . .

He had reserved that. His thoughts having come to Elizabeth gravitated about her for some time. How *little* Elizabeth understood him!

That thought became intolerable. Before all other things he must set that right. He realised that there was still something for him to do in life, his struggle against Elizabeth was even yet not over. He could never overcome her now, as he had hoped and prayed. But he might still impress her!

From that idea he expanded. He might impress her profoundly—he might impress her so that she should for evermore regret her treatment of him. The thing that she must realise before everything else was his magnanimity. His magnanimity! Yes! he had loved her with amazing greatness of heart. He had not seen it so clearly before—but of course he was going to leave her all his property. He saw it instantly, as a thing determined and inevitable. She would think how good he was, how spaciously generous; surrounded by all that makes life tolerable from his hand, she would recall with infinite regret her scorn and coldness. And when she sought expression for that regret, she would find that occasion gone for ever, she should be met by a locked door, by a disdainful stillness, by a white dead face. He closed his eyes and remained for a space imagining himself that white dead face.

From that he passed to other aspects of the matter, but his determination was assured. He meditated elaborately before he took action, for the drug he had taken inclined him to a lethargic and dignified melancholy. In certain respects he modified details. If he left all his property to Elizabeth it would include the voluptuously appointed room he occupied, and for many reasons he did not care to leave that to her. On the other hand, it had to be left to someone. In his clogged condition this worried him extremely.

In the end he decided to leave it to the sympathetic exponent of the fashionable religious cult whose conversation had been so pleasing in the past. "*He* will understand," said Bindon with a sentimental sigh. "He knows what Evil means— he understands something of the Stupendous Fascination of the Sphinx of Sin. Yes—he will understand." By that phrase it was that Bindon was pleased to dignify certain unhealthy and undignified departures from sane conduct to which a misguided vanity and an ill-controlled curiosity had led him. He sat for a space thinking how very Hellenic and Italian and Neronic, and all those things, he had been. Even now—might one not try a sonnet? A penetrating voice to echo down the ages, sensuous, sinister, and sad. For a space he forgot Elizabeth. In the course of half an hour he spoilt three phonographic coils, got a headache, took a second dose to calm himself, and reverted to magnanimity and his former design.

At last he faced the unpalatable problem of Denton. It needed all his newborn magnanimity before he could swallow the thought of Denton; but at last this greatly misunderstood man, assisted by his sedative and the near approach of death, effected even that. If he was at all exclusive about

Denton, if he should display the slightest distrust, if he attempted any specific exclusion of that young man, she might —*misunderstand*. Yes—she should have her Denton still. His magnanimity must go even to that. He tried to think only of Elizabeth in the matter.

He rose with a sigh, and limped across to the telephonic apparatus that communicated with his solicitor. In ten minutes a will duly attested and with its proper thumb-mark signature lay in the solicitor's office three miles away. And then for a space Bindon sat very still.

Suddenly he started out of a vague reverie and pressed an investigatory hand to his side.

Then he jumped eagerly to his feet and rushed to the telephone. The Euthanasia Company had rarely been called by a client in a greater hurry.

So it came at last that Denton and his Elizabeth, against all hope, returned unseparated from the labour servitude to which they had fallen. Elizabeth came out from her cramped subterranean den of metal-beaters and all the sordid circumstances of blue canvas, as one comes out of a nightmare. Back towards the sunlight their fortune took them; once the bequest was known to them, the bare thought of another day's hammering became intolerable. They went up long lifts and stairs to levels that they had not seen since the days of their disaster. At first she was full of this sensation of escape; even to think of the underways was intolerable; only after many months could she begin to recall with sympathy the faded women who were still below there, murmuring scandals and reminiscences and folly, and tapping away their lives.

Her choice of the apartments they presently took expressed the vehemence of her release. They were rooms upon the very verge of the city; they had a roof space and a balcony upon the city wall, wide open to the sun and wind, the country and the sky.

And in that balcony comes the last scene in this story. It was a summer sunsetting, and the hills of Surrey were very blue and clear. Denton leant upon the balcony regarding them, and Elizabeth sat by his side. Very wide and spacious was the view, for their balcony hung five hundred feet above the ancient level of the ground. The oblongs of the Food Company, broken here and there by the ruins—grotesque little holes and sheds—of the ancient suburbs, and intersected by shining streams of sewage, passed at last into a remote diapering at the foot of the distant hills. There once had been the squatting-place of the children of Uya. On those farther slopes gaunt machines of unknown import worked slackly at the end of their spell, and the hill crest was set with stagnant wind vanes. Along the great south road the Labour Company's field workers in huge wheeled mechanical vehicles were hurrying back to their meals, their last spell finished. And through the air a dozen little private aëropiles sailed down towards the city. Familiar scene as it was to the eyes of Denton and Elizabeth, it would have filled the minds of their ancestors with incredulous amazement. Denton's thoughts fluttered towards the future in a vain attempt at what that scene might be in another two hundred years, and, recoiling, turned towards the past.

He shared something of the growing knowledge of the time; he could picture the quaint smoke-grimed Victorian city with its narrow little roads of beaten earth, its wide common-land, ill-organised, ill-built suburbs, and irregular enclosures; the old countryside of the Stuart times, with its little villages and its petty London; the England of the monasteries, the far older England of the Roman dominion, and then before that a wild country with here and there the huts of some warring tribe. These huts must have come and gone and come again through a space of years that made the Roman camp and villa seem but yesterday; and before those years, before even the huts, there had been men in the valley. Even then—so recently had it all been when one judged it by the standards of geological time—this valley had been here; and those hills yonder, higher, perhaps, and snow-tipped, had still been yonder hills, and the Thames had flowed down from the Cotswolds to the sea. But the men had been but the shapes of men, creatures of darkness and ignorance, victims of beasts and floods, storms and pestilence and incessant hunger. They had held a precarious foothold amidst bears and lions and all the monstrous violence of the past. Already some at least of these enemies were overcome. . . .

For a time Denton pursued the thoughts of this spacious vision, trying in obedience to his instinct to find his place and proportion in the scheme.

"It has been chance," he said, "it has been luck. We have come through. It happens we have come through. Not by any strength of our own. . . .

"And yet . . . No. I don't know."

He was silent for a long time before he spoke again.

"After all—there is a long time yet. There have scarcely been men for twenty thousand years—and there has been life for twenty millions. And what are generations? What are generations? It is enormous, and we are so little. Yet we know—we feel. We are not dumb atoms, we are part of it— part of it—to the limits of our strength and will. Even to die is part of it. Whether we die or live, we are in the making. . . .

"As time goes on—*perhaps*—men will be wiser. . . . Wiser. . . .

"Will they ever understand?"

He became silent again. Elizabeth said nothing to these things, but she regarded his dreaming face with infinite affection. Her mind was not very active that evening. A great contentment possessed her. After a time she laid a gentle hand on his beside her. He fondled it softly, still looking out upon the spacious gold-woven view. So they sat as the sun went down. Until presently Elizabeth shivered.

Denton recalled himself abruptly from these spacious issues of his leisure, and went in to fetch her a shawl.

THE MAGIC SHOP

I HAD seen the Magic Shop from afar several times; I had passed it once or twice, a shop window of alluring little objects, magic balls, magic hens, wonderful cones, ventriloquist dolls, the material of the basket trick, packs of cards that *looked* all right, and all that sort of thing, but never had I thought of going in until one day, almost without warning, Gip hauled me by my finger right up to the window, and so conducted himself that there was nothing for it but to take him in. I had not thought the place was there, to tell the truth—a modest-sized frontage in Regent Street, between the picture shop and the place where the chicks run about just out of patent incubators—but there it was sure enough. I had fancied it was down nearer the Circus, or around the corner in Oxford Street, or even in Holborn; always over the way and a little inaccessible it had been, with something of the mirage in its position; but here it was now quite indisputably, and the fat end of Gip's pointing finger made a noise upon the glass.

"If I was rich," said Gip, dabbing a finger at the Disappearing Egg, "I'd buy myself that. And that"—which was The Crying Baby, Very Human—"and that," which was a mystery, and called, so a neat card asserted, "Buy One and Astonish Your Friends."

"Anything," said Gip, "will disappear under one of those cones. I have read about it in a book.

"And there, Dadda, is the Vanishing Halfpenny—only they've put it this way up so's we can't see how it's done."

Gip, dear boy, inherits his mother's breeding, and he did not propose to enter the shop or worry in any way; only, you know, quite unconsciously he lugged my finger doorward, and he made his interest clear.

"That," he said, and pointed to the Magic Bottle.

"If you had that?" I said; at which promising inquiry he looked up with a sudden radiance.

"I could show it to Jessie," he said, thoughtful as ever of others.

"It's less than a hundred days to your birthday, Gibbles," I said, and laid my hand on the door-handle.

Gip made no answer, but his grip tightened on my finger, and so we came into the shop.

It was no common shop this; it was a magic shop, and all the prancing precedence Gip would have taken in the matter of mere toys was wanting. He left the burthen of the conversation to me.

It was a little, narrow shop, not very well lit, and the door-bell pinged again with a plaintive note as we closed it behind us. For a moment or so we were alone and could glance about us. There was a tiger in *papier-mâché* on the glass case that covered the low counter—a grave, kind-eyed tiger that waggled his head in a methodical manner; there were several crystal spheres, a china hand holding magic cards, a stock of magic fish-bowls in various sizes, and an immodest magic hat that shamelessly displayed its springs. On the floor were magic mirrors; one to draw you out long and thin, one to swell your head and vanish your legs, and one to make you short and fat like a draught; and while we were laughing at these the shopman, as I suppose, came in.

At any rate, there he was behind the counter—a curious, sallow, dark man, with one ear larger than the other and a chin like the toe-cap of a boot.

"What can we have the pleasure?" he said, spreading his long, magic fingers on the glass case; and so with a start we were aware of him.

"I want," I said, "to buy my little boy a few simple tricks."

"Legerdemain?" he asked. "Mechanical? Domestic?"

"Anything amusing?" said I.

"Um!" said the shopman, and scratched his head for a moment as if thinking. Then, quite distinctly, he drew from his head a glass ball. "Something in this way?" he said, and held it out.

The action was unexpected. I had seen the trick done at entertainments endless times before—it's part of the common stock of conjurers—but I had not expected it here. "That's good," I said, with a laugh.

"Isn't it?" said the shopman.

Gip stretched out his disengaged hand to take this object and found merely a blank palm.

"It's in your pocket," said the shopman, and there it was!

"How much will that be?" I asked.

"We make no charge for glass balls," said the shopman, politely. "We get them"—he picked one out of his elbow as he spoke—"free." He produced another from the back of his neck, and laid it beside its predecessor on the counter. Gip regarded his glass ball sagely, then directed a look of inquiry at the two on the counter, and finally brought his round-eyed scrutiny to the shopman, who smiled. "You may have those, too," said the shopman, "and if you *don't* mind, one from my mouth— *So!*"

Gip counselled me mutely for a moment, and then in a profound silence put away the four balls, resumed my reassuring finger, and nerved himself for the next event.

"We get all our smaller tricks in that way," the shopman remarked.

I laughed in the manner of one who subscribes to a jest. "Instead of going to the wholesale shop," I said. "Of course, it's cheaper."

"In a way," the shopman said. "Though we pay in the end. But not so heavily—as people suppose. . . . Our larger tricks, and our daily provisions and all the other things we want, we get out of that hat. . . . And you know, sir, if you'll excuse my saying it, there *isn't* a wholesale shop, not for Genuine Magic goods, sir. I don't know if you noticed our inscription—the Genuine Magic shop." He drew a business-card from his cheek and handed it to me. "Genuine," he said, with his finger on the word, and added, "There is absolutely no deception, sir."

He seemed to be carrying out the joke pretty thoroughly, I thought.

He turned to Gip with a smile of remarkable affability. "You, you know, are the Right Sort of Boy."

I was surprised at his knowing that, because, in the interests of discipline, we keep it rather a secret even at home; but Gip received it in unflinching silence, keeping a steadfast eye on him.

"It's only the Right Sort of Boy gets through that doorway."

And as if by way of illustration, there came a rattling at the door, and a squeaking little voice could be faintly heard. "Nyar! I *warn* a' go in there, Dadda, I WARN 'a go in there. Ny-a-a-ah!" and then the accents of a down-trodden parent, urging consolations and propitiations. "It's locked, Edward," he said.

"But it isn't," said I.

"It is, sir," said the shopman, "always—for that sort of child," and as he spoke we had a glimpse of the other youngster, a small, white face, pallid from sweet-eating and over-sapid food, and distorted by evil passions, a ruthless little egotist, pawing at the enchanted pane. "It's no good, sir," said the shopman, as I moved, with my natural helpfulness, doorward, and presently the spoilt child was carried off howling.

"How do you manage that?" I said, breathing more freely.

"Magic!" said the shopman, with a careless wave of the hand, and behold! sparks of coloured fire flew out of his fingers and vanished into the shadows of the shop.

"You were saying," he said, addressing himself to Gip, "before you came in, that you would like one of our 'Buy One and Astonish your Friends' boxes?"

Gip, after a gallant effort, said "Yes."

"It's in your pocket."

And leaning over the counter—he really had an extraordinarily long body—this amazing person produced the article in the customary conjurer's manner. "Paper," he said, and took a sheet out of the empty hat with the springs; "string," and behold his mouth was a string-box, from which he drew an unending thread, which when he had tied his parcel he bit off—and, it seemed to me, swallowed the ball of string. And then he lit a candle at the nose of one of the ventriloquist's dummies, stuck one of his fingers (which had become sealing-wax red) into the flame, and so sealed the parcel. "Then there was the Disappearing Egg," he remarked, and produced one from within my coat-breast and packed it, and also The Crying Baby, Very Human. I handed each parcel to Gip as it was ready, and he clasped them to his chest.

He said very little, but his eyes were eloquent; the clutch of his arms was eloquent. He was the playground of unspeakable emotions. These, you know, were *real* Magics.

Then, with a start, I discovered something moving about in my hat—something soft and jumpy. I whipped it off, and a ruffled pigeon—no doubt a confederate—dropped out and ran on the counter, and went, I fancy, into a cardboard box behind the *papier-mâché* tiger.

"Tut, tut!" said the shopman, dexterously relieving me of my headdress; "careless bird, and—as I live—nesting!"

He shook my hat, and shook out into his extended hand two or three eggs, a large marble, a watch, about half-a-dozen of the inevitable glass balls, and then crumpled, crinkled paper, more and more and more, talking all the time of the way in which people neglect to brush their hats *inside* as well as out, politely, of course, but with a certain personal application. "All sorts of things accumulate, sir. . . . Not *you*, of course, in particular. . . . Nearly every customer. . . . Astonishing what they carry about with them. . . ." The crumpled paper rose and billowed on the counter more and more and more, until he was nearly hidden from us, until he was altogether hidden, and still his voice went on and on. "We none of us know what the fair semblance of a human being may conceal, sir. Are we all then no better than brushed exteriors, whited sepulchres——"

His voice stopped—exactly like when you hit a neighbour's gramophone with a well-aimed brick, the same instant silence, and the rustle of the paper stopped, and everything was still. . . .

"Have you done with my hat?" I said, after an interval. There was no answer.

I stared at Gip, and Gip stared at me; and there were our distortions in the magic mirrors, looking very rum, and grave, and quiet. . . .

"I think we'll go now," I said. "Will you tell me how much all this comes to? . . .

"I say," I said, on a rather louder note, "I want the bill; and my hat, please."

It might have been a sniff from behind the paper pile. . . .

"Let's look behind the counter, Gip," I said. "He's making fun of us."

I led Gip round the head-wagging tiger, and what do you think there was behind the counter? No one at all! Only my hat on the floor, and a common conjurer's lop-eared white rabbit lost in meditation, and looking as stupid and crumpled as only a conjurer's rabbit can do. I resumed my hat, and the rabbit lolloped a lollop or so out of my way.

"Dadda!" said Gip, in a guilty whisper.

"What is it, Gip?" said I.

"I do like this shop, Dadda."

"So should I," I said to myself, "if the counter wouldn't suddenly extend itself to shut one off from the door." But I didn't call Gip's attention to that. "Pussy!" he said, with a hand out to the rabbit as it came lolloping past us; "Pussy, do Gip a magic!" and his eyes followed it as it squeezed through a door I had certainly not remarked a moment before. Then this door opened wider, and the man with one ear larger than the other appeared again. He was smiling still, but his eye met mine with something between amusement and defiance. "You'd like to see our showroom, sir," he said, with an innocent suavity. Gip tugged my finger forward. I glanced at the counter and met the shopman's eye again. I was beginning to think the magic just a little too genuine. "We haven't very much time," I said. But somehow we were inside the showroom before I could finish that.

"All goods of the same quality," said the shopman, rubbing his flexible hands together, "and that is the Best. Nothing in the place that isn't genuine Magic, and warranted thoroughly rum. Excuse me, sir!"

I felt him pull at something that clung to my coat-sleeve, and then I saw he held a little, wriggling red demon by the tail—the little creature bit and fought and tried to get at his hand—and in a moment he tossed it carelessly behind a counter. No doubt the thing was only an image of twisted india-rubber, but for the moment——! And his gesture was exactly that of a man who handles some petty biting bit of vermin. I glanced at Gip, but Gip was looking at a magic rocking-horse. I was glad he hadn't seen the thing. "I say," I said, in an undertone, and indicating Gip and the red demon with my eyes, "you haven't many things like *that* about, have you?"

"None of ours! Probably brought it with you," said the shopman—also in an undertone, and with a more dazzling smile than ever. "Astonishing what people *will* carry about with them unawares!' And then to Gip, "Do you see anything you fancy here?"

There were many things that Gip fancied there.

He turned to this astonishing tradesman with mingled confidence and respect. "Is that a Magic Sword?" he said.

"A Magic Toy Sword. It neither bends, breaks, nor cuts the fingers. It renders the bearer invincible in battle against anyone under eighteen. Half-a-crown to seven and sixpence, according to size. These panoplies on cards are for juvenile knights-errant and very useful—shield of safety, sandals of swiftness, helmet of invisibility."

"Oh, Dadda!" gasped Gip.

I tried to find out what they cost, but the shopman did not heed me. He had got Gip now; he had got him away from my finger; he had embarked upon the exposition of all his confounded stock, and nothing was going to stop him. Presently I saw with a qualm of distrust and something very like jealousy that Gip had hold of this person's finger as usually he has hold of mine. No doubt the fellow was interesting, I thought, and had an interestingly faked lot of stuff, really *good* faked stuff, still——

I wandered after them, saying very little, but keeping an eye on this prestidigital fellow. After all, Gip was enjoying it. And no doubt when the time came to go we should be able to go quite easily.

It was a long, rambling place, that showroom, a gallery broken up by stands and stalls and pillars, with archways leading off to other departments, in which the queerest-looking assistants loafed and stared at one, and with perplexing mirrors and curtains. So perplexing, indeed, were these that I was presently unable to make out the door by which we had come.

The shopman showed Gip magic trains that ran without steam or clockwork, just as you set the signals, and then some very, very valuable boxes of soldiers that all came alive directly you took off the lid and said—— I myself haven't a very quick ear and it was a tongue-twisting sound, but Gip— he has his mother's ear—got it in no time. "Bravo!" said the shopman, putting the men back into the box unceremoniously and handing it to Gip. "Now," said the shopman, and in a moment Gip had made them all alive again.

"You'll take that box?" asked the shopman.

"We'll take that box," said I, "unless you charge its full value. In which case it would need a Trust Magnate——"

"Dear heart! *No!*" and the shopman swept the little men back again, shut the lid, waved the box in the air, and there it was, in brown paper, tied up and—*with Gip's full name and address on the paper!*

The shopman laughed at my amazement.

"This is the genuine magic," he said. "The real thing."

"It's almost too genuine for my taste," I said again.

After that he fell to showing Gip tricks, odd tricks, and still odder the way they were done. He explained them, he turned them inside out, and there was the dear little chap nodding his busy bit of a head in the sagest manner.

I did not attend as well as I might. "Hey, presto!" said the Magic Shopman, and then would come the clear, small

"Hey, presto!" of the boy. But I was distracted by other things. It was being borne in upon me just how tremendously rum this place was; it was, so to speak, inundated by a sense of rumness. There was something vaguely rum about the fixtures even, about the ceiling, about the floor, about the casually distributed chairs. I had a queer feeling that whenever I wasn't looking at them straight they went askew, and moved about, and played a noiseless puss-in-the-corner behind my back. And the cornice had a serpe·· ·ine design with masks—masks altogether too express·.   for proper plaster.

Then abruptly my attention was caught by one of the odd-looking assistants. He was some way off and evidently unaware of my presence—I saw a sort of three-quarter length of him over a pile of toys and through an arch—and, you know, he was leaning against a pillar in an idle sort of way doing the most horrid things with his features. The particular horrid thing he did was with his nose. He did it just as though he was idle and wanted to amuse himself. First of all it was a short, blobby nose, and then suddenly he shot it out like a telescope, and then out it flew and became thinner and thinner until it was like a long, red, flexible whip. Like a thing in a nightmare it was! He flourished it about and flung it forth as a fly-fisher flings his line.

My instant thought was that Gip mustn't see him. I turned about, and there was Gip quite preoccupied with the shopman, and thinking no evil. They were whispering together and looking at me. Gip was standing on a stool, and the shopman was holding a sort of big drum in his hand.

"Hide and seek, Dadda!" cried Gip. "You're He!"

And before I could do anything to prevent it, the shopman had clapped the big drum over him.

I saw what was up directly. "Take that off," I cried, "this instant! You'll frighten the boy. Take it off!"

The shopman with the unequal ears did so without a word, and held the big cylinder towards me to show its emptiness. And the stool was vacant! In that instant my boy had utterly disappeared! . . .

You know, perhaps, that sinister something that comes like a hand out of the unseen and grips your heart about. You know it takes your common self away and leaves you tense and deliberate, neither slow nor hasty, neither angry nor afraid. So it was with me.

I came up to this grinning shopman and kicked his stool aside.

"Stop this folly!" I said. "Where is my boy?"

"You see," he said, still displaying the drum's interior, "there is no deception——"

I put out my hand to grip him, and he eluded me by a dexterous movement. I snatched again, and he turned from me and pushed open a door to escape. "Stop!" I said, and he laughed, receding. I leapt after him—into utter darkness.

Thud!

"Lor' bless my 'eart! I didn't see you coming, sir!"

I was in Regent Street, and I had collided with a decent-looking working man; and a yard away, perhaps, and looking extremely perplexed with himself, was Gip. There was some sort of apology, and then Gip had turned and come to me with a bright little smile, as though for a moment he had missed me.

And he was carrying four parcels in his arm!

He secured immediate possession of my finger.

For the second I was rather at a loss. I stared round to see the door of the magic shop, and, behold, it was not there! There was no door, no shop, nothing, only the common pilaster between the shop where they sell pictures and the window with the chicks! . . .

I did the only thing possible in that mental tumult; I walked straight to the kerbstone and held up my umbrella for a cab.

"'Ansoms," said Gip, in a note of culminating exultation.

I helped him in, recalled my address with an effort, and got in also. Something unusual proclaimed itself in my tail-coat pocket, and I felt and discovered a glass ball. With a petulant expression I flung it into the street.

Gip said nothing.

For a space neither of us spoke.

"Dadda!" said Gip, at last, "that *was* a proper shop!"

I came round with that to the problem of just how the whole thing had seemed to him. He looked completely unamaged—so far, good; he was neither scared nor unhinged, e was simply tremendously satisfied with the afternoon's ntertainment, and there in his arms were the four parcels.

Confound it! what could be in them?

"Um!" I said. "Little boys can't go to shops like that every ay."

He received this with his usual stoicism, and for a moment was sorry I was his father and not his mother, and so ouldn't suddenly there, *coram publico*, in our hansom, kiss im. After all, I thought, the thing wasn't so very bad.

But it was only when we opened the parcels that I really egan to be reassured. Three of them contained boxes of oldiers, quite ordinary lead soldiers, but of so good a quality s to make Gip altogether forget that originally these parcels ad been Magic Tricks of the only genuine sort, and the fourth ontained a kitten, a little living white kitten, in excellent ealth and appetite and temper.

I saw this unpacking with a sort of provisional relief. I ung about in the nursery for quite an unconscionable ime. . . .

That happened six months ago. And now I am beginning o believe it is all right. The kitten had only the magic natural o all kittens, and the soldiers seem as steady a company as ny colonel could desire. And Gip——?

The intelligent parent will understand that I have to go autiously with Gip.

But I went so far as this one day. I said, "How would you ike your soldiers to come alive, Gip, and march about by hemselves?"

"Mine do," said Gip. "I just have to say a word I know efore I open the lid."

"Then they march about alone?"

"Oh, *quite*, Dadda. I shouldn't like them if they didn't do hat."

I displayed no unbecoming surprise, and since then I hav
taken occasion to drop in upon him once or twice, unan
nounced, when the soldiers were about, but so far I hav
never discovered them performing in anything like a magica
manner. . . .

It's so difficult to tell

There's also a question of finance. I have an incurabl
habit of paying bills. I have been up and down Regent Stree
several times, looking for that shop. I am inclined to think
indeed, that in that matter honour is satisfied, and that, sinc
Gip's name and address are known to them, I may very we'
leave it to these people, whoever they may be, to send i
their bill in their own time.

THE VALLEY OF SPIDERS

TOWARDS midday the three pursuers came abruptly round a bend in the torrent bed upon the sight of a very broad and spacious valley. The difficult and winding trench of pebbles along which they had tracked the fugitives for so long expanded to a broad slope, and with a common impulse the three men left the trail, and rode to a low eminence set with olive-dun trees, and there halted, the two others, as became them, a little behind the man with the silver-studded bridle.

For a space they scanned the great expanse below them with eager eyes. It spread remoter and remoter, with only a few clusters of sere thorn bushes here and there, and the dim suggestions of some now waterless ravine to break its desolation of yellow grass. Its purple distances melted at last into the bluish slopes of the farther hills—hills it might be of a greener kind—and above them invisibly supported, and seeming indeed to hang in the blue, were the snow-clad summits of mountains—that grew larger and bolder to the northwest-ward as the sides of the valley drew together. And westward the valley opened until a distant darkness under the sky told where the forests began. But the three men looked neither east nor west, but only steadfastly across the valley.

The gaunt man with the scarred lip was the first to speak. "Nowhere," he said, with a sigh of disappointment in his voice. "But after all, they had a full day's start."

"They don't know we are after them," said the little man on the white horse.

"*She* would know," said the leader bitterly, as if speaking to himself.

"Even then they can't go fast. They've got no beast but the mule, and all to-day the girl's foot has been bleeding——"

The man with the silver bridle flashed a quick intensity of rage on him. "Do you think I haven't seen that?" he snarled.

"It helps, anyhow," whispered the little man to himself.

The gaunt man with the scarred lip stared impassively. "They can't be over the valley," he said. "If we ride hard——"

He glanced at the white horse and paused.

"Curse all white horses!" said the man with the silver bridle, and turned to scan the beast his curse included.

The little man looked down between the melancholy ears of his steed.

"I did my best," he said.

The two others stared again across the valley for a space. The gaunt man passed the back of his hand across the scarred lip.

"Come up!" said the man who owned the silver bridle, suddenly. The little man started and jerked his rein, and the horse hoofs of the three made a multitudinous faint pattering upon the withered grass as they turned back towards the trail. . . .

They rode cautiously down the long slope before them, and so came through a waste of prickly twisted bushes and strange dry shapes of horny branches that grew amongst the rocks, into the level below. And there the trail grew faint, for the soil was scanty, and the only herbage was this scorched dead straw that lay upon the ground. Still, by hard scanning, by leaning beside the horses' necks and pausing ever and again, even these white men could contrive to follow after their prey.

There were trodden places, bent and broken blades of the coarse grass, and ever and again the sufficient intimation of a footmark. And once the leader saw a brown smear of blood where the half-caste girl may have trod. And at that under his breath he cursed her for a fool.

The gaunt man checked his leader's tracking, and the little man on the white horse rode behind, a man lost in a dream. They rode one after another, the man with the silver bridle led the way, and they spoke never a word. After a time it came to the little man on the white horse that the world was very still. He started out of his dream. Besides the minute noises of their horses and equipment, the whole great valley kept the brooding quiet of a painted scene.

Before him went his master and his fellow, each intently leaning forward to the left, each impassively moving with the paces of his horse; their shadows went before them—still, noiseless, tapering attendants; and nearer a crouched cool shape was his own. He looked about him. What was it had gone? Then he remembered the reverberation from the banks of the gorge and the perpetual accompaniment of shifting, jostling pebbles. And, moreover——? There was no breeze. That was it! What a vast, still place it was, a monotonous afternoon slumber. And the sky open and blank, except for a sombre veil of haze that had gathered in the upper valley.

He straightened his back, fretted with his bridle, puckered his lips to whistle, and simply sighed. He turned in his saddle for a time, and stared at the throat of the mountain gorge out of which they had come. Blank! Blank slopes on either side, with never a sign of a decent beast or tree—much less a man. What a land it was! What a wilderness! He dropped again into his former pose.

It filled him with a momentary pleasure to see a wry stick of purple black flash out into the form of a snake, and vanish amidst the brown. After all, the infernal valley *was* alive. And then, to rejoice him still more, came a breath across his face, a whisper that came and went, the faintest inclination of a stiff black-antlered bush upon a crest, the first intimations of a possible breeze. Idly he wetted his finger, and held it up.

He pulled up sharply to avoid a collision with the gaunt man, who had stopped at fault upon the trail. Just at that guilty moment he caught his master's eye looking towards him.

For a time he forced an interest in the tracking. Then, as they rode on again, he studied his master's shadow and hat and shoulder appearing and disappearing behind the gaunt man's nearer contours. They had ridden four days out of the very limits of the world into this desolate place, short of water, with nothing but a strip of dried meat under their saddles, over rocks and mountains, where surely none but these fugitives had ever been before—for *that!*

And all this was for a girl, a mere wilful child! And the

man had whole cityfuls of people to do his basest bidding—girls, women! Why in the name of passionate folly *this* one in particular? asked the little man, and scowled at the world, and licked his parched lips with a blackened tongue. It was the way of the master, and that was all he knew. Just because she sought to evade him. . . .

His eye caught a whole row of high plumed canes bending in unison, and then the tails of silk that hung before his neck flapped and fell. The breeze was growing stronger. Somehow it took the stiff stillness out of things—and that was well.

"Hullo!" said the gaunt man.

All three stopped abruptly.

"What?" asked the master. "What?"

"Over there," said the gaunt man, pointing up the valley. "What?"

"Something coming towards us."

And as he spoke a yellow animal crested a rise and came bearing down upon them. It was a big wild dog, coming before the wind, tongue out, at a steady pace, and running with such an intensity of purpose that he did not seem to see the horsemen he approached. He ran with his nose up, following, it was plain, neither scent nor quarry. As he drew nearer the little man felt for his sword. "He's mad," said the gaunt rider.

"Shout!" said the little man and shouted.

The dog came on. Then when the little man's blade was already out, it swerved aside and went panting by them and past. The eyes of the little man followed its flight. "There was no foam," he said. For a space the man with the silver-studded bridle stared up the valley. "Oh, come on!" he cried at last. "What does it matter?" and jerked his horse into movement again.

The little man left the insoluble mystery of a dog that fled from nothing but the wind, and lapsed into profound musings on human character. "Come on!" he whispered to himself. "Why should it be given to one man to say 'Come on!' with that stupendous violence of effect. Always, all his life, the man with the silver bridle has been saying that. If *I* said it——!" thought the little man. But people marvelled when the master was disobeyed even in the wildest things. This half-caste girl seemed to him, seemed to everyone, mad—blasphemous almost. The little man, by way of comparison, reflected on the gaunt rider with the scarred lip, as stalwart as his master, as brave and, indeed, perhaps braver, and yet for him there was obedience, nothing but to give obedience duly and stoutly. . . .

Certain sensations of the hands and knees called the little man back to more immediate things. He became aware of something. He rode up beside his gaunt fellow. "Do you notice the horses?" he said in an undertone.

The gaunt face looked interrogation.

"They don't like this wind," said the little man, and dropped behind as the man with the silver bridle turned upon him.

"It's all right," said the gaunt-faced man.

They rode on again for a space in silence. The foremost two rode downcast upon the trail, the hindmost man watched the haze that crept down the vastness of the valley, nearer and nearer, and noted how the wind grew in strength moment by moment. Far away on the left he saw a line of dark bulks—wild hog perhaps, galloping down the valley, but of that he said nothing, nor did he remark again upon the uneasiness of the horses.

And then he saw first one and then a second great white ball, a great shining white ball like a gigantic head of thistledown, that drove before the wind athwart the path. These balls soared high in the air, and dropped and rose again and caught for a moment, and hurried on and passed, but at the sight of them the restlessness of the horses increased.

Then presently he saw that more of these drifting globes—and then soon very many more—were hurrying towards him down the valley.

They became aware of a squealing. Athwart the path a huge boar rushed, turning his head but for one instant to glance at them, and then hurling on down the valley again. And at that, all three stopped and sat in their saddles, staring into the thickening haze that was coming upon them.

"If it were not for this thistledown——" began the leader.

But now a big globe came drifting past within a score of yards of them. It was really not an even sphere at all, but a vast, soft, ragged, filmy thing, a sheet gathered by the corners, an aërial jelly-fish, as it were, but rolling over and over as it advanced, and trailing long, cobwebby threads and streamers that floated in its wake.

"It isn't thistledown," said the little man.

"I don't like the stuff," said the gaunt man.

And they looked at one another.

"Curse it!" cried the leader. "The air's full of it up there. If it keeps on at this pace long, it will stop us altogether."

An instinctive feeling, such as lines out a herd of deer at the approach of some ambiguous thing, prompted them to turn their horses to the wind, ride forward for a few paces, and stare at that advancing multitude of floating masses. They came on before the wind with a sort of smooth swiftness, rising and falling noiselessly, sinking to earth, rebounding high, soaring—all with a perfect unanimity, with a still, deliberate assurance.

Right and left of the horsemen the pioneers of this strange army passed. At one that rolled along the ground, breaking shapelessly and trailing out reluctantly into long grappling ribbons and bands, all three horses began to shy and dance. The master was seized with a sudden, unreasonable impatience. He cursed the drifting globes roundly. "Get on!" he cried; "get on! What do these things matter? How *can* they matter? Back to the trail!" He fell swearing at his horse and sawed the bit across its mouth.

He shouted aloud with rage. "I will follow that trail, I tell you," he cried. "Where is the trail?"

He gripped the bridle of his prancing horse and searched amidst the grass. A long and clinging thread fell across his face, a grey steamer dropped about his bridle arm, some big, active thing with many legs ran down the back of his head. He looked up to discover one of those grey masses anchored as it were above him by these things and flapping out ends as a sail flaps when a boat comes about—but noiselessly.

He had an impression of many eyes, of a dense crew of squat bodies, of long, many-jointed limbs hauling at their mooring ropes to bring the thing down upon him. For a space he stared up, reining in his prancing horse with the instinct born of years of horsemanship. Then the flat of a sword smote his back, and a blade flashed overhead and cut the drifting balloon of spiderweb free, and the whole mass lifted softly and drove clear and away.

"Spiders!" cried the voice of the gaunt man. "The things are full of big spiders! Look, my lord!"

The man with the silver bridle still followed the mass that drove away.

"Look, my lord!"

The master found himself staring down at a red smashed thing on the ground that, in spite of partial obliteration, could still wriggle unavailing legs. Then when the gaunt man pointed to another mass that bore down upon them, he drew his sword hastily. Up the valley now it was like a fog bank torn to rags. He tried to grasp the situation.

"Ride for it!" the little man was shouting. "Ride for it down the valley."

What happened then was like the confusion of a battle. The man with the silver bridle saw the little man go past him slashing furiously at imaginary cobwebs, saw him cannon into the horse of the gaunt man and hurl it and its rider to earth. His own horse went a dozen paces before he could rein it in. Then he looked up to avoid imaginary dangers, and then back again to see a horse rolling on the ground, the gaunt man standing and slashing over it at a rent and fluttering mass of grey that streamed and wrapped about them both. And thick and fast as thistledown on waste land on a windy day in July, the cobweb masses were coming on.

The little man had dismounted, but he dared not release his horse. He was endeavouring to lug the struggling brute back with the strength of one arm, while with the other he slashed aimlessly. The tentacles of a second grey mass had entangled themselves with the struggle, and this second grey mass came to its moorings, and slowly sank.

The master set his teeth, gripped his bridle, lowered his head, and spurred his horse forward. The horse on the ground rolled over, there was blood and moving shapes upon the flanks, and the gaunt man, suddenly leaving it, ran forward towards his master, perhaps ten paces. His legs were swathed and encumbered with grey; he made ineffectual movements with his sword. Grey streamers waved from him; there was a thin veil of grey across his face. With his left hand he beat at something on his body, and suddenly he stumbled and fell. He struggled to rise, and fell again, and suddenly, horribly, began to howl, "Oh—ohoo, ohooh!"

The master could see the great spiders upon him, and others upon the ground.

As he strove to force his horse nearer to this gesticulating, screaming grey object that struggled up and down, there came a clatter of hoofs, and the little man, in act of mounting, swordless, balanced on his belly athwart the white horse, and clutching its mane, whirled past. And again a clinging thread of grey gossamer swept across the master's face. All about him, and over him, it seemed this drifting, noiseless cobweb circled and drew nearer him. . . .

To the day of his death he never knew just how the event of that moment happened. Did he, indeed, turn his horse, or did it really of its own accord stampede after its fellow? Suffice it that in another second he was galloping full tilt down the valley with his sword whirling furiously overhead. And all about him on the quickening breeze, the spiders' air-ships, their air bundles and air sheets, seemed to him to hurry in a conscious pursuit.

Clatter, clatter, thud, thud—the man with the silver bridle rode, heedless of his direction, with his fearful face looking up now right, now left, and his sword arm ready to slash. And a few hundred yards ahead of him, with a tail of torn cobweb trailing behind him, rode the little man on the white horse, still but imperfectly in the saddle. The reeds bent before them, the wind blew fresh and strong, over his shoulder the master could see the webs hurrying to overtake. . . .

He was so intent to escape the spiders' webs that only as

his horse gathered together for a leap did he realise the ravine ahead. And then he realised it only to misunderstand and interfere. He was leaning forward on his horse's neck and sat up and back all too late.

But if in his excitement he had failed to leap, at any rate he had not forgotten how to fall. He was horseman again in mid-air. He came off clear with a mere bruise upon his shoulder, and his horse rolled, kicking spasmodic legs, and lay still. But the master's sword drove its point into the hard soil, and snapped clean across, as though Chance refused him any longer as her Knight, and the splintered end missed his face by an inch or so.

He was on his feet in a moment, breathlessly scanning the onrushing spiderwebs. For a moment he was minded to run, and then thought of the ravine, and turned back. He ran aside once to dodge one drifting terror, and then he was swiftly clambering down the precipitous sides, and out of the touch of the gale.

There under the lee of the dry torrent's steeper banks he might crouch, and watch these strange grey masses pass and pass in safety till the wind fell and it became possible to escape. And there for a long time he crouched, watching the strange grey ragged masses trail their streamers across his narrowed sky.

Once a stray spider fell into the ravine close beside him— a full foot it measured from leg to leg, and its body was half a man's hand—and after he had watched its monstrous alacrity of search and escape for a little while, and tempted it to bite his broken sword, he lifted up his iron-heeled boot and smashed it into a pulp. He swore as he did so, and for a time sought up and down for another.

Then presently, when he was surer these spider swarms could not drop into the ravine, he found a place where he could sit down, and sat and fell into deep thought and began after his manner to gnaw his knuckles and bite his nails. And from this he was moved by the coming of the man with the white horse.

He heard him long before he saw him, as a clattering of

hoofs, stumbling footsteps, and a reassuring voice. Then the little man appeared, a rueful figure, still with a tail of white cobweb trailing behind him. They approached each other without speaking, without a salutation. The little man was fatigued and shamed to the pitch of hopeless bitterness, and came to a stop at last, face to face with his seated master. The latter winced a little under his dependant's eye. "Well?" he said at last, with no pretence of authority.

"You left him?"

"My horse bolted."

"I know. So did mine."

He laughed at his master mirthlessly.

"I say my horse bolted," said the man who once had a silver-studded bridle.

"Cowards both," said the little man.

The other gnawed his knuckle through some meditative moments, with his eye on his inferior

"Don't call me a coward," he said at length.

"You are a coward like myself."

"A coward possibly. There is a limit beyond which every man must fear. That I have learnt at last. But not like yourself. That is where the difference comes in."

"I never could have dreamt you would have left him. He saved your life two minutes before. . . . Why are you our lord?"

The master gnawed his knuckles again, and his countenance was dark.

"No man calls me a coward," he said. "No. . . . A broken sword is better than none. . . . One spavined white horse cannot be expected to carry two men a four-days' journey. I hate white horses, but this time it cannot be helped. You begin to understand me? . . . I perceive that you are minded, on the strength of what you have seen and fancy, to taint my reputation. It is men of your sort who unmake kings. Besides which—I never liked you."

"My lord!" said the little man.

"No," said the master. "*No!*"

He stood up sharply as the little man moved. For a minute

perhaps they faced one another. Overhead the spiders' balls went driving. There was a quick movement among the pebbles; a running of feet, a cry of despair, a gasp and a blow. . . .

Towards nightfall the wind fell. The sun set in a calm serenity, and the man who had once possessed the silver bridle came at last very cautiously and by an easy slope out of the ravine again; but now he led the white horse that once belonged to the little man. He would have gone back to his horse to get his silver-mounted bridle again, but he feared night and a quickening breeze might still find him in the valley, and besides he disliked greatly to think he might discover his horse all swathed in cobwebs and perhaps unpleasantly eaten.

And as he thought of those cobwebs and of all the dangers he had been through, and the manner in which he had been preserved that day, his hand sought a little reliquary that hung about his neck, and he clasped it for a moment with heartfelt gratitude. As he did so his eyes went across the valley.

"I was hot with passion," he said, "and now she has met her reward. They also, no doubt——"

And behold! Far away out of the wooded slopes across the valley, but in the clearness of the sunset distinct and unmistakable, he saw a little spire of smoke.

At that his expression of serene resignation changed to an amazed anger. Smoke? He turned the head of the white horse about, and hesitated. And as he did so a little rustle of air went through the grass about him. Far away upon some reeds swayed a tattered sheet of grey. He looked at the cobwebs; he looked at the smoke.

"Perhaps, after all, it is not them," he said at last.

But he knew better.

After he had stared at the smoke for some time, he mounted the white horse.

As he rode, he picked his way amidst stranded masses of web. For some reason there were many dead spiders on the ground, and those that lived feasted guiltily on their fellows. At the sound of his horse's hoofs they fled.

Their time had passed. From the ground, without either a wind to carry them or a winding sheet ready, these things, for all their poison, could do him no evil.

He flicked with his belt at those he fancied came too near. Once, where a number ran together over a bare place, he was minded to dismount and trample them with his boots, but this impulse he overcame. Ever and again he turned in his saddle, and looked back at the smoke.

"Spiders," he muttered over and over again. "Spiders! Well, well. . . . The next time I must spin a web."

THE TRUTH ABOUT PYECRAFT

HE SITS not a dozen yards away. If I glance over my shoulder I can see him. And if I catch his eye—and usually I catch his eye—it meets me with an expression——

It is mainly an imploring look—and yet with suspicion in it.

Confound his suspicion! If I wanted to tell on him I should have told long ago. I don't tell and I don't tell, and he ought to feel at his ease. As if anything so gross and fat as he could feel at ease! Who would believe me if I did tell?

Poor old Pyecraft! Great, uneasy jelly of substance! The fattest clubman in London.

He sits at one of the little club tables in the huge bay by the fire, stuffing. What is he stuffing? I glance judiciously and catch him biting at a round of hot buttered teacake, with his eyes on me. Confound him!—with his eyes on me!

That settles it, Pyecraft! Since you *will* be abject, since you *will* behave as though I was not a man of honour, here, right under your embedded eyes, I write the thing down—the plain truth about Pyecraft. The man I helped, the man I shielded, and who has requited me by making my club unendurable, absolutely unendurable, with his liquid appeal, with the perpetual "don't tell" of his looks.

And, besides, why does he keep on eternally eating?

Well, here goes for the truth, the whole truth, and nothing but the truth!

Pyecraft—— I made the acquaintance of Pyecraft in this very smoking-room. I was a young, nervous new member, and he saw it. I was sitting all alone, wishing I knew more of the members, and suddenly he came, a great rolling front of chins and abdomina, towards me, and grunted and sat down in a chair close by me and wheezed for a space, and scraped for a space with a match and lit a cigar, and then addressed me. I forget what he said—something about the matches not lighting properly, and afterwards as he talked he kept stopping the waiters one by one as they went by, and telling them about the matches in that thin, fluty voice he has. But, anyhow, it was in some such way we began our talking.

He talked about various things and came round to games. And thence to my figure and complexion. "You ought to be a good cricketer," he said. I suppose I am slender, slender to what some people would call lean, and I suppose I am rather dark, still —— I am not ashamed of having a Hindu great-grandmother, but, for all that, I don't want casual strangers to see through me at a glance to *her*. So that I was set against Pyecraft from the beginning.

But he only talked about me in order to get to himself.

"I expect," he said, "you take no more exercise than I do, and probably you eat no less." (Like all excessively obese people he fancied he ate nothing.) "Yet"—and he smiled an oblique smile—"we differ."

And then he began to talk about his fatness and his fatness; all he did for his fatness and all he was going to do for his fatness; what people had advised him to do for his fatness and what he had heard of people doing for fatness similar to his. "*A priori*," he said, "one would think a question of nutrition could be answered by dietary and a question of assimilation by drugs." It was stifling. It was dumping talk. It made me feel swelled to hear him.

One stands that sort of thing once in a way at a club, but a time came when I fancied I was standing too much. He took to me altogether too conspicuously. I could never go into the smoking-room but he would come wallowing towards me, and sometimes he came and gormandised round and about me while I had my lunch. He seemed at times almost to be clinging to me. He was a bore, but not so fearful a bore as to be limited to me; and from the first there was something in his manner—almost as though he knew, almost as though he penetrated to the fact that I *might*—that there was a remote, exceptional chance in me that no one else presented.

"I'd give anything to get it down," he would say—"anything," and peer at me over his vast cheeks and pant.

Poor old Pyecraft! He has just gonged, no doubt to order another buttered teacake!

He came to the actual thing one day. "Our Pharmacopœia," he said, "our Western Pharmacopœia, is anything but the last word of medical science. In the East, I've been told——"

He stopped and stared at me. It was like being at an aquarium.

I was quite suddenly angry with him. "Look here," I said, "who told you about my great-grandmother's recipes?"

"Well," he fenced.

"Every time we've met for a week," I said—"and we've met pretty often—you've given me a broad hint or so about that little secret of mine."

"Well," he said, "now the cat's out of the bag, I'll admit, yes, it is so. I had it——"

"From Pattison?"

"Indirectly," he said, which I believe was lying, "yes."

"Pattison," I said, "took that stuff at his own risk."

He pursed his mouth and bowed.

"My great-grandmother's recipes," I said, "are queer things to handle. My father was near making me promise——"

"He didn't?"

"No. But he warned me. He himself used one—once."

"Ah! . . . But do you think——? Suppose—suppose there did happen to be one——"

"The things are curious documents," I said. "Even the smell of 'em. . . . No!"

But after going so far Pyecraft was resolved I should go farther. I was always a little afraid if I tried his patience too much he would fall on me suddenly and smother me. I own I was weak. But I was also annoyed with Pyecraft. I had got to that state of feeling for him that disposed me to say, "Well, *take* the risk!" The little affair of Pattison to which I have alluded was a different matter altogether. What it was doesn't concern us now, but I knew, anyhow, that the particular recipe I used then was safe. The rest I didn't know so much about, and, on the whole, I was inclined to doubt their safety pretty completely.

Yet even if Pyecraft got poisoned——

I must confess the poisoning of Pyecraft struck me as an immense undertaking.

That evening I took that queer, odd-scented sandalwood box out of my safe and turned the rustling skins over. The gentleman who wrote the recipes for my great-grandmother evidently had a weakness for skins of a miscellaneous origin, and his handwriting was cramped to the last degree. Some of the things are quite unreadable to me—though my family, with its Indian Civil Service associations, has kept up a knowledge of Hindustani from generation to generation—and none are absolutely plain sailing. But I found the one that I knew was there soon enough, and sat on the floor by my safe for some time looking at it.

"Look here," said I to Pyecraft next day, and snatched the slip away from his eager grasp.

"So far as I can make it out, this is a recipe for Loss of Weight. ("Ah!" said Pyecraft.) I'm not absolutely sure, but I think it's that. And if you take my advice you'll leave it alone. Because, you know—I blacken my blood in your interest, Pyecraft—my ancestors on that side were, so far as I can gather, a jolly queer lot. See?"

"Let me try it," said Pyecraft.

I leant back in my chair. My imagination made one mighty effort and fell flat within me. "What in Heaven's name, Pyecraft," I asked, "do you think you'll look like when you get thin?"

He was impervious to reason. I made him promise never to say a word to me about his disgusting fatness again whatever happened—never, and then I handed him that little piece of skin.

"It's nasty stuff," I said.

"No matter," he said, and took it.

He goggled at it. "But—but——" he said.

He had just discovered that it wasn't English.

"To the best of my ability," I said, "I will do you a transla-tion."

I did my best. After that we didn't speak for a fortnight. Whenever he approached me I frowned and motioned him away, and he respected our compact, but at the end of the fortnight he was as fat as ever. And then he got a word in.

"I must speak," he said. "It isn't fair. There's something wrong. It's done me no good. You're not doing your great-grandmother justice."

"Where's the recipe?"

He produced it gingerly from his pocket-book.

I ran my eye over the items. "Was the egg addled?" I asked.

"No. Ought it to have been?"

"That," I said, "goes without saying in all my poor dear great-grandmother's recipes. When condition or quality is not specified you must get the worst. She was drastic or noth-ing. . . . And there's one or two possible alternatives to some of these other things. You got *fresh* rattlesnake venom?"

"I got a rattlesnake from Jamrach's. It cost—it cost——"

"That's your affair, anyhow. This last item——"

"I know a man who——"

"Yes. H'm. Well, I'll write the alternatives down. So far as I know the language, the spelling of this recipe is particu-larly atrocious. By the bye, dog here probably means pariah dog."

For a month after that I saw Pyecraft constantly at the club and as fat and anxious as ever. He kept our treaty, but at times he broke the spirit of it by shaking his head despond-ently. Then one day in the cloakroom he said, "Your great-grandmother——"

"Not a word against her," I said; and he held his peace.

I could have fancied he had desisted, and I saw him one day talking to three new members about his fatness as though he was in search of other recipes. And then, quite unexpec-tedly his telegram came.

"Mr. Formalyn!" bawled a page-boy under my nose, and I took the telegram and opened it at once.

"For Heaven's sake come.—Pyecraft."

"H'm," said I, and to tell the truth I was so pleased at the rehabilitation of my great-grandmother's reputation this evidently promised that I made a most excellent lunch.

I got Pyecraft's address from the hall porter. Pyecraft inhabited the upper half of a house in Bloomsbury, and I went there so soon as I had done my coffee and Trappistine. I did not wait to finish my cigar.

"Mr. Pyecraft?" said I, at the front door.

They believed he was ill; he hadn't been out for two days.

"He expects me," said I, and they sent me up.

I rang the bell at the lattice-door upon the landing.

"He shouldn't have tried it, anyhow," I said to myself. "A man who eats like a pig ought to look like a pig.'

An obviously worthy woman, with an anxious face and a carelessly placed cap, came and surveyed me through the lattice.

I gave my name and she opened his door for me in a dubious fashion.

"Well?" said I, as we stood together inside Pyecraft's piece of the landing.

"'E said you was to come in if you came," she said, and regarded me, making no motion to show me anywhere. And then, confidentially, "'E's locked in, sir."

"Locked in?"

"Locked himself in yesterday morning and 'asn't let anyone in since, sir. And ever and again *swearing*. Oh, my!"

I stared at the door she indicated by her glances. "In there?" I said.

"Yes, sir."

"What's up?"

She shook her head sadly. "'E keeps on calling for vittles, sir. '*Eavy* vittles 'e wants. I get 'im what I can. Pork 'e's 'ad, sooit puddin', sossiges, noo bread. Everythink like that. Left outside, if you please, and me go away. 'E's eatin' sir, something *awful*."

There came a piping bawl from inside the door: "That Formalyn?"

"That you, Pyecraft?" I shouted, and went and banged the door.

"Tell her to go away."

I did.

Then I could hear a curious pattering upon the door, almost like someone feeling for the handle in the dark, and Pyecraft's familiar grunts.

"It's all right," I said, "she's gone."

But for a long time the door didn't open.

I heard the key turn. Then Pyecraft's voice said, "Come in."

I turned the handle and opened the door. Naturally I expected to see Pyecraft.

Well, you know, he wasn't there!

I never had such a shock in my life. There was his sitting-room in a state of untidy disorder, plates and dishes among the books and writing things, and several chairs overturned, but Pyecraft——

"It's all right, o' man; shut the door," he said, and then I discovered him.

There he was right up close to the cornice in the corner by the door, as though someone had glued him to the ceiling. His face was anxious and angry. He panted and gesticulated. "Shut the door," he said. "If that woman gets hold of it——"

I shut the door, and went and stood away from him and stared.

"If anything gives way and you tumble down," I said, "you'll break your neck, Pyecraft."

"I wish I could," he wheezed.

"A man of your age and weight getting up to kiddish gymnastics——"

"Don't," he said, and looked agonized. "Your damned great-grandmother——"

"Be careful," I warned him.

"I'll tell you," he said, and gesticulated.

"How the deuce," said I, "are you holding on up there?"

And then abruptly I realized that he was not holding on at all, that he was floating up there—just as a gas-filled bladder might have floated in the same position. He began a struggle to thrust himself away from the ceiling and to clamber down the wall to me. "It's that prescription," he panted, as he did so. "Your great-gran——"

"*No!*" I cried.

He took hold of a framed engraving rather carelessly as he spoke and it gave way, and he flew back to the ceiling again, while the picture smashed on to the sofa. Bump he went against the ceiling, and I knew then why he was all over white on the more salient curves and angles of his person. He tried again more carefully, coming down by way of the mantel.

It was really a most extraordinary spectacle, that great, fat, apoplectic-looking man upside down and trying to get from the ceiling to the floor. "That prescription," he said. "Too successful."

"How?"

"Loss of weight—almost complete."

And then, of course, I understood.

"By Jove, Pyecraft," said I, "what you wanted was a cure for fatness! But you always called it weight. You would call it weight."

Somehow I was extremely delighted. I quite liked Pyecraft for the time. "Let me help you!" I said, and took his hand and pulled him down. He kicked about, trying to get foothold somewhere. It was very like holding a flag on a windy day.

"That table," he said, pointing, "is solid mahogany and very heavy. If you can put me under that——"

I did, and there he wallowed about like a captive balloon, while I stood on his hearthrug and talked to him.

I lit a cigar. "Tell me," I said, "what happened?"

"I took it," he said.

"How did it taste?"

"Oh, *beastly!*"

I should fancy they all did. Whether one regards the ingredients or the probable compound or the possible results, almost all my great-grandmother's remedies appear to me at least to be extraordinarily uninviting. For my own part——

"I took a little sip first."

"Yes?"

"And as I felt lighter and better after an hour, I decided to take the draught."

"My dear Pyecraft!"

"I held my nose," he explained. "And then I kept on getting lighter and lighter—and helpless, you know."

He gave way suddenly to a burst of passion. "What the goodness am I to *do?*" he said.

"There's one thing pretty evident," I said, "that you mustn't do. If you go out of doors you'll go up and up." I waved an arm upward. "They'd have to send Santos-Dumont after you to bring you down again."

"I suppose it will wear off?"

I shook my head. "I don't think you can count on that," I said.

And then there was another burst of passion, and he kicked out at adjacent chairs and banged the floor. He behaved just as I should have expected a great, fat, self-indulgent man to behave under trying circumstances—that is to say, very badly. He spoke of me and of my great-grandmother with an utter want of discretion.

"I never asked you to take the stuff," I said.

And generously disregarding the insults he was putting upon me, I sat down in his armchair and began to talk to him in a sober, friendly fashion.

I pointed out to him that this was a trouble he had brought upon himself, and that it had almost an air of poetical justice. He had eaten too much. This he disputed, and for a time we argued the point.

He became noisy and violent, so I desisted from this aspect of his lesson. "And then," said I, "you committed the sin of euphuism. You called it, not Fat, which is just and in-glorious, but Weight. You——"

He interrupted to say that he recognised all that. What was he to *do?*

I suggested he should adapt himself to his new conditions. So we came to the really sensible part of the business. I suggested that it would not be difficult for him to learn to walk about on the ceiling with his hands——

"I can't sleep," he said.

But that was no great difficulty. It was quite possible, I pointed out, to make a shake-up under a wire mattress, fasten the under things on with tapes, and have a blanket, sheet and coverlet to button at the side. He would have to confide in his housekeeper, I said; and after some squabbling he agreed to that. (Afterwards it was quite delightful to see the beautifully matter-of-fact way with which the good lady took all these amazing inversions.) He could have a library ladder in his room, and all his meals could be laid on the top of his bookcase. We also hit on an ingenious device by which he could get to the floor whenever he wanted, which was simply to put the *British Encyclopædia* (tenth edition) on the top of his open shelves. He just pulled out a couple of volumes and held on, and down he came. And we agreed there must be iron staples along the skirting, so that he could cling to those whenever he wanted to get about the room on the lower level.

As we got on with the thing I found myself almost keenly interested. It was I who called in the housekeeper and broke matters to her, and it was I chiefly who fixed up the inverted bed. In fact, I spent two whole days at his flat. I am a handy, interfering sort of a man with a screwdriver, and I made all sorts of ingenious adaptations for him—ran a wire to bring his bells within reach, turned all his electric lights up instead of down, and so on. The whole affair was extremely curious and interesting to me, and it was delightful to think of Pyecraft like some great, fat blow-fly, crawling about on his ceiling and clambering round the lintel of his doors from one room to another, and never, never, never coming to the club any more. . . .

Then, you know, my fatal ingenuity got the better of me. I was sitting by his fire drinking his whisky, and he was up in his favourite corner by the cornice, tacking a Turkey carpet to the ceiling, when the idea struck me. "By Jove, Pyecraft!" I said, "all this is totally unnecessary."

And before I could calculate the complete consequences

of my notion I blurted it out. "Lead underclothing," said I, and the mischief was done.

Pyecraft received the thing almost in tears. "To be right ways up again——" he said.

I gave him the whole secret before I saw where it would take me. "Buy sheet lead," I said, "stamp it into discs. Sew 'em all over your underclothes until you have enough. Have lead-soled boots, carry a bag of solid lead, and the thing is done! Instead of being a prisoner here you may go abroad again. Pyecraft; you may travel——"

A still happier idea came to me. "You need never fear a shipwreck. All you need do is just slip off some or all of your clothes, take the necessary amount of luggage in your hand, and float up in the air——"

In his emotion he dropped the tack-hammer within an ace of my head. "By Jove!" he said, "I shall be able to come back to the club again."

The thing pulled me up short. "By Jove!" I said, faintly. "Yes. Of course—you will."

He did. He does. There he sits behind me now, stuffing—as I live!—a third go of buttered teacake. And no one in the whole world knows—except his housekeeper and me—that he weighs practically nothing; that he is a mere boring mass of assimilatory matter, mere clouds in clothing, *niente*, *nefas*, the most inconsiderable of men. There he sits watching until I have done this writing. Then, if he can, he will waylay me. He will come billowing up to me. . . .

He will tell me over again all about it, how it feels, how it doesn't feel, how he sometimes hopes it is passing off a little. And always somewhere in that fat, abundant discourse he will say, "The secret's keeping, eh? If anyone knew of it—I should be so ashamed. . . . Makes a fellow look such a fool, you know. Crawling about on a ceiling and all that. . . ."

And now to elude Pyecraft, occupying, as he does, an admirable strategic position between me and the door.

THE NEW ACCELERATOR

CERTAINLY, if ever a man found a guinea when he was looking for a pin it is my good friend Professor Gibberne. I have heard before of investigators overshooting the mark, but never quite to the extent that he has done. He has really this time at any rate, without any touch of exaggeration in the phrase, found something to revolutionise human life. And that when he was simply seeking an all-round nervous stimulant to bring languid people up to the stresses of these pushful days. I have tasted the stuff now several times, and I cannot do better than describe the effect the thing had on me. That there are astonishing experiences in store for all in search of new sensations will become apparent enough.

Professor Gibberne, as many people know, is my neighbour in Folkestone. Unless my memory plays me a trick, his portrait at various ages has already appeared in *The Strand Magazine*—I think late in 1899; but I am unable to look it up because I have lent that volume to someone who has never sent it back. The reader may, perhaps, recall the high forehead and the singularly long black eyebrows that give such a Mephistophelian touch to his face. He occupies one of those pleasant detached houses in the mixed style that make the western end of the Upper Sandgate Road so interesting. His is the one with the Flemish gables and the Moorish portico, and it is in the room with the mullioned bay window that he works when he is down here, and in which of an evening we have so often smoked and talked together. He is a mighty jester, but, besides, he likes to talk to me about his work; he is one of those men who find a help and stimulus in talking, and so I have been able to follow the conception of the New Accelerator right up from a very early stage. Of course, the greater portion of his experimental work is not done in Folkestone, but in Gower Street, in the fine new laboratory next to the hospital that he has been the first to use.

As everyone knows, or at least as all intelligent people know, the special department in which Gibberne has gained so great and deserved a reputation among physiologists is the action of drugs upon the nervous system. Upon soporifics, sedatives, and anæsthetics he is, I am told, unequalled. He is also a chemist of considerable eminence, and I suppose in the subtle and complex jungle of riddles that centres about the ganglion cell and the axis fibre there are little cleared places of his making, glades of illumination, that, until he sees fit to publish his results, are inaccessible to every other living man. And in the last few years he has been particularly assiduous upon this question of nervous stimulants, and already, before the discovery of the New Accelerator, very successful with them. Medical science has to thank him for at least three distinct and absolutely safe invigorators of un-rivalled value to practising men. In cases of exhaustion the preparation known as Gibberne's B Syrup has, I suppose, saved more lives already than any lifeboat round the coast.

"But none of these things begin to satisfy me yet," he told me nearly a year ago. "Either they increase the central energy without affecting the nerves or they simply increase the available energy by lowering the nervous conductivity; and all of them are unequal and local in their operation. One wakes up the heart and viscera and leaves the brain stupefied, one gets at the brain champagne fashion and does nothing good for the solar plexus, and what I want—and what, if it's an earthly possibility, I mean to have—is a stimulant that stimulates all round, that wakes you up for a time from the crown of your head to the tip of your great toe, and makes you go two—or even three to everybody else's one. Eh? That's the thing I'm after."

"It would tire a man," I said.

"Not a doubt of it. And you'd eat double or treble—and all that. But just think what the thing would mean. Imagine yourself with a little phial like this"—he held up a bottle of green glass and marked his points with it—"and in this precious phial is the power to think twice as fast, move twice as quickly, do twice as much work in a given time as you could otherwise do."

"But is such a thing possible?"

"I believe so. If it isn't, I've wasted my time for a year. These various preparations of the hypophosphites, for example, seem to show that something of the sort. . . . Even if it was only one and a half times as fast it would do."

"It *would* do," I said.

"If you were a statesman in a corner, for example, time rushing up against you, something urgent to be done, eh?"

"He could dose his private secretary," I said.

"And gain—double time. And think if *you*, for example, wanted to finish a book."

"Usually," I said, "I wish I'd never begun 'em."

"Or a doctor, driven to death, wants to sit down and think out a case. Or a barrister—or a man cramming for an examination."

"Worth a guinea a drop," said I, "and more—to men like that."

"And in a duel again," said Gibberne, "where it all depends on your quickness in pulling the trigger.'

"Or in fencing," I echoed.

"You see," said Gibberne, "if I get it as an all-round thing it will really do you no harm at all—except perhaps to an infinitesimal degree it brings you nearer old age. You will just have lived twice to other people's once——"

"I suppose," I meditated, "in a duel—it would be fair?"

"That's a question for the seconds," said Gibberne.

I harked back further. "And you really think such a thing *is* possible?" I said.

"As possible," said Gibberne, and glanced at something that went throbbing by the window, "as a motorbus. As a matter of fact——"

He paused and smiled at me deeply, and tapped slowly on the edge of his desk with the green phial. "I think I know the stuff. . . . Already I've got something coming." The nervous smile upon his face betrayed the gravity of his revelation. He rarely talked of his actual experimental work unless things were very near the end. "And it may be, it may be— I shouldn't be surprised—it may even do the thing at a greater rate than twice."

"It will be rather a big thing," I hazarded.

"It will be, I think, rather a big thing."

But I don't think he quite knew what a big thing it was to be, for all that.

I remember we had several subsequent talks about the stuff. "The New Accelerator" he called it, and his tone about it grew more confident on each occasion. Sometimes he talked nervously of unexpected physiological results its use might have, and then he would get a bit unhappy; at others he was frankly mercenary, and we debated long and anxiously how the preparation might be turned to commercial account. "It's a good thing," said Gibberne, "a tremendous thing. I know I'm giving the world something, and I think it only reasonable we should expect the world to pay. The dignity of science is all very well, but I think somehow I must have the monopoly of the stuff for, say, ten years. I don't see why *all* the fun in life should go to the dealers in ham."

My own interest in the coming drug certainly did not wane in the time. I have always had a queer twist towards metaphysics in my mind. I have always been given to paradoxes about space and time, and it seemed to me that Gibberne was really preparing no less than the absolute acceleration of life. Suppose a man repeatedly dosed with such a preparation: he would live an active and record life indeed, but he would be an adult at eleven, middle-aged at twenty-five, and by thirty well on the road to senile decay. It seemed to me that so far Gibberne was only going to do for anyone who took his drug exactly what Nature has done for the Jews and Orientals, who are men in their teens and aged by fifty, and quicker in thought and act than we are all the time. The marvel of drugs has always been great to my mind; you can madden a man, calm a man, make him incredibly strong and alert or a helpless log, quicken this passion and allay that, all by means of drugs, and here was a new miracle to be added to this strange armoury of phials the doctors use! But Gibberne was far too eager upon his technical points to enter very keenly into my aspect of the question.

It was the 7th or 8th of August, when he told me the distillation that would decide his failure or success for a time was going forward as we talked, and it was on the 10th that he told me the thing was done and the New Accelerator a tangible reality in the world. I met him as I was going up the Sandgate Hill towards Folkestone—I think I was going to get my hair cut; and he came hurrying down to meet me—I suppose he was coming to my house to tell me at once of his success. I remember that his eyes were unusually bright and his face flushed, and I noted even then the swift alacrity of his step.

"It's done," he cried, and gripped my hand, speaking very fast; "it's more than done. Come up to my house and see."

"Really?"

"Really!" he shouted. "Incredibly! Come up and see."

"And it does—twice!"

"It does more, much more. It scares me. Come up and see the stuff. Taste it! Try it! It's the most amazing stuff on earth." He gripped my arm and, walking at such a pace that he forced me into a trot, went shouting with me up the hill. A whole charabancful of people turned and stared at us in unison after the manner of people in charabancs. It was one of those hot, clear days that Folkestone sees so much of, every colour incredibly bright and every outline hard. There was a breeze, of course, but not so much breeze as sufficed under these conditions to keep me cool and dry. I panted for mercy.

"I'm not walking fast, am I?" cried Gibberne, and slackened his pace to a quick march.

"You've been taking some of this stuff," I puffed.

"No," he said. "At the utmost a drop of water that stood in a beaker from which I had washed out the last traces of the stuff. I took some last night, you know. But that is ancient history, now."

"And it goes twice?" I said, nearing his doorway in a grateful perspiration.

"It goes a thousand times, many thousand times!" cried Gibberne, with a dramatic gesture, flinging open his Early English carved oak gate.

"Phew!" said I, and followed him to the door.

"I don't know how many times it goes," he said, with his latch-key in his hand.

"And you——"

"It throws all sorts of light on nervous physiology, it kicks the theory of vision into a perfectly new shape! . . . Heaven knows how many thousand times. We'll try all that after—— The thing is to try the stuff now."

"Try the stuff?" I said, as we went along the passage.

"Rather," said Gibberne, turning on me in his study. "There it is in that little green phial there! Unless you happen to be afraid?"

I am a careful man by nature, and only theoretically adventurous. I *was* afraid. But on the other hand there is pride.

"Well," I haggled. "You say you've tried it?"

"I've tried it," he said, "and I don't look hurt by it, do I? I don't even look livery and I *feel*——"

I sat down. "Give me the potion," I said. "If the worst comes to the worst it will save having my hair cut, and that I think is one of the most hateful duties of a civilised man. How do you take the mixture?"

"With water," said Gibberne, whacking down a carafe.

He stood up in front of his desk and regarded me in his easy chair; his manner was suddenly affected by a touch of the Harley Street specialist. "It's rum stuff, you know," he said.

I made a gesture with my hand.

"I must warn you in the first place as soon as you've got it down to shut your eyes, and open them very cautiously in a minute or so's time. One still sees. The sense of vision is a question of length of vibration, and not of multitude of impacts; but there's a kind of shock to the retina, a nasty giddy confusion just at the time if the eyes are open. Keep 'em shut."

"Shut," I said. "Good!"

"And the next thing is, keep still. Don't begin to whack about. You may fetch something a nasty rap if you do. Remember you will be going several thousand times faster than you ever did before, heart, lungs, muscles, brain—everything —and you will hit hard without knowing it. You won't know it, you know. You'll feel just as you do now. Only everything in the world will seem to be going ever so many thousand times slower than it ever went before. That's what makes it so deuced queer."

"Lor'," I said. "And you mean——"

"You'll see," said he, and took up a measure. He glanced at the material on his desk. "Glasses," he said, "water. All here. Mustn't take too much for the first attempt."

The little phial glucked out its precious contents. "Don't forget what I told you," he said, turning the contents of the measure into a glass in the manner of an Italian waiter measuring whisky. "Sit with the eyes tightly shut and in absolute stillness for two minutes," he said. "Then you will hear me speak."

He added an inch or so of water to the dose in each glass.

"By the bye," he said, "don't put your glass down. Keep it in your hand and rest your hand on your knee. Yes—so. And now——"

He raised his glass.

"The New Accelerator," I said.

"The New Accelerator," he answered, and we touched glasses and drank, and instantly I closed my eyes.

You know that blank non-existence into which one drops when one has taken "gas." For an indefinite interval it was like that. Then I heard Gibberne telling me to wake up, and I stirred and opened my eyes. There he stood as he had been standing, glass still in hand. It was empty, that was all the difference.

"Well?" said I.

"Nothing out of the way?"

"Nothing. A slight feeling of exhilaration, perhaps. Nothing more."

"Sounds?"

"Things are still," I said. "By Jove! yes! They *are* still. Except the sort of faint pat, patter, like rain falling on different things. What is it?"

"Analysed sounds," I think he said, but I am not sure. He glanced at the window. "Have you ever seen a curtain before a window fixed in that way before?"

I followed his eyes, and there was the end of the curtain, frozen, as it were, corner high, in the act of flapping briskly in the breeze.

"No," said I; "that's odd."

"And here," he said, and opened the hand that held the glass. Naturally I winced, expecting the glass to smash. But so far from smashing it did not even seem to stir; it hung in mid-air—motionless. "Roughly speaking," said Gibberne, "an object in these latitudes falls 16 feet in the first second. This glass is falling 16 feet in a second now. Only, you see, it hasn't been falling yet for the hundredth part of a second. That gives you some idea of the pace of my Accelerator." And he waved his hand round and round, over and under the slowly sinking glass. Finally he took it by the bottom, pulled it down and placed it very carefully on the table. "Eh?" he said to me, and laughed.

"That seems all right," I said, and began very gingerly to raise myself from my chair. I felt perfectly well, very light and comfortable, and quite confident in my mind. I was going fast all over. My heart, for example, was beating a thousand times a second, but that caused me no discomfort at all. I looked out of the window. An immovable cyclist, head down and with a frozen puff of dust behind his driving-wheel, scorched to overtake a galloping charabanc that did not stir. I gaped in amazement at this incredible spectacle. "Gibberne," I cried, "how long will this confounded stuff last?"

"Heaven knows!" he answered. "Last time I took it, I went to bed and slept it off. I tell you, I was frightened. It must have lasted some minutes, I think—it seemed like hours. But after a bit it slows down rather suddenly, I believe."

I was proud to observe that I did not feel frightened—I suppose because there were two of us. "Why shouldn't we go out?" I asked.

"Why not?"

"They'll see us."

"Not they. Goodness, no! Why, we shall be going a thousand times faster than the quickest conjuring trick that was ever done. Come along! Which way shall we go? Window, or door?"

And out by the window we went.

Assuredly of all the strange experiences that I have ever had, or imagined, or read of other people having or imagining, that little raid I made with Gibberne on the Folkestone Leas, under the influence of the New Accelerator, was the strangest and maddest of all. We went out by his gate into the road, and there we made a minute examination of the statuesque passing traffic. The tops of the wheels and some of the legs of the horses of this charabanc, the end of the whip-lash and the lower jaw of the conductor—who was just beginning to yawn—were perceptibly in motion, but all the rest of the lumbering conveyance seemed still. And quite noiseless except for a faint rattling that came from one man's throat! And as parts of this frozen edifice there were a driver, you know, and a conductor, and eleven people! The effect as we walked about the thing began by being madly queer and ended by being—disagreeable. There they were, people like ourselves and yet not like ourselves, frozen in careless attitudes, caught in mid-gesture. A girl and a man smiled at one another, a leering smile that threatened to last for ever-more; a woman in a floppy capelline rested her arm on the rail and stared at Gibberne's house with the unwinking stare of eternity; a man stroked his moustache like a figure of wax, and another stretched a tiresome stiff hand with extended fingers towards his loosened hat. We stared at them, we laughed at them, we made faces at them, and then a sort of disgust of them came upon us, and we turned away and walked round in front of the cyclist towards the Leas.

"Goodness!" cried Gibberne, suddenly; "look there!"

He pointed, and there at the tip of his finger and sliding down the air with wings flapping slowly and at the speed of an exceptionally languid snail—was a bee.

And so we came out upon the Leas. There the thing seemed madder than ever. The band was playing in the upper stand, though all the sound it made for us was a low-pitched, wheezy rattle, a sort of prolonged last sigh that passed at times into a sound like the slow, muffled ticking of some monstrous clock. Frozen people stood erect; strange, silent, self-conscious-looking dummies hung unstably in mid-stride, promenading upon the grass. I passed close to a poodle dog suspended in the act of leaping, and watched the slow movement of his legs as he sank to earth. "Lord, look *here!*" cried Gibberne, and we halted for a moment before a magnificent person in white faint-striped flannels, white shoes, and a Panama hat, who turned back to wink at two gaily-dressed ladies he had passed. A wink, studied with such leisurely deliberation as we could afford, is an unattractive thing. It loses any quality of alert gaiety, and one remarks that the winking eye does not completely close, that under its drooping lid appears the lower edge of an eyeball and a line of white. "Heaven give me memory," said I, "and I will never wink again."

"Or smile," said Gibberne, with his eye on the lady's answering teeth.

"It's infernally hot, somehow," said I. "Let's go slower."

"Oh, come along!" said Gibberne.

We picked our way among the Bath chairs in the path. Many of the people sitting in the chairs seemed almost natural in their passive poses, but the contorted scarlet of the bandsmen was not a restful thing to see. A purple-faced gentleman was frozen in the midst of a violent struggle to refold his newspaper against the wind; there were many evidences that all these people in their sluggish way were exposed to a considerable breeze, a breeze that had no existence so far as our sensations went. We came out and walked a little way from the crowd, and turned and regarded it. To see all that multitude changed to a picture, smitten rigid, as it were, into the semblance of realistic wax, was impossibly wonderful. It was absurd, of course; but it filled me with an irrational, an exultant sense of superior advantage. Consider the wonder of it! All that I had said and thought and done since the stuff had begun to work in my veins had happened, so far as those people, so far as the world in general went, in the twinkling of an eye. "The New Accelerator——" I began, but Gibberne interrupted me.

"There's that infernal old woman!" he said.

"What old woman?"

"Lives next door to me," said Gibberne. "Has a lapdog that yaps. Gods! The temptation is strong!"

There is something very boyish and impulsive about Gibberne at times. Before I could expostulate with him he had dashed forward, snatched the unfortunate animal out of visible existence, and was running violently with it towards the cliff of the Leas. It was most extraordinary. The little brute, you know, didn't bark or wriggle or make the slightest sign of vitality. It kept quite stiffly in an attitude of somnolent repose, and Gibberne held it by the neck. It was like running about with a dog of wood. "Gibberne," I cried, "put it down!" Then I said something else. "If you run like that, Gibberne," I cried, "you'll set your clothes on fire. Your linen trousers are going brown as it is!"

He clapped his hand on his thigh and stood hesitating on the verge. "Gibberne," I cried, coming up, "put it down. This heat is too much! It's our running so! Two or three miles a second! Friction of the air!"

"What?" he said, glancing at the dog.

"Friction of the air," I shouted. "Friction of the air. Going too fast. Like meteorites and things. Too hot. And, Gibberne! Gibberne! I'm all over pricking and a sort of perspiration. You can see people stirring slightly. I believe the stuff's working off! Put that dog down."

"Eh?" he said.

"It's working off," I repeated. "We're too hot and the stuff's working off! I'm wet through."

He stared at me. Then at the band, the wheezy rattle of whose performance was certainly going faster. Then with a tremendous sweep of the arm he hurled the dog away from him and it went spinning upward, still inanimate, and hung at last over the grouped parasols of a knot of chattering people. Gibberne was gripping my elbow. "By Jove!" he cried. "I believe it is! A sort of hot pricking and—yes. That man's moving his pocket-handkerchief! Perceptibly. We must get out of this sharp."

But we could not get out of it sharply enough. Luckily, perhaps! For we might have run, and if we had run we should, I believe, have burst into flames. Almost certainly we should have burst into flames! You know we had neither of us thought of that. . . . But before we could even begin to run the action of the drug had ceased. It was the business of a minute fraction of a second. The effect of the New Accelerator passed like the drawing of a curtain, vanished in the movement of a hand. I heard Gibberne's voice in infinite alarm. "Sit down," he said, and flop, down upon the turf at the edge of the Leas I sat—scorching as I sat. There is a patch of burnt grass there still where I sat down. The whole stagnation seemed to wake up as I did so, the disarticulated vibration of the band rushed together into a blast of music, the promenaders put their feet down and walked their ways, the papers and flags began flapping, smiles passed into words, the winker finished his wink and went on his way complacently, and all the seated people moved and spoke.

The whole world had come alive again, was going as fast as we were, or rather we were going no faster than the rest of the world. It was like slowing down as one comes into a railway station. Everything seemed to spin round for a second or two, I had the most transient feeling of nausea, and that was all. And the little dog which had seemed to hang for a moment when the force of Gibberne's arm was expended fell with a swift acceleration clean through a lady's parasol!

That was the saving of us. Unless it was for one corpulent

old gentleman in a Bath chair, who certainly did start at the sight of us and afterwards regarded us at intervals with a darkly suspicious eye, and finally, I believe, said something to his nurse about us, I doubt if a solitary person remarked our sudden appearance among them. Plop! We must have appeared abruptly. We ceased to smoulder almost at once, though the turf beneath me was uncomfortably hot. The attention of everyone—including even the Amusements' Association band, which on this occasion, for the only time in its history, got out of tune—was arrested by the amazing fact, and the still more amazing yapping and uproar caused by the fact, that a respectable, over-fed lapdog sleeping quietly to the east of the bandstand should suddenly fall through the parasol of a lady on the west—in a slightly singed condition due to the extreme velocity of its movements through the air. In these absurd days, too, when we are all trying to be as psychic and silly and superstitious as possible! People got up and trod on other people, chairs were overturned, the Leas policeman ran. How the matter settled itself, I do not know—we were much too anxious to disentangle ourselves from the affair and get out of range of the eye of the old gentleman in the Bath chair to make minute inquiries. As soon as we were sufficiently cool and sufficiently recovered from our giddiness and nausea and confusion of mind to do so we stood up and, skirting the crowd, directed our steps back along the road below the Metropole towards Gibberne's house. But amidst the din I heard very distinctly the gentleman who had been sitting beside the lady of the ruptured sunshade using quite unjustifiable threats and language to one of those chair-attendants who have "Inspector" written on their caps. "If you didn't throw the dog," he said, "who *did?*"

The sudden return of movement and familiar noises, and our natural anxiety about ourselves (our clothes were still dreadfully hot, and the fronts of the thighs of Gibberne's white trousers were scorched a drabbish brown), prevented the minute observations I should have liked to make on all these things. Indeed, I really made no observations of any scientific value on that return. The bee, of course, had gone. I looked for that cyclist, but he was already out of sight as we came into the Upper Sandgate Road or hidden from us by traffic; the charabanc, however, with its people now all alive and stirring, was clattering along at a spanking pace almost abreast of the nearer church.

We noted, however, that the window-sill on which we had stepped in getting out of the house was slightly singed, and that the impressions of our feet on the gravel of the path were unusually deep.

So it was I had my first experience of the New Accelerator. Practically we had been running about and saying and doing all sorts of things in the space of a second or so of time. We had lived half an hour while the band had played, perhaps, two bars. But the effect it had upon us was that the whole world had stopped for our convenient inspection. Considering all things, and particularly considering our rashness in venturing out of the house, the experience might certainly have been much more disagreeable than it was. It showed, no doubt, that Gibberne has still much to learn before his preparation is a manageable convenience, but its practicability it certainly demonstrated beyond all cavil.

Since that adventure he has been steadily bringing its use under control, and I have several times, and without the slightest bad result, taken measured doses under his direction; though I must confess I have not yet ventured abroad again while under its influence. I may mention, for example, that this story has been written at one sitting and without interruption, except for the nibbling of some chocolate, by its means. I began at 6:25, and my watch is now very nearly at the minute past the half-hour. The convenience of securing a long, uninterrupted spell of work in the midst of a day full of engagements cannot be exaggerated. Gibberne is now working at the quantitative handling of his preparation, with especial reference to its distinctive effects upon different types of constitution. He then hopes to find a Retarder with which to dilute its present rather excessive potency. The Retarder will, of course, have the reverse effect to the Accelerator; used alone it should enable the patient to spread a few seconds over many hours of ordinary time, and so to maintain an apathetic inaction, a glacierlike absence of alacrity, amidst the most animated or irritating surroundings. The two things together must necessarily work an entire revolution in civilised existence. It is the beginning of our escape from that Time Garment of which Carlyle speaks. While this Accelerator will enable us to concentrate ourselves with tremendous impact upon any moment or occasion that demands our utmost sense and vigour, the Retarder will enable us to pass in passive tranquillity through infinite hardship and tedium. Perhaps I am a little optimistic about the Retarder, which has indeed still to be discovered, but about the Accelerator there is no possible sort of doubt whatever. Its appearance upon the market in a convenient, controllable, and assimilable form is a matter of the next few months. It will be obtainable of all chemists and druggists, in small green bottles, at a high but, considering its extraordinary qualities, by no means excessive price. Gibberne's Nervous Accelerator it will be called, and he hopes to be able to supply it in three strengths: one in 200, one in 900, and one in 2000, distinguished by yellow, pink, and white labels respectively.

No doubt its use renders a great number of very extraordinary things possible; for, of course, the most remarkable and, possibly, even criminal proceedings may be effected with impunity by thus dodging, as it were, into the interstices of time. Like all potent preparations it will be liable to abuse. We have, however, discussed this aspect of the question very thoroughly, and we have decided that this is purely a matter of medical jurisprudence and altogether outside our province. We shall manufacture and sell the Accelerator, and, as for the consequences—we shall see.

THE STOLEN BODY

MR. BESSEL was the senior partner in the firm of Bessel, Hart, and Brown, of St. Paul's Churchyard, and for many years he was well known among those interested in psychical research as a liberal-minded and conscientious investigator. He was an unmarried man, and instead of living in the suburbs, after the fashion of his class, he occupied rooms in the Albany, near Piccadilly. He was particularly interested in the questions of thought transference and of apparitions of the living, and in November, 1896, he commenced a series of experiments in conjunction with Mr. Vincey, of Staple Inn, in order to test the alleged possibility of projecting an apparition of oneself by force of will through space.

Their experiments were conducted in the following manner: At a pre-arranged hour Mr. Bessel shut himself in one of his rooms in the Albany and Mr. Vincey in his sitting-room in Staple Inn, and each then fixed his mind as resolutely as possible on the other. Mr. Bessel had acquired the art of self-hypnotism, and, so far as he could, he attempted first to hypnotise himself and then to project himself as a "phantom of the living" across the intervening space of nearly two miles into Mr. Vincey's apartment. On several evenings this was tried without any satisfactory result, but on the fifth or sixth occasion Mr. Vincey did actually see or imagine he saw an apparition of Mr. Bessel standing in his room. He states that the appearance, although brief, was very vivid and real. He noticed that Mr. Bessel's face was white and his expression anxious, and, moreover, that his hair was disordered. For a moment Mr. Vincey, in spite of his state of expectation, was too surprised to speak or move, and in that moment it seemed to him as though the figure glanced over its shoulder and incontinently vanished.

It had been arranged that an attempt should be made to photograph any phantasm seen, but Mr. Vincey had not the instant presence of mind to snap the camera that lay ready on the table beside him, and when he did so he was too late. Greatly elated, however, even by this partial success, he made a note of the exact time, and at once took a cab to the Albany to inform Mr. Bessel of this result.

He was surprised to find Mr. Bessel's outer door standing open to the night, and the inner apartments lit and in an extraordinary disorder. An empty champagne magnum lay smashed upon the floor; its neck had been broken off against the inkpot on the bureau and lay beside it. An octagonal occasional table, which carried a bronze statuette and a number of choice books, had been rudely overturned, and down the primrose paper of the wall inky fingers had been drawn, as it seemed for the mere pleasure of defilement. One of the delicate chintz curtains had been violently torn from its rings and thrust upon the fire, so that the smell of its smouldering filled the room. Indeed the whole place was disarranged in the strangest fashion. For a few minutes Mr. Vincey, who had entered sure of finding Mr. Bessel in his easy chair awaiting him, could scarcely believe his eyes, and stood staring helplessly at these unanticipated things.

Then, full of a vague sense of calamity, he sought the porter at the entrance lodge. "Where is Mr. Bessel?" he asked. "Do you know that all the furniture is broken in Mr. Bessel's room?" The porter said nothing, but, obeying his gestures, came at once to Mr. Bessel's apartment to see the state of affairs. "This settles it," he said, surveying the lunatic confusion. "I didn't know of this. Mr. Bessel's gone off. He's mad!"

He then proceeded to tell Mr. Vincey that about half an hour previously, that is to say, at about the time of Mr. Bessel's apparition in Mr. Vincey's rooms, the missing gentleman had rushed out of the gates of the Albany into Vigo Street, hatless and with disordered hair, and had vanished in the direction of Bond Street. "And as he went past me," said the porter, "he laughed—a sort of gasping laugh, with his mouth open and his eyes glaring—I tell you, sir, he fair scared me!—like this."

According to his imitation it was anything but a pleasant laugh. "He waved his hand, with all his fingers crooked and clawing—like that. And he said, in a sort of fierce whisper, '*Life.*' Just that one word, '*Life* !'"

"Dear me," said Mr. Vincey. "Tut, tut," and "Dear me!" He could think of nothing else to say. He was naturally very much surprised. He turned from the room to the porter and from the porter to the room in the gravest perplexity. Beyond his suggestion that probably Mr. Bessel would come back presently and explain what had happened, their conversation was unable to proceed. "It might be a sudden toothache," said the porter, "a very sudden and violent toothache, jumping on him suddenly-like and driving him wild. I've broken things myself before now in such a case. . . ." He thought, "If it was, why should he say '*life*' to me as he went past?"

Mr. Vincey did not know. Mr. Bessel did not return, and at last Mr. Vincey, having done some more helpless staring, and having addressed a note of brief inquiry and left it in a conspicuous position on the bureau, returned in a very perplexed frame of mind to his own premises in Staple Inn. This affair had given him a shock. He was at a loss to account for Mr. Bessel's conduct on any sane hypothesis. He tried to read, but he could not do so; he went for a short walk, and was so preoccupied that he narrowly escaped a cab at the top of Chancery Lane; and at last—a full hour before his usual time—he went to bed. For a considerable time he could not sleep because of his memory of the silent confusion of Mr. Bessel's apartment, and when at length he did attain an uneasy slumber it was at once disturbed by a very vivid and distressing dream of Mr. Bessel.

He saw Mr. Bessel gesticulating wildly, and with his face white and contorted. And, inexplicably mingled with his appearance, suggested perhaps by his gestures, was an intense fear, an urgency to act. He even believes that he heard the voice of his fellow experimenter calling distress-fully to him, though at the time he considered this to be an illusion. The vivid impression remained though Mr. Vincey awoke. For a space he lay awake and trembling in the dark-ness, possessed with that vague, unaccountable terror of unknown possibilities that comes out of dreams upon even the bravest men. But at last he roused himself, and turned over and went to sleep again, only for the dream to return with enhanced vividness.

He awoke with such a strong conviction that Mr. Bessel was in overwhelming distress and need of help that sleep was no longer possible. He was persuaded that his friend had rushed out to some dire calamity. For a time he lay reasoning vainly against this belief, but at last he gave way to it. He arose, against all reason, lit his gas and dressed, and set out through the deserted streets—deserted, save for a noiseless policeman or so and the early news carts—towards Vigo Street to inquire if Mr. Bessel had returned.

But he never got there. As he was going down Long Acre some unaccountable impulse turned him aside out of that street towards Covent Garden, which was just waking to its nocturnal activities. He saw the market in front of him—a queer effect of glowing yellow lights and busy black figures. He became aware of a shouting, and perceived a figure turn the corner by the hotel and run swiftly towards him. He knew at once that it was Mr. Bessel. But it was Mr. Bessel trans-figured. He was hatless and dishevelled, his collar was torn open, he grasped a bone-handled walking-cane near the ferrule end, and his mouth was pulled awry. And he ran, with agile strides, very rapidly. Their encounter was the affair of an instant. "Bessel!" cried Vincey.

The running man gave no sign of recognition either of Mr. Vincey or of his own name. Instead, he cut at his friend sav-agely with the stick, hitting him in the face within an inch of the eye. Mr. Vincey, stunned and astonished, staggered back, lost his footing, and fell heavily on the pavement. It seemed to him that Mr. Bessel leapt over him as he fell. When he looked again Mr. Bessel had vanished, and a policeman and a number of garden porters and salesmen were rushing past towards Long Acre in hot pursuit.

With the assistance of several passers-by—for the whole street was speedily alive with running people—Mr. Vincey struggled to his feet. He at once became the centre of a crowd greedy to see his injury. A multitude of voices competed to reassure him of his safety, and then to tell him of the behaviour of the madman, as they regarded Mr. Bessel. He had suddenly appeared in the middle of the market screaming *"Life! Life!"* striking left and right with a blood-stained walking-stick, and dancing and shouting with laughter at each successful blow. A lad and two women had broken heads, and he had smashed a man's wrist; a little child had been knocked insensible, and for a time he had driven everyone before him, so furious and resolute had his behaviour been. Then he made a raid upon a coffee stall, hurled its paraffin flare through the window of the post office, and fled laughing, after stunning the foremost of the two policemen who had the pluck to charge him.

Mr. Vincey's first impulse was naturally to join in the pursuit of his friend, in order if possible to save him from the violence of the indignant people. But his action was slow, the blow had half-stunned him, and while this was still no more than a resolution came the news, shouted through the crowd, that Mr. Bessel had eluded his pursuers. At first Mr. Vincey could scarcely credit this, but the universality of the report, and presently the dignified return of two futile policemen, convinced him. After some aimless inquiries he returned towards Staple Inn, padding a handkerchief to a now very painful nose.

He was angry and astonished and perplexed. It appeared to him indisputable that Mr. Bessel must have gone violently mad in the midst of his experiment in thought transference, but why that should make him appear with a sad white face in Mr. Vincey's dreams seemed a problem beyond solution. He racked his brains in vain to explain this. It seemed to him at last that not simply Mr. Bessel, but the order of things must be insane. But he could think of nothing to do. He shut himself carefully into his room, lit his fire—it was a gas fire with asbestos bricks—and, fearing fresh dreams if he went to bed, remained bathing his injured face, or holding up books in a vain attempt to read, until dawn. Throughout that vigil he had a curious persuasion that Mr. Bessel was endeavouring to speak to him, but he would not let himself attend to any such belief.

About dawn, his physical fatigue asserted itself, and he went to bed and slept at last in spite of dreaming. He rose late, unrested and anxious, and in considerable facial pain. The morning papers had no news of Mr. Bessel's aberration—it had come too late for them. Mr. Vincey's perplexities, to which the fever of his bruise added fresh irritation, became at last intolerable, and, after a fruitless visit to the Albany, he went down to St. Paul's Churchyard to Mr. Hart, Mr. Bessel's partner, and so far as Mr. Vincey knew, his nearest friend.

He was surprised to learn that Mr. Hart, although he knew nothing of the outbreak, had also been disturbed by a vision, the very vision that Mr. Vincey had seen—Mr. Bissel, white and dishevelled, pleading earnestly by his gestures for help. That was his impression of the import of his signs. "I was just going to look him up in the Albany when you arrived," said Mr. Hart. "I was so sure of something being wrong with him."

As the outcome of their consultation the two gentlemen decided to inquire at Scotland Yard for news of their missing friend. "He is bound to be laid by the heels," said Mr. Hart. "He can't go on at that pace for long." But the police authorities had not laid Mr. Bessel by the heels. They confirmed Mr. Vincey's overnight experiences and added fresh circumstances, some of an even graver character than those he knew—a list of smashed glass along the upper half of Tottenham Court Road, an attack upon a policeman in Hampstead Road, and an atrocious assault upon a woman. All these outrages were committed between half-past twelve and a quarter to two in the morning, and between those hours—

and, indeed, from the very moment of Mr. Bessel's first rush from his rooms at half-past nine in the evening—they could trace the deepening violence of his fantastic career. For the last hour, at least from before one, that is, until a quarter to two, he had run amuck through London, eluding with amazing agility every effort to stop or capture him.

But after a quarter to two he had vanished. Up to that hour witnesses were multitudinous. Dozens of people had seen him, fled from him or pursued him, and then things suddenly came to an end. At a quarter to two he had been seen running down the Euston Road towards Baker Street, flourishing a can of burning colza oil and jerking splashes of flame therefrom at the windows of the houses he passed. But none of the policemen on Euston Road beyond the Waxwork Exhibition, nor any of those in the side streets down which he must have passed had he left the Euston Road, had seen anything of him. Abruptly he disappeared. Nothing of his subsequent doings came to light in spite of the keenest inquiry.

Here was a fresh astonishment for Mr. Vincey. He had found considerable comfort in Mr. Hart's conviction: "He is bound to be laid by the heels before long," and in that assurance he had been able to suspend his mental perplexities. But any fresh development seemed destined to add new impossibilities to a pile already heaped beyond the powers of his acceptance. He found himself doubting whether his memory might not have played him some grotesque trick, debating whether any of these things could possibly have happened; and in the afternoon he hunted up Mr. Hart again to share the intolerable weight on his mind. He found Mr. Hart engaged with a well-known private detective, but as that gentleman accomplished nothing in this case, we need not enlarge upon his proceedings.

All that day Mr. Bessel's whereabouts eluded an unceasingly active inquiry, and all that night. And all that day there was a persuasion in the back of Mr. Vincey's mind that Mr. Bessel sought his attention, and all through the night Mr.

Bessel with a tear-stained face of anguish pursued him through his dreams. And whenever he saw Mr. Bessel in his dreams he also saw a number of other faces, vague but malignant, that seemed to be pursuing Mr. Bessel.

It was on the following day, Sunday, that Mr. Vincey recalled certain remarkable stories of Mrs. Bullock, the medium who was then attracting attention for the first time in London. He determined to consult her. She was staying at the house of that well-known inquirer, Dr. Wilson Paget, and Mr. Vincey, although he had never met that gentleman before, repaired to him forthwith with the intention of invoking her help. But scarcely had he mentioned the name of Bessel when Doctor Paget interrupted him. "Last night—just at the end," he said, "we had a communication."

He left the room, and returned with a slate on which were certain words written in a handwriting, shaky indeed, but indisputably the handwriting of Mr. Bessel!

"How did you get this?" said Mr. Vincey. "Do you mean?——"

"We got it last night," said Doctor Paget. With numerous interruptions from Mr. Vincey, he proceeded to explain how the writing had been obtained. It appears that in her *séances*, Mrs. Bullock passes into a condition of trance, her eyes rolling up in a strange way under her eyelids, and her body becoming rigid. She then begins to talk very rapidly, usually in voices other than her own. At the same time one or both of her hands may become active, and if slates and pencils are provided they will then write messages simultaneously with and quite independently of the flow of words from her mouth. By many she is considered an even more remarkable medium than the celebrated Mrs. Piper. It was one of these messages, the one written by her left hand, that Mr. Vincey now had before him. It consisted of eight words written disconnectedly "George Bessel . . . trial excav^n" " . . . Baker Street . . . help . . . starvation." Curiously enough, neither Doctor Paget nor the two other inquirers who were present had heard of the disappearance of Mr. Bessel—the news of it appeared only in the evening papers of Saturday—and they had put the message aside with many others of a vague and enigmatical sort that Mrs. Bullock has from time to time delivered.

When Doctor Paget heard Mr. Vincey's story, he gave himself at once with great energy to the pursuit of this clue to the discovery of Mr. Bessel. It would serve no useful purpose here to describe the inquiries of Mr. Vincey and himself; suffice it that the clue was a genuine one, and that Mr. Bessel was actually discovered by its aid.

He was found at the bottom of a detached shaft which had been sunk and abandoned at the commencement of the work for the new electric railway near Baker Street Station. His arm and leg and two ribs were broken. The shaft is protected by a hoarding nearly 20 feet high, and over this, incredible as it seems, Mr. Bessel, a stout, middle-aged gentleman, must have scrambled in order to fall down the shaft. He was saturated in colza oil, and the smashed tin lay beside him, but luckily the flame had been extinguished by his fall. And his madness had passed from him altogether. But he was, of course, terribly enfeebled, and at the sight of his rescuers he gave way to hysterical weeping.

In view of the deplorable state of his flat, he was taken to the house of Doctor Hatton in Upper Baker Street. Here he was subjected to a sedative treatment, and anything that might recall the violent crisis through which he had passed was carefully avoided. But on the second day he volunteered a statement.

Since that occasion Mr. Bessel has several times repeated this statement—to myself among other people—varying the details as the narrator of real experiences always does, but never by any chance contradicting himself in any particular. And the statement he makes is in substance as follows.

In order to understand it clearly it is necessary to go back to his experiments with Mr. Vincey before his remarkable attack. Mr. Bessel's first attempts at self-projection, in his experiments with Mr. Vincey, were, as the reader will remember, unsuccessful. But through all of them he was concentrating all his power and will upon getting out of the

body—"willing it with all my might," he says. At last, almost
against expectation, came success. And Mr. Bessel asserts
that he, being alive, did actually, by an effort of will, leave his
body and pass into some place or state outside this world.

The release was, he asserts, instantaneous. "At one moment I was seated in my chair, with my eyes tightly shut, my
hands gripping the arms of the chair, doing all I could to
concentrate my mind on Vincey, and then I perceived myself outside my body—saw my body near me, but certainly
not containing me, with the hands relaxing and the head
drooping forward on the breast."

Nothing shakes him in his assurance of that release. He describes in a quiet, matter-of-fact way the new sensation he
experienced. He felt he had become impalpable—so much he
had expected, but he had not expected to find himself enormously large. So, however, it would seem he became. "I was
a great cloud—if I may express it that way—anchored to my
body. It appeared to me, at first, as if I had discovered a
greater self of which the conscious being in my brain was
only a little part. I saw the Albany and Piccadilly and Regent
Street and all the rooms and places in the houses, very minute
and very bright and distinct, spread out below me like a little
city seen from a balloon. Every now and then vague shapes
like drifting wreaths of smoke made the vision a little indistinct, but at first I paid little heed to them. The thing that
astonished me most, and which astonishes me still, is that I
saw quite distinctly the insides of the houses as well as the
streets, saw little people dining and talking in the private
houses, men and women dining, playing billiards, and drinking in restaurants and hotels, and several places of entertainment crammed with people. It was like watching the
affairs of a glass hive."

Such were Mr. Bessel's exact words as I took them down
when he told me the story. Quite forgetful of Mr. Vincey, he
remained for a space observing these things. Impelled by
curiosity, he says, he stooped down, and with the shadowy
arm he found himself possessed of attempted to touch a man
walking along Vigo Street. But he could not do so, though his

finger seemed to pass through the man. Something prevented his doing this, but what it was he finds it hard to describe. He compares the obstacle to a sheet of glass.

"I felt as a kitten may feel," he said, "when it goes for the first time to pat its reflection in a mirror." Again and again, on the occasion when I heard him tell this story, Mr. Bessel returned to that comparison of the sheet of glass. Yet it was not altogether a precise comparison, because, as the reader will speedily see, there were interruptions of this generally impermeable resistance, means of getting through the barrier to the material world again. But, naturally, there is a very great difficulty in expressing these unprecedented impressions in the language of everyday experience.

A thing that impressed him instantly, and which weighed upon him throughout all this experience, was the stillness of this place—he was in a world without sound.

At first Mr. Be sel's mental state was an unemotional wonder. His thought chiefly concerned itself with where he might be. He was out of the body—out of his material body, at any rate—but that was not all. He believes, and I for one believe also, that he was somewhere out of space, as we understand it, altogether. By a strenuous effort of will he had passed out of his body into a world beyond this world, a world undreamt of, yet lying so close to it and so strangely situated with regard to it that all things on this earth are clearly visible both from without and from within in this other world about us. For a long time, as it seemed to him, this realization occupied his mind to the exclusion of all other matters, and then he recalled the engagement with Mr. Vincey, to which this astonishing experience was, after all, but a prelude.

He turned his mind to locomotion in this new body in which he found himself. For a time he was unable to shift himself from his attachment to his earthly carcass. For a time this new strange cloud body of his simply swayed, contracted, expanded, coiled, and writhed with his efforts to free himself, and then quite suddenly the link that bound him snapped. For a moment everything was hidden by what appeared to be whirling spheres of dark vapour, and then through a momentary gap he saw his drooping body collapse limply, saw his lifeless head drop sideways, and found he was driving along like a huge cloud in a strange place of shadowy clouds that had the luminous intricacy of London spread like a model below.

But now he was aware that the fluctuating vapour about him was something more than vapour, and the temerarious excitement of his first essay was shot with fear. For he perceived, at first indistinctly, and then suddenly very clearly, that he was surrounded by *faces* ! that each roll and coil of the seeming cloud-stuff was a face. And such faces! Faces of thin shadow, faces of gaseous tenuity. Faces like those faces that glare with intolerable strangeness upon the sleeper in the evil hours of his dreams. Evil, greedy eyes that were full of a covetous curiosity, faces with knit brows and snarling, smiling lips; their vague hands clutched at Mr. Bessel as he passed, and the rest of their bodies was but an elusive streak of trailing darkness. Never a word they said, never a sound from the mouths that seemed to gibber. All about him they pressed in that dreamy silence, passing freely through the dim mistiness that was his body, gathering ever more numerously about him. And the shadowy Mr. Bessel, now suddenly fear-stricken, drove through the silent, active multitude of eyes and clutching hands.

So inhuman were these faces, so malignant their staring eyes and shadowy, clawing gestures, that it did not occur to Mr. Bessel to attempt intercourse with these drifting creatures. Idiot phantoms, they seemed, children of vain desire, beings unborn and forbidden the boon of being, whose only expressions and gestures told of the envy and craving for life that was their one link with existence.

It says much for his resolution that, amidst the swarming cloud of these noiseless spirits of evil, he could still think of Mr. Vincey. He made a violent effort of will and found himself, he knew not how, stooping towards Staple Inn, saw Vincey sitting attentive and alert in his armchair by the fire.

And clustering also about him, as they clustered ever about all that lives and breathes, was another multitude of these vain voiceless shadows, longing, desiring, seeking some loophole into life.

For a space Mr. Bessel sought ineffectually to attract his friend's attention. He tried to get in front of his eyes, to move the objects in his room, to touch him. But Mr. Vincey remained unaffected, ignorant of the being that was so close to his own. The strange something that Mr. Bessel has compared to a sheet of glass separated them impermeably.

And at last Mr. Bessel did a desperate thing. I have told how that in some strange way he could see not only the outside of a man as we see him, but within. He extended his shadowy hand and thrust his vague black fingers, as it seemed, through the heedless brain.

Then, suddenly, Mr. Vincey started like a man who recalls his attention from wandering thoughts, and it seemed to Mr. Bessel that a little dark-red body situated in the middle of Mr. Vincey's brain swelled and glowed as he did so. Since that experience he has been shown anatomical figures of the brain, and he knows now that this is that useless structure, as doctors call it, the pineal eye. For, strange as it will seem to many, we have, deep in our brains—where it cannot possibly see any earthly light—an eye! At the time this, with the rest of the internal anatomy of the brain, was quite new to him. At the sight of its changed appearance, however, he thrust forth his finger, and, rather fearful still of the consequences, touched this little spot. And instantly Mr. Vincey started, and Mr. Bessel knew that he was seen.

And at that instant it came to Mr. Bessel that evil had happened to his body, and behold! a great wind blew through all that world of shadows and tore him away. So strong was this persuasion that he thought no more of Mr. Vincey, but turned about forthwith, and all the countless faces drove back with him like leaves before a gale. But he returned too late. In an instant he saw the body that he had left inert and collapsed—lying, indeed, like the body of a man just dead —had arisen, had arisen by virtue of some strength and will beyond his own. It stood with staring eyes, stretching its limbs in dubious fashion.

For a moment he watched it in wild dismay, and then he stooped towards it. But the pane of glass had closed against him again, and he was foiled. He beat himself passionately against this, and all about him the spirits of evil grinned and pointed and mocked. He gave way to furious anger. He compares himself to a bird that has fluttered heedlessly into a room and is beating at the window-pane that holds it back from freedom.

And behold! the little body that had once been his was now dancing with delight. He saw it shouting, though he could not hear its shouts; he saw the violence of its movements grow. He watched it fling his cherished furniture about in the mad delight of existence, rend his books apart, smash bottles, drink heedlessly from the jagged fragments, leap and smite in a passionate acceptance of living. He watched these actions in paralysed astonishment. Then once more he hurled himself against the impassable barrier, and then, with all that crew of mocking ghosts about him, hurried back in dire confusion to Vincey to tell him of the outrage that had come upon him.

But the brain of Vincey was now closed against apparitions, and the disembodied Mr. Bessel pursued him in vain as he hurried out into Holborn to call a cab. Foiled and terror-stricken, Mr. Bessel swept back again, to find his desecrated body whooping in a glorious frenzy down the Burlington Arcade. . . .

And now the attentive reader begins to understand Mr. Bessel's interpretation of the first part of this strange story. The being whose frantic rush through London had inflicted so much injury and disaster had indeed Mr. Bessel's body, but it was not Mr. Bessel. It was an evil spirit out of that strange world beyond existence, into which Mr. Bessel had so rashly ventured. For twenty hours it held possession of him, and for all those twenty hours the dispossessed spirit-body of Mr. Bessel was going to and fro in that unheard-of middle world of shadows seeking help in vain.

He spent many hours beating at the minds of Mr. Vincey

and of his friend Mr. Hart. Each, as we know, he roused by his efforts. But the language that might convey his situation to these helpers across the gulf he did not know; his feeble fingers groped vainly and powerlessly in their brains. Once, indeed, as we have already told, he was able to turn Mr. Vincey aside from his path so that he encountered the stolen body in its career, but he could not make him understand the thing that had happened: he was unable to draw any help from that encounter. . . .

All through those hours the persuasion was overwhelming in Mr. Bessel's mind that presently his body would be killed by its furious tenant, and he would have to remain in this shadow-land for evermore. So that those long hours were a growing agony of fear. And ever as he hurried to and fro in his ineffectual excitement innumerable spirits of that world about him mobbed him and confused his mind. And ever an envious applauding multitude poured after their successful fellow as he went upon his glorious career.

For that, it would seem, must be the life of these bodiless things of this world that is the shadow of our world. Ever they watch, coveting a way into a mortal body, in order that they may descend, as furies and frenzies, as violent lusts and mad, strange impulses, rejoicing in the body they have won. For Mr. Bessel was not the only human soul in that place. Witness the fact that he met first one, and afterwards several shadows of men, men like himself, it seemed, who had lost their bodies even it may be as he had lost his, and wandered, despairingly, in that lost world that is neither life nor death. They could not speak because that world is silent, yet he knew them for men because of their dim human bodies, and because of the sadness of their faces.

But how they had come into that world he could not tell, nor where the bodies they had lost might be, whether they still raved about the earth, or whether they were closed for ever in death against return. That they were the spirits of the dead neither he nor I believe. But Dr. Wilson Paget thinks they are the rational souls of men who are lost in madness on the earth.

At last Mr. Bessel chanced upon a place where a little crowd of such disembodied silent creatures was gathered, and thrusting through them he saw below a brightly-lit room, and four or five quiet gentlemen and a woman, a stoutish woman dressed in black bombazine and sitting awkwardly in a chair with her head thrown back. He knew her from her portraits to be Mrs. Bullock, the medium. And he perceived that tracts and structures in her brain glowed and stirred as he had seen the pineal eye in the brain of Mr. Vincey glow. The light was very fitful; sometimes it was a broad illumination, and sometimes merely a faint twilight spot, and it shifted slowly about her brain. She kept on talking and writing with one hand. And Mr. Bessel saw that the crowding shadows of men about him, and a great multitude of the shadow spirits of that shadow land, were all striving and thrusting to touch the lighted regions of her brain. As one gained her brain or another was thrust away, her voice and the writing of her hand changed. So that what she said was disorderly and confused for the most part; now a fragment of one soul's message, and now a fragment of another's, and now she babbled the insane fancies of the spirits of vain desire. Then Mr. Bessel understood that she spoke for the spirit that had touch of her, and he began to struggle very furiously towards her. But he was on the outside of the crowd and at that time he could not reach her, and at last, growing anxious, he went away to find what had happened meanwhile to his body.

For a long time he went to and fro seeking it in vain and fearing that it must have been killed, and then he found it at the bottom of the shaft in Baker Street, writhing furiously and cursing with pain. Its leg and an arm and two ribs had been broken by its fall. Moreover, the evil spirit was angry because his time had been so short and because of the pain— making violent movements and casting his body about.

And at that Mr. Bessel returned with redoubled earnestness to the room where the *séance* was going on, and so soon as he had thrust himself within sight of the place he saw one of the men who stood about the medium looking at his watch as if he meant that the *séance* should presently end. At that a great number of the shadows who had been striving turned away with gestures of despair. But the thought that the *séance* was almost•over only made Mr. Bessel the more earnest, and he struggled so stoutly with his will against the others that presently he gained the woman's brain. It chanced that just at that moment it glowed very brightly, and in that instant she wrote the message that Dr. Wilson Paget preserved. And then the other shadows and the cloud of evil spirits about him had thrust Mr. Bessel away from her, and for all the rest of the *séance* he could regain her no more.

So he went back and watched through the long hours at the bottom of the shaft where the evil spirit lay in the stolen body it had maimed, writhing and cursing, and weeping and groaning, and learning the lesson of pain. And towards dawn the thing he had waited for happened, the brain glowed brightly and the evil spirit came out, and Mr. Bessel entered the body he had feared he should never enter again. As he did so, the silence—the brooding silence—ended; he heard the tumult of traffic and the voices of people overhead, and that strange world that is the shadow of our world—the dark and silent shadows of ineffectual desire and the shadows of lost men—vanished clean away.

He lay there for the space of about three hours before he was found. And in spite of the pain and suffering of his wounds and of the dim damp place in which he lay; in spite of the tears—wrung from him by his physical distress—his heart was full of gladness to know that he was nevertheless back once more in the kindly world of men.

THE DREAM

A Dream of Armageddon

THE man with the white face entered the carriage at Rugby.
He moved slowly in spite of the urgency of his porter, and
even while he was still on the platform I noted how ill he
seemed. He dropped into the corner over against me with a
sigh, made an incomplete attempt to arrange his travelling
shawl, and became motionless, with his eyes staring vacantly.
Presently he was moved by a sense of my observation, looked
up at me, and put out a spiritless hand for his newspaper.
Then he glanced again in my direction.

I feigned to read. I feared I had unwittingly embarrassed
him, and in a moment I was surprised to find him speaking.

"I beg your pardon?" said I.

"That book," he repeated, pointing a lean finger, "is about
dreams."

"Obviously," I answered, for it was Fortnum-Roscoe's
Dream States, and the title was on the cover.

He hung silent for a space as if he sought words. "Yes,"
he said at last, "but they tell you nothing."

I did not catch his meaning for a second.

"They don't know," he added.

I looked a little more attentively at his face.

"There are dreams," he said, "and dreams."

That sort of proposition I never dispute.

"I suppose——" he hesitated. "Do you ever dream? I
mean vividly."

"I dream very little," I answered. "I doubt if I have three
vivid dreams a year."

"Ah!" he said, and seemed for a moment to collect his
thoughts.

"Your dreams don't mix with your memories?" he asked

888

abruptly. "You don't find yourself in doubt; did this happen or did it not?"

"Hardly ever. Except just for a momentary hesitation now and then. I suppose few people do."

"Does *he* say——" he indicated the book.

"Says it happens at times and gives the usual explanation about intensity of impression and the like to account for its not happening as a rule. I suppose you know something of these theories——"

"Very little—except that they are wrong."

His emaciated hand played with the strap of the window for a time. I prepared to resume reading, and that seemed to precipitate his next remark. He leant forward almost as though he would touch me.

"Isn't there something called consecutive dreaming—that goes on night after night?"

"I believe there is. There are cases given in most books on mental trouble."

"Mental trouble! Yes. I dare say there are. It's the right place for them. But what I mean——" He looked at his bony knuckles. "Is that sort of thing always dreaming? *Is* it dreaming? Or is it something else? Mightn't it be something else?"

I should have snubbed his persistent conversation but for the drawn anxiety of his face. I remember now the look of his faded eyes and the lids red stained—perhaps you know that look.

"I'm not just arguing about a matter of opinion," he said. "The thing's killing me."

"Dreams?"

"If you call them dreams. Night after night. Vivid!—so vivid . . . this"— (he indicated the landscape that went streaming by the window) "seems unreal in comparison! I can scarcely remember who I am, what business I am on. . . ."

He paused. "Even now——"

"The dream is always the same—do you mean?" I asked.

"It's over."

"You mean?"

"I died."

"Died?"

"Smashed and killed, and now, so much of me as that dream was, is dead. Dead for ever. I dreamt I was another man, you know, living in a different part of the world and in a different time. I dreamt that night after night. Night after night I woke into that other life. Fresh scenes and fresh happenings—until I came upon the last——"

"When you died?"

"When I died."

"And since then——"

"No," he said. "Thank God! That was the end of the dream. . . ."

It was clear I was in for this dream. And after all, I had an hour before me, the light was fading fast, and Fortnum-Roscoe has a dreary way with him. "Living in a different time," I said: "do you mean in some different age?"

"Yes."

"Past?"

"No—to come—to come."

"The year three thousand, for example?"

"I don't know what year it was. I did when I was asleep, when I was dreaming, that is, but not now—not now that I am awake There's a lot of things I have forgotten since I woke out of these dreams, though I knew them at the time when I was—I suppose it was dreaming. They called the year differently from our way of calling the year. . . . What *did* they call it?" He put his hand to his forehead. "No," said he. "I forget."

He sat smiling weakly. For a moment I feared he did not mean to tell me his dream. As a rule I hate people who tell their dreams, but this struck me differently. I proffered assistance even. "It began——" I suggested.

"It was vivid from the first. I seemed to wake up in it suddenly. And it's curious that in these dreams I am speaking of I never remembered this life I am living now. It seemed as if the dream life was enough while it lasted. Perhaps—— But I will tell you how I find myself when I do my best to recall it all. I don't remember anything clearly until I found myself sitting in a sort of loggia looking out over the sea. I had been dozing, and suddenly I woke up!—fresh and vivid—not a bit dreamlike—because the girl had stopped fanning me."

"The girl?"

"Yes, the girl. You must not interrupt or you will put me out."

He stopped abruptly. "You won't think I'm mad?" he said.

"No," I answered; "you've been dreaming. Tell me your dream."

"I woke up, I say, because the girl had stopped fanning me. I was not surprised to find myself there or anything of that sort, you understand. I did not feel I had fallen into it suddenly. I simply took it up at that point. Whatever memory I had of *this* life, this nineteenth-century life, faded as I woke, vanished like a dream. I knew all about myself, knew that my name was no longer Cooper but Hedon, and all about my position in the world. I've forgotten a lot since I woke—there's a want of connection—but it was all quite clear and matter of fact then."

He hesitated again, gripping the window strap, putting his face forward and looking up to me appealingly.

"This seems bosh to you?"

"No, no!" I cried. "Go on. Tell me what this loggia was like."

"It was not really a loggia—I don't know what to call it. It faced south. It was small. It was all in shadow except the semicircle above the balcony that showed the sky and sea and the corner where the girl stood. I was on a couch—it was a metal couch with light striped cushions—and the girl was leaning over the balcony with her back to me. The light of the sunrise fell on her ear and cheek. Her pretty white neck and the little curls that nestled there, and her white shoulder were in the sun, and all the grace of her body was in the cool blue shadow. She was dressed—how can I describe it? It was easy and flowing. And altogether there she stood, so that it came to me how beautiful and desirable she was, as though I had never seen her before. And when at last I sighed and raised myself upon my arm she turned her face to me——"

He stopped.

"I have lived three-and-fifty years in this world. I have had mother, sisters, friends, wife, and daughters—all their faces, the play of their faces, I know. But the face of this girl —it is much more real to me. I can bring it back into memory so that I see it again—I could draw it or paint it. And after all——"

He stopped—but I said nothing.

"The face of a dream—the face of a dream. She was beautiful. Not that beauty which is terrible, cold, and worshipful, like the beauty of a saint; nor that beauty that stirs fierce passions; but a sort of radiation, sweet lips that softened into smiles, and grave grey eyes. And she moved gracefully, she seemed to have part with all pleasant and gracious things——"

He stopped, and his face was downcast and hidden. Then he looked up at me and went on, making no further attempt to disguise his absolute relief in the reality of his story.

"You see, I had thrown up my plans and ambitions, thrown up all I had ever worked for or desired for her sake. I had been a master man away there in the north, with influence and property and a great reputation, but none of it had seemed worth having beside her. I had come to the place, this city of sunny pleasures, with her, and left all those things to wreck and ruin just to save a remnant at least of my life. While I had been in love with her before I knew that she had any care for me, before I had imagined that she would dare— that we should dare, all my life had seemed vain and hollow, dust and ashes. It *was* dust and ashes. Night after night and through the long days I had longed and desired—my soul had beaten against the thing forbidden!

"But it is impossible for one man to tell another just these things. It's emotion, it's a tint, a light that comes and goes. Only while it's there, everything changes, everything. The thing is I came away and left them in their Crisis to do what they could."

"Left whom?" I asked, puzzled.

"The people up in the north there. You see—in this **dream**, anyhow—I had been a big man, the sort of man men come to trust in, to group themselves about. Millions of men who had never seen me were ready to do things and risk things because of their confidence in me. I had been playing that game for years, that big laborious game, that vague, monstrous political game, amidst intrigues and betrayals, speech and agitation. It was a vast weltering world, and at last I had a sort of leadership against the Gang—you know it was called the Gang—a sort of compromise of scoundrelly projects and base ambitions and vast public emotional stupidities and catchwords—the Gang that kept the world noisy and blind year by year, and all the while that it was drifting, drifting towards infinite disaster. But I can't expect you to understand the shades and complications of the year—the year something or other ahead. I had it all—down to the smallest details—in my dream. I suppose I had been dreaming of it before I awoke, and the fading outline of some queer new development I had imagined still hung about me as I rubbed my eyes. It was some grubby affair that made me thank God for the sunlight. I sat up on the couch and remained looking at the woman and rejoicing—rejoicing that I had come away out of all that tumult and folly and violence before it was too late. After all, I thought, this is life—love and beauty, desire and delight, are they not worth all those dismal struggles for vague gigantic ends. And I blamed myself for having ever sought to be a leader when I might have given my days to love. But then, thought I, if I had not spent my early days sternly and austerely, I might have wasted myself upon vain and worthless women, and at the thought all my being went out in love and tenderness to my dear mistress, my dear lady, who had come at last and compelled me—compelled me by her invincible charm for me—to lay that life aside.

"'You are worth it,' I said, speaking without intending her to hear; 'you are worth it, my dearest one; worth pride and praise and all things. Love! to have *you* is worth them all together.' And at the murmur of my voice she turned about.

"'Come and see,' she cried—I can hear her now—'come and see the sunrise upon Monte Solaro.'

"I remember how I sprang to my feet and joined her at the balcony. She put a white hand upon my shoulder and pointed towards great masses of limestone, flushing, as it were, into life. I looked. But first I noted the sunlight on her face caressing the lines of her cheeks and neck. How can I describe to you the scene we had before us? We were at Capri——"

"I have been there," I said. "I have clambered up Monte Solaro and drunk *vero Capri*—muddy stuff like cider—at the summit."

"Ah!" said the man with the white face; "then perhaps you can tell me—you will know if this was indeed Capri. For in this life I have never been there. Let me describe it. We were in a little room, one of a vast multitude of little rooms, very cool and sunny, hollowed out of the limestone of a sort of cape, very high above the sea. The whole island, you know, was one enormous hotel, complex beyond explaining, and on the other side there were miles of floating hotels, and huge floating stages to which the flying-machines came. They called it a pleasure city. Of course, there was none of that in your time—rather, I should say, *is* none of that *now*. Of course. Now!—yes.

"Well, this room of ours was at the extremity of the cape, so that one could see east and west. Eastward was a great cliff—a thousand feet high, perhaps—coldly grey except for one bright edge of gold, and beyond it the Isle of the Sirens, and a falling coast that faded and passed into the hot sunrise. And when one turned to the west, distinct and near was a little bay, a scimitar of beach still in shadow. And out of that shadow rose Solaro straight and tall, flushed and golden crested, like a beauty throned, and the white moon was floating behind her in the sky. And before us from east to west stretched the many-tinted sea all dotted with sailing boats.

"To the eastward, of course, these little boats were grey and very minute and clear, but to the westward they were little boats of gold—shining gold—almost like little flames.

And just below us was a rock with an arch worn through it.
The blue sea-water broke to green and foam all round the
rock, and a galley came gliding out of the arch."

"I know that rock," I said. "I was nearly drowned there.
It is called the Faraglioni."

"*I Faraglioni?* Yes, *she* called it that," answered the man
with the white face. "There was some story—but that——"

He put his hand to his forehead again. "No," he said, "I
forget that story.

"Well, that is the first thing I remember, the first dream I
had, that shaded room and the beautiful air and sky and that
dear lady of mine, with her shining arms and her graceful
robe, and how we sat and talked in half-whispers to one another. We talked in whispers not because there was anyone
to hear, but because there was still such a freshness of mind
between us that our thoughts were a little frightened, I think,
to find themselves at last in words. And so they went softly.

"Presently we were hungry and we went from our apartment, going by a strange passage with a moving floor, until
we came to the great breakfast-room—there was a fountain
and music. A pleasant and joyful place it was, with its sunlight and splashing, and the murmur of plucked strings. And
we sat and ate and smiled at one another, and I would not
heed a man who was watching me from a table near by.

"And afterwards we went on to the dancing-hall. But I
cannot describe that hall. The place was enormous—larger
than any building you have ever seen—and in one place there
was the old gate of Capri, caught into the wall of a gallery
high overhead. Light girders, stems and threads of gold, burst
from the pillars like fountains, streamed like an Aurora across
the roof and interlaced, like—like conjuring tricks. All about
the great circle for the dancers there were beautiful figures,
strange dragons, and intricate and wonderful grotesques
bearing lights. The place was inundated with artificial light
that shamed the newborn day. And as we went through the
throng the people turned about and looked at us, for all
through the world my name and face were known, and how
I had suddenly thrown up pride and struggle to come to this

place. And they looked also at the lady beside me, though hal
the story of how at last she had come to me was unknown o
mistold. And few of the men who were there, I know, bu
judged me a happy man, in spite of all the shame and dis
honour that had come upon my name.

"The air was full of music, full of harmonious scents, ful
of the rhythm of beautiful motions. Thousands of beautifu
people swarmed about the hall, crowded the galleries, sat i
a myriad recesses; they were dressed in splendid colours an
crowned with flowers; thousands danced about the great circl
beneath the white images of the ancient gods, and gloriou
processions of youths and maidens came and went. We tw
danced, not the dreary monotonies of your days—of thi
time, I mean,—but dances that were beautiful, intoxicating
And even now I can see my lady dancing—dancing joyously
She danced, you know, with a serious face; she danced wit
a serious dignity, and yet she was smiling at me and caressin
me—smiling and caressing with her eyes.

"The music was different," he murmured. "It went—
cannot describe it; but it was infinitely richer and more varie
than any music that has ever come to me awake.

"And then—it was when we had done dancing—a ma
came to speak to me. He was a lean, resolute man, very so
berly clad for that place, and already I had marked his fac
watching me in the breakfasting hall, and afterwards as w
went along the passage I had avoided his eye. But now, as w
sat in an alcove, smiling at the pleasure of all the people wh
went to and fro across the shining floor, he came and touche
me, and spoke to me so that I was forced to listen. And h
asked that he might speak to me for a while apart.

"'No,' I said. 'I have no secrets from this lady. What d
you want to tell me?'

"He said it was a trivial matter, or at least a dry matter
for a lady to hear.

"'Perhaps for me to hear,' said I.

"He glanced at her, as though almost he would appeal t
her. Then he asked me suddenly if I had heard of a great an
avenging declaration that Evesham had made. Now, Eves

ham had always before been the man next to myself in the leadership of that great party in the north. He was a forcible, hard, and tactless man, and only I had been able to control and soften him. It was on his account even more than my own, I think, that the others had been so dismayed at my retreat. So this question about what he had done reawakened my old interest in the life I had put aside just for a moment.

"'I have taken no heed of any news for many days,' I said. 'What has Evesham been saying?'

"And with that the man began, nothing loth, and I must confess even I was struck by Evesham's reckless folly in the wild and threatening words he had used. And this messenger they had sent to me not only told me of Evesham's speech, but went on to ask counsel and to point out what need they had of me. While he talked, my lady sat a little forward and watched his face, and mine

"My old habits of scheming and organising reasserted themselves. I could even see myself suddenly returning to the north, and all the dramatic effect of it. All that this man said witnessed to the disorder of the party indeed, but not to its damage. I should go back stronger than I had come. And then I thought of my lady. You see—how can I tell you? There were certain peculiarities of our relationship—as things are I need not tell you about that—which would render her presence with me impossible. I should have had to leave her; indeed, I should have had to renounce her clearly and openly, if I was to do all that I could do in the north. And the man knew *that*, even as he talked to her and me, knew it as well as she did, that my steps to duty were—first, separation, then abandonment. At the touch of that thought my dream of a return was shattered. I turned on the man suddenly, as he was imagining his eloquence was gaining ground with me.

"'What have I to do with these things now?' I said. 'I have done with them. Do you think I am coquetting with your people in coming here?'

"'No,' he said; 'but——'

"'Why cannot you leave me alone. I have done with these things. I have ceased to be anything but a private man.'

"'Yes,' he answered. 'But have you thought?—this talk of war, these reckless challenges, these wild aggressions——'

"I stood up.

"'No,' I cried. 'I won't hear you. I took count of all those things, I weighed them—and I have come away.'

"He seemed to consider the possibility of persistence. He looked from me to where the lady sat regarding us.

"'War,' he said, as if he were speaking to himself, and then turned slowly from me and walked away.

"I stood, caught in the whirl of thoughts his appeal had set going.

"I heard my lady's voice.

"'Dear,' she said; 'but if they have need of you——'

"She did not finish her sentence, she let it rest there. I turned to her sweet face, and the balance of my mood swayed and reeled.

"'They want me only to do the thing they dare not do themselves,' I said. 'If they distrust Evesham they must settle with him themselves.'

"She looked at me doubtfully.

"'But war——' she said.

"I saw a doubt on her face that I had seen before, a doubt of herself and me, the first shadow of the discovery that, seen strongly and completely, must drive us apart for ever.

"Now I was an older mind than hers, and I could sway her to this belief or that.

"'My dear one,' I said, 'you must not trouble over these things. There will be no war. Certainly there will be no war. The age of wars is past. Trust me to know the justice of this case. They have no right upon me, dearest, and no one has a right upon me. I have been free to choose my life, and I have chosen this.'

"'But *war*——' she said.

"I sat down beside her. I put an arm behind her and took her hand in mine. I set myself to drive that doubt away—I set myself to fill her mind with pleasant things again. I lied to her, and in lying to her I lied also to myself. And she was only too ready to believe me, only too ready to forget.

"Very soon the shadow had gone again, and we were hastening to our bathing-place in the Grotta del Bove Marino, where it was our custom to bathe every day. We swam and splashed one another, and in that buoyant water I seemed to become something lighter and stronger than a man. And at last we came out dripping and rejoicing and raced among the rocks. And then I put on a dry bathing-dress, and we sat to bask in the sun, and presently I nodded, resting my head against her knee, and she put her hand upon my hair and stroked it softly and I dozed. And behold! as it were with the snapping of the string of a violin, I was awakening, and I was in my own bed in Liverpool, in the life of to-day.

"Only for a time I could not believe that all these vivid moments had been no more than the substance of a dream.

"In truth, I could not believe it a dream for all the sobering reality of things about me. I bathed and dressed as it were by habit, and as I shaved I argued why I of all men should leave the woman I loved to go back to fantastic politics in the hard and strenuous north. Even if Evesham did force the world back to war, what was that to me? I was a man with the heart of a man, and why should I feel the responsibility of a deity for the way the world might go?

"You know that is not quite the way I think about affairs, about my real affairs. I am a solicitor, you know, with a point of view.

"The vision was so real, you must understand, so utterly unlike a dream that I kept perpetually recalling trivial, irrelevant details; even the ornament of a book-cover that lay on my wife's sewing-machine in the breakfast-room recalled with the utmost vividness the gilt line that ran about the seat in the alcove where I had talked with the messenger from my deserted party. Have you ever heard of a dream that had a quality like that?"

"Like——?"

"So that afterwards you remembered details you had forgotten."

I thought. I had never noticed the point before, but he was right.

"Never," I said. "That is what you never seem to do with dreams."

"No," he answered. "But that is just what I did. I am a solicitor, you must understand, in Liverpool, and I could not help wondering what the clients and business people I found myself talking to in my office would think if I told them suddenly I was in love with a girl who would be born a couple of hundred years or so hence, and worried about the politics of my great-great-great-grandchildren. I was chiefly busy that day negotiating a ninety-nine-year building lease. It was a private builder in a hurry, and we wanted to tie him in every possible way. I had an interview with him, and he showed a certain want of temper that sent me to bed still irritated. That night I had no dream. Nor did I dream the next night, at least, to remember.

"Something of that intense reality of conviction vanished. I began to feel sure it *was* a dream. And then it came again.

"When the dream came again, nearly four days later, it was very different. I think it certain that four days had also elapsed in the dream. Many things had happened in the north, and the shadow of them was back again between us, and this time it was not so easily dispelled. I began I know with moody musings. Why, in spite of all, should I go back, go back for all the rest of my days to toil and stress, insults and perpetual dissatisfaction, simply to save hundreds of millions of common people, whom I did not love, whom too often I could do no other than despise, from the stress and anguish of war and infinite misrule? And after all I might fail. *They* all sought their own narrow ends, and why should not I —why should not I also live as a man? And out of such thoughts her voice summoned me, and I lifted my eyes.

"I found myself awake and walking. We had come out above the Pleasure City, we were near the summit of Monte Solaro and looking towards the bay. It was the late afternoon and very clear. Far away to the left Ischia hung in a golden haze between sea and sky, and Naples was coldly white against the hills, and before us was Vesuvius with a tall and slender streamer feathering at last towards the south, and the ruins of Torre Annunziata and Castellamare glittering and near."

I interrupted suddenly: "You have been to Capri, of course?"

"Only in this dream," he said, "only in this dream. All across the bay beyond Sorrento were the floating palaces of the Pleasure City moored and chained. And northward were the broad floating stages that received the aëroplanes. Aëroplanes fell out of the sky every afternoon, each bringing its thousands of pleasure-seekers from the uttermost parts of the earth to Capri and its delights. All these things, I say, stretched below.

"But we noticed them only incidentally because of an unusual sight that evening had to show. Five war aëroplanes that had long slumbered useless in the distant arsenals of the Rhinemouth were manœuvring now in the eastward sky. Evesham had astonished the world by producing them and others, and sending them to circle here and there. It was the threat material in the great game of bluff he was playing, and it had taken even me by surprise. He was one of those incredibly stupid, energetic people who seem sent by heaven to create disasters. His energy to the first glance seemed so wonderfully like capacity! But he had no imagination, no invention, only a stupid, vast, driving force of will, and a mad faith in his stupid idiot 'luck' to pull him through. I remember how we stood out upon the headland watching the squadron circling far away, and how I weighed the full meaning of the sight, seeing clearly the way things must go. And then even it was not too late. I might have gone back, I think, and saved the world. The people of the north would follow me, I knew, granted only that in one thing I respected their moral standards. The east and south would trust me as they would trust no other northern man. And I knew I had only to put it to her and she would have let me go. . . . Not because she did not love me!

"Only I did not want to go; my will was all the other way about. I had so newly thrown off the incubus of responsibility: I was still so fresh a renegade from duty that the daylight clearness of what I *ought* to do had no power at all to touch my will. My will was to live, to gather pleasures and make my dear lady happy. But though this sense of vast neglected duties had no power to draw me, it could make me silent and preoccupied, it robbed the days I had spent of half their brightness and roused me into dark meditations in the silence of the night. And as I stood and watched Evesham's aëroplanes sweep to and fro—those birds of infinite ill omen—she stood beside me watching me, perceiving the trouble, indeed, but not perceiving it clearly—her eyes questioning my face, her expression shaded with perplexity. Her face was grey because the sunset was fading out of the sky. It was no fault of hers that she held me. She had asked me to go from her, and again in the night time and with tears she had asked me to go.

"At last it was the sense of her that roused me from my mood. I turned upon her suddenly and challenged her to race down the mountain slopes. 'No,' she said, as if I jarred with her gravity; but I was resolved to end that gravity, and made her run—no one can be very grey and sad who is out of breath—and when she stumbled I ran with my hand beneath her arm. We ran down past a couple of men, who turned back staring in astonishment at my behaviour—they must have recognised my face. And halfway down the slope came a tumult in the air, clang-clank, clang-clank, and we stopped, and presently over the hill-crest those war things came flying one behind the other."

The man seemed hesitating on the verge of a description.

"What were they like?" I asked.

"They had never fought," he said. "They were just like our ironclads are nowadays; they had never fought. No one knew what they might do, with excited men inside them; few even cared to speculate. They were great driving things shaped like spear-heads without a shaft, with a propeller in the place of the shaft."

"Steel?"

"Not steel."

"Aluminium?"

"No, no, nothing of that sort. An alloy that was very common—as common as brass, for example. It was called—let me see——" He squeezed his forehead with the fingers of one hand. "I am forgetting everything," he said.

"And they carried guns?"

"Little guns, firing high-explosive shells. They fired the guns backwards, out of the base of the leaf, so to speak, and rammed with the beak. That was the theory, you know, but they had never been fought. No one could tell exactly what was going to happen. And meanwhile I suppose it was very fine to go whirling through the air like a flight of young swallows, swift and easy. I guess the captains tried not to think too clearly what the real thing would be like. And these flying war machines, you know, were only one sort of the endless war contrivances that had been invented and had fallen into abeyance during the long peace. There were all sorts of these things that people were routing out and furbishing up; infernal things, silly things; things that had never been tried; big engines, terrible explosives, great guns. You know the silly way of the ingenious sort of men who make these things; they turn 'em out as beavers build dams, and with no more sense of the rivers they're going to divert and the lands they're going to flood!

"As we went down the winding stepway to our hotel again, in the twilight, I foresaw it all: I saw how clearly and inevitably things were driving for war in Evesham's silly, violent hands, and I had some inkling of what war was bound to be under these new conditions. And even then, though I knew it was drawing near the limit of my opportunity, I could find no will to go back."

He sighed.

"That was my last chance.

"We didn't go into the city until the sky was full of stars, so we walked out upon the high terrace, to and fro, and—she counselled me to go back.

"'My dearest,' she said, and her sweet face looked up to me, 'this is Death. This life you lead is Death. Go back to them, go back to your duty——'

"She began to weep, saying, between her sobs, and clinging to my arm as she said it, 'Go back—Go back.'

"Then suddenly she fell mute, and, glancing down at her face, I read in an instant the thing she had thought to do. It was one of those moments when one *sees*.

"'No!' I said.

"'No?' she asked, in surprise, and I think a little fearful at the answer to her thought.

"'Nothing,' I said, 'shall send me back. Nothing! I have chosen. Love, I have chosen, and the world must go. Whatever happens I will live this life—I will live for *you*! It—nothing shall turn me aside; nothing, my dear one. Even if you died— even if you died——'

"'Yes?' she murmured, softly.

"'Then—I also would die.'

"And before she could speak again I began to talk, talking eloquently—as I *could* do in that life—talking to exalt love, to make the life we were living seem heroic and glorious; and the thing I was deserting something hard and enormously ignoble that it was a fine thing to set aside. I bent all my mind to throw that glamour upon it, seeking not only to convert her but myself to that. We talked, and she clung to me, torn, too, between all that she deemed noble and all that she knew was sweet. And at last I did make it heroic, made all the thickening disaster of the world only a sort of glorious setting to our unparalleled love, and we two poor foolish souls strutted there at last, clad in that splendid delusion, drunken rather with that glorious delusion, under the still stars.

"And so my moment passed.

"It was my last chance. Even as we went to and fro there, the leaders of the south and east were gathering their resolve, and the hot answer that shattered Evesham's bluffing for ever took shape and waited. And all over Asia, and the ocean, and the South, the air and the wires were throbbing with their warnings to prepare—prepare.

"No one living, you know, knew what war was; no one could imagine, with all these new inventions, what horror war might bring. I believe most people still believed it would be a matter of bright uniforms and shouting charges and triumphs and flags and bands—in a time when half the world drew its food supply from regions ten thousand miles away——"

The man with the white face paused. I glanced at him, and his face was intent on the floor of the carriage. A little railway station, a string of loaded trucks, a signal-box, and the back of a cottage, shot by the carriage window, and a bridge passed with a clap of noise, echoing the tumult of the train.

"After that," he said, "I dreamt often. For three weeks of nights that dream was my life. And the worst of it was there were nights when I could not dream, when I lay tossing on a bed in *this* accursed life; and *there*—somewhere lost to me—things were happening—momentous, terrible things. . . . I lived at nights—my days, my waking days, this life I am living now, became a faded, far-away dream, a drab setting, the cover of the book."

He thought.

"I could tell you all, tell you every little thing in the dream, but as to what I did in the daytime—no. I could not tell—I do not remember. My memory—my memory has gone. The business of life slips from me——"

He leant forward, and pressed his hands upon his eyes. For a long time he said nothing.

"And then?" said I.

"The war burst like a hurricane."

He stared before him at unspeakable things.

"And then?" I urged again.

"One touch of unreality," he said, in the low tone of a man who speaks to himself, "and they would have been nightmares. But they were not nightmares—they were not nightmares. *No!*"

He was silent for so long that it dawned upon me that there was a danger of losing the rest of the story. But he went on talking again in the same tone of questioning self-communion.

"What was there to do but flight? I had not thought the war would touch Capri—I had seemed to see Capri as being out of it all, as the contrast to it all; but two nights after the whole place was shouting and bawling, every woman almost and every other man wore a badge—Evesham's badge—and there was no music but a jangling war-song over and over again, and everywhere men enlisting, and in the dancing halls they were drilling. The whole island was awhirl with rumours; it was said, again and again, that fighting had begun. I had not expected this. I had seen so little of the life of pleasure that I had failed to reckon with this violence of the amateurs. And as for me, I was out of it. I was like a man who might have prevented the firing of a magazine. The time had gone. I was no one; the vainest stripling with a badge counted for more than I. The crowd jostled us and bawled in our ears; that accursed song deafened us; a woman shrieked at my lady because no badge was on her, and we two went back to our own place again, ruffled and insulted—my lady white and silent, and I aquiver with rage. So furious was I, I could have quarrelled with her if I could have found one shade of accusation in her eyes.

"All my magnificence had gone from me. I walked up and down our rock cell, and outside was the darkling sea and a light to the southward that flared and passed and came again.

"'We must get out of this place,' I said over and over. 'I have made my choice, and I will have no hand in these troubles. I will have nothing of this war. We have taken our lives out of all these things. This is no refuge for us, Let us go.'

"And the next day we were already in flight from the war that covered the world.

"And all the rest was Flight—all the rest was Flight."

He mused darkly.

"How much was there of it?"

He made no answer.

"How many days?"

His face was white and drawn and his hands were clenched. He took no heed of my curiosity.

I tried to draw him back to his story with questions.

"Where did you go?" I said.

"When?"

"When you left Capri."

"South-west," he said, and glanced at me for a second. "We went in a boat."

"But I should have thought an aëroplane?"

"They had been seized."

I question him no more. Presently I thought he was beginning again. He broke out in an argumentative monotone:

"But why should it be? If, indeed, this battle, this slaughter and stress *is* life, why have we this craving for pleasure and beauty? If there *is* no refuge, if there is no place of peace, and if all our dreams of quiet places are a folly and a snare, why have we such dreams? Surely it was no ignoble cravings, no base intentions, had brought us to this; it was Love had isolated us. Love had come to me with her eyes and robed in her beauty, more glorious than all else in life, in the very shape and colour of life, and summoned me away. I had silenced all the voices, I had answered all the questions—I had come to her. And suddenly there was nothing but War and Death!"

I had an inspiration. "After all," I said, "it could have been only a dream."

"A dream!" he cried, flaming upon me, "a dream—when, even now——"

For the first time he became animated. A faint flush crept into his cheek. He raised his open hand and clenched it, and dropped it to his knee. He spoke, looking away from me, and for all the rest of the time he looked away. "We are but phantoms," he said, "and the phantoms of phantoms, desires like cloud shadows and wills of straw that eddy in the wind; the days pass, use and wont carry us through as a train carries the shadow of its lights—so be it! But one thing is real and certain, one thing is no dreamstuff, but eternal and enduring. It is the centre of my life, and all other things about it are subordinate or altogether vain. I loved her, that woman of a dream. And she and I are dead together!

"A dream! How can it be a dream, when it has drenched a living life with unappeasable sorrow, when it makes all that I have lived for and cared for, worthless and unmeaning?

"Until that very moment when she was killed I believed we had still a chance of getting away," he said. "All through the night and morning that we sailed across the sea from Capri to Salerno, we talked of escape. We were full of hope, and it clung about us to the end, hope for the life together we should lead, out of it all, out of the battle and struggle, the wild and empty passions, the empty arbitrary 'thou shalt' and 'thou shalt not' of the world. We were uplifted, as though our quest was a holy thing, as though love for one another was a mission. . . .

"Even when from our boat we saw the fair face of that great rock Capri—already scarred and gashed by the gun emplacements and hiding places that were to make it a fastness—we reckoned nothing of the imminent slaughter, though the fury of preparation hung about in puffs and clouds of dust at a hundred points amidst the grey; but, indeed, I made a text of that and talked. There, you know, was the rock, still beautiful for all its scars, with its countless windows and arches and ways, tier upon tier, for a thousand feet, a vast carving of grey, broken by vine-clad terraces and lemon and orange groves and masses of agave and prickly pear, and puffs of almond blossom. And out under the archway that is built over the Marina Piccola other boats were coming; and as we came round the cape and within sight of the mainland, another string of boats came into view, driving before the wind towards the south-west. In a little while a multitude had come out, the remoter just specks of ultramarine in the shadow of the eastward cliff.

"'It is love and reason,' I said, 'fleeing from all this madness of war.'

"And though we presently saw a squadron of aëroplanes flying across the southern sky we did not heed it. There it was —a line of dots in the sky—and then more, dotting the south-eastern horizon, and then still more, until all that quarter of the sky was stippled with blue specks. Now they were all thin little strokes of blue, and now one and now a multitude would heel and catch the sun and become short flashes of light. They came, rising and falling and growing larger like some huge flight of gulls or rooks or such-like birds, moving with a marvellous uniformity, and ever as they drew nearer they spread over a greater width of sky. The southward wing flung itself in an arrow-headed cloud athwart the sun. And then suddenly they swept round to the eastward and streamed eastward, growing smaller and smaller and clearer and clearer again until they vanished from the sky. And after that we noted to the northward and very high Evesham's fighting machines hanging high over Naples like an evening swarm of gnats.

"It seemed to have no more to do with us than a flight of birds.

"Even the mutter of guns far away in the south-east seemed to us to signify nothing. . . .

"Each day, each dream after that, we were still exalted, still seeking that refuge where we might live and love. Fatigue had come upon us, pain and many distresses. For though we were dusty and stained by our toilsome tramping, and half-starved and with the horror of the dead men we had seen and the flight of the peasants—for very soon a gust of fighting swept up the peninsula—with these things haunting our minds it still resulted only in a deepening resolution to escape. Oh, but she was brave and patient! She who had never faced hardship and exposure had courage for herself—and me. We went to and fro seeking an outlet, over a country all commandeered and ransacked by the gathering hosts of war. Always we went on foot. At first there were other fugitives, but we did not mingle with them. Some escaped northward, some were caught in the torrent of peasantry that swept along the main roads; many gave themselves into the hands of the soldiery and were sent northward. Many of the men were impressed. But we kept away from these things; we had brought no money to bribe a passage north, and I feared for my lady at the hands of these conscript crowds. We had landed at Salerno, and we had been turned back from Cava, and we had tried to cross towards Taranto by a pass over Monte Alburno, but we had been driven back for want of food, and so we had come down among the marshes by Pæstum, where those great temples stand alone. I had some vague idea that by Pæstum it might be possible to find a boat or something, and take once more to sea. And there it was the battle overtook us.

"A sort of soul-blindness had me. Plainly I could see that we were being hemmed in; that the great net of that giant Warfare had us in its toils. Many times we had seen the levies that had come down from the north going to and fro, and had come upon them in the distance amidst the mountains making ways for the ammunition and preparing the mounting of the guns. Once we fancied they had fired at us, taking us for spies —at any rate a shot had gone shuddering over us. Several times we had hidden in woods from hovering aëroplanes.

"But all these things do not matter now, these nights of flight and pain. . . . We were in an open place near those great temples at Pæstum at last, on a blank stony place dotted with spiky bushes, empty and desolate and so flat that a grove of eucalyptus far away showed to the feet of its stems. How I can see it! My lady was sitting down under a bush resting a little, for she was very weak and weary, and I was standing up watching to see if I could tell the distance of the firing that came and went. They were still, you know, fighting far from each other, with those terrible new weapons that had never before been used: guns that would carry beyond sight, and aëroplanes that would do—— What *they* would do no man could foretell.

"I knew that we were between the two armies, and that they drew together. I knew we were in danger, and that we could not stop there and rest!

"Though all these things were in my mind, they were in the background. They seemed to be affairs beyond our concern. Chiefly, I was thinking of my lady. An aching distress filled me. For the first time she had owned herself beaten and had fallen a-weeping. Behind me I could hear her sobbing, but I would not turn round to her because I knew she had need of weeping, and had held herself so far and so long for me. It was well, I thought, that she would weep and rest and then we would toil on again, for I had no inkling of the thing that hung so near. Even now I can see her as she sat there, her lovely hair upon her shoulder, can mark again the deepening hollow of her cheek.

"'If we had parted,' she said, 'if I had let you go.'

"'No,' said I. 'Even now, I do not repent. I will not repent; I made my choice, and I will hold on to the end.'

"And then——

"Overhead in the sky flashed something and burst, and all about us I heard the bullets making a noise like a handful of peas suddenly thrown. They chipped the stones about us, and whirled fragments from the bricks and passed. . . ."

He put his hand to his mouth, and then moistened his lips.

"At the flash I had turned about. . . .

"You know—she stood up——

"She stood up, you know, and moved a step towards me——

"As though she wanted to reach me——

"And she had been shot through the heart."

He stopped and stared at me. I felt all that foolish incapacity an Englishman feels on such occasions. I met his eyes for a moment, and then stared out of the window. For a long space we kept silence. When at last I looked at him he was sitting back in his corner, his arms folded, and his teeth gnawing at his knuckles.

He bit his nail suddenly, and stared at it.

"I carried her," he said, "towards the temples, in my arms —as though it mattered. I don't know why. They seemed a sort of sanctuary, you know; they had lasted so long, I suppose.

"She must have died almost instantly. Only—I talked to her—all the way."

Silence again.

"I have seen those temples," I said abruptly, and indeed he had brought those still, sunlit arcades of worn sandstone very vividly before me.

"It was the brown one, the big brown one. I sat down on a fallen pillar and held her in my arms. . . . Silent after the first babble was over. And after a little while the lizards came out and ran about again, as though nothing unusual was going on, as though nothing had changed. . . . It was tremendously still there, the sun high and the shadows still; even the shadows of the weeds upon the entablature were still—in spite of the thudding and banging that went all about the sky.

"I seem to remember that the aëroplanes came up out of the south, and that the battle went away to the west. One aëroplane was struck, and overset and fell. I remember that —though it didn't interest me in the least. It didn't seem to signify. It was like a wounded gull, you know—flapping for a time in the water. I could see it down the aisle of the temple —a black thing in the bright blue water.

"Three or four times shells burst about the beach, and then that ceased. Each time that happened all the lizards scuttled in and hid for a space. That was all the mischief done, except that once a stray bullet gashed the stone hard by—made just a fresh bright surface.

"As the shadows grew longer, the stillness seemed greater.

"The curious thing," he remarked, with the manner of a man who makes a trivial conversation, "is that I didn't *think* —I didn't think at all. I sat with her in my arms amidst the stones—in a sort of lethargy—stagnant.

"And I don't remember waking up. I don't remember dressing that day. I know I found myself in my office, with my letters all slit open in front of me, and how I was struck by the absurdity of being there, seeing that in reality I was sitting, stunned, in that Pæstum Temple with a dead woman in my arms. I read my letters like a machine. I have forgotten what they were about."

He stopped, and there was a long silence.

Suddenly I perceived that we were running down the incline from Chalk Farm to Euston. I started at this passing of time. I turned on him with a brutal question, in the tone of "Now or never."

"And did you dream again?"

"Yes."

He seemed to force himself to finish. His voice was very low.

"Once more, and as it were only for a few instants. I seemed to have suddenly awakened out of a great apathy, to have risen into a sitting position, and the body lay there on the stones beside me. A gaunt body. Not her, you know. So soon —it was not her. . . .

"I may have heard voices. I do not know. Only I knew clearly that men were coming into the solitude and that that was a last outrage.

"I stood up and walked through the temple, and then there came into sight—first one man with a yellow face, dressed in a uniform of dirty white, trimmed with blue, and then several climbing to the crest of the old wall of the vanished city, and crouching there. They were little bright figures in the sunlight, and there they hung, weapon in hand, peering cautiously before them.

"And farther away I saw others and then more at another point in the wall. It was a long lax line of men in open order.

"Presently the man I had first seen stood up and shouted a command, and his men came tumbling down the wall and into the high weeds towards the temple. He scrambled down with them and led them. He came facing towards me, and when he saw me he stopped.

"At first I had watched these men with a mere curiosity, but when I had seen they meant to come to the temple I was moved to forbid them. I shouted to the officer.

"'You must not come here.' I cried. 'I am here. I am here with my dead.'

"He stared, and then shouted a question back to me in some unknown tongue.

"I repeated what I had said.

"He shouted again, and I folded my arms and stood still. Presently he spoke to his men and came forward. He carried a drawn sword.

"I signed to him to keep away, but he continued to advance. I told him again very patiently and clearly: 'You must not come here. These are old temples and I am here with my dead.'

"Presently he was so close I could see his face clearly. It was a narrow face, with dull grey eyes, and a black moustache.

He had a scar on his upper lip, and he was dirty and unshaven. He kept shouting unintelligible things, questions, perhaps, at me.

"I know now that he was afraid of me, but at the time that did not occur to me. As I tried to explain to him, he interrupted me in imperious tones, bidding me, I suppose, stand aside.

"He made to go past me, and I caught hold of him.

"I saw his face change at my grip.

"'You fool,' I cried. 'Don't you know? She is dead!'

"He started back. He looked at me with cruel eyes. I saw a sort of exultant resolve leap into them—delight. Then, suddenly, with a scowl, he swept his sword back—*so*—and thrust."

He stopped abruptly.

I became aware of a change in the rhythm of the train. The brakes lifted their voices and the carriage jarred and jerked. This present world insisted upon itself, became clamorous. I saw through the steamy window huge electric lights glaring down from tall masts upon a fog, saw rows of stationary empty carriages passing by; and then a signal-box, hoisting its constellation of green and red into the murky London twilight, marched after them. I looked again at his drawn features.

"He ran me through the heart. It was with a sort of astonishment—no fear, no pain—but just amazement, that I felt it pierce me, felt the sword drive home into my body. It didn't hurt, you know. It didn't hurt at all."

The yellow platform lights came into the field of view, passing first rapidly, then slowly, and at last stopping with a jerk. Dim shapes of men passed to and fro without.

"Euston!" cried a voice.

"Do you mean——?"

"There was no pain, no sting or smart. Amazement and then darkness sweeping over everything. The hot, brutal face before me, the face of the man who had killed me, seemed to recede. It swept out of existence——"

"Euston!" clamoured the voices outside; "Euston!"

The carriage door opened admitting a flood of sound, and a porter stood regarding us. The sounds of doors slamming, and the hoof-clatter of cab-horses, and behind these things the featureless remote roar of the London cobble-stones, came to my ears. A truckload of lighted lamps blazed along the platform.

"A darkness, a flood of darkness that opened and spread and blotted out all things."

"Any luggage, sir?" said the porter.

"And that was the end?" I asked.

He seemed to hesitate. Then, almost inaudibly, he answered, "*No.*"

"You mean?"

"I couldn't get to her. She was there on the other side of the temple—— And then——"

"Yes," I insisted. "Yes?"

"Nightmares," he cried; "nightmares, indeed! My God! Great birds that fought and tore."

THE END